Souls Collide

NEF HOUSE PUBLISHING

Souls Collide (Where We Begin)
Copyright © 2025 L.S. River

ISBN: 978-1-965393-09-3

DEDICATION

This journey was often a solitary one, but I was never truly alone.

To my children, Alabama and Romeo, thank you for inspiring me to be the best version of myself and for reminding me to chase my dreams, no matter how impossible they might seem. I'm sorry for the moments I missed while writing this story, but know that every word was written with you in my heart. I love you endlessly, and I'll always keep doing my best for you.

To my husband, thank you for caring for our children when I was lost in the world of words. I hope one day you'll look at this book and feel proud.

To my dearest friend, Samia, thank you for standing by me from day one, for cheering me on in the way only a true friend can.

To my parents, with all my love. To my brothers and my sister, the best siblings a girl could ever hope for. And to my nephews, Alessio and Andrea—my first babies—thank you for believing in me long before I believed in myself.

A special thanks to Seb, for making fictional worlds feel real.

And to Stuart, my editor, thank you for believing in this story, and in me, the French girl who dared to dream of publishing in English.

And finally, to those who never believed in me: thank you, too. I'm so glad I never listened.

« Elle était belle à faire chialer les roses, à les faire faner de honte de s'être crues si importantes sans s'être aperçues que sur Terre, en même temps qu'elles, Maïssane avait poussé. Pas de chance, les roses »

Tristan Koëgel

"She was so beautiful she could make roses cry, make them wither in shame for ever believing themselves important, blind to the fact that, on this Earth, Maïssane had bloomed beside them. Tough luck, roses."

Tristan Koëgel

Souls Collide

WHERE WE BEGIN

L.S. RIVER

CHAPTER 1
Delilah

"I am done."

What is the limit to a person's capacity for enduring pain and suffering? I've been through it all. God alone knows how much I've traversed the pathways of Hell in my lifetime. Although I'm only twenty-six years old, I feel like I'm over eighty.

So, this is it—my last night on Earth. I've made up my mind that at 3:03 a.m., I'll jump from the Rigel building. I read somewhere that at 3:03, the world goes quiet, just for a moment. Shadows and light blend together, and in the silence, hidden truths come out like soft whispers from the stars. They said 3:03 is a special time, a "mirror hour" that connects us to the universe and those looking for peace. And that's what I want—peace for my mind, my heart, and my soul.

My heart feels heavy, yet strangely hollow. It used to be alive with hope, but now there's only an empty silence. I thought things would get better, that pain would give way to beauty. But I was wrong. I wasn't dreaming of something as simple as peace—I imagined life like a perfect melody, where every note fits, creating harmony that brings meaning. That vision kept me grounded, kept me believing.

Now I'm broken—not just my heart, but my soul, my dreams, all shattered by the villains of my story. I'm so tired, exhausted from carrying the weight of it all. I just want to be free from the pain. For a brief moment, I tasted what it was like to live a normal, happy life. I've never wanted fame or fortune, just simple joys, real moments.

That's all I ever needed to feel whole. But now even that feels out of reach.

I just wanted to be . . . happy. And it lasted only a second. An intense second of my life. Now it's all gone. Though I wasn't given the choice of birth, nor was I given the direction of my life, I am going to choose my final departure. I *am* leaving. I left places so many times, I left people behind, I left many lives I lived, and yet it all went back to the same end. So, I decided that this would be the End. I tried to start over, and I failed. Now the only option left is . . . to commit suicide. I want to fly, so I'm going to jump. I've already hit rock bottom in theory, so I'm going for it in practice.

So that's what it's like to feel dead inside?

For my very last night, I decided I'll become another version of myself. There's a high-end bar within a luxurious hotel that's very elitist and fancy. I pass by it every day on my way to work and always imagined how women would spend their Friday nights there. I went to the bank and withdrew all the money I managed to save, which amounted to $450.82. I then went to a store and bought the most beautiful black dress that hugs my tight waist, accentuating delicate curves, with a sumptuous décolleté showcasing hot cleavage. For the very first time in twenty-six years, I went to a salon to get the most amazing blow-dry, and I adorned one side of my hair with a gold pin. I put on natural makeup but insisted on red lips for a more dramatic look. Yes, for my last night on planet Earth, I look elegant and feminine.

Now I have $313.51 left that I intend to spend on nice, expensive alcohol in that posh bar. I didn't forget to buy a piece of paper and a pen to write my final goodbyes.

I'm now back at my apartment on Rockaway Avenue in Brownsville, New York City. When I first got the keys to this place, I felt so happy, so hopeful, so eager to finally start a life that would belong solely to me. To live the promise of freedom from the past and the hope for a shiny yet simple future. It's a small place with one bedroom that I barely decorated. Tiny but very practical and a little cozy. I'm expected to leave this place by the end of next week. Guess that will no longer be a problem. I've gathered the few belongings I have into a box addressed to Ashley, my dearest little sister. Even though we don't share blood, she *is* my sibling at heart. I saw her for the last time over five months ago. She was ready for her new life and willing to never look back. I understood all too well her wishes, even if the things she left included me.

Touching the contents of the box with the edge of my fingertips, I replay all my memories in my mind, creating scenarios that would have led me to different ends. Now that everything is packed and the place is clean, I'm finally ready to go.

"Goodbye, sweet place. Even though I can't stay here anymore and the last memory I have here is too painful, I choose to remember only the first day I saw you. May your next tenant be happier than I ever was or could have been." I lock the door for the last time, put the keys under the doormat, and leave.

~

Friday, May 6, 2022, 7:00 p.m.

I open the door of Orion and am instantly amazed. The space feels both grand and cozy. A soft violet carpet beneath my feet gives a sense of comfort, while the tall walls, decorated with stained glass windows, remind me of a church.

In the center, the bar stands out with its sleek U shape, made of dark, polished wood that gives off a feeling of luxury. Behind it, shelves filled with fine spirits sparkle behind glass, each bottle showing off wealth. The black walls have small lights that add a sense of style.

Columns draped with white, black, and purple flowers stand near the bar, bringing a poetic touch to the otherwise exclusive space. Around the bar are private corners with comfortable leather seats, offering quiet places away from the crowd. It's a place where the rich come to relax, where luxury is everything, and only a select few can enter. To the right, double doors lead to the hotel connected to the bar. Behind the left column is a sign pointing to the restrooms. I find an open seat, feeling a bit uneasy, and glance at the beautiful blonde barmaid.

I do not belong here. I don't belong anywhere.

"Hi, um, good evening . . . miss?" I stammer. "Sorry, I'm not great at this. Can I get a drink, please?"

The barmaid turns to me with a smile. "You can call me Jenna. What can I get you?" I notice her neat black pants and blazer—pretty stylish for a bar. But what do *I* want to drink? *I have no idea.*

"I know this sounds weird, but I honestly don't know what to order. I've never really been the one to order. Can you just . . . give me something worth trying before I die?" I say, trying to make it sound casual, though I know how dark that sounds. She laughs, but it feels genuine, like she's not put off by my awkwardness.

"You got it. Trust me, I'll make you something good," she says, and heads off.

I watch her go and pull out some paper and a pen from my bag. I start scribbling down my thoughts, trying to make sense of everything. I don't know if this letter will ever be read, but I need to write it to free my soul, to explain my journey, to share without fear how I was born, how I lived, what I did and what was done to me—that led me to this moment. I wonder if there's a Heaven. *Will I go there?*

Anyway, I want to explain to those who brought me into this world why I chose to leave it.

"Here you go!" Jenna's voice snaps me back to the present. She places a glass in front of me, brown with ice and a slice of orange. "Tell me what you think." I take a sip. It's smooth, bitter but sweet at the same time.

"Mmm, I like it! What is this?"

"It's a *Negroni.* Campari, vermouth, and gin. Classic Italian. I thought you might be Italian?"

I chuckle, shaking my head.

"Nope, just plain old American."

"With that hair and those eyes, I could've sworn you had some Italian in you," she says with a teasing smile.

"Careful, or I might think you're hitting on me," I joke. She laughs even more, shaking her head.

"No worries. You're gorgeous, but I'm more into bad boys than beautiful women. But a 'thank you' would've been nice!" she adds with a wink. I laugh again and it *feels* good.

"Alright, thank you. I didn't expect to be laughing tonight, so . . . thanks for that."

"You're welcome," she says. "What's your name, anyway? If I may ask."

"You may, I'm Delilah," I reply, feeling a little lighter. "And thanks for the compliment."

"Delilah in New York City! Kind of rare around here, pretty cool."

She's clearly referring to the Plain White T's song. "Well, compared to Jenna, I guess it is," I say with a teasing grin. "Kidding, of course! Don't mind me, sometimes I think I'm funnier than I actually am."

Jenna grins. "No, you're good. Definitely my coolest customer tonight."

I'm surprised by how good that makes me feel.

"Well, the night is still young," I say softly, as the weight of everything starts to creep back in. The beginning of the end. *How poetic.*

Jenna heads off to help someone else, leaving me alone, but for a brief moment, I feel . . . okay.

I focus on getting my thoughts down on paper.

Dear Universe,
Whoever or whatever you may be, you gave me what people call the gift of life, and here I'll explain to you why I choose to give it back. Life

was never a gift to me, it was a burden. You gave me to the Ferris family in the first place, but they never loved me.

They never wanted me either. My "mother" always used to remind me what an accident I was, and how I had become responsible for the turbulent relationship she shared with my "father," how I was responsible for his wrath and violence towards her for only the fault of being born. I grew up under total violence, both physical and psychological. I was beaten, battered, humiliated, starved, punished under a freezing water jet, most of the time locked in darkness for days surrounded by my own waste, with nothing and no one to help me. All of this until the age of ten.

I have never earned their empathy, neither from them nor from my two big brothers. They were strangers to me. They sometimes allowed me to go to school thanks to a state allowance for a third child, but because I was a fast learner and starved for knowledge, they soon denied me that right. I used to sneak out whenever I had the opportunity, and they cared so little about me, thinking I was still in the basement, that they never thought to check. I spent ten years crying every fucking night. The little girl I was died when . . .

"Are you a writer or something?" a young man asks, startling me as I'm focused on my writing. He looks handsome, rich, and elegant—everything someone might find attractive. But I'm as interested in men as I am in learning about bees, which is to say, not at all.

"Hi, no, I'm not," I say, trying to sound cold so he'll get the hint. He doesn't.

"I'm Jack. Can I buy you a drink?"

"I already have one, thanks," I reply, showing him my Negroni. *What a weird name for a drink.*

"Then let me get you another. Don't worry, I can afford it," he says with a big grin, trying to impress me with his money. If only he knew how little I cared.

"Okay, big guy, I'm not interested. I'm kind of in the middle of something and would prefer not to be disturbed. There are plenty of other people here who would love to hear about you, but I'm not one of them." I say it as politely as I can while making it clear I'm annoyed.

"Whatever . . ." he mutters under his breath, and walks away. I'm fine with that.

Just then, Jenna returns, and judging by her face, she's shocked.

"What just happened? Why would you reject him? He was so handsome and clearly rich! Do you have a boyfriend or something?" she asks.

"No, no boyfriend. I'm just not looking for anything with anyone. I just want to sit here, write, have a few drinks, and leave. I really don't want to meet anyone tonight, and I'd rather not talk about it, please." I try to sound polite. Her face softens, and I'm relieved that she seems to understand.

"Alright, no problem. If you need help getting rid of any more guys, just give me a wink, and I'll step in," she says with a smile. I appreciate the offer, but instead of saying anything, I just nod.

I go back to my letter, but as I read what I've written, the sadness of my past overwhelms me. I try to remember something happy from those days and think about Ms. Winnie, my old schoolteacher. She was always so kind, making her students laugh, and it always worked. I find myself laughing out loud at one of those memories.

"What's so funny, sweetheart?" I look up to see another handsome man trying to start a conversation. Okay, maybe I'll have a little fun. After all, this is my last night.

"Oh, hi. I was just laughing because I had this huge booger stuck in my mouth for a while, and I was challenging myself to see how long I could keep it there before swallowing it. Pretty funny, right?" I say, fake laughing.

"This is a pretty sexy thing to say. There could have been something else you swallowed. I've got some ideas if you're interested," he replies with a grin. Wait, what? Eww! That's not how I meant it to sound!

"First of all, that's disgusting. I'd rather deal with the boogers in my throat than anything that could come out of you," I start to say, but he interrupts me.

"Speaking of your throat . . ." he says, cutting me off. That's it.

"Oh my god, just leave me alone. You're disgusting, and you're making me sick," I snap at him. He looks shocked but walks away quickly.

At that moment, Jenna comes back, and I tell her what just happened. We both laugh so hard that it feels like the first time I've laughed in ages. *How sad is that?*

Another woman calls Jenna over for drinks, so she leaves, and I return to my letter.

After about an hour—and six more men bothering me—I head to the bathroom. The bar is really fancy. Even the bathrooms are beautiful, and the place smells amazing. I take a moment to appreciate how chic it all is before heading back to my seat with my letter in hand.

Fifteen minutes later, a new bartender approaches me. *Where's Jenna?*

"Would you like a refill, miss?" he asks. *Nope, not Jenna.*

"Oh, Jenna has been helping me. Is she gone?" I ask, a little sad I didn't get to say goodbye.

"No, she's just on her break. She'll be back in about ten minutes. But I'd be happy to help with anything you need," he says. I take a closer look at him. He's small and thin, wearing black slacks, a white dress shirt, and a blazer like Jenna. He has stunning green eyes and chestnut hair slicked back neatly. He looks fine, but I'd rather wait for her.

"Thank you, but I'll wait for Jenna. I'm in no rush," I say. He nods and walks away.

So, where was I?

. . . I remember thinking that living with the Ferris family was hell on earth. How stupid I was to think so. Actually, I was just naïve, so

innocent. I was only a child . . . But because this is my very last night, because I want to free my soul before I go, I'm going to revisit the worst days of my existence in great detail. Memories I wish I could have erased so badly but never was able to. And now I'm going to revisit the content of my nightmares. I have to reopen that memory box and empty it.

The truth is I was sold by my own parents. They were so in debt they were threatened with eviction when a man said he knew people who were interested in buying children. It was a sort of black-market adoption system. They didn't think twice about selling me to them for $80,000. I heard that conversation and cried. I cried so hard and then, and only then, I started to really experience the horror of fear in the extreme. I did not want to stay, but I did not want to leave.

I ran to school to warn everyone I could about my future departure, praying for a good soul to help me get out of that situation. I gathered the courage to talk and told everything to my teacher. But she must have thought I was searching for attention or something. It led me to think that I was . . . invisible. I remember that day when they came to pick me up and . . .

"Hey, I'm back. Nolan told me you only wanted me to serve you. I'm so honored!" Jenna laughs, clearly pleased by what I said. I laugh along with her.

"Well, I usually don't like to talk to people, but you seem nice, so . . ." I say with a shrug.

"Thank you! Do you want another drink? You've had three Negronis already, and you're not even tipsy. Want to try something different?"

"I told you that I don't trust people, but tonight is an exception, so go ahead and surprise me."

"I know you said you didn't want questions, but are you, like, okay? Are you looking for something specific tonight?" she asks carefully, unsure how I'll react.

My first instinct is to shut down. My body tenses up, and I frown. I can't answer her. I can't even speak. I'm frozen.

"Okay, sorry. Don't mind me. Just know, if you ever need someone to talk to, I'm here for you. I'll go make that cocktail," she says, clearly feeling awkward about my silence.

"Thank you," I whisper.

In another life, I would've loved to be her friend. She's been nothing but kind, making me feel at ease in a place where I don't belong. She did nothing wrong. It's me. I'm the one who's broken. I know my heart is dead inside. I don't feel anything except sadness—just deep waves of sorrow. I'm trying so hard to be "lighter," to somehow balance the weight of my heavy yet hollow heart. For once, I want to feel something fun. It sounds contradictory, but I need it tonight. I need the balance.

By the end of tonight, after all, I'll be joining the stars.

"Here! It's a cosmopolitan. Have you ever had one before?" Jenna says, handing me a drink with an olive on top.

"Did you choose the olive as if you're offering me an olive branch?" I ask, grinning, trying to shake off my dark mood.

"How did you know?!" She laughs again.

"Just a wild guess."

"Is it working?"

"Yup," I say, bringing the glass to my lips. It tastes good—better than the Negroni. Different. Lighter. Exactly what I needed. *Well done, Jenna.*

"To answer your question, no, I've never had a cosmopolitan before. I like it."

"Do you live here in New York?" she asks, and I'm not sure where she's going with this.

"Yes, and I'll die here in this city," I reply. It's an inside joke, one only I can understand. She doesn't get it, thankfully.

"Yeah, I get it," she says. *No, you don't.* "Who wouldn't want to live here, right? But how are you a New Yorker and never had a cosmo before?" she asks, genuinely surprised.

Well, I've lived in New York for ten years, but I only really experienced the city for only a few months. Does that make me a New Yorker? I don't know. *I never will.*

"There's a first time for everything, I guess?" I say vaguely. It works. I think she's trying not to push, and I appreciate that even more.

For the next forty-five minutes, I write more than I expected. I have fun chatting with Jenna. Nolan tries to join in on the jokes, and though I'm hesitant, I let him. A few more men hit on me—too many. I've never thought of myself as unattractive. I know I'm beautiful on the outside; I wouldn't have survived at The Rex if I wasn't. But beauty has always just been a tool. Nothing more. Eric used to tell me how beautiful I was to him . . .

Speaking of which . . .

. . . and that's how I met him. Eric. Before that night, whenever I thought about Eric, it was always with the purest form of love, comfort, warmth, and happiness. My savior. My everything.

It was about two weeks after Ashley left The Rex to have a chance at happiness with Paul. My heart was yet again broken when she wished to keep contact from afar. It was too painful for her to look at me and see what we've been through. And I understood her decision. I understood it all too well. But it put me into a loneliness that no one ever knew was possible.

Until him. Eric really only came to The Rex to accompany Marty, his best friend, a detective trying to solve an investigation. I was twenty-five, he was forty-one. That age gap never bothered me in the least. No, because Eric became my friend before he became anything else. He really wanted to know me, to finally understand what had happened to me.

He needed to understand why I would talk the way I did. Why I would act the way I acted. How I could be so cold yet so warm. How I could possibly wear the biggest smile while having the saddest eyes. That's what he told me. And for weeks, he pursued me. Not with the idea of having sex with me (that happened later), but to feed his curiosity.

For weeks, he tried to talk to me. He was so nice, so delicate, so careful. I could only fall for him. He got me. I told him everything a few weeks after we met. And he decided to help me.

He literally saved me. From my past and my present. He offered me what I thought never existed: hope. I fell in love with him. I am still in love with him despite everything. But Eric was married . . .

"Hey, Delilah, you're crying. How can I help you?" Jenna interrupts me. I was so deep in the memory of him—how happy I was and how it all fell apart. I can't answer. I can't speak. I can't think. I feel like I can't even breathe. I know her hands are on my arms, trying to comfort me, but I don't feel anything.

"Hey, my shift ends at 4:00 a.m. What do you say we go to my place after? We could eat ice cream and drink more tequila," she suggests.

"I won't be here at 4:00 a.m.," I say with a sigh, resigned.

"You know what? I can call my boss and leave now. Nolan can cover for me. We can leave right away if you want. I know we don't really know each other, but I have a good feeling about you. I can tell something's wrong, and I just want to help," she insists. I think I appreciate the gesture. The alcohol starts hitting me. I feel like I'm softening, at least toward her.

"That's not necessary. Thanks, but I'd rather stay here, have more of your amazing cocktails, finish my paper, and then . . . leave," I say, keeping it vague. Only I know the weight of my words and what they truly mean.

"Fair enough," she says simply. I know she wants to say more but doesn't. I appreciate it.

I try to get back to writing, but thinking about Eric tears me apart. Every sentence reminds me of the pain. I've read this part over and over, but each time feels like I'm living it again. Tears fill my eyes, and the memories are squeezing the air out of my lungs. I need a break.

So I take a look around, focusing on the décor, the lighting, and the intricate patterns on the mosaic windows. I trace their shapes with my eyes, imagining the softness of the flowers nearby, their scent wrapping around me like a hug. I imagine myself taking a flower and tucking it behind my ear, as if everything were okay. But reality hits, and the familiar sadness returns. Joy feels so far away, just out of reach. I tear my gaze away, desperate to focus on something else.

I start watching the people around me. I study their interactions, their body language, the way they look at each other. Every conversation tells a story. Some people look frustrated, others content, a few happy. Some might be in love. There's laughter, drinks, and people truly living their lives. And then there's me, alone in the middle of it all.

I wonder what it would be like to have someone, to be in a long-term relationship. What would it feel like to know someone so well, to trust them completely? To have someone who would always be there for you, to share your life with? To fall asleep and wake up next to someone, knowing they'd answer your call no matter what, because to them, you are their special someone?

"So, how's it going? I didn't see you writing much in the last twenty minutes. Need some inspiration? I can totally be your muse," Jenna says, interrupting my thoughts. I've had three or four drinks by now. I'm not too tipsy, but I feel light-headed. It's nice. I feel so relaxed, I play with the idea of being mysterious, and it makes me laugh a little to myself.

"Well, Jenna, this story is hard. I'm struggling with my emotions, and it's tough to get through," I say, half laughing, half serious. The alcohol is definitely getting to me now.

"Let me get you some appetizers. It's on the house, honey. That'll help," she offers.

"Can't say no," I reply, my voice higher than usual.

"Yeah, I figured," she says with a smile, then walks away. I gather what's left of me and reopen that box filled with memories of Eric.

. . . With Eric, I shared what I can only describe as a true love story. I knew he was married at the beginning of our "friendship"; it was never about turning things into love. No, he was protective of me. He was older and so reassuring. He truly wanted to help me, and he did. But once, after he got me the apartment, we went to celebrate, and he kissed me.

We knew we shouldn't have crossed that line, we knew it was wrong, we knew! But we just couldn't help it. We were drawn to each other. I did not want to believe it would last, I didn't want to create any drama because, truth be told, I was so scared to lose him that I accepted everything he was able to give me. His friendship was so important to me . . .

He kept saying that it was different with his wife, that he was not even sure he loved her anymore. He told me there was no passion between them. Then, obviously, he told me he would leave her, that he wanted to marry me and be with me. And for the very first time, I had a glimpse of hope for the future. I could visualize myself healed from the past, happily married, living a simple life. The dream of a lifetime.

He got me an apartment, my very own first home. He got me a job as a secretary in a local print store. I can remember that day so vividly. He was supposed to leave his wife and come move in with me. Have a future with me . . .

As I write, my mood completely shifts. It's like I'm looking at everything from a distance, like I've stepped away from the past. And I start laughing. Laughing hard at how stupid I used to be. What made me cry an hour ago now makes me laugh. Why didn't I stop it? I guess it's because what he promised was more than I ever imagined. I lived in darkness, and he showed me the light. I thought love was just an idea, but he made me believe it was real. I was always treated like an object, and he treated me like a princess—a damsel in distress, really. But I never wanted to be weak, never wanted to be a victim. Yet here I am, at my weakest, ready to do something I can't take back.

Jenna comes back with a plate of fancy food.

"Here you go, girl! Enjoy this, it'll help you get sober. I can see alcohol cheers you up, but be careful, you don't want to get hooked," she says.

"Believe me, Jenna, I won't," I reply.

"Good for you! You know your limits. By the way, that smile looks good on you. Wanna talk about what's on your mind?"

"No, thanks," I say, keeping it short. I take a bite of what looks like a mozzarella stick. It's delicious. I eat the shrimp, too, realizing I've never tasted anything this good before.

"This is amazing! I don't even want to know how much this costs," I say with my mouth full.

"Told you, it's on the house," Jenna says.

We're getting more familiar with each other, and she talks to me like we're friends. She doesn't know how much it means to me. For a second, I think maybe opening up to the right person could be good, but I quickly push that thought away.

Honestly, I have no intention of changing my decision. What's done is done. But I can't help wondering—what if I survive until tomorrow? What would I do? I can't keep my job because Eric's wife might find out if I stay. I'll have to quit. I can't keep my apartment because Eric doesn't want his name on a lease that's not theirs. But what if I find another job? Another place to live? Could I forget and move on? *No, I can't forget the anonymous letter, the threat . . .*

But if I put that aside, what would be my options? Maybe Jenna could help me get a job as a waitress. Maybe I could crash at her place for a bit. What would life be like then? I'd work with a nice woman, look for an apartment, and maybe get another secretary job.

I'd never be with a man again, though. Eric was the only one, and it would stay that way. I'll never love again, never want to be touched by anyone else. Just Eric. The rest are strangers.

Could I live without love?

I imagine a life without love. Every day would feel empty, like a hollow routine. No tender touches, no loving words, just silence. Could I live like that? Could I survive on memories of Eric alone? A loveless life is cold, something I've always known. But now it's different. I've tasted love. Knowing that, could I live without it?

Some people think "one-night stands" are enough. I've had sex with Eric, twice, but I've never had any orgasm. He took my virginity, and I gave it willingly, but the sex wasn't great. Our connection was. Our bond felt sacred, and pleasure didn't matter as much as being together. When we were together, it was always gentle, delicate. I've never made myself come. I always thought it was because I was broken—my heart, my soul, and eventually, my body.

But as I dream, reality slams back. The letter. The threat. I'd never put anyone in danger just through them knowing me. It's only a matter of time before they find me. But by then, I'll be gone. Tonight is mine, and after that, it's over.

"Hey, I've been watching you. Can I get you a drink?" a man asks as I zone out.

"Thanks, but no thanks. I'm not—"

"She's waiting for her boyfriend. If I were you, I'd leave this seat empty. He doesn't like to share," Jenna interrupts, saving me from more awkwardness.

"Yeah, exactly what she said," I say, chuckling at the word "boyfriend."

"My bad, have a good night," the guy says, and walks off.

"Thanks, I owe you," I tell Jenna.

"I saw the look on your face and figured you needed an out. But damn, he was gorgeous! One of our richest clients, too! I won't ask, but I'll never get it," she says, throwing up her hands.

~

I finish all the food. I'm stuffed, and the alcohol buzz is fading. Jenna brings me another cosmo, and I get back to my letter. I manage to write another page. I watch the people around me, guessing what they're talking about and laughing to myself.

"I think your boyfriend ditched you. I'm Logan. What can I get you this time?" The same guy from earlier sits next to me again. This is the third time. *Shit, Jenna's not here.*

"He's busy with work, but he'll be here soon. So I suggest you leave," I say, trying to sound convincing.

"Sweetheart, I've been watching you for an hour. You're alone. Give me a chance. I can make your night better," he insists.

"Even if I were alone, which I'm not, I'm still not interested. Again, no thanks."

"Oh, come on, don't be a—"

"Sorry, babe, I'm late," a man interrupts, wrapping his arms around me from behind and kissing the top of my head. I don't even have time to look at him. I can only smell him—he smells incredible. He hugs me tight.

What the fuck!

CHAPTER 2

Nate

Friday, May 6, 2022, 3:00 p.m.

Today sucks. From the moment I woke up, everything's gone wrong. First off, I woke up next to some woman I didn't even realize was still in my bed. I thought she'd left last night, but somehow, she ended up staying. I don't even know her name—didn't care to learn it.

I only do one-night stands and I'm always up-front about it, hoping it'll scare them off. It never does. If anything, it draws them in more. I expect them to leave before morning, but this one didn't get the memo. So there she is, trying to have a "getting to know each other" moment—*Fuck no*. I tried to nicely show her the door, but she didn't take the hint. I had to call security, and that whole fiasco made me late to work, which never happens.

In the ten years I've been CEO of Williams Holdings, I always get there before everyone and leave after everyone. I've made it my rule to outwork them all. My father, grandfather, and great-grandfather made millions with the company. I made *billions*. They ran a national company; I expanded it worldwide. Whether it's in the U.S., U.K., Singapore, Japan, or even India, we're leading the market. That's *my* doing. *I* built this.

Was this my dream, though? Absolutely not. I was always the smart kid—the best in my private school. But my passion was science. I excelled in it, and all my professors pushed me toward astrophysics.

I've always had a deep love for the universe—more than just curiosity. It's a respect for the unknown, a reverence for the mysteries out there. Since I was a kid, I found peace in the night sky. The stars spoke to me, inviting me to explore beyond our world. Learning about space wasn't just knowledge—it felt like victory. I wanted to discover new things, unlock the secrets of the cosmos. That's what astrophysicists do—they're the detectives of the universe. They figure out how stars are born, how galaxies collide, and they share their discoveries with the world. *That was supposed to be my life.*

But my dad got caught in a sex scandal, so he turned to then-twenty-four-year-old me to take over Williams Holdings. I begged him to let my younger brother Nick *also known as Satan*—do it. I didn't want this life. But I was the good son, the smart one, the hard worker, the one everyone respected.

My brother always wanted to compete with me, but all I ever wanted was to be close to him, to bond, to be real brothers. It never happened. Eventually, I gave up trying. I still made him COO, but that just means I'm constantly cleaning up his messes. Because he always fucking screws up.

Which brings me to the next reason today is a disaster. I was working on closing a huge deal with the Hudson family, who never partner with anyone outside their own. After months of negotiation, I was close. Then Nick begged me to let him take over. And e's my one weak spot. I can say "fuck no" to anyone else, but not to him. So I trusted him, and now the deal's off. Why? Because Jake took Jeannie Hudson, their precious daughter, out, slept with her, and then ghosted her. Her dad, predictably, lost it and kicked me out of the deal. Now I'm sitting in my office, trying to fix this mess.

"Nate, you have to fire him," James, my CFO and best friend, says. "This is the fourteenth deal he's screwed up in eighteen months. We're going to take a huge hit for this."

James is one of the brightest minds I've ever known. We met at Harvard and became very good friends almost instantly. I trust him like no one else. When I was handed the company, I immediately asked him to join me. He gave me a "yes" in a heartbeat and helped me make it an empire. If I listen to anyone, it would be him.

But with Jake? I need to think carefully.

"James, it's not that simple. I'll talk to him first," I say.

"He won't listen. He'll give some lame excuse and screw up again. He's not even in his office, and lunch was over two hours ago."

"Tell my assistant to bring him here the minute he shows up. I'll deal with him. Now, I've got a ton of shit to do," I say, dismissing him.

James nods and leaves.

For the next hour, I work while listening to scientific podcasts to calm down.

Then I get an email, and my heart starts racing.

From: *Charlotte Jones*
To: *Nathan Williams*
Subject: *Let's meet up*
Date: *May 6, 2022, 4:30 p.m.*

Hey stranger, how are you? How's the passionate life of a CEO? How's business going? I have been thinking about you so much lately, knowing it's almost been three months since we last spoke, so I thought, hey? Let's meet up? I'm in San Marcos, Guatemala. There's only a two-hour time difference, so will you be available later, say around 7 PM for you and 5 PM for me? Our usual Skype session would be nice. What do you think?

I miss you, Nate.

Charlotte Jones

Charlotte . . .

Charlotte is the love of my life. We've been together since we were twenty-one. Our relationship has always been easy, really comfortable. We've known each other forever. She's from my world — an heiress to the biggest American jewel company. We went to school together and were always hanging out. James joined us later. We didn't fall in love right away, even though I thought she was the most beautiful woman I'd ever seen. It didn't start like that.

One day, she told me she'd been feeling something for me and needed to be honest. I was too shocked to respond. Our parents pushed us together, James too, and things just fell into place. I gave in to her charm and fell in love later. She understood me, just like I understood her. We were the same. I didn't have to say a word — she knew what I was thinking, and I knew her just as well.

When we turned twenty-three, she told me she was struggling with who she was. She needed time to travel, to live a different life than the one she was always expected to have. She knew she'd take over Jones Diamond eventually, out of love and duty to her family. She's the only heir. But before stepping into her father's shoes, she needed time for herself, to live outside the U.S.

Around the same time, my father's sex scandal hit the news, and I knew I'd have to take over the family business. I begged her to stay, and she did.

When she turned thirty, I proposed. She said, "Yes, but not yet." She told me how much she needed that long trip, to find herself, to see if she could live on her own, relying on no one but herself. I understood her too well. I was living a life I didn't want, and if I had the chance to do something else, I'd take it. I wasn't that lucky, but Charlotte was. I couldn't stop her. I didn't even try. I supported her, helped her pack, but it shattered me.

We agreed to take a break while she was gone. We'd stay single, check in every three months, and never tell each other who we were with. And when she came back, we'd go straight to City Hall and get married that same day. It's been fifteen months now, and she's still not ready to come back.

That's why I stick to one-night stands. No repeats, no attachments. I pick women I know I'll never fall for—usually shallow ones, so it's only about sex. My second rule: I avoid any woman who interests me.

If I find a woman interesting, funny, or fascinating, I walk away. I might be single, but my heart belongs to Charlotte. No one else will ever have it. But sex? That's different. I love sex. I fuck a lot. And I have a type. I only sleep with tall blondes, like Charlotte. I'm six foot one, and I prefer tall women—usually supermodels. These women travel all the time, and they're too busy for a relationship, which suits me perfectly. But no matter what, before, during, and after, I think about Charlotte. Always. And every single time, I come to the same conclusion: *she's the one.*

I type back:

From: *Nathan Williams*
To: *Charlotte Jones*
Subject: *Can we dirty meet virtually?*
Date: *May 6, 2022, 4:33 p.m.*

Hey beautiful,
I would love to see your wonderful face again. I miss you so much, Charlie; it's crazy. Business is business, as usual, but I want to skip that shit and hear everything about you. 7 PM is good for me; I'll make time for you, always.
Love,

Nathan Williams, CEO of Williams Holdings, Inc.

From: *Charlotte Jones*
To: *Nathan Williams*

Subject: *No dirty shit, you know the rule*
Date: *May 6, 2022, 4:38 p.m.*

We are not supposed to flirt, Nate . . . But that's a date! Yayyy! Can't wait to see those crazy blue eyes of yours . . .

Charlotte Jones

From: *Nathan Williams*
To: *Charlotte Jones*
Subject: *You were just flirting, Charlie . . .*
Date: *May 6, 2022, 4:42 p.m.*

*You can't make up rules and not follow them, Charlie.
See ya ;)*

Nathan Williams, CEO of Williams Holdings, Inc.

Funny thing is, when I was with Charlotte, our sex life was . . . *normal?* We weren't into anything wild. We both come from prestigious families, surrounded by very privileged people. There were still rules to respect, proper behavior. That's how it was with Charlotte, and it worked for us. But, to be honest, I became a *munwhore.* The more sex I had, the more depraved I got. I developed some pretty specific tastes.

We make a rule not to talk about our sex lives. I know she's sleeping with others, but I don't need the details. Still, I sometimes imagine what it'll be like when we're together again. I can't wait to do to her what I've done to others. I wonder if she'll respond the same way. Maybe she's changed like I have? Who knows?

I feel lighter after thinking about all that when I hear a knock at the door.

"Come in," I say. Jake walks in, and here we go.

"So, I was summoned by the big boss, huh? Well, here I am," he says, almost proudly.

"Cut the shit, Jake. You really fucked up this time."

"Oh, come on. Don't tell me this is about the Hudson thing. She came on to me, I give her what she wants. It's not my fault I don't wanna marry her, *bro*," he says, dripping with sarcasm. He stares at me, blue eyes locked with blue eyes. That's all we share, just the color of our eyes. And right now, I know I can't show him mercy. I've never given anyone the opportunity to contradict me, to fight me, or to mess with me.

"I don't wanna hear it. You fucked up. We could lose a ton of money because of what you did. But I won't be making the call here. The board will decide if you get demoted or kicked out. Whatever they choose, I'll back them. I'm not protecting you again. You're twenty-nine, time to grow up. Clear your desk and go home. You'll get the report once the decision's made. Now, get out of my office." I say it calm and steady, like a river, showing no emotion. He'll know I'm done with him.

"You serious right now? You know they'll fire me, Nate! You can't let them do this! I'm your *brother!*"

"You've never acted like one. It's over, Jake. Get the hell out of my office."

"I get it. The golden boy. That's what you've always wanted, huh? To get me out of the way, finally. You've got the company, the glory, the family's love, but that wasn't enough. Now you wanna cut me out too? Fucking bastard. But don't think I'll go quietly, brother. You'll see me again," he says, now pacing, arms flailing. *He's panicking.* But I don't give him the satisfaction of correcting him. He always twists things in his favor. No point in saying anything. I just give him a small nod toward the door.

"I look forward to it. Dinner at Mom's on Sunday, remember?"

"Fuck you, Nathan," he spits before storming out.

People who don't know me think I'm cold. People who know me a little think I've been numb since Charlotte left. People who really know me—well, that's just me—know how much it kills me to see Jake like this. But I don't show it. No one could ever guess I'm not okay. I wear a mask that's stuck to my face. And I smile.

I call James to tell him about Jake. The bastard is pleased. Then I get back to work.

Lots to deal with on my desk.

I look at the clock—6:15. Forty-five minutes left. I've been counting the minutes until I can talk to her, see her, love her. But then James barges in, unannounced.

"Hey, man, you okay? Can I talk to you for a sec?" He looks like hell. He's my best friend, so I make time.

"Sure, what's up? You look awful."

"Hayley broke up with me. I feel like shit. But I don't wanna sound like a wuss, and I don't wanna talk about it here. I need to unwind. I wanna take you to Orion tonight. I need a change of scenery. I'll explain, I promise," he says. *Hum, no.*

"I wish I could, but I'm meeting with Charlie in forty-five minutes. Tomorrow, I'm all yours."

"Don't ditch me for a phone call, man. I really need a friend. I was there when Charlotte left you, remember? I was by your side. Now I need you to do the same for me. Just tonight, please!" he begs.

"You're playing dirty. I haven't seen her in three months! You can't ask me that, James!" I say, getting a little angry because deep down, I know he's right.

He's the one who got me through losing Charlotte. He helped with the company too. I shouldn't even be hesitating. *But it's Charlotte, for fuck's sake!*

"Can you ask her if she's free tomorrow? You've waited ninety days, one more won't kill you. I really need you tonight. I'll meet you at Orion in less than an hour, okay? Don't make me beg. I've no pride left after the last two hours of my life," he pleads. Fuck.

"I'll email her. But this is the last time I'm ditching her for you, got it?" I say, not happy about it.

"First and last. Thanks, man. I'll see you at Orion," he says, and leaves.

Shit.

I open my inbox and try to come up with an excuse, so she doesn't think she's not my priority.

From*: Nathan Williams*
To: *Charlotte Jones*
Subject: *Unexpected meeting*
Date: *May 6, 2022, 6:25 p.m.*

Hey sweetheart,

I'm so, so sorry. I have to reschedule our Skype session. I have an emergency board meeting about some shit Jake did (I'll tell you more about it. No, he did not calm the fuck down). I tried to arrange things so they wouldn't need me, but it's impossible. Can we speak tomorrow, please?

Nathan Williams, CEO of Williams Holdings, Inc.

From: *Charlotte Jones*
To: *Nathan Williams*
Subject: *Fine by me*
Date: *May 6, 2022, 6:28 p.m.*

It's totally fine. Tomorrow is perfect, same time :) I hope your situation will be better with your brother. I'll be thinking about you. See you tomorrow

Charlotte Jones

Now I feel guilty.

Even though I'm tempted to reply to her "I'll be thinking about you" with something kinky, it was never like that with Charlotte.

Deep down, I fear she wouldn't have responded the way I wanted her to. So, I just send a quick thank you and get back to some important files before heading to Orion. It's not far, but I ask Tyler, my driver, to take me so I can respond to a few more emails on the way.

James and I are regulars at Orion. It's a bar connected to the Rigel Hotel, a fancy high-end spot where powerful people can relax without being watched. I always have a private seat there. I'm a famous personality in the business, so no need to let my arrival be known.

Orion is nice, though I've seen better. Honestly, it's the name that draws me in—anything related to the stars, and I'm game. No one really knows about my love for astronomy except my family, James, and Charlotte, of course. But the place has a good vibe. The décor is dark and poetic, with plush leather seating.

It's a prestigious spot, no doubt, but I've grown used to places like this. I've been to grander, more breathtaking venues. Still, I enjoy the familiar feel—the soft light from the chandeliers, the quiet hum of conversation, the weight of a drink in my hand. It's a sanctuary, a place where I can forget the pressures of work for a bit and just enjoy a drink with a friend.

When Tyler pulls up to the entrance, I'm still buried in my emails, so he gives me a moment to realize we've arrived. I didn't have time to go home and change, but I doubt they'll mind my Brioni three-piece suit.

I get out of the car, tell Tyler goodbye, and let him know I'll call when I'm ready to leave. The doorman opens the door to Orion for me, and I step inside.

~

Friday, May 6, 2022, 7:30 p.m.

As I enter the bar, a hostess approaches me right away.

"Good evening, Mr. Williams. Your seat will be ready in less than two minutes. You can wait here or head to the bar, where your favorite whiskey will be waiting for you. Which do you prefer, sir?" she asks.

"I don't mind standing here, thank you. Mr. Kingston will join me shortly," I reply.

She smiles and leaves.

Only then do I look around. The alcoves are almost full, and I recognize many of the regulars. My eyes drift to the bar, where I spot a woman I've never seen before. I only see her profile: delicate nose, red lips, and a cascade of brown hair falling on her back, held by a golden pin. She's wearing a black dress that stops mid-thigh, showing off her light curves. She's stunning. And alone. *Is she . . . writing? On a piece of paper?*

"Mr. Williams, your seat is ready. Will you follow me?" The hostess returns, and I lose sight of the woman at the bar until I reach my alcove, which faces the back of the beautiful brunette.

As I sit, the barmaid hands me my glass of Bowmore whiskey. I thank her and pull out my phone to let James know I've arrived.

I take a sip, savoring the rich, smoky flavor, but my gaze keeps drifting back to *her*. I can only see her back and that long, shiny brown hair covering her dress. Her waist is slim, her hips perfect. Every now and then, she glances around, giving me quick glimpses of her profile. She really is gorgeous. And yet I know I won't approach her. I won't try to fuck her. She's too . . . *captivating*. Something about her feels off-limits.

As I wait for James, I keep watching her, curious about what she's doing. The most surprising thing is that she's writing with a pen and paper. Is she working? Does she not have an office? At least a laptop? Is she a student? But even students use computers now, don't they? So many questions swirl in my mind.

Then she laughs. *Alone.* How intriguing. Maybe she's drunk? But what kind of student works on a paper while boozing up? She looks too classy for that. It's gotta be something else. As I sit there wondering, I text James, who doesn't seem to be in any rush to join me for that drink.

Nate: *Where the fuck are you?*

James: *I'll be there soon, dealing with something, and then I'll come.*

Nate: *I didn't want to go out tonight; you made me. I had better plans, yet I'm stuck in this fucking bar waiting for your fucking ass. Being evasive? Come on!*

James: *I'll tell you everything once I'm there. Go talk to some nice blonde in the meantime.*

Nate: *Fuck you.*

James: *I love you too. See ya in a bit.*

What the fuck is going on tonight?

I watch her again, drawn to her like a magnet. Then I notice Brett Stiles, heir to one of the biggest oil companies in the country—rich, powerful, influential, and handsome. *Damn, I'm screwed.*

He's walking toward her, probably offering her a drink. Wait, she's turning him down? He's insisting, but now the barmaid steps in. Gorgeous is laughing, but Brett isn't. The barmaid does most of the talking while Gorgeous goes back to her writing. Brett leaves, thank God. The barmaid returns to her duties, and Gorgeous acts like nothing happened.

What the fuck?

I've never seen Brett Stiles get rejected by a woman. Married women would throw themselves at him. Is Gorgeous taken? I need to stop thinking about this.

I open my email and try to focus on work. But the questions pile up. Why did the barmaid step in? What is Gorgeous writing? Why would she turn down someone like Brett? I can't deal with this right now. I focus on my emails. Williams Holdings is what matters, not this woman.

But I can't concentrate.

I've never been in this situation before. I've never had to chase a beautiful woman. It sounds arrogant, but it's just the truth. I've never been so captivated by someone, either.

When I was with Charlotte, no woman ever tempted me. I didn't let them. I've always been closed off to feelings, keeping myself only for Charlotte. Thinking about her keeps me grounded, focused on my ultimate goal—getting her back and being together forever.

It's 8:15 p.m., and I've been here for forty-five fucking minutes. Still no sign of James. Why haven't I left? Because I can't stop watching her. I've seen at least eight guys try to hit on her, and they all get shut down, helped by the barmaid. And she keeps writing. I can't stop wondering what she's writing. Who even writes on paper these days?

I have to see her up close. That's it. The restrooms are on the other side of the bar. If I walk over there, I'll get a closer look at her face. It's not weird to go to the bathroom after two whiskeys and two waters, right? I actually do need to go. I just need to make sure I don't stare at her.

"Just go to the restroom like a normal guy. Don't act like a creep. Take a piss, and on the way back, sneak a quick look at her. Keep it cool," I mutter to myself. Damn, why am I so anxious?

I get up and head to the restroom, careful not to walk too close to her. I do what I have to do, then take a deep breath before leaving. When I step out, I finally see her.

In the soft glow of the bar's light, she stands out—a striking figure, almost otherworldly in her beauty. Her long brown hair, pinned with a gold clip, flows down her back like silk. Her light-brown eyes, highlighted with a touch of eyeliner, give her gaze a sharp, feline intensity. Her red lips curve slightly, as if she were hiding a secret smile.

Those lips . . . God, that mouth.

She's so fucking beautiful. Her black dress hugs her curves just right, elegant but not revealing too much. It's enough to leave a lot to the imagination. And my imagination is going wild.

But it's not just her looks. There's something more, something about her that pulls me in. It feels like the universe lined up just to bring us to this moment. I can't take my eyes off her. She's the most beautiful woman I've ever seen—a goddess among mortals, a vision that I can't forget. I feel like I've discovered something rare, like a hidden gem in the vastness of the cosmos.

And as I stand there, spellbound by her presence, I just know that I will never forget this moment.

As I stand there, mesmerized by her beauty, I find myself unable to look away, drawn to her like a moth to a flame.

As I stand there, lost in the depths of her gaze, I know with a certainty that surpasses reason—I am seriously, deeply, and ultimately fucked up.

What the hell have I gotten myself into?

I stand frozen for what feels like an eternity before I force myself back to my table. I need to be closer to her, just to feel her presence. My heartbeat quickens the closer I get. She doesn't even notice me, doesn't see me at all. I'm invisible to her, but she's all I can see.

I walk past her and hear her speak to the barmaid. *Her voice . . .* it's soft, like a symphony echoing in my soul. She isn't saying anything important, but the sound of her voice captivates me. It's as if she existed in her own world, untouched by everything around her. And I'm completely enchanted by just the sound of her voice.

Leaving her behind feels like torture, but I drag myself back to my seat. I sit down, unable to move, think, or do anything.

"Who are you, Gorgeous?" I mutter to myself. I try calling James again, but he doesn't pick up. Yet I'm not going anywhere.

Then she stands up, runs her hands over her dress to smooth it out. I'm fucking jealous of her hands. She says something to the barmaid, grabs her purse, and puts her papers inside. *Shit, is she leaving?* I really hope not. But she's walking toward the restroom, not the exit.

What the fuck is wrong with me?

Do I stand up and join her?

Shit, I have to summon every fiber of my being to resist the urge to rise and follow her. Every fiber of my body begs for me to join her in that confined space that is the restroom.

I want to follow her, I'd be behind her, and as she's closing the door, she'd see me, she'd recognize me, her breathing would intensify, her magnificent breasts would rise and fall with her heartbeat. She'd raise her head to meet my gaze and open her alluring fucking mouth in an O shape. I wouldn't be able to resist. I'd lean in and kiss her, slow at first, tasting and testing. She'd open up for me, I'd slide my tongue inside that mouth of hers. I'd put my hand on her waist, push her to the wall, encircling her with my arms.

She'd put her fantastic legs around my waist, and I'd start mouthfucking her. I'd put my hand on her calf, sliding slowly toward her thighs, teasing her. She'd grind against me all the more. I'd feel the heat from her pussy on my very erect cock, still in our clothes. I'd slide my hand to her core, sliding a finger between her folds, reaching her clit, and then she'd moan my name, and I'd . . .

My phone buzzes, snapping me out of my fantasy.

> **James:** *I'm sorry I'm late, wait for me.*
> **Nate:** *Please know, that in my entire life so far, never have I wished to see you more than right fucking now. I'm fucked up man, I'll tell you when you're here.*
> **James:** *Haha, are women throwing themselves at you and you don't know how to push them off your dick?*
> **Nate:** *Believe me when I say: I FUCKING WISH!*
> **James:** *Wow, that's a first.*

He can't come fast enough.

There she is. She comes out of the restroom, as beautiful as ever, looking around as if making sure no one followed her. Maybe? *I'd protect you, Gorgeous.*

As I watch her come out of the restroom, everything seems to slow down. She moves with a quiet grace that doesn't seem to fit in this dark place. Every step she takes looks elegant in its own way. She doesn't seem to notice the attention she's getting from everyone, completely lost in her own world as she walks back to her seat.

I can't stop looking at her, totally captivated. She seems both confident and a bit unsure, which somehow makes her even more interesting. And fuck, she's perfect.

Honestly, the most beautiful woman I've ever seen—Charlotte included.

That thought alone should make me get up and leave. I should just walk out, tell James to screw himself. I've been sitting here for almost an hour, trapped in my own head. I know I should leave, forget this night ever happened. I should pray I never see her again, never find out her name or what she tastes like. I should just go.

But I just can't. *I just fucking can't.*

Something inside me says if I leave, something bad will happen. I have no idea why I feel this way. This has never happened to me before. But I can't leave until I know she's okay.

She's back on her stool now, flipping her hair behind her, pulling out her pen and papers from her purse. She starts writing again.

I sip my drink, watching her. Why is she using a pen and paper in this day and age? Maybe writing by hand feels more personal, more real. Maybe it calms her. Or maybe she likes the idea of having something solid, something lasting, instead of just typing on a screen. Who knows?

And then there's Logan fucking Danes. He's a big shot in the media business, and he's known for being good with women. Nobody says no to him. Yeah, he has charm, sure, but does he seriously think trying to hit on her for the third fucking time will work? What the fuck?

Where's Blondie barmaid who usually helps her out? And now Logan's starting to look pissed. I try to see her reaction. I stand up and move closer so I can hear better. She looks nervous.

He's pushing too hard. She's fucking panicking. He's fucking insisting.

What do I do? What do I do? What do I do? Get out of the bar, get out of the fucking bar, get out of the motherfucking bar, get out of the damn motherfucking bar NOW!

Fuck me, I can't, I have to . . . *shit.*

I decide to follow my fucking instincts instead. *Let's go.* I get closer to her and then begins the scene I was fucking fantasying about for over an hour:

"Sorry, babe, I'm late," I say, wrapping my arms around her waist from behind and kissing the top of her head. She doesn't pull away. Her hair smells like lavender, and she grabs my hands, holding them tight. *Yes, baby, I'm here. I've got you, keep touching me.*

I can't even begin to understand what is going on. All I know is, for the first time in forever, I feel like I can finally . . . *breathe.*

What the fuck?

CHAPTER 3
Delilah

"Hey, baby, it's okay, I kept myself busy."

I don't even try to understand what's coming out of my mouth. I'm shocked. I grab his hands and hold them tight so he won't leave. He feels good. I turn to look at him, and he's, without a doubt, the most beautiful man I've ever seen.

He's dressed in a perfectly tailored suit that fits his figure effortlessly. There's a mystery about him, a pull I can't explain. His face is sharp and flawless, almost unreal, like a statue, drawing me in without effort.

It's not just the clothes—it's *him*. He radiates quiet strength, more than just a man.

As I hold him, I feel like I'm in the presence of something rare, someone powerful.

Our eyes meet, and his soft smile sends a rush through my body. His blue eyes, intense like lightning, seem to see right into me. I've never felt so drawn to a stranger, but being near him brings an unexpected calm. He moves closer, his touch gentle, and I feel an undeniable connection between us. When he reaches out, I take his hand without hesitation, letting myself be carried away by his charm.

"Oh, hey, Williams, right? Sorry, my mistake, I thought she was . . . never mind, man, I apologize," Logan says, clearly panicked. He looks really intimidated by . . . *Williams?*

That's his name, right?

As Logan leaves, I turn into William's still-holding arms. Now . . . he's smiling.

"Okay, pretty boy, thanks for your help, you can go now," I say. But as I speak, he looks at me, silent, analyzing me. *Weird.*

"Hello? Earth to Williams? Do we even pronounce the 's' at the end? Sorry if I mispronounced," I say, a little embarrassed by his silence. He's still looking into my eyes, tracing the contour of my face, settling on my lips. *Okay, that's sexy as fuck.*

Focus, Delilah.

"Actually, I'm Nate. Nate Williams. Yes, we pronounce the 's,' by the way. And you are?" he says as he takes the stool next to mine.

"Thanking you for rescuing me and wishing you a good night . . . *Nate*," I say with a smile, so he doesn't feel offended or something. But he doesn't move, intensifying his gaze on me. He's studying me in complete silence.

"So, you know my name, but I can't know yours? Sounds unfair, don't you think?" he says, his voice taking on a wonderful tone.

"You *don't* want to know my name. You *don't* want to know who I am, and you sure as fuck *don't* want to stay seated next to me. Go away, pretty boy. Don't waste your time, I'm not game," I say, trying to push him away. I mastered that skill years ago. I'll use it tonight, *one last time.*

"I beg to differ, baby. I *do* want to know your name, I *do* want to know more about you, and I sure as fuck *do* want to stay seated next to you," he says, chuckling. Things are getting complicated. He's getting close, familiar even. I don't feel like I dislike it, but I don't feel like I should keep talking to him. *Broken-hearted bitch me.*

"Can we forget the whole thing and pretend we never talked? You can walk away, and I won't look at you while you do it. Please?"

"Not a chance," he says, straight-faced.

"I beg your pardon?"

"What's your name? I'm not here to cause drama or give you a hard time, I swear. I'm just curious, that's all. You know my name. Let me know yours, and the mystery's solved," he says, flashing one of the most exquisite smiles I've ever seen. He's using a tone that adds a humorous twist to the conversation, which I appreciate. *He's charming.*

"Delilah," I cave, easily. What's a name? He saved me, after all. I can give a little.

"You don't play fair, Delilah," he says, still roaming with his gaze all over me. And in this act, I feel like he's giving me . . . *power?*

"How come, *baby?*" Aaaaand now is when I should stop drinking. But honestly, he's giving me something to think about. The lightness of this conversation soothes my heart, my body, and my soul, somehow, in a way I can't explain. The humor allows me to approach this final evening with ease, freeing my mind from its demons, simply by giving me a somewhat normal conversation with a stranger who seems . . . *kind.*

I don't know if it's the alcohol or something else about him, but I start to wonder—why stop here? Since I'm laughing, still alive, and maybe even "healing," why not continue this exchange with this Nate Williams before saying goodbye to this world? *It won't hurt my eyes.*

He smiles at my reply, then pulls my stool closer, making our legs touch. The closeness is sweet and spicy. Things are heating up, but I don't care. I've got nothing left to lose. If things are heading this way, let's just fucking go.

"How come? You can't be the most gorgeous woman in the room—in all rooms combined—inviting sin among even the strongest men, with the most beautiful name, the purest name in history. You're so fucking gorgeous it hurts. Your name's biblical and sexy at the same time. It's intriguing, just like you."

"And do you really need to be that close to my face while insulting me?" I say, grinning.

"I'd be closer if you'd let me," he murmurs, leaning in as if to bite my cheek. I manage to pull his head away, laughing hard. So is he.

"Get off!" I say, still laughing. Nate smoothly rests his hands on my thighs, just behind my knees. The gesture feels natural, and it doesn't bother me. I won't try to understand why. Nate is pure sexiness.

Still, I can't control what I say or how I act. I'm possessed by old demons, and my true nature comes out. It kills me to be this way, but thankfully, I won't have to endure it much longer.

"Seriously, Nate," I say, regaining composure. "You look really, *really* handsome. Beautiful, even. I'd bet good money no woman turns you down. Do you even need to talk to women? They must throw themselves at you. Look around—plenty of women here tonight. Just go and let me be, okay? It was nice, though. Thank you for this, but I'd like to get back to my thing, *alone*." I put my hands on top of his. And again, he looks deeply into my eyes, and I do the same. His eyes are such a deep light blue, like shards of ice. They pierce through the soul with their cold beauty, serene yet powerful. My heart skips a beat.

"I don't see them, nor do I want to. I have no interest in looking anywhere but at you. What's your deal, Delilah?" His voice is filled with concern. That bothers me.

Okay, time to part ways.

"Okay, enjoy the rest of your night, Nate," I say, pushing his hands away, closing myself off. He seems to realize I'm about to tell him to fuck off.

"Wait, no, I'm sorry, I didn't mean to offend you. Let's start over. Hi, I'm Nate. I think you're beautiful, and I'd like a chance to share a drink with you," he says, holding out his hand.

"Nice try, pretty boy. Hey, I'm Delilah. I'm the least interested woman here. I'm boring as shit, probably more damaged than anything. Oh, and I'm only looking for a husband. Will you marry me, Nate?" I reply, hoping to scare him off, but it backfires.

"Let's go to Vegas," he says, dead serious, making me burst out laughing. He laughs too.

"What's your deal?" I ask, regaining control.

"No, no," he tuts, shaking his head, "you can't ask me that if you can't answer it yourself, babe."

"Will you stop with the 'babe' already? I wasn't asking like you were. I mean, why are you still here with me when you could be over there with someone more like . . . you?" I say, pointing toward the alcoves and then at him. He's doing that deep-eye thing again.

Ice-blue eyes.

"What do you mean, someone like me?"

"You know . . . You look so . . ." I say, making a happy face. "And then look at me, I look so . . ." I make a sad face.

"What? Beautiful? Gorgeous? Alluring? Sexy as hell? Take your pick, baby," he says seriously. I laugh hard, and he seems to like it, because his hands return to my waist, feeling natural again. Before I know it, my hands are on his strong arms. *I like those.*

"You're saying this because you want to fuck me, *baby*," I say, using a voice I didn't know I had. The tension between us is thick.

"No, Delilah. I *really* want to fuck you. It's becoming a need the more time passes. But I meant what I said," he says, caressing my thighs while locking eyes with me.

"How is this conversation even real?" I ask, still close to him. I barely recognize myself.

"As real as it gets, babe."

"Are you going to keep calling me that?"

"All night long. But in my head, I called you Gorgeous." *What?*

"Care to explain?" I ask.

"I didn't just see you now, Delilah. I've been watching you for over an hour. Not in a creepy way, but from my usual seat over there. I only saw your back, but I was drawn to you. The woman writing. The woman not noticing anyone. Not even me," he says, frowning.

"It's not about you. It's not even about them. It's . . . complicated," I manage, feeling unsure.

"You don't have to explain," he says, his voice softer.

"Thank you. But honestly, I'd prefer to be alone. It was fun, though. You'll never know how much it eased my mind. But I'm not looking for anything with anyone. No offense."

"None taken. Is the barmaid your friend?" he asks, switching the topic, catching me off guard.

"No, I just met her. She's been nice. Why?"

"Because every time a guy tried to approach you, she stepped in. I thought she was looking out for you."

"Oh, yeah, she knows I want to be left alone tonight."

The more I say it, the less I believe it. My heart wants to keep talking to him, to "open up." But my body shuts down, controlled by old traumas. I want to tell him to stay, that he's giving me the lightness I need. But I push him away, hating myself for it.

Nate looks at me like he's trying to figure me out, and it makes me uncomfortable, off-balance.

"Don't try to solve a mystery where there's nothing. There's nothing, Nate. Stop wasting your time," I say, colder than I mean to.

"If you knew me, you'd know I value my time. If I'm here with you, it means I think it's time well spent," he says with a grin.

Ugh. I can't fight it. I smile, genuinely.

"And so you called me Gorgeous."

"And so I called you Gorgeous, obviously. But Delilah is sexier."

I have to laugh.

This is nice. He's getting closer, his hands on my thighs again, and it feels . . . *hot.*

"Do you plan to keep your hands on my thighs?" I ask, amused.

"Baby, I'm fighting every urge to keep them from wandering elsewhere."

Ouch, dangerous. Let's play with him a little. I have nothing left to lose.

"Like onto someone else?" I tease. He leans in, lips near my ear, grasping my waist tight like he's holding back, sending a shiver through me.

"Like onto your pussy, baby. I want my hands all over you. I want to wet my fingers on your tongue, then slide them down to your pussy. I'd tease your clit with my thumb, then slip a finger inside, making you moan my name and beg for more until you're starving for my big cock. Am I clear enough on wanting just *you*, or do you need more details?" *Okay. I'm really turned on now. Let's see where this goes.*

"So, you think you have a big cock?" I ask.

"Let's get out of here and find out," he says, standing and taking my hand.

"Not so fast, pretty boy. I never said I was convinced," I say, sitting back down. He exhales in frustration, then laughs.

"You're teasing me, baby," he says, hugging me, resting his head on my neck. It feels nice, not awkward. I don't feel the need to push him away. *This is surreal.*

"I wasn't the one caressing your thighs and whispering about sex," I laugh.

"Feel free to touch me all you want. Here, take my ear, whisper something dirty," he says, leaning his ear toward my lips.

Let's play. I use my sexiest voice.

"Not. Going. To. Happen. I told you, I'm not what you're looking for. There are plenty of willing women here. Take that big cock and have fun," I say, biting his earlobe for extra spice.

"I only heard you talking about my cock. I'm hard, baby. Put me out of my misery, please," he says, pouting. I giggle. He's funny, I'll give him that.

I spot Jenna from across the bar. She gives me a curious look. I wink to let her know I'm okay. She flashes me a big thumbs-up and goes back to work.

"You're funny. But even though I'm not getting naked with you, I should tell you—I'm no good in bed. You'd be disappointed," I admit. He looks at me like I just told a huge lie, which I didn't.

"Bullshit."

"Nope. Sad but true."

"If you give me the honor of proving you wrong, I'd die a happy man," he whispers, and presses a kiss to my cheek. This may look like a normal gesture, something barely noticeable, almost meaningless, but it makes my heart race. I feel it for the first time in forever. I don't dwell on it and push the thought away. Still, I feel the blush creep onto my face. *Embarrassing . . .*

"Oh, come on! I'm giving you a way out here!" I laugh, trying to hide my embarrassment.

"But I want a way *in!*" he insists, using a childlike voice, grabbing my waist again.

"I don't let people in," I respond with a sad smile.

"Who's the motherfucker responsible for your sadness? Give me a name, I'll handle it," he demands, his tone turning serious.

"It's not just a man, it's more complicated. I can't explain it. Want me to sing it?" I ask playfully.

"Be my guest," he challenges, clearly not believing me. He must think I won't go through with it.

And then, without even thinking, I start singing Benson Boone's song, just the chorus, deliberately changing a few words. I don't even think about it; I just let my soul cry as I sing:

I'm still holdin' on to everything that's dead and gone
I don't wanna say goodbye, 'cause this one means forever
And I'll be in the stars and this shit never felt so far
There I'll be alone between the heavens and the embers
Oh, it hurts so hard
For a million different reasons
They took the best of my heart
And left the rest in pieces

I know I can sing. I know I have a beautiful voice, but I've never *felt* like I had one. When I open my eyes, I'm met with a very moved Nate. He's quiet for a minute, so I decide to break the silence.

"Feel free to interpret it however you like, but I'm not offering more. That's all I have to say."

"I'm speechless. You have the most beautiful voice I've ever heard in my entire life. I'm spellbound."

"Thank you," I reply, and I mean it.

"I take it you don't want to share your story with me."

"It's not about you," I respond, the words heavy.

"What if I share a bit of my story with you? Would that help?" he asks.

"I doubt it. I'm not sure I'm interested in you sharing your story either," I say, chuckling.

"Well, I'm taking a shot. Here goes. I'm Nathan Williams, but my friends and family call me Nate. I'm thirty-three. Born and raised in New York. I have an evil little brother, an overbearing mother, a problematic father. I run the family business, but it's not what I wanted. I've always been into science, a proper nerd, if I may say so. I'm passionate about the universe, the cosmos, the stars, all of it. I studied it as much as I could, but I was forced to go to law school and then business school. I excelled, obviously, but now I just listen to astrophysics podcasts and donate to research programs. Now everyone's on my ass to run for the senatorial campaign, and I couldn't care less. So?"

I laugh as he spills all this information in ten seconds flat. He sounds interesting, but something is still missing.

"What about women?"

"No, no, baby. Give me some info about you, and then I'll share the rest," he says with a wide grin. *Bastard.*

"Okay, let me think . . . I'm Delilah Rose. I'm twenty-five, though I was supposed to turn twenty-six in a few weeks. I have no family; I won't go into detail. Well, I had Ashley, who I considered a sister, but she's gone. Anyway, I work as an assistant in a print store, boring, I know. I've been in New York for a while. No formal education, though not by choice. I've always been smart. I like singing, but you already knew that.

That's pretty much it."

I'm surprised I reveal that much. I realize how different we are, coming from two separate worlds. It would never work between us, and that comforts me. He looks at me with suspicion.

"Why did you say you were supposed to turn twenty-six?" *Shit. How do I dodge this?*

"Alcohol," I reply, raising my drink. He doesn't buy it, but he lets it slide.

"You're quite the mystery, Delilah. I want to know more," he says softly.

"And you're full of surprises, Nathan. I really thought you'd bail after my story. Why are you still here? Are you that desperate to fuck me that my story didn't scare you off?"

"First, I *do* want to fuck you, very much. I will fuck you good, believe me. Second, your story doesn't scare me at all. I don't care about your past. I'm intrigued at best, but that doesn't change the fact that I want you."

"I told you, I'm not good at sex," I admit, exhaling.

"I beg to differ. I don't even want to think about the asshole who had you before, but I can tell you, he didn't do it right. The woman always comes first, at least three times, before the guy even thinks about it. And I do, baby." He smirks, giving me a wink. *Cocky bastard.*

This shouldn't work on me, but it does. No one's ever spoken to me this directly, and I actually like it. He takes my hand and kisses it.

"Sweet." I smile. Then he licks my hand, and when I try to pull it away, he holds on firmly.

"Gross!" I laugh out loud.

"Let's get out of here. My driver's waiting. We can be at my place in ten minutes, or would you rather we go to yours?"

"Driver? I knew you were rich, but not that rich!"

"I don't show all my cards at once."

"And the fact that I'm broke doesn't bother you? I could be a gold-digger."

"You're no gold-digger, baby," he says, completely assured.

"And how would you know that?"

"Because we'd already be at my place. We'd be fucking in the restroom by now even. That's a gold-digger."

"I could be playing hard to get," I tease, making him laugh.

"A real gold-digger would know exactly who I am and what I'm worth. No one plays hard to get with me. Too dangerous of a gamble."

"I hate to break it to you, babe, but you're so full of yourself."

"And I want you to be so full of myself too. Trust me, it feels good," he says, pulling me into his arms, pretending to bite my neck. I burst out laughing at the boldness.

"Delilah," he says, suddenly serious.

"Yes?" I reply, still amused.

"I want to kiss you." *He. Did. Not.*

"You already kissed my hand. Isn't that enough?" Now it's his turn to laugh.

"Not even close."

The truth is, I *want* to kiss him too. But the last person I kissed was Eric, and it broke me. He left his mark on me—on my body, my heart, my soul. And I wish, oh how I wish, to wash it all away. I'm freeing my soul tonight. Might as well free my body too, right?

"I'll tell you what, Nathan. I'm not going to kiss you out of lust or attraction or even because you asked me to. I'm going to kiss you because I think it could heal a part of me that is desperate to be mended. Right now it's with you, but it could have been with someone else. But, God knows why, you seem perfect for the job. And willing. Just a kiss, though!" I don't even finish my last sentence before Nate already stands up and positions himself between my legs. He grabs me by the waist, pulling me flush against him, then holds my head in both hands.

"It could have only been me. I'll gladly heal every part of you that needs me right now. No going back, baby. Ready? Damn, I'm not even sure I'll be able to stop." I nod to show him I agree.

He leans into me, keeping his eyes open, staring into mine. He parts his lips and then closes them on mine. When our lips meet, something happens. A connection, I think—a tie, maybe, something magnetic, a strange force surrounds us. And I close my eyes. He kisses me, slowly at first, as if he were savoring me or even making sure this is real. He holds my face, caressing my cheeks with his thumbs. The kiss is slow, soft even. My heart races, and I dare to touch him. I place my hands on his, silently begging him not to stop. Not to let me go.

I want to die, but right now, I want to live. I'm certain he feels it because he presses me to open, and I gladly do. His tongue glides into my mouth, dancing with mine. He deepens the kiss. It's erotic for sure, but it's . . . more. His hand moves to my waist, pulling me even closer, and I feel him. He is hard. I can't help but moan into his mouth, unable to hold it back. He loves it, and now he's devouring my mouth while I grind against him. My hands in his hair, our connection deepens. I dare to think it's even more intense than it ever was with Eric. I dare to think this is the first time in my life I'm truly met with lust, desire, craving—hunger.

I don't want to stop. I can't stop. I won't stop. In my head, I sing. I don't know what or even why, and I'm not trying to understand. I let myself be. And damn, it feels good.

Then he releases me, and I instantly miss him. I don't know him, I don't love him, but his body is somehow connected to mine, and I already miss it.

"Delilah, let's get out of here, I beg you, let's get out of here." Shit! I hadn't even realized we're still at the bar, and everyone around us must have seen what just happened. Oh my God, he must feel so embarrassed. *Shit, I've gone too far.*

"I'm so sorry, I forgot about this place and the people. I'm sorry, you must feel embarrassed as hell," I say, my face heating up.

"I don't give a damn about what's around us, but Delilah, if I'm not inside you within five minutes, things are really going to be embarrassing for me," he replies, glancing at his crotch. I burst out laughing. Yes, tonight is surreal in every way.

I stay close to him to hide his erection.

"I'm sorry, baby, your mouth is covered with red lipstick," I laugh, trying to clean the contour of his lips with my thumb. The gesture feels so intimate, even comforting.

It's hard to explain.

"Let them see," he murmurs, removing my hand. I laugh again.

"Wait, did you say five minutes? I thought you lived ten minutes from here."

"I'll tell my driver to drive faster. I'll take you in the car first, then I'll take you in my bed. All night. I want to smell you on my sheets for the next ten weeks." That makes me giggle like a schoolgirl. Really. He looks at me with the biggest smile.

"Nate, it's not a good idea. I have other plans. It was just a kiss. A really good one, but I told you, I have no intention of pushing things further."

"What other plans?" he asks, looking upset. *Shit, I have to stop this. I have to stop him.*

"Things that are my business only. You should go back to your booth and enjoy the rest of your night the way you planned it," I say coldly.

"Why are you pushing me away? What have I done?"

"I told you, it's not about you. We had fun, now the moment is gone," I reply, frustrated.

"This is bullshit, Delilah. What just happened was incredible. Don't even try to deny it. Give me some credit here."

"It's not about you."

"Then what the hell is this about?" he asks, frowning as he tries to understand. But no one can.

"Don't pretend my existence means something to you. You just want to fuck me. That's flattering, though, thank you. You brought some lightness to my heavy night. I appreciate it, but now I need to be alone."

"For reasons far beyond me, I can't. You don't want to talk to me anymore, fine. But I'll stay here until you leave and make sure you're safe," he says, returning to his drink as if nothing happened.

"You're overreacting. I don't need protection. I just need to be left alone." I'm getting more exasperated.

"I'll stop talking, but I won't leave. You need me, I can feel it. I'm not going anywhere," he says, putting some distance between our stools.

He waves Jenna over, and she arrives almost instantly.

"I'll have another whiskey, please. And a plate of your best food. And whatever Delilah wants is on me," he adds.

"Of course, sir. I'll be right back," she says, winking at me.

"I don't need your charity," I mutter, my voice low.

"It's not charity, it's called being a gentleman," he replies, grinning from ear to ear.

"Damn. Gold-diggers must have trained you well," I quip. He laughs, and it clears the air a little.

"You're something else, baby, I'll give you that. I miss you, by the way." He pouts.

Okay, he's cute.

"You don't know me, so you can't miss me," I say sarcastically.

"And yet, I do."

"I'm right here," I point out, gesturing at myself. He stretches his arm, trying to reach me but fails. I laugh at the ridiculousness of it all. I need to think about something else.

"Nathan, tell me something about the stars," I ask, inviting him to sit closer to me. He does so immediately, resting his elbow on the bar, leaning toward me, and I mimic his pose.

"Stars have different colors that show how hot they are. Blue stars are the hottest, and red ones are cooler. It's the opposite of what we usually think. Our Sun, which is yellow, is somewhere in the middle," he says with a smile.

"Wow, that's so interesting! How does a star start?" I ask, and he lights up.

"Stars form from huge clouds of gas and dust in space. These clouds get pulled together by gravity, and as they squeeze tighter, the center gets really hot. When it gets hot enough, the gas inside starts to smash together, creating a ton of energy. That's when a star is born, and it can keep burning for millions or even billions of years, depending on how big it is," he explains, bringing the universe to life before my eyes.

It's impressive.

"How could you possibly know all this?" I ask, astonished. This man becomes more intriguing by the second. He just shrugs.

"Do you think we join them after we die?" I ask.

"I don't know, baby," he responds, placing his hand on my thigh. The gesture feels so natural. Familiar.

"So, am I red, or am I blue?" I tease, trying to lighten the mood.

"You're a bit of red and a bit of blue," he replies with a smile.

"So, I'm purple, then."

"Fits you perfectly. Purple is the color of ambiguity and balance. It's a mix of warm red and cool blue, symbolizing the balance between opposing forces or emotions. Just like you. You're hot and cold. One moment we're making out, the next you're pushing me away," he says, pouting.

"That's unfair! Accurate, but still unfair. What's your color?"

He pauses, thinking.

"People who don't know me might say black, but I'd call myself navy," he replies before counting on his fingers. "First: authority and strength. Second: seriousness and stability. And third: sophistication and elegance," he finishes with a sly smile. *Cute.*

"Full of yourself," I say, raising my glass. He opens his mouth to respond, but I cut him off.

"No, I won't be full of yourself," I laugh.

"A man can dream, I guess." He takes my hand, kissing it again.

Then I hear it. This song. It's the most beautiful thing I've ever listened to. It's more than music, it's poetry. It's playing as background noise, but that doesn't do it justice. It should be heard by thousands, listened to while dreaming. My heart feels heavier. Nate notices, tightening his grip on my hand.

"What's going on, baby?" he asks, concerned.

"It's just this song. I love it," I say softly.

"What's it called?"

"'Saturn' by Sleeping At Last. Every time I hear it, I feel like I'm in a trance." We stop everything to listen until the song ends.

"It's beautiful. We'll listen to it again at my house in the Hamptons. At night, you can see the stars like you're in the middle of nowhere. It's magical. We'll drink wine, I'll play the song through the speakers, and we'll watch the sky together," he says, dead serious.

"A bit ahead of yourself, aren't you?" I tease him.

"Stop pretending already. You know that this"—he gestures between us—"this is happening."

"This"—I gesture back—"ends tonight."

"Give me your phone," he says seriously. *What the hell?* He doesn't know, but I'll tell him the truth.

"I don't have a phone," I say.

"You're messing with me, right?"

"I swear I'm not," I say, smiling.

"Where's your phone, Delilah?" he demands.

"I left it behind," I say. He looks behind me, even though I'm on a backless stool.

"Open your purse, you little liar." I hand him my purse, and he rummages through it, finding nothing.

"Stop messing with me, or I'll check your boobs for it," he says, almost annoyed. I laugh and stand between his legs, arms wide open.

"Okay, officer, search me. I swear I don't have any drugs. Please, be gentle. I'm fragile," I joke, smiling. He laughs, cursing under his breath before starting his "search." He palms my breasts, taking his time, massaging them, and I feel a rush of desire. My nipples harden, and unexpectedly, Nate kisses the top of my cleavage. I don't pull away, I press my hand on his neck, urging him to continue. He groans, grabs my waist, and raises his head to kiss me deeply. I wrap my arms around his neck, and he grips my ass, pressing me closer to him. I moan, unable to help it, and I bite his lower lip, smiling.

"Nate, people are watching," I whisper, though I'm part of the reason for the show.

"Ask me if I care," he murmurs against my lips. I laugh again.

"Where's your phone, Delilah?" he whispers.

"Left behind," I repeat.

"Behind what?"

"Everything. I don't need it anymore. Please, don't ask me any more questions, Nate. I won't give you answers," I say, my voice shaking. I can't control anything anymore.

"I'm sorry for the wait," Jenna says, "here's your food. The kitchen was closed, but I made them reopen for you." She appears just in time, saving me. *She's an angel.*

"Thank you," we both say at the same time. We look at each other and smile.

"Eat with me," Nate suggests. "You've been drinking; it'll help sober you up." I've known hunger my whole life, and I've learned never to refuse food.

"Thanks," I say, winking at him. As he lowers his head to eat, Jenna mouths, "Are you okay?" I mouth back, "I'm great." She smiles and walks away. I'm ready to keep talking tonight.

"Baby, what does the universe mean to you?" I ask, popping a shrimp into my mouth. He smiles, clearly liking that I called him "baby." I like it too, especially since this is my last night here. I want it to be memorable. He pauses for a moment, then dives into his response with passion.

"It's huge, beautiful, and way bigger than we can ever imagine. Out there, beyond our planet, there are stars, galaxies, and all sorts of incredible things. When I think about us humans, we're so tiny compared to the universe. Our lives are short, and our problems might seem big to us, but in the grand scheme of things, they're really small.

"Looking at the night sky feels like staring into infinity. The stars twinkle, and it's just breathtaking. It reminds me that our worries are just a tiny part of something much bigger. I love taking a moment to appreciate it all—soaking in the sun, gazing at the stars. It helps me remember that life is amazing, and we're lucky to be here.

"When I'm overwhelmed, I just look up and remind myself that there's so much more to life than what's happening right in front of me. We're just tiny specks in this vast universe, and that's okay. Life is amazing, even when it doesn't feel like it. Does that answer your question?"

His words hit me straight in the heart. *Does he know what I'm about to do?* I take a moment to look at him, absorbing his beauty—not just physically, but his spirit. He's incredible. There's something about him, an aura. He can be intimidating, hilarious, cocky, and then turn into this deep, spiritual guy. It's like a whole world lives inside his mind. He's truly extraordinary, and I'm blown away.

"You're an amazing man, you know that?" I say.

"I can do a lot more amazing things, my babe," he replies, biting my arm, making me squeak.

"Ouch! Eat your food, not my arm! And I'm not your *babe*, you fool," I say, laughing.

"I know a part of you I'd rather eat. Your pussy, if you need me to spell it out. You're mine; you just don't know it yet. This is happening, baby," he says, mouth full of food.

"You have a way with words. One minute you're being all poetic, and then boom, dirty talk about eating me out. Great job seducing me into bed, baby."

"I'm sorry, but I can't stop picturing you naked at the end of my bed while I'm on my knees, giving you the best experience of your life."

He closes his eyes, lost in the scene he's describing. "Shit, I'm so hard right now. It's time for you to realize we're leaving this place and going straight to the Hamptons for the weekend. No need for clothes or toiletries. We'll be naked the whole time. I've got a spare toothbrush and everything." He's funny. I'm not sure if he's serious, but I'll play along.

"You just want to go upstate to look at the stars, huh?"

"Along with the obvious reason—fucking you to the brinks of madness—yes, I want to look at the stars with you," he says, locking eyes with me.

"I feel like I should tell you something that might change your mind about the Hamptons."

"You can try, but you're coming with me," he says confidently, making me laugh.

"I have digestive issues. After eating, I usually end up stuck in the bathroom for a while. I poop like no one else. It's embarrassing, but it's the truth. Still think I'm sexy?" I ask with a grin. He bursts out laughing, slapping the bar. I can't help but laugh too, hitting his arm playfully.

"Stop laughing at me! It's true!" I say, pretending to be offended. He stands up and hugs me from behind, resting his arms on my chest. I tilt my head to meet his gaze, and he smiles before kissing me softly. It feels so natural, like we've kissed a thousand times.

"You couldn't be cuter if you tried. And yes, I still think you're sexy. The sexiest woman I know, for sure. Your honesty is beautiful, even if you're talking about shit. I have six bathrooms at my place, so you'll be comfortable. Just leave some toilet paper for me," he jokes, and I slap his arm again. He laughs and hugs me tighter. It feels so good. Then he faces me, taking a deep breath.

"Let's go, baby. Come on."

In another life, I'd follow him without a second thought. I'd open up to him, give him everything. I'd go to the Hamptons and have the best time of my life. But that's not my reality. We've been laughing like life is easy, and I've been pretending I'm someone I'm not. He only sees the tip of the iceberg. If he knew what's underneath, he'd run.

"Don't, Delilah," he says, snapping me back to reality.

"Don't what?"

"Don't overthink this. Stop looking for reasons to fight it. Do you have your ID?" he asks, and I can't help but wonder why.

"Why do you need my ID? Do you think I'm underage or something?" He laughs, but I'm not joking.

"No, it's for my security team. I need to make sure you're not a serial killer or something," he says with a wink. *A security team?*

"You have a security team? Why?"

"It's cute that you don't know who I am. I'm Nathan fucking Williams. I own half this city. I'm worth billions. I run Williams Investments and might run for Senate someday. I don't take risks, so I have security around me all the time. I need your ID for a quick background check. It'll only take a few minutes. But know that I trust you." *Wow. I could be under his protection for two more days, right?*

I give Nate my ID, he snaps a photo of it with his phone, and I think he's sending it to his head of security. He takes a quick look at it—Mr. Officer is back in town—then he gives it back to me.

"Do you do that with all your fuck dates?"

Now he's frowning. *What did I say wrong?*

"You're not just a fuck date, Delilah. I don't see you that way. To answer your question, no, I don't usually run background checks. I usually fuck women at a hotel, it lasts less than an hour, then I leave. Sometimes, when I'm too drunk, I forget and bring them back to my penthouse, but my head of security handles everything. I've never brought a fuck date to my house in the Hamptons, though."

"Well, you're right, I'm not your fuck date because you won't fuck me. I'm staying here, but if you wanna leave, it was nice meeting you, Nathan fucking Williams," I say, grinning.

"I'm two seconds away from putting you over my shoulder, slapping that magnificent ass of yours, and getting the fuck out of here. Don't push me, Delilah." He growls, and I laugh out loud, literally. But I stop when I realize he's not laughing.

"What makes you think I want to come with you?"

"The way you look at me, the way you smile, the way I make you laugh, the way I make you shiver, the way you mouthfucked me, the way you talk to me, the way you allowed yourself to call me 'babe,' the way your nipples spike through that fucking dress, the way you told every man you encountered to fuck off—every one of them but me, the way you sang to me, the way you hold me . . . Should I keep going?" *How is this even real?*

"But I'm . . . fucked up! You can't possibly be serious about getting anywhere near me. You seem like a smart man, please take some time to reconsider."

"Okay." He stands still, eyes rolling to the ceiling. The action takes only two seconds. "Done. I've thought about it, and I came up with the same conclusion. I wanna go to the Hamptons with you, fuck you, then drop you back at your apartment. Where do you live?"

I need to escape his question, so I redirect the conversation. "Wait, you want me to go to the Hamptons just to fuck? For forty-eight hours? What if I'm hungry?" I say, pretending to be panicked but secretly amused by the situation.

"I'll feed you, smart-ass. With my cock. Can't risk my toilets being occupied all weekend."

"You son of a bitch!" I smack his chest, and we laugh together.

"Relax, you'll get actual food. Plus my cock, obviously."

"Nate, I've never given a blow job before. Ever," I say as I exhale. He looks at me like he's analyzing me.

"Is that because you've never wanted to? Or because you don't feel comfortable with it? I'll never force you to do anything, baby. You know that, right?"

"No, it wasn't any of that. I don't know, the opportunity just never came up. I have very limited experience with sex, and I told you, I suck at it. And yes, I know, you're respectful. Don't worry," I say, waving my hand at him.

"Now I'm curious. Babe, how come you got involved sexually with a man and never had to go down on him? Don't give me details about him, though. I already feel like breaking his teeth," he says, pressing his fingers against his nose. He's cute.

Possessive much, but cute.

"Because it was never like that. It wasn't about having sex; it was truly about making love, I guess? I don't know . . ."

"You can be making love and suck a man's dick, baby. One does go with the other. Okay, I don't want to ask, but I have to know a little. How many guys have you had sex with?"

Do I tell him? Do I really intend to go further with him? No, stay focused, Delilah. Tell him. Be honest. The man will leave, and you'll finally rest in peace.

Literally.

"One," I say bluntly.

"One?! Are you shitting me right now? Delilah, you are the sexiest woman I've ever seen. You're so beautiful it physically hurts. I'm fucking blown away by your beauty, and the more I talk to you, the more I want to do very dirty things to you. You can fucking sing! Babe, are you lying to me for some reason?" he asks, incredulous.

"No, I'm not. Although, thank you, that was very nice of you to say all those things about me," I say, blushing a little bit. Eric always hid his thoughts, but I knew he loved me. He didn't have to say anything—I understood it all. At The Rex, men were crude, they looked at me like I was meat. I never took their "compliments" seriously because they never meant anything. But Nate is totally different.

"I meant every word," he says. God, why does he have to have such beautiful blue eyes? It's unfair for the world. "How many times did you have sex with the fucker?"

"Twice," I answer honestly, with no shame at all. "Why would you call him a fucker?"

"Baby, any man who dares lay his eyes on you is a fucker. The one who actually got to touch you? I have even stronger words, but I'm trying to be polite here. When was the last time?"

"Um, I don't know, over a month or so. Does it matter to you?" I ask, looking him straight in the eyes.

"You know what? I'll be completely honest. I like experienced women. I like women who know what they want sexually, and I like sex in a specific way. I don't do virgins. I don't do 'limited-experience' women. I've never even hit on a woman. I know how bad that sounds, but it's the truth. Tonight is something I've never experienced before. I've never been this attracted—and I mean the scientific definition—by a woman this much. I've never begged for sex the way I've been doing tonight. And now the idea that someone touched you makes me sick. That's never happened before. The fact that you've only been fucked twice? Huge turn-on. Go figure, I can't explain it." He stops mid-sentence. "Hold on, wait a second . . . did you come during those two times?" His question surprises me after everything he's said.

"Um, no. I didn't. It wasn't about that, I told you."

His eyes widen.

"You're telling me that I'll be the first to make you come?" he says, in complete disbelief.

"Um, I don't know if I *can* come," I say, unsure.

"Oh, you *will*. You fucking will. On my fingers, on my tongue, and on my cock. Let's get the fuck out of here. I can't keep having this conversation, I'm literally about to come in my pants," he says, grabbing my hand to pull me up, but I push him away.

"I didn't say I was convinced. I'm having fun talking, but I'm not willing to leave, Nate. I told you, I have plans."

I think I just startled him. He sits back down.

"What are your plans, Delilah? Please, enlighten me. But know that I'm not going anywhere without you. What are your fucking plans now? You don't even have a damn phone on you!" Now he's pissed. Little does he know I've experienced men who threatened me, beat the shit out of me. I'm not in the least intimidated. I keep a straight face.

"My plans are none of your business. This is a public space. Feel free to stay here until it closes, I don't care. You don't scare me, Nate. I've met more dangerous men who did worse things to me. Don't try to raise your voice at me, it won't work."

He scowls at me, clearly displeased. "First of all, your plans *are* my business. Second, I will never try to scare you or intimidate you. I want to satisfy you, make you smile. Third, you should give me a list of every fucker who's ever laid a hand on you and start seeing me as a very dangerous man when it comes to those who deserve my wrath." *He can't know. He can't know. I can't tell him. I can't put him at risk. I just can't.*

A shaky "whatever" is all I manage to say. He cups my face with both hands, looking deep into my eyes.

"I'm not just any guy. Now, finish your food. We'll go after." He speaks with all the intensity in the world.

"What part of 'I'm not willing to leave' did you not understand? If I let you fuck me in the restroom, will you leave me alone?" I ask coldly, though it's unwilling. He doesn't know how badly I want to go with him. He doesn't know how much I want to escape my life. He'll never know. But I keep pushing him away. I don't know how to act differently. He's mad at me, I see it. I feel it. Icy blue eyes, staring at me. And now I think he's going to leave.

"I'm not even answering you. I won't give credit to your bullshit . . . You know what, Delilah? I won't fuck you. Not tonight, not tomorrow, not ever. But you *are* coming with me. I'll just fucking wait until you do. You'll come to the Hamptons, you'll have an amazing time. You'll enjoy the beach, the fireplace, the stars, the food—everything. I'll treat you like a fucking queen. We'll talk, but I won't force you to say anything you don't want to. Then, on Sunday night, not too late because we work on Monday, I'll drop you off at your apartment." *Huh, interesting.*

"And if I want to fuck?" I reply. A massive deviation from the subject, but I like teasing him. It helps ease my sorrow.

"For fuck's sake, Delilah," he says, hiding his head in his hands. I laugh again. This time, he laughs with me, just a little.

"Purple, right?" I say, winking at him.

"And all its fucking shades. God, you're infuriating, but you're funny. How did you get here? Do you have a car parked somewhere?" he asks.

"No, I took the subway."

"In that dress? Fuck, baby, that's not safe! Do you have a car?"

"Yeah, I had one. I still own it, though I won't be using it anymore."

"Is it broken? Do you need help fixing it?" He's digging, but I can't tell him.

"Something like that. I don't have enough money to get it fixed anyway," I say with a shrug.

"What kind of car is it, and where is it parked? I'll have someone fix it over the weekend while we're away. Where do you live?" he says, pulling out his phone.

"That won't be necessary, but thank you, I appreciate the thought," I say, trying to end the conversation.

"You're playing a dangerous game with my sanity, baby. Just give me the fucking address. Do you have the car keys with you?"

"No, I don't. They're in the apartment."

"Then give me the keys to your apartment. I'll give them to my head of security. I'll introduce him to you so you'll know he's not a criminal or something. He'll go into your apartment to get your car keys."

Okay. How do I tell him without telling him? Truthfully, I don't care what he thinks of me because I don't plan on sticking around long enough for it to matter.

"I don't have the keys to my apartment," I say, shrugging again. Nate narrows his gaze at me.

"Why don't you have the keys to your apartment, Delilah?"

"I don't plan on going back there. I got a letter saying I was evicted. I can't keep the place, so I left." So far, that's true.

"Were you evicted because you couldn't pay your rent?" he asks, carefully.

"Nope," I answer truthfully again. But I can't explain the real story behind that answer.

"I'm this close to murdering your landlord. Give me his fucking name and your fucking address. Why would you leave your apartment and your car keys inside? Wait . . . hold on." He stops, thinking. "Where were you planning on sleeping tonight? If you can't afford to fix your car, then you wouldn't be able to afford a night in this hotel. So where were you planning to sleep?"

"Among the stars," I say vaguely. Thank God, he doesn't get it.

"What the fuck does that even mean?" He's growing more frustrated with me.

"Why are you still here? Am I not fucked up enough for you already?"

"Nice try, baby. Were you going to crash at a friend's place?" he asks, pressing the issue.

"Can you leave me alone, Nate? Please?"

"Not a chance. Oh, look!" he says, showing me his phone. "I just got your background check. I have your address. It's only a matter of time before I get your landlord's number. Care to explain before he receives my wrath?" He smirks, clearly pleased with himself.

Shit.

"Wow, I must really look fuckable for you to go this far," I say, rolling my eyes.

"I'll go further, even without fucking you, baby. You have one minute before I call."

"What did you say earlier? Let me think . . . Oh right, I remember: 'I won't force you into saying things you don't want to say.' Wow, you're right. I *can* trust you. Thank you, baby, for your undeniable patience. I'm touched," I answer, sarcasm dripping from every word.

"Smart-ass. Nice try. But that was before I found out you're fucking homeless."

"You're being ridiculous. You've known me for two seconds and you think that gives you the right to change the course of my life? You want to be my savior, don't you? Well, been there, done that, and guess what? It fucking doesn't work. It always ends badly for *me*. You're a nice guy, a smart one. Give yourself some credit and get the fuck out of here. Good job ruining things," I say, closing myself off. I'm really pissed now.

"You think that little speech is going to push me away? It only makes me want you more. Go ahead, be pissed at the guy who's trying to do something in your fucking best interest."

"Oh, so you think you're the first one to try? Again, been there, done that. He tried, he failed, I cried, I broke, I got up, I'm here, and I'll move on. Life goes on. Mind your own business," I snap, now truly angry. He just laughs.

"You met the wrong guy, baby. I'm Nathan fucking Williams. I own this fucking city. I even own its people. No one, ever, gets in my way. You better remember that."

"Is that a threat?" I ask, almost bored.

"Towards every fucking bastard who ever mistreated you, yes, it is."

"Wow, the list is pretty long. You better have the time."

"I have money. I have people," he says, shrugging one shoulder.

"Wow, I didn't know you were the master of the universe. Why would you go to such lengths for a girl you met in a bar?" I ask, genuinely curious.

"Because I said so. I just feel like it. You have less than thirty seconds to explain your living situation, or I'm calling your landlord," he says, dead serious.

I can't let him call Mrs. Lee. If she makes any connection with Eric's wife, it'll destroy him. After everything that happened, I don't hate Eric. I don't wish him any harm. He's going to be a father, for God's sake. His wife is pregnant. I can't leave this world with a huge mess. *Fucking Nate.* I have no way out here.

"The apartment's lease wasn't in my name. My former 'hero' got it for me. He's the guy I was briefly involved with. He's married. He asked me to leave because he was afraid his wife would find out. I told him it was fine and that I had other options. He gave notice for me because he thought I was okay with everything. I packed my stuff and left, and now here I am. Satisfied?" I say boldly.

"What are your other options?"

"To finish my drink and enjoy the rest of my night," I reply, nonchalant.

"You're coming with me. End of discussion. Where's your coat?" he asks, and it makes me giggle.

"I don't have one."

"For fuck's sake, Delilah. It's freezing outside! I won't pressure you into saying anything else. You'll just follow me, and we'll figure things out."

"You think I trust you with this? There's nothing *to* figure out."

"I'm not giving you options."

"Please, master, may I finish my food and drink before I kneel to suck your big dick?" I say, sarcastically, stuffing more food into my mouth.

"You're killing me. You don't even know what you're doing to me right now," he sighs, and I see my chance to change the topic.

"What about women?" I ask.

"What about them?" he replies, confused.

"When you told me about yourself, you forgot to mention

women. You made a deal with me to tell you things about myself, so I think it's only fair you tell me about women. Plus, you know about Eric now."

"Eric? That's the name of the married guy?"

"Don't change the subject. What about women?" I press him.

"I don't date. I don't do relationships. I fuck, a lot, but that's it. I don't have time for anything more," he answers honestly.

"So, you just want to fuck me, right?"

"Yes. And help you too. I know you're not a virgin, but it feels like you're giving me the honor of teaching you a thing or two about sex. Seems only fair that I help you in return." He makes it sound like a fair deal.

"Okay, I see your point. So, if I follow you to the Hamptons for the weekend and come back here on Sunday night, and realize that I want more with you, that'll be an issue, right ? So, wouldn't be better to let me stay here and spare my little broken heart from falling in love with you in the Hamptons? I'm fragile, you know. Vulnerable, even. Can't take the risk of breaking me more, can ya?" I say, playing him a bit, feeling smart.

"Nice try. You're not going to fall in love with me. We'll keep sex and feelings separate. You'll have a good time, I promise. Then you'll go back to your life a little more loaded," he says, winking at me.

"With your cum?" I tease, smiling.

"Delilah, for fuck's sake, please . . . I'll punish you for this," he groans, putting his face in his hands.

"Punish me? Because I've been a baaad girl?" I reply in a cocky voice, teasing him even more. He's too easy, and it's way too much fun.

"Okay, that's enough, we're leaving." That makes me burst out laughing, hard.

"Okay, okay, I'll stop. I'm sorry. I really just want to finish my food, though, please," I say, trying to buy more time.

I'm genuinely considering his proposition. What's the real risk?

Sure, he's handsome, funny, and kind when he wants to be, and so far, he's given me something I desperately needed: lightness. But I know I won't fall for him, and that gives me comfort. He has a security team, so I don't think I'll be in any danger, and neither will he. Going to the Hamptons—probably in a beautiful house—will let me witness some beauty, even in my misery.

I know I won't change my mind about my plan to end it all. The weight of my pain outweighs any glimmer of hope for my nonexistent future. I trusted Eric when he offered me a chance at a better life, and that was my first mistake. I *won't* trust Nate. He can't save me, because I can't save myself. It's already over. It's been over since the moment I was born. Nate won't fall for me either, obviously, so he won't miss me when I'm gone.

He doesn't even realize how much this night means to me. Having sex with him will wash away all traces of Eric. I'll finally be . . . *free*. What's wrong with spending two more days to see the stars with him? It's just a forty-eight-hour delay. I *can* do this. After all, the week ends on Sunday. So will my life, apparently. *What do I do?*

"What were you writing earlier, gorgeous?" he asks, pulling me out of my thoughts.

"Nothing important." I really don't want to talk about it.

"Was it for work?" he presses.

"No." I try to cut him off.

"Can I read it?"

"Absolutely not."

"To whom were you writing?"

"The universe." He laughs at my reply, clearly thinking I'm joking. *Little does he know . . .*

"And here I come, master of the universe in person. Don't you think it's a sign?" he says, smiling wide. The thought makes me chuckle.

Ouch!

"Nate?"

"Yes, baby?"

"I have to go to the bathroom."

He bursts out laughing. I laugh with him, but I'm not kidding.

"I swear, it's true. I have a stomachache," I say.

"You're so cute. Weird, but cute. I'll come with you," he says, standing up and offering me his hand.

"No way! This is embarrassing! I don't want you to hear me. I'll be fast, I promise," I say, pushing his hand away.

"If you think I'm letting you slip away, you're wrong. I'll come with you, wait for you, and laugh at you," he says, grabbing me by the waist. I slap his chest at his words.

"Nate! You're unbelievable! Fine, let's go. Maybe this part of me will gross you out enough that you'll leave and I'll never see your beautiful face again," I say, playfully grabbing his chin like he's a five-year-old boy.

"Not a chance," he says, kissing the tip of my nose.

We make our way to the restroom, Nate's hand warm on my back, sending a shiver through me. A small line awaits us, and he stands close behind, wrapping his arms around me, resting his head on mine, and softly kissing my hair. I lean into him, holding him tight. He's so much bigger than me, and for those few minutes, he teases me about my stomach, his laughter filling the air.

"People are going to think we're having sex in the bathroom, you know," I say, somewhat seriously.

"Ask me if I care," he replies, and I roll my eyes.

I finally get inside and take a moment to look around. It smells nice, like lavender. The stall is clean and well-decorated, with a chic ambiance. Who knew a bathroom could be this . . . nice?

"Toilets for rich people are really incredible," I call out through the door. I hear him laugh.

"Wait until you see mine in the Hamptons. You okay?"

"It hurts a little, but I'm used to it. Don't worry. But, Nate, if you hear anything, please pretend you didn't." I can't help but laugh at the situation.

"Impossible."

"I thought you said you were a gentleman?"

"The best of them," he replies, laughing again.

I manage to finish quickly, a record time for me. *What a mess.* I clean up, spray the air freshener heavily, and step out. Nate is waiting for me, leaning against the sink, phone in hand. When he looks up, a broad smile spreads across his face, and I can't help but smile back. Despite everything, I feel . . . *good.*

"That took you long enough," he says as I walk over to wash my hands.

"What? I've never been that fast before. You can't be serious," I say, pretending to be offended. He laughs as I dry my hands.

Out of nowhere, Nate's strong arms encircle my waist, pulling me close. My heart races as he lifts me effortlessly onto the sink, my legs parting instinctively to accommodate him. His body presses against mine. The heat between us intensifies with each passing second. I gasp in surprise as he positions himself between my parted legs. His lips claim mine in a passionate kiss that sends shivers down my spine. Every nerve in my body tingles with the urgency of his touch, and I melt into his embrace, completely taken aback yet filled with an overwhelming sense of joy and desire. He deepens the kiss with his tongue, slow dancing with mine. His hands catch my breasts, making me moan his name.

"Keep making that sound, baby, see where it goes. You're so fucking gorgeous," Nate murmurs while grabbing my ass to push me flush against him. I start grinding him, seeking relief. I'm breathless. Nate lowers the top of my dress, the part covering my breasts, exposing them. He begins to take my nipple into his mouth, sucking, licking, and then biting it. It stings at first, but he licks it right after, soothing the pain and adding ten thousand times more pleasure. I moan again. His other hand wanders lower. He reaches my panties, crooks them with his finger, putting them aside, then caresses my slit. I'm dreaming. Pleasure overwhelms me, and I urge him to touch me more.

"You are fucking wet, Delilah, and I haven't done anything yet. You're soaking, and it's all for me, baby," he teases, his finger at my entrance.

I move around his finger, circling, craving any release.

"Oh, you want it, baby? Do you want to come on my hand, beautiful?" he says in a sexy voice. I melt by the second. I nod.

"Use your words, Delilah, what do you want?" he whispers against my lips. I grab his lower lip with my teeth.

"I want to come on your hand, *master*," I say, teasing him. He can't always have the upper hand here. That does him in.

"Fuck, baby, now you're getting fucked. Are you on the pill?"

Shit, no. I'm not. I shake my head, biting my lips.

"Shit, I don't have any condoms with me. Well, baby, you'll have to settle for my hand. I'll make it up to you, I promise," he says, kissing me once again.

This time, I return the passion he gives me. I encircle his neck with my arms, embracing him in a captivating hug. I kiss him as if it were the last day of my life. Ironic given the context, but it doesn't matter. I don't give a shit. In that moment, I dedicate myself to him with an unnamed devotion, letting myself be guided by his warmth, his light, and above all, his expertise.

He touches my clit and then pushes one finger inside me. *Oh my God!*

"How are you so fucking tight? I can't fucking wait for you to squeeze my cock with your pussy, baby. Shit, I love it." The pressure of his thumb on my clit grows stronger, and he adds another finger inside me. Then I feel something. It's coming like a wave, filled with ultimate pleasure. I feel a bolt of electricity teasing me. I accelerate my movements around Nate's fingers, increasing the pace, barely breathing, I can feel it.

What's happening?

"That's right, baby, you're gonna come in less than a minute. Keep going, baby, your breath is turning me on right now. Your cheeks are blushing, you're fucking gorgeous. My cock has never been this hard. It's all for you, baby, take it all," he says, licking my lips, my tongue, biting me. And then again, I feel the wave coming. The electricity is more than teasing this time.

It feels like the air before a thunderstorm, charged with anticipation and possibility. With each touch, each caress, the feeling intensifies, a current running through me, awakening every nerve ending in my body. His fingers work magic down there, but so does his mouth on mine. Both combine to make me explode. Heat surges through me, starting deep within and spreading like wildfire. It's like being struck by lightning, my body trembling with the sheer force of it. Waves of pleasure wash over me, consuming me completely.

I must be loud, because Nate covers my mouth with his hand. I have no fucking clue what just happened. *Did I orgasm?* I blacked out completely.

Nate is laughing now. He takes his fingers into his mouth, licking them, licking my orgasm.

Shit, that's hot as fuck.

"You're so fucking beautiful when you come, baby. So fucking perfect. You taste delicious, Delilah. But you're loud, and I don't need any lawsuits for exhibitionism. How was your first orgasm?" he asks sincerely.

"Hmm?" I can't seem to find words. Now he's laughing harder.

"That good, huh? Let's get out of here. Be a good girl, and I'll give you another one in the car," he says, attempting to readjust my dress by pulling on it to restore its normal shape.

"I feel like I should thank you. I'm literally seeing stars right now," I say, laughing.

"I can think of a few ways to thank me," he says, winking. God, he's beautiful.

We get out of the restroom, people staring at us. We look at each other and burst out laughing.

This night is surreal.

"Can I take you home for the weekend now?" Nate asks me,

with a weary expression, eager to leave this place and finally go stargazing, I suppose. After what happened, I don't even need to think about my answer.

"Sure, baby, let's go." As I say it, he suddenly picks me up, spinning us around as if we've just won the lottery. I giggle loudly.

"Thank you, baby, thank you! I have everything ready, I called my housekeeper, she stocked the pantry and the fridge, the sheets have been changed, and I asked for some clothes for you. Don't worry about a thing, we'll have an amazing weekend, you'll see," he rambles, sounding all cute.

"I'd like to pay half for the tab, please. I have some money on me," I say because it's important to me to cover for myself. I know he has money, but I need to show that I'm not a damsel in distress or anything.

"Over my dead body. It's already taken care of. The car is outside," he says, gesturing toward the exit.

I take a look inside my purse, no special reason, then take Nate's hand. He's much, much bigger than me, and he feels incredibly warm. I glance up at the ceiling, not even sure why. But I feel . . . *okay.* I'm fine with this. I'll be back Sunday night. *It's just a little delay.*

"Wait, Nate, I just want to say goodbye to Jenna, if you don't mind." I have to thank her. She's been an angel, and I need her to know that it meant something to me, in my own words. *I hope she'll be here on Sunday.*

"Sure," he says simply, kissing the top of my head, then resting his arms over my shoulders. How quickly we've become so intimate is both completely understandable and inexplicable—logical and absurd at the same time. We make our way to the bar, always touching one another, and find Jenna.

"Hey, Jenna, I'm gonna go now. I just . . . um, I wanted to thank you for, um, everything. You weren't just a barmaid, but . . . more. Anyway, thank you so much. It meant a lot to me. Will you be working here on Sunday night?" I ask, with Nate looking at me like I've grown two heads.

"Oh, Delilah! It was my pleasure! I had fun with you! I do work on Sunday night, I start at 6 p.m. and go until 2 a.m. Will I see you?" she asks, a huge, genuine smile on her face.

"I'll be there! I guess I'll see you Sunday, then. Wait, I forgot—here," I say, pulling out fifty dollars for the tip. I hand her the money, but she pushes my hand away.

"I'll never take a dime from you, honey. Plus, Mr. Williams already tipped me very generously. Thank you, sir, again," she says, directing her gaze at Nate. He nods, that's it. *Rude?*

Anyway, I tell her I'll see her in two days, and we head for the door.

Once we reach the exit, Nate stops, faces me, and takes off his jacket, placing it on my shoulders.

"The car is right outside, but it's cold out there. I don't want you to get sick," he says, kissing me softly.

Who the hell is Nathan Williams? How does he switch personalities in two seconds? He's being perfect. I came here with a heavy heart, but I leave with a light one, thanks to him. *Forty-eight hours, Delilah.*

When we step onto the sidewalk, I see a limo in front of us, but I don't make the connection.

"Where's your car?" I ask, looking around.

"Right here, baby," he says, opening the door of the limo. Holy shit!

"Are you serious? This is your car? I've never been inside a limo before! Shit, Nate, this is huge!" I exclaim, jumping on the street, grinning like a kid, and then jumping onto Nate, wrapping my legs around his waist like a little girl. He catches me, a bit startled, but laughs with me. I can't believe I'm living this moment. Right now, I decide to be very grateful, for once. *I'm getting into a limo!*

"You're so fucking cute, baby. If a limo impresses you this much, the rest of the weekend might give you a heart attack," he says, laughing and kissing me between words.

"Oh my god, okay, I'm ready, let's go!" I can't contain my joy. Let's see what these forty-eight hours will be like. Only I know what's coming after.

But for now, I choose not to give a fuck.

CHAPTER 4

Nate

Delilah settles inside the limo, jumping all around, amazed by the car that has taken me to work every day for the past ten years or so. I'm so used to luxury that I'm no longer in awe, but her reaction is the cutest. She wears the biggest smile, and it's magnificent. She's beautiful in every way.

I'm not used to befriending people outside my world. All my relationships, whether in love, sex, friendship, or business, come from my circle of privilege. From the moment I saw her, I knew she was different.

She probably has multiple personalities, but does that turn me off? Not even close. She's fascinating—funny, smart, sensitive, infuriating, and, yeah, maybe a little crazy. I knew I should've stepped back a million times, but I *felt* something. Call it gut instinct or whatever; I just knew something was wrong. I can't even explain it—I just knew if I left her, like she wanted, something bad could have happened. I'm no hero. I don't usually care about anything beyond my own world, but with her? Something kept pulling me in, and I always trust my gut. It's gotten me to the top so far.

Anyway, I'm not thinking about what comes before or after this. I'll make sure Anders has someone keeping an eye on Delilah when our weekend's over, but for the next forty-eight hours, she's mine. Just for me. We just hit the road, and I hand her some water from the minibar. She's amazed by all the little things. *It's cute.*

"Do you own the car or do you rent it?" she asks, curiosity lighting up her voice.

"Don't insult me, baby," I reply, giving her a playful wink. I can't stand the distance between us, so I grab her hand and pull her onto my lap, which makes her laugh. *I have to touch her.*

"No, but seriously, it's yours? Like, you paid for it?" She sounds almost incredulous, her eyebrows lifting as she looks around.

"Mmmh," I murmur into the crook of her neck, enjoying the warmth of that spot.

My hands rest on her thigh as I encircle her with my arms. She feels so good in my grasp.

"Did you grow up in a castle as well?" she asks, and I laugh. Luxury is a foreign concept to her. It'll be my pleasure to introduce her to it.

"If you ask me a question, you gotta let me ask you one too."

"I'll stop asking questions, sorry." Not quite the reaction I expected.

"No, I want you to ask me anything, but I really want to ask you questions too. Communication, baby," I say.

"Hard no for me, sorry. Plus, you got me into coming with you. That should be enough. We should make a list of rules for this weekend, what do you think?" she suggests, suddenly more guarded.

How can she be hugging me like we're old-time lovers and then shut me out? The funny thing is, *I'm* usually the one acting this way toward women. I almost want to call each and every one of them to apologize. But I'm intrigued by her "rule proposition."

"Hit me," I say, leaning in, curious.

"First rule for me, no more personal questions. Your turn," she declares in a firm tone. *I don't like that rule.*

"No falling in love, obviously," I say, which makes her laugh. Hard. *Too hard.*

"That's a done deal. Another rule, I'd like for you to NOT help me with my living situation. And my car. I want you to drop the subject, please."

"Nonnegotiable," I answer, my voice flat. That's a hard no. "I told you, you offer me something and I offer something in return. You offered me your inexperience to remedy, and I offer you my help with your car and apartment. That's it. Don't see anything more in it than there is. It means nothing to me," I say. And it's true. I'm not falling for her. Far from it. But I do want to fuck her. She seems nice and in need. Why can't I help her a little? It's not like I can't afford it.

"Believe me, I know. But you'd only be wasting your time and your money. Which brings me to my third and last rule. After Sunday night, you forget about me. You forget my name, my face, my voice, everything. You have to promise to never, ever look back and try to find me, to learn how I might be or something. Are we clear about that?" she asks, her eyes locked on mine, serious as hell. *What the fuck?*

I didn't plan to stay in touch with her. I just want to enjoy the weekend, nothing more. She's funny, sexy as fuck, and there's something between us—a pull, like a magnet, drawing us together. That much is obvious. But right now, her rejection stings. I'm used to being the one who walks away, not the other way around. I've never been rejected before—this is a first. And damn, it hurts, even though I don't want anything more with her. But now I can't even control what's coming out of my mouth.

"And what if I want to?" I ask, my voice steady but pointed. Her reaction is immediate. She jumps off my lap like I just threatened her life. *What the actual fuck?*

"Oh no, Nate, you can't . . . you can't. You have to promise me you won't try anything after Sunday. Can you pull up the car, please? I think I've just changed my mind. I'd like to go back, please." *What the hell just happened?*

"Delilah, it's fine, it's okay, I promise I won't try to look for you directly or indirectly. But I don't understand you. And what makes you so sure you won't want a repeat?"

"It's not about you." Okay, I've heard that too many times tonight. It's starting to piss me off.

"Sounds like it's more and more about me."

"Ugh, this was such a bad idea. I'm sorry, I should just go. Pull up the car and I'll find my way back by myself, don't worry." *Wait, what? No!*

I grab her waist and pull her back onto my lap, wrapping her in my arms, breathing her in. She relaxes almost instantly. I realize I have to play by her rules if I want to enjoy this weekend, but I'm sure as hell that this topic isn't off the table.

"I'll stop, I'm sorry. I was messing with you. Let's enjoy our weekend and then part ways friendly, even if that sentence is hard to say and hear. But I promise I won't care about you after our time together. Sounds cool?" I say, trying to smooth things over.

She laughs, her tension melting away.

"Sounds perfect," she says, pressing a bit tighter against me.

"Delilah, if you want to ask me any questions, it's fine. I'll answer, and I won't ask any in return, okay?" I offer.

"No, that's fine. Don't take this the wrong way, but I don't want to know more. I just want to . . ." She pauses, thinking for a moment before taking a deep breath. ". . . live a little more. I don't just want to live, but live differently, just for a moment. See what it's like. How it'd feel. But this is nice," she says. I think she's implying she wants to experience life outside her usual constraints, just for now.

"I see. Like *Pretty Woman?*"

"Which pretty woman?" she asks, genuinely puzzled.

"No, not *which* pretty woman, I was making a reference to the movie."

"What movie?"

"*Pretty Woman,*" I say, frowning.

"Never watched it. Never heard of it, sorry," she says with a shrug.

"Babe, it's a classic! I know you're twenty-six, but . . . still!"

"First, I'm twenty-*five*. Second, I didn't see a lot of movies in my life." She tries to move off my lap.

"Get your sweet ass back here! You told me you'll be turning twenty-six in a few weeks, so you're practically twenty-six," I say, keeping her close. She laughs at my persistence.

"If you say so," she replies, taking off her shoes and stretching her little toes. *Cute.*

"Give me your feet, I'll massage them," I say, grabbing her feet. She tries to push me away, but I'm stronger.

"You can't massage my feet! You don't know me! This is weird!"

"I gave you an orgasm less than an hour ago, I think I know you enough," I say as I massage her tiny foot. The woman is petite. Exactly the kind I wouldn't be having sex with. But with her? *Shit.* I start to massage her, and she obviously relaxes in an instant.

She really enjoys the massage I give her because she moans. And her moans? HUGE. FUCKING. TURN. ON!

"Keep making those sounds with that mouth of yours, Delilah. Let's see where it takes you," I say, my voice low, urging her on.

She lets out another soft moan, eyes closed, relaxing completely against the backseat.

"I know I should care right now, but damn, your hands are doing magic." Her tone drips with satisfaction. She's so fucking gorgeous. I can't resist, so I place her foot on my hard cock so she can feel just how turned on I am. She gasps, startled by the gesture, which makes me chuckle. But then, without hesitation, she starts rubbing me with her bare foot, and I feel like I'm going to explode.

"Baby, if you keep this up, I'm gonna come in my pants. My dick is screaming to get out. Jesus, *fuck!*" I groan, feeling overwhelmed by the sensation. She laughs at my reaction, and I can't help but think she's the cutest thing.

"Don't mind me, get it out, free it," she says, her voice sultry and teasing, waving her hand at me as if to give permission. *Damn, the things I'm going to do to her soon.*

"I don't have any condoms. Stop tempting me," I warn, scowling playfully. Her laughter grows louder, clearly amused.

"So what? Is fucking my pussy the only way for you to come?" Her innocent tone clashes with the boldness of her words, and I realize she has no clue what she's doing to me. I'm barely hanging on there.

"Delilah . . ." I exhale, trying to regain control. "No, fucking your pussy isn't the only way I *will* come. But you've never given head before, right? I'm guessing your ass is untouched too . . . *Fuck,* just thinking about your untouched ass is driving me crazy." I pause to catch my breath, feeling the heat rising in my chest.

"You could use your hand. It won't take long. But I won't ask you for anything unless you want to."

I can feel my climax building just from talking about it, and it's electrifying as fuck.

"I'm willing to try. Let's get it out and see what I'm more comfortable with." Her words send a rush of desire through me. She's so sexy, so gorgeous, yet so innocent. It's pure lust, and I realize I've never wanted anyone as much as I want her. *I'm fucking obsessed.*

I unzip my pants, push down my boxers, and take my cock out, stroking myself to find some relief. Delilah's eyes widen in shock as she watches me.

"Nate, you're huge! It'll never fit inside me! I don't . . . I don't even think it'll fit in my mouth! Or in my hands!" Her disbelief is like music to my dick, and it throbs at her words.

"It *will* fit, baby. You'll have my cock inside your pussy, your mouth, and your perfect ass. Shit, I'm so turned on right now. Give me your hand," I say, almost desperate. She places her hand on my cock, and just the feel of her touch makes me feel like a teenager again. She begins to caress the head of my cock, kneading my girth, and I know I won't last for shit.

"Then what do I do next?" she whispers. Her inexperience adds fuel to the fire.

"You stroke it, baby, from top to bottom. Yeah, just like that. Slowly at first. Don't rush, take your time. Your hand is perfect, baby, keep going." She follows my directions so well, and it's driving me insane. I moan her name, losing control.

"Would it be better if I kneel between your legs?" she asks, her voice tentative but filled with desire.

I lift my head, eyes wide with excitement.

"Come here, beautiful." I position her between my legs. She stares at my cock like it's something divine. She keeps stroking me, then opens her mouth as if unsure of how to start. God, she's so fucking perfect.

"You wanna suck me, baby?" I ask, and she nods, but I want more than just a nod.

"Use your words, gorgeous. What do you want to do to me?"

"I want to suck your dick," she says, and that almost sends me over the edge.

"Fuck, I swear I almost came. You're such a good girl, Delilah. Now, put your tongue out and lick the head." She obeys, her tongue gently flicking across my cock, and I grip her hair, guiding her.

"Yeah, just like that, baby. You like it, don't you? Such a good girl. Now, keep your hand moving like this, that's perfect." She keeps her focus on the head, licking every inch, her tongue warm and soft. She's delicate but also eager. It's fucking incredible.

But I need more.

"Now, spit on my cock," I tell her. She raises her head, clearly taken aback.

"Excuse me?"

"You heard me. Spit on my cock, baby. Now." Without hesitation, she does it, her spit dripping onto me. It's so fucking hot.

"Rub it all around with your hands. And if there's not enough, you spit again, beautiful." She follows, coating my cock with her saliva, and it feels amazing.

"Now, open your mouth and suck me, but keep looking me in the eyes." She takes me in, her mouth enveloping my cock, and the way she moans as she does is driving me wild.

"You like that, don't you, baby? Such a slut for me already. Keep going, take it all, it's yours." She moans louder, taking me deeper, and I can't help but smile.

"My sweet, sweet Delilah likes being called a slut, doesn't she? Spit again and suck me deeper." She listens so well, like she was made to follow orders in the bedroom. *But I want more.*

"You're doing so great, baby, but I want you to go even deeper. Gag for me, baby. Suck my cock until you can't take it. Let me reach your throat." She goes for it, gagging as she takes me in, tears forming at the corners of her eyes. She's absolutely breathtaking.

"Okay, I'll try. Wait a second, I need to breathe a little," she says, laughing softly. I lean in, kissing her tenderly before she goes back to work and opens her mouth for me again. I'm done for. She sucks me like the fucking pro she's not.

"Don't forget to use your hand at the base. That's right, just like that. Good girl, baby, keep going," I manage to instruct her, though I can barely speak anymore. She's sucking me like the good slut that she is, and I'm about to come any second. My breathing is erratic, and I know I have to warn her.

"Baby, if you don't want me to come in your mouth, you should stop now. I'm ten seconds away from losing it." She meets my eyes, a playful smile on her lips, and takes me even deeper. *Fuck, Delilah is perfect.*

"If you want me to come in your mouth, don't swallow. I want to see my cum in your mouth." She nods and goes back to work, her tongue warm and slick, her hand firm as she jerks me off. I'm on the edge, and my entire body tightens as the wave crashes over me.

My body seizes in that moment, every nerve on fire, my muscles clenching as I come hard, spilling everything into her mouth. The pleasure is overwhelming, and time feels like it slows down as I ride the wave of my orgasm. I'm lost in the moment, nothing else matters. I'm panting while Delilah watches me, waiting for her next order.

"Open your mouth, beautiful," I barely manage to say, still catching my breath. She opens wide, showing me my sperm in her mouth, her tongue playing with it. *Fuck, that's fucking hot.* I trace my finger along her lips, spreading it all.

"Swallow for me, baby." She obeys, swallows it and licks her lips afterward, looking like an enchantress. Just as she tries to move off me, I grab her waist and pull her onto my lap to straddle me.

"So, how was it? Did I do okay?" She can't be asking me that right now.

"Baby, that was the best fucking blow job I've ever had! You did a perfect job, and for a first, shit, it feels like you're a fucking pro. I don't even remember my name right now," I say, and it's the god-damn truth. That makes her giggle.

"Thank you, Nathan fucking Williams," she responds, winking at me. I laugh a little and then firmly handle her waist, pulling her into a hard, long kiss.

"I guess we're even now," she says, breaking our kiss.

"We're not even close to even. You fucking sucked my dick as if it's your last meal on Earth, baby, inside my limo. I only finger-fucked you in a public restroom. I owe you more," I respond, ca-ressing her thighs.

As the car hits the highway, heading toward our destination, our embrace gets more intense. Every touch jolts through me, ev-ery kiss hints at what's coming next. In this moment, there's no past or future, only now—filled with her perfume and the soft sound of her breath on my skin. We give in fully to the pull be-tween us.

We know we can't have sex, not without protection, but we still tease each other, laughing, even pouting out of frustration. Honestly, it's the most fun I've had in ages.

Yeah, I'm definitely fucked.

During the ride, Delilah and I stay close. We talk easily, avoiding anything too personal but still covering a lot of ground. We laugh a lot, and in these moments, it feels like there's an unspoken bond between us. What really hits me is how familiar she feels, like I've known her for years. I touch her like she's an old lover, talk to her like nothing can break us. I don't know how to explain it.

Still, the more we talk, the clearer it becomes how different we are. We come from two completely different worlds, and I know this would never work in real life. So, I decide to enjoy every second of this dream.

At some point, Delilah falls asleep with her head on my lap, and I stroke her hair.

She looks peaceful, and so fucking beautiful it hurts.

While she sleeps, I text Linda, my housekeeper, making sure everything is ready—plus a little surprise for Delilah—before we arrive.

A short while later, I feel her stirring, her eyes opening softly. *That gorgeous woman . . .*

"Hey sleepyhead, we're almost there, beautiful," I say, caressing her cheek. She smiles at me, and my heart skips a beat.

"How long was I asleep? I never fall asleep like this, usually," she says, stretching.

I take a look at my watch.

"Almost an hour, tops. You were so peaceful I let you sleep."

"Thank you, though I feel like I slept eight hours straight. I'm all rested! I've never needed a lot of sleep to feel fresh and good," she says with a smile that makes her glow.

"Well, that's good, because I have a surprise for you at the house," I reply, grinning wide. I hope she'll love it.

Tyler tells me that we've entered the property, parks the limo, and opens the door for us. I thank him and take Delilah's hand in mine. It is after midnight, but the lights outside are bright enough to see my house. As she steps out of the car, her eyes widen, taking it all in.

"You can't be fucking serious, Nate. *This* is your house?" she asks, pointing at the property.

I laugh at her reaction.

"Yes, baby, that's my house."

Hand in hand, we stand on the sandy path leading to my house, and a surge of pride hits me. The mansion glows under the moonlight, standing tall as a true symbol of Hamptons luxury. Even at this hour, lights shine warmly, casting a beautiful contrast against the quiet beach.

Delilah's eyes widen, taking it all in. The place may be big and grand, but there's a warmth here that makes it feel like home. The porch lights glow softly, and as we approach, she squeezes my hand a little tighter, as if to reassure herself this is real.

I guide her up the steps, each one bringing us closer as the house's details come into focus—the intricate carvings, the wide arches. At the large double doors, I pause, smiling at her.

"Welcome, sweet Delilah," I whisper as we walk inside. Her smile lights up her face. She's at a loss for words.

"Holy shit," she whispers again and again as I show her the first floor.

We start in the foyer, where there's a double staircase and a round table in the middle. The soft lights show off the brown, white, and beige colors of the house.

Then I take her to the kitchen. The marble countertops shine under the lights, and the steel appliances are sleek and modern. I watch her, and she's clearly amazed. The smell of fresh coffee mixes with vanilla from the candles. Linda did a great job.

"I've always wanted to really learn how to cook," Delilah says, running her hand across the stove. "I think I was good. It's sad I couldn't stick with it."

"It's never too late," I say, wrapping my arms around her and kissing her neck. She nods, and I drop the subject, not wanting her to shut down.

Next, I show her the large bathroom with its cool marble floors. The rain shower and the bathtub in the middle make the space feel luxurious. Delilah looks around, quiet, just taking it in.

Then we go to the living room. A big cream-colored sofa sits in front of a crackling fireplace warming the room. There's modern art on the walls, giving it a stylish look. A whole wall facing the backyard is made of windows, letting the moonlight shine through. The sound of waves crashing far away makes everything feel calm.

"I have a surprise for you," I say as I hug her, feeling the need to stay close.

"Another surprise?" she laughs. "This place is already amazing. I feel so lucky to be here, Nate. I don't need anything else. You could let me sleep on the couch, and I'd be cool with it," she says, making me laugh.

We step outside into the backyard. The air is cool, but Delilah is still wearing my vest to keep herself warm. The sky is full of stars, perfect for the surprise I planned. Linda has turned the backyard into a romantic heaven.

In the center of the yard, a large, plush mattress sits draped in white linens. Hundreds of candles surround it, casting a gentle glow. Rose petals scattered over the bed and ground add a touch of romance. Fairy lights hang around the edges, giving the whole scene a magical vibe.

Next to the bed, there's a table with a bottle of Domaine de la Romanée-Conti, one of the best wines money can buy. Its rich aroma mixes with the night air and promises indulgence. A plate of cheeses, fresh strawberries, and dark chocolate truffles sits nearby, tempting with perfect flavors.

The highlight is the Celestron CGX-L telescope, perfectly placed for stargazing. I love astronomy, so I spared no expense.

I take a moment to admire Linda's work. She and her team did an amazing job bringing my last-minute idea to life. Everything is perfect, from the candles to the rose petals. I feel proud and grateful.

Delilah's reaction is just what I hoped for. Her eyes go wide, and she covers her mouth in disbelief. She turns to me, clearly moved.

"Nate, this is . . . I don't even know what to say," she whispers, her voice trembling.

I smile, pulling her close.

"I'm glad you like it. I wanted it to be special."

She hugs me tightly, her face pressed against my chest.

"It's perfect. Thank you."

I pull out my phone to thank Linda and snap a picture of the scene. When I look back at Delilah, she still seems amazed, and it makes me smile.

"I'm speechless. I have no words," she says, her eyes glistening with tears. My heart skips a beat. I wrap my arms around her from behind, resting my head in the crook of her neck. She holds me tight, and it feels so natural, like we've done this a hundred times.

"I hope that's a good thing, gorgeous," I say softly.

"It is, thank you. So much. This is all just so . . . unexpected. Tonight is unexpected. *You* were unexpected," she admits.

"Likewise, baby. Come on, I want to show you something." I take her hand and lead her to the telescope. I point it at a special constellation—Orion. I take a quick peek and then offer it to her.

"Here, gorgeous, take a look."

"I don't even know where to look! What am I supposed to see?" she says, clearly overwhelmed.

I guide her eye to the scope.

"Right here." She looks in.

"It's beautiful, but am I looking at something specific?"

"Do you recognize the constellation?"

"Will you kick me out if I say I have no fucking idea what it is?" she says, and I laugh, tightening my hold on her waist. I'm getting hard. *Again.*

"That's Orion, baby."

"It's amazing," she says, and she tilts her head, inviting me to kiss her. So, I do.

There's comfort in the kiss, like I've known her forever. It feels like we're reuniting, like I missed her. She opens up to me, and I go deeper. She's so beautiful, and for the first time in a long time, I feel like I'm exactly where I'm supposed to be, right here with her under the stars. *I don't want to let go.*

"Want to eat something or have a drink?" I ask, guiding her to the mattress.

"I usually don't drink, but tonight's an exception. How did you set all this up? When did you plan it? Wait . . . were you supposed to be here with someone else?" she asks, wide-eyed. *She's so damn cute.*

"I've never brought anyone here, except my mom. I texted my housekeeper while you were asleep in the car."

"And she did all this by herself? Wow, I hope you pay her well."

"She has a team, and yeah, I pay them well," I say, pulling her onto the bed with me. I roll on top of her, and she laughs. God, I love that sound. She opens her legs naturally, and I simply look at her. Her smile is like a dream. Her eyes shine like the stars, telling a story I can't quite figure out. I take in her perfect face, her delicate nose, the texture of her skin.

"God, you're beautiful," I manage to say, and I've never meant it more than I do now.

"Your charm's going to get you somewhere, alright," she says, laughing. She has no idea how serious I am. "Thank you for all of this. I can't believe you put it together so fast with just a text."

"Baby, I'm Nathan fucking Williams. Remember it . . . Remember me."

Before she can respond, I kiss her deeply. She grips my hair, grinding her body against mine. I'm so close to losing it, I need to pull back. I want to know more about her, but we don't have much time. I break the kiss and sit on her legs, taking a deep breath.

"Shit, I want to fuck you so bad, but I also want to take my time. Let's have a drink first, okay?" I say. She smiles, and damn, that smile drives me crazy.

"I'm no expert, so you lead and I follow," she says. I pour two glasses of wine and hand her one.

"To what do we toast?" I ask.

"To Orion," she replies. *She couldn't be more perfect if she tried.*

"To Orion and the unexpected."

We sit comfortably on the mattress, legs tangled together, drinking and eating. Delilah asks about the stars, and I start talking about what I love most. I show her a star map on my phone, and she listens, asking questions.

Talking to her is easy, effortless. She shouldn't feel this familiar, and yet I'm drawn in. *And to know that I will devour every inch of her during the whole weekend . . .*

"Will we sleep out here?" she asks, pulling me from my thoughts.

"If you want to, but I also have a bedroom. The weather's nice for now, but it could get really cold," I say, kissing her lightly.

"I'd rather sleep in the bedroom, if you don't mind. I should've told you before, I fall asleep in my bed but wake up somewhere else almost every night. I'd hate to wake up in the sea over there," she laughs.

"No shit?"

"I swear, but I never remember it."

"I'll keep you close. Let's go upstairs."

I take her hand, leading her inside. I can't wait to fall into bed with her and get lost inside her.

As we step into the master bedroom, her eyes widen, and her smile stretches across her face.

"Oh my God, that bed is huge! I've never slept in one like this."

She jumps on it like a kid, and I can't help but laugh. She's adorable. I stand back, watching her. It's hard to believe this is real. How can we connect like this? I'm usually so closed off, but with her, I'm completely open. *What did she do to me?*

She walks over, wrapping her arms around my waist.

"Is everything okay?" she asks, looking into my eyes. I don't know what to say, so I kiss her. I kiss her like it's all that matters, and I let go of everything else.

She cups my face, and I grab her hips, pulling her closer. I need to know she's with me, that she feels the same. I try to break the kiss to speak, but it's impossible.

"Baby, we don't have to do anything. Tell me what you want. Tell me, I'll give it all to you, beautiful," I say, almost panting. She opens her beautiful eyes and looks at me. I could come just from that look.

"I want you to teach me how to forget everything for a moment. I want you to teach me how to fly," she whispers. At that precise moment, she has me. I take her in a real hug, a very comforting one, and I don't know if that embrace comforts me more than it's meant to comfort her.

"Don't move, angel," I say in her ear. I take my phone out and connect it to the sound system, playing her song, "Saturn" by Sleeping at Last. The same song we heard in the bar earlier. I have to admit, this song is really, really beautiful.

And I take her back to our kiss, moving to the rhythm of the song. Our dance is intense, passionate, and I feel devoted to her. I take off my suit jacket from her shoulders while she unbuttons my shirt.

Usually, when I fuck a woman, it's in a rush. The rush to fuck and come, good but fast; I don't even kiss that much. I always make a woman come first and enjoy doing it, but I never forget my own aim. Right now is totally different. It's a completely different story.

It's *unrushed*. We take our time, we savor each other. Knowing that I will probably never see her again after Sunday night breaks me and soothes me at the same time. I know I can't see her again, not after what we're experiencing here. It has to remain a temporary exception and nothing else, nothing more. *So I dive deep.*

I take the hem of her dress and slowly take it off, caressing the delicate curve of her perfect body, touching the softness of her skin with my fingertips. I put the dress on the floor, and we exchange a long look. We're barely breathing, but we don't need to talk. I understand what she wants, what she's asking. *But that body of hers . . .*

"Your body is . . . Damn, baby, you're probably the most beautiful woman on the whole planet. You are so beautiful."

I turn her around, pressing my cock against her ass, my hand on her shoulder, caressing her. I kiss her neck as if it were my final task on earth. My hands slowly reach her hips, and I put my right hand on her belly.

"Close your eyes, baby. Tell me what you see," I whisper. She does as she's told, imagining.

"I see the stars," she replies.

"That's because we're among them, angel mine. Nothing else exists," I say, sliding my hand inside her panties to touch her core. She gasps a little but doesn't pull back. She's so hot. I take my time, just caressing her slit with my middle finger, playing with her anticipation. She puts her hand on the back of my head. Little does she know we're only starting . . . *Damn, she's so wet already.*

"Baby, you're dripping . . . I haven't done anything yet."

"I can feel you against my ass too. You're hard, and I haven't done anything yet either," she says, pushing her ass against my cock, teasing me. *Fuck. Me.* I bite her ear in response to her teasing. Now it's my turn to tease her, and that is one of my specialties.

I put my thumb on her clitoris, circling it, toying with it while playing with her entrance with my middle finger. Delilah is panting, leaning her head back on my chest, begging for more.

"Yeah, feel it, baby. Move on my hand, beautiful. Soon enough it'll be my cock."

"I want to . . . ah . . ." she says, barely breathing, seeking relief.

"You want to come, gorgeous?" I say, playing with her incoming orgasm.

"Yes, please, Nate." She moans as I give her wet kisses on her neck and increase my pace.

"I'll give anything to you," I say as I take my free hand and put it under her bra, playing with her tit, pinching it, caressing it while

I push a finger inside her. I feel her warmth, her wetness, and she's fucking tight.

I add another finger inside her and mimic the moves my dick is craving for, while playing with her clit. She's squirming on my hand, turning me on, and I'm panting with her. I feel her body contracting as she's coming, and I give it all to her.

"Come for me, baby," I whisper in her ear. Then I lick her earlobe and gently bite it.

There she goes, and I try to keep my eyes open to watch her come. *Damn, what a sight.* Her mouth makes the shape of a perfect O, her cheeks flushed, her body contracting, and then the most exquisite sound comes out of her mouth. I'm this close to losing it. *I have to fuck her. Now.*

"Babe, I need to be inside you real fast, or it'll be very embarrassing for me real soon," I say. She turns back to me, barely out of her orgasm, and throws herself at me, wrapping her legs around me, her mouth on mine. I'm surprised for the first three seconds. Then I take hold of her, my hands on her perfect ass, and throw her on the bed.

I take off my shirt, tossing it to the ground, and when I raise my head to look at Delilah, I have to take a second to contemplate the siren in front of me. Still in her black underwear, on her elbows, legs open, one knee up. *Fuck. Me. Where was this woman before?*

"Baby, you are a siren, a goddess, a nymph, you are so beautiful. I can't believe only one fucker was lucky enough to have you. There should have been more," I say, feeling a strange anger in me. *How weird.* I don't like that thought one bit, but it makes her laugh. I take off my pants under her perfect gaze; she's fucking me with her eyes. When I take off my underwear, I stand in front of her, naked and extra erect. She deliberately licks her perfect lips.

"You like what you see?" I say, smirking.

"'Like' isn't strong enough a word, but I fear it won't fit inside me."

"It *will* fit, baby," I say, bending on top of her, covering her body with mine, kissing her fiercely. I kneel us up, pulling her onto me, never breaking our kiss. She puts her arms around me, holding me close while my hands caress her back. I undo her bra, freeing her perfect round breasts. Without thinking, I immediately put her tits in my mouth, licking every inch, nibbling. The smell of her skin is intoxicating. I give both just as much time and energy, the same treatment. Delilah is moaning and grinding on my dick. I can't wait any longer, so I break the kiss, panting heavily. I hold her head in my hands and lock eyes with her.

"Baby, there are plenty of things that I'd like to do to you, with you, but I'm too horny and too close. I have to be inside you right now before I lose it, but I swear to

God I will make it up to you, okay? Please don't be mad at me, baby . . ."

"That's more than okay. I honestly don't know how much more I can take. I need you now," she says, closing her lips on mine, and I'm done for. I put her down, my hand on her breasts, stroking down her flat stomach, reaching the hem of her panties, hooking them with my fingers and slowly taking them off, revealing a naked Delilah in front of me . . . she's a vision. *Her beauty is beyond compare.*

"You like what you see?" she says, smirking, imitating me. That makes me laugh with nerves.

"Oh baby, 'like' isn't strong enough a word," I say, lifting an eyebrow to match her smirk. God, she's too sexy. I reach out to the drawer of the nightstand, open it, and take a condom out of its box. I tear off the wrapper with my teeth and roll the condom onto my penis. I don't remember the last time I was this hard in my life, if ever. I raise my gaze to Delilah, and if I'm not mistaken, I think she's anxious.

I say, "I'll take it slow, I'll be gentle, I promise. If it's too much, you tell me, okay?" I say, and she nods.

I lean into her and kiss her, slow at first, but I feel the heat in me, I feel every inch of my body calling for her, craving her entrance to seal this connection between us. It's not something I can control, nor something I can escape. *I have to get inside.* The urge in my body grows stronger as I feel her hands roaming on my back, hesitating, and her lips on mine, her tongue insistent in a heated dance.

Before I can think about it, I slowly push the tip of my dick inside her, but the contact against her warmth, even with the condom barrier, is overwhelming. Delilah gasps.

"You're okay, baby? Does it hurt?" I ask.

"No, but . . . you're huge." *Oh, sweet, sweet Delilah . . .*

"I'll stretch you, gorgeous. You are so beautiful, I don't remember being this hard for anyone," I say, pushing a little more inside her. I feel her adjusting to my girth, her tightness is alluring. The self-control I have right now not to come should be rewarded.

I move back and forth inside her, getting more and more in, Delilah moans, and *oh my God,* that sound will be the death of me.

"I'm halfway in, baby," I say, kissing her nose. I don't move so she can keep adjusting to my size and I can restrain my orgasm.

Shit, what the fuck is happening to me.

"I want more," she whispers in my ear, moving her hips up to meet me, gripping my biceps with her hands. And now I'm gone. I catch her mouth with mine, deepening the kiss. She opens for me, not only her mouth but her body too. I feel her legs opening up, and then I'm *fully* inside her. I can barely breathe.

In that moment, as we finally come together, it feels like somewhere up in the night sky, there's a force that recognizes how strong our connection is. Her lips touch mine, and in that gentle kiss, time seems to stop. It's like we're the only two people in the world, caught up in a dance of passion and desire. The way her hands move on my skin sparks a fire in me I never knew was there. As our bodies move together, I feel a deep sense of wholeness, like I've finally found where I belong.

In that embrace, I'm completely captivated by her and by the beauty of this moment.

It feels like we're floating among the stars, two souls connected beyond anything else. It's pure magic, where the lines between us and the universe blur, and for that brief moment, I feel truly alive, floating among the stars.

"Nate, I feel like I'm gonna come," she says, pulling me back to reality. I didn't realize I was increasing my pace, holding her by the waist, my head in her neck, breathing her in. I have no idea how I did that. That's never happened to me before.

Now, I think I'm going to come too. *Ladies first, always.*

"Are you okay? Is it good for you?" she asks, a bit panicked. *Oh sweet Delilah . . .* I lock eyes with her while I thrust deep into her.

"Baby, I'm in a trance right now. The fact that my dick is buried deep inside your tight pussy gives me shivers. I've never enjoyed sex this much, and we're only doing missionary style. I won't last for shit, but I want you to come first. You're a goddamn delight. I'm gonna have you in every way I can until Sunday night. This was just a preview, baby."

That makes her smile, but I feel her moving along with me, hurrying me to give her relief, all the while feeling my own climax rising. I capture her lips with my teeth, like an animal, then put my thumb on her clit to accelerate her orgasm.

I have to come, I have to let it go. It's urging me like never before. I feel her flat stomach touching mine as our rhythm goes; every touch of this woman is arousing. I feel her contracting.

"Come, angel, come for me. I'm right there with you," I say between wet kisses. I'm an animal right now, I can't help it. I thrust like a beast into her, both of us very loud, all sweaty. I feel her legs rising, giving me more room inside her. And then we both feel it; we literally explode at the same time. I feel her pussy contracting all around my cock, milking every inch of it, while I release everything, until the very last drop.

We don't speak for about two minutes, both needing to understand what just happened. I'm still deep inside her, unwilling to come out. We're both breathless, speechless. I raise my gaze to meet hers, and when our eyes lock, we smile at each other, giggling. She's beauty personified; I've never seen someone so beautiful before. I automatically put my head in the crook of her neck, my hands in her perfect hair, still on top of her, deep inside her. I give her sweet kisses as I run my nose over every inch of her skin, enjoying her hand caressing my biceps.

"I have a question that might be stupid," she says, piquing my curiosity. I raise my head to see her beautiful face.

"Ask it anyway."

"Is . . . well, is sex like this for everyone?" *Where is she going with this?*

"What do you mean?" I ask, wincing.

"Well, I've had sex like twice before you, and it was never this . . . *intense.* I've never blacked out like this. I've never even *come* during sex. This, what we just did, well, it was really . . . *good,* like I felt all parts of my body. I was so deep into it that I completely stopped thinking to just . . . feel you, feel me. Does that make sense? Is sex like this with every woman you fuck?" she asks. Her innocence will be the death of me.

"No, it's not. Usually, to ejaculate the way I just did takes a lot of very, very dirty work, a lot of time, and I'm never sure it will come out the right way. But what just happened here is totally new for me too. I can't explain," I admit.

"And do you always stay this long inside a woman after sex?" she says, laughing, mocking me for sure.

I try to thrust into her to feel her again, and I swear I'm getting a little hard again.

"You don't like it, baby? You want me out already?" I say, licking her cheek like the animal I've become since I met her sweet ass. She tries to push me away, laughing hard, pretending not to like my gesture. So I keep licking her face, biting her when I can.

"Oh my God, you're gross! What's the matter with you?" she manages to say while laughing hard, pushing me away, breaking our connection. I feign death by the loss of her, putting my hand on my forehead and the other one on my dick, making some weird agonizing sound. It makes her laugh even more, and she pushes me, kicking me out of the bed.

Delilah's laugh is intoxicating; I can't help but laugh with her. I want to record that sound. She comes to the edge of the bed to witness her own joke. I see her beautiful face again, she offers me her hand to help me get up, but I take it and pull her down with me. I catch her and hold her close. We look into each other's eyes. *God, she really is beautiful.*

"You know you still have your condom on, right?" she says, smirking at me.

"Take it off," I say, offering her access with my hip. She doesn't even hesitate. I feel her becoming more comfortable with me. She delicately puts her hand on my dick, slowly taking off the condom. The movement is arousing as fuck. Never has a woman taken a condom off my penis, and right now, I don't even know why. Everything is so different with this woman. I watch her, mesmerized yet again.

"I think a thank-you is in order here, don't you think?" *That smart mouth of hers . . .*

"Thank you, gorgeous," I say, giving her a quick kiss.

The room is dark, with only the soft moonlight shining across her face. We're lying on the floor, our bodies pressed together, the cool wood beneath us contrasting with the warmth between our skin. Her light-brown eyes meet mine, and the intensity of the emotion takes my breath away.

I reach out. My hand trembles as I cup her face, my thumb traces her jaw. Her skin feels soft, and a shiver runs through me.

Her lips part, inviting me closer. With a tilt of her head and the closing of her eyes, I feel the pull toward her. That's all I need.

I move in and kiss her gently at first, but soon the kiss deepens. Her lips are warm, her tongue meets mine in a dance that feels ancient. Each touch sparks something primal within me, and every kiss deepens our connection. Our fingers tangle in each other's hair, holding on as if we were afraid to let this moment slip away.

Her heartbeat matches mine, and in that moment, it feels like we're merging, not just physically but emotionally. It's more than just passion. It's something more . . . *beautiful.*

When we pull back, both of us breathless, I rest my forehead against hers. Our eyes lock, and again, no words are needed to speak something only we could understand.

"You really have such beautiful eyes," she says. That makes me smile.

"Not as much as you," I murmur back.

"That's debatable. No, but really, just a look and you can have all the women you want."

"I didn't have you with my eyes."

"I'm not . . . common. If I can say it like that," she says, unsure.

"That I see. You are uncommon but in the most beautiful way, I guess."

"Flattery," she replies, waving her hand at me. I catch it, then kiss it.

"You're beautiful," I say, and God don't I mean it.

"I have to say that if I were a gold-digger, you'd be so screwed." And I laugh at her comment.

"Let's go back to bed, you'll be more comfortable than on the floor," I say.

"I've slept on a floor for years, I think I'll manage. You, on the other hand? Not so much," she says, laughing, but there's absolutely nothing funny about that anecdote. I frown at her because I need an explanation.

"Don't ask." She cuts me off. "I need to pee first, then I'll join you in bed." I hate it because I already know it's too soon to win this battle, but I won't give up.

I get up and help her as well. Once we stand, I take her beautiful head in my hands and look deeply into her bright eyes.

"One day, you will tell me everything, and I will hear it all, and I'll make it all better."

"You can't," she whispers.

"You seem to forget something here, baby," I say. She frowns at me as if not understanding anything. "I'm Nathan fucking Williams; there is nothing I can't do." She smiles the saddest smile, looking down. I kiss her head, and then she goes to the adjoining bathroom.

I pick up the used condom on the floor, tie it, and join her in the bathroom to put it in the trash bin. She's on the toilet seat when I enter and seems surprised to see me.

"What?" I say, a bit surprised by the look on her face.

"I'm peeing!" she says, in shock, I guess.

"So?" I don't understand her reaction; there's absolutely nothing wrong with her peeing in front of me.

"Well, it's weird! We don't know each other well; it's really intimate."

"Oh, come on! After what just happened between us? I think we're pretty intimate. I don't mind seeing you pee. You look gorgeous anyway, I don't care."

She rolls her eyes at me. Then, she cleans herself, and I hold her from behind, taking her by surprise. She melts into my embrace while washing her hands.

"I'm all sweaty. You don't mind if I take a quick shower?" she asks.

"No, but you don't mind if I join you?"

"Says he, Mister *I-Enter-the-Room-While-You-Pee*."

I bite her shoulder in response. She playfully slaps me on my chest, and I laugh with her.

"I've never taken a shower with a man before," she confesses.

"I already want to marry you; you don't have to try to convince me anymore," I reply, mocking her.

"Oh, shut up," she says, half laughing while tying up her hair.

If I had said that to any woman before her, they would have surely held me to my word. Not Delilah.

I open the shower screen and turn on the water. I make sure it's warm enough before inviting her in.

"Come here, beautiful," I say, offering her my hand, and she takes it. I hold her close and guide us under the shower.

"I don't want to wet my hair, I just want to clean the sweat off my body."

"I'll do it."

"You want to clean me?" she says, almost shocked by my offer.

"Yes," I say firmly.

I put some body wash in my hands, then take my time cleaning her from head to toe. Her body is incredible. Every inch of her is perfection, her skin smooth, her curves delicate, and her breasts perfectly shaped. She is flawless, even though I spot a few scars here and there. I slip my hand between her thighs, and her breathing quickens. I gently clean and massage her folds, aroused the entire time. I can't resist pushing a finger into her warm pussy. She's still tight, and I see her squirm. *Shit, maybe I was too rough.*

"Are you sore?"

"Just a little. I'll be fine, don't worry," she says, kissing me lightly on the lips.

"I'm sorry," I reply, my voice low.

"Don't be. I hope to God you'll do the very same thing to me again. I really enjoyed everything you did," she says, teasing me with her closeness.

"Fine. Let me finish what I started here," I say because I really want to wash her beautiful legs, her feet, her ass. So I continue, and Delilah seems very pleased. I can't help but kiss parts of her body while I clean her.

"Can I wash your body too?" she asks. That makes me smile. I like that she wants to touch me. I like that she wants to try things she hasn't done before.

"Of course. Here," I say, handing her the body wash. I watch her smile grow wider and wider at the thought of washing me. I love seeing her smile. I feel completely relaxed now.

Life is unexpected in so many ways. Never in a million years would I have thought it would be possible to spend the weekend here, in the Hamptons, with a woman I know from nowhere, taking a shower together at whatever time of the night it is. And I just decide to let everything else go. Only this moment counts. This feels like a dream, and I'll wake up Sunday night. That's it.

Delilah is taking great care in her task, washing every part of me. It makes me smile, and we exchange knowing glances, but now I feel her hesitating.

"You know you can clean my dick, right?" I say, teasing her.

"I know, I just don't want to turn you on more than you already are," she replies with a giggle.

"Whether you touch me or not, I'll still be turned on, baby. Go ahead, do it. I know you want to."

"Okay," she says.

And what a mistake it was.

Her touch feels magical, her hesitancy is a turn-on. I tilt my head, almost asking for more without realizing it. She laughs softly and washes my legs and every part of me. Once we're done, I take the shower jet and rinse our bodies. I step out first, grabbing a towel and wrapping it around my waist, then hand one to Delilah. I give her a hug and kiss the tip of her nose.

"Do you have clean boxers I can use for tonight? And maybe a T-shirt?" she asks.

"If I play my cards right, you won't need any," I say with a smirk.

"I don't like going to bed naked, but that doesn't mean you can't take them off later."

"Sure, whatever you want, babe. Come on."

I head to the dressing room, grab a pair of boxers and a T-shirt, and hand them to her.

When I come back to the bedroom after brushing my teeth, she's in my T-shirt, her legs bare, and my heart skips a beat. There's something primal about seeing her in my clothes. She looks beautiful and natural, her smile lighting up everything inside me.

She slips into bed, pulling the covers over her, and I quickly join her. Without thinking, I pull her close as I hug her tight and kiss her, my hands moving all over her body.

"You're a cuddler!" she says, running her hands through my hair.

"I usually am not, but I'll make an exception for this weekend."

"Does that mean you don't like it?" she asks, curious.

"I don't think it's about liking it or disliking it. I just don't do it nor do I think about it. Does that make sense?"

"Yeah, it does. But do you like it now?" she asks, making me laugh.

"What do you think?" I press her body against my erection, and she gasps.

I capture her mouth with mine, get on top of her, holding her hands and entwining our fingers. It feels like more than just a make-out session, but I'm not thinking, I'm just doing. The connection between us grows more intense. I want her more than anything, but I stop myself.

"Baby, you're sore, and I don't want to hurt you. Let's give your body some time before we go again," I say, breathless.

"I know, but . . . I want you," she whispers, looking sexy as fuck.

"I can give you what you need, baby. Do you trust me?" I ask, looking deeply into her glowing eyes in the moonlight. She nods, giving me permission. I take off her T-shirt first.

I kiss her deeply, my mouth consuming hers as she grinds against me. I trail kisses down her body, starting at her ear and moving lower.

"You're going to see the stars again, gorgeous," I promise, biting her earlobe. I move to her neck, my hand gliding along her side, down to her perfect breasts.

"You have the most beautiful boobs I've ever seen," I say before I lick, bite, and kiss them, then kiss my way down to her flat stomach. I notice her shivering, hot for me, craving my touch, and I'm ready to reward her.

I play with the waistband of the boxers she's wearing. She shifts, as if to say, "Please take them off," but I want to tease her. I lick just above the underwear, my fingers toying with the band.

"Nate, please," she moans. It's music to my dick.

"Say my name again, baby. It's so beautiful coming from your sexy mouth," I say, completely on fire.

"Nate, please, I need you," she moans again, moving her hips closer to my face. *If only she knew . . .*

"Damn right you do. Only I can give you what you need, baby. Be patient, I'll give it all to you. I'm hard as fuck for you right now."

I slowly pull down the boxers, the smell of her pussy frying my brain.

"Nate, I've never . . . well, no one has ever, you know . . ."

"You're offering me something priceless, baby. Don't worry, you'll love it," I say, kissing her lips lightly.

Then I go down, placing my head between her legs, my hands on her hips. I start kissing her inner thighs, getting closer to her core, teasing her. Her breathing speeds up, her body shakes, and her scent drives me wild. I inhale deeply, feeling intoxicated by her. I force myself to slow down, licking her from the bottom to the top. She tastes incredible, a mix of sweet and salty. I take my time, playing with her clit and kissing her deeply.

She screams my name, and I nearly lose control. I can't help but touch myself just a little. She's too much, pure heaven. I insert one finger, testing her soreness. She's so tight that I have to close my eyes to focus. I spend extra time on her clit, and she's clearly loving it, begging for more. I feel her tightening around my finger. She's close, and I give her everything I have.

I've never gone down on a woman like this before, but with Delilah, it feels like my mission to give her the orgasm of her life.

She grips my hair, pulling me closer, and I love every second of it. She's losing it, completely overwhelmed, and I'm not stopping.

Sweet, sweet Delilah is hot as fuck.

"Nate, baby, I'm gonna . . ." She doesn't finish, but I know it's happening now.

She comes on my tongue, and I lick up her cum, making sure I leave her dry. I want to remember her taste for the rest of my days. Her screams are everything to me. I don't even know how I'll sleep without some release, but I won't fuck her. She's still too fragile.

I go back up to kiss her sweet lips and share her taste with her, giving her what she just gave me. Fuck, can she kiss. She doesn't miss a beat; she devours my mouth, and I'm so focused on the kiss that I almost jolt when I feel her hand on my cock.

"Easy, baby. It's not about me here," I say, taking her hand in mine and giving a slight kiss on the tip of her fingers.

"I know, but I want to please you too," she says, looking at me with those eyes. She's all flushed after her orgasm, and I don't know if she can be more beautiful than she is right now.

"I know, beautiful, but you're sore, and if I fuck you now, it'll be more complicated for the next forty-eight hours. Just rest your delicious pussy, and it'll be better for both of us. I'll be fine, don't worry."

"Have you ever gone to sleep with an erection like this? Doesn't that keep you from falling asleep?" That makes me laugh. *She's so innocent.*

"No, I have never. Which is why I'm going to take a quick but very cold shower. I'll be back in no time, believe me," I say, kissing her firmly on the lips before going to the bathroom.

It takes me less than ten minutes to feel like myself again, and when I get back to bed, Delilah is lying on her back, looking at the ceiling, thinking, I guess. I join her under the covers and automatically envelop her with my body.

"What were you thinking about?" I ask.

"How my day started and how my day is ending. It's 3:05 a.m., and I'm . . . here," she replies, lost deep in her thoughts.

"Is that a bad thing? What did you plan on doing in the first place? If you hadn't met me, I mean."

"I wanted to see the stars. And I kinda did," she says, turning her head to look me in the eyes. Her lips are saying one thing, but her eyes are telling me something completely different.

"Alone?" I ask, scared to know that someone else might claim her. But again, she smiles the saddest smile.

"Always have been, always will be. We come into this world alone, and we leave it the same way."

I give some thought to her reply. It's deep; it has to mean more than she intends.

There is a deep sensitivity in this woman, veiled by an invisible shield through which no one can enter. She pushes away all the souls around her, retreating into loneliness, and I, the luckiest bastard of them all, have the chance, here and now, to share what I believe to be a rare moment of her opening up, allowing me to witness her existence.

There is something magical in our exchange. Uncommon, really. A strange, magical atmosphere surrounds us here.

"Solitude is just a step in life, not its whole. Happiness doesn't grow in isolation; it thrives in the warmth of companionship and love, whether it's from friends, family, or a lover. People find their greatest joy with each other, as partners, teammates even, in life's ups and downs. What was true before doesn't have to stay that way. Life changes, often for the better when we look back, as we open ourselves to new connections and the deep bonds that give our lives meaning."

"Happiness? Happiness is a concept, Nate. Don't tell me you believe in that bullshit."

"I do, baby. What do you mean by 'happiness is a concept'?"

"Happiness is just a fleeting idea, a cruel trick the world plays on us. How can people believe in something so brief and fragile?

People hold on to the idea of happiness like fools, stupid, stupid fools, not seeing how easily it can disappear. In my experience, believing in such a fragile and imaginary thing is a mistake I can't afford to make again."

"I take it you don't believe in silver linings, huh?" I say, to lighten the mood.

"Do you consider yourself a smart man, Nate? It's a real question, no pun intended."

"I wouldn't be where I'm at if I weren't, so yes, I'm a smart man. Why?"

"Then consider yourself smarter by remembering what I just told you," she states.

"I think someone here needs to learn how to dance in the rain. I thought I made you happy tonight," I reply, pouting.

"You did! But there's a difference between being happy for a moment and happiness."

"Enlighten me," I say.

She lies back, looking at the ceiling as if searching for her words, sighing.

"Happiness is an unreachable ideal. Being happy for a moment is like a brief flicker of light in endless darkness, a cruel tease. But happiness, as a concept, suggests something lasting and profound, something I believe doesn't truly exist. I'm driven by darkness, so yeah, I think happiness is a lie we tell ourselves to endure the unendurable. It's an illusion people chase thinking it's a permanent condition when in reality, it's just moments of temporary relief we call 'being happy.' Does that enlighten you?" she says, turning her head to look me in the eye.

Her melancholia is something. I don't understand how this beautiful woman, with such a radiant smile, with this much tenderness in her gestures and a laugh that could really warm anyone's cold heart, can be this much haunted by darkness. This woman is a mystery I can't wait to solve. But I have to remember to go easy with her, as I don't want to risk her shutting down on me again. So I decide humor might be better to lighten the mood, though I will talk about this with her some other time, later.

"So I *did* make you happy," I say, smiling at her, enveloping her in my arms. She laughs and hugs me back. She yawns, and it's my cue that I should give her some rest.

"Sleep, baby. Tomorrow is another day," I say, kissing the tip of her nose, and she closes her eyes.

"Good night, Nate. Thanks for tonight."

"Thank *you* for tonight, gorgeous. Sleep well."

I can feel her drifting away to sleep. Her breathing slows a little, but I can't manage to close my eyes. I want to look at her. I want to see her. I want to know her. She's a broken soul that needs help to get back to life again. For the next forty-eight hours, it'll be my mission to make her smile, laugh, feel free, feel good, feel . . . happy.

The only thing I hope is that it'll be enough. Not for her, but for *me*. I pray that at the end of my time with her, I'll be able to forget about her. I hope the mystery will be solved and that I'll be able to live like none of this ever happened. I need to have faith in myself. I need to believe that this is just a moment suspended in time. I'll do everything I can to not involve my heart in this.

I keep watching her sleep, the moonlight making her face glow softly, like she's wrapped in a halo. Her hair spreads across the pillow like a dark cloud, framing her pale skin in a way that makes her look almost otherworldly. My heart flutters at the sight of her, a wild, uncontrollable dance in my chest. Her beauty pulls me in, making my pulse quicken and my thoughts scatter. In this quiet moment, I'm completely mesmerized by her, unable to look away, as if the universe had conspired to bring this perfect vision into my life. This perfect angel touched by shadow. I settle myself in the crook of her neck, breathe her in, holding her extra tight. I finally shut my eyes. I laugh to myself.

Yes . . . I'm completely fucked.

CHAPTER 5

Delilah

I feel the light.

It's blinding me. I open my eyes slowly, but I don't recognize a thing. Where am I?

Then I hear music coming out of a speaker, I think. I turn over and then I see him. *Okay, I remember.* He put on "Let's Do It Again" by J Boog, and he's dancing, naked, looking at me. I can't help but burst out laughing. What the fuck is this? He's fucking singing the lyrics of the song, and I think I'm gonna pee on myself because right now, he's so funny.

"Nice to nice to know ya, let's do it again, how we did it on a one night staaaaand," he sings to me. Dancing, his penis going all over the place. He is, by far, the most beautiful man ever living on this Earth. He has everything, everywhere. I'm enjoying his six-pack, large, broad shoulders, strong biceps, legs to kill, the smile — damn, his smile . . . Perfect white teeth, and his icy blue eyes were meant to end me. I won't even start on his massive dick.

"You can't be serious right now," I say, while he keeps dancing and singing, and I can't help but enjoy this incredible moment out of time.

"She looking pretty real nice, lightly remote, she got the perfect body type. Being with you is like being in paradise. Boog never seen a girl that can live up to da hype, ayy, ayy, ayy." He keeps singing and I think I'm crying right now; he can't be real. He can't be a huge business-man, all CEO-like, and be this carefree, almost like a teenager. He jumps on me, but I protect myself with the cover. He reaches for my neck, still singing.

"How we did it on a one-night stand, girl, I wanna be more than a friend to ya." He takes off the cover and sits on me.

"If I were you," I say, "I'd remove myself from there. I'm two seconds away from peeing on myself."

"Pee on me, baby, give it to me, go on," he says, looking almost too serious for my liking.

"Eww, gross, no way!"

He takes me in his arms, my legs around his waist, and stands up.

"Where are you taking me?" I ask in his ear.

"My girl wants to pee; I go by her orders." He enters the bathroom, with me still wrapped around him, then sits me on the toilet seat and stands there, facing me.

"First of all, 'my girl'? I don't think so. Second of all, you can't be serious about staying here watching me pee. This is intimate! How come this doesn't repulse you?"

"During our time together, you *are* my girl. Get used to it. Watching you pee excites me. I like seeing you carefree with me, with no boundaries. I could fuck you here. You can't repulse me, get used to it too."

I cover my face with my hands. He can be so embarrassing, but I think his charm almost overtakes his weird behavior. *Almost . . .*

"Please tell me you're joking," I say, still hiding behind my hands, catching a glimpse of him through my fingers. The bastard is smiling.

"I am . . . almost. What do you want for breakfast? We can eat here or we can eat out," he says, still facing me, as if all of this were normal.

"Out where?" I ask, resigned, not wanting to pay too much attention to the situation.

"Wherever you wish. Linda filled the pantries with food before we arrived, and there are some nice places downtown where we can have a decent breakfast."

"Well, if there's food here, I can make us something. I'd like to try that beautiful kitchen of yours."

"Sure, if you want to. Let's see if there's anything you need." He stops mid-sentence to think, I suppose. Then he laughs, shaking his head.

"What?" I ask.

"You're so different. If I were to ask any woman to stay in to eat or go out, they'd jump at the idea of going out, to some very luxurious establishment, spending a good deal of my money. But you, you prefer to stay in, to cook for us. I've never done that with a stranger. If we can still call ourselves that."

"I'm still not used to the outside life. I've never been to a restaurant to eat. Plus, your house is beautiful, and you have food, so why would anyone choose to go out? And by the way, you still standing here watching me pee doesn't qualify as 'stranger' anymore," I say, cleaning myself. I go to the sink to wash my hands and then I see his reflection through the mirror. He's frowning. *What again?*

"What?" I ask.

"Again, were you in prison? Like in a cell?"

"If your question is 'were you in a detention center after a sentence declared by a judge,' the answer is no. I told you this already, I'm not a criminal."

"I wasn't implying that you were. I'm just trying to understand what you meant by 'not used to the outside life.'"

"I meant nothing. Can I borrow one of your shirts, please?" I hope he won't try to dig up the subject anymore.

Sometimes I say things without giving much thought to it. I don't mean to tease him or anything, but finding the right balance between faking normalcy as if I were not who I truly am and "breaking free" from . . . everything, well, it's hard. It's even harder with him, somehow. But I should know better than to trust anything, whether it comes from within me or from the outside.

Nate gives me a light-blue button-down shirt that feels like heaven on my skin. The material of this shirt is so soft, it's amazing.

"Out of curiosity, how much does this cost?" I ask.

"I don't know, around a thousand dollars or so, why?" *Holy shit.*

"For a shirt?" I reply, astonished.

"I'm Nathan fucking Williams," he says back, laughing.

"The material is so soft, it feels so comfortable, but now I'm scared I'll stain it or ruin it! Do you have something less . . . expensive?"

"You're cute. You can keep it. I have a hundred of those here, back in my penthouse, and in my office as well. Plus, you can call it a souvenir," he says, raising his eyebrows at me, being all smart-ass.

"No, that's fine. I don't plan on doing anything much after our encounter. I'll try to protect it and give it back in excellent condition," I reply, playing smarter. He doesn't answer, but sighs and shakes his head as if I were a child. That makes me laugh, and I follow him downstairs to the kitchen.

I didn't really take a look at the house last night. I was deep in an "out-of-this-world" experience, not believing what happened to me, that I looked without seeing. I remember it being beautiful, but now? It's magnificent. It's huge, so white and clean.

"Delilah?" he says, bringing me back to reality.

"Yes?"

"What were you just thinking? I was asking you what you wanted for breakfast."

"Oh, right, sorry. Well, show me where the food is, and I'll make us something."

The pantry is filled with so many things that look almost too delicious; I won't even start on what's in the fridge. Everything looks fresh and good. I take everything I need to make the perfect breakfast: salmon and avocado bagel, bacon, and eggs Benedict. I'll make some homemade orange juice and a sweet side with homemade chocolate chip muffins.

I go around like the place is mine while Nate prepares some

good coffee and sets the table. He puts a song on the speaker, and we go on dancing and cooking together. The mood is light, joyful even; I'm not used to this. Nate is touchy-feely, very affectionate, always a hand on me whenever he's near, a stolen kiss whenever he can, and I have to say that I like it.

Usually I hate it when people touch me. Even with Eric, we were never touching each other. With Nate, it's another story. Maybe it's because I don't plan on living, maybe it's because our time is limited. I truly feel like time stopped when we met, so when we'll part, time will start again. Then and then only, I'll stop it . . . for good. And in the meantime? Fuck it. Let's just enjoy what life has never given me: peace. And I smile.

When everything is set and ready, we sit down and begin to eat.

"Where did you learn how to cook? This is delicious. Thanks, babe," he says, mouth full.

"You're welcome. Well, actually, I learned it in my previous job, and then when I got my apartment, I had to cook with minimal food. YouTube helped me really enjoyed doing it."

"You used to work in a restaurant?"

"Sort of."

I don't know how to tell him about The Rex. I'm not ashamed of it, I don't really care what he may think of me, but talking about me makes me uncomfortable. Yet maybe if I told him, it would add another reason for him to let me go after Sunday. It's another way to push away people, and that brings me peace. And that's exactly why I hate myself a little more.

"I used to work at The Rex," I say, looking at his reaction. He seems to think.

"The private gentlemen's club? You worked at their restaurant?"

"Yes, but not just. I was a stripper. And a waitress, and everything else. Except the sex part. I got covered for that," I say.

"Do you feel okay talking about it?"

I have to think about his question. Maybe if I don't speak about Ashley or Eric. *Yeah, that should be okay.*

"I guess I could be."

"How did you end up there?" *Wrong question.*

"Pass." Hard no.

He's rolling his eyes at me, but that makes me laugh.

"Okay. How did you get covered for the sex part?" I guess this one's okay.

"I stole from the cashier to pay off a med student. He came to run our weekly blood tests to see if we were clean enough to perform, and all my blood tests came back with tons of fake sexual diseases. Then we became friends, and he kept doing it for free. I could strip to make money and do the rest too, which includes cleaning, cooking, bartending, waitressing, et cetera."

"Why would your boss keep you if you couldn't perform sex with clients?"

"Not to be pretentious, but it was because I'm a very good dancer and I'm really beautiful. And I could sing, too. Men kept asking for me, and they were extra turned on to know they could never touch me. Go figure," I say, biting my muffin.

"Already have," he replies with a huge grin on his face. "Were men respectful to you?"

"They had to be if they wanted to keep their membership. Girls are protected; there's security, and there are weekly self-defense classes. The boss took care of his girls. He knew his business could only work if the girls were okay."

"For how long did you work there? Were you happy? Why did you leave?" His eagerness to know more makes me giggle. He's funny.

"I worked there for almost eight years or so. I was never happy, but compared to my previous life, it was like Disneyland. I still dreamed of leaving that place one day. I held on from day one till the end. I was freed."

"Freed?" he asks, confused.

"You can't get out of The Rex if you don't pay your worth to the boss. That was in the contract. I won't go into details, but it was Eric who set me free."

"Are the women prisoners of some sort?"

"Oh, no. Most of them are happy to live there. Compared to the streets or prison, it's a very good life. Most of them didn't understand why I chose to leave."

"Do you still see them? The girls?"

"No. But if I were to see one of them, I'd be delighted to catch up, I guess. It was another life, though. One I wish not to revisit, if you know what I mean," I say, and he pauses.

"And so you can dance," he says, almost disbelieving me.

"And so I can dance," I reply, smiling.

"I'm gonna need proof," he says, giving me a wink.

"I hope you have enough cash."

"Oh baby, you obviously don't know who you're talking to. I'd empty my bank account right now if need be."

"We'll see. So, what are we gonna do today?"

"I thought we could go walk on the beach, then eat out and get back here, watch some movies, chill, fuck, and repeat."

I burst out laughing at his honesty, him saying this as if saying the sky is blue. I like the fact that he doesn't mince his words with me.

"Sounds perfect. But I don't have anything to wear."

"Linda got you some clothes in my closet upstairs. I'll show you, come with me."

He takes me by the hand and leads me upstairs to his dressing room. As he opens the wardrobe, I see all the clothes he got for me. There's at least enough to go for six months. This is way too much. Dozens of sundresses, countless pairs of shoes, jeans, shirts, even coats and sweaters! All beautiful for sure, but this is not right.

"First, how does she know my size? Second, it can't all be for me! You know that I'll never come back here and that I'll never see you again after tomorrow, right?" He looks offended by what I just said, but he can't be serious. I don't want him to think I'd want to . . . *stay.*

"I know, but you don't have to be mean about it. I told her to buy anything for every season just in case the weather wasn't nice. It's all for you. You can take it all to your place. You know that I have money, right?"

"I won't take any of it. I won't need it. But thank you. You can keep it and use it for another woman you'll pick up in a bar," I say, laughing, to lighten the mood.

I feel like he's somehow hurt by my words, and it wasn't my intention, but I can't help it. I don't know how to be nice, I don't know how to not push people away, I just don't know. I don't want to think. I'm tired of thinking. I'm tired of it all.

Then, out of nowhere, Nate takes me in his arms, hugging me close, as if he knew I needed to calm down a little. And it works. He kisses the top of my hair and takes my face in his hands.

"Wear anything you want. Put on a sweater just in case, because there's some wind at the beach. We'll leave when you're ready," he says, closing the discussion with a light kiss on my lips. I nod and then he goes to get ready.

I don't take too much time to get dressed. I put on a lavender sundress, black flat sandals, and a blue sweater on top of it. I effortlessly tie up my hair, wash my face, no makeup—never liked it—and I'm good.

I go downstairs to meet him. Nate is insanely hot. Blue jeans on, beige sweater, white sneakers, and a face to die for. I spin around like a teenager to show him my outfit, and he's obviously pleased. Then he sighs.

"I guess what they say is true," he says.

"About what?" I ask back, confused.

"That Times Square can't shine as bright as you," he replies with a wink. I puff at him, rolling my eyes. He laughs at his own joke, which is cute, and then we're out the door.

We walk for less than five minutes to reach the beach. On the way, Nate shows me the surroundings, as a tour guide might do, telling me stories about the Hamptons. I listen to it all, holding his hand all the time, never breaking away. The landscape is breathtaking.

We walk along the golden sands of the Hamptons beach, the sun warm on my skin and a soothing breeze rustling the dune grasses. The clear blue sky stretches above, while seagulls call and swoop over the sparkling ocean waves. The scene is perfect, with charming beach houses lining the shore and wildflowers blooming nearby, filling me with peace and comfort.

And that's a fucking first for me. I stop to take a look at Nate and find myself smiling.

"What?" he asks.

"Wanna swim?" I dare him, knowing the weather is not that warm. But I decided I would live a little more, so why not live to the fullest? I've never been to the beach before. Let's find out what the ocean is like.

"You've gotta be crazy to think we'd go in the ocean."

But I don't let him finish as I take off my dress, leaving only my panties on, without an ounce of care in the world about being half-naked on an almost deserted beach. Nate's eyes widen.

"Delilah!" he tries to warn me, but it's too late.

I run towards the ocean. I run and then I feel it. The ocean, the ice-cold water on my frozen skin. The feeling runs through my body, down my spine, from the roots of my hair to the tips of my fingers and throughout my whole body. I breathe the air and it feels so pure. I feel the water and it feels as electric as it does soft, and then I truly feel it, my soul. I feel everything, I feel *me*, the one who I thought was dead. Me, who thought I had nothing left inside. I feel . . . alive. I laugh, I laugh so hard, as I feel the joy of my being here. I'm surprised to feel Nate's arms around me, him laughing as hard as I do.

"You're fucking crazy! The water is fucking cold," he says, and then I decide to push him deeper in the water. But he has more strength than I, so he takes me instead, throwing me into the water, and I don't even remember when was the last time in my whole damn life I laughed that hard. I have to wonder if this is real.

We fight like children in the blue water, gentle waves around us pushing us even closer toward each other. Nate takes me in his arms, his embrace is everything right now. I feel protected. There are so many things I wish I could tell him right now. I want to thank him for giving me that incredible feeling I've never felt before: peace. I want to thank him for offering me the experience of truly living before I go. I want to thank him for allowing me into his world, seeing the world through his magnificent eyes, seeing the beauty of things. Even though there is no hope left for me, even though I no longer consider myself a living being, I want to thank him for pretending I am.

But words don't come out. They're stuck in my body, in my own cell. So instead, I grab his head with both of my hands and I kiss him. Deeply. I force him to open up for me and he does. I don't even feel the cold water, nor the wind around me. All I feel is this growing flame inside of me, I feel the same flame inside of him. We're on fire, we're burning, the sweetest burn of all, and boy does he kiss me back with the same fervor.

I put my legs around his waist, holding him extra close, feeling all of him. I was born to live this moment. When the time comes to shut my eyes forever, I'll think about this. About the time I was reborn in the ocean, and instead of being caught by the arms of my mother, I was caught by the arms of my flame. My Nate. And I tell him all this through my kiss. I hope he'll know what I meant, I hope he'll know he offered me everything, I hope he'll know he was the reason my heart felt at peace and no longer at war.

So I mark him with my mouth, my tongue, my teeth, all of it, and he happily joins me as I feel his powerful body all around mine.

We break our kiss, resting our foreheads against each other. We breathe, we don't speak, I can't speak. So I raise my gaze to meet his, and I smile. He's so beautiful. He has the most magnificent light-blue eyes that are transcending my soul. When he looks at me with those eyes, I feel every part of me, from my hair to my toes. I feel it all.

"We're gonna get pneumonia if we stay here, baby," he finally says.

"Don't know what you're talking about. I'm on fire here, *baby*," I reply, widening my eyes as I mimic his endearment. He starts to get us out of the water, never putting me down, and we regain the beach.

"If you're on fire here, I wonder how you'd feel in a warmer sea."

"Which one are you thinking about?" I ask, curious.

"Beaches in Bora Bora are exceptional. The water is as warm as a bath and the colors are sublime. From the blue of the sea and the white of the beach sand to the green of the trees, it's all gorgeous."

"And to think I'll never see any of it. You'll show me pictures of it later," I say as we get dressed, and now I feel the fucking cold.

"I can take you there." *What is he talking about?*

"Take me where?" I reply.

"Bora Bora." *Oh, okay.* That makes me laugh, as I guess it's a joke. *Right?*

"Very funny," I say, rolling my eyes. But Nate grabs my elbow to bring me back to him, forcing me to look at him.

"I can take you there, Delilah."

"Okay, smart boy, how much time to go back and forth from here to Bora Bora?"

"I have a jet, so around twenty-three hours or so to go and come back from and to New York, why?"

"But we have like thirty hours or so left together, which means a very expensive yet stupid idea to go through this much just to take a peek in the water, don't you think?"

He seems to think, but before he opens his mouth, I cut him off.

"Thought so. Let's get back, I'm freezing. Plus, you said going in Bora Bora's water was like going inside a bath, and I've never taken one before. I saw you have a huge bathtub in your house; it'll be like going to Bora Bora! You can show me pictures of that place in the bathtub, that'll be great!" I say, excited about the idea.

Nate is looking at me all funny.

"What?" I ask, because I have no idea what he may be thinking right now.

"I feel like I've said this a thousand times already, but you are nothing like any woman I've ever met in my entire life. If I had offered anyone the opportunity to go to Bora Bora, they'd jump at the occasion in a heartbeat, no thinking. But you? You'd rather take a bath in my house? Unbelievable. Worst of all, you're not even joking about this shit. You seem to be all excited for . . . a fucking bath. I just don't get it."

"Well, maybe the problem isn't me being excited for a bath, but you not associating yourself with the right people," I fire back, sticking out my tongue, but he grabs me in his arms in a playful embrace.

When we arrive at the house, we go straight to the bathroom adjoined to the master bedroom. While Nate is preparing a hot bath for both of us, I take a moment to clean up the room because I cannot handle any mess.

When I get back to Nate, he's already naked, waiting for me, with what might be the girliest bath ever seen. A lot of bubbles, candles, and a wonderful scent of vanilla.

He settles in first and offers me a hand. The temperature of the water is perfect, the vanilla smell is amazing, and the man that goes with it is . . . also perfect.

We lie down together, my back to his front, his arms around my breasts, and then I just relax. Completely. We talk for a while, he shows me pictures of his property in Bora Bora—and okay, the place looks like heaven—we're cuddling, appreciating the simple yet perfect moment we're sharing.

"So you've never taken a bath before?"

"No, just showers. Never been in a bathtub before. This is an amazing first, thank you."

"You're most welcome. I'd like to see your shower when I take you back to your place tomorrow. Just to see." *That's a no.*

"You won't. You'll drive me straight back to where we met, if that's okay with you, of course."

"Why do you want to go back to Orion?" *How can I say it without saying it . . .*

"Unfinished business." I stay extra vague.

"Can I come?" *What?*

I turn around to face him. "Why would you?"

"To get more time, I guess. Is that so bad?"

"Yes, it is. It wasn't part of our deal. Let's not ruin this, please," I say, almost begging. *If he's there, I'll never jump.* The thought crosses my mind and I immediately push it away.

He holds me tight, back in my original position, his head in my neck, breathing me in. He doesn't speak for a moment.

"Is there someone you're meeting there tomorrow?" he asks, almost in a whisper. As if he were scared of asking. A meeting with someone: no. A meeting with my fate: yes. But he can't know. I don't answer, I don't speak, I can feel myself shutting down. That is what I do best, but right now, I hate myself for it.

"Delilah, please tell me the truth. Is there someone else?" he asks more firmly in my ear.

"That's not any of your business, Nate. We have a deal: forty-eight hours and that's it. Then we forget we ever existed. I'm too hot now, I'm going to—" I'm trying to get up to leave him and this discussion, but he grabs me by the arm, pulling me back into his embrace.

"Not so fast. I need this answer from you, Delilah. Are you involved with someone else? Because right now, it feels a lot like you have a boyfriend and you're cheating on him with me, and then you'll get back to him as if none of this ever happened. This is beyond disrespectful; I think I have a right to know the truth. The more I know you, the more difficult it is to believe a woman like you is single. So again, are you involved with another man, Delilah?"

This is hilarious. On every level. He can't be serious. This is beyond ridiculous. But I'll gladly play him.

"Would you have looked away if I were? Would you have brought me here if you knew I belonged to another man?" I answer in all sincerity.

"Don't even try to play me, Delilah. I'm not a man you can fool easily. I'm not joking here. Answer me," he says, and I have to admit he can be intimidating. Little does he know, I have met way worse than him.

"Now what are you going to do, Nathan?" I tease him, deadpan.

He holds me closer, taking my face in his hands. The contrast between his menacing look and the delicacy of his hold on me is almost disturbing.

"You'll call him, you'll tell him you're over him. And I'll come back with you to make sure he understands the situation. You. Are. Mine," he says. I tut.

"Let's get something very clear here, Nate. I. Don't. Belong. To. Anyone. No one has a hold on me anymore. I'm a free bird, and I'll die a free one. What is happening here will stop right now if you don't understand clearly what I say. The fact that you think I lied to you when you are no one to me is insulting enough to push me further into wrath mode," I reply, being fully mean to him. *Who the hell does he think he is?*

I stand up and get out of the bathtub, grabbing a towel, but then I feel him taking my hand, turning me to him, our bodies colliding. He looks me straight in the eyes, holding a threat larger than his silence. But then I can feel it. This palpable tension between us, this magnetism that only forces us closer and closer. This intense chemistry is almost tangible. We stand no chance against it.

I don't even know who starts first. All I know is that I'm now breathing in his mouth, holding him tight as if holding on to life, backed up against the wall, moaning like the whore he thought I was ten seconds ago. And damn, can he kiss me with that same passion, touching me everywhere. I'm drawn to him; my body is craving his. I don't even know how we got from fighting to making out like two horny teenagers.

Nate takes me in his arms and goes to the bedroom, where he throws me on the bed. He doesn't take a moment to look around or take a breath; he jumps on me, and I welcome him. It feels like I was dying from thirst, and he was the water. He ascends with kissing, going from my mouth to my breasts and then . . . *there*. Oh my God. He's worshipping me with his tongue. He's doing magic to me. I feel his finger pushing inside me, and I love every bit of this. But when I feel myself on the verge of my orgasm, he stops and gets back to my mouth, making me taste myself like yesterday, and damn, that's just too sexy for me.

"Open your mouth," he says, and I do as I'm told. Then he spits his saliva in my mouth. We look deeply into each other's eyes.

"Swallow," he orders more than asks. And I do it. He's so fucking sexy that this is fucking turning me on. He kisses me again like I'm made of glass, taking extra care not to be brusque.

"Do you trust me?" he asks, still looking at me with those icy blue eyes. I don't even think, I just want more of this.

"Yes," I answer, fully meaning it.

"Stand up," he says, kissing me again. "Do you know what a safeword is?" he asks as he caresses the sides of my body, up and down, with both of his hands, giving me light kisses at the base of my neck. The feeling is beyond incredible.

"No," I answer.

"When it's too much for you, you use your safeword, and I'll instantly stop whatever I'm doing. Pick a word, Delilah."

"Delilah? I guess we're done with endearments. Too bad, I started to like it," I reply, laughing a little, but then he slaps my butt, hard enough to make me stop immediately.

"Don't start with your smart mouth. You'll get your endearments after I'm done. Pick a word." Ooh, he's being dominating.

After everything I've been through, I know my natural reaction would be to get the hell out of here. But I feel the complete opposite. I'm drawn to him; I want even more of it. His spanking turned me the fuck on.

I liked it . . . *How is that even possible?*

"Orion," I say.

"Good girl," he says, looking me straight in the eye.

"Will you spank me again?" I whisper to him.

"Who allowed you to speak?" Damn . . . I have to put an end to my way of thinking. I'll try to dig up how the hell I'm enjoying every bit of this when I'm supposed to hate it later. For now, I just stop and play by the rules.

"Sorry, sir."

"Good. Now, hear me, Delilah: in this bedroom, you'll obey me, you'll do what I say. Don't forget your safeword."

He leaves the room for two minutes or so and comes back with ropes and a . . . *what?* He takes both my hands and ties them with the rope, and then he literally attaches me to the fucking hook hanging from the ceiling. I didn't even see it there. Then he takes my feet and ties them to the bedposts one by one. I'm unable to move, naked, and mesmerized by him. With his finger, he slightly caresses my pussy, testing me. I'm so turned on I feel like I'm about to die.

"You're dripping. Do you like this, Delilah? Being all tied up, completely at my mercy?"

"Yes, sir," I answer. And he intensifies his touch on me. Taking my nipple into his mouth, playing with his tongue and his teeth. The thin line between pain and pleasure is incredible. I've never felt this way. *Never.* He steps away, taking that thing in his hand. "Do you know what this is, Delilah?"

"No."

"It's a riding crop. I'll use it on you. Whenever you feel it's too much, you use your safeword. I know that you're new at this, so don't think too much. I'll go easy on you even if you deserve to be well-punished." *What ?*

"Punished for what ? What the fuck are you talking about ?" I say, but then he slaps me on my pussy. It hurts, but it feels so oddly . . . *good.* Then he looks right in my eyes.

"For pretending that this means nothing," he says, and I shut my eyes.

Then—then I feel it. He caresses me with the crop, from my mouth to my arms, my breasts, my stomach, my pussy, then my legs and feet. He gets back up, and I see how hard he is. This is turning him on real bad. The veins of his penis are showing like I've never seen before. *Damn . . . So fucking hot.* Then he hits me with the crop, which makes me jump.

"Stop looking at my dick. You don't deserve to have it."

"Damn, here I thought I was a good girl," I say back, fully teasing him. And I shouldn't have. He hits me harder on the nipples, then licks both and finishes them with a bite, making me moan like hell. I look at him and I know—oh God, how I do know—I made him laugh inside. And that ignites in me the ultimate pride.

"Don't move. Oh, that's right . . . you can't!" he says, and then he leaves the room laughing at his own joke, bastard. I feel like I'm on fire. I miss his touch, I miss his eyes, I miss his smell, I hate the fact that he left me here, hanging, craving for him.

Fortunately, he comes back less than two minutes later. My relief frightens me. He kisses me with fierce intensity, forcing me to open up for him. The kiss is hot, passionate . . . violent.

Then I'm surprised when I feel something cold on my left boob. I jump, still kissing him. *What the fuck?* Is that . . . *ice*?

"Do you know why I put ice there?" he asks, his lips never leaving mine. I shake my head. He steps back an inch to look deep into my eyes.

"To match your cold heart. Your fucking dark heart," he says. He obviously doesn't know who he's playing with.

"I don't have a dark heart, Nathan. I have a black one."

His eyes darken at my reply. *Good.* He puts his hand on my neck. He doesn't strangle me, but I feel his hold, his domination over me, and I submit.

"Wanna play poets now, huh? Try to call me Nathan again, and I swear you'll regret it." I don't even have time to answer before he kisses me with urgency, pressing his body to mine. I seek friction, I shamelessly grind on him, needing some release. Then, out of nowhere, he puts the ice on my pussy. *Fuck.*

The contrast between the cold ice and my hot core is electrifying. He grabs my hair with his other hand, pulling it down, making my head rise. He literally licks my face and bites my cheeks. I'm his toy right now, but does that bother me? Absolutely not. But I can't wait any longer.

"Nate, please," I beg.

"No," he says simply, pushing two fingers inside me. *Oh my God.* He fucks me with his fingers, but that's far from being enough for me. I want more, I *need* more.

"I'll be nice, I promise." He can make me say anything right now, I need him.

I feel his hands undoing the rope, freeing my hands, finally. It hurts a little, but nothing unbearable. Then he unties my feet, and when I'm freed, I try to jump on him, but he pushes me away. His eyes are dark, his face serious, and that doesn't sit well with me. I want him.

"Kneel," he orders, and boy, do I obey like a bitch.

"Open your mouth." I do as I'm told.

"Now suck me like I taught you to." And I don't even think, I execute orders. Happily. I do it the same way he showed me to, back in his limo. I spit on his cock, spread my saliva all around his big dick, and I suck it like the good whore that I apparently become. I hear him moan my name, louder and louder, and I intensify my task, massaging his balls, my tongue on his head, baring my teeth, probably giving him more pleasure than he ever had.

He holds my head, pulling my hair from time to time, thrusting into my mouth. I look him straight in the eye the whole time. This is extra perfect. I feel his cock contracting, he's on the verge of coming. I don't think, I just want to please him, I want him to be satisfied with me, I want him to thank me.

"Your fucking perfect warm mouth is going to make me fucking come, Delilah."

Perfect. He thrusts even harder and it gives me chills. I love every bit of this blow job.

And I feel it. He jerks off in my mouth, tons of sperm, and I remember not to swallow. When he takes out his penis, I open my mouth to show him his work. He kneels in front of me, eyes wide open, mesmerized.

"Stick out your tongue," he asks, barely breathing. I take my tongue out, drooling, his sperm running down my mouth. He puts his index finger in my mouth, caressing my tongue and then spreading his cum on my neck and on my breasts. The act is so hot, so fucking sexy, I'm so turned on.

"I have to take another bath now," I say.

"No, keep my cum on you. I'll be hard again in five minutes tops, then I'll fuck you with my mark on your fucking perfect body." That makes me laugh hard.

"Sorry to disappoint, but I don't want to risk any of your soldiers going discreetly inside me, and risking any bad omen."

If he managed to stay serious for the past hour or so, it all falls apart now. He bursts out laughing, falling on his back right on the floor, and I join him.

"Yeah, that's right, get my kid in your tummy, that'll keep you next to me for a very long time," he says, snorting. His joke isn't even funny, but he cracks me up anyway.

"Fuck you, that'll never happen," I reply, slapping him on the chest. He lies down, sighing, looking at the ceiling.

"That's right, I forgot," he says.

"Forgot what?" I reply, getting on top of him.

"That you were a cold-hearted bitch."

I slap him harder, which makes him laugh even more. I know he's not being insulting, just a playful bastard.

"Better that than a gold-digger, don't you think?"

He stops to think about my reply, which is slightly concerning.

"No, I'd rather you be a gold-digger."

I know he's joking. For sure. *Obviously.* I gotta get away with this.

"You can't be serious. Anyway, I'm starving and I'm frustrated. You've fed me with your cock; now please feed me with food."

"Wait, kiss me a little." And I don't even have time to respond as he grabs my mouth with his, in a tender at first but quickly passionate kiss, his hands roaming everywhere, and I'm so turned on he has to make me come or I'll explode real fast.

"I'm hard again, babe, let's go." *What the fuck?*

"Nate, you can't play with me like this. I don't want to eat anymore, I want to fuck!" If I were to go back in time and tell myself I'd ever be able to say something like that, I wouldn't have believed it. Impossible. But with him? Totally different story.

"I was going to say let's go on the bed, you nympho. Already addicted to my cock, I see," he says, grinning. *Bastard.*

"Looks like the cold-hearted bitch has found the perfect jerk," I say, and he laughs as he pushes me on the bed. He jumps on me and gets back to kissing me. And eventually, he fucks me good for I don't know how long, as time completely stops whenever our bodies become one.

~

It's past five in the afternoon. We're lying on the couch, watching some movies Nate considers "classic." We've spent the day at home. I cooked, he helped, we fucked a lot, we laughed even more, and now we're cuddled up on the couch watching TV. I've never had a day like this before. It feels so . . . *good.* I wonder if I feel this lighthearted because I know I'm about to shut it all down very soon. Or is it him that's . . . calming me? The line is so blurred.

He does have this aura, this beautiful light above his head that tells me I can trust him. And even though I will never trust anyone ever again, I want to at least pretend to. I want to imagine that I can. With him. Nate is really tall with a very athletic body, and he's dominant. He acts as if he were protecting me, and I didn't even know how much I needed this. There is something about him. His physique, his mind, his intelligence, I don't know. I can't tell which is it that calms me. Or is it just the fact that I'm leaving this world for good.

As I feel his hands on my back, caressing me as if it were out of habit, it becomes clearer and clearer. I rest my head on his chest and I kiss it.

"Do you want to go out tonight? Have dinner in some fancy place, maybe go dancing if you want?" he asks. I raise my head to meet his beautiful blue eyes and I smile.

"Far be it from me to make you spend money on me, but I've never eaten in a fancy restaurant, except for Orion last night. And I've never been out dancing, as I always *was* the one dancing for work. And I decided that I'd take the opportunity to live fully as if I were to die soon. Lead me and I'll follow," I say, smiling. It's like I haven't stopped smiling since I met him.

"Sure, baby. I'm happy to spend money on us. Let's go get ready, we'll leave in an hour," he says. *Us . . .*

I'm getting ready, but my mind is somewhere else. Before I met Nate, I always thought that what I had with Eric was extra special. I thought our "relationship" was passionate, that the love we shared was endless, infinite, pure, real, strong . . . It didn't last at all. We kissed three months after we first met, and he left me two months after we first kissed. But he belonged to someone else. He was never meant to be mine from the beginning. But I think I loved him.

Yet the more time I spend with Nate, the more obvious it becomes that Eric and I did not have the connection I thought we had. This alone should make me feel better after everything we've been through, but it doesn't. *We were never close . . .*

I can't say why I'm this close to Nate. Is it because he's beautiful? Is it his beauty that draws me to him? Is it our sexual attraction? Is it because I don't give a fuck anymore about anything, now that I've decided to end my own life? Is it because the whole thing is surreal?

I stand in front of the mirror, my hands lightly tracing the silk of the red dress I chose. It clings to my silhouette, the fabric soft against my skin, the thin straps resting delicately on my shoulders. The dress is mid-thigh length with a beautiful décolleté that reveals just a hint, enough to feel elegant without overdoing it. I brush my long brown hair, letting it fall naturally, and apply the same red lipstick I wore the first time I met Nate.

As I look at my reflection, a wave of emotion washes over me. I've never dressed up like this for myself before. It was always for work, for something I hated at The Rex, where I had to look a certain way but felt empty inside. This dress, this moment, is different. It's for *me*. Yes, a part of it is for Nate because I'm grateful for what he's given me, but mostly, it's for me. For once, I'm making myself beautiful to enjoy the night, to savor the freedom and the sense of self-worth that's blossoming inside me. This is a first, and it feels incredibly empowering. And then it hits me: no, the last time I made myself beautiful, it was to go to die. Now I'm making myself beautiful because I'm about to go to . . . *live.*

Nate passes next to me to grab a watch on the dresser as I rearrange my hair, and I can't help it. I grab him by the neck and kiss him softly on the lips, caressing his cheeks lightly with the palms of my hands. I feel his arms immediately around my waist. His warmth, his size, his smell—everything is intoxicating where he's concerned. The embrace feels natural, comfortable, easy even. I feel like I've known him for so long, my body instantly responds to his. I put my hand in his hair to rearrange a lock of hair that's falling on his forehead.

"You're okay, baby? I really like it when you're tender like this."

"Don't get used to it, big boy." I say, pinching his nose as if he were a child. I add, "I'm ready whenever you are," and he slaps me on the way.

"Let's go, gorgeous mine," he replies.

"I don't think that 'gorgeous mine' is good English," I tease him as we get downstairs.

"It is to me. And if I say it is, then it just is."

"Oh, excuse me, I forgot that you were the master of the universe," I fire back.

"Mmmh, master of that gorgeous body, for sure," he says, taking me in his arms, putting his head in the crook of my neck. I have to say that the gesture is extremely relaxing. I gladly welcome him in my arms, fully enjoying this embrace.

We arrive at the restaurant, one Nate told me he knows well. The heavy, gilded doors of the restaurant swing open, and I step into a world I've only seen in movies. My breath catches as I take in the opulence that surrounds me. The colors of the room are rich and vibrant, with deep reds and gleaming golds. Velvet curtains drape elegantly from the ceiling, glowing softly under the ambient lights that cast a romantic shimmer across the room. It's an Italian dream, filled with the mouth-watering scent of freshly made pasta and the soft, inviting melody of a piano playing in the corner.

I can hardly believe I'm here. This place is worlds away from where I come from. As I walk further in, I feel a wave of emotions. Amazement, excitement, and a tinge of unease ripple through me. This isn't my world, but it's Nate's. Nate, who moves through these surroundings with effortless grace, a regular in this bastion of elegance. His presence beside me is reassuring. With his hand on the small of my back, he guides me to our table.

It's set with pristine white linens, crystal glasses, and silverware that gleams under the chandeliers' light. Nate pulls out my chair, and I sit, still overwhelmed by the sheer beauty of the place. He sits right next to me, his eyes twinkling with amusement as he watches me take it all in. Despite the grandeur, there is an unexpected comfort in the way he makes me feel. I know I am *not* falling in love with him, but I deeply appreciate the gift he's giving me tonight—this exceptional moment, this taste of a life so different from my own.

As we talk, I find my gaze drifting to the small stage in the corner. A pianist plays a gentle tune, and next to him stands a mic, inviting anyone brave enough to share their voice. I wonder what it would be like to sing here, to let my voice mingle with this place. It's a fleeting thought, but it stays with me, adding another layer to this surreal experience.

Nate speaks of his world—his business, his travels, his life of privilege, his possible candidacy for Senate, and even more things about the universe, the planets, the stars. And though I listen, a part of me is acutely aware of how different we are. He belongs to this world of luxury while I'm just a visitor, a temporary guest. Our time together is limited, and in some ways, that's a good thing. It keeps us both grounded, aware of the realities that await us outside these golden walls.

Yet, even as I tell myself this, I can't help but feel a pang of sadness. Sharing this night with Nate, I realize that letting him go will mean losing something I thought was dead in me, a part that has dared to dream, to step into a world I never thought possible. Our lives are too different to ever truly intertwine, but for now, I am content to savor this moment, to bask in the glow of an evening that feels almost like a fairy tale.

Nate reaches across the table and takes my hand, his touch warm and steady.

"Are you enjoying yourself, beautiful?" he asks, his voice low and sincere. I smile, squeezing his hand.

"More than you know," I reply.

And in that moment, I am truly grateful. It feels like pure magic. We talk and laugh for a while. The food is too great to be real, and a part of me wishes I could learn the recipes. *That won't happen.*

I tell him more about my life at The Rex, intentionally avoiding some details, and Nate, being a gentleman, lets it go.

"Take off your panties," Nate commands suddenly, his voice low and dangerous.

"What?" I blink, heat spreading across my cheeks. "Excuse me?"

"You heard me." His gaze locks onto mine, unrelenting, daring.

I look around quickly, making sure no one is close enough to hear us.

"I need them. What's gotten into you?"

"I'll give them back," he promises. "I just need to have them. Now."

"Are you drunk?" I murmur, trying to keep my voice steady.

"Drunk on you," he growls softly, eyes darkening. "Now, be a good girl and take them off."

A thrill rushes through me, hot and wicked. My pulse hammers wildly as I weigh his words. *What the fuck? Okay, Nate. Let's see where this goes.*

I glance around one last time. The low lighting and the buzz of conversation around us give me a thin veil of privacy, enough to dare. Slowly, I slide my hands beneath my dress, feeling the hem brush against my thighs as I grip the edges of my panties. My heart races as I start to pull them down. The silky fabric clings to my skin, the movement slow and deliberate, making the air around us crackle with heat. Each inch I lower them, I feel my arousal heightening, my skin tingling with awareness.

Nate's eyes never leave me. His breathing deepens, nostrils flaring slightly. He looks like a predator, completely focused on his prey. The intensity of his gaze makes my whole body tighten, every nerve on fire. I can see his fingers twitch, his jaw tense as if he were keeping himself from grabbing me right here.

My heart is racing as I ball up the delicate material and, with trembling fingers, slide it across the table to him.

He takes them, his hand closing around the soft lace. His chest rises and falls in heavy breaths as he looks at me, eyes blazing. Slowly, he brings the panties to his nose, and then . . . he inhales deeply.

A low, guttural sound rumbles from his throat. His eyes flutter shut, lips parting as if savoring every part of my scent. I bite down on my lower lip, feeling a fresh wave of wetness between my thighs. Watching him—completely lost in the smell of me—sends a wild rush of heat straight to my core.

"Fuck, Delilah . . ." His voice is rough, almost a growl. "I need to fuck you right now."

I burst into laughter, my body still shivering with need.

"Slow down, boy. Now, give them back—I don't like being this exposed."

"Let me." He doesn't wait for my answer. He slides out of his seat, eyes never leaving mine, and I know—*oh God*, I know I'm done for.

"What? No . . . Nate—" I whisper-shout, but he cuts me off with a stern look, gently pushing my hands aside.

"Shh, let me take care of you," he murmurs, voice low and thick with desire.

Before I can protest, I feel his hand on my ankle. The touch sends a shock wave through my body, making my breath hitch. He moves slowly, deliberately, sliding the lace back up my leg, his fingers brushing my bare skin. My pulse pounds in my ears as his hand travels higher, each inch bringing a new rush of heat. My thighs part instinctively, craving more, aching for his touch.

When he reaches my hips, he pauses, fingers playing with the lace. He drags them slowly over my core, the faintest pressure making me gasp. He pulls them into place with agonizing slowness, his fingers grazing me through the thin fabric, just enough to make my back arch.

"Nate . . ." I breathe, barely able to form words. My body is on fire, every nerve screaming for him.

"Like that?" he whispers, his voice dripping with dark satisfaction. His lips brush against the sensitive skin of my neck, a fleeting caress that leaves me shuddering.

I nod, swallowing hard, fighting to keep my composure. He stands up, eyes dark and dangerous, and I can see the strain in his posture, the raw need he's barely holding back.

He leans in, his lips brushing my ear, his breath hot and teasing.

"I'm going to fuck you so hard you won't remember your own name."

I shiver, caught between fear and excitement, every cell in my body begging for more.

"We'll see," I whisper, meeting his gaze, feeling a reckless thrill course through me.

"Mmm," he murmurs, eyes devouring me.

The waiter comes back faster than expected and Nate orders us some desserts, as if nothing happened, and again I trust him with the choice of food.

I take another look at the beautiful place, my eyes resting on the stage. Nate notices and puts a hand on my thigh.

"You wanna go sing, baby?" he asks in a dare.

"I used to sing at The Rex, so I'm not shy about it," I counter.

"Then go ahead," he says, smirking. Well, why not one last time? So I stand up and go straight to the pianist. The old man gives me his most beautiful smile as he sees me coming towards him.

"*Buonasera, signorina,* how can I help you?" he says, with the most elegant Italian accent. Wearing a fine tux, the man couldn't look better if he tried.

"Hi, I wanted to know if I could join you and sing?"

"*Si, signorina,* what song do you want to sing?"

"I'd like, if it's possible of course, to sing Adele, 'A Million Years Ago.' Do you know it?" This song has a way of breaking my heart a little more, and I think I need a reminder of who I am in this world where I don't belong. The lyrics speak to me, even if they don't relate to what happened to me; they still ring true to my mental state.

"I'm a very talented pianist. I'll find the partition on my iPad and I'll play it. Can you give me five minutes and come back?"

"Of course, sir, thank you so much!" I say, squeezing his arm. He looks so nice. I get back to Nate and decide to play him a bit.

"So?" he asks.

"No, he doesn't know how to play with someone who sings, so I didn't want to bother him any further. That's fine, I'll sing to you when we get home," I say as I regain my seat.

"I'd love that. You singing when we get home, I mean. We could watch the stars again, what do you think?"

I know I said the word "home" first, but hearing it come out of his mouth, that beautiful, delicious mouth of his, it's just . . . different. *Home, us* . . . What is going on with me?

I nod because I'm incapable of saying anything. I just can't speak. Yet again, I so badly wish I could tell him how much it means to me that he brought me some form of truce I never thought was accessible. I wish I could tell him how grateful I am. And I think he knows by the look on his face. I feel like he understands me.

As I turn my head, I see the pianist giving me a sign, inviting me to join him. I stand up, pretending to go to pee so Nate wouldn't find out my ruse. I go on stage, and that feels really . . . good. The mic and I are great friends.

"Ready, *signorina?*"

"As I'll ever be." And he plays the first note of that beautiful melody.

When I hear it, I feel the music taking me, taking full possession of my body, what's left of my heart and my soul. I'm no longer me, I'm no longer here; I'm just the notes, the melody, and my voice. That's when I begin to sing.

I open my eyes and they find Nate's. He's surprised. *Good.* But then I go back to my other self, the servant of the melody, and I join it and completely let go. God, how good that feels.

But then, as I sing the chorus, I hear people clapping their hands. I open my eyes and see them. They're looking intensely at me, they must be really enjoying my performance. Then I see Nate's eyes. He's mesmerized by the song, so I close my eyes again and go back to oblivion as I let my voice explore the musical notes.

> . . . I wish I could live a little more
> Look up to the sky, not just the floor
> I feel like my life is flashing by
> And all I can do is watch and cry
> I miss the air, I miss my friends
> I miss my mother, I miss it when . . .

And then the music ends. I reopen my eyes and see all the people standing up, applauding me. This is no new experience, but it's always gratifying. And then I see Nate. He seems to be moved by my performance, his eyes a bit gloomy. He doesn't smile. He's just shocked, I think?

"Your voice is a gift, *signorina*. It'll be my pleasure to accompany you again anytime you wish. What's your name, if I may ask?" the pianist says.

"The pleasure was all mine. I'm Delilah."

"Beautiful name for a beautiful lady! I'm Giovanni. Don't ever stop singing, *bellissimu*. Your voice is a gift," he says, kissing the back of my hand. His words go straight to my soul because he, and the rest of them, don't know that I'm likely to never sing again, and never be heard either.

I smile at him, thank him before going back to Nate. I don't say a word and neither does he.

I'm pleased to see that my dessert has arrived. I wouldn't be able to tell what it is, but man, I can say it looks delicious. I take a bite and oh my God, it's the sweetest thing I've ever had in my life. Which is not a high bar. I raise my gaze and see Nate: he hasn't touched his dessert, he's watching me intently.

"What?" I ask. He shakes his head in disbelief.

"You're amazing," he says, and I give him a little wink as a thank-you.

"Not as much as this. Taste it and tell me," I say, cutting him a piece and feeding him directly. I use my thumb to clean the side of his mouth.

"Yes, this tastes good, but you taste better. I know what I'm talking about," he says, winking at me. "The song you just sang, are the lyrics a reflection of your story?"

"This is too personal. But, to answer you without telling you, yes and no." I do understand his curiosity, obviously. But I can't share this part of my life. I can't speak out about what happened to me. I don't want to offend him because so far, this night has been nothing but perfect. The whole day was fucking perfect. I have no desire to ruin it. I take his hand and entwine our fingers to show him that I'm not shutting off.

"Where to now?" I ask, because we've finished our dinner.

"Wherever you want. I thought about going to a club, having some drinks, then going back home to watch the stars and end this beautiful night by burying myself deep, deep inside you for hours. But if you have other ideas that still include me deep, deep inside you, I'm game, babe." It amazes me how our conversations can go from deep and meaningful to light and comical. Of course, his reply makes me giggle.

"I'm game too, baby," I say as I lean into him to give him a slight kiss on the lips. "You know, I still have some money from last night, since you paid for my drinks, and I sure as hell don't have enough to cover for this meal, but I can participate, at least." It's not that I don't want him to think I'm some kind of gold-digger. I won't live long enough to care about that. It's just that, I don't know, he's been so nice that I want to give back a little. But that only makes him laugh.

"As long as you're with me, I've got you covered. It's cute you thought I would let you, though. Plus, as I recall, you will effectively cost me a small fortune."

"What are you talking about?"

"You said that I needed a lot of cash to watch you strip for me. I'll show you just how much I'm willing to give to watch you do so."

"Then we'd better go home now," I say, using my most seductive voice. That turns him on plenty, I can see it in his eyes.

He doesn't even respond; he stands up, takes my hand, and leads us toward the exit.

Outside, his driver is ready to pick us up. We don't even need to wait, and that treatment, that luxury, that life is so beyond my understanding.

I thought I'd be dead by now. *Dead.* And here I am, getting out of a beautiful restaurant where I ate a delicious dinner. I'm wearing the most beautiful dress, I'm picked up by a fucking driver, and last but not least, the most handsome man I've ever seen is holding my hand. A man that has shown me nothing but respect, a man that has no agenda, a man that has no will nor power to hurt me. A man that is showing me a vision of what life could have been. He's genuine, authentic, funny, so nice. I can't believe I'm living this moment right now. All thanks to him. But I will thank him with everything I have and everything I am, for it is going to be the last thing I'll ever do.

We go inside the limo and head back to his house. *Home,* as he called it. The second I dare to have a hint of hope, I shut it off completely. I just can't do it. All I want from now on is to enjoy the rest of the hours that are offered to me. I want him, I want everything with him, just for our time.

The rest doesn't exist. The rest is irrelevant.

CHAPTER 6

Nate

D elilah and I drive straight home. I can't keep my hands to myself the whole time, and neither can she—to my utmost liking.

This night has been incredible so far. And it has only just begun. When we were at the Italian restaurant and she sang, I can't
even begin to describe how I felt. Truth be told, she has a fucking
gift. Her voice is one of the most powerful I've ever heard in my entire life. During the whole performance, she seemed possessed by
the music, and dare I say, haunted by the lyrics. It took me time to
understand it was connected to whatever she's been through in her
past, but I concluded that Delilah has been through hell and back.

She must have had a very hard life. I can hear it through her unspoken words, see it in her sad eyes, and feel it through her broken soul. Yet I sense a sliver of hope for her. I know she's not done
yet, and somehow, she's looking for a way out of it all. I think she
just doesn't know how. Even though I don't know what happened
to her, and even though I fear she won't ever tell me anything, I
want to try to help her. I know that we just met, yet I have a feeling
about her that tells me to just go for it.

We arrive at home, and I tell Delilah to wait for me in the kitchen
as I go to the cellar to take out a very good bottle of champagne to
celebrate us. When I get back to her, the second she sees me, she
smiles. And damn, her smile illuminates the dark. I show her the
bottle of Dom Pérignon as I start to open it.

"You shouldn't waste a good bottle of champagne on me, Nate. I
wouldn't be able to tell the difference from a cheap one," she says.
Pfff, little does she know . . .

"I don't have 'cheap,' baby. And it's my pleasure to treat you right," I say, but she rolls her eyes. I can only guess that, sadly, no one ever treated her like what she's worth. Anyway, I want to get back to business with this fine goddess of mine wearing the devil's dress.

"So, about that dance, how do you want to proceed?" I swear that just saying it makes me hard as fuck.

"Do you have a pole?" Shit, she's too much for me. *I'm* too much for people, usually, but with her? Damn.

"I can have it settled within ten minutes," I say, and I don't even waste any time as I text Linda to get a team to settle it immediately.

"Where do you want it?" she asks. *Interesting . . .*

"You're the pro here, baby. You tell me where it would be more . . . intense."

"Well, opposed to what you may think, the best place would be your office, a place where you feel powerful, master-of-the-universe-like. My clients always ask me to come and perform in their office, and I've never said yes to anyone. I guess I could make an exception for you," she says, winking at me.

Thinking that some motherfucking bastard has ever had a private dance makes me want to destroy everything and kill them all. But the idea of her in my office is beyond tempting. I will have her there for sure, *one day.* Even if she's not ready to hear it, she will. But I still have a home office here, as in all my properties. I text Linda to have it settled there. She informs me that it'll be done in less than thirty minutes, which is already twenty-nine minutes too many. Knowing that I'll be the first (dare I hope the only) one to have her makes me harder in a way I never thought was possible. *What the fuck did she do to me?*

"Usually I have special outfits for my performances, but I'll manage with what you bought me, sir." For fuck's sake, I'm afraid I'll lose it too soon. She's so fucking sexy, so fucking gorgeous. I can't wait to fuck the shit out of her. I have to control my compulsion, regain some composure, and try to act normal. If I can.

"Keep talking like that to me, gorgeous mine, and the night will be very, very long for your sweet ass," I say, grabbing her by her thighs, putting her on the countertop, and kissing the fuck out of her. I can't help but glide my hands under her provocative dress, reaching her panties. I need her, right now, so much. But she breaks the kiss.

"You wanna play a little?" she asks with the most beautiful smile I've ever seen. I gotta say I'm intrigued.

"Play?"

"Well, you'd be a client, just like at The Rex. I'll give you what I gave them, nothing less, nothing more. You'll have to play pretend."

"Like roleplay?" She couldn't be more perfect if she tried. I love roleplays. I live for them. In my fucking home office, with her, God, how am I going to survive this?

"What are the rules, baby?"

"First things first, do you have enough money to afford me?"

"What's your price?"

"Fifteen thousand dollars."

I burst out laughing. If she thought that this was an obscene amount of cash, she got me real wrong.

"Baby, you could have said $150K, and I would have thought it wouldn't be enough. I'll give you $150K for your dance," I reply.

"I only accept cash. You can't call me 'baby.' I'm Delilah, and that's just it. If you're not happy about this, I invite you to have another dancer. During the performance, you can't touch me, ever. You keep your hands to yourself, and if not, I'll call security, and you'll lose your membership." She replies in all seriousness. That only rises my excitement, and I wonder how I would have reacted if I saw her at The Rex first. I'll play with her.

"How much do I have to pay to fuck you, *Delilah?*" And damn, I'm dead serious.

"You can't afford it."

"I beg to differ. Try me," I dare her.

"Ten million dollars if you want to touch me. A hundred million to fuck me. Take it or leave it," she replies stone-faced. If this is real, then it really is hilarious. I have to realize that this is the truth because she couldn't have faked her inexperience. No one has fucked her before, except that Eric, so she really was a virgin stripper. Shit, that turns me on even more, if possible.

"Damn, you are expensive. Let's get the dance done, see if you are that good that I'd want to fuck you after. Believe me, I *can* afford it."

"Have you ever had a lap dance before? Do you know what you like?"

"I have. Can't say I remember it well, but nothing that expensive for sure. And I like your body on me, to answer your question," I say. She gets down from the countertop and puts space between us. *I miss her.* How could I miss her? I take her hand and bring her into my embrace again as I circle her waist with my arms.

"Where are you going?" I ask in a harsh tone, playing with her. That makes her giggle a lot. I like that sound.

"I need to get ready! I want you to be satisfied, but without my equipment, I fear you might not like it. I have to try to find appropriate clothes and underwear to impress you. And it's been months since I've done it, so . . . I won't take $150K, but $50K instead. Deal?"

That makes me chuckle. *Sweet, sweet Delilah.* I put my hand on her ass and press her to my cock.

"Feel that, baby? Indeed, I want you. I want you in every way I can. I'm about to lose my shit just by looking into your eyes. Imagine how I'll feel when I see you dance in front of me. You could wear a sack and it would be the same to me. You will ravish me, baby, don't worry," I say in her ear, finishing my sentence with a gentle bite on her cheek. She laughs at my gesture as she tries to get out of my embrace, but I hold her tighter, just a bit.

"I don't want you to stress out about this, okay?" I say, looking deeply into her wonderful eyes.

"Okay, yes, thank you. Let me go get ready and tell me when it's done. The bar installation, I mean," she replies. But then that reminds me . . .

"I would text you to tell you it's ready, but you obviously don't have a phone. Baby, we need to clear up that situation. How am I supposed to drop you back to Orion at night without a phone? What if something happens? How would you call for help?" I ask, frowning. She gets out of my grasp, and I know she'll try to shut me out. When we first talked about it, we were at the bar. I had to be careful not to scare her. But now she knows me, she knows I don't want any harm. Now it's time to talk a little. *Just a little.*

"You're not supposed to care. Let's not ruin this, okay? I'll go get ready. Just wait for me to come back, and if it's not here then, I'll put on a robe to hide the surprise," she says, kissing me quickly on the lips. I don't like it. The businessman I am wants to force this deal, but with her, I know better. This night is nothing short of perfect, so just for now, I'll agree, but I will talk to her about this. I give her a bit of a nod, and then she leaves.

Less than thirty minutes later, the team has installed the bar in my home office, finishing as Delilah comes down dressed in a robe that was in my closet. Even wearing this, she looks alluring as fuck.

"The room is ready," I say almost in a dare. A smile appears at the corner of that beautiful mouth of hers. She's pleased. *Oh baby, what are you going to do to me?*

"Get in. I'll be there in two minutes. Do you have the money for my service? By the way, give me your phone so I can put on the music through the speakers of the house, please," she says, using that sexy voice. Fuck me, the show hasn't even begun and I'm already over the edge.

I give her the phone and instruct her on how to use it. She thanks me, and I nod because I can't find the words in front of this much beauty and sexiness. That makes her smile, and I get to my home office, where I settle down in my desk chair, waiting for her to come in.

The night envelops the room in a cloak of shadows and antici-pation. This place, usually my fortress of control, now buzzes with electric tension, and I see the pole standing there, gleaming under the soft light as a witness to my sudden, reckless desire.

The door opens, and Delilah steps in, her silhouette framed by the dim light from the hallway, still wearing the robe that clings to her curves, hinting at the beauty beneath. My heart pounds in my chest, my mouth dry as she glides toward the pole, her hips moving with effortless grace. She drops the robe with casual ele-gance, revealing a lithe body adorned in a delicate silk-and-lace black bodysuit that leaves little to the imagination.

Delilah moves with a charm that is both intoxicating and terrify-ing. Her hips sway gently, each step calculated to draw me deeper into her spell. I've never seen a woman move like this—so fluid, so utterly in control of her own body. Her long, dark hair cascades over her shoulders, framing her face in a way that makes her look both fierce and delicate.

The first notes of "You Don't Own Me" fill the room, and she grips the pole, her movements fluid and mesmerizing. She dances with a refined sensuality that leaves me breathless, each spin and twirl a hypnotic display of raw, unbridled femininity. I've had lap dances before, countless times, but they all blur into insignificance now, erased from memory by Delilah's captivating performance. This moment, I know, will be etched in my mind forever.

She joins the lyrics, her voice barely audible over the music but resonating in my chest like a second heartbeat.

"You don't own me," she mouths, her eyes locking onto mine, daring me to look away. But I can't. I'm caught, hypnotized, com-pletely under her spell. I've known her for barely twenty-four hours, but it feels like I've been waiting my whole life for this moment.

Her eyes lock onto mine again as she makes the sexiest pause ever on the pole, the burning intensity sending shivers down my spine. My entire body reacts, every nerve alive and tingling. She moves with a grace that defies gravity, her skin glistening under the light. Her touch on the pole is deliberate, each caress a silent promise of what could be. As she ascends it, her legs wrapping around it, I can see the strength in her movements, the control she exerts over every muscle. She climbs higher, her body an artful display of fluid, sinewy power. She reaches the top, holding herself upside down with just her thighs, and descends slowly, each controlled slide down the pole sending waves of heat through my body.

She lands softly, her feet barely making a sound. Her eyes meet mine again, a flicker of a smile playing at the corners of her mouth. She knows exactly what she's doing to me. She starts to walk toward me, her hips swaying with each step, the song still playing in the background. She's coming to me, coming to get me.

"Don't forget the rules. You can't touch me. You can't have me. After the dance, I leave. If you want more, you pay. You understand, sweetheart?" she says in that sexy voice of hers. I am so fucking hard for her already. I love to play with her. I pray this won't be the last time.

"I understand," I mumble.

"Good," she says, smiling, and gets back to dancing. For me.

And she sings along, louder, her voice a haunting melody of defiance and independence.

"*You don't own me, don't say I can't go with other boys,*" she croons, her gaze piercing through me. Jealousy gnaws at my insides. She used to be a stripper, and the mere thought of other men witnessing her like this, having her like this, drives me to the edge of madness. I want to be the only one to see her, to touch her, to know her. My desire for her is unlike anything I've ever felt, a primal need that courses through my veins.

"You won't go with any other boys, gorgeous mine, only me," I say back to her, using almost a menacing tone, but I don't even know how I can manage to speak right now. She just smiles as she keeps dancing. She's so fucking sexy. She looks me in the eye, all proud of herself as I know that she knows exactly what she's doing to me. But there's a story behind those eyes, a life I'm desperate to uncover.

Who are you, Delilah? Why haven't I met you before? Why has the universe brought us together only now?

I've never felt this way before, never desired a woman with such an all-consuming intensity. How did I, Nathan Williams, the man who always has everything under control, find myself so utterly enthralled by a woman I met just twenty-four hours ago?

She dances closer, her body a symphony of sensuality. My breath catches as she straddles me, her warmth seeping through my clothes, igniting a fire that threatens to consume me. Her rule was clear—no touching.

It's a rule I'm struggling not to break as she grinds against me, every movement a tantalizing tease. I'm so hard, my cock is urging me to act on it, but I can't. I respect the roleplay here, but I'm on the verge of losing my composure, my hands trembling with the effort to keep them at my sides.

Delilah's fingers trail over my chest, leaving a burning path in their wake. She kneels before me, her mouth so close to my throbbing desire, barely an inch away from my dick. I can almost feel her breath against it, but she never touches, driving me closer to insanity. She then touches herself during her dance, her hands gliding over her own skin, and I feel a surge of jealousy toward her fingers, wishing it were my hands exploring her body. She mouths, *"I'm young and I love to be young, I'm free and I love to be free, to live my life the way I want, say and do whatever I please,"* and I hear that wonderful voice she tries to hide.

Oh baby, say and do whatever pleases you.

Her scent envelops me, a heady mix of perfume and my own cologne. Her wearing something that's mine along with something uniquely her is incredibly satisfying. Then she turns, her back to me, and straddles my lap again in the reverse cowgirl position. Her head is on my chest, giving the most perfect view of her exquisite rounded breasts, perfect and inviting, and I lose my mind. The feel of her skin, smooth and warm, against my lips is almost too much to bear. She dances around, her ass moving against my throbbing erection, and I'm blown away by the sight and feel of her.

Now she sits up, leaning forward, and I catch a glimpse of her perfectly rounded ass. The sight sends a jolt of electricity through me, igniting fantasies of what I'd like to do to her. My desire for her is an ache, a need that feels insatiable. I want to possess her, to claim her as mine, but I'm powerless in her presence.

"Keep dancing like that, Delilah. I love it. This is perfect, you're perfect," I manage to say, breathless.

She stands up to face me, brings her breasts to my face, her scent and the softness of her skin overwhelming my senses. I'm hyper-aware of every part of my body, every pulse of my heart-beat. I've never wanted a woman this much, never felt so power-less in the face of desire.

"I'm free, and I love to be free," she sings, and I can't help but be-lieve her. She embodies the lyrics, her confidence and indepen-dence shining through every move she makes.

My heart races, my breath coming in short, ragged gasps. I'm on the verge of losing it, of crossing that line and breaking her rules. But I can't. I won't. She's transformed me in this moment, showing me a world of desire and restraint that I never knew ex-isted. Her smile, the knowing curve of her lips, tells me she under-stands exactly what the fuck is going on. She leans back and I'm drawn to her. I follow her moves, wanting to grab her with my mouth, but she's the pro here, she keeps me at bay, and I feel the frustration in me. She smiles as she moves her way in perfect har-mony with the music.

"You don't own me," she sings again, her voice a siren's call. Our eyes lock, and I see a flicker of something in her gaze—vulnerabil-ity, perhaps, or maybe a recognition of the power she holds over me.

Finally, the song fades, and she rises, her movements slow and deliberate. She retrieves her robe, the spell she cast over me beginning to wane but not breaking entirely. As she slips it back on, she looks at me one last time, her eyes revealing nothing and everything all at once.

I've never questioned my life the way I do now, watching her. Everything I thought I knew about desire, about control, is being rewritten. My mind is a storm of wonder and fascination. I want to know everything about her but she remains an enigma, a mystery. I'm left in the aftermath, my body thrumming with a desire that might never be sated. I'm ready to spend every dollar I have just to touch her, just to feel her skin against mine. But I know it's more than that. It's about her. It's about the way *she* makes me feel, the way she's broken down my defenses and laid bare my soul.

Here, in my own sanctuary of power, I'm powerless before her. My body still hums with the sensation of her touch, my skin burning where she's been. I'm spellbound, completely and utterly captivated by this woman who I can't quite have. I've never wanted a woman this much, never felt so powerless in the face of desire. I'm willing to uncover the secrets she hides so well. But as she walks away, I know she's slipping through my fingers, a fleeting dream I might never fully grasp.

And it breaks me. I'll never be the same again.

What did you do to me, Delilah?

She left the room and I can't even form a coherent thought in my head. I shake my head and feel deeply relieved as I hear the door open. Delilah enters my office, extremely happy, wearing the biggest smile. *How beautiful . . .*

"So, how was it? Did you like it?" she asks. I laugh hard at her question. How serious can she be right now?

"Baby, I'm done for. Come here," I say as I open my arms to welcome her. To my delight, she jumps on my lap, excited as shit, giggling around. She's so pleased with herself, and that makes me really, really happy.

"I haven't done this in months and I've never enjoyed it, always hated it. But that one? That dance? I loved every bit of it. I'm so happy I got to do it for me once in my life. Well, no, it was for you, of course, but I felt like I did it for me too! I loved it! Thank you, baby. You'll never know how much this means to me, how much it healed a part of me that was really, severely wounded. Thank you so much, baby," she says, kissing me.

But that only makes me wonder even more. The thought of a part of her being "severely wounded" makes my heart break and makes me mad. The fact that she thinks that *I* did something to heal her while she was the one humanizing me? Damn, that's really interesting. The fact that she thinks she owes me something while it's the complete other way around is confusing as shit. I won't even try to elaborate on why my heart skipped a bit when she called me baby. *Twice.*

"Baby, you're so wrong. I'm the one who's supposed to thank you. That really was incredible. I'm so hard for you. I want you so much, baby. I can't hold on any longer, but I want you to know that you're the one who brought me something I never knew existed. You deserve your money, let me give it to you," I say, caressing her soft hair, and she bursts out laughing.

"No, I don't want your money. It was just for the roleplay. I thought it was funny to play you and get you thinking I only wanted money from you, like the gold-digger joke, remember?"

"Well done, but still, the money is yours. You deserve every cent."

"I won't need it, but thank you. Use it well for me, okay? So, I take it you want to get in my panties now, huh?" she says.

She's not even real. Why would she refuse the money? Why won't she need it? Some might think I'd try to talk more on that, but right now? I'm only focused on the *you-want-to-get-into-my-panties* part, and later, I hope, I'll have a chance to question her on this particular topic.

So I grab her by the waist and put her on my desk. I spread her fucking alluring legs, settle between them and kiss the fuck out of her. I take the robe off her shoulders and I don't even have time to undress her completely. Instead, I just push aside the bodysuit at her entrance, take out the condom I had prepared in my pocket, put it on, then slide right in. *Damn . . .*

"You're so wet, baby. What am I gonna do with you?"

"Fucking me is a very good start," she replies. That makes me laugh, but I'm so focused on her exquisite body, on her moans, on her hold on me . . . I reluctantly get out of her, put her down, then turn her around. I put my hand on her head and grab her by the waist.

"Lean for me, baby. I'm taking you from behind. That ass got me so fucking hard, shaking under my eyes."

I don't let her respond as I thrust deep into her pussy from behind. And I thrust like I've never done before. And then I completely stop thinking. Once she and I are connected this way, that happens. I literally stop thinking. Nothing around us exists, nothing matters but us, nothing lives but our desire.

Delilah's voice brings me back to reality, and I try to hear what she's saying. Then I understand she's about to come. I feel it around my cock, I hear it through her heartbeat, so I put my fingers on her clit to heighten her orgasm. She doesn't last for shit, she explodes on my fingers and all around my dick. Feeling her pussy contracting all over me only brings me to my own orgasm as I blow it all, to the very last drop of cum I have.

I can barely breathe as I fall onto her back, both of us half on my desk.

"Baby?" she asks in a barely audible voice.

"Yes?" I reply, panting.

"I think I wanna go dancing, see what it's like. Do you think we still can?" That came out of nowhere. She makes me laugh, as always. *What an incredible woman.*

"You could ask me anything right now, I'd give it all to you. If go dancing you wish, then go dancing you will," I say, kissing her shoulders. I get out of her, throwing the used condom in the trash under the desk.

I take Delilah in my arms, her circling my neck, and she laughs hard, which makes me laugh hard too. Then we go to the dressing room inside the master bedroom. I choose some nice black slacks with a fine white button-down shirt and my vintage Rolex that belonged to my great-grandfather. Delilah chooses an emerald minidress that fits her perfectly. A bit revealing, but she looks so beautiful in it that I don't dare say a thing. She lets her hair fall onto her back like a cascade, adds a slight touch of makeup. Delilah's a natural beauty, she doesn't need any. And the most perfect detail: the gold leaf pin in her hair, just like when we first met. I help her put on a nice pair of black strappy heels, kissing each foot, and then off we go.

We arrive at the Ermont. Stepping into the club, I'm not impressed by the elegance of the place—I've been here many times. What stands out tonight is the wonder in Delilah's eyes. She looks around, taking in every detail of this exclusive spot.

The air is warm, with a faint scent of exotic wood and the distant sound of the ocean. The grand entrance opens up to a space that feels like a hidden paradise. Palm trees and soft lighting give it a Bali-like vibe, an exotic touch right in the Hamptons.

Inside, the atmosphere is as chic and luxurious as ever. The crowd, dressed in designer outfits, moves to the music, a mix of modern beats and classic tunes. The lights above cast a warm glow, making everything shine. Delilah slips her hand into mine, and I glance at her, captivated by her excitement. She starts to sway to the rhythm of the music, catching a few admiring glances from people around us.

We pass the bar. Delilah's eyes widen, and I can't help but smile at how amazed she is.

When we step out onto the terrace, the vibe changes to

something even more magical. The wooden floor feels steady underfoot, and twinkling string lights add a soft glow. Lush plants—ferns, palms, and flowering vines—surround us, making it feel like a jungle escape. The sound of the ocean mixes with the music, creating a soothing backdrop.

Out here, the crowd is more spread out. Couples sit at intimate tables, and small groups chat away. The mood is relaxed and cozy, the perfect balance with the lively energy inside.

Delilah can't contain herself. As soon as we step onto the terrace, she starts dancing again, her movements fluid and natural. She pulls me into her rhythm, and for a moment, I'm lost in her world. Her joy is infectious, and I find myself grinning, utterly captivated by her. Seeing this place through her eyes, it feels new and wonderful. The night is young, and with Delilah by my side, it promises to be unforgettable.

Watching her, I realize how much I adore showing her my world, seeing it afresh through her wonder. I dance with her as if no one were around, as if time had stopped and people had disappeared. It's only her and me. It's just us. The rest completely fades away.

It's almost two in the morning, but I feel like it's still early, and I know it's going to be a night to remember. Again, I find myself lost in her eyes, our bodies close as we dance, as I make her sway and laugh hard. I'm crushing on her, on her beauty, on her wonder, on her charm, everything. I'm charmed.

I love everything about this night, this day, this whole damn time together. We drink a bit, to the point where I feel buzzed and I can't stop laughing. We spent our time dancing, teasing each other on the dance floor. A lot of it is me keeping at bay the men looking toward my Delilah, but mostly, we laugh. Hard. And God, how good that feels.

After a few hours at the club, we decided it was time to go and watch the stars together. *One last time.* I don't want to ruin the mood and the light air between us, so I keep that thought to myself. I text Linda to have everything ready and settled before we arrive and then ignore my phone again, as I want to enjoy every second we have together.

But as we're getting closer and closer, the mere thought of not seeing her anymore breaks me a little. I don't know if I'm enjoying myself this much because we both know our time is limited, or if it's because we really do have a special connection here.

Will I be able to go back to my life and pretend none of this ever happened? Will I survive the loss of her? A woman I just met?

~

We finally arrive back home. I asked Linda earlier to set up the same scenery as yesterday with the telescope, the candles, the bed, the bottle of red wine, and some appetizers, which she did perfectly, as always. We step into the backyard, and my eyes are drawn solely to Delilah. Despite having seen the décor yesterday, she seems overwhelmed by it once more. I can sense her gratitude, but she has no idea that it is *I* who feel the most blessed.

I capture another picture of the scene, this time with Delilah at its heart. I know this weekend will be etched in my memory forever, that I will never forget her. Even when I'm old and gray, I'll cherish this memory and the lessons she imparted. Still, I want a tangible reminder to ensure it was real, not just a dream.

Delilah poses like the goddess she is, her wide smile and sparkling eyes illuminated by her beautiful green dress, her hand gesturing towards the bed. My heart aches with her beauty.

"You really didn't have to do this, but thank you, again. I wish I had more words coming out of my mouth to tell you . . . I just . . . I . . . ugh . . . Thank you," she says, confused, almost frustrated she hasn't found what she *thinks* are the right words. I can sense that she's not comfortable with speaking, so instead, I take her in my arms, hold her extra tight, and kiss the top of her head.

"My utmost pleasure, baby. I'll do anything to make you smile. Come, I'll show you some cool things in space," I say, winking at her.

The rest of the night begins with Delilah and me seated on the bed, drinking some fine Château Margaux 2015, and to my surprise, we finish the whole bottle by ourselves. So now we're a bit drunk, but damn, do we laugh a lot. And it feels so good to be this . . . *carefree.*

I never share moments like this in my everyday life, as I have to prioritize my reputation, which means extreme control in public. When I go out with my friends, most of them business partners, I always have limits. When I'm intimate with a woman, it's always just to have dirty, meaningless sex I'm eager to get over with.

But with Delilah, everything is different. We're alone, she doesn't come from my world, she doesn't judge me, she doesn't care who I am or what I do. And I so want her to feel happy and good that I put extra effort into liberating myself with her because I want her to trust me. And now, here we are, laughing hard because I'm incapable of forming a normal sentence as I try to explain what we're about to see in the sky.

I laugh a little too loudly as I fumble with the telescope under the starlight. Delilah stands beside me, her eyes wide with curiosity, the cool night air brushing against us.

"Alright, alright," I say, finally getting the telescope aligned correctly. "Here we go, the star of the show . . . well, not a star, but you get the point." I giggle at my own joke, my buzz making everything seem extra amusing. Delilah leans in, peering through the eyepiece.

"What am I looking at again?" she asks, her voice filled with wonder.

"That, my sweet Delilah, is Saturn," I say, trying to sound as dramatic as possible. "Although it's lower in the sky, it's visible before dawn, and tonight we're in luck." I fine-tune the focus with a delicate touch, the rings of Saturn coming into sharp, breathtaking clarity.

"You see those rings? They're made of ice and rock, and they make Saturn one of the most distinctive planets in our solar system."

She gasps softly, mesmerized by the sight. I lean in closer, enjoying our moment.

"Saturn is the sixth planet from the Sun and the second largest in our solar system, right after Jupiter. It's a gas giant, mostly made up of hydrogen and helium. Pretty cool, huh?" She nods, still staring into the telescope.

"It's beautiful," she murmurs.

"It really is," I agree, my voice softening at the sight of her. "This telescope is incredible. It can magnify Saturn's rings so much that you can see the gaps between them, like the Cassini Division. Those rings are made up of billions of particles, ranging in size from tiny grains to massive chunks. They reflect sunlight, which is why they're so visible," I say. I pause, taking a sip from my glass, the alcohol making me feel warm and loose.

"Saturn has over eighty moons, but the most famous one is Titan. It's actually bigger than the planet Mercury. Titan has lakes and rivers of liquid methane and ethane. Can you imagine?" I say in complete wonder. Delilah finally looks up from the telescope, her eyes shining.

"I had no idea," she says, her smile radiant in the dim light. I laugh again, a deep, joyful sound.

"There's so much out there, Delilah. So much to see, so much to learn. Nights like this . . . they make you feel small, but in the best way possible."

She leans into me, and for a moment, we just stand there, gazing up at the sky. The universe feels vast and mysterious, but with Delilah by my side, it also feels a lot less lonely.

"Can I ask you a question?" she asks, serious.

"Sure."

"Why can't you quit your job to become an astrophysicist or something? You seem to know everything, and you look so passionate about all this. What holds you back?" she asks. *How to answer that question . . .*

"So many things. Loyalty towards my family, loyalty towards

my business partners, a sense of responsibility towards all my employees from all around the world. My company wouldn't be what it is without me. My little brother, Jake, would be very happy to watch me step down from my CEO position, but I fear he'd ruin the company my great-grandfather built, and all my work with it, burn to ashes. I can't afford to disappoint millions of people, including my family, just because I'm too selfish. Do I wish things were different? Absolutely. But I'm a man of my word. So I guess looking through a telescope from time to time has to be enough. There are many answers to your question . . ." I say, sighing and looking at the beautiful night sky. When I turn my head to see Delilah, I see her watching me, thinking about what I told her, I guess.

"What?" I ask.

"You're a wonderful man, Nathan fucking Williams. I hope you know that. And I hope everyone knows that too," she says, and I'm very, very pleased by her comment. I want her so much right now, and I feel the need to lighten the mood too.

"You say that because you want my big dick inside you," I say as I grab her by the waist and throw her on the mattress. She laughs really hard—alcohol playing a good part in this—and I can't help but laugh again with her.

"Your ability to discuss such a deep, meaningful topic and then switch to such crude and light language knows no bounds," she replies, chuckling between my bites on her face. I've never bitten and licked a woman's face this much. Come to think of it, I think Delilah is the first woman I tried to eat this much in my life. But again, she's so delicious.

We've spent a great amount of time in the backyard. I wouldn't be able to tell what time it is, as time really seems to have stopped since I met her, but at some point, we regain the master bedroom, where we prolong our night under the sheets.

We fuck as though it was our final night on Earth, our passion a desperate dance against the menacing yet inevitable dawn.

We explore each other's bodies with the fervor of painters crafting a masterpiece, eager to capture every stroke and nuance in our memory. Our kisses speak the words our voices cannot, a silent language of longing and horrific farewell.

Knowing this will be the last time I fall asleep with her in my arms shatters me in ways I never thought possible.

Delilah is sleeping now, tired from all the sex, a vision of serenity, her dark hair framing her angelic face. Her breathing is a soothing lullaby, a rhythm that brings me peace.

When we wake up, it will be the last time we wake up together. It was part of our deal, a clear understanding that our time was limited, finite, that we were never meant to be, never meant to last in the harsh light of the real world. We were never meant to stand a chance.

So I dream, clinging to the fantasy, wishing to never wake up.

CHAPTER 7
Delilah

I feel something on me. A hand, I think, so I open my eyes. The sunlight is coming into the room. I turn around and see Nate still asleep, naked, his front pressed against my back. His hand is unconsciously caressing my thigh. I get closer to him, enjoying his warmth, his affection, his company. I raise my hand and try to reach the back of his head, stroking his hair with my fingers. Naturally, he glides his hand from my thigh to my boob, and I instantly feel his erection in my ass. We've had a lot of sex; I've seen him more times naked than dressed, and yet his size still amazes me. I find myself smiling again. Then reality hits me hard. This is the last time I'll ever wake up. But what a beautiful way to start a day that is going to end it forever.

Nate kisses me right under my ear. It tickles, but in the most amazing way.

"Good morning, babe," he says.

"Good morning to you too," I say, grinding him with my ass. In response, he bites my shoulder and slaps my butt. I jump in surprise and turn around to face him. I see his tired eyes opening; the perfect shade of light blue around his irises is a huge turn-on. He kisses me lightly on the lips, and I melt against him.

"So, what have you planned for us today?" I say almost in a whisper.

"Let's just stay here a little more. I'm not ready," he says in a serious tone, his voice gravelly this early. I understand all too well what he means.

"Okay," I agree. Then I take all of him in my arms, holding him strong, almost as if I were holding on to him. We stay like this for a while, not daring to speak. I don't even know how to say what I want to say. I can't even formulate a thought as everything blurs in my mind.

Because I can't find the words, I take his head in my hands and kiss him. I force him to open, and he does it so well. I feel his hands roaming on my body; the feeling is exquisite, warm, sensual. And then I decide to explore what it means to take the lead. Nate is a natural dominant. He always has control in the bedroom and I love it, really, but just for once, I wanna see what it's like, to have control.

I get on top of him. I take his hands in mine, entwining our fingers just above his head as I deepen our kiss. The passion between us is tangible, the heat under those sheets is scorching in the best way. Then I make a trail of kisses from his mouth to his ear; I feel like I'm on fire.

"Do it, baby. Show me how you want me," he says, panting. His hips dance the same moves as mine. I spread my legs to straddle him and take an appreciative look at the strong body before my eyes.

"I can feel the perfect warmth of your pussy right on my cock. Keep grinding me, baby, keep masturbating on my cock."

"That mouth of yours will lead you somewhere, alright," I say, smirking. He catches me by the waist, moving under me, intensifying the friction between my clit and his penis. I love the sensation, so I keep doing it, feeling everything in my body.

"Come on, baby, come on my big cock, spread all your cum on me; I'll lick it all off you after."

Even though I love the feeling of my clit on his penis, I need more, I need him, all of him.

"It's not enough, I need you inside me," I say, breathless. Nate offers me an exaggerated smile, putting his hands behind his head.

"My baby wants to ride me, huh? Come on, cowgirl, show me what you can do. I never let women do it usually, but for you, I'll make an exception," he says.

But now I feel a slight pinch in my chest. I don't like his comment one bit. What's wrong with me?

Everything's fucking wrong with me.

I say, "Give me a condom, dirty mouth. Keep thinking about what you do with other women while you fuck me, and I'll try not to think about other men too much myself." I dare him, using a very confident voice I didn't know I had. He bursts out laughing, then sits up to face me, eye to eye.

"Jealous much?" he says, mocking me. But he doesn't leave time to respond as he grabs my head and kisses me hard. "Me too," he says, looking deeply into my eyes.

"I wasn't being jealous; I was being funny."

"Yeah, go try to convince someone else," he says. I roll my eyes, not wanting to give too much thought to this conversation.

I'm so driven by desire that the only thing I want to do is connect with him on a level that has no words.

I roll the condom on his large penis, taking time to tease him. Nate's breathing accelerates; I see shivers down his arms, and the fact that I, Delilah, am responsible for his pleasure gives me so much more power than I ever possessed.

"Go on, baby, climb me. I'm so ready to be inside you. You're so beautiful," he says, urging me on. I'm loving every second of this.

I put the tip of his cock at my entrance, stroking him in the meantime to prepare him, then start to push onto him. The feeling of his penis is incredibly satisfying; this very moment when I make him enter me is extremely delectable. I start to shift to adapt to his size, while Nate grabs me by the hips, using his strength as if he weren't able to control himself any longer. I push even more, getting him deeper, and the action makes me moan his name.

"That's right, baby, keep going. You're so perfect," he moans back.

I'm so turned on that I feel how wet I am, how he'll be able to fill me almost easily. Then I start to move, back and forth, and that kind of pleasure is extremely good. I can't help but continue.

"Oh my God, Nate, this is incredible, move with me," I plead. And so he does, he moves along with me, setting a united rhythm, accentuating the beautiful connection between us. I'm on top of Nate, moving rhythmically, feeling the intense pleasure building with every thrust. Our breaths are ragged, bodies slick with sweat. He grabs my hips, guiding me as I ride him, his eyes dark with desire.

"Baby, I can come just with the vision of your boobs bouncing all around," he says.

"Oh no, don't come just yet, please," I beg, stopping my movement to prevent his ejaculation. He starts to chuckle and takes me, turning us around so now I'm on my back. I laugh at his gesture, but he silences me with a kiss.

"I've never been this into a woman, Delilah. You turn me on so bad, it's hard to restrain myself. But I'll always put *you* first, beautiful. *Always*," he says.

And, against all expectations—because I'm supposed to know better—his words bring me comfort, relief even. It's not supposed to be this way. I'm not supposed to feel anything. I'm supposed to be dead. *Stick to the plan, Delilah*

"*Always* ends tonight," I say while opening up my legs to him. He is about to fuck me, but he stops at my words. He looks deep into my eyes and pauses.

"*Always* never ends," he says. Again, he doesn't leave me time to answer as he thrusts into me with fierce rage. But damn, don't I love his power over me. I love it when he uses his strength in bed. Why do I ever love it this much? I decide not to answer him; I don't want to think anymore, I just want to be. I just want to really live a little more.

"The feel of you, Delilah. I won't last; we need to change position," he says, never losing a minute as he turns me around and puts me on all fours. "You have the most perfect ass, baby. I'm going to have it, I hope you know."

"Whatever you want right now, you can have it all," I reply, all sincere. I'm so entranced by our sexual exchange that I'll gladly give him what he wants.

"Open your mouth," he says, so I do.

"Suck my fingers," he orders, and that I do too. He puts his wet fingers on my pussy, caressing me, turning me on even more.

Then I feel his mouth on my back, right above my butt, leaving wet kisses right until my black hole. I've never had someone touch me there. The feeling is sensual, good, intense. I feel his tongue on me, licking my anus while caressing my clit with his hand. I'm almost overwhelmed with pleasure; I'm on the verge of losing all traces of control. Then he pushes delicately, one finger in my ass. It's very tight, that I can feel, but I do not dislike it. On the contrary.

"How does that feel, baby?"

"Different, but not bad."

"Just relax," he says softly. "If you want me to stop, just tell me."

"No, no. Don't stop, I wanna know what it's like," I reply.

"That's my girl. I'm gonna add another finger," he says, kissing my butt cheek before adding another finger, stretching me gently. I cry out; the sensation is intense, but I find myself relaxing into it, curious about what's to come. Nate takes his time, ensuring I'm comfortable before he positions himself at my entrance. I find myself pushing against his fingers, increasing the pace with him. I want more.

"I think you're ready for my cock. Your body was made for mine; we fit perfectly, baby. All your body wants me in," he says, and I could question his choice of words as if they had a double meaning. I could, but I won't.

"Okay. Be gentle, please. You have such a huge penis I fear it might hurt."

"I won't hurt you," he says in a soft voice. I take a deep breath, trusting him completely.

"Are you ready?" he asks, his voice a comforting anchor.

"Yes," I breathe, eager to feel him. I hear him spit on his cock—damn, that's fucking hot—then pushes in slowly, inch by inch, allowing me to adjust to the fullness. The initial pressure is sharp, but he pauses, giving me time to get used to him. He's so gentle, his hands caressing my back and hips, soothing me.

"Talk to me, Delilah. How does it feel?" he asks, his voice filled with concern and care.

"It's . . . intense," I manage to say, surprised by the mix of sensations. "But I like it." He moves slowly, his thrusts controlled. As my body adjusts, the discomfort fades, replaced by a growing pleasure that takes me by surprise. I moan, pushing back against him, encouraging him to go deeper.

"God, Nate," I gasp, "this feels . . . amazing." His hands grip my hips more firmly, his thrusts becoming more confident.

"You're incredible, baby. Just relax and enjoy it."

I do as he says, letting the sensations wash over me.

While he thrusts, Nate puts his fingers on my pussy, massaging my clit, and the pleasure builds, wave after wave, until it crashes over me in a powerful orgasm that leaves me quaking and breathless. Nate's movements become more urgent, driving us both to the edge. He groans, his own climax overtaking him as he fills me completely.

As we collapse onto the bed, our bodies spent and satisfied, I turn to look at him, barely breathing, with a smile on my face. Nate chuckles softly, brushing a strand of hair from my face.

"Did you like it?"

"I'm still processing what just happened. Is it always like this?" I ask.

"I've experienced it before, but it was never this good. So I guess no, it's not always like this," he says, kissing me lightly on the lips. I'm so tired that I feel my eyes closing, drifting easily into sleep.

~

I sleep for almost an hour. When I wake up, Nate is still next to me, watching me sleep. Things are almost weird between us; I think it's because we're hours away from bidding farewell to each other, and neither of us is really comfortable with that yet. Of course I wish we had more time, but it is what it is. Nate is going back to work tomorrow, and I'll be . . . *Actually, I won't be.*

Anyway, there are things we don't say. Thoughts we don't express, like a silent understanding that we can't betray. But I feel it in his gaze; I can see his brain working from here.

"Let's not ruin this, okay?" I say, caressing his beautiful face. He simply nods. I think he's scared to tell me things I might fear to hear. But I'm happy he remains silent.

We get up, take a shower together, enjoy a nice breakfast that I prepare with love, and now we're cleaning the kitchen, trying to decide what to do for our last day.

"I thought we could go to Sag Harbor's village, eat there, then take a long walk, enjoy the place before we come back here, fuck again real good—I'm not done with your ass yet, nor your pussy, by the way, nor your mouth . . . well, any of you, really—then get nicely dressed to go out and have a nice dinner before I bring you back to Orion. What do you think?"

I burst out laughing at his sheer honesty, which I've come to like so much. It makes me laugh, it makes me smile, and God, I needed this.

"Sounds perfect. I'll be ready in less than ten minutes."

"I'll get ready with you; we can get dressed together."

We go back upstairs, get ready together in less than fifteen minutes. I wear a beautiful white dress in cotton gauze; it hugs my breasts and waist perfectly and flares out gracefully from the waist, creating a flowing, airy effect. It ends at mid-thigh, adding a playful and charming touch to its overall cute design. Nate wears a simple pair of blue jeans paired with a navy-blue polo and stylish white sneakers, creating a casual yet polished look.

We leave the house to go downtown, and once again, I don't think I've ever seen such a beautiful place. As we stroll down Main Street in Sag Harbor, I am utterly captivated by the charm surrounding me. The quaint, historic buildings line the street, their facades adorned with vibrant flowers and signs. The scent of fresh coffee and pastries wafts from cozy cafés, mingling with the salty breeze from the nearby harbor. Everywhere I look, there are picturesque boutiques and art galleries, each more inviting than the last. The whole scene feels like a painting come to life, and I can't help but be amazed by the enchanting allure of this idyllic town. All the while, Nate holds my hand, kisses my hair from time to time, and describes the place we're walking through.

Later, we have lunch in one of the beautiful restaurants downtown. We share a pizza and drink some red wine that buzzes me and makes me laugh harder at Nate's stupid jokes.

Afterwards, we take a walk near the harbor with two Italian ice creams. I choose strawberry and Nate picks lemon, but we end up finishing each other's.

Now we're walking hand in hand, talking about everything and nothing. The sun is still high in the sky, leaving the most perfect shade of light blue.

Everything around us is beautiful, magical. Everything seems to be . . . *alive.*

But in my heart, there's a raging tempest, lightning strikes, and heavy rain. I'm a bird trying to fly, dancing under the storm, going through the clouds to catch a glimpse of the light. But as I try to fly higher, I fall deeper under the unbeatable rain.

And my eyes are disconnected from my body, as if my vision weren't connected to the right world. My own eyes lie to me.

Now I'm facing Nate, who's all beautiful, thoughtful, and so fucking nice, surrounded by the beauty of his environment. And then there's me, drowning in chaos. *What do I do?*

I try to smile to hide what's inside, but Nate can see right through me.

"What's wrong, baby?"

"Nothing. I'm thinking about work tomorrow," I lie.

"Let's not think about it just yet. Let's enjoy a little more," he says, caressing my face and kissing me on the lips.

We walk for a while before we get back to the house. We follow

Nate's schedule: we have a lot of sex, take a shower, and now we're getting ready to eat out.

Naturally, I put on my black dress from Friday night, brush my hair, let it cascade over my shoulders, and put my golden laurel pin in my hair. I apply the same red lipstick, take my purse, and I see my unfinished letter. My heart breaks all over again just at the sight of it.

I look just the same as before I came here. I thought my heart was lighter, yet I feel it heavier than ever before. Saying farewell to Nate will be hard, but inevitable.

Nate joins me in the foyer as I put on my strappy black sandals. He stops when he sees me.

"Everything okay?" I ask.

"Why are you dressed just like Friday?"

"Because it's mine, and this is the only thing I have, and I'm not coming back," I say almost dismissively.

"I bought you tons of clothes. Can't you pick another outfit? Why wear this again? Don't get me wrong, you look gorgeous, but I just don't understand."

"There is *nothing* to understand. I told you I won't accept the clothes and that you could reuse them for another woman. I won't need them. Anyway, can we go?" I say, closing the subject. I don't want to tell him because I don't want to think about what I'm going to do.

"Fine. I'll deliver them to your address."

"Good luck with that." I smirk back.

"Fuck, I forgot you have no place to live anymore. Where are you going to sleep tonight?"

"None of your business. Remember the part of our deal where we say goodbye and you never think of me again," I say, my voice pretending I don't care. Nate looks very much upset, his eyes dark with anger. The frown on his face only makes me laugh a little.

"I won't fight you now. Let's go out and eat and enjoy our night together," he says, resigned.

"Yeah, let's do that."

We leave the house hand in hand, as always. The tension in the car is thick, but we manage small talk, exchanging kisses here and there.

We arrive at a cozy restaurant on a quiet corner, its warm amber lights spilling out into the evening. Nate leads me to a secluded table by the window, our knees brushing under the table, an unspoken connection that lingers.

We order quickly—duck confit for me, filet mignon for Nate—and share a bottle of red wine. Each sip feels like a warm embrace, easing the tension between us.

We avoid heavy topics, choosing instead to laugh about old jokes and share stories. Nate's eyes sparkle in the dim light, his smile pulling me closer. It feels like a normal date, as if we were pretending the future is as bright as the lights around us.

For a moment, I let myself believe in this illusion. It feels good. But as the hours pass, the inevitable goodbye looms larger. My heart aches with each passing minute. I cherish Nate's presence, trying to hold on to every second, hoping to remember this night forever.

I smile to myself, wondering if, when I'm gone, I can watch over him from the clouds, silently cheering for his success, health, and the love that will fill his life.

But as the night goes on, a deep sadness settles over me. The realization that our time is almost up is painful, and the weight of my decision presses heavily on my heart.

I want Nate to have a beautiful life, even if it means I can't be part of it.

Eventually, we have to leave. We stand, our hands lingering, reluctant to part. The drive back to New York stretches out like a dark, endless road. Tears sting behind my eyes as we walk to the waiting limo in silence, the cool night air brushing my cheeks.

As the limo glides through the darkened streets, an unspoken understanding passes between us. Nate turns to me, his eyes filled with a mixture of passion and desperation. I move closer, and without a word, our lips meet in a kiss that is both tender and fervent. The urgency of our desire ignites, and we find ourselves lost in each other, like only we know how to be.

Nate's hands roam my body with a familiarity and affection that bring shy tears to my eyes. I return his touches with equal passion, needing to feel him, to connect one last time. The partition between us and the driver goes up, giving us privacy, and we waste no time.

Our clothes are discarded hastily, and soon I find myself beneath him on the plush leather seats. The limo's interior is dimly lit, creating an intimate cocoon around us. Nate's touch is both gentle and demanding, his kisses trailing fire along my skin. When he enters me, it's with a slowness that speaks of reverence, of a need to make this moment last. We move together, our bodies a seamless blend of passion and affection. Each thrust, each gasp, each whisper is a testament to the depth of our connection.

The world outside ceases to exist once more as we pour every ounce of us into our final act. Our breaths mingle, our hearts beat in sync, and for those precious moments, we are one. The pleasure builds and crests, a wave that carries us both to the brink of ecstasy and back.

As our climaxes wash over us, we hold each other close, savoring the lingering warmth of our shared passion. The limo continues its journey, the city lights flickering past like distant stars. We lie entwined, the reality of our imminent separation a distant whisper for just a while longer.

In the afterglow, I look at Nate, my heart heavy yet full. I hope he can't see the sorrow in my eyes, the finality of my thoughts. The journey is a blur of emotions, a mix of gratitude for the moments we shared and a deep, abiding grief for what will never be.

The world outside is dark, but inside the car, with Nate by my side, there's a tragic beauty to it all. The things I felt were pure, even if they were bound by the chains of despair. And now I hold on to the hope that somewhere, somehow, my spirit will find peace, and I will watch over Nate, my heart forever intertwined with his—a silent guardian gazing from the heavens.

The limo parks, and the sound of the motor turning off sends shivers through me. Nate is the first to get out, and again, the sound of the car door slamming against the vehicle makes me jump. I don't want to leave; I don't want to say goodbye.

Please, somebody help me.

Nate opens the door for me, offering his hand, and I take it. We're now facing each other, looking deeply into each other's eyes. I can't speak as I feel tears coming up. I don't think I'll be able to hide them from him.

Nate seems to think as he watches me watching him.

"Does it have to be this way?" he asks in a whisper.

"We agreed on that," I say, my voice almost shaking.

"Why do we have to say goodbye?" he asks in despair.

"Because that's how things are meant to be," I say, shivering.

"Will you remember me?"

"I wish for you to *not* remember me," I plead.

"I'll always remember you, Delilah. I'll always remember us," he says, but he doesn't give me time to answer.

Nate stands before me, the night air cool against my flushed cheeks, the distant hum of the city a faint backdrop to our farewell. His eyes, those deep, captivating eyes, search mine as if trying to memorize every detail. I can see the pain there, the same anguish that churns within me making it almost impossible to breathe.

He steps closer, and I feel his warmth enveloping me. His hands cup my face, his touch soft, almost reverent. I close my eyes, leaning into his palms, savoring the sensation one last time. His thumbs stroke my cheeks, and I can't help but let out a small, shuddering breath. I feel the tears welling up, threatening to spill over, but I fight them back, not wanting to blur this moment.

Nate's lips find mine, and the world around us fades into nothingness. The kiss is soft at first, a tender brush that speaks of unspoken words and unfulfilled dreams. His mouth moves against mine with a desperation that mirrors my own, a silent plea to hold on just a little longer. I taste the salt of our shared sorrow, and it breaks something deep inside me.

It's way harder than I thought it would be.

I wrap my arms around his neck, pulling him closer, needing to feel every inch of him pressed against me. His arms encircle my waist, holding me tightly as if he couldn't bear to let go. The kiss deepens, growing more intense, more passionate, as if we could pour all our emotions and heartache into this final embrace.

His fingers tangle in my hair, and I feel the tremor in his hands, the barely contained emotion. I press myself closer, my body molding to his, trying to memorize the feel of him, the scent of him, the very essence of him. Our breaths mingle, ragged and heavy, and I feel the first tear slip down my cheek.

Nate breaks the kiss, his forehead resting against mine, our breaths mingling in the cold night air. His eyes are glistening with unshed tears, and the sight of his pain nearly undoes me. I bite my lip, trying to hold back the sob that threatens to escape.

"We'll be okay," he murmurs, his voice barely audible. "Somehow."

A choked sob escapes my throat silently, and I clutch him tighter, burying my face in the crook of his neck.

"Yeah," I whisper, though I don't believe it. "Somehow."

We stand there, the world around us forgotten. I can feel the dam breaking. Nate's hand strokes my back, trying to soothe me, but it only makes the pain sharper, more acute. I pull back just enough to look at him, admire him a little more.

"This is goodbye," I say, my voice trembling.

Please fight, please fight, please fight.

He nods, but I can see the doubt in his eyes, the fear of losing me, I think. I rise on my tiptoes and press one last, lingering kiss to his lips, pouring all my unsaid feelings and hopes into it. When we finally part, I step back, the loss of his touch a physical ache.

Nate reaches out, his fingers brushing mine one last time before he lets his hand fall to his side. I turn away, my heart shattering with every step. One tear escapes, and I don't bother to wipe it away. I feel his gaze on my back, a burning imprint that will stay with me forever.

As I walk away, I whisper a silent prayer, hoping that somehow, somewhere, we will find our way back to each other, in another life, maybe, or another dimension, I don't know. The night swallows me up, and I feel the weight of our final goodbye settles over me like a dark, suffocating shroud.

I approach the double doors of Orion, and in a flash I remember the first time I opened them, forty-eight hours ago. *What a difference . . .* I turn around to see if Nate has already left, but no. He's still there, all magnificent, standing straight next to the limo, making sure I go safely. I smile at him, waving my hand softly to say goodbye one last time. He smiles back, but stand there waiting for me to go in.

So, I go.

CHAPTER 8

Nate

I *fucking let her go.*

Watching her walk away from me was something I wasn't ready for. I can't believe our time together has come to an end.

I watch her, in all her beauty, walking away with such elegance that only she possesses. How am I going to turn away and live my life as if none of this ever happened?

She refused all the help I offered, she declined my money—which is a first in the history of all the Williams family—she refused the phone I gifted her—which I still don't get why—and finally, she didn't take anything from me, not even my vest. I couldn't insist.

As time passed with her, I started to realize how and why all of this was a bad idea. She's not from my world; she's too damaged for me, I know it. She's too secretive, too broken, too cynical, she's just . . . too much.

I can't be with a woman like this. I can't be with any woman at all.

When we arrived back at Orion, I had a thought that had never once crossed my mind since meeting Delilah: *Charlotte.* Why didn't I think of her before?

Not only has Charlotte left my mind this weekend, but she's also left my heart. I didn't think of her. I didn't picture her face, nor did I think of her in any other way. I was so drawn to Delilah that I completely forgot about my Charlotte. I feel ashamed because I betrayed her. I was supposed to talk to her yesterday, and I didn't.

I reluctantly turn on my phone, and I'm overwhelmed by the

number of emails and text messages I received. I don't dare open the ones from Charlotte.

What the fuck did I do?

Before arriving at Orion tonight, I intended to go inside with Delilah; I planned on following her and staying with her. But the second I thought about Charlotte, I changed my mind. It fucking broke me, but thinking about Charlotte gave me all the reasons I shouldn't ever see Delilah again.

We're too fucking different, we have nothing in common. The woman has an unbreakable shield around her, and I don't have the time nor the room in my heart to do something about it. But as I keep repeating the reasons not to see Delilah again, the voice inside me keeps pleading to go back to her.

I miss her. I fucking miss her, and knowing I won't see her again is destroying me.

"Where to, sir?" my driver, Tyler, asks. Where the fuck do I go?

"Home, Tyler, thanks."

"Of course, sir," he says, starting the car.

The further we go, the harder the pain becomes. Being away from her after being inseparable for forty-eight hours is unbearable. I take my phone out to call Anders, my head of security. He picks up the phone after one ring.

"Anders, I wanted to make sure you've set up a security team for Ms. Rose starting now."

"Yes, sir. I'm at Orion myself. I'm seeing her right now—black dress, dark hair, and a golden pin on the side. I have two other men here as well. Everything is under control; you don't need to worry."

Fuck, he can see her, he can see her beauty. I'm so fucking jealous I'm not the one there with her. My heart aches with this fucking situation.

"Fine. Make sure she's safe and that she gets home safely. Keep me posted." I don't give him time to answer as I hang up the phone.

I'm completely lost. I know I'm making the right decision. I know it's best for both of us to never get involved with each other, and that we should only feel grateful we got to experience a beautiful moment suspended in time. As long as it stays this way, we can be okay. If we were ever to actually be together, it would be doomed. We are incompatible. So why the fuck do I feel like I lost a part of me? Why do I feel like the world is crashing down on me? I put my head in my hands, revisiting every memory we had. I'm so lost.

"Everything okay, sir?" Tyler asks. *No, I'm not okay.*

"I've been better," I say.

"She was pretty," he says.

Tyler has been my driver for almost ten years; he was also my father's driver for over twenty-five years. I've basically known him my whole life. He became a true friend. I respect him a lot, which is why I won't get mad at him for getting too personal.

"Yeah, she was," I say, sighing. I don't even know what to say. Not to me, not to him.

"It's been quite a long time since I saw you smiling this much. It was good to see you like this."

He's fucking right. When was the last time I smiled this much? And for real? Delilah was such a breath of fresh air. Even though she was cold and hot, even though she had the ability to switch moods in a second, even though she closed off too many times and it angered me, I can't help but think the positives outweighed the negatives.

But we just . . . *can't.*

"Things are complicated. We're different, we don't come from the same world. It's better off this way."

"Neither do we, yet that doesn't mean we can't enjoy each other's company, am I right?"

I see his point, but it's just not the same. I just remain silent, and I think Tyler understands what I need.

The limo glides smoothly over the darkened streets of

Manhattan, the city lights blurring into streaks of neon and amber through the tinted windows. I lean back into the plush leather seat, my eyes staring blankly at the passing skyscrapers, though my mind is far from here. Tyler, ever silent and professional, focuses on the road ahead, leaving me alone with my tumultuous thoughts.

We've just returned from the Hamptons, a place that now feels both magical and cursed. I still can't believe I left Delilah at Orion. It's still burned into my mind: her silhouette as she stood under the garish hotel lights, her expression a mixture of hurt and resignation. My chest tightens, a physical ache that's almost unbearable. I keep telling myself that I can't see her again, not after these forty-eight hours that have changed everything. Yet I feel like I've torn my own heart out and left it with her.

Then my mind drifts again: *Charlotte.* The name slices through my thoughts like a knife, sharp and relentless. How could I have forgotten her? The love of my life, the one I promised to wait for. She's been gone for eighteen months on her solitary world tour, and we agreed to be on a break. But I never expected to feel this way about someone else. Never expected Delilah. *My sweet, sweet Delilah . . .*

Guilt washes over me, a heavy, suffocating wave. Charlotte and I have made a promise, a promise I intended to keep. Yet with Delilah, I felt something raw and powerful, a magnetic pull that was impossible to resist. I didn't think about Charlotte once during my time with Delilah. Not once. And now the realization of that betrayal makes me feel ashamed again.

But it's more than shame. It's confusion. My heart is torn between two women, each holding a piece of my soul. Charlotte, with her classy, elitist ways and our shared history, and Delilah, who awakened a passion in me I didn't know existed. The incredible passion I shared with Delilah, a stranger who has become so much more, is unlike anything I've ever felt. Yet there's an unsolved mystery about her, her reluctance to open up to me, to accept any of my gifts. It's killing me. What is she hiding? Why does she keep me at arm's length even when we shared such intensity?

I run a hand through my hair, exhaling sharply. What does this mean? Have I moved on from Charlotte, or is this just temporary madness, a distraction from the loneliness of her absence? The thought is almost too painful to contemplate.

"Tyler," I say, my voice breaking the heavy silence. He glances at me in the rearview mirror, his eyes calm and understanding. "Can you take the long way home?" I need to think things through. He nods without a word, adjusting our route.

I close my eyes, trying to picture Charlotte—her laughter, her warmth, the way she looked at me like I was her entire world. But then, unbidden, Delilah's face appears, her light-brown eyes filled with an intensity that matched my own. The connection we shared was undeniable, a fire that burned brightly and fiercely. It makes Charlotte seem like a distant memory, a faded photograph in the back of my mind.

Everything tells me that I shouldn't be with Delilah, that I was right to leave. Yet inside, I feel broken, empty. Everything feels wrong. How can I feel this way about Delilah when Charlotte is the love of my life? How can I reconcile these two parts of myself? The limo continues its journey through the city, and I know I can't run from these questions forever. At some point, I'll have to face the truth.

For now, I let myself be lost in the liminal space between what was and what is, hoping that somewhere along this long, winding drive, I might find some clarity. *I'm so fucked.*

Again, I take out my phone to call Anders. I just need to know she's okay.

Professional as always, he picks up the phone immediately.

"How is she?" I ask urgently.

"She seems okay, I think. She's writing a letter right now, and sometimes she talks to the blonde barmaid—nothing to report for now."

For fuck's sake. I'm so fucking jealous I'm not with her. Why is she still writing? Why is she replaying everything from Friday night?

"If anyone else tries to talk to her, call me," I say, hanging up the phone.

What are you thinking about, baby?

I can't believe I let her go. What the fuck do I do? Should I go back to her?

No, absolutely not. I have to stop this madness. I just need to go home and get a good night's sleep. Tomorrow is another day, another start, another beginning. I just need tonight to be over, and only then will I feel a little better.

I'm suddenly caught by reality when I feel my phone buzzing. The first fucking thing that comes to mind is: Delilah? No, it's just James. Shit, I have to get this.

"Williams," I say.

"Don't fucking 'Williams' me! Where the fuck have you been? Anders told us you were okay, just on 'off mode.' What the fuck, bro?"

"Says the guy who stood me up on Friday night," I reply. *Thank God he did.*

"I'm sorry. Hayley was at my place, and I tried my best to talk to her, to keep her, but she still dumped me. I forgot to call you back; I was a mess. Anyway, where the fuck have you been? What does 'off mode' mean?" he says, his voice filled with concern. Usually, I would've paid attention to his story, but right now? I don't give two shits. All I can think about is my "off mode" . . . *My Delilah.*

"I had to retreat a while to think things through about Jake and his future agenda. I had my dear mother on the phone for an argument I would've gladly avoided had I been given the chance. All this shit got to my head, so I went to the Hamptons to study the stars a little, too," I lie. I bluff, even. One of my many talents as the successful businessman I am. I can't tell anyone what happened. I'll take this secret to the grave.

"Yeah, shit, I forgot about your evil little brother. Have you scheduled a meeting with the board? Do you have any information on what Jake plans to do next?" he asks.

Shit, I really forgot about all this. I really have to get back to business.

"I'll tell you the details when I see you."

"Okay, no problem. We can have lunch tomorrow if you want. By the way, did you see Charlotte?"

That one hurts. I feel like my ear is bleeding when I hear her name. I feel my heart contracting in a very ugly way. I really need to get over this.

"No, she couldn't." I lie. *Again.*

"Oh, man, you must have been bummed. Anyway, you'll be fine. Where are you now? Wanna go have a drink?" The last time James wanted us to go have drinks, I met Delilah instead. The weight on my heart is very heavy.

"Thanks, but I have to decline. I need to get back home and sleep. I'll see you at the office," I say, and hang up the phone.

I really like James. He's my best friend and the best business partner anyone could wish for. Normally, I tell him everything. He's never judged me, nor would he ever do so. We've been best friends for over ten years, and I intend to keep him in my life, both professionally and personally.

Yet . . . he's not only my friend. He's Charlotte's friend as well. Even though he pushes me to entertain meaningless sex with plenty of women, he keeps reminding me to enjoy it while I can before me and Charlotte tie the knot together. He stands for our relationship because we were actually a trio. I know he sees Charlotte like a sister and genuinely loves her.

So, if I mention meeting another woman and being completely under her spell, making me question the true nature of my feelings for Charlotte? Well, not only would he be disappointed, but he'd also be sad and mad at me. And I'd understand him. I would agree with him. Still, I'm not ready for anyone to tell me what a mistake it was to meet Delilah.

The truth is, it wasn't a mistake; it was a delight. A privilege. I know James would never approve, even though I don't live my life according to people's approval, whoever they might be. Yet I'm not sure I want to ruin everything by creating any drama. My relationship with Delilah is mine to protect. I'll forever live with the memory of us. *Why is it so hard?*

"Sir, we're almost there. Would you like to take another detour, or do you feel like going home?" Shit. I don't know. I can't seem to think straight.

"No, just keep driving, please. I'm not . . . ugh," I say, sighing, resting my head in my hands. I'm not sure what to do.

"It's fine, sir. I'll keep driving. If you need any piece of advice, I'll be happy to help you. Just like I've been for the past ten years, and just like I was for your father before. I'm an old man, but I still have my head," Tyler says. I laugh at his comment. I really appreciate the man. He's devoid of any judgment or ill intentions. I can't speak to anyone about this, but he's seen Delilah, so he might have an opinion.

"You're no old man! You're like seventy or something, and you're in good shape. Anyway, what do you want to tell me, Tyler?"

"Depends, what do you want to hear?" Ah, the wise man is back.

"The truth, always."

He pauses to reflect on what he's about to say.

"She seemed genuine. I felt like she was a good person. I saw you two together from afar the whole time, not just in the limo. I heard her too. What a voice. She's very beautiful, her natural beauty is rare nowadays. Her laugh was indeed intoxicating. You seemed to be more . . . yourself with her, if I may say. You laughed a lot; you were really relaxed. I don't think I've ever seen you like this, even when you were just a boy.

"But she had a shadow over her head. Something really dark within her, to my eye. Can't say where it's from, but it was there. You two are very different. She doesn't come from your world, and neither do you come from hers. Looking at you two was like looking at the Sun and the Moon sitting next to each other. Something rare and truly beautiful. But we all know the Moon and the Sun can't sit next to each other.

"And then there's Ms. Jones. I know you didn't mention her, but I know your history. You might be thinking of her too."

Wow, I'm blown away, as always, by his reflection. He's absolutely right in every way possible. Delilah has a dark side; we, together, can't coexist . . . and there's Charlotte.

"I guess Delilah and I were just an eclipse, then. Rare, beautiful, incredible . . ."

"What kind of eclipse, sir?"

"What do you mean?" I ask.

"You're the secret scientist here, tell me. What kind of eclipse?"

"Well, there's a solar eclipse; this happens when the Moon passes between the Earth and the Sun, completely blocking the Sun's light and casting a shadow on Earth. A lunar eclipse happens when the Earth is directly between the Sun and the Moon, causing the Earth's shadow to completely cover the Moon."

"I guess you have your answer in that sentence."

"I'm not sure I understand," I say, which makes him laugh.

"You see, an eclipse is when the Sun and the Moon, two very different things, come together in a rare and beautiful alignment. For a brief moment, they create something extraordinary, something that captures the attention of everyone who sees it. Trust me. You and Delilah, you're like the Sun and the Moon. You come from different worlds, different paths. When you come together, it's magical, but it's also fleeting. There's something so special about your connection, yet it seems almost impossible to hold on to.

"But then there's Charlotte's shadow over you. It's like the Earth in a lunar eclipse, casting a shadow and creating darkness. It's a reminder that even in the most perfect alignments, there are obstacles. But remember, an eclipse also brings hope. It's a sign that even the most impossible situations can create moments of incredible beauty.

"That's something you should remember and be grateful for, even if we don't know who's the Sun and who's the Moon in your story. Maybe Delilah is the Moon, mysterious and captivating, and you, Nathan, you're the Sun, bright and full of energy. Or maybe it's the other way around. The important thing is that when you come together, you create something rare and wonderful. I truly believe that's what happened.

"It may seem impossible for you to be together all the time, just like the Sun and the Moon can't stay in an eclipse forever. But don't lose hope, son. Even the brief moments of alignment show that it's possible. Keep fighting for those moments, and maybe, just maybe, you can find a way to overcome the shadows and be together, whether it's now or somewhere in the future. Maybe you first need to put light on the shadow over your own head before trying the impossible."

"You mean Charlotte," I clarify.

"Only you know," he replies.

He's giving me something to think about.

"You're a wise man, Tyler."

"Ha, another word for 'old man,' I suppose." That makes me laugh.

I shake my head and take another look at the city lights outside the window. My thoughts naturally drift to Delilah—what is she doing, what is she thinking about, is she okay, why can't we be together right now, why can't I go back to her, why won't she let me be there for her . . . so many questions without answers.

I don't know what to do.

We've been driving for almost half an hour in Manhattan. I

haven't tried to call Anders again; he hasn't reached out to me either, and I think it's for the best. He and his team are going to watch over her for as long as needed, and I just have to step back. Tomorrow I'll ask someone to deal with her living situation, and I'll keep my distance until I forget about her. I've made my decision; it's only for the best.

"Tyler, I'm ready to go home now," I say, not entirely convinced.

"That's your call, sir," he simply says.

"You don't agree?"

"It's not my place to agree with that. Only yours, sir."

"Well, I need to go home and sleep and clear my head. Tomorrow is a new day, and I think this is only for the best," I say.

"Alright, sir, we'll be there in ten."

When we arrive in front of my building on Park Avenue, I take a deep breath before getting out of the car.

The last time I was here was before going to work last Friday. I didn't know about the existence of the exquisite and mysterious Delilah Rose. And now I realize how I no longer resemble the Nate Williams from last Friday. I feel different. So different.

I left this place completely in love with a woman who now feels like a distant memory. I left unaware of the existence of a woman who today has turned my world upside down.

I left feeling like the most powerful man in the country, on top of the world. I come back feeling powerless, at my lowest point.

I left knowing I had everything I could ever need, yet I come back incomplete, missing something . . . *someone.*

This is what forty-eight hours with a woman has brought me. I don't dare imagine if it had been more, and how much worse I would have felt.

That only reassures me that I made the right decision. I won't see her again. I'll think about her every day—that I know—but I'll do my best not to think too much. I left her fate in competent hands that'll take care of her, and I bow in retreat. That's just it.

The doorman of my building opens the door for me.

"Good evening, Mr. Williams. Welcome back! I hope you had a good time upstate."

"Good evening, Suresh, thank you," I respond, not going into details about the trip. *Delilah* . . .

I put my card in to call for my private elevator, and I'm afraid to enter it. Getting inside will mean stepping outside of my time with her.

I can't believe I did this.

CHAPTER 9

Delilah

"You sure you don't want something stronger?"

"Hmm, no thank you, I need my head clear," I reply to Jenna.

I've been here for almost an hour now. I haven't drunk too much; I've been keeping my sorrow close, unable to put it aside. I've been writing quite a lot, but mostly, I've been hurting.

The light of this night is Jenna. She was genuinely happy to see me come back, though little does she know the real reason why I returned. She wanted to know everything about my time with Nate.

Nate . . . I told her I couldn't share much because he's Nathan Williams, and his private life has to stay private. She understood, but I've been itching to share some parts with her.

We got to know a little more about each other, more her than me, and I came to the conclusion that in another life, Jenna and I could have been close friends.

"There's another man coming your way," she whispers to me. *Shit. Not again.*

"Help me out of it," I beg.

"Count on me, baby," she winks. *Baby* . . .

I feel the man approaching, so I straighten on my stool to face him.

"Good evening. I wondered if I could offer you another drink? I'm Andrew."

"Hey, sorry, I'm not available, so I have to decline your offer, but thanks," I reply, smiling, always polite.

"I don't see a ring on your finger, so I'm guessing your boy-friend isn't around."

"No, but her *girlfriend* is. Hi, I'm Jenna." Oh my God, she's the fucking best!

"Yeah, that's right, she's my girlfriend. Have a good night, Andrew," I say simply.

"Alright, good night, ladies," he replies with a polite smile. Jenna and I laugh at our little act, sharing another fleeting moment of "joy." But it feels good anyway. I needed this.

Orion looks the same, yet it feels different. It's still a showcase of wealth and elegance, but the last time I was here, I met *him*.

I hear the rich voices and the sound of clinking glasses fill the air as I sit at that polished bar, feeling like an outsider, yet again. It's only been an hour since I said goodbye to Nate, yet it feels like he's still here, a shadow that haunts my thoughts. I can still smell him on me.

Men keep approaching me, all of them eager to impress with their sharp suits and tales of success, as if I gave a fuck about any of it. They are well-dressed, confident, and powerful, but to me, they're all like shadows. Their words are empty, their presence dim. Compared to Nate, they fade into the background, unable to shine.

Nate was pure light. His beauty, his grace, his very essence ra-diated a warmth and brilliance that these men can't touch. He was charming and funny, his charisma unmatched. I sip my drink and think about how he changed my life.

In just forty-eight hours, he left a mark on me that will last long beyond my death. He was an experience, a force of nature. I'm so lost in memories of him, remembering his smile, his touch, the way he made me feel alive. He brought light into my dark, dark world, if only for a short time. But I'm still grateful for those moments, even though they were brief. He showed me a glimpse of some-thing beautiful and real. *How I miss him . . .*

All these men—if not all men—with their bullshit can't com-pare. They try to impress me, but they don't understand. Nate wasn't just another man. He gave me something real, something I will hold on to as I face the darkness ahead.

My heart aches with the loss, but I'm also filled with gratitude. For a brief moment, I experienced true beauty and light. Nate was a gift, a brief but brilliant star in my life.

As I finish my drink, I know that no one else will ever measure up to him.

He didn't insist. He didn't try to hold me back, he didn't try to follow me, he didn't make a speech to convince me to stay. Not only do I think he knew it wouldn't have worked, but I believe he finally understood how broken I was and how much he didn't have the time, nor the energy, to try to bear with me.

He must have realized how fucked up I was and how stupid it would have been to be with me. Maybe he even got tired of me already. That wouldn't surprise me one bit.

People can't live with me, people can't love me.

Do I blame him, though? Absolutely not. I understand him; I'd even cheer his decision not to push it with me. I've always been trash while he was always . . . magnificent.

I felt him change when we arrived at Orion, I felt him disconnect from me. That's why I tried to be cold, despite my tears betraying my true feelings.

Deep down, I have to admit that I wanted him to insist. I wanted him to break through my unbreakable shield, I wanted him to *want* me. I wanted him. But he left, and he was so beyond right to. I'll never blame him, I'll never hold it against him. I hope he never learns I'm dead by suicide. I hope he never learns I'm dead at all.

I have finished my letter, but I feel like I have to mention Nate in it. To thank him so if he comes to know what happened, at least he'll have something to know he wasn't responsible for any of it. On the contrary, he freed me. So I take my pen again.

. . . This is the last part of my letter, and the last part of my life. I don't even know how to begin to write about what I've experienced in

the past forty-eight hours. His name is Nate Williams, and he's an angel among humans.

I met him last Friday, the day I originally planned on killing myself. Meeting Nate was like dancing in the sky with the stars. He came
into my life and brought a light I hadn't seen before.

From the very first moment, everything changed. His smile, his
kindness, his very presence, his passion for the universe, his sense of
humor—it was all so beautiful. Nate showed me what it feels like to be
alive, he showed me what it's like to live and not just survive. He was a
bright star in my darkest nights.

Nate had a profound and meaningful impact on me. He made me
laugh so hard, made me feel special, made me feel desired, and gave me
hope, even if it was fleeting. I wish I had told him why I was thanking him. I so desperately wish I could have told him everything, but
I couldn't. I guess I just wanted him to know how thankful I was he
showed me that, for some people, there is still light in this world.

We shared a physical connection that was more than just intimacy.
He freed me from old trauma. Through our connection, old scars began
to heal. For the first time ever, I felt empowered and strong. His touch
and care made me feel whole like I never had before.

We didn't even do anything out of the ordinary. We ate ice cream
at the harbor, took baths together, walked along the beach, and went to
restaurants. What others might see as mundane was extraordinary for
me. Each simple moment with Nate was filled with a joy and peace I
had long forgotten.

I don't blame him for leaving at all. I pushed him away because I
knew I couldn't be saved. I was already doomed. No one and nothing
could have changed my fate—I was too far gone. But I am grateful for
the moments we shared. Nate was a beautiful fire in my life, and I will
always remember him for that, even from above.

I wish him love and happiness. He deserves everything good. He deserves all the joy, peace, and love that life can offer. My only hope is
that he finds true happiness and lives his life to the fullest . . .

I feel the tears on my cheeks as I pour out my memories with Nate. I thought I'd feel lighter coming back here, but I feel heavier than ever. Losing him is extra hard—harder than I ever thought possible.

"Hey, Delilah, you're crying! Please, tell me how I can help you," Jenna says, her voice filled with empathy.

"If I don't see him again, would you please tell him he was perfect? That he never did anything wrong, and that I hope he's happy?" I say, sobbing. I need to make sure someone will pass on my message.

"Of course I will. He's a regular here, you know. You might see him again. I could call you when I see him. Stop crying, come on," she says, approaching to hug me. I really dislike people's touch, but as it's my last night, I choose not to give a fuck and accept the hug she offers. She's soothing me, caressing my back, and I appreciate it.

"I don't want to see him. I'm not going to see him. I just want him to know that he was perfect in every way."

"Of course, honey, I'll tell him, I promise. What do you need? It's on the house," she says, smiling, comforting me.

"I'll have another Cosmo, please. Thank you," I reply. She nods and goes behind the bar again.

We keep talking, I keep drinking. Jenna tells me more about her life, that she's always been a good girl, growing up in a loving family, born and raised in New York. She was never good at school and is happy to work at Orion, where she feels at home. She never dates the right guys but doesn't consider herself unfortunate.

The more she tells me about her life, the more I envy her. I envy her innocence of the dark world, the perversion of men, the violence, the crassness, and the disdain. I envy her for having such a simple life. To someone like me, her life is like a dream—a life I'd be eager to wake up to every fucking morning.

When she starts to mention her great relationship with her mother, I have to find a way to change the subject. I've never known the love of a family, least of all from a *mother*. Being an adult today, with hindsight, makes me think about what a family is—or is supposed to be. What a bond implies, what should be a mother's love and protection . . . *protection, what a joke.*

Anyway, that's just another layer to my pain. I'm hurt that I never got to have a family, to experience it. I've never given it much thought, but as I'm about to end it all, I realize how hurtful it was to never have been able to be loved by a family. *And I never will be.*

Then it hits me, my sadness. I feel so sad, so hurt . . . The parents, my adolescence held in captivity, the escape, The Rex, Ashley, fucking Eric, the fucking letter, the happiness Nate tried to show me but couldn't . . . It's too much. I want it to end; I *need* it to end. *Now*. It's now or never. I take a look at the time—it's almost 11:30 p.m. Fuck 3:03 a.m., I can't wait any longer. I'm too far gone. I just have to go.

I see Jenna, and my eyes water instantly. How do you say good-bye when this one means forever?

"Hey, you okay? Need another drink or a hug?" she asks, trying to make me smile, again. *I'm so sorry, Jenna.*

"No, I'm fine, I'm just a bit drunk, I guess. I'm going upstairs to meet someone I know. If I don't come down, well, again, thank you, Jenna. For tonight, for last Friday too. I felt like I almost met a friend, and it meant a lot to me. You are such a beautiful soul."

"Delilah! Why do I feel like this is a farewell?" she says, worried.

"Because it is," I reply, my voice trembling. I'm literally saved as a client asks for her service.

"I'll be back in a second. Please don't go, I'll be right back," she pleads.

"Okay," I lie.

I look around and no one is paying attention, so I choose this moment to go. *It'll be over soon.* I walk toward the double entry to the hotel lobby, go straight to the elevator, and press the button to the top.

During the elevator ride, since I'm not alone, I remain calm, determined. Then the doors open. I get out and find the service stairs. *Please let the door be open, please, please, please . . .* Yes! I almost run up the staircase, reaching the rooftop.

I step onto the roof, and the cool night air hits me. Below, the city spreads out, glowing and alive. Lights everywhere—skyscrapers shining, streets filled with cars moving like rivers of it. The Empire State Building stands tall, its white tip cutting through the dark sky. Neon signs flash, painting the streets with color. It feels like the whole city is awake, buzzing.

But I feel nothing. I stand here, watching the city live, and inside, I'm already gone. Empty. The noise, the lights, the life—none of it reaches me. I'm cold, not from the wind, but from the hollow feeling inside. The stars above seem distant, and even the moon, so bright, feels so far away.

I step closer to the edge, and the noise fades. I look out at all the life below so full of energy, and I wonder how it feels to be a part of it. I can't remember anymore. All I feel is the darkness inside me, heavy and endless.

The lights of the city shine, but I'm lost in my own shadow. *It's time.*

The cold air bites at my skin, but I hardly feel it. My eyes, drawn up to the night sky, begin to blur with tears. I try to hold them back, but it's no use. The tears start to fall, first slowly, then faster, streaming down my face.

I clench my fists, my knuckles white, as the sobs wrack my body. I can't stop the tears. They pour out of me, each one a drop of my sorrow and pain. My shoulders shake, and my chest tightens with the force of my crying. The sounds of the city fade away, and all I can hear are my own sobs echoing in the night.

"I'm so, so sorry," I cry. But only I can hear.

The memories of Nate flood my mind. His smile, his touch, the light he brought into my life. It all feels like too much, too heavy to bear. The sadness is overwhelming, a tidal wave of emotion that crashes over me again and again and again. I cry harder, my breath coming in ragged gasps, my heart feeling like it might burst from the pain.

"I can't do it anymore, I'm so sorry," I cry again, louder.

I drop to my knees. The rough surface of the rooftop is digging into my skin, but I don't care. I'm lost in my pain, consumed by it. The tears blur my vision, and I can barely see the stars above anymore. Each sob tears me apart from the inside, leaving me feeling more broken and alone.

I cry for the little Delilah. I failed her. I failed the child I once was—I promised her a chance at happiness, and I never made it. I cry for Ashley, my baby sister, for the horrible story we shared, for the ones we'll never have again. I cry for Eric, for everything we never were, for everything I thought was true but turned out to be in my own head. The tears keep coming, unstoppable, as if they carried all the pain I've been holding inside.

"It's too hard, I can't, I just can't live anymore, I'm so sorry," I cry out. I look up at the sky, searching for an answer as I cry.

Is there anyone out there? Lord, is there someone? I need someone . . .

The city around me is a silent witness to my heartbreak. The buildings stand tall and indifferent, the lights continue to flicker, and the stars above remain distant and cold. I cry until there are no more tears left, until my body is exhausted and my heart feels empty.

I'm scared. I'm so, so scared.

I walk over to the edge, drawn to the void that mirrors my heart. I don't know if I can do this.

Please, give me a sign. Anything, please.

I step down from the edge, fall onto my knees, and stay like this for I don't know how long. I'm so tired. I just don't know what to do and how to do it. Maybe I should wait for the right hour—shit, I don't have a watch. I should probably get back to the bar and wait for the right time. Yes, that's the right decision. It's too early—that's why it doesn't feel right. I clear my face with my hand, waiting for the tears to stop, and once I feel my face is back to normal, I head back down.

I open the door, get down the stairs, reach the elevator, and step in. The ride is long as it stops for people on almost every level. The building has ninety-eight floors; it really *is* long.

I reach the hotel lobby and open the double doors to the bar. When I do, I'm literally in shock. I can't even breathe as I try to understand what the fuck is happening right now.

How is this possible? How could it be? Why?

"Nate? What are you doing here?" I say, my voice barely audible. *He's here—oh my God, he's really here.*

"Where were you?" he asks, his tone a bit menacing. *Oh, I missed him so.*

"But . . . why are you here?" I really need to know. *Did he come back for me?*

"Don't play with me, Delilah, where the fuck were you?" he insists. He really is angry, judging by the expression on his face. *He can't know—it's impossible.*

"Where do you think I was?"

"Blondie barmaid told me you went upstairs to meet someone. Don't fucking play with me, Delilah, where the fuck were you?" His voice grows louder, harder. I'm so relieved he doesn't suspect anything.

"I wasn't—I just needed fresh air and silence, so I went up by myself. Now I feel better, so I'm back. Now your turn—what are you doing here?"

"I don't believe you," he says.

"I don't think I've ever given you reasons to doubt me. Plus, if I recall, we weren't supposed to see each other again. I'm not lying when I say I needed fresh air and silence and to be completely alone." That was a beautiful way to tell the truth without saying it. "Again, why are you here?" I insist.

"What do you think?" he answers.

"I have no idea, hence my question."

"I came back for you. For us. I can't let you go, and I can't be without you. Not anymore," he says in a softer voice. And my heart skips a beat.

I can feel everything contracting in me. He's here, my Nate, again. When I was at my lowest, I begged for a sign, and here he is. *Could it be?* I start to open my mouth to speak, but he cuts me off.

"I know what you're going to say, but hear me out, baby, please. I truly believe that what we have is special. I've never felt this way before, and I think it's enough to pursue it a little. Just step by step. We can take our time—that's why I want you to come with me."

"To come with you?" I ask, uncertain.

"Yes, to my penthouse. I know you have no place to live, so you can come with me until you're back on your feet, all while exploring a little more of what we have."

"But Nate, that doesn't make sense," I say, frowning.

"You know what doesn't make sense? Black holes. Black holes are regions of space where gravity is so strong that nothing, not even light, can escape. Their behavior, especially what occurs inside the event horizon, surpasses our current understanding of the laws of physics. It literally doesn't make sense, and yet here they are. Just because we can't understand it doesn't mean they don't exist," he says.

This can't be real.

"Okay, what about neutron stars? These extremely dense objects result from the collapse of large stars and defy our understanding of matter. A teaspoon of neutron star material would weigh billions of tons! Does this shit make sense? Absolutely not. Yet it's true. We *are* true, baby. Come with me."

"Nate, let's be serious for a moment, please," I beg, putting my head in my hands.

I have lost all ability to think straight. I was seconds away from jumping off the building, crying like I've never cried before, and a minute later, here he is—Nate, in all his glory, offering me a hand. I'm so lost, I'm so vulnerable, weak, and defenseless. *Could it be?*

Nate takes my hand, freeing my face, and looks me in the eyes.

"Come with me, baby. We'll find a way. We'll figure things out. If it helps, just tell yourself it's temporary, just so you can get back on your feet. And only then we'll talk about us again. Let's make a new deal."

"Because we respected the first one so well, huh?" I tease him. *I missed him so much.*

"God, how I missed this smart mouth," he says, grabbing my face to kiss me.

Nate's lips are on mine before I even realize it. The world blurs as he pulls me close, his hands cupping my face. His touch sends sparks through my body, and I gasp against his mouth, overwhelmed by the feeling.

His kiss is urgent, filled with a need that matches my own. I taste him, breathe him in, and I feel like I'm coming back to life. His stubble brushes against my skin, grounding me in the reality of this moment—a reality I thought I'd never experience again.

I cling to him, my fingers tangling in his hair, not wanting to let go, ever. His arms wrap around me, strong and secure, and I feel warmth spreading through me, a lightness I haven't felt in so long. It's like breaking through the surface after being underwater.

Every part of me responds to his touch. My heart races, my skin tingles, and I melt into him, losing myself in the kiss. His lips move against mine, and I breathe him in, all of him. He rekindles the flame in me that I thought was extinguished forever. He breaks the kiss too soon for my liking, so I try to reach back, but he stops me.

"Come with me, baby. Please, come with me. I know you can feel this thing between us, just like I do. Please, sweet Delilah, come with me," he begs.

That's just it—I can't say no. There's this force, this magnetism between us that defies the law of gravity. It's palpable, it's strong, it's there . . . *Could it be?*

"Okay," I say, my voice barely audible. I'm still not sure if it's the right thing.

"Let's go to your place first to take your belongings and bring them home." *Home . . .*

"I don't want to go back there. I can't."

"Do you want me to send someone?" he offers instead.

"No, that's not necessary. I don't have anything that matters."

"Okay. I have someone bringing your clothes back from the Hamptons; that should be good for now."

"More than good, yes. I'm so tired, Nate," I admit, hiding my face against his chest as he holds me tight and kisses the top of my head.

"I know, baby. Let's go home."

Nate takes my hand and leads us to the limo waiting outside. The air is cool on my skin, the city lights shining around us. New York is alive tonight. *So am I.*

"Very happy to see you again, Ms. Rose," the driver says to me, bowing, his hat to his chest. *How nice of him.*

"Thank you so much. Tyler, right?" I reply, mirroring his smile.

"That's right," he says before going back to the driver's seat. Nate opens the door for me, and we settle inside the car.

Even this place is already so familiar to me. I can't believe I'm back here. We hit the road, and I realize something terrible.

"Shit, I didn't say goodbye to Jenna! I have to go back."

"No need. I have her number; you can text her or call her whenever you like. By the way, here, take this," he says, offering me a brand-new iPhone. "Don't even think of saying no. Take it. I've already set it up, and Jenna's number is inside."

"Thank you," I say simply.

"Now, I have to explain a few things about me," he says, his tone serious.

"You scare me. Go on."

"You don't know it, but I'm quite famous. Plus, I might be a candidate for the Senate in a few months, so I have to move around with security, always. At the penthouse, four armed men have their own wing. They live with me, though I don't see them. They're

there just in case. Whenever I go somewhere, there's a car following me and security guys who go wherever I go. That will include
you too. You'll have your own security team, and that's nonnegotiable. We're meeting them tomorrow morning before going to
work."

I think about what he says, and it only eases my mind more. I'll
feel better, protected. That feels good. Nothing can happen to him,
and nothing can happen to me.

"Right, okay. You've thought of everything," I say, almost
timidly.

"I'm serious about this. About *us*," he replies firmly.

"I know, but I need to take things one day at a time. I'm still
uncertain about my future, so I need to take it slow. I'm still confused," I admit.

"Of course, baby," he says, kissing the side of my head. "What
time do you need to be at work tomorrow?" he asks.

Shit, I completely forgot about work. I thought I'd never set foot
there again.

"You do work, right?" he asks, suspiciously.

"No, yeah, I do, I just forgot about it with everything. Usually,
I'm there by 8:30. Why?"

"Your security team will be there at 7:30. We'll leave together.
I'll drop you off at work, and then I'll go to my office."

"Okay," I whisper. This feels like too much, but I can't seem to
gather rational thoughts. I'm still a bit lost within myself. I'm exhausted. Nate feels it, so he takes me in a warm embrace that gives
me a brief illusion of relief.

A few minutes later, we arrive on the street where Nate lives.
Where I'll be living?

For how long?

We step out of the car, and I recognize where we are: Park
Avenue. Damn, never in a million years would I have thought
I'd end up here. I take a look around and see tall, elegant build-
ings stretch up on either side, their windows softly glowing. The

prestigious building in front of me has a sleek glass facade that shimmers with reflections of the city lights. I guess it's Nate's building. The atmosphere around us feels almost peaceful. Warm streetlights illuminate the sidewalk, and the rustle of leaves in the breeze adds a touch of calm. The distant hum of traffic and the occasional honk of a horn create a lively, constant backdrop. Taking a deep breath, I squeeze Nate's hand a little tighter, and we both walk toward the grand entrance.

"Welcome back, Mr. Williams, and Ms.?" the doorman asks. He looks very nice, with what I suppose is a genuine smile. I don't have time to answer before Nate starts to speak.

"Ms. Rose. She'll be living here with me. I expect her to have a copy of my elevator card and her name already listed as a resident."

"Of course, sir. It's already been taken care of. I'll give it to you right away," he says. Then turning to me: "I'm delighted to meet you, Ms. Rose. I'm Suresh. Should you require anything at all, please do not hesitate to call me at any time. I would be more than happy to assist you." *Wow.*

"Thank you so much," I say. *I need time to process this.*

Nate opens the doors of the elevator, explaining to me that it's a private one, meant only for us to use. He lives on the top floor, and I already feel dizzy, though it has nothing to do with the fear of heights.

The doors slide open, revealing Nate's penthouse. *Holy shit!* I step out into the foyer, my breath catching in my throat. The space is bathed in warm shades of beige and light wood, exuding a serene, understated elegance. The floor is a flawless expanse of polished oak, leading my eye to the expansive living area beyond.

Every piece of furniture looks like it belongs in a design magazine: sleek, modern lines, plush fabrics, and an air of quiet luxury. A large, low sofa in a soft beige anchors the room, flanked by armchairs in complementary tones. A glass coffee table, minimalist in design, holds a few carefully chosen art books and a vase of fresh lilies, their fragrance subtly mingling with the crisp air. *Oh my . . .*

The walls are adorned with tasteful, abstract art. Windows stretch from floor to ceiling, offering a breathtaking view of the city lights twinkling far below. The sheer height and scale of it all make me feel both awestruck and microscopic.

Despite the opulence, I can't shake the feeling of being out of place. I've never been surrounded by such luxury—except for the Hamptons, but that was only for a short time, so I didn't really care that much. Now it feels almost surreal to be here. I move hesitantly, afraid to touch anything, as if I might leave a mark on this pristine sanctuary.

Nate must sense my unease. He steps beside me, his hand warm and reassuring on my back.

"It's okay," he says softly, his voice a balm to my frayed nerves. "You'll get used to it."

"I'm not supposed to," I reply in a whisper, but he just rolls his eyes at me.

His words are comforting, but the strangeness of it all still lingers. I turn to him, searching his eyes for the certainty I lack. He smiles a gentle, knowing smile that melts some of my apprehension.

"It's just walls and furniture," he continues.

"To me, it isn't. But it's really beautiful," I admit.

I take a deep breath, trying to absorb his reassurance. The initial awe and discomfort begin to blend together into a tentative acceptance. I allow myself to sink into the plushness of the nearest chair, feeling its softness embrace me. Nate's presence beside me is a steadying force, grounding me amidst the overwhelming luxury.

Nate leads me through the penthouse, starting with the living area and then heading toward the kitchen. It's sleek and modern, with shiny white countertops and cabinets that match the light wooden floors. A large marble island sits in the center, perfect for cooking or eating. The appliances are all stainless steel, reflecting the soft light from a pendant lamp above. I can't help but picture myself learning recipes here.

Next, we walk to the master bedroom. It's a peaceful and luxurious space. I'm really impressed. The king-sized bed is covered in crisp white linens, and large windows offer a stunning view of the city lights. There's a chaise lounge in the corner and a spacious walk-in closet. *Damn . . .*

As we move through these rooms, I feel a mix of awe and unease. Everything is so perfect and far from what I know. Nate notices and stops, smiling warmly.

"Hey, I want you to feel at home here, Delilah," he says. "This is our space now."

Our . . . I simply nod to him, unable to find words.

The genuine kindness in his eyes starts to ease my worries. I take a deep breath and begin to imagine what it might be like to belong in this beautiful place with him, just for a second. *Could it be?*

As it's already late, Nate and I take a quick shower. The clothes from the Hamptons arrived sometime during the night, so I have PJs to put on. Then we settle in his bed, both of us exhausted. I didn't have time to process things, nor do I find the time to do it. I'm just overwhelmed by . . . all of it. My failed attempt at suicide has resulted in me going to sleep here, with him—again. *What does this all mean?*

"I can see your brain working from here. Share it with me," Nate says, lying beside me on his shoulder.

"It's just . . . a lot. I can't seem to process things just yet," I admit.

"I know you're not ready to . . . open up to me on certain topics regarding your past and what happened to you. And that's okay, for now. I won't pressure you. I want you to trust me. I want you to see me as someone you can rely on. It'll take time, for sure. But when the day comes, I'll be there for you, baby. I'll listen, and I'll help the best I can. I'm so happy that you're here with me. I couldn't picture myself going to sleep without you next to me," he says, and I exhale.

"Thank you. But it can't last." I answer.

"It'll last for as long as we decide it will. It could be for three days, three weeks, three months—no one knows, nor can we predict it. Let's just appreciate every moment that's offered to us. That's just it," he says, and I pause.

"Can you do something for me, Nate, please?" I say out of the blue.

"Anything."

"Make me forget. I beg you, make me forget like only you know how to," I plead. I'm desperate for him to make me stop thinking in the only way that's been working for me, for us.

He doesn't even need to ask, as he knows what I want, what I need. He kisses me like it is the first time he tastes my lips. He holds me with just the right amount of strength, speaks to me with words only he knows how to express, and fucks me with the intensity only we know is infinite. And I love every second of it.

Only then do I fall asleep . . . *No, wait a second.*

"Nate?"

"Yes?"

"Why did you come back?"

"Because, somewhere deep inside me, I feel you're worth fighting for."

And then I fall asleep . . . *at peace.*

CHAPTER 10

Nate

I hear my alarm buzzing. It feels like it's way too fucking early. Shit, it's already 5:30 a.m. I have to get up, but then I turn my head and see the most beautiful sight ever—her, lying next to me. My sleeping beauty. She's so tired; I don't have the heart to wake her just yet. So I kiss her head lightly, careful not to disturb her.

I'm so relieved to know she's here with me. I know she's hiding something dark, something deep, but I'm willing to wait.

I head to my personal gym to go through my usual morning routine, all the while thinking about last night and how everything unfolded.

When I came home last night, when the elevator doors slid open, and I saw my apartment—my supposed "home"—nothing looked familiar. I felt like I was out of place, out of time. The thought of "moving on" was unbearable. I knew right then that I could never pretend this never happened. There's something about this woman I can't shake off . . . *yet*. I feel it in my gut that letting her go would be a huge fucking mistake. I just need more time to figure it out, to resolve the mystery surrounding her, help her get back on her feet, and then—only then—I'll let her go.

Charlotte is still enjoying her world tour; she doesn't seem to be in any hurry to come back just yet. And for the first time since she left, I'm happy about it. By the time Charlotte gets home, Delilah will be long gone, for sure.

I didn't manage to talk to Charlotte. I don't have the courage to face her, to hear her voice, to explain. I'm just . . . I'm not ready. The time isn't right. I'll deal with all this later.

For forty-five minutes, I work out in my gym, then take a quick shower, get dressed, and text the new security team to be ready to meet us in an hour. Delilah told me she has to be at work by 8:30 a.m., so there's still time for her to get ready.

All her clothes from the Hamptons arrived late last night, and I made sure everything was put in place. When I open the bedroom door, I see Delilah on the bed, her eyes open, staring at the ceiling.

There's something dark that follows her—I can see it. I want to know what it is, but she seemed shaken up last night. "Make me forget," she said, and I sensed her pain. I did what we do best, and the whole time I tried hard to convince myself I was soothing her when really, she was soothing me. Her touch is a balm to my soul.

But now she seems haunted—again. I sit on the bed next to her.

"Good morning, baby. You okay?" I ask. She sits up and stares blankly. I squeeze her hand, and she sighs.

"I guess I'm a little lost. I'm struggling. To be honest, I don't know if I should accept your offer to 'get back on my feet' or just go away." *Okay, she's talking, she's being honest.* I don't like what she's saying, but still, she's talking, and that's a good start.

"Let's just try it for a week or two. It'll take a little time to adjust, but I want to be here for you. You'll go to work, you'll come back here, we can hang out together, and when you have enough money saved up, then you can start looking for a new apartment. I'll back you up. Once you get everything in order, you'll be better. And in the meantime, I get to spend more time with you. It's a win-win situation," I reply simply.

"Looks like I win more than you in this situation," she chuckles.

"Baby, me inside you every fucking day is a bigger win. Don't compete with me, you'll lose," I wink at her.

"Mister Presumptuous is back in town, I see. What makes you think I'll let you fuck me every day?"

"Are you challenging me, gorgeous? Trust me, you'll beg for this," I say, gesturing at my body. That makes her laugh, and I instantly feel at ease.

"Okay, let's try this. We'll talk again in two weeks to review the situation," she says, teasing.

"Good. Now, get your ass up so I can introduce you to your security team."

Delilah wakes up in all her beautiful nakedness, and I have to give a slap to my all-too-enthusiastic dick. I show Delilah the shower and all the products she may need, then show her the new wardrobe in my dressing room. She looks a bit overwhelmed, so I hug her from behind.

"It's just clothes, baby. Don't overthink it," I say, kissing the top of her head. She squeezes me, and I just know she means thank you in her own way.

"I'll wait for you downstairs," I say, giving a light slap on her behind. She gasps and then smiles at me. God, she's so fucking beautiful.

After a while, Delilah comes downstairs, and I hand her a cup of coffee. She's wearing a high-waisted gray skirt suit and a cream-white blouse, her hair tied back in a ponytail. There's just a hint of makeup on her face, and she has on black pumps. She looks so . . . professional. It's strange to see her like this, and it's almost even more exciting. She smiles and thanks me for the coffee, and then we proceed with introducing her to the security team.

"This is Sophia and Ben. They'll be with you twenty-four seven, but you won't see them—they're discreet. I've already added their numbers to your favorite contacts in your phone," I say as they shake hands.

"Um, I don't know if they're allowed to come to work with me . . ." she says.

"Ms. Rose," Sophia replies, "there is no need for concern. We will be stationed in front of your building during your work hours. Should you require anything, please feel free to call us without needing to speak, and we will come up immediately." *Good.*

"Oh, okay, that should do it," Delilah replies shyly.

"Around what time do you leave work?" I ask her.

"Um, around five-ish. Depends on the amount of work I have."
Shit, that's early.

"Okay. Well, I, for sure, won't be done at the office by then, but we'll meet at home later tonight."

"Yeah, sure, no problem."

"Tyler will drive us to work, and he'll come back to get you. If there's anything, you call me."

I check the time—it's eight o'clock, and I'm already two hours late for work.

We drink our coffee and have some small talk about how everything runs inside the building and the penthouse. I give her the codes and the card for the entrances. I know it's a lot of information, but she'll get there.

Then we're out the door.

It's a short drive to Delilah's office, so I don't have much time to chat. Tyler parks in front of her building, and I take Delilah's hand in mine.

"Whatever you need, you call me, I'll answer. I can't wait to see how this goes," I say, hiking her skirt up a little.

"Okay, so I guess I'll see you tonight?"

"Oh, it's no guess—you *will* see me tonight," I say, pulling her onto my lap, not wanting to let her go just yet. I kiss her perfect mouth, and then she goes. I watch her enter the building and check that her team is right behind her.

I arrive at the office and feel all the glances directed toward me. I'm used to it, but these seem different.

What's up with everyone?

I reach my floor and head to the desk of Chloe, my PA, to run through the day's schedule.

"Where were you, and why didn't you answer your phone?" she asks, almost aggressively.

"Last time I checked, I wasn't obligated to explain my private matters to you," I reply.

Chloe stands there, her blonde hair cascading over her

shoulders. Her sharp green eyes seem to catch every detail. She's tall, with an elegance that turns heads, but I've never felt any attraction toward her. She's been my PA for almost a year now, and she's the best I've ever had. Her ability to juggle tasks and prioritize is unmatched. We've developed a rhythm, a seamless way of working together that makes everything run smoothly.

Over time, we've become almost friendly. She speaks a bit too freely sometimes, her comments bordering on personal. It's a delicate balance, but one that somehow works. Despite her occasional oversteps, her professionalism and competence are undeniable. She makes my chaotic life manageable, and for that, I'm grateful. But now she's overstepping.

"Why wouldn't you answer me? The board decided on your brother's case, but you were just too busy with something that I obviously know nothing about. You know you can tell me everything, right?"

"Just because I can doesn't mean I have to. Just run through the day with me, and I'll check the rest," I say.

It takes less than five minutes to go over today's meetings, and then I'm off to my office.

I have to open the mail concerning Jake, but I dread the outcome, whatever it is. Here goes . . .

Dear Members of Williams Holdings,

Following the recent events that have come to light, we regret to inform you that Mr. Jake Williams has been terminated from his position as Chief Operating Officer (COO) of Williams Holdings, effective immediately. After thorough deliberation during the board meeting held on May 6th, 2022, it was concluded that Mr. Williams's actions have severely compromised the reputation and integrity of our company. Such conduct is unacceptable and not in line with the values and standards we uphold at Williams Holdings.

To ensure a smooth and orderly transition, Mr. Williams will remain with the company in a non-decision-making capacity until a new COO is appointed. During this period, Mr. Williams will not be permitted to participate in any decisions or strategic planning activities. His role will be strictly limited to assisting with the handover process to facilitate continuity in operations.

We are committed to maintaining the highest levels of professionalism and integrity within our organization and will take all necessary measures to restore confidence and trust among our stakeholders.

We appreciate your understanding and cooperation during this transitional period. Should you have any questions or require further clarification, please do not hesitate to contact the Board Secretary.

Thank you for your attention to this matter.

Sincerely . . .

Shit . . .

I know it's the right decision, and I know things at the company will only get better, but a part of me feels for Jake. He never managed to succeed at anything. I've tried my best, but now there's nothing more I'm willing to do. He has to grow up on his own and realize that he needs to work.

And now I fucking have to study all the possible candidates for the COO position. *Fuck me . . .*

I need a little distraction. I haven't heard from Delilah for almost three hours. I hate that I've turned into a schoolboy for her.

Nate: *How's my girl's day going?*
Delilah: *Missing me already, huh?*
Nate: *Woman, you have no idea. So, how's it going?*
Delilah: *Ugh, I hate my job, so the day is quite long, but I manage. How's yours?*
Nate: *Long and painful.*
Delilah: *How can I help?*
Nate: *A picture of your tits should do.*

Delilah: *Haha, funny. Wait until tonight; I might be very accommodating . . .*

Nate: *I'll hurry to get home early.*

I hear someone knocking on my door and I raise my head.

"Come in."

Then I see James entering my office. It feels like I haven't seen him in ages. The last time I saw him, I hadn't met Delilah yet. It feels like years have passed between those two events."What the hell, man?" he says, all agitated.

"What?" I answer, unaffected.

"What the fuck happened to you on Friday? Why haven't you answered your fucking phone? And why didn't you come to meet me last night?"

That's a lot of questions. I can't answer them all. I'm not ready to talk about Delilah just yet. She's my beautiful little secret.

"Nothing happened. I told you, I needed some air and some distance from all the Jake shit," I say, maintaining my usual indifference.

"Bullshit, I know you, and I know when something's off."

"Get to the point, James."

"Okay, so Jake's out, finally, but I wanted to know how you're handling things and if you've had time to look at the COO applications."

"No, not yet. Do you have any suggestions?" I ask, hoping he has someone in mind already.

"Yeah, I have some good candidates. Let's go to lunch, and we'll discuss them."

We leave the office and head to one of our favorite lunch spots near Bryant Park on 6th Avenue. As we walk, we review Jake's case and the ways he might seek revenge against us. Throughout the meal, I successfully avoid discussing the reason for my weekend disappearance, focusing instead on evaluating candidates for the COO position.

James's eyes are on me, filled with unasked questions about my absence. I stay firm, not revealing anything about Delilah. But James, being James, cuts straight to the heart of the matter.

"She called me," he says. I know exactly who he means. Talking about her and our situation still makes me uncomfortable.

"What did she say?" I ask, trying to keep my tone neutral.

"She said you blew her off and never answered her emails or calls. She was worried. I told her you were fine, that Jake was just occupying too much of your headspace, and that she had nothing to worry about. So you lied to me."

"What do you mean?" I ask, locking eyes with him.

"Did you blow her off to go fuck some supermodels in the Hamptons?"

"No," I say, my gaze unwavering. "I blew her off for *you*, but *you* blew me off, so I got bored and left. I rested well, and now I'm back."

And I appreciate you putting me first, but since I didn't come, why not call her back? That's not like you at all. I'm trying to understand."

"There's nothing to understand. Let's get back; I have tons of shit to do."

James remains silent, and I don't give him time to dwell on his thoughts as I pay the bill and head back to work.

~

I'm in my office trying to focus on the crisis with the Hudsons when my mother calls, again. Shit, I have to deal with her at some point.

"Mother," I answer, trying to keep my voice calm.

"Nathan, what on Earth have you done to your poor little brother? Why didn't you come to dinner on Sunday? Why did you turn off your phone? And why haven't you called me back already? I'm about to have a heart attack!" *Such a drama queen.*

"Mother, if you want information about what your *poor little son* did, I suggest you call him. I don't have time for this, I'm really busy. I didn't come because I suddenly became extra busy, thanks to your other son. Now, please, what do you need?"

"Don't speak to me that way. I only want what's best for both of you. I'll come to your place tonight to discuss this." *Shit, Delilah. No!*

"I won't be there tonight, but we can have lunch tomorrow if you want. Today is really not the day, I'm overloaded with work."

"Fine, see you tomorrow," she says, and hangs up.

My mother has always been overprotective of Jake because of his inability to achieve anything in his goddamn life. She knows I'm a big boy, that I can handle anything, so she doesn't play the "sweet mommy" role with me. But she remains intrusive, always wanting to know every detail about how I live my life. It's incredibly frustrating. She can never know about Delilah, or she might just have that heart attack she mentioned earlier.

My sweet Delilah . . . I need to hear her voice, to know she's okay. I hope she's smiling. With a surge of longing, I call her. The phone rings once, twice, and on the third ring, she answers.

"Hey, baby," I say, unable to hide my enthusiasm.

"Hi, baby, what's up?" she replies playfully, and the sound of her cheerful voice is a balm to my soul.

"I just wanted to hear your voice. Come on, sing to me," I urge her, teasing. She bursts out laughing, and it's the most delightful sound I've ever heard.

"A song for a song?" she teases.

"Are you bargaining with me, babe? I'm still waiting for that picture, by the way. Come on, sing for me," I coax, grinning wider as her laughter rings out again.

And then she sings, her voice soft yet powerful:

There I was again tonight
Forcing laughter, faking smiles
Same old tired, lonely place
Walls of insincerity, shifting eyes and vacancy

Vanished when I saw your face
All I can say is, it was enchanting to meet you

No, baby, it was enchanting to meet *you*.
"Your turn," she challenges. Alright, an easy one.

Hey there, Delilah, what's it like in New York City?
I'm a thousand miles away, but girl, tonight you look so pretty
Yes, you do
Times Square can't shine as bright as you, I swear it's true

I pour my heart into it, and she bursts out laughing again. *Oh. My. God,* that sound is doing things to me.

"That was good, baby, you nailed it! Shit, my boss is coming, gotta go. Call you later."

"I'll wait," I say, reluctantly hanging up.

That woman is just . . . *fuck*, she's such a light. One with a huge train of shadows, but all I see is her light and how it warms my heart. I can't wait to go home and take her in my arms. And then do very, *very* dirty things to her.

The day drags on, each minute stretching longer than the last. I still haven't heard from Jake, but I know him. I know he'll return with a vengeance, thinking he can outsmart me. Jake might fancy himself a predator, but he's nothing more than a kitten playing at being a tiger. Me? I'm a lion, poised and ready.

I focus on the pile of important files demanding my attention, sifting through each document with meticulous care. The quiet hum of the office is interrupted by the sharp ring of my phone. Delilah's name flashes on the screen.

"Hey." Her voice is a soothing balm among the chaos.

"Hey, you," I reply, leaning back in my chair. "What's up?"

"I'm about to head to your apartment," she says, a hint of hesitation in her tone. "I've finished work. I don't know how to ask Tyler if he's there. I'm so not used to this . . ."

"It's okay," I reassure her. "I'll text him right now to let him know. You'll get used to it, don't worry. Whenever it feels like too much, just talk to me, okay?" I shoot a quick text to Tyler, letting him know Delilah is on her way.

I glance at the clock. It's 5:30, but there's still a mountain of work to conquer.

"I'm not done yet, so I'll meet you at home."

"Okay, no problem. It'll give me time to cook dinner."

"You don't have to," I say, feeling a pang of guilt. "I can order in if you want, or ask Fran, the housekeeper, to make dinner for us."

"Oh no, I'd love to cook, don't bother anyone. Oh, I see Tyler. Okay, I'll get in the car. Talk to you when you're there."

"Okay, babe. See you soon."

She hangs up, and the office feels a bit quieter without her voice.

The day's tasks pull me back into their relentless grip, but my mind wanders to Delilah and the warmth of home.

Now it's almost seven o'clock, and I'm ready to leave. For the first fucking time in my life, I'm leaving work before eight. Usually, I stay until nine or ten, but today is different. Today, Delilah is waiting for me at home. I take my briefcase, lock my office door, and meet Chloe's gaze.

"What are you doing? You have no meetings planned," she questions, confusion etched on her face.

"I'm going home. You can leave for the day too. Thank you," I reply, keeping my tone brisk and professional.

"Why?"

"Why what?" I ask, genuinely puzzled by her curiosity.

"Why are you going home now?"

"Chloe, that's none of your business. I'd hate to fire you, so please remember your place," I respond, perhaps a bit too harshly, but she needs to understand boundaries.

"Okay, okay," she says, holding up her hands in surrender.

"Goodbye, Chloe."

"Goodbye, *sir*." I ignore whatever intention lies behind that last word.

Tyler is already waiting when I leave the building, and we head straight home. The drive is smooth, but my anticipation builds with each passing moment.

When I open the door, a wave of satisfaction washes over me as I hear Delilah singing, her voice a soothing melody that fills the apartment. She's in the kitchen, the aroma of dinner making my stomach rumble.

"Hey," I call out, letting her know I'm home.

"Hey," she answers, coming straight into my arms. I hug her extra tight, savoring the warmth and comfort she brings. "I've made lasagna, and it's ready. I hope you're hungry."

"I'm hungry for many things, baby," I murmur, my hand wandering down to her. I feel her warmth through the fabric of her panties, a sensation that sends a jolt of desire through me.

"Oh, but that's for dessert, Mr. Williams," she teases, her voice a sultry whisper. If I was hard before, I'm rock solid now. *Damn, woman.*

"You're good," I say with a cocky grin. She laughs—a light, carefree sound—and leads me to the kitchen table. We settle in for a nice dinner, the comfort of home and the promise of the night ahead making this moment perfect.

During dinner, we talk and laugh a lot, as if this were an old habit for us. I feel incredibly at ease talking to her. I tell her about James, Jake, and my mother, and she seems genuinely interested in everything I say.

"Wow, looks like you have a lot to work on with all this," she says, her eyes wide with empathy.

"I know."

"Plus my being here . . . Are you sure that's still okay?" she asks, tucking a lock of hair behind her ear. *God, she's so fucking adorable.*

"Delilah, do you know what kept me going through this fucking day?" I ask, leaning in a bit. She shakes her head in response.

"Knowing that when I got home, you'd be here. The mere idea of you being here when I get back gave me all the energy in the world to get through all this shit. It's not just *'okay'* that you're here, it's fucking necessary for me now. Don't ask me why—I don't fucking know."

She smiles at my answer, looking down at her plate, clearly at a loss for words. So, I decide to lighten the mood a little.

"Plus, knowing that I'll be deep inside you wasn't bad for my mental health either," I say, grinning. Well, that's also the truth, to be honest. She laughs, a beautiful, melodic sound, and I feel like everything is finally in place. *Finally.*

"I thought you would have changed your mind by now," she says. "You know, come to your senses. But I've thought about it all day, and I want to give it a try. I've turned the whole thing upside down, and I just came to the realization that maybe, I don't know, things happen for a reason, and whatever is supposed to happen to me will happen. Whether it's good or bad. I've been through hell and back, and I think this might be a chance for me to . . . try again."

"Try what again?" I ask, a bit confused.

"Life," she says, shrugging. I keep listening, trying to understand what she's implying.

"I'll work, save money, and then I'll look for an apartment. I will pay you back for everything you're giving me."

"No need," I say. I stay silent because there are some things she said that don't sit well with me.

With Delilah, I know better than to push things. She just needs time. She needs time to trust me, and I'll do anything to prove to her that she can.

We finish dinner, and Delilah insists on doing the dishes, but I won't have it, so I help her. It's the first time I've ever done it. It all feels so domestic, but in the very best way. I've never done this with Charlotte.

We lived together, but at the time, I was buried in work, and so was she. We never had time just for ourselves at home. We would finish work past ten in the evening, go straight to a fancy restaurant—most of the time to join our friends—then go back to our apartment, fuck—sometimes, if we weren't too tired—and then fall asleep and repeat. If we ate at home, it was only because we were sick. It never felt this . . . *right*. How have things changed so much in such a short period of time?

"Wanna watch a movie?" Delilah asks, pulling me out of my thoughts.

"Sure, I'd snuggle with you, baby," I answer all too happily.

"I said *movie,* but good to know you're still you," she replies, laughing. I take her in my arms, resting my hands on her fine ass.

"Let's grab a shower first. Together, if you need clarification," I say, winking at her.

"Of course," she says, rolling her eyes, which makes me laugh.

We go upstairs and shower quickly, but I manage to tease her under the water. She laughs most of the time, and we make out, touching each other *a lot.* I love every bit of this moment. Then Delilah puts on a set of black-and-white satin pajamas. She looks so gorgeous in them, but I can't shake the image of undressing her out of my head.

Patience, boy, everything will come to those who wait!

Then we get down and settle on the couch. Delilah chooses the movie *Forrest Gump,* and we watch it. Well, "watch" is a bit of a stretch, knowing that my mission is to get in her panties. Which I do.

She's focused on the movie for a while, but has to abandon it at some point, faced with a very horny man who has very roaming hands.

Of course, she finishes the movie bent over the couch with my dick deep inside her, screaming my name all around the place. *I could get used to this life.*

As we get ready for bed. I leave the bathroom and take a moment to observe her. I stand at the entrance, one shoulder against the doorframe, crossing my arms. She's taking off the pillows, arranging the bed to get in, folding all the clothes, tidying up. She's fucking cute. I feel extremely lucky to be here with her. I just had her, but I want even more of her.

"What?" she asks as she realizes I'm watching her.

"Nothing, I just like having you here."

"Don't get used to it," she teases. That makes me laugh on the outside, but I feel a little cry on the inside.

I grab her arm and pull us onto the bed. I plug in my phone, set my morning alarm, and then turn to her beautiful, angelic face.

"Thank you," she says, caressing my stubble.

"What for?"

"Everything."

I kiss her gently on the lips. I turn her around, her back to my front, and spoon her.

"This is nice," she whispers.

"Wait until the middle of the night when I wake you up to really appreciate the definition of 'nice,'" I say, and she bursts out laughing. I just love that sound. My heart squeezes a little.

Fuck, this is just day one.

CHAPTER 11
Delilah

It's been over two weeks since I moved in with Nate, and time feels like it's slipping through my fingers. How can I describe my life since then? I don't know yet. I'm still trying to figure it out. I don't dare to dream, to hope, or to even think. Since that day, I've been taking it one step at a time, just to see where things lead.

Do I still want to join the stars? *Yes.* Yes, because it all feels so unreal and impossible. I still have moments where I sink into darkness, doubt, and fear. I still have panic attacks, but I manage to "handle" them. Or at least I try to. Sometimes it's hard to breathe and pretend everything is okay. My mind is still a battlefield where my demons try to drag me down.

But then I take a deep breath, look up at the sky, and I feel *him*. Nate has been so supportive. Our life together is simple yet amazing. I wake up in his arms, we get ready together and even go to the gym together. We text and call each other all day, and I'm always the first one home. I cook dinner, and I've gotten really good at it. When Nate comes home, I jump into his arms like a little girl. We have amazing sex and talk a lot. He makes me laugh so hard. I'm so grateful for everything he does for me.

We've had a few fights, of course—we both have tempers—but overall, living together is really nice. Despite the challenges, I find myself feeling thankful for Nate and everything he's offering me.

I've seen Jenna a couple times after work for coffee. We text all the time, and she's easy to be around, like everything is, I don't know, *normal?* Her friendship is starting to become important to me. She doesn't know my story, but I mostly talk about Nate and my job, and so far, it works.

Now I'm at work, and I can't focus. Today, nothing seems to matter, and I know I can't stay here. I've been searching for a new job, but no responses yet. This place still haunts me; it's my last connection to my previous life, to what I need to escape. Fate, however, has different plans for me today.

I see my boss, Mr. Berard, striding toward me. I know he's about to reprimand me for my lack of productivity, but I just can't muster the energy to care anymore.

"Ms. Rose, you are to come to my office in five minutes," Mr. Berard announces, his tone dripping with authority.

"What about?" I ask, trying to sound innocent. He doesn't bother to respond, just gives a dismissive huff. That's the final straw for me.

"I asked you a question," I repeat, this time with a sharper edge to my voice.

"You're not allowed to speak just yet, Ms. Rose. I suggest you revisit your tone before addressing me," he retorts, clearly taken aback by my defiance. *Oh, for fuck's sake.*

"You can't tell me that I'm not allowed to speak. With all due respect, you're out of line," I snap back.

"Ms. Rose, if you want to be jobless, please continue," he dares me. Little does he know, living with Nathan Williams has taught me a thing or two about standing my ground. I've heard him over the phone during business calls enough times. Channeling Nate's confidence, I decide to give Mr. Berard a taste of his own medicine. *This one's for you, babe.*

"I advise you never speak to me like that again if you want to keep breathing. I won't tolerate such behavior. I'm not just any woman, I'm Delilah fucking Rose."

"Are you threatening me?" he asks, incredulous. I can't help but let out a small laugh.

"Yes," I reply, deadpan.

Five minutes later, I'm on my way home. Of course, I got fired on the spot, but damn, it felt exhilarating. This was fun. Finally free from the chains of my old life, I head home, ready for whatever comes next.

I decide not to tell Nate just yet. I want to see his face when I share what happened and how it all went down. I call him, and as always, he answers after the first ring.

"Hey baby," he purrs over the phone. Damn, his voice still sends shivers down my spine.

"Hi babe, just wanted to let you know that I finished work early and have the rest of the day off. I'm heading home," I say, trying to keep my tone casual.

"Really? It's only 2:00 p.m."

"I know. I'll use this time to clean the house," I tell him. "You know we have a cleaning lady, right?"

"Yes, but I do it better. No offense," I say with a smirk.

"None taken. Fire her and hire a better one," he suggests.

"No, she's nice. I just like to do it my own way. Nobody can beat me at this." Damn, Nate's confidence must be rubbing off on me. I hear him laugh again, and it makes me even prouder of my little victory.

"Okay, I'll see if I can get out of the office to join you," he says.

"To clean with me?" I ask, teasing.

"No, to fuck with you."

"Of course," I say, laughing hard. "Okay, call me when you know."

"See you soon," he replies, and then he hangs up.

I arrive home and proceed with the cleaning of the year. I can't stand dirt and mess. I need everything to shine, and damn him for having such a huge apartment—sorry, *penthouse*—with so many windows and surfaces to clean.

I grab the cleaning supplies and start working on the penthouse.

Cleaning feels like therapy, like I'm bordering on OCD. The scent of lemon cleaner fills the air, and I meticulously polish the surfaces, losing myself in the rhythm of the motions.

But as I clean, the demons in my head begin to stir. The job I hated is now gone, and I know I had to leave it to break free from my past. Yet doubt creeps in.

Will I ever find another position? I have no education, no degree, and very limited experience. The thought gnaws at me as I scrub the kitchen counter until it gleams.

I need to find a job, fearing Nate will throw me out. Even though he's been the nicest person to me, grounding me, helping me, cheering for me, I can't shake the fear.

What if he gets tired of me? What if he realizes I'm not worth the trouble? The fear of abandonment, the recurring theme in my life, grips me hard. I wipe down the windows, but the view outside blurs as my eyes fill with unshed tears.

Chaos has always been a part of my existence. I've clawed my way out, and Nate has been my anchor, my steady rock. The thought of disappointing him terrifies me. I know it's irrational, that he wouldn't be pissed about the job, but I can't manage to be realistic. The fear is too deep, too consuming. My dark thoughts drag me down.

What if I'm not good enough? What if I fail again? I move to the living room, vacuuming the carpet with methodical precision, trying to banish the doubts.

My mind races as I dust the bookshelves. Each book is a reminder of what I lack, the knowledge I never gained. I try to focus on the task at hand, but the fear is relentless.

I continue cleaning, every movement a desperate attempt to find some sense of control. The penthouse sparkles, but inside, I feel more broken than ever. I need to believe in myself, to trust that I can make it. But as I move to the bedroom, straightening the sheets with trembling hands, I wonder if I'll ever silence the demons in my head. The fear of abandonment lingers, threatening to pull me back into the chaos I'm fighting so hard to escape.

My phone buzzes, and "Handsome CEO" flashes on the screen. Nate did this. He changes it from time to time.

"Hey," I answer, my voice tinged with a bit of stress.

"Hey, have you finished cleaning the house?" he asks.

"I never really finish cleaning, but yeah, the house is done."

"Great. I'm off work and heading home," he says, his tone playful.

"Did you wait until I was done to come home?" I ask, scolding him lightly, though I can't help but laugh.

"I did, but I have the best cleaning task for you, baby."

"Oh, let me guess—clean your dick with my tongue after you come hard, right?"

"See! I taught you so well, baby. We're so good together already!" he says, sounding like a proud schoolboy. His playful tone makes me laugh even harder, soothing my dark mood.

"Okay, hurry up," I say before hanging up the phone.

As I put the phone down, a small smile plays on my lips. The apartment is spotless, every surface gleaming, but my mind remains cluttered with doubts and fears. Cleaning is my therapy, a way to control the chaos, but today, even that hasn't chased away the shadows.

Nate comes home, and as usual, I run to him and jump into his arms, wrapping my legs around his waist. I hold him tight, and he supports me effortlessly, his strong arms encircling my back.

"Nate, do you like me?" I murmur against his shoulder, too embarrassed to meet his eyes.

"Of course I like you, sweetheart," he answers, his voice soothing as he speaks into my hair.

"Would you *still* like me if I were unemployed?" I ask, my voice uncertain. His laughter surprises me, a deep, genuine sound that reverberates through his chest. He tilts my head, searching for my eyes and meeting them with his warm, reassuring gaze.

"Of course I'd still like you. What happened?" he asks, caressing my cheek with one hand. I climb down from his embrace and take a deep breath, ready to explain everything. I recount how I got fired earlier, how his influence gave me the courage to stand my ground.

Nate bursts out laughing as I finish the story, his laughter shaking his whole body.

"So, I take it you're *not* throwing me out because I'm out of a job?" I ask, half joking, half serious.

"What? No, absolutely not. Get rid of that shit in your head, Delilah. I'll never throw you out. This is your home too now," he says firmly.

I nod, relief washing over me.

"Do you have any leads on another job yet?" he inquires.

"Well, no. I've been applying everywhere, but nobody wants me. I don't blame them; I have no education and very limited experience. But I learn fast, and . . . Ugh, I hate this," I say, hiding my face behind my hands. Nate gently pulls my them away.

"It's okay, baby. We'll figure it out. Take some time to think about what you want to do next."

"It's not about what I *want* to do. I don't have options here. If only I had a degree . . ." I trail off, frustration seeping into my voice.

"Why don't you go back to school? I'm sure there are programs where you can catch up, even by correspondence. Take the time to do some research, and I'll see what I can do," he suggests. That, is a very interesting idea.

"I'd love that! Do you think it's possible?" I say, excitement bubbling up as I jump around.

"Of course it is. Plus, if I recall, you are 'Delilah fucking Rose.' There's nothing you can't do," he says, winking at me.

"Speaking of which," I say, grabbing him by the waistband of his expensive suit pants. I unfasten his belt and kneel before him.

"That was about damn time," he says, and the rest is history.

After two hours of amazing sex, we now lie in bed, talking about everything and nothing. The soft sheets are cool against our skin, and the hum of the city outside our window creates a soothing backdrop. It's incredibly relaxing, a perfect end to a passionate afternoon. Nate turns to me, his eyes sparkling with a spontaneous idea. He suggests we go out for coffee.

A knot of anxiety forms in my stomach. I rarely leave the house except for work, and though I've gone out for coffee with Jenna, the outside world, with its bustling streets and crowds, still kind of freaks me out. But then I look at Nate, his reassuring smile, his calm presence, and of course, his dominance. With him by my side—and our security team too—I decide to face my fears and just go.

I slip into a dress that makes me feel both comfortable and elegant. It's long and flowing, with a delicate floral pattern. The sleeves are long, since it's not that hot outside, and the neckline dips into a daring yet classy V shape. I choose sandals for comfort on the busy streets of New York City.

Nate, ever the picture of sophistication, puts on a fine navy suit that contrasts beautifully with his bright-blue eyes, making them even more striking.

As we walk hand in hand, I feel a mix of nervousness and anticipation. The city is alive with energy, and Nate's presence beside me is a comforting anchor. He begins to talk about New York, sharing stories of his childhood and the places he loves. His voice is filled with warmth and excitement, and I find myself captivated by his tales. He doesn't realize how happy it makes me to hear about his good fortune, to know he grew up in a healthy environment. Not all of us were that lucky.

His stories make the city feel a little less daunting, a little more familiar. I take a deep breath, letting the sounds and sights of New York wash over me.

"So, where are you taking me?" I ask, curiosity tinged with a hint of impatience as we stroll down the street.

"Greenwich Village," he replies with a nostalgic smile, his eyes glinting with memories. "There's a café I used to go to after school. All the girls hoped to catch me there, try to steal a kiss. Ahh, those were the good old days," he teases, his voice carrying a playful lilt. I roll my eyes and playfully slap his chest.

"Oh, go fuck yourself!" I laugh, the sound echoing lightly in the air. His mischievous grin widens, and in one swift, cheeky move, he grabs me by the ass and nips at my ear, sending a shiver down my spine.

"There's just one girl I want now," he whispers, in that sexy, seductive voice of his. I don't want to respond, I don't want to think about it too much—I just want to enjoy this moment as if it were my last, so I lean into him.

"Delilah?" I hear a different, all-too-familiar voice, and suddenly, shock overtakes my whole being. *How?*

I open my eyes, raise my gaze, and see him.

"Delilah, *Dios mio*, that's you! What the fuck, *hermosa*, where have you been?"

"Sam," I exhale. Nate immediately steps in front of me as if to protect me, giving Sam a very dark look. But Sam doesn't even notice—he must be in shock, seeing me here.

"I could hug you right now, but I know how much you hate human contact. Delilah, what the hell—we thought you were dead!" he exclaims.

"I was," I whisper. Technically, that's true. Nate squeezes my hand, searching for my eyes. "I'm sorry, Sam," I say, half smiling because it's Sam, and he's been one of my best friends. He fucking saved me, too.

"*Hermosa*, please come here," he says, opening his arms to me. I go, reluctantly—because yes, I don't like it when people touch me. *But it's Sam . . .*

He holds me extra tight, and even though it's awkward, I think it's okay. Nate grabs my hand, pulling me back to him.

"What the fuck?" Nate asks, clearly confused.

"Right, Nate, this is Sam. I've talked to you about him—he's the one who covered for me at The Rex. Sam, this is, well . . . he's, um—"

"Nathan Williams. Nice to meet you, and thank you for helping my girl out back then," Nate says, extending his hand. Hearing him introduce himself as *"Nathan"* feels strange.

"Samuel Hernandez," Sam replies, shaking Nate's hand before turning his gaze back to me. "Damn, baby girl, now I have a crush," he jokes, making me laugh. I notice Nate smiling too, pleased by the compliment.

"Okay," he says, "you have to tell me what happened to you. I've called you like a thousand times."

"I changed my number," I admit.

"Well, give it to me. I'm late for my shift at the hospital, but I'll come back tomorrow," he says, pulling out his phone.

"Sammy, no one can know I'm here. No one can know you've seen me, and you can't give my number to anyone," I say firmly, making my condition clear. Truth is, I've missed him so much. I want to see him, but I need to remain, well . . . *dead*.

"If you leak that information," Nate interrupts, "I'll personally make you regret it. And believe me, you won't like it one bit," he says in a menacing tone that sends chills through both of us.

"Oh my God, of course not! Delilah's my friend—I'd never betray her. But *Dios mio*, that was ho-ot," Sam says, breaking the tension, and I laugh again as I give him my phone number.

Then he says, "I have to ask, Delilah. What if Ashley—"

"Don't." I cut him off sharply. I can't. It's too much. I feel the emotion rising, and suddenly, I'm overwhelmed by sadness all over again. Nate feels it too and pulls me into his strong arms.

"Okay, I'm sorry. I won't. I promise," Sam says, surrendering. "I fucking have to go. I'll call you tomorrow morning, and you better pick up! You look so beautiful, Delilah. I missed you, *mi hermosa*."

"You too," I reply, and I mean it. Sam runs off, hurrying to catch his bus, and I watch him disappear into the crowd.

"Well?" Nate asks, his eyes wide with curiosity.

I just sigh.

"I'll explain. Let's just have that coffee first."

We arrive at the vintage coffee shop on 8th Avenue, a hidden gem that radiates a charming sixties vibe. The décor is a delightful mix of light blue and pink, with checkered floors and retro posters adorning the walls. Vinyl records and classic jukebox tunes add to the nostalgic atmosphere. I can't help but smile as we settle into a cozy booth in the back, its cushions a soft, faded pink.

Nate slides in across from me. As we take in the surroundings, a waitress on roller skates glides over to our table. Her uniform is a cute pastel-blue dress, complete with a frilly apron, and her blonde curls bounce with every movement. She looks straight at Nate, her eyes widening with unmistakable interest.

"Hi there, what can I get for you?" she asks, her gaze fixed on him. I can practically see her heart fluttering.

"Two coffees, black, no sugar please," Nate replies, his voice steady and polite. He doesn't seem to notice her obvious attempts at flirting. She writes down the order, but her eyes never leave his face.

"Anything else?" she purrs, batting her eyelashes. It's as if I didn't even exist. *Ugh, stupid woman.*

I feel a twinge of annoyance but quickly push it aside. I understand all too well her reaction. Nate has that effect on women. He's handsome, exudes power, and has that effortless charm that draws people in. Still, it irritates me.

"No, that's all for now," he says, glancing at me with a smile. The waitress reluctantly skates away, defeated.

I take a deep breath, trying to steady my nerves. I'm anxious about what I have to tell Nate, but I know I have no way out. I owe him that much. I sip my water, the cool liquid doing little to calm my racing heart.

"So, this place is amazing," I say, trying to delay the inevitable confession. "This is where the girls used to try to get your attention, huh?"

He chuckles. "Yes. It hasn't changed much," he replies, leaning back in the booth. His eyes are warm, focused solely on me, completely oblivious to the waitress and her antics. That pleases me more than I care to admit.

The waitress returns with our coffees, placing Nate's cup in front of him with an extra flourish, and mine in front of me with barely a glance.

"Enjoy," she says, her tone slightly deflated.

Nate thanks her without looking up, his attention still on me. I can't help but smile, feeling a bit more confident. I wrap my hands around my coffee cup, savoring the warmth.

"I don't know where to begin," I say, my voice getting unsteady. He leans in, concern etched on his face.

"You can tell me anything, sweetheart," he says softly. His sincerity gives me the courage to continue.

"Okay, ask me a question, and I'll see how to answer it. That okay?" I say, trying to keep my voice steady. He nods, his eyes serious.

"Why did he think you were dead?" he asks. *Shit.* That question hits me like a punch to the gut. I stay silent for a moment, not wanting to dredge up those horrible memories.

Then I try to find the words.

"Because I . . . left," I say, my voice barely above a whisper.

"Go on," he encourages gently.

"I wanted to disappear. I stopped answering my phone, and I . . . well, I was in a very dark place. I just wanted to shut everything out, somehow. And I, well, I just . . . I couldn't tell anyone that." I struggle to keep my voice from breaking. "And then I met you," I continue, words tumbling out in a rush. "I thought it was a great opportunity to be . . . reborn." I exhale deeply. "Sorry," I add, feeling embarrassed.

"No need to apologize, baby. But why didn't he come to your workplace to find you?" he asks, his brow furrowing.

"Oh, no one knew where I worked. Eric kept it a secret. I just told people I found a job in Brooklyn, but that wasn't true."

"Did he know Eric?" he asks, a note of disgust in the name, which makes me laugh a little.

"Yes, but they weren't close. Even if he had asked Eric for information, Eric wouldn't have said anything. That I know for sure. Plus, Sam knows how fucked up I am, so it must not have been a surprise that I . . . disappeared."

"How long have you known Sam? I take it you trust him? What does he do?" he inquires, his curiosity piqued.

"I've known him for almost eight years. I do trust him, in my own way. He's the one who faked my blood tests. We became friends. He's from Venezuela, came to the U.S. to become a doctor. He's an intern at Harlem Hospital and works extra jobs, like at The Rex, to pay the bills. He's the only male friend I have because I hate how men look at me, and him being gay, well, let's say that was no problem for me," I say, chuckling.

"Does he know your story?" Nate asks softly.

"Yes," I confess. I know Nate wants to know it too, but I just can't bring myself to share it.

"Why him and not me?" His voice is tinged with hurt.

"It has nothing to do with you, Nate. I had to tell him. I needed his help and his friendship. I was a terrified kid at the time, scared shitless. Fuck, I was just a child. Please don't make me talk more," I beg, tears welling up in my eyes. I see the hurt in Nate's eyes, and it breaks me to be the cause of it, but I just can't.

"I'm so sorry, Nate. I just . . . can't."

"It's okay, I'll wait until you trust me. I won't push you. You can invite Sam over if you want, but we'll have to do a background check first," he says, trying to comfort me.

"Of course. Thank you, baby, thank you," I say, standing up to join him. I wrap my arms around him and give him a deep, lingering kiss on his plush, perfect lips, hoping he can feel how much I appreciate his patience and understanding. Then he looks at me with those gorgeous ice-blue eyes of his, a smile playing at the corner of his lips, and I can feel the butterflies fluttering in my stomach. He's so beautiful it hurts.

"Now, tell me what's up at Williams. How are things turning out with your brother?" I ask genuinely. I've become fascinated by Nate's stories, like they're a show and I can't wait to watch the next episode.

Nate has told me everything about his feud with his brother Jake. It's a complicated mess that weighs heavily on his shoulders. He told me that Jake was evicted from his COO job at Williams after messing up a crucial deal with one of New York's richest families, the Hudsons. Despite this, Nate is still trying to manage the deal, hoping to salvage something from the wreckage.

He tells me that Jake still goes to the office, even though he's not allowed to be part of any decision-making. This ongoing power struggle seems to only fuel Jake's hatred for Nate, and I think it eats away at Nate's feelings.

Nate attends family brunch on Sundays, but I don't go with him, since no one knows I exist—something I appreciate a lot. He tells me about his mother being her usual annoying and intrusive self, always poking her nose into his business, making unwelcome comments and suggestions. I already dislike her very much. His father, on the other hand, is too busy to care about anything happening within the family. He's absorbed in his own world, and I conclude that he's leaving Nate to navigate the family dynamics alone. I hate that too.

The feud with Jake, Nate says, isn't just about the job; it's about something deeper, a simmering resentment that has built up over the years. Nate hasn't had a proper discussion with Jake since everything blew up, but he knows his brother is plotting revenge. Jake's bitterness drives him, and Nate is constantly on edge, trying to stay one step ahead, to cut the ground from under Jake's feet before he can strike.

As I sit across from Nate, I can see the strain in his eyes, the weariness in his posture. He tries to mask it with a brave face, but the burden is great. He confides in me, letting me into this complicated, painful part of his life. I listen, my heart aching for him, wishing I could do more to help.

In this moment, I realize how much I care for Nate and our relationship. His struggles, his pain—they've become part of my own world. I want to support him, to be there for him.

As the afternoon light fades, casting a warm glow over the room, I reach out and take Nate's hand. It's a silent promise that he's not alone, that I'll stand by him through whatever comes next. We sit there, connected by more than just the coffee we share, bound by the unspoken understanding that only we can truly understand.

Then we go back home, and once we're inside, Nate leads me to his office, where I sit on his lap while he opens his computer. We start doing some research together about a study program where I can take a shot at the SATs and maybe attend college via correspondence. Nate knows way more about these things than I do, so I trust him completely when he says one program is good and another is trash. We decide together to apply for several distance learning programs. But then I take a look at the cost, and *holy shit*.

"Nate, there's no way on Earth I can afford any of this! We have to find another solution."

"The fact that you think you'd pay anything is cute. Don't worry, that's on me."

"On you?!" I practically shriek. "Nate, this is way too much for me!"

"Delilah, if it makes you feel better, just tell yourself you'll pay me back."

"HOW?!" I ask in disbelief.

"Blow jobs," he says, a mischievous grin spreading across his face.

"Nate, please be serious for a second," I beg, pinching the bridge of my nose.

"I assure you with all my being that I am," he says, half smiling. He's just being cocky, as always, but I like it. "Delilah, I think it's time I tell you how much money I actually have," he adds, which makes me burst out laughing.

"No need, I've seen your closet. I know you're rich. But still, it feels wrong for you to pay for my education. Feels like you're my sugar daddy," I say, laughing as I realize what I just said. But Nate's smile only widens.

"Oh, for the love of God, Nathan!" I groan, but that only makes him laugh harder.

"Baby, just think of me as a bank. I loan you the money, and you'll pay me back once you have a steady job, okay?"

"Will you let me pay you back with actual money?"

"Fuck no," he says, deadpan, and we laugh together. I have to drop the subject because he'll win. He always does.

We prepare dinner together, for once. I love how much of a team we've become. His friendship means the world to me. We laugh and talk as we chop vegetables and stir pots, enjoying the time together.

After dinner, I insist we watch *Titanic*. I love that movie, even though it always makes me cry. As we watch, tears stream down my face, and Nate finds it cute. He smiles at me, amused by my reaction.

Later, in the shower, I can't help myself and belt out that beautiful song, "My Heart Will Go On," at the top of my lungs. When I finish, I open my eyes to see Nate leaning against the sink, arms crossed, watching me.

"What?" I ask.

"That voice of yours, baby," he says, clearly amazed. "Hearing you sing that song was more emotional than the whole damn movie itself."

"Can't be," I reply, stepping out of the shower. I dry off, feeling both vulnerable and warm. I don't know if it's the movie or the events of the day, but tonight feels different.

In the bedroom, there's a shift in the air. We don't just have our usual dirty, sweaty sex that I love so much. Tonight, every touch is gentle, every kiss filled with emotion. Nate doesn't call me his "good little slut"; instead, he tells me I have a beautiful soul.

It's supposed to scare me. I'm not supposed to like it, let alone love it. But I do. I *really* do.

Every moment is tender, every connection is deeper. It's a night that makes us feel closer than ever before.

No, tonight, we don't just have good, dirty, sweaty sex.

Tonight, we make love.

CHAPTER 12
Nate

I hear my alarm buzzing and wake up to shut it off, wanting nothing more than to go back to the sleeping beauty beside me. Except this morning, she's not here. *What the fuck?*

"Delilah," I call out, thinking she might be in the bathroom, but no answer. I get up and start looking for her. I shout her name again, but still no response. *Where the fuck is she?*

I search the whole house and finally find her in my home office, sitting behind my desk, wearing my shirt. She has her headphones on, which is probably why she didn't hear me.

She's working on her SATs again. A few weeks ago, after she got fired from her job, I made a few calls—and yeah, some bribes—to get her a test date in following weeks. Since then, she's been working her ass off, studying like crazy. I've helped her a little, but the woman was right: she's a fast learner. Her brain works so well that I know Delilah can and will conquer the world.

She's still looking for a part-time job, but I've made some arrangements. She's starting at Williams the day after tomorrow. I won't see her much at work, since I'm up on the top floor with the executives, and she'll be on the twenty-seventh floor with the marketing team as a project assistant.

I haven't told her yet because I need to talk to James first. He's completely in the dark about the whole Delilah situation. But honestly, I'm glad things played out like this. It gave us time to figure out how to live together, to learn more about each other, to build a trusting relationship before making anything public. I don't want to hide anymore, but I won't introduce her as my girlfriend either. We haven't had that conversation, and that's fine. We both know this situation is temporary, even though we haven't set an end date. We have time, and we're just taking it one step at a time.

I do care about her a lot, though.

Every time I leave for work, it kills me because I just want to stay in with her. And every hour I'm at the office, I check the time, waiting until I can leave and go back to her. I long for her. I call her ten times a day just to hear her voice. What kind of lovesick school-boy have I become? I don't even know. She just lights up every-thing, all the time.

When I get home, she always jumps into my arms like we hav-en't seen each other in days, and I love it. She cooks, she cleans, she sings, she laughs, she talks, she listens, she cuddles—it's all the lit-tle things about her that keep me hooked.

I love her ambition, her resilience. I know she's still fighting in-ner demons, but I'm by her side. I'll always be there. She's fight-ing to get better, sometimes she wins, sometimes she sinks, but she's brave. Something tells me Delilah isn't just a survivor. She's a warrior.

I love how she tries to mimic me, to stand her ground, and I give her advice to help. I can't wait to see how Delilah is going to change the world. She's already changed mine—for the better.

I stand there, leaning against the entrance of my office, waiting for her to notice me. Luckily, she does, and as always, she smiles when she sees me. The most beautiful sight I've ever seen.

"Hey," she says, taking off her headphones.

"I didn't hear you come in."

"That's alright," I say, stepping inside. I lift her out of the chair, sit down, and pull her onto my lap, kissing her neck.

"What are you studying?" I ask.

"Math. I know it's one of the subjects you mastered in school, so I want to be good at it too," she says, flashing me that smile.

"Good grace, outshine me, baby." My hand slides into her wet panties. "How are you already so wet, baby?" I ask as my fingers glide down her slit to her clit.

She rests her head on my shoulder, opening up to me. *That's my girl.*

"Well, I don't think you realize what you do to me—coming in here, bare-chested, with that sexy morning voice, kissing my neck. I couldn't resist. I'm only human," she teases, making me chuckle.

"Don't ever try to resist, Delilah," I murmur as I capture her mouth with mine. I kiss her slowly at first, pacing myself against her hot pussy. I feel my cock hardening, and that's it—I need her. I pull down my boxers to free myself and tease her entrance.

"Baby, condom," she says. *Fuck.*

"I want to go bare," I plead.

"I'm not on the pill," she pants, and I know she's close. She needs me as much as I need her.

"That's it. I'm booking a doctor's appointment today," I warn her.

"Mmmh, boss. Yes, Mr. Williams, I'll go, I promise," she answers in that sexy, dirty voice that drives me crazy. She knows exactly how to undo me.

"And what am I supposed to do with this now?" I ask, gesturing to my cock.

She laughs and leans into me. "Masturbate. I want to watch you do it." *Oh, dirty, dirty girl.*

"You're such the perfect little whore for me, aren't you? Sit on the desk, spread those gorgeous legs. And take off my shirt—I want to see you naked." She does as she's told, perfect as always.

"Is this good for you, Mr. Williams?" she asks, wide open, completely naked, sprawled across my desk, propped up on her elbows.

"Touch yourself like the good slut that you are for me. Show me how you like it."

She starts stroking her pussy and gives herself pleasure. I grip my shaft firmly.

"I need some lube. How are you going to give it to me, baby?" I ask, teasing. She sits up, leans toward me, and I think she's going to put my cock in her mouth, but instead, she spits on it. That nearly finishes me off. I'm so fucking turned on by this goddess.

"My sweet, sweet Delilah has turned into a kinky fan. Damn," I say, completely in awe. She goes back to touching herself, focusing on her clit, her eyes glued to my cock the whole time. It's sexy as fuck.

"Don't come," I order.

"It's harder when I do it myself. It's easier when you use *your* hand," she says.

"That's right, baby. Only *I* can give you pleasure. Keep going, but don't come," I bark, and she nods. I love dominating her—it's my favorite thing in the world right now.

But then I see her breathing quicken, her panting growing heavier.

"Not yet, Delilah."

"Please, Nate," she begs.

"No," I say more firmly. The sight of her right now, spread before me, is mind-blowingly incredible. Then I feel my release building.

"Now, Delilah. Come now."

"Kiss me, kiss me, kiss me," she cries, and I grab the back of her neck with my free hand, pulling her into a kiss as we both scream into each other's mouths, her body convulsing as she comes and I empty myself. *Wow.*

She collapses onto the desk, arms dangling off the sides. I clean myself up with some tissues, then climb on top of her, scattering her paperwork everywhere—but who cares right now?

"That was sexy as shit, Delilah," I say, grabbing her face for another kiss. We stay like that for what feels like forever, laughing like a couple of damn teenagers.

Then I glance at the time on her phone. Shit, I'm late for work.

"Come shower with me. I have to go."

"You go, babe, I have to finish this. I'll shower later," she says as she starts to clean the mess we've made. Even her fucking OCD is cute.

"Okay," I say, kissing the top of her hair before I go get ready.

Thirty minutes later, and Delilah's still working on her school papers. I go in to say goodbye, give her a firm kiss on her lips, and reluctantly leave.

Today is the day I have to tell James. I don't know how he'll react. I want his support, but I don't need it. If he doesn't approve of Delilah, that'll be his problem, not mine. It won't change a thing. But I'll be disappointed.

Chloe comes into my office, unannounced, which I don't appreciate. I raise my gaze, questioning her without the need to say a word.

"Hey, I just wanted to know if we could have lunch together," she asks, almost sweetly.

"Business lunch?" I ask.

"Um, no, I thought it could be personal."

"Why?" I ask, not understanding where this is going.

"Well, you've been kind of absent for over a month, and I want to know more about you, and for you to know more about me, so I can support you through whatever you're obviously going through."

"No need," I answer simply. No need to elaborate. I don't waste my time.

"Well, we could at least have fun, don't you think?" she asks boldly.

"Go back to your desk, Chloe. Don't bother me with insignificant requests next time. I'm a busy man. Close the door on your way out."

I don't even look at her, as I have more important emails to go through. I only hear the gentle slam of the door.

My phone buzzes, and then I see "Hottest Bitch Who Sings Better Than Celine" appear on the screen. That's one of our games lately; we switch each other's names on our phones, and that one makes me laugh hard.

Delilah: *I'm trying, I swear I'm trying hard, baby, but science is shit.*

I burst out laughing at her text.

Nate: *What part are you studying, hottest bitch who sings better than Celine?*
Delilah: *I knew you'd laugh at that one, Mister Cocksplendid. The shit about how hydrogen atoms combine to form helium, releasing energy in the process and stuff.*
Nate: *I'll teach you this weekend, babe, that's easy.*
Delilah: *Says the master of the universe . . .*
Nate: *No, says Cocksplendid.*
Delilah: *Okay, you cracked me up with that one. Call me when you have time.*
Nate: *I will. I miss you.*

She doesn't reply to my text.

We don't talk about these things between us, and I know it still makes her uncomfortable. That's fine, I'll be the bigger man. I'm not afraid to tell her I miss her.

She just needs to hear it. I know she misses me too; she just can't admit it yet.

I press the button on the intercom to reach Chloe.

"Tell Mr. Kingston to come to my office," I demand.

"Okay," she replies, her voice flat. I might have hurt her feelings earlier. *If only I cared . . .*

Five minutes later, James strolls in. "Hey, what's up, man?" he asks.

"Are you free tonight?"

"No way! I've been begging you for a night out for over a month, and you're finally ready to get out of your cave? Does that mean the Jake matter is solved?" he asks, excitement lighting up his face. James thinks the reason I've been distant is Jake, but it isn't. Well, not entirely.

"Yes, I want to talk to you about it, but not here. So?"

"Of course! Let's go to Orion," he suggests, our usual hangout spot. But *fuck no*, Orion belongs to me and Delilah now. I don't want to go there without her.

"No, I was thinking of that new Italian restaurant in Soho. I'll make the reservation. We leave at six."

"Six? I won't be done by then. I have tons of work."

"Yeah, but I'm the boss, so you'll be fine."

"Damn, I love my job. I'll be at your door at six, then," he says with a grin, and leaves the office.

I tell Chloe to make the reservation for me. Then I go back to my work, the weight of unspoken words hanging in the air.

As I get lost in my work for hours, my mind drifts to my beautiful Delilah and how I'm going to make her come on my dick when I get back to her.

Shit, I forgot to tell her I'll be out tonight. The only times I leave her alone are for my family's brunch on Sundays. She never seems bothered by it; she spends that time cleaning the entire house because on weekdays she's too busy studying.

I grab my phone and call her. She answers after the first ring. *Good girl.*

"Hey, took you long enough to call. Everything okay?" she asks, a hint of worry in her voice.

"Sorry, everything's fine. Just a lot of work. Anyway, I wanted to tell you I'll be out with James tonight, right after work. I don't know when I'll be back."

"Okay. Oh, wait! What will you eat?" she asks. She's just too fucking cute. The way she cares for me is so damn endearing. I really, *really* like this woman. I laugh at her concern.

"I'll eat at the restaurant. I'll send you a picture of my dish so you can relax," I say, mocking her. I hear her giggle, and my heart skips a beat.

"Okay, sure. Thanks for telling me."

"Of course, baby."

I can sense her hesitation; she wants to say something.

"Go on, what is it?"

"Um, I just . . . I wanted to know if, you know, if there will be, um, women that you might, um, end up with . . ." *What the fuck?*

"Come again?"

"No, but that's okay. I mean, you don't owe me any explanation—"

"No, that's not okay!" I bark at her. "I'm not going to fuck someone else, Delilah. The fact that you even think that's okay pisses me the fuck off," I say, losing my shit.

"Hey, I'm not one of your employees that you can bark at whenever you want!" she says, raising her voice.

"No, you're fucking not," *yet,* "but that's not the point. How could you possibly be okay with me fucking another woman, Delilah?"

"I'm *not* okay with it! I just wanted to discuss this with you so you know I expect honesty. If you ever want to fuck someone else, tell me before it happens, so we can stop fucking and just stay friends without ruining our friendship! But you're just so upset that we can't even talk!"

"You're the one being ridiculous! I don't like your suggestions at all. No, I'm not going to fuck another woman. For fuck's sake, I don't even want to *look* at them, least of all fuck them! It's just *you,* Delilah. Fuck!" I say, then pause . . . "And just so we're clear, YOU ARE NOT ALLOWED TO LOOK AT OTHER MEN!" I shout through the phone.

"I DON'T EVEN LIKE PEOPLE! How would I look at men when I fucking despise them?! You're the one who used to fuck around with no strings, not me! So calm the fuck down!" she yells back, matching my volume.

"That was *before* you!" I snap.

"Okay!" she shouts again. We stay silent for what feels like forever.

"I'm sorry," she says, her voice barely audible. I have to remind myself that she doesn't know how to do this. She's never been in a relationship; she doesn't know how to do any of it. I have to be patient with her.

"It's fine. Keep despising men, by the way. I like it," I say, trying to lighten the mood. She giggles, and I feel a wave of relief.

"You go have fun. I'll enjoy some chick flick that you never want to watch with me. I'll bake brownies. I'm going to have the night of my life," she says, and I know she's sincere. She's a simple girl with basic needs, and that makes me melt for her even more. I'd rather be home with her than at that fucking restaurant, but I need to talk to James, so I stick to my plan.

"The night of your life, huh? I'm hurt," I tease.

"Figure of speech, baby."

"Keep studying English, gorgeous."

"That I'll do. You'll call me back?" she asks, unsure.

"I'll call you back, I'll kiss you back, I'll fuck you back, Delilah." I almost say "forever," but I know that would freak her out. She laughs again, and that sound soothes me.

"Good," she says.

"Good. See you soon, baby." We hang up together. *What a woman.* I exhale. Then I hear a knock on my door.

"What?" I ask through the door, and Chloe appears.

"I heard you scream. I wanted to make sure you were okay."

"I'm fine," I answer curtly. She stands there, expecting me to elaborate. I give her a look that says, "What?" She's pushing my patience.

"Fine, don't talk to me," she mutters, and leaves. If she thinks I'll chase after her, she's in for more disappointment today.

Later in the day, I prepare for an important call with our investors in Tokyo—one of the most critical meetings of the month. The challenge brings me back to life. I love playing with big money, and these guys are my best prey.

But then, unannounced—yet again—the fucking door to my office opens, and I'm surprised to see *him*.

"Hey, little brother," I say, not even glancing up as I keep preparing for my meeting.

"We need to talk," he says, already angry. I swear the guy was born an anger ball.

"*We* don't need to talk. *I* need to get ready for my meeting, and *you* need to leave," I say, my voice steady as water, already bored with the exchange.

"I heard you named a new COO. How could you, Nate?"

I raise my gaze to him, questioning his tone.

"I don't owe you any explanation. Get out, Jake. I'm busy," I say.

"I'm not leaving until you tell me what the fuck you've done and how you're going to fix this! You can call security; I don't give a fuck," he shouts, losing his temper again. I laugh at his charade.

"You think I need security to remove you from my office?" I reply with a huge grin. I know Jake hates it, but I've always been bigger and stronger than him. There's really no fight. But he's too scared to be humiliated in front of the other execs on the floor by my own hands, so he backs down. *How disappointing.*

"This is not over, Nate. You better watch your back," he dares to warn me. But I just burst out laughing as he leaves my office.

I know for sure that Jake is plotting against me. He's been meeting with other powerful people in the city, especially potential candidates for the Senate next year—potential opponents for me. He's looking for information on me, but he's too naive to realize that the people he meets with report back to me. So I will show him no more kindness. *Not anymore.*

The only thing I fear is Jake finding out about Delilah.

I really need to talk to James. Delilah is my only weakness in this game. I know I'm about to "out" us without really doing it, but I'll protect her with everything I have.

The thing is, we've been living together for over a month now, and I know she *trusts* me—not with her past, but with everything else. I *completely* trust her. I have a feeling that neither Jake nor anyone else could ever turn her against me. Because it's us against the world. And no one can get close to Delilah. I've made sure of that. Her safety is my number one priority now.

James and I arrive at the new Italian restaurant in Soho around eight o'clock, later than planned because work was a beast today. The place is chic, very New York-like, with luxurious touches every-where—but nothing I haven't already seen. I know Delilah would have loved it here. It's dark, with touches of light from the big chan-deliers, giving it an almost gothic vibe that's pretty cool. *I miss her.*

We each order a scotch and settle into the sophisticated mood of the place. We relax easily; James has been my best friend for years, so the jokes come naturally between us.

We discuss business for hours, the conversation flowing as smoothly as the drinks and food. I discreetly send a picture of my cacio e pepe to Delilah. She's so jealous she promises to nail the recipe just so I can tell her that hers is better. I'll always tell her hers is better. *She's* better, period.

Then James brings up the new COO he's found, who sounds competent, a good fit for our team. He seems confident in his choice, and I trust his judgment. Even though I have the final word on appointments, James knows the fact that I share some of my power with him is meaningful. I trust the man with my life.

Eventually, the conversation shifts to Jake, obviously. I tell James about what I've discovered regarding his plans for revenge—who he's been meeting with, what he's plotting. James listens intently, his brow furrowing. He asks questions, and we go back and forth, strategizing. I think we've found a solid plan.

But as we talk, I feel a knot of unease in my stomach. I know I need to tell James about Delilah, but the words aren't coming eas-ily. We've been here for hours, and now is the time to speak, but I'm struggling to find the right way to say it.

James orders another round of digestifs, then looks at me expectantly, and I know I can't put it off any longer. The words are on the tip of my tongue, but I hesitate, feeling the weight of what I'm about to reveal. *Fuck, let's just do this.*

"I've met someone," I say, looking him in the eye.

"What kind of someone are we talking about?" he asks, unsure.

"I've met a woman," I say evenly.

"I'm not sure what you're telling me, man.""Remember last month when you stood me up at Orion?" I ask.

"Yeah," he replies.

"When I went into the bar, the first thing I saw was her. I swear she's the most beautiful woman I've ever met. I didn't want to talk to her—I even hurried you to come because I was so deeply drawn to her. Then some fucker tried to bother her, and I stepped in." James is listening closely now, and I just keep going.

"She kept dismissing me, didn't want anything to do with me, but I couldn't walk away. I just *couldn't.* Then I begged her to come with me to the Hamptons so we could be alone for just forty-eight hours, and then we'd part ways. That was the deal, and we did it. Our weekend was magical. It made me forget everything about the outside world.

"But then I dropped her off at Orion two days later. When I got home, I felt like I was suffocating. I couldn't just forget about her. I couldn't let her go. The thing is, she's fucked up. She's got demons inside her, always on the verge of breaking. She's got a dark past I know nothing about." I realize it's the first time I'm talking about Delilah to another living soul, and I take the opportunity to get it off my chest.

"She had nowhere to go, no one to hold on to. She was haunted by . . . sadness. But on the other side, she was—is—this beautiful, incredible woman who laughs a lot. She has this great sense of humor. I swear, sometimes I'm this close to peeing on myself from laughing at her jokes. She's so loving and caring. She's vivid, she has a bright mind, and she soothes me like no one else. She's always moving around, always doing stuff—cleaning the whole damn house all the time. And she cooks, man, can she cook! And she fucking sings, too. Her voice is like a miracle. She's sexy as fuck, and the sex—fuck—the sex is phenomenal. I've never enjoyed sex as much as I do with her. She was almost a fucking virgin when we met.

"Anyway, I made her come home with me. We've been living together for a month now, and James, I swear to you, I've never been this fucking happy in my entire life. The whole Jake thing doesn't even hurt because I'm too focused on being happy with her. She's sexy, funny, witty, bitchy even—she's perfect," I say and exhale, waiting for his reaction. I can see he's stunned.

"You *live* with her?" he asks.

"Yes," I reply.

"Wow, okay, I have to ask this, Nate. What about Charlotte?"

That question hits me right in the chest, and I feel my heart break a little. I sigh.

"Charlotte won't be back just yet. I'm trying to figure things out with Delilah first, and then I'll see what happens."

"Delilah? That's her name?"

"Yes," I answer.

"She sure has a beautiful name," he says.

"Just say it, James."

"You can't ruin what you have with Charlotte. You guys have a plan—"

"We did. But both Charlotte and I knew there was a risk of meeting someone else one day. I'm not the one who had to leave, she is! Don't you dare blame me, James," I fire back, not liking one bit what he implied. He raises both hands in surrender.

"I'm sorry, you're right. But, I have to ask—don't you think she might be with you because of who you are and what you're worth?" he asks. I laugh at his question.

"Don't insult me. I've met my fair share of gold-diggers to know she's not one of them," I reply. Then I hear my phone ring.

"Speak of the devil," I say. I answer the phone. "Hey, babe."

"Hey, I'm so sorry to bother you while you're out, but I need you to explain to me how the alarm system works. I wanted to go to bed, but I don't know how to set it," she says.

"Baby, it's okay. Go to bed. I'll ask one of the security guys to set it."

"No, I don't trust them. Usually, you're the one who does it, and I trust you, but now I can't remember how you do it," she says, and I sense her starting to panic.

"Babe, accept the FaceTime request, and I'll show you," I say, and she instantly does. *Fuck me,* she's so beautiful—I miss her. I guide her through the alarm system until she's calm.

"Good, it's done," she says. "Phew. Thank you. I'm going to sleep now. Don't forget to put it back on when you get home, please."

"Don't worry, gorgeous. I'll take care of it. I'm not staying out much longer. I just told James about you," I say, looking into James's eyes, but he's still too stunned to say anything.

"Oh, okay. I hope it went well. Tell him how much I love your money and you should be fine," she says, making me laugh. Even James cracks a smile. I hang up and turn back to him.

"You're falling for her," he says, matter-of-factly.

"Hard," I admit simply. It's just the truth. I'm falling for her, and I know that there's no going back.

I keep talking about Delilah—her previous job, her studies, even about Sam, who sometimes comes over to the apartment to see her. I tell him how I arranged for her to work part-time at the office and about the possibility of Jake trying to use her for revenge, if he dares.

James reassures me, and we go back and forth on the different ways Jake might act. He gives me the green light—not that I needed it—to hire Delilah and, of course, swears he'll keep his mouth shut about her. Deep down, I know he's not thrilled with any of it, but he's my friend, and he's being supportive despite his reluctance. I appreciate him even more for that.

We leave the restaurant together. Tyler drops James off first—he lives on Park Avenue too, just a few buildings away from mine—and then I get home.

I remember to reset the alarm. When I reach the kitchen, I'm surprised to see a batch of homemade brownies with a note on top.

> *Couldn't keep them for myself. Hope you like them. xoxo,*
> *—D*

The cutest woman ever. And damn, the woman is also the best cook. I know a few ways of thanking her.

I head upstairs, straight to the shower, and get ready for bed. Delilah is fast asleep on her side, looking like a fallen angel. My heart squeezes in my chest at the sight of her.

I slip under the covers and spoon her from behind. My cock is suddenly all too happy to see her, but she's sleeping and tired, and I don't have the heart to wake her up.

She stirs under the sheets, opening one eye, and I reassure her.

"It's me, baby. I'm home," I whisper, and she immediately relaxes against me. The fact that I'm the one who brings her peace is exhilarating. She's so perfect.

I close my eyes, thinking that right now, here with her, is the best goddamn place in the world.

~

I'm jolted awake by a noise in the bedroom. *What the fuck?* I check the time—three in the morning. *What the actual fuck?* I reach for Delilah, but she's not next to me. I sit up and see her sitting beside the bed, her ass on the floor.

"Baby, what are you doing?" I ask, but she doesn't move—like she can't hear me. I get closer and see her staring blankly, mumbling something. *What the fuck is going on?*

"Baby, come back to bed," I say again, but she doesn't respond. She mumbles more, and her words become clearer.

"Ashley, go hide," she whispers. It hits me—Delilah once told me she sleepwalks.

She's dreaming. What do I do? But I don't have time to react; she keeps talking.

"Ashley, please hide inside the closet. They'll hurt you, Ashley . . . Don't worry about me. I'm strong, the beating doesn't hurt me. Please, go hide, Ashley . . . No, please," she mumbles. Fury boils inside me.

"Ashley, when they come, don't look, okay? Hide and think of something else . . . Don't worry about me. These are just bruises, I can handle it . . . Ashley, go hide, I beg you . . ." She keeps talking in her sleep, and I pray this is just a nightmare and not her past. I feel her fear—she's fucking terrified, but she's still trying to reassure her little sister.

What happened to you, Delilah?

Her pain is killing me. She gasps in surprise, utterly afraid, and I'm powerless over a fucking dream. My heart aches for her.

"It's okay, Delilah, it's just a dream," I manage to say, even though she can't hear me.

"They're coming, Ashley. Go hide and don't look at me, okay . . . Stop crying, baby girl. I'll be fine. I'm used to the beating. They can't hurt me, Ashley . . . They're here . . . Go, Ashley, go!" she whisper-shouts into the empty room.

"Oh my god, oh my god, oh my god . . . Mara, it's okay." she says, but I can see the pain inside her, and it makes me want to kill everyone responsible for this. *Who the fuck is Mara?*

"They're coming . . ." she says, still in her sleep, and I can't stand the pain in my chest anymore, feeling my heart beat.

"I'll burn them all, Delilah, this is it. Whoever hurt you, I'll burn them all, baby, I promise," I whisper, my voice weak, feeling a tear slide down my cheek.

"It's okay, Mara. You're used to this. You'll be fine."

"I'll burn them all, Delilah. Whoever it is, I'll avenge you, my love," I tell her, my voice breaking.

She starts shaking like someone is strangling her. I see the pain in her eyes—it's too fucking much. I can't take it anymore. I gently lift her into my arms and bring her back to bed. The second she feels me, she falls into a deep sleep, no longer shaking.

What's your story, Delilah?

I hurt for her. I ache for her. Whatever happened to her was darker than I ever thought.

I grab my phone and text my head of security to hire a private investigator to dig into Delilah's past. I need to know who hurt her, so I can fucking burn them to the ground.

My beautiful Delilah, I'll avenge you, baby. I promise.

I can't go back to sleep. I can't even shut my eyes. I feel like I have to stay awake, to watch over her, make sure she's okay. I can't help but run my fingers through her hair, trying to soothe her, even though she's unconscious. She's become too precious to me. I'll fight for her. I'll fight with her.

Like I said, it's us against the world.

CHAPTER 13
Delilah

I wake up feeling a little shaken, though I don't know why. Maybe it was a bad dream, but I can't remember any details. I sit up and realize the bed is empty. Nate must have already left for work.

I stretch and get out of bed, then walk to the bathroom and turn on the shower. The warm water feels good against my skin, washing away the last bits of sleep and the strange unease I woke up with.

After my shower, I put on my comfy clothes: soft sweatpants and an old T-shirt. They feel like a hug—warm and familiar. As I get dressed, I wonder about my schedule for the day, thinking about the tasks I need to complete.

I walk to the kitchen and see Nate drinking his coffee, looking at me like I've done something wrong, but I have no idea what it could be.

"Good morning to you too," I say, taking a coffee.

But Nate remains silent, his eyes fixed on me, scrutinizing.

"What's wrong with you? Why aren't you at work?" I ask. He exhales, struggling to find words.

"You had a dream last night," he finally says.

"Okayyy, and?"

"You talked in your sleep. And you weren't in bed."

"I'm a sleepwalker, so?" I reply.

"We've been sleeping together for over a month now, and you've never had an episode of sleepwalking," he counters. His words hang in the air, heavy with unspoken concerns.

"I know. Usually, I'd never wake up where I fall asleep. Well, until I met you. But I don't understand what's wrong," I say, genuinely puzzled.

"You scared the shit out of me, Delilah." His voice quivers. I immediately go to him, wrapping my arms around his tense body, trying to reassure him. He hugs me back fiercely.

"I'm sorry, I don't have any control over it."

"Do you know what might trigger it?" he asks, looking for answers.

"Well, no. Last night, I watched *The Princess Diaries* and then went to bed. I guess I was startled by the alarm thing, but everything seemed fine after that. So no, I don't understand," I explain, searching my memory for any clue.

He looks down, contemplating, then raises his gaze. "You talked about Ashley," he says. I freeze, unable to speak.

"You told her to go hide, that they couldn't do anything to you because you were too strong. Then you got scared because someone was strangling you." His eyes bore into mine, but I can't process his words. It's a dark place for me.

"It was just a dream," I murmur, knowing I sound unconvincing.

"The hell it was. I see you, Delilah. I think it's time you tell me something," he insists, his tone delicate but firm. I move around the kitchen island, resting my elbows on the cool marble. I take another sip of coffee, stalling for time.

"You mentioned someone named Mara," he continues. Panic flares inside me. Nate tries to approach, but I back away, overwhelmed.

"I'm not going to work until we talk about this. I want to be there for you, support you in any way I can, but I need to know more about what happened. Let me in, Delilah."

I look into his big, beautiful, icy eyes and take a deep breath. "Before I tell you, you need to know that this part of my life means nothing to me now. I don't care that it happened. I'm fine, you understand?" I assert firmly.

"Yes," he replies.

"Ashley is my little sister, you know that. Not by blood, but she *is* my little sister. I haven't seen her in six months, and she doesn't want to see me because I remind her too much of what we've been through. And you got a glimpse of it in my sleep," I say, watching him closely.

"She abandoned you?" he asks, almost disgusted.

"She didn't *abandon* me, she just had a chance at a better life. Seeing me was too hurtful, like a reminder of everything we'd been through. And I understand it, I do."

"Just because you understand it doesn't mean it's right. Baby, she left you," he replies, a trace of anger in his tone.

"Please, I can't talk about Ashley. I'm willing to share something, but don't push it."

"Okay, go on," he says, and I take a deep breath. I look up, then face him. "I wasn't born Delilah Rose," I confess. Nate doesn't flinch.

"My birth name is Mara Ferris, though I lost that name at the age of ten," I say, my voice shaking. Nate's compassionate gaze encourages me to continue.

"My 'parents'—I hate that word—had me by accident. They didn't want a little girl after two boys, so they locked me up in the basement. I lived in darkness, never seeing the light of day. I didn't have a bed, a blanket, or even a pillow. Just an old, rusty sink surrounded by filth for as long as I can remember. Sometimes, if I was lucky, they threw food scraps down the stairs, like feeding a dog. And I ate right from the dirty floor. When the father was furious, he'd come down and take it out on me. But I survived," I recount, my voice steadying with resolve.

"They were poor, but they discovered the state gave an allowance for the third child, so guess who was finally able to go to school? Me. The sun burned my skin, people scared me, but I adapted. I'm a fast learner; I became smart. But they hated me more for it, so my schooling was intermittent at best. Because they had to see me more, even though I still wasn't allowed in the house—just the basement—their hatred grew. They became . . . meaner. More evil. But the only mistake I ever made was being born. Soon I wasn't really allowed to go to school, but they forgot about me sometimes, so I escaped just to go learn. That was my life until I was ten. By then, they were desperate." Nate listens, his eyes filled with hurt and rage.

"What happened when you were ten?" he asks gently.

"They became really poor," I say unevenly.

"And?"

"And I was sold." His face twists in shock.

"What do you mean 'sold'?" he demands.

"They met someone who offered them cash for a child. They didn't think twice about it." I'm surprised to feel a tear running down my cheek. Nate sees it and rushes to me.

"Fuck, baby, I'm so sorry," he says, pulling me into his arms, holding me tight.

"I'm okay, Nate, it's okay" I try to reassure him.

"It's not okay, Delilah. This is horrific," he insists, fury in his voice.

"It's irrelevant today. I survived," I say, almost proudly.

"Wait a minute, where does Ashley fit into this?" he asks, not letting it go.

"I'm not ready to share that yet. But it was after," I admit, knowing he understands.

"I have so many questions," he says.

I'm not ready . . . Please, I don't want to talk about my past anymore. I just . . . I can't, please," I say, looking down at my feet. He lifts my chin, forcing me to meet his gaze, then plants a soft kiss on my lips.

"I'll wait. Thank you for sharing a little. I wish I knew earlier so I could have been gentler with you."

"But that's exactly what I don't want. I love that you're rough and tough with me. You have no idea how much you've healed me by being you. If you change, I'd rather leave."

"No, no, don't worry, I won't change a thing, I promise," he says, caressing my hand.

"Good. Now, go to work. I believe you have urgent matters with your brother," I remind him.

"You're more important," he says, melting my heart. But I can't quite admit it yet, so I playfully slap his chest. He understands and doesn't push it.

I start to prepare breakfast, seeing that Nate has no will to go to work. I take the time to appreciate his presence. We're eating at the table when Nate tells me about his discussion with James, then suddenly changes the subject.

"I think I know what triggered your sleepwalking," he says, and I feel amused by his sudden realization.

"Okay, I'm listening."

"You didn't feel safe last night without me by your side. You freaked out about the alarm, and I think it brought you back to a dark place," he says. I'm surprised by how perceptive he is and how right he might be.

"That could be it. I don't know."

"But there might be times when I come home late, and I don't want you to be scared," he says, his concern clear.

"I'll be fine, don't worry."

"I'll always worry, that's just a fact. But I have a surprise for you. Go get ready, we're leaving in ten minutes," he says.

"Wait, what? What do you mean?"

"You can't ask questions until we're there. Go on, we have to go."

"But what about work?"

Right now, I don't give two shits about work. Come on, let's go." His excitement is contagious. I thought he might want to get rid of me, but no. I still have to fight my inner demons, but still!

I don't waste a minute. I put on a nice pair of jeans, a white crop top, and a black leather jacket. I slip on my Stan Smiths, let my hair fall loose, skip the makeup, and head downstairs.

"I'm ready!" I shout, and we leave. Nate grabs a blanket, which is odd, but it gets even weirder when he presses the button for the parking lot instead of the ground floor.

"Where are we going?" I ask.

"We won't need Tyler today," he says with a grin.

"What?"

"Wait and see, babe," he says, grabbing my ass and pulling me against him. I feel all of him, and I'm relieved that my little confession didn't trouble him.

When we arrive at the parking lot, I'm amazed by all the luxury cars parked there.

"Wow, you have one of these?"

"Baby, please, give me some credit. I own all of these," he says with a smirk.

"What the fuck?" I mutter in disbelief. "Damn, I really need to dig deeper into this gold-digger thing," I tease him. That earns me a playful slap on the ass, and I giggle until we stop in front of the car we're about to take.

My eyes widen as I take in the sight. It's bright red, almost glowing, even in the dim lighting. The sleek curves and sharp lines make it look like something straight out of a movie. I can see my reflection in its glossy surface.

Nate walks beside me, a small smile playing on his lips. He holds the keys with a sense of pride.

"What kind of car is this?" I ask, my voice barely above a whisper.

"It's a *Ferrari SF90 Stradale.* Do you like it?"

"Like it? It's amazing," I reply, still in awe. I walk around the car, my fingers trailing lightly over the smooth, cool metal. The headlights are piercing, like eyes.Nate opens the door for me, and I slide into the passenger seat. The interior is just as impressive. The seats are soft leather, and everything looks high-tech. I glance at Nate as he gets in, feeling a mix of excitement and nervousness.

He starts the car, and the engine roars to life. The sound is powerful, almost like a growl. I can't believe I'm sitting in a car like this, about to go for a ride with Nate.

As we pull out of the parking lot, I look over at him, a smile spreading across my face.

"This is incredible," I say, feeling the thrill of the moment.

Nate chuckles and nods.

"Hold on tight," he says, and we speed off. Once we hit the highway, I have to grip my seat because this thing moves fast. I laugh a lot, and Nate enjoys every bit of it. His hand stays on my thigh the whole time. The intimacy is perfect.

"May I know where we're going now?" I ask.

"Soon," he promises. He turns on the radio, and I can't help but sing loudly, letting go of everything because, for the first time in a long time, I feel . . . happy. *But for how long?*

After an hour of driving, Nate and I arrive at a place I can't quite figure out yet. We're in the countryside, outside of New York City. The landscape is beautiful, with rolling hills and fields stretching out as far as I can see. The air is fresh, and everything feels peaceful. I already know I love this place.

"We're here," Nate says, pulling into a driveway.

I look around, still unsure.

"Where exactly is here?" I ask.

He smiles and gets out of the car, coming around to open my door.

"It's a dog breeding establishment. We're here to pick up a dog."

"What? Seriously? No kidding?" I ask, almost too happy.

"Yeah, no kidding. That way, when I'm not there, you won't be totally on your own."

"I love this idea! Okay, yeah, let's go! Oh my god!" I say, jumping into his arms.

Nate's smile is everything to me.

We walk toward the building, and I'm starting to feel intrigued.

Inside, the place is clean and organized. Puppies are everywhere, each one in a small pen with a price tag in front of it. They are all highbred, perfect and pristine.

As I look around, something feels off. A pang hits my chest. These puppies are adorable, but the idea of buying one feels wrong. I shift uncomfortably.

Nate notices and his face shows concern.

"What's wrong?" he asks, his voice soft.

I take a deep breath.

"It just feels wrong to buy a dog instead of adopting one that might be in greater need, don't you think?" I ask, hesitant.

Nate looks at me, understanding dawning in his eyes. He nods slowly.

"It's okay," he says. "We can go to a shelter if that makes you feel better."

A wave of relief washes over me, and I jump into his arms again, hugging him tightly.

"Thank you," I whisper.

Nate turns to the salesman and says, "We won't need a dog here after all."

We head back to the car, and Nate pulls out his phone, showing me some addresses of nearby dog shelters. It's another hour drive, but neither of us minds. We're too excited about adopting a dog.

During the drive, we talk about work and my studies. Nate tries to teach me science while driving, which amuses me. We can't seem to break contact, always touching each other. This time, it's me resting my hand on his muscular leg, my head on his shoulder, while we listen to some good old country music until we finally arrive at the shelter.

My heart feels lighter as we step out of the car. I know this is the right thing to do.

We arrive at the shelter, and my heart sinks. The place is small and old, with chain-link fences and concrete floors. The animals inside look desperate, their eyes following us as we walk in. The air is filled with a mix of barks, meows, and the scent of animal fur.

As I look around, my heart breaks. Each dog here is looking for a family, just like I once wished for. I can see myself in their eyes— longing for love and a place to belong.

"Nate, I really want to adopt a dog today," I tell him, my voice steady despite the sadness I feel.

A volunteer with a name tag that says "Jordan" approaches us with a warm smile.

"Welcome to Paw's Heart. Let me give you a tour and tell you more about our animals," she says.

We agree and follow her through narrow aisles, past cages filled with dogs of all shapes and sizes.

As we walk, Jordan explains how the shelter helps animals from all over the country. My eyes land on a big dog with only one eye. He has brown and black fur and looks at me with a soulful gaze. My heart skips a beat.

"Who is this?" I ask, pointing to the dog.

Jordan looks at him and smiles sadly.

"That's Cowboy. He's three years old. He was abandoned in the woods and lost his eye. No one wants him because of that." *What the fuck?*

Without thinking, I open the gate and step into Cowboy's cage. The big dog comes to me immediately, his tail wagging furiously. He nudges my hand with his nose, eager for attention. I kneel down, and he licks my face, his whole body shaking with excitement. He has my whole heart now.

Jordan continues, "Cowboy is bonded with another dog. We call him Sheriff. He's a little mixed breed, part Chihuahua and part dachshund. We can't separate them, I'm sorry." *Oh, poor babies.* Sheriff comes to me too, all playful and perfect!

I look at Nate, feeling a mix of emotions.

"I want them both," I say firmly.

Nate looks at the two dogs, then back at me.

"Are you sure?" he asks, his brow furrowed. I feel a pang of hurt at his question.

"Don't judge them by their appearance, Nate. They need us," I say, my voice breaking. Nate's face softens, and he smiles fondly.

"What my girl wants, my girl gets," he says, turning to Jordan. "We'll take them both."

"Oh, fabulous! I'll get the paperwork ready. They are great dogs, I swear. I'm happy for them, but sad that I won't see them anymore," Jordan says, clearly emotional.

My heart leaps with joy. I jump into Nate's arms and give him a big kiss on the lips.

"Thank you, thank you, thank you!" I squeal, hugging him tightly.

Before we leave, we buy everything the dogs need at the shelter, and Nate gives more money than expected. My heart melts.

As we get back to the car, we wonder if Cowboy will fit in the backseat. Nate has thought ahead and placed a blanket over the seat. Cowboy squeezes in, and everyone is relieved. "Please don't hesitate to come back or email us any updates on the dogs. I'll miss them," Jordan says. I squeeze her arm, promising we'll keep in touch. Then I turn back to Nate.

"You're so thoughtful, baby," I say, circling my arm around his waist, and he kisses the top of my head.

We take the road back home, Cowboy and Sheriff nestled comfortably in the backseat. I feel like I'm living a dream, realizing how lucky I am to have Nate by my side.

"Thank you for making this happen," I say softly, looking at Nate as he drives. He glances at me and smiles.

"Anything for you, baby."

I lean back in my seat, feeling happier than I ever thought possible. This is our little family now, and I couldn't be more grateful.

Don't get too attached, my inner voice warns. *It'll disappear one day, it always does. He'll leave you and take the dogs with him.*

~

We arrive back home and introduce the dogs to the apartment. We play with them, feed them, and promise them they'll be happy with us. I can't stop smiling.

"The dogs' names are Cowboy and Sheriff, for fuck's sake," Nate says, shaking his head with a playful smile.

"I know!" I scream, delighted.

Wherever I go, the dogs follow. I love them so much already.

Nate heads to his home office to make some work calls while I take over the kitchen to make chicken stir-fry. I keep my study notes nearby and check them from time to time. Two birds, one stone. All while talking with the boys, as Nate calls them.

I set the table and call for Nate to come eat. As we settle in, still cheerful from the day we've had, Nate grabs my hand.

"I have something to tell you," he says. I tilt my head.

"I've talked it over with James, and starting tomorrow, you'll come work at Williams as a project assistant with the marketing team—part-time so you still have time to study."

"What?" I blink, taken aback.

"You won't be working directly with me. I'm on the executive floor—the ninetieth floor. You'll be on the twenty-seventh. I had HR prepare your contract. You'll have a training session with Ailly Harris. Everything's been taken care of." I'm stunned.

"Wait, what?" My voice comes out louder than I intended.

"Baby, I know you want to work. It's fine if you'd rather stay here, but I think it would be good for you to work again. My company is one of the best in the world. We treat people right. That's my number one requirement. I think you'll be great there."

"But, Nate—"

"No, listen to me." He squeezes my hand gently.

"I truly believe you have a bright mind. I see you every day. I see how fast you learn, how dedicated you are to your tasks. I see how passionate you are when I talk about my job, and I want that for you. I can't wait for the world to see Delilah Rose conquer it. I know deep down that you can do it, baby. I believe in you." I'm speechless. His confidence in me is overwhelming.

"Please accept my proposition. If you don't like it after giving it a fair try, we'll find something else. I promise."

"Is this real?" I ask, not just about the job, but about . . . everything.

Nate smiles, his eyes warm and reassuring.

"Yes, it's real. All of it."

I look at him, feeling a mix of emotions—gratitude, affection and a bit of fear.

"Okay," I finally say, squeezing his hand.

"I'll give it a try."

Nate pulls me into a hug, and I feel the weight of his belief in me.

"You won't regret it, Delilah. You're going to do amazing things," he says, and I pause to watch and admire him.

"You're the best person I know," I say quietly.

"You too, baby. But wait until we're in the bedroom to show me how I'm the best," he teases, and I giggle. Nate is still Nate, after all.

"Shut up and eat your food before it gets cold."

Yes, ma'am."

We eat dinner as Nate tells me more about the job. It's a challenge, but I'm ready to take it on. Apparently, I'll be coordinating project plans and tracking progress, acting as a bridge between the marketing team and other departments. I'll create and update documentation, help with marketing materials, and support campaign execution. Monitoring quality and gathering feedback will also be part of my role, along with administrative tasks like scheduling meetings and liaising with vendors. Most importantly, I'll be learning and growing in a fast-paced, collaborative environment.

It sounds scary, but just like Nate says, I'm Delilah fucking Rose, and there's nothing I can't do.

After dinner, we decide to walk the dogs. The security team is never far from us, and I feel much safer knowing that. We have a lot of fun, throwing balls for the dogs and running around with them. The boys love it.

"So, I take it no one can know we live together," I say as we walk.

"I'm not hiding you," Nate replies, looking me in the eye.

"Okay, well, I'm not much of a talker anyway, so problem solved. Plus, I won't be seeing you much, since we'll be on different floors."

"We'll run into each other sometimes. And I want that lap dance in my office. You have no idea how many times I've fantasized about fucking you on my desk."

"Nate!" I gasp, half-mortified but secretly pleased that he's fantasized about me.

"Don't start playing the prude," he teases.

"I'm not," I say, raising an eyebrow. "I did fantasize about giving you head under your desk."

The words have barely left my mouth before Nate sweeps me up into his arms, grabbing my ass. I laugh so hard it hurts.

"Damn woman, I'm fucking hard. You *will* suck my big cock in my office," he growls playfully. I laugh even harder as we make our way back toward the building, with Sheriff insisting on being carried in my arms, too tired to walk. *My little pup.*

It's nighttime when we get back home from walking Cowboy and Sheriff. The dogs are still adjusting to their new home and the rules we're teaching them, like not entering the bedroom. Nate is firm on that rule, and I understand why.We laugh as we take off their leashes, watching them settle down in their area.

"Good boys," Nate says, giving each of them a pat before heading upstairs. I follow him, feeling a sense of contentment wash over me.

In the bathroom, we stand side by side, brushing our teeth. It's such a simple thing, but it makes me feel grounded and at peace. I glance at Nate in the mirror, toothpaste foam at the corners of his mouth, and I can't help but smile. These quiet, ordinary moments with him mean so much to me.

As I brush my teeth, I think about everything Nate has given me—stability, security, companionship. He's my rock, and I feel so grateful.

We finish up and head to the bedroom. I fluff the pillows and straighten the blankets, getting the bed ready. Nate watches me with a small smile, and I feel warmth spread through my chest. I love these simple tasks, these moments that make up our life together.

Until when?

Once the bed is ready, we climb in. I lie on my side, facing Nate, watching him. He's beautiful, not just on the outside but inside too. His soul, his heart—that's what fascinates me. He's kind, strong, and always there for me. As I think about all of this, I feel overwhelmed by the depth of my feelings for him.

No, stop it, Delilah. Stop it. You'll break your heart.

Nate catches me staring, and a huge grin spreads across his lips. He's always been a bit cocky, but I love that about him. Without wasting any time, I start taking off my clothes, then his. My hands move quickly, eager to feel his skin against mine.

"Attagirl," he says, clearly pleased, making me laugh.

I take in his magnificent body, savoring every inch as I kiss his skin. I love the warmth of it under my lips and tongue.

"You're so beautiful," I tell him, smiling as the roles are reversed. "Your body is a wonderland."

"That's yours, baby," he says.

Until when?

I continue my trail of kisses all over Nate's body as I hear his breathing quicken. We come together, our bodies pressing close. His hands explore every inch of me, and I do the same to him. Our breaths mingle, hearts beating in sync. The sensations are over-whelming, every touch sending waves of pleasure through me.

"You're so fucking perfect. I'm so hard for you, Delilah," Nate groans.

His lips find mine, and we kiss deeply, passionately. Our move-ments become more urgent, more desperate. I wrap my legs around him, pulling him closer.

Nate grabs a condom from the nightstand and hands it to me.

"Roll it on," he commands, and I do it.

"Good girl," he murmurs, sending chills down my spine. He enters me, and I gasp, feeling complete. We move together, each thrust bringing us closer to the edge.

The room fills with the sounds of our lovemaking—soft moans, whispered words.

"You take my cock so well, baby," he says, his dirty talk exhilarating.

I look into Nate's eyes, seeing the passion and desire there, and I feel a surge of emotion. I match his rhythm, fucking him with the same intensity he gives me. It's my way of thanking him, of show-ing him how much he means to me.

"I'm gonna come, Nate," I gasp.

"I'm there too," he pants, both of us nearing the edge. He takes my hands in his, pinning them above my head, our fingers inter-twined. I move with him, matching his rhythm.

We reach our climax together, our bodies trembling with the force of it.

"Fuck, Delilah," he groans into my mouth. I hold him close, feeling his warmth, his heartbeat against mine. "*This* is my favorite place in the whole goddamn world," he whispers in my ear.

"Mine too. I mean your bed, not your dick." I laugh, lightening the mood.

"*Our* bed," he corrects me, and I fall silent. I can't respond. The words are too heavy.

We stand up and head to the bathroom to clean up before

returning to bed. As we lie there, spent and satisfied, I know this is where I'm meant to be.

At least for now.

~

I wake to the feel of Nate's hand on my cheek. I blink my eyes open and see his beautiful face.

"Hey, you," I murmur, realizing he's already dressed, nearly ready to leave.

"Hi, baby. I gotta go to work early—I have an important meeting—but you still have time. Don't worry. I guess I'll see you at the office," he says, winking.

"Oh, okay. Well, I'm already up, so I better go get ready and take my time preparing for today," I say, getting out of bed.

I walk him to the door, and we kiss goodbye before Nate leaves.

Then I hop into the shower, trying not to stress about my first day at Williams. I still don't know how we're going to act if we run into each other. Will we pretend we don't know each other? We discussed it last night and decided to play it by ear, but Nate saying *"I'm not hiding you"* gave me chills. I try not to overthink it and push the thought aside.

Stepping into the dressing room, I see a range of gorgeous office outfits. I pick a light-gray skirt suit paired with a classy white blouse, pull out white lacy underwear and stockings. After straightening my hair, I apply a touch of makeup. I want to look presentable, even pretty. I can't embarrass Nate.

I prepare a nice breakfast, pack the leftovers from last night into a lunchbox, and make myself a coffee to go. I text Tyler, telling him I'll be downstairs in ten minutes. He replies that he's already here. *Perfect*. I feel the stress building, but I know I'll manage—I always do.

Less than twenty minutes later, Tyler drops me at the entrance of the building, and I have to catch my breath at the sight. *Damn*.

I stare up at the tower, nervous and thrilled. The building is enormous, with countless floors of shiny glass windows reflecting the morning sun. At the top, bold letters spell "Williams Holdings Inc." I've never seen anything so grand.

As I walk closer, the building becomes even more imposing. Sleek revolving doors guard the entrance, and people in business attire rush in and out, looking important and busy. It's hard to believe Nate is the CEO of this place. I've always seen him as just Nate, but now I realize how powerful he must really be. This building, this company—it's all his responsibility.

I take a deep breath, trying to calm my racing heart. Today is my first day here, and I want to make a good impression. My palms are sweaty, and tension knots my shoulders.

I hope everything goes well. I hope I don't mess up.

When I enter the building, the lobby is just as grand as the exterior—marble floors, modern art on the walls, and a huge chandelier hanging from the ceiling. It's overwhelming. Clutching my bag tighter, I head toward the reception desk.

"Good morning," I say, trying to sound confident. "I'm Delilah Rose. It's my first day—I'm supposed to go to the twenty-seventh floor."

The receptionist smiles warmly and directs me to the elevators. As I ride up, I think about Nate again. How does he handle all this? How does he manage to lead something so big? A surge of admiration for him rushes through me. He's not just a normal guy—he's remarkable.

The elevator doors open, and I step out into my new workplace. This is it. I straighten my shoulders, take another deep breath, and walk forward, ready to start.

I see another receptionist and introduce myself again.

"Oh, right. Yes, I'm Susan. Let me call Ms. Harris—she'll come to get you. You can wait over here," she says. I thank her and wait.

Less than two minutes later, a tall woman in a bright-red suit approaches me.

"Delilah Rose?" she asks in a Southern accent.

"Yes, that's me," I reply, smiling as I take her in. She's stunning.

Her red suit fits her slender body perfectly, exuding style and power. Her dark, straight hair falls neatly over her shoulders, framing her high cheekbones, big brown eyes, and full lips painted red to match her outfit. Her skin is smooth and coffee-toned, making the red suit pop even more. She looks powerful and elegant, her presence commanding the attention of everyone around. The contrast between her Southern accent and her stylish appearance is striking.

Ailly Harris leads me to her office, which is small but charming, and explains all the job responsibilities Nate had already filled me in on. I nod, understanding everything.

"I'm so happy they hired someone. I was overloaded with work! You'll be working with me as a team, part-time, so we can share the tasks," she says, clearly relieved.

"I hope they told you I'm a beginner, and I'll need to learn everything from scratch. Is that okay?" I ask.

"We all have to start somewhere, hun. Fine by me, I'll train you. You don't mind sharing this office with me? I think it'll be better for us to work this way, since we'll be sharing projects," Ailly says in her accent, which I'm starting to love.

"It's no problem for me, don't worry."

"Okay, good! Let's go, I'm gonna give you a tour," she says with a big smile on her face.

Ailly leads me around, introducing me to everyone. Damn, there are a lot of people to work with. I have to keep my nerves in check. She explains that we'll mainly work on the twenty-seventh floor, but sometimes we'll go from the twentieth to the thirtieth floor.

For over two hours, we visit all ten floors to meet everyone. Then she surprises me.

"Now, because it's your first day and all new employees get introduced to the executives, we'll go to the ninetieth floor to meet some of them. But we won't be returning there. You gotta act cool, though—those are some scary people," she warns me.

"Define scary," I say, amused.

"Well, the most important people work there. We're still waiting for the new COO, but there's the CFO, Mr. Kingston. He's scary— you don't want to talk to him, trust me." *That's James.* "And most of all, there's the CEO, Mr. Williams. He's the scariest. Don't look at him. I don't think we'll meet him, but if you do, don't talk. Okay?" *What?!*

"What? He's not . . . nice?" I mumble.

"Hell no. I mean, he got this company to the top of the world, and I hear he's a respectable man who keeps his word. But he's scary as hell. No one dares to look at him. I've seen him, and I know what I'm talking about." *That's impossible.*

"Okay," I say, just as the elevator doors open to the executive floor. And again—*damn.*

The place is like nothing I've seen before. It's luxurious and white, almost like an art gallery but without any artwork. The floors are spotless, the walls gleaming, and everything looks sleek and modern. The people here look serious, focused, and move with purpose. There's a quietness in the air, a sharp contrast to the noise and hustle of the other floors. I'm shocked by how clean and polished everything is. It's overwhelming, but I'm determined to make a good impression.

Ailly introduces me to all the personal assistants, but we don't meet any of the executives, since they're "in a meeting," according to their schedule.

"Last but not least, we're going to meet Chloe Lenly. She's Mr. Williams's PA. Don't get offended by her attitude; the woman's a bitch to everyone. Don't take it personally," Ailly warns me.

"Why is she a bitch?" I ask, bemused.

"No one knows, but the rumor says she's in love with the boss." *Excuse me?*

We arrive at Chloe's desk, and I see her. She has long, blonde hair that falls in soft waves around her face. Her eyes are a striking blue-green, giving her a captivating look.

She has high cheekbones and a well-defined jawline, making her face look sculpted. Her lips are full and naturally red. Chloe is tall and slender, moving with grace and confidence. She's stunning. I can't believe Nate works this closely with her without wanting to fuck her—or at least thinking about it.

She has a dark, almost menacing expression, seeming hostile and annoyed by our presence before we even speak.

"Mr. Williams is not available," she says dismissively. *Bitch!*

"Chloe, I'm here to introduce you to our new employee in the marketing team. This is Delilah Rose. Delilah, this is Chloe Lenly, Mr. Williams's PA."

"Nice to meet you," I say, trying to remain polite and professional. She doesn't bother to respond, going back to her computer. We leave the damn place.

Back at our office, Ailly shows me how everything works—the computers, the software, the files, all of it. Then it's lunchtime.

"Wanna go out to eat?" she offers.

"Actually, I brought a lunchbox, if that's okay," I reply, a little embarrassed.

"No problem! Let's go to the thirty-first floor. We've been there already—it's the cafeteria floor, where you can heat up your food, grab coffee, and there are vending machines if you're still hungry." Ailly says she'll buy food and join me.

As we eat, she tells me more about her background—how her mother came to the States from Congo to raise her on her own. How she fought hard to succeed in school and then worked her way up to being employed at Williams seven years ago. I don't say much, and she notices my discomfort but doesn't push for details.

We return to our office, where Ailly continues teaching me everything I need to know about the projects the team is working on. She tells me she has a meeting and suggests I take some time to review what I've learned so far. There's a lot to take in.

While I'm deep in the files, I hear a knock on the door.

"Come in," I say.

A man steps in, and I look up. He's tall and athletic, dressed in a tailored suit. His dark-brown hair is short and a bit messy, and his green eyes are intense and captivating. He has a defined jawline, accented by a bit of stubble, giving him a rugged look. His presence commands attention. I wince, puzzled.

"Delilah Rose?" he asks.

"Yes?" I reply, still unsure.

"I'm James Kingston," he says simply. *Oh, James!*

I smile and rise to my feet, pleased to finally meet him. He casually sits on the desk.

"I came here to have a little chat," he says, his tone serious, which troubles me.

"Okay," I say, waiting.

"I'm sure Nate has told you we've been best friends for years," he starts, and I nod.

"Nate is my best friend, and I have his best interests at heart. I don't have anything against you, and from what he's told me, I think under different circumstances, we could have been friends."

I don't like where this is going.

"But I've known him for a long time, and given how complicated things are right now, I know that your presence is a distraction he doesn't need." I can't find the words to respond, but I know he's right.

"You've taken his focus away from urgent matters. I'm not blaming you, and if Nate says you're a great person, I trust his judgment. But now is not the right time. He's lost interest in things that matter because of you. I know a bit about your past, and I don't think I'm wrong when I say that you two don't stand a chance. That's why your presence here isn't welcome."

His words hit me hard, but I keep a smile plastered on my face. I won't show how much it hurts.

He pulls out a small notepad from his pocket and starts writing something.

"I believe this should be enough," he says, handing me a check for five million dollars.

What the actual fuck?

"Should be enough for what?" I ask.

"To disappear," he says, looking straight into my eyes. I stare back, trying to process what he's saying. "You have enough here to go away, start a new life, and never come back. I'll even give you a letter of recommendation for another job."

"So, you're okay with parting with five million dollars? You're fine not having that money in your bank account anymore?" I ask, incredulous.

"I have a lot more, Ms. Rose," he replies, almost dismissively.

Huh.

"Can you make another one without my name on it, please? I have another identity," I lie.

"Of course," he says, laughing like I've just confirmed something he already suspected. He tears up the previous check and writes a new one.

"Can you give me until the end of the week?" I ask.

"Yes, that's fine. As long as you're gone by then." His words cut deeper than I expected. He leaves the office, and I feel a tear slide down my cheek.

It's his best friend.

I somehow manage to get through work, avoiding Nate's texts, pretending everything is fine when inside, I'm falling apart. The worst part? Today is my fucking birthday.

You're trash, Delilah. Everyone knows it. Nobody wants you. You need to leave.

CHAPTER 14

Nate

I haven't heard from her yet. I think she's trying to make a good impression by not picking up her phone, as if she were proving she's not easily distracted. It's commendable, but I want her to prioritize me, just like I prioritize her. It's almost four o'clock; she was supposed to be done working hours ago, since she's only part-time, but she hasn't called.

So, I assume she's still here.

I decide to check if everything's okay. I tell Chloe I'll be back. She tries to ask where I'm going, but I leave her question unanswered.

I reach the twenty-seventh floor, a place I rarely visit, and as soon as people see me, they almost stop what they're doing. They all stare, but I'm used to it. I have more important matters to attend to.

Then I see her, in the middle of the open workspace, surrounded by her team members. She looks focused, professional, her outfit impeccable, and my mind instantly fills with very, very dirty thoughts. I have to calm myself to avoid showing my excitement to everyone.

She notices me approaching. Her eyes widen, and she subtly shakes her head, almost as if telling me to back off. *I don't like that.*

I keep walking. When I reach the group, everyone stops, and I can see the fear in their eyes. Nothing new. Addison Rutherford, the manager, comes over to greet me

"Good afternoon, Mr. Williams. To what do we owe the pleasure?" she asks politely.

"I was curious to see how things are going down here," I reply. She gives me an update on their ongoing project, and I'm pleased to hear everything's on track. But my real focus is on Delilah, who hasn't even glanced at me.

"There are some faces I don't recognize," I say, prompting introductions of everyone. My eyes land on Ailly Harris, knowing she'll be working closely with Delilah.

"And, this is the newest member of our team, Delilah Rose. She just started today," Addison says, and I extend my hand toward Delilah. When our skin touches, there's an undeniable spark, something magnetic pulling us together. I try to lean in, but she steps back. *I don't like that.*

"When is your tour of the building scheduled?" I ask her, but before she can answer, Ms. Harris steps in.

"We already had the tour this morning, sir," she says.

"I've been in my office all morning and didn't see you. Care to explain?" I ask, my tone harsher than I intended. But I don't care.

"Your assistant told us you were busy, *sir*," Delilah responds, that sharp wit of hers showing. I love her smart mouth.

"I'm always busy, but I *make time* for important things," I say, emphasizing her absence.

"Again, sir, we *were* there, but your assistant said we couldn't see you," she insists, and all eyes are on us now. No one—and I mean no one—has ever spoken to me like this in my own office. And my dick enjoys the show far too much. I pull out my phone and call Chloe, putting her on speaker.

"Did two women visit this morning for the new recruit's tour of the executive floor?" I demand.

"I don't recall, why?" Chloe answers nonchalantly.

I glance at Delilah, who looks disgusted.

"So, you think I lied?" she asks, her voice full of disdain. I can see the panic in everyone's eyes at her response.

"Chloe, go to my office. We're going to have a little chat." I hang up without waiting for her reply. "If you'll excuse me, I have to go. Keep up the good work on the project," I say to Addison before giving Delilah one last glance. She quickly averts her gaze.

When I get back to my office, Chloe is already there, waiting.

"Why didn't you inform me when the new recruit came for her tour, as per protocol?" I ask.

"Because you never care about new recruits. I didn't even remember them coming," she responds casually.

"Next time, you ask me. Now, get back to work, Chloe." She leaves, smiling as if nothing happened.

I text Delilah, asking her to come to my office once she's done working, but there's no response.

Why is she upset with me?

Back at my desk, I stare at the mountain of tasks ahead. I review financial reports, oversee major transactions, and ensure our global operations are running smoothly. Today, I'm particularly focused on a potential merger with a tech company in Japan. The details are complex, but that's what I love about this job—numbers, projections, strategies. It all makes sense to me.

I send a few emails, approve budgets, and take a quick call with our London office about a new investment opportunity. It's all routine, but it's what keeps the company thriving. Just as I'm about to dive into another report, Chloe buzzes me.

"Mr. Williams, the Los Angeles team needs to speak with you. It's urgent."

I nod and open my computer for the video call. The screen lights up, showing the familiar faces of the L.A. team. They look tense.

"Good afternoon, everyone. What's the urgent matter?" I ask, leaning forward.

"Good afternoon, Mr. Williams," says Jerry, the head of the L.A. office. "We have a situation with the Atlantica project. There are complications with city regulations, and our permits might be delayed. This could push our timeline back by months."

I frown. This project is critical to our West Coast expansion. "What kind of complications, John?"

"We're facing new environmental regulations that weren't part of the original assessment. We need to meet with city officials to negotiate, but we need someone with your authority to ensure they take us seriously," John explains.

"Why wasn't this anticipated?" I ask, trying to keep my frustration in check.

"The regulations were updated recently, and our local consultants missed it. We found out just yesterday," John replies apologetically.

I take a deep breath.

"Alright. Set up the meetings with the city officials. I'll fly out and handle it personally. We can't afford delays on this project."

"Thank you, Mr. Williams. Your presence will make a big difference," John says, visibly relieved.

The call ends, and I lean back in my chair. I realize I'll need to be in Los Angeles for at least four days. The thought of being away from Delilah and the dogs doesn't sit well with me.

I'll ask Delilah to come with me. The dogs will love the California sun, and I'll love having her by my side.

I have Chloe send James to my office so we can prepare for the L.A. trip. While I'm waiting, I review the financial reports for the Atlantica project.

The door opens, and James walks in, calm as always.

"Hey, man," he says, dropping into the chair across from me. "What's up?"

"We have a situation in L.A.," I begin, and then explain the whole deal.

James nods, understanding the gravity of the situation. We both turn our attention to the problem at hand, going through the details of the new regulations and the impact on our timeline and budget.

After a while, I look up from the papers.

"Looks like we have to leave in two days to handle this," James agrees.

"Yeah, better get ahead of it before it gets worse." I hit the intercom. "Chloe, call the pilot and tell him to get the jet ready for Sunday morning."

"Got it, Mr. Williams," she replies promptly.

Turning back to James, I ask, "By the way, have you had the chance to meet Delilah yet? She had the tour of the office this morning."

"No, I haven't had the pleasure yet."

I feel a slight unease but push the thought aside.

"Well, you'll meet her soon enough."

We need to get back to work and stay at the top of our game. James leaves.

~

Later in the day, the buzzer of the intercom goes off.

"Yes," I answer.

"Mr. Williams, there's a young woman here claiming you requested her presence, but she's not on your calendar."

That must be Delilah, but just in case.

"What's her name?" I ask.

"Delilah Rose," she answers. *Finally.*

"Let her in."

Delilah walks into my office, and it's strange to see her here, but it makes me happy.

Her eyes widen as she takes in the space.

"You can't be serious," she says, laughing. I missed that laugh.

"What?" I ask with a grin.

"Your office is like . . . I mean, do you really need all that space? Look at the view! Damn, no wonder you think you're the master of the universe," she teases.

I pull her into my arms, holding her tight, but she hides her face in my chest. Something feels off. Delilah stays in my arms, not letting go, while I try to see her face, but she keeps it buried.

"What's wrong?" I ask softly into her hair.

"Nothing," she whispers.

"Delilah," I warn her playfully.

"Nothing, it's just a lot to take in and I don't always have words . . . you know," she admits. I like that she opens up little by little.

"I know. How was your day? Why didn't you answer me all day?"

"My phone was in my purse; I didn't take it out. The day was okay. Ailly is great. I have a lot of work for the weekend to prepare for next week, and I have to study, too," she says, exhaling.

"Well, I thought you could come study in my office in the afternoon after you finish working downstairs."

"No, I want to get home to the dogs. I don't want them to feel left out," she says, and I understand that her attitude with the dogs reflects what she's been missing her whole life.

"Okay," I say simply. She looks tired, and I still feel like something is off. I want to push it, but knowing Delilah, she'd just shut me out. She's not ready. I have to give her more time.

"Anyway, I was coming to tell you I was heading home," she says.

"I still have a lot of work to do, but I won't be late, okay?" I say, and she smiles. I love her smile.

"By the way, you have to tell me who cleans this floor. I want to be able to clean the same way. I'm jealous." I find her OCD endearing.

"I thought no one could beat you at cleaning."

"Oh yeah, shit, I forgot. Rub more of that arrogance of yours on me so I can get back to this," she says, making me laugh hard.

I grab her and rub my face all over her body, and she laughs at my playful gesture. I take her mouth in mine, trying to deepen the kiss, but she steps back.

"Stop it! I really have to go!" she says, laughing as she heads to the door. I slap her behind before she leaves, and then she's out of sight.

This new life with her is priceless. It's unique, it's fulfilling. I can't imagine a life without her in it anymore.

I get back to my desk when the door swings open, and Chloe walks in.

"Who was *she*?" she asks, her tone curious but tinged with something else.

"*She* was none of your business," I reply, keeping my voice steady.

"I saw her this morning. Why would she come back to see you? Why didn't I know about it? We used to talk, remember?" she presses. The truth is, Chloe and I have developed a sort of friendship because of her hard work. I don't want another PA, so I try to be gentler.

"Chloe, I'm really busy right now. Who I see is really none of your concern. I'm facing real challenges here and I don't need you to fight me, I need you to support me. Period." I'm trying to keep my frustration in check.

"Okay, I understand," she says, sounding resigned.

"Good, now please, go back to work. You have to finish writing the conclusions of today's meeting with the board."

"I'm on it. You'll have it before six."

"Good," I say, redirecting my eyes to my computer. Chloe understands that it's her cue to leave.

It's almost eight when I get home. Since Delilah moved in, I've always tried to come before six, but today I just couldn't.

When I reach the foyer, I shout the usual "honey I'm home" that I've come to love so much, but instead, Sheriff and Cowboy jump on me, telling me how happy they are to see me. I pat them both, because I'm happy to see them too. I'm waiting for Delilah to come and jump on me, but she doesn't.

I go to the kitchen and I see her studying on the kitchen island. It smells incredibly good. I come around her and hug her from behind.

"Hey, baby."

"Hey," she says, squeezing my arms. "Dinner's ready, I've made spaghetti and meatballs. Wanna eat now?" "Baby, you've worked all day and you're studying. You didn't have to cook dinner, you could have ordered in," I say, kissing her head.

"You don't like my cooking?" she asks, shockingly. I laugh.

"I love your cooking, but I don't want you to feel obligated. But thank you." I say as I seat down at the table. Delilah joins me with the dishes. It really smells enticing.

Delilah tells me all about her workday, what she thinks of the place, how she felt people were, and the project she'll be working on. I feel in her voice that she's excited, she likes the job. Even though she still feels unfavorable toward humans in general, I can see that she puts effort into work relationships.

"Babe, I forgot to tell you, we have to go to L.A. on Sunday. I have an important meeting to attend. We'll take the boys too. It's only for four days tops," I say, but then I see literal fear in her eyes.

"I can't go to L.A.," she says.

"Why not?"

"I hate the West Coast," she says, and I feel like there's more to her story.

"Care to share why?" I ask, hesitant.

"No," she sighs, and I get it.

"Well, I *have* to go there. I promise you'll be fine. You can stay at the hotel if you want."

"No, I have too much work. I can't miss this first week. I've built a routine with studying, and I don't want the pups to move around too much—they just arrived. I think I'll be fine. I have security, and the dogs, so there's no reason to panic," she says.

"I don't want to be away from you for that long. Can't you at least think about it?" I say, taking her hand in mine.

"We'll be fine, I promise."

We finish dinner and head upstairs; we're both exhausted. We get ready for bed and settle in. I try to take her to cuddle as usual, but she retreats. *What the fuck?*

"Nate, we can't have sex," she blurts out.

"Excuse me?" I ask, surprised.

"I just got my period."

"So?" I ask again.

"Well, we can't have sex while I'm on my period."

"Because it hurts? Do you have cramps?"

"No, it doesn't hurt."

"Then why?" I ask.

"Well . . . it's . . . you know . . . *intimate*," she says, as if it were obvious.

"Define intimate," I demand.

"It's just . . . something that . . . I don't know, like what a husband and wife would do. Not . . . um, friends," she says. *That one stings.*

"You're my girlfriend, Delilah," I say flatly.

"I'm not your girlfriend," she replies defiantly.

"Go try to convince someone else. . . . So, you wanna get married now?" I ask, grinning.

"What? Nooo!" she says, smacking me with a pillow, making me laugh.

"Come on, I don't mind your period. I've never done it before, and I'd like to try it with you."

"We're not having sex," she says firmly, and I smile, loving the challenge of fucking her on her period.

Then she asks, "Can I tell you something?" I nod.

"Your PA is a bitch. A very, very gorgeous and hot one," she says, making me laugh hard.

"You're hotter," I say, pulling her closer by the waist.

"Did you sleep with her?" she whispers.

"No, I didn't," I say, wanting to calm her jealousy.

"Have you ever wanted to?"

"Never." I say. "I like that you're jealous."

"Oh, fuck you!" She smacks my chest. I catch her hand and kiss it.

"People at work . . . they're scared of you," she confesses.

"I know, I'm a scary man," I say, a little too proudly.

"It makes me sad," she says quietly.

I don't like the sound of that. "Why?"

"Because . . . they think you're someone they shouldn't even look in the eye. I heard someone say you were mean and relentless. They see you as cold, emotionless. It hurts because that's not true," she says, and I watch her, feeling a flood of emotions for her.

She continues, "You're not that man. You're the best human I know. You're so, so beautiful, Nate. People at work have no idea who you really are. They see a facade, a mask you wear to keep everything running smoothly. But I *see* you. I see the man behind the mask." Her words catch me off guard. I stay quiet, letting her speak.

"Your soul is beautiful," she says softly, her eyes steady. "You're like this calm ocean, strong and kind. When I was lost, you reached out and gave me a place to belong."

She moves closer, eyes locked on mine. "Your mind is incredible." She smiles, her voice sincere. "You see things most people don't, and you always find the best way forward. Your mind isn't just smart—it's thoughtful, too."

She takes my hand, her touch warm. "And your heart, Nate. That's the best part of you. You care so deeply, even if you don't show it. Your kindness is steady, and your love is strong. You've healed me in ways I never thought possible."

Overwhelmed, I pull her close. She rests her head on my chest, and I feel peace wash over me. Her words make me feel seen in a way I can't explain.

I pull her into my arms, holding her close, letting the weight of her words sink in.

I run my fingers through her hair, feeling a peace wash over me. Her declaration moves me more than I can express. It's like she's stripped away all my layers and shown me the person I want to be.

As we lie there, I realize how lucky I am to have her. Delilah sees me in a way no one else ever has, and her understanding gives me the strength to face whatever comes next. She is my anchor, my solace. With her by my side, I feel ready to conquer the rest of the world.

I drift toward her and kiss her, and the kiss deepens, grows more passionate, like it's the first time I've ever kissed this beautiful woman. My hands roam over her body, touching her everywhere, and I move on top of her as she spreads her legs. We don't speak; we can't. Our need is too urgent. Delilah digs her nails into my back, and I silently hope she leaves a mark. Our tongues are on fire, and we can't pull away. I feel her grinding against me, and every nerve in my body lights up.

"I really need to be inside you, Delilah. Please, baby," I beg.

"Okay," she whispers, and we quickly strip off our clothes. I grab a condom, put it on while she takes out her tampon—which is a huge turn-on for me—and I slide into her.

The feel of her, of *us*, is overwhelming.

Don't worry, baby, I'll be your husband," I joke, and she laughs, but I can't shake the idea.

Because it feels so right.

One thing I've heard about a woman on her period is that everything gets more intense—every touch, every sensation. Delilah is no exception. Her body is electric, hyper-responsive to my every move. Each gasp, each plea for more pulls me deeper into her until I lose all sense of myself in her desire. The fact that she's on her period doesn't bother me at all; if anything, it draws me closer. There's something raw, something primal about it. It makes me feel like we're connecting on a level far beyond the physical. Like we're transcending the boundaries of who we usually are, becoming something much more.

She was right—this *is* intimate, something only two people who are truly close would share. It's a bond I know I could never have with anyone else. With Delilah, it feels natural, perfect. There's a comfort in that intimacy that I've never felt before. It's like we're in our own world, where nothing else exists but us.

Afterward, when we're both spent, we stumble to the shower. The hot water cascades over us, washing away the evidence of our passion. We stand there for a moment, just letting the warmth surround us, and I feel this deep satisfaction—not just physically, but emotionally. Delilah moves quickly to strip the bed and change the sheets, with a kind of quiet efficiency that I find utterly adorable. She's practical, but there's something endearing about the way she does it, like she's taking care of us, making sure our space is clean and comfortable.

Once the bed is made, we crawl back in, lying there facing each other, our breathing still a little uneven. I reach out and brush a strand of hair away from her face, my fingers lingering on her cheek.

"It didn't hurt?" I ask softly, my voice full of concern.

"Not in the least. It felt really good, thank you," she replies, her eyes shining with sincerity. I lean in and kiss the tip of her nose, a small, tender gesture that makes her smile.

As we lie there, I can't help but feel a wave of contentment. This is more than just sex—it's an unspoken connection, a level of trust and closeness I never imagined possible. With Delilah, everything feels right, like I'm exactly where I'm supposed to be.

"You're most welcome," I reply, watching as she turns onto her back and stares up at the ceiling with that distant, lost look in her eyes. It's like the weight of the world has suddenly pressed down on her, and it makes my heart tighten in my chest.

"What's wrong, baby?" I ask softly, my hand trailing gently over her stomach. She opens her mouth, hesitates, like she's struggling to find words. The silence stretches, almost unbearable, until she finally speaks, her voice barely a whisper.

"Today is my birthday . . ."

My mind races, and all I can think is, *what the fuck?*

"What?" I sit up straight, shock jolting through me.

"It's not a big deal," she says, avoiding my eyes. "I've never celebrated it. Only Ashley knows . . ."

"Did she call you today?" I ask, trying to keep my voice steady, not wanting her to see how much this is hitting me. Delilah closes her eyes, and it cuts me deep.

"It doesn't matter," she whispers. But it *does* matter. It fucking matters, and guilt gnaws at me for not knowing. And to top it off, I have to leave tomorrow morning.

Fuck. Where the hell is her sister in all this?

"It *is* important," I say, pulling her closer.

"I'm sorry I didn't know. Happy birthday, Delilah. I'll make it up to you, I promise." I kiss her everywhere I can, trying to coax that beautiful laugh out of her, and it works, but there's a heaviness in the air that won't lift.

"I don't want you to," she murmurs, her voice thick with emotion. "I don't even know why I told you. I couldn't care less about it."

"And yet . . ." I joke, making her laugh, but the smile fades just as quickly, replaced by a seriousness that chills me.

"Twenty-six years ago, I was born, and that was the day I faced my first rejection," she says, her voice flat, detached. "The mother hated me from the start. She told me so many times that this 'special' day was the day she wished I'd be gone. It's this fucking cycle that keeps going still today. I was defenseless then. I'm trying not to be now." She exhales, her words hanging in the air like a dark cloud. This is the most she's ever opened up about her past, and it's tearing me apart to hear it.

"Why do you call her 'the mother'?" I ask, treading carefully, not wanting to push too hard but needing to understand, to connect with her.

"I never called her anything," she says with a bitter edge to her voice. "I just heard her role in the house was 'the mother.' And her name, of course. But she was just that."

"What was her name?" I ask, genuinely curious now. She looks at me, and a small, almost sardonic smile plays at the corner of her lips.

"Delilah," she says, and I frown, trying to process this twist. She sees the confusion on my face and lets out a tired sigh.

"I'll tell you the rest another day. Can I sleep now? I'm so tired," she asks, yawning like the weight of everything has drained her completely. I don't want to push her, but there are so many fucking questions spinning in my head.

"Sure, baby," I whisper as I spoon her, holding her as tightly as I can without crushing her. I kiss her hair, breathing in her scent, and vow to never let her go.

What is your story, Delilah?

CHAPTER 15

Delilah

Nate left this morning. Our goodbyes were painful. Neither of us could let go. I felt his warmth, the steady beat of his heart against mine, and I wanted to cry so badly. But I held it in—I didn't want him to feel guilty or worry about me while he's gone. He promised he'd call all the time, but even that didn't seem like enough. I hate that he's gone, and I already miss him so much. This weekend was beyond incredible.

Once the door closed behind him, the apartment felt eerily quiet. Even the dogs seemed sad. But I took a deep breath and reminded myself that I had a lot to do today. I started with my SAT studies, gathering my books and settling at the kitchen table. Sunlight streamed through the windows, creating a warm, inviting atmosphere. I dove into my work, focusing on math problems and science. And now I'm done.

Switching gears, I remind myself I have work to do for Williams. Ailly gave me a stack of files to review, and they won't read themselves. I move to the living room, sitting cross-legged on the floor, spreading the files around me. I take detailed notes, highlighting key points and jotting down questions for later. It's a lot of work, more than I expected, and I feel a bit overwhelmed. But I push through, determined to finish.

In the afternoon, I take a short break and make myself a cup of tea. The apartment is still quiet, and I find myself missing Nate more than ever. Just as I'm about to get back to work, my phone rings. It's Jenna. I smile as I answer.

"Hey, Jenna!" I say.

"Hey, beautiful!" Just the sound of her voice makes me cheerful. "I just finished my shift. How are you?"

"I'm alright, just working on some projects and studying. But hey, since you're off, why don't you come over for dinner tonight? I'll make something good."

"Dinner sounds amazing! I'd love to come over. What time?"

"How about seven?"

"Perfect. Send me the address, and I'll see you then."

"Great! Sending it now. See you later." I hang up, feeling a bit lighter. I've never had a close girlfriend before. I've always thought of Ashley as my baby sister, someone I needed to protect, so I spared her from my worries. But Jenna and I have been getting close, texting a lot, joking around, and it gives me a little more faith in people.

I call the head of security and the doorman to inform them that Jenna will be arriving around seven. It's protocol—Nate insists on it, and I feel safer because of it.

Now I glance around the apartment. Time to tidy up a bit before Jenna arrives. I start in the living room, picking up stray papers and straightening the cushions on the couch. As I move to the kitchen, I hear it—the whisper of my demons, creeping into my thoughts.

Nate will forget about you. He'll come to his senses and realize you're not worth it.

I try to ignore it, focusing on scrubbing the counters and sweeping the floor. But the voice persists, louder, more insistent.

He's too good for you. He'll leave you behind.

I grit my teeth, pushing the thoughts away, knowing they're not true but struggling to silence them. I move to the bedroom, making the bed and putting away laundry. The voice follows, echoing in my mind.

You're just a burden. He'll find someone better, someone less troubled.

After finishing the cleaning, I take a deep breath. I need to stay busy, keep the demons at bay. I head to the kitchen and start preparing dinner. I decide to make homemade lasagna—a recipe Nate loves.

I gather the ingredients: fresh pasta sheets, ricotta cheese, mozzarella, Parmesan, ground beef, onions, garlic, and tomatoes. I start by making the sauce, finely chopping the onions and garlic before sautéing them in olive oil. The warm smell fills the kitchen. Once the onions are soft, I add the ground beef, breaking it up with a wooden spoon as it browns.

He didn't call because he's not thinking about you.

Next, I add the crushed tomatoes, stirring them into the meat and letting it simmer. While the sauce cooks, I prepare the cheese mixture. In a bowl, I mix the ricotta with grated Parmesan, an egg, and some chopped parsley. I set it aside and begin layering the lasagna.

When he comes back, he'll tell you he doesn't want you anymore. You'll have to quit your job and leave the apartment—just like before.

I spread a thin layer of sauce on the bottom of the baking dish, then add a layer of pasta sheets. I spread a generous amount of the ricotta mixture over the pasta, followed by shredded mozzarella. I repeat the layers, finishing with a thick topping of mozzarella and Parmesan, then cover the dish with foil and place it in the oven, setting the timer for forty-five minutes. As it bakes, I clean up the kitchen, washing the dishes and wiping down the counters. The voice in my head has quieted, the act of cooking soothing my nerves.

Finally, the timer goes off. I remove the foil and let the lasagna bake for another ten minutes, allowing the cheese to turn golden and bubbly. The apartment smells amazing, and I can't wait for Jenna to arrive.

Just as I'm taking the lasagna out of the oven, Tony, one of the security guards, informs me that she's here. I tell him to let her up and thank him before he leaves.

I set the dish on the counter and go to greet Jenna, but the dogs start barking like crazy. Good—they're protective.

"Hey, come on in," I say, stepping aside. Jenna knows I'm not a fan of physical contact, so she keeps her distance. But the dogs? They have other plans and rush toward her.

"Hey, oh my gosh! You have dogs?!" she says, her voice turning playful.

"It's a long story—I'll tell you about it later," I say, trying to wrangle the boys.

"Oh my god, I've never been inside a penthouse in my life! This place is incredible!" she shrieks with excitement, and I can't help but laugh.

"Want a tour?" I ask, grinning mischievously.

"Of-fucking-course!" she says, blinking in amazement. We laugh together as I show her around. Every now and then, she curses in disbelief at the size and beauty of the place.

"It smells amazing in here."

"Thanks! I made lasagna. I hope you're hungry," I say, winking.

"Starving! It's been such a long day."

We sit down at the table, and I serve generous portions. Jenna takes a bite and closes her eyes, savoring the flavor.

"This is amazing, Delilah. You've outdone yourself."

"Thanks. I'm glad you like it. Nate's the only one who's ever tasted my cooking."

We chat and laugh as we eat, and the demons in my mind fade into the background.

For tonight, at least, I feel at peace. The day has been long and challenging, but having Jenna here makes it all worth it. I know there will be more hard days ahead, but moments like this give me hope.

"So, besides work and studying, how are things going?" she asks.

"Can I tell you a secret?"

"I know you don't trust people, but I swear I'll never betray you. I've been betrayed by friends in the past, and that's just not who I am. I hope one day you'll see that," she says, and I feel like she's being honest. Tonight, I want to hold on to hope, so I decide to open up.

"Nate's best friend, James—he came to my office on Friday and made me a proposition," I say, noticing her curiosity piquing.

"Aaaaand?" she urges me.

"He asked me to leave Nate, leave the city, and never come back because I was a burden to Nate and a distraction from his business. He even offered me a check to start a new life."

"What the fuck? Are you serious? What a piece of shit! How much did he offer?" she asks, eyes wide.

I take a deep breath and just say it.

"Five million dollars."

"WHAAAAAT?" she screams, and I can't help but laugh at how comical her reaction is. I stand up, take the check out of my purse, and show it to her.

"Holy shit, I don't even want to touch it—I feel like it's going to burn me! Wait, it's not addressed to you—it's blank. Why?"

"I asked him to leave it blank."

"Why?" she asks, incredulous.

"Because I'm not going to cash the check," I say.

"Attagirl! So, what are you going to do?" she asks, still buzzing with curiosity.

I take another deep breath.

"I've been searching online for a charity that helps abused women. I think I found one."

"How are you going to do it?" she asks, still not grasping my plan.

"I'm going to pretend to be James Kingston's PA and tell the charity that my boss wishes to make a huge donation on his behalf."

Jenna bursts out laughing.

"That's genius! If you need any help, just call, and I'll be there." I thank her, knowing I may actually need her help with this.

"Can I ask you a question?" she says, and while I usually

hate being asked questions, I decide to make an effort. I nod in response.

"I just kinda have to ask . . . Five million dollars is a huge amount of money. Why turn it down?"

I can't tell if she's implying that I've fallen in love with Nate, which I haven't, or that staying with him would mean more money, given how rich he is. Little does she know, I never use his money. I barely have enough in my bank account to get through the week while I wait for my paycheck. But I decide to answer truthfully, for once.

"I don't want the money because I finally feel like I have a second chance at life.

"This new job is incredible, and it's fulfilling me in ways I never thought possible. Having Nate with me, even if it's temporary, even if it doesn't last . . . I don't want to be the one to end it. I want to enjoy every second of it because I don't know when it'll be the last. He gives me more than anyone could ever expect, and it's not about the money. His presence, his kindness, his friendship— that's everything to me.

"I'm not naive—I know it won't last. It's like . . . a perfect day at the beach when the sun is high, the weather is perfect, and you're having the time of your life. You know the sun will eventually set, and the darkness of the night will take over. That's inevitable. I'm at the beach right now, and I know the night will come, but I'll stay until I can't anymore. Besides, I have nowhere else to go."

I see Jenna's eyes welling up just a little, and I keep going.

"Plus, I'm tired of men controlling my life, telling me what to do—especially when money is involved. It takes me back to dark places. So, what better way to use this money than for something good?" I say, taking a sip of my wine.

"I don't even know what to say," she says softly.

"Wanna take the dogs out?" I ask, knowing my babies need a walk.

"Sure, fresh air will be good," she replies.

"Just a heads-up—I have a security team that follows me everywhere, since Nate is a public figure in the business and political world. Is that okay?"

"Of course," she says.

We take the dogs out, walking toward Central Park, laughing the whole way as I tell her all about Sheriff and Cowboy. She melts, thinking Nate is the greatest guy in the world, and I have to agree with her. I check my phone, but still no message from him.

He doesn't want to talk to you. He's figuring out how to get rid of you.

"So, what's going on with you?" I ask, eager to change the subject.

Jenna and I walk back to the apartment, and as usual, Sheriff wants to be carried, so I scoop him up and continue walking with him in my arms. The night sky begins to show as we stroll, the dogs happily trotting beside us. The distant hum of traffic fills the air, and I glance over at Jenna, who seems lost in thought.

"Hey, Jenna, what's going on? You seem a bit off. If you don't want to answer, that's fine—I understand," I say.

Jenna sighs and looks down, kicking a small pebble along the path.

"It's nothing, really," she mumbles.

I nudge her gently with my elbow.

"Come on, you can tell me. What's bothering you?" I say, using a baby voice as if Sheriff were talking to her.

She takes a deep breath and looks at me, her eyes filled with uncertainty.

"Okay, well . . . There's this regular customer at the bar. He's been hitting on me a lot lately. At first, I thought it was just harmless flirting, but now I'm not so sure."

I raise an eyebrow. "Really?"

Jenna hesitates before continuing.

"His name is Chase. He comes in almost every night, usually sits at the bar, orders a whiskey, and chats with me. He's charming, funny, and seems genuinely interested in getting to know me."

I smile encouragingly.

"That doesn't sound so bad. What's the problem?"

We turn the corner onto our street, and Jenna's expression grows more serious.

"The problems—plural—are, first, he's older. I'm twenty-nine, and he looks like he's around forty. He's very attractive and powerful, and I'm just . . . a barmaid. I love my job, but feeling inferior bothers me. And every guy I fall for turns out to be a jerk. I don't think I'm ready for another relationship just yet. I've been hurt too many times."

I feel a pang of compassion for her. I know how hard it is to open up and trust someone new.

"I'm sorry, Jenna. I get it. What happened with the last guy?"

She sighs again, clearly reluctant to relive the memory.

"His name was Kyle. He was sweet at first, but as soon as things got serious, he changed. He became distant, made secretive phone calls, and told me many times I wasn't pretty enough. He made me feel worthless. One day, I went to his place unannounced, and he was screwing two women right in front of me. He threw me out and went back to his business. It broke me."

We reach the penthouse, and I unlock the door. As we step inside, I turn to her, my heart aching for her.

"I'm really sorry you went through that. You deserve so much better."

Jenna nods, her eyes downcast. "I know, but it's hard to believe that sometimes. It's like I'm drawn to the wrong guys. And it's not even the first time."

We take off our shoes and settle on the couch. The dogs curl up at our feet, and I turn to Jenna, determined to offer her some comfort.

"When history repeats itself, it really sucks. I'm not the one to tell you to open up and start trusting people again. Maybe you should just enjoy the flirting, maybe even have sex with him and leave it at that. I don't know."

She looks at me, her eyes filled with doubt. "It's . . . not such a bad idea. The man *is* attractive," she admits.

I think for a moment, choosing my words carefully.

"You can't be sure of him, not completely. But you could take things slow, get to know him better without rushing into any-thing. And trust your instincts. If something feels off, listen to that feeling."

Jenna nods slowly, considering my advice.

"I guess you're right. Maybe I should give it a chance, but keep my guard up."

I smile, relieved that she's open to the idea. "Exactly. Just take it one step at a time. And please know, I'm here for you. If you ever need to talk or need some crappy advice, I'm just a call away." She laughs, some of the tension leaving her shoulders.

"Thanks, Delilah. It means a lot to know I have your support. And your crappy advice."

We spend a good amount of time talking, sharing stories, and laughing. Jenna tells me more about Chase and how he makes her laugh with his silly jokes. I see the glimmer of hope in her eyes—the possibility that, maybe this time, things will be different.

My phone buzzes, and I start looking all around for it, as it's buried in the couch. "What's going on?" Jenna asks, amused.

"I can't find my damn phone, and it's buzzing," I say, and we search the couch cushions. Jenna finds it first and bursts out laughing.

"*Irresistible CockForce Hubs* is calling," she says, grinning as she hands it to me. I laugh at Nate's joke as I pick up the phone.

"Hey," I answer.

"Took you long enough, *Cowboy and Sheriff Dirty Mama*—sexy as shit, by the way," Nate purrs over the phone. The man just knows how to melt me.

"Took *you* long enough. Why are you just calling me now?" I ask, trying not to sound too worried.

"James kept me busy. He really wanted me to focus while we

prepped for tomorrow's meetings. But I've been thinking about you all day, baby," he says in that playful tone of his.

"Well, I've been busy too—reviewing files for work, studying, cleaning the house. I invited Jenna over, made homemade lasagna, we walked the dogs out, and now we're talking on the couch."

"Say hi to her for me. It's great that you're having a girl's night. But does that mean you didn't think about me at all today?" he asks, mockingly offended, and I laugh.

"You know I'll never admit it," I tease, my voice turning sultry.

"Keep talking to me like that, baby. Go on."

"You're such a perv."

"Wait till we meet again. I'll show you perv."

"Promises, promises . . ." I tease back.

"Challenge accepted. Is Jenna staying over?"

"Hold on," I say, covering the phone and turning to Jenna. "Wanna stay the night?" I ask, and she pauses to think.

"Yeah, sure. As long as you give me some spare clothes," she says.

I get a little too excited and put the phone back to my ear. "Yeah, she's staying," I tell Nate.

"Alright, don't have too much fun without me. Call me when you're in bed," he demands, and I agree before hanging up.

"You guys are cute," Jenna says, but I'm uncomfortable discussing the nature of my relationship with Nate. I push the thought aside, like always.

"I have to be at work tomorrow by 8:30. Is that alright for you?" I ask.

"That's perfect. I'll leave at the same time for my morning run," she says. "So, I guess tonight's a slumber party," Jenna adds with a grin.

"A what?" I reply, confused.

"A slumber party. It's a sleepover where we wear cozy pajamas, eat junk food, have pillow fights, girl talk, paint our nails—you know."

No, I don't know. I've never had a slumber party, never had a childhood like that. I never had the chance to be a teenager, never had friends like that. I've never been . . . *normal.* I wouldn't even be able to define "normal." That's how messed up my life has been. I feel this wave of anger and sadness all at once, realizing I never got the chance to be a normal kid—and I never will. Time has passed. Jenna is just being friendly, completely unaware of my past, but being confronted with my life like this? It hurts.

Jenna notices the switch in my mood.

"Hey, we don't have to do anything. I was just being silly, I'm sorry," she says, almost mortified. It saddens me more because it's not her—it's me. It's always me. Usually, Nate calms me down, but he's not here. The void of his absence feels enormous. I need to hear his voice.

"No, it's okay. It's just me. You didn't do anything wrong. I just need to talk to Nate for a second," I say, excusing myself and heading to his home office.

I dial his number, and he answers almost immediately.

"Hey, babe, did—" he starts, but I cut him off.

"I'm having a moment," I whisper, my voice barely audible.

"Okay, breathe, baby, just breathe, and talk to me. I'm right here." *No, you're not.*

But I can't tell him that, so I just take a few deep breaths before I speak.

"I'm fucked up, Nate," I admit.

"We all are, baby. What triggered it?" His voice is soft, reaching the broken parts of me.

"It's stupid," I say.

"It's okay, you can tell me."

"Jenna said we were having a slumber party, and I didn't know what that even meant. She explained it, and . . . I felt like shit. I've never had one. I've never had a girlfriend. I never had a childhood. They stole my teen years. I was never . . . carefree. And it angered me. It hurt. I'll never get that time back; it's too late. I'm too old.

I'm just . . . sad. I'm sorry." I exhale, realizing I'm upset over something that feels so trivial.

"I understand. I'm sorry you feel like this. Remember when you told me how upset you were with people who didn't see me for who I really am? I'm feeling the same way right now. Hearing you say that you felt like shit—it hurts me. You are *so* much more than you think you are, baby. My greatest wish is for you to see yourself through my eyes. You're beautiful, Delilah. You're even more beautiful because of what you've been through, not despite it. You're the strongest, most resilient person I know. I'm in awe of you."

I'm speechless. His words soothe me deeply.

He continues, "Use this night to get your revenge. Have a slumber party like you're fourteen and innocent. I just wish I could see your beautiful face."

"Thank you, Nate. I feel a lot better now."

"Anytime, baby. Send me some pictures so I can feel like I'm part of the party," he says in that sexy voice that only he can pull off.

"I sure will. I better get back to Jenna—poor girl freaked out when she saw my mood shift," I say.

Nate laughs, and just as I'm about to hang up, I hear him again. "Delilah?"

"Yes?"

"Thank you for telling me. I'll always answer. I'll always be here."

I can't speak—it's too much for me. Nate gets it. He says good night and hangs up.

I return to Jenna, trying to reassure her. She looks at me with concern.

"I'm sorry, Jenna. It's not you, it's me. I'm . . . I'm just fucked up."

"I didn't mean to upset you," she says softly.

"You didn't. I promise. Sometimes I just have these . . . moments.

But I'm okay now. Let's have that slumber party," I say, attempting a smile.

"Are you sure?" she asks, still worried.

"Yeah, I'm sure. Let's have some fun tonight." I feel more determined now. I won't let my past ruin this night—not for Jenna and not for myself.

We throw on Nate's pajamas. They're oversized, plush, and ridiculously comfy. We're laughing so hard as we bake cookies and brownies in the kitchen. There's even popcorn, so everything feels perfect. Jenna picks a movie, *PS. I Love You,* and we grab every blanket and pillow we can find to make the couch cozier.

As the movie plays, I can't help but cry. The story is heartbreaking—a woman receiving letters from her late husband that guide her through her grief and help her find joy again.

Tears blur my vision. I try to blink them away, but they spill over.

"He writes letters to her," I say, my voice breaking. "Even after he's gone, he finds a way to keep her going. It's like he knew she'd need him, even from beyond. It's beautiful and heartbreaking all at once."

Jenna, her own eyes wet with tears, nods. "I know, right? It's so sad and beautiful at the same time," she says, handing me a tissue. We both laugh a little through the tears, trying to lighten the mood. It's such a strange mix—crying and laughing together.

I can't help but think about Nate. The apartment feels so empty without him. I miss his presence, his voice, his touch . . . everything. A deep fear settles in my chest as I think about losing him. What if something happens? What if he doesn't come back? The thought terrifies me.

The movie ends with the woman finding peace, moving on with her life, but it leaves me feeling raw and vulnerable. The story lingers in my mind, stirring up my own emotions. Jenna wipes her eyes and laughs softly.

"God, that movie always makes me cry. How about you?"

I nod, trying to smile through my tears. "Yeah, it really got to me. It's so powerful." Jenna reaches over and squeezes my hand.

"We needed a good cry, didn't we?"

"Yeah, I guess we did," I say, grateful for her understanding. But inside, my thoughts are still with Nate. I glance at my phone on the coffee table and feel a sudden urge to reach out to him. But I hesitate. I've never let myself admit how much I miss him. I feel exposed, fragile. The loneliness and fear are overwhelming.

I take a deep breath, pick up my phone, and open our text thread. My fingers hover over the keyboard. I feel a lump in my throat, my heart pounding. Finally, I gather the courage and type out a simple message: *I miss you.*

I stare at the words for a moment, my thumb hovering over the send button. Then, with another deep breath, I hit send.

I feel a mixture of relief and anxiety as I watch the message disappear. I put the phone down and try to focus on cleaning up, but my mind races. I just told Nate I miss him—something I've never fully admitted to myself, let alone to him.

My phone buzzes. I look down at it.

> **Delilah:** *I miss you.*
> **Nate:** *I miss you more.*

A huge smile spreads across my face. Jenna notices and nudges me gently.

"Hey, you okay?"

"I'm perfect," I answer, and it's the truest thing I've ever said.

Later, I show Jenna to the guest room. She seems utterly satisfied. We bid each other good night, and I thank her for everything. I take a moment to say good night to the dogs. It breaks my heart to leave them downstairs.

As I climb the stairs and open the door to the bedroom, a surge of loneliness hits me. I *hate* it. The room feels cold, unwelcoming, and sad. Everywhere I look, I search for him, hoping he'll suddenly appear. *Why is it so difficult?*

I pull out my phone and FaceTime him. I tell him I want to get ready for bed with him, even if it's just over the phone. He tells me I'm beautiful and that he misses my face, and I melt even more. We brush our teeth together, get the bed ready, and the whole time, Nate tells me about his day in L.A. I share the details of the movie with him. Then we get into bed.

"Are you still on your period?" he asks, frowning.

"Yes, why?" I answer.

"That means no phone sex. I take it you can't touch yourself," he says, rolling his eyes, and I burst out laughing.

"You really are a perv."

"Yeah, but you like me anyway."

"I don't—"

"Go convince someone else," he says, cutting me off. I laugh again.

"Three days to go, baby," he says.

"Three days . . ." I answer. God, I miss him.

Nate hangs up the phone. Then I hear something at the door. I get up and see Cowboy and Sheriff have managed to come upstairs. I'm feeling too lonely to push them away. They climb onto the bed, and only then do I manage to shut my eyes.

~

I wake up on Monday with a heavy heart. Nate's absence is like a hole in my chest. I drag myself out of bed and stumble to the kitchen. *I miss him.*

As I make my coffee, Jenna comes into view, already dressed and ready to leave for her morning run. She's late, so I don't hold her back. She says she'll call, and I say okay.

When I go back to the kitchen, I realize there's a flower delivery. My heart skips a beat. I take the bouquet of roses inside, my hands quivering. There's a note attached. I unfold it and read:

It killed me not to see your eyes when I opened mine.
I miss you,
—*Nate.*

My heart melts. I hold the note to my chest and close my eyes, feeling a wave of unwelcome feelings wash over me.

It won't last, he'll tire of you, he'll leave you, you're trash.

The rest of Monday goes by in a rush. I'm overloaded with work until two. Papers pile up on my desk, emails flood my inbox, and my phone keeps ringing. I barely have time to breathe, but I push through, determined to get everything done.

In the afternoon, I study at home. I've prepared all the books I need to work on English and history. I focus on my goal, but my mind keeps drifting back to Nate. He kept his word and calls me whenever he can. His voice is a lifeline, but his absence is still a constant ache.

~

Tuesday arrives, and with it, another flower delivery. This time, the note says:

I feel like I left my heart at home with you.
I miss you even more than the day before.
—*Nate.*

I feel butterflies in my chest as I read his words. I don't want to dig up the thoughts of how I feel and why I feel this way. It's too overwhelming.

Tuesday looks like Monday, but harder. My demons rush back, filling my mind with insecurities and doubts. I dread the thought of Nate leaving me, of being left on my own again. But I manage to push those thoughts aside. They're still there, for sure, but I have so many things to be grateful for—Nate aside—that I try to remind myself of all the blessings. First and foremost, the dogs. They bring me so much: they brighten my life with true love, comfort, and a deep sense of belonging.

Then there's my relationship with Ailly, my coworker, which is getting better. We have lunch together, we laugh a lot and genuinely enjoy each other's company. We work well together, and I start to look forward to seeing her in the morning.

Even my relationship with Sam is growing. We see each other for coffee, we catch up on his life at the hospital and his passion for his work. I love listening to his stories. We never mention my past or any connection to it. Our friendship, which was solid before, becomes even more meaningful.

And of course, Jenna, a wonderful soul I met during the darkest of my days. She's funny, she's real, she never judges anyone. The woman has her heart on her sleeve. I love opening up to her a little. It's getting less scary than it ever was.

Yet, despite opening up to people, my heart still feels empty without Nate. I ache for his return. I long for him. We talk for at least an hour every night, we text each other during the day, we send each other pictures of what we're doing, and of course, Nate being Nate, he sends me dirty texts, and I love doing it too. I miss him. I want him. It was too soon for us to be apart for this long.

~

Now it's Wednesday, and I'm at my desk with Ailly. We dive into our tasks, brainstorming ideas for our latest project, bouncing ideas off each other and laughing at our sillier suggestions. We break for lunch and head to the cafeteria, where we continue our conversation over food.

"Ailly," I say, my tone a bit too serious.

"Yeah?" she answers.

"Do you know the name of Mr. Kingston's PA?" I ask.

"Her name is Adaline Fairmont. Why?"

I know that right now she's in L.A. as part of the business team, but I'm looking for a way to get to her emails.

"I need to do something, but I'm going to need some help doing it," I say.

"Okay, hun, tell me."

"I need access to her email address and her office phone." Ailly looks really surprised by my comment, but she doesn't tell me not to do it.

"Delilah, I'm going to tell you two things. First, yes, I can get access to her mail and her phone through the company software. And second, you better have an excellent reason for this and tell me about it if you want my help," she says, her tone serious. I can't tell her the whole truth, but I can tell her some of it.

"I have some money I'd like to donate to a charity called The Voices of Women

Shelter. That charity helps women victims of abuse, most of whom are in great danger. They might need help finding a roof, food, a job, freedom from their abusers, and the list goes on. They're trying to build a new center to welcome more women, but they don't have enough funds to keep going. But I'm no one to make the donation, and I don't want to draw attention to myself.

"I've done some research, and Mr. Kingston donates a lot to charity. I figured that if I can reach The Voices of Women Shelter pretending to be Mr. Kingston's PA, on his behalf, they won't question the money and will just take it," I say.

Ailly is stunned completely. She's starting to know me well enough not to ask further questions, and she accepts the challenge.

We spend almost two hours on the task, getting into Adaline Fairmont's file. We write the email, and Ailly almost has a heart attack at the size of the donation, but the plan is in motion. Later, I ask Tyler to go with me to the shelter, where I meet with Jonathan Cellone, the president of The Voices of Women. I pretend to be James's PA, and it all works out. They cash the check. And I feel free.

Later, I go back home. I barely have time to study, as I have to take care of the boys, clean the house, and make dinner.

Nate calls. We talk about our day, but I don't mention any of my plans—I don't want him to ever know. We laugh, and we talk sweet. Both of us can't wait for tomorrow to come. I can't wait to see him again.

He'll come back only to leave you. You'll never be enough.

CHAPTER 16

Nate

Today is the day I'll finally see her again.

I sit in a small café with James, sipping my coffee. The past four days in L.A. have been a whirlwind. We came here to deal with the Atlantica project, specifically the environmental issues that have been holding everything back. It's been a challenge, but I managed to turn things around.

On the first day, I met with the L.A. team. They seemed nervous, unsure. They all knew my reputation. I walked into the room, and it went silent. Everyone's eyes were on me. I started by outlining the issues and my expectations. I don't tolerate incompetence.

Everyone knows this. As I spoke, I saw them sit up straighter, paying close attention.

The main problem is the environmental impact study. It's flawed, incomplete. The local authorities are all over it. I assigned tasks, delegated responsibilities. I made it clear that failure is not an option. By the end of the first day, the team was already working harder, faster. They fear the consequences of letting me down.

On the second day, I met with the environmental consultants. They tried to argue, to push back. I didn't let them. I used facts, data, and a strong presence to make my point. They fell in line. We came up with a revised plan that meets the regulations. I oversaw every detail, ensuring there were no mistakes.

The third day was about execution. The team worked nonstop. I moved between them, checking progress, answering questions, keeping everyone on track. My dominance in the room was clear. No one dared to question me. By the end of the day, the revised study was complete. We submitted it to the authorities, and it was approved within hours.

On the fourth day, today, I feel a mix of triumph and exhaustion. The project is back on track, but my mind is elsewhere. I miss Delilah. I miss her so much it hurts. She finally opened up and said, "I miss you." It might not seem like much, but I know how hard it was for her to say it. It's a battle she won, and it means everything to me.

I wish she were here with me in L.A. I think about how we could have spent our evenings after work. We could have visited the Getty Center, admired the art and the gardens. We could have walked along Santa Monica Pier, watched the sunset over the ocean. I imagine us driving up the Pacific Coast Highway, stopping at Malibu for a quiet dinner by the beach. It would have been perfect, like our time in the Hamptons.

The memories of the Hamptons flood back. The beach walks, the quiet dinners, the way she smiled in the sun, how she sang to me. I wanted to recreate that here, show her the beauty of L.A., not just work. The Griffith Observatory, with its stunning views of the city and the stars, or a peaceful afternoon at the Huntington Library, strolling through the gardens. I wanted to share these moments with her.

But instead, I'm here in this café with James. He has to stay another day in L.A. to finalize some details. I'm waiting for my private jet to be ready. I look at him, and I can see he's exhausted too, but he's done well. He respects me, and I know he appreciates my leadership. We're a great team.

"You did good," James says, breaking the silence.

"Thanks," I reply, taking another sip of coffee. "It was a team effort." James laughs, shaking his head.

"Yeah, right. They were scared out of their minds."

I smile, knowing he's right. Fear is a tool I use well. It gets results. But now, as I sit here, all I can think about is getting back to Delilah and the dogs. I need to see her, hold her. The city seems empty without her. Every achievement here feels hollow because she's not with me to share it.

The café is small, quiet. The aroma of fresh coffee fills the air. Outside, the sun is setting, casting a warm glow over the city. I watch people pass by, living their lives, and I feel a pang of longing. I want to be home.

"Look at this woman. Damn, she's hot," he says, but I don't bother looking. I'm not interested.

"Wanna have some fun before you go?" he says, and I give him a very dark look. I feel disgusted by what he's implying, and it's not the first time. Every day for the past four days, James has made suggestions about fucking some women, just like we used to before Delilah, but fuck, things have changed now.

"Oh, come on, man, don't tell me you're not even a little tempted!" he pushes.

"No, you sick fuck, I'm not. What's the matter with you? No wonder Hayley threw your ass out," I say, anger in my tone.

"That's a low blow. But men are men, we have needs."

"Needs I intend to fill with the gorgeous brunette waiting for me at home, fucker," I fire back. James doesn't respond, and I see the unease in his face.

"What?"

"Nothing. I just hope you'll be okay, and if you want me to come back to New York earlier, I'll do it." I'm puzzled.

"Why would I want you to come back to New York earlier?"

I see embarrassment in his eyes, and I have to say, I'm curious. I glare at him, waiting for him to elaborate.

"I was just saying, man, I didn't mean anything by it," he says.

Something is off, I feel it. I'm never wrong with my instincts. But I won't dig into the subject right now. We finish our coffee, talking about other things, avoiding my personal life.

"Are you ready to head to the airport?" James asks, pulling me out of my thoughts.

"Yeah," I say, standing up. "Let's get going."

We leave the café, and I call my driver. The car arrives quickly, and we head to the airport. James will stay behind to handle the final details, but my mind is already on the flight back. I picture Delilah waiting for me, the smile on her face when she sees me.

It's what keeps me going.

At the airport, my private jet is ready. I say goodbye to James, thanking him for his hard work. He nods, understanding. As I board the plane, I feel a sense of relief. Each mile that brings me closer to Delilah is a weight lifting off my shoulders.

The jet will take off in twenty minutes, so it's time I call my girl. She answers after the first ring.

"Hey, gorgeous," I say.

"Hey, you," she answers.

"I'll be landing at 4:30 p.m. New York time. With traffic, I think I'll be home around five. I expect you to be naked on our bed, legs wide open," I say, dead serious. Delilah bursts out laughing, and I love that sound.

"Actually, baby, I'm sorry, but I won't be there . . . I have a meeting to attend. Ailly insisted I be there to learn more, and I agreed. I'm so sorry."

"Cancel it."

"I can't! I'm so sorry, but I'll make it up to you, I promise."

"Delilah, I haven't seen you in four days, for fuck's sake. I'm not delaying our reunion. You call Ailly and tell her you can't be there, end of story."

"Wow, I wonder who's the boss in that company."

"Don't start being a smart-ass, Delilah. I just need to see you."

"I promise I'll make it fast. I'll try to leave the meeting before everyone," she says. But I'm hurt. I don't like the fact that she doesn't prioritize me. I want to be the center of her world.

"Okay, I guess I'll see the boys first, have some boy time, because the lady of the house doesn't have enough time for us," I say. But she just laughs even harder. We talk a little more, but then it's time for takeoff, so we hang up.

I take a sip of my scotch, looking out the window as the plane takes off. The city lights fade below me, and I close my eyes, thinking of her again. The past four days have been tough, but knowing I'll see her soon makes it all worth it. I can't wait to be home.

New York City is just a few hours away, along with my office and the mountain of work that's surely piling up there. The hum of the engines is soothing, almost making me forget about the pressures of being the CEO of Williams Holdings.

My laptop is open on the small table in front of me. I've been going through emails, trying to stay on top of things. Suddenly, a new email notification pops up. It's from James. The subject line reads, "Urgent." *Interesting.*

I open the email and quickly scan its contents. My pulse quickens as I read about Jake's latest attempt to undermine me. He's been meeting with the regulatory official who almost shut down our Atlantica project in Los Angeles. The same official who's known for being particularly difficult and prone to bribery. James discovered that Jake has been trying to use this connection to create legal roadblocks for us, hoping to damage the company's reputation and my leadership. *Fucker.*

To make matters worse, Jake took advantage of my absence to show up at the office and try to organize a board meeting without me. He's telling the board members that I'm too focused on other ventures and not paying enough attention to the business, hoping to sway them to his side. I close my eyes for a moment, taking a deep breath. Jake has always been a thorn in my side, but this is a new low, even for him. He's willing to sabotage our projects and hurt the company just to get back at me. I can't let him get away with this. I need to act fast to stay ahead of his schemes.

I open another email, this one from Danny, my PR manager. He's been working on a new campaign to highlight our latest achievements and future plans. *Perfect.* I type a quick response, telling her to expedite the campaign and ensure that our key investors get a preview. This will remind them of our recent successes and our solid plans for the future.

Next, I type an email to Chloe. She came with us to L.A., but as an assistant, she flies commercial in business class. I ask her to arrange a meeting with our most important investors and the board as well. It's time for payback. Then I draft a detailed email to our investors, outlining the company's recent accomplishments and our strategic vision. I make sure to emphasize my personal commitment to the company and my dedication to its continued success, adding links to some of our recent press releases and media coverage, which highlight our achievements and positive outlook.

I hit Send and lean back in my seat, feeling a bit more at ease. But I'm not done yet. I need to make sure Jake's words don't leave a lasting impression. I start drafting another email, this one to my legal team. I ask them to quietly look into Jake's recent activities and gather any evidence that could show he's acting against the company's best interests. If he's violating any agreements or laws, I want to know about it.

But I need more than just legal leverage. I need to show Jake that I'm always a step ahead. I'll instruct my team to prepare a comprehensive report detailing our compliance with all regulations and our proactive measures for the Atlantica project. This will not only counter any potential accusations from Jake's side but also bolster our standing with the regulatory bodies. Jake may be my brother, but I won't let him ruin everything I've worked so hard to build. Williams Holdings is my legacy, and I'll protect it at all costs.

I'm not going to let him get away with this.

By the time I finish, the plane is beginning its descent. I look out the window again, seeing the skyline of New York City come into view. It's a sight that always fills me with a sense of purpose. I see the limo coming into view as the jet stops, Tyler behind the wheel. I gather the rest of my things and head to the door. When it opens, my heart skips a beat.

What the fuck?

I see Delilah in front of the car, looking way too beautiful for this world. I fucking missed her. She's taking my damn breath away. She stands effortlessly, her white tank top contrasting with the soft pink of her high-waisted skirt, her casual white sneakers hinting at a laid-back vibe. She looks way too proud of herself for fooling me.

As I get down the jet stairs, Delilah starts to run toward me, so I run a little toward her too. Then she jumps on me, wrapping her legs around my waist and crashing her lips onto mine. We don't even open our mouths for a while—we just need to connect, to feel each other. As she clings to me, I catch her beautiful head in my hands, brushing her hair away from that gorgeous face.

"I missed you so much," she whispers, her voice trembling with emotion.

"I missed you too, baby," I say, my voice thick with longing. I pull back slightly to look into her eyes. They're filled with tears, but she's smiling.

"Four days was too much," she says, scolding me.

"Never again," I promise.

Our lips meet in a hot, passionate kiss. It's deep and intense, conveying all the longing we feel for each other. Her hands grip my shoulders, and I can feel her heart beating fast against my chest. My hands roam her back, holding her as close as possible.

We kiss for what feels like forever, neither of us wanting to let go. When we finally pull back, we're both breathless. I press my forehead against hers, closing my eyes for a moment to savor the feeling of having her in my arms again.

"I can't believe you're here," she says, her fingers brushing my cheek. "It felt like an eternity."

"I know," I reply, my hands resting on her hips. "Every day without you was torture."

She smiles and kisses me again, softer this time, but just as full of passion.

"Welcome home," she whispers.

"I'm not home yet," I reply.

"I hope I didn't overstep by showing up here. I just missed you too much, and I didn't want to overthink it. I called Tyler and told him I wanted to surprise you, and he agreed. I hope I didn't, you know . . . overstep," she says, anxious.

"Please feel free to overstep like this anytime," I say, laughing.

We stand there for a moment, wrapped up in each other, letting the world fade away. Finally, I set her down gently, but I keep her close, my arm around her waist. Together, we walk toward the car waiting nearby.

Tyler stands by the limo, a respectful distance away. He opens the door for us, and I help Delilah in before sliding in beside her. Tyler closes the door and gets behind the wheel, ready to take us home.

But as soon as the door closes, all I can see is Delilah. There's this pull, this magnetic force between us. It's irresistible, and I don't even think about resisting, nor do I want to. I grab her, pulling her onto my lap. Our lips collide, and the kiss is fierce, needy.

I can't get enough of her. My hands tangle in her hair, pulling her closer, deeper into the kiss. Her fingers dig into my shoulders, then slide down my chest, clutching at my shirt. It's been too long. I've missed this. I've missed her.

I break away just long enough to catch my breath, my forehead resting against hers.

"You have no idea how much I've missed you," I murmur, my voice rough with longing. "Every damn second I was away, all I could think about was this. You. Us." Delilah's eyes are dark with desire, her lips slightly swollen from our kiss.

"Nate," she breathes, and it's all the encouragement I need. My hands move to her hips, guiding her as she presses against me. Our lips meet again, and it's even more intense this time. I kiss her like a man starved, tasting, exploring. Her tongue tangles with mine, and I can feel the desperation in her touch, mirroring my own, her moans matching my groans. My hands slide under her skirt, gripping her thighs, feeling the smooth skin beneath my fingers. I've missed the way she feels, the way she fits against me.

"I hope you're wet for me, baby, because I'm fucking hard for you," I whisper in her ear, biting her earlobe as I glide my hand under her panties. Drenched. *Perfect.*

She pulls back just long enough to whisper, "I'm on the pill." *What?*

Her words hit me like a shot of adrenaline. I'm thrilled, not wasting a second. My fingers hook into her underwear, tearing them off in one swift motion. My belt is next, and I push down my boxers, the need for her overwhelming.

I slide inside her, bare, and the sensation is pure ecstasy. The feel of her is beyond anything I've ever experienced. We often hear about the so-called "golden pussy," and I've met my fair share of women, but this one is diamond. I need to buy her a diamond to go with her pussy. But I know it's not just the feel of her sex that brings me to my knees. It's *her*—her familiar, exquisite scent, her smile, her eyes. Damn, her eyes. It's her broken soul, her heart, and all of her. I'm overwhelmed by everything I feel right now.

As I'm deep inside her, I lean into her ear.

"Now I'm home," I murmur, the words quiet, charged with the longing I've carried since we've been apart. She doesn't answer, probably bewildered by my admission, but I let her be.

I grip her hips, guiding her movements.

"God, I missed you," I say, my voice husky. "Missed feeling you like this. Missed the way you fit me, how well you fit me."

Delilah's breath hitches, and she starts to move, matching my rhythm.

"You feel so good," I groan. "Better than I remembered. So tight, so perfect, always milking my cock the right way."

Her fingers dig into my shoulders, and she lets out a soft moan.

"Please don't stop," she begs, and it's all the encouragement I need.

I thrust harder, my hands roaming over her body, needing to feel every inch of her.

"You're mine, Delilah. Every part of you," I growl, my lips brushing against her neck. "I want you more than ever."

The limo glides through the city, but we're lost in each other. I whisper dirty promises in her ear, telling her how I plan to keep her up all night, how I'm going to make up for all the time we've lost. Her responses are breathy, urging me on, and it's a heady mix of desire and raw need.

We move together, the world outside completely forgotten. I'm home, right here, inside her, and nothing else matters.

I don't last for shit. Delilah comes on my dick, and this time, I can feel her pussy contracting all around my cock. I feel everything, I can't control it, I groan as I come hard inside her. I'm fucking spent, but then I step back to admire my work.

"You have no idea how much I've fantasized about seeing my cum dripping out of your pussy, babe. Fuuuuuck, that's so sexy," I say. "I've marked you," I add, grinning like a teenager. Delilah bursts out laughing.

We finally make it to the penthouse, and I have to admit I'm a little moved. The dogs run to me as if I were their favorite human, greeting me like I'm some sort of hero. The delicious scent of an appetizing dinner fills the air, and of course, my girl is next to me, never breaking contact because the need to touch, to connect, is so much greater.

We spend a quiet evening together, as we usually do. We eat at the table, enjoying the amazing lamb shank Delilah made. She's an incredible cook, and tonight's dinner doesn't disappoint. We pair the meal with a good bottle of wine from the cellar, a rich red that complements the flavors perfectly.

As we eat, we talk, sharing stories from our time apart. Delilah's laughter is infectious, and I find myself grinning at her animated retelling. She tells me about a funny incident at work, and I share a few amusing moments from my recent trip. The conversation flows easily, filled with warmth and joy.

After dinner, we decide to take the dogs for a walk near Central Park.

"I hope the dogs are happy," she says.

"Why wouldn't they be?"

"Well, I guess I just meant, you know, living in an apartment so high up, having to take an elevator to go out . . . I don't know, I guess I've always pictured dogs in a backyard. It's stupid. Let's forget about it," she says.

"That's not stupid at all," I reply, but we both drop the subject and move on.

The evening air is cool and refreshing, and the park is beautifully quiet at this hour. We stroll along the pathways, the dogs happily trotting beside us. The city lights twinkle in the distance, creating a serene backdrop for our walk.

As we walk, my thoughts turn to Jake. I've been worried about him, and I feel the need to warn Delilah. Jake can be dangerous in his own way, and she needs to be careful around him when they finally cross paths. I feel a protective instinct surge within me, determined to keep her safe from any harm. But as long as she trusts me, I know nothing can truly hurt her.

Finally, we end our evening in the comfort of our bedroom, lying in our bed. The lights bathe everything in a warm glow. Delilah snuggles close to me, her head resting on my chest. I stroke her hair, feeling a deep sense of contentment.

When I look at her, I can hardly believe my luck. Meeting Delilah feels like a once-in-a-lifetime chance, and I'm grateful every day. She's incredible—beautiful inside and out, with a sublime heart and a charm that captivates me completely.

"Nate?" she says, pulling me from my reverie.

"Yes?" I answer.

"Don't worry about Jake and me. I'm not scared."

"You have no reason to be. I won't let anything happen to you or to us. I just need you to trust me."

"I do," she whispers, raising her gaze to meet mine, and I can see her sincerity. "Besides," she continues, "I've met men way more dangerous than 'Jake Williams,'" she says with a laugh. "We'll be okay," she adds, but it doesn't sit well with me.

"Care to explain?" I ask, but then Delilah falls silent. She doesn't want to share, and I can tell she doesn't know how to find the words without hurting me. I know her too well.

"It's okay," I say, caressing her hair.

She exhales. "Sometimes I say things without thinking, and they just leave my mouth without control. But sometimes, there are things I want to say, but I can't find the words. I overthink, and my fears take over, and I remain silent. I hate it. I hate that part of me. I don't mean to tease you. I'm sorry," she says, sighing.

It's a trait I've noticed before, this internal battle she faces. The duality struggles she tries to handle. Delilah hates physical contact—or at least human touch—but at the same time, she has this great need for affection from me. She describes herself as cold and distant, someone with not just a dark heart but a black one. Yet Delilah is the most caring person I know. She always looks after me, making sure I'm okay, and her love for the dogs is something else entirely.

This need to speak without holding back and the simultaneous need to remain silent is one of her great battles. And here I am, playing my role, helping, supporting, and protecting her. Damn, I embrace this role in my life—the role *of* my life.

I kiss her softly to show her how much I appreciate her opening up a little more to me tonight.

We end the evening in the best way possible, a way only she and I understand. In our lasting embrace, our souls come closer, seeking the peace found in the depths of our bodies. These quiet moments, where time stands still, reveal a deeper connection. Our bodies, moving together, find comfort in each other's warmth.

Yes, tonight, once again, we make love.

CHAPTER 17
Delilah

I hear a knock on my door at the office, sharp and insistent. Ailly is busy with the marketing team, but I already know who that is.

"Come in," I say, my voice steady. *Let the show begin.*

The door swings open, revealing a man with steely eyes and a hard-set jaw.

"Delilah. I'm surprised to see you here," he says, his tone sharp.

"I'm not sure I understand why, Mr. Kingston," I reply, feigning innocence.

"Oh, I think you do. See, apparently, I donated five million dollars to The Voices of Women Shelter. We had an agreement!" he says, his voice laced with anger. *Good.*

"Wow, that's generous. You must be such a good man, Mr. Kingston. But I don't recall any agreement between the two of us. It's the first time I see you in person." I respond, keeping my voice calm but mocking.

"Stop fucking with me!" he shouts, his face contorting with rage. Little does he know, I've faced scarier people in my life.

"Oh, I'm sorry, sir, but I have no idea what you're talking about. Are you sure I'm the person you wanted to speak with?" I say, my performance deserving of an Oscar.

"I gave *you* the fucking money!" he yells, his fury fully unleashed.

"That's ridiculous. I have never seen you before now. Least of all received any money from you. I would have remembered; five million dollars is quite an amount," I say with a wink.

"Stop fucking with me!" he interrupts, cutting me off. I laugh, a calculated move that only enrages him more.

"Mr. Kingston, you just told me you've donated money to help women. Not all men are that generous. Do you have any idea how many women's lives you are going to save? Thanks to your money? Do you know how many women will finally break free from their abusers? Thanks to you? They'll escape the clutches of men who control their choices and their lives. Thanks to you, those men won't have power over them anymore. They'll finally breathe. All thanks to *you*, Mr. Kingston. I only wish I had that much money to help people too." I hold his gaze, unwavering, standing my ground.

He must know that living with Nathan fucking Williams has made me resilient. He doesn't respond. Instead, he turns on his heel and slams the door behind him. I smirk, satisfaction coursing through me. *Good job, Delilah.*

I know he won't have the balls to face Nate and tell him the truth about offering to pay me to disappear. It's disappointing, especially coming from him. I can't believe this man is Nate's closest friend, trusted confidant, and right hand in business. It feels like a huge betrayal.

Since Nate returned from his business trip to L.A. last week, his schedule has been relentless. He's been tied up with managing Jake's issues, which seem never-ending, and helping me prepare for my SATs, which are just around the corner. Our days are a blur of meetings, study sessions, and endless to-do lists. Despite the chaos, we always find moments for each other and the dogs. No matter how busy we get, we make time for a quick coffee break or a late-night chat. So, I haven't had much time to worry about the James situation.

Ailly enters the office in a much gentler manner than James.

"Hey, go grab your purse. We're having lunch with the team and the managers outside. We'll discuss the next steps for the launch," she says in that wonderful Southern accent of hers. But, shit, I haven't been paid yet. I have zero money. Funny enough, I live in a penthouse, fucking with a billionaire, and have zero cents in my bank account.

"Um, do I have to go?" I ask, unsure.

"Yeah, I know you have trouble with human relations, but this one you'll have to deal with. I'll be with you, don't worry," she says. She's right, and I'm surprised she already knows that about me. Still, shit!

"Um, I need to go to the restroom real quick. I'll be back in five," I say, and she agrees. I run to the elevator and press for the ninetieth floor. I only have one way out.

I reach Nate's office, but I'm stopped by his PA, Chloe.

"Where do you think you're going?" she asks, looking disgusted at the sight of me.

"I need to see Nate for five minutes, okay?" I say, asserting myself.

"Nate? Since when are you on a first-name basis? You can't call him Nate! Mr. Williams is busy."

"Don't make me call him. You'll regret it," I warn her. She sighs, exasperated. *What a bitch.*

"Mr. Williams, Ms. Rose is here to see you, *unannounced.*"

"Send her in," he says. I flash her a grin. That's how it's done.

I walk in and see Nate. He's too damn handsome to resist, even though we had sex this morning. It always feels like it's never enough. I wrap my arms around his waist and look up at him.

"I'm sorry to bother you," I say, my voice sweet.

"Never apologize for it," he says, kissing me and putting his hands on my ass. He's possessive, and I love it.

"Listen, I need to ask you something embarrassing," I say. He looks at me and nods.

"Okay, I don't have a lot of time, but go ahead."

"Well, the team and managers invited me to lunch to discuss the project, and . . . I haven't been paid yet. I don't have any money in my bank account. I'm sorry to ask, but do you think I could borrow some money?"

"What the fuck?" he says, clearly upset. *Shit.*

"I know I've always said I wasn't interested in you for your money, and me asking now might seem confusing—"

"How come you have no money? Why am I just finding out about this now?"

"Well, I didn't need money before now, so there was no reason to mention it. But my paycheck will arrive in a day or two, and I'll pay you back—"

"I don't want you to pay me back, Delilah!" he says, now furious.

"Nate, please, they're waiting for me. I'm late. I swear we'll talk more later, okay?" I beg.

Nate pulls out his wallet and hands me a credit card.

"Keep it until I solve the problem. It's unlimited, so don't hold back. I'm really pissed, Delilah. The fact that my girl has no money while I have all the money in the world is unacceptable," he says.

"Thank you. I'm sorry. We'll talk about this tonight," I say, giving him a quick kiss.

I head to the door but turn back.

"By the way," I say, "your PA is a bitch." Then I'm out the door. I don't even glance at said bitch as I run to the elevator and head straight to the ground floor, where everyone is waiting for me.

I walk with the team to a nearby restaurant, a cozy little place called The Urban Frost on Fulton Street. I see Sophia and Ben, my security, following behind, but as professional as ever; no one notices them.

The restaurant has a modern vibe, with exposed brick walls and large windows letting in plenty of natural light. Potted plants are scattered around, giving it a welcoming atmosphere.

We settle at a long wooden table near the back, away from the bustling front. I sit next to Ailly, trying to look relaxed, but inside, I feel uneasy. I'm not used to being surrounded by so many people, and socializing has always been tough for me. But I know I need to make an effort, especially in a professional setting like this.

As we browse the menu, the conversation quickly turns to work. One of the managers, Matthew, brings up the upcoming project we're all working on.

"So, the new investment initiative is set to launch next month. We need to finalize the marketing strategy," he says, looking around the table.

Addison, the head of the marketing team, nods.

I chime in, trying to contribute despite my nerves. "We need to focus on our target demographics and make sure our message is clear. We're aiming to attract both individual and corporate investors. Ailly and I have started analyzing how a strong social media presence could really boost our visibility."

Everyone nods, and I feel a small wave of relief. Speaking up in these situations is hard, but important.

The discussion continues, with ideas bouncing around about ad campaigns, partnerships with financial influencers, and the importance of a user-friendly website.

As we eat, I try to stay focused on the conversation, but my mind drifts to how hard it is for me to be sociable. I pick at my salad, listening. The others talk so easily, laughing and joking between serious discussions. I envy their ability to connect so effortlessly.

Lunch goes on, and the plates gradually empty. I start to feel a bit more at ease, having managed to participate without completely retreating into my shell. The waiter brings the check, and there's a moment of fumbling as everyone reaches for their credit cards. I do the same, pulling out Nate's card and handing it to the waiter with the others.

I reflect on the lunch—it was hard, but I managed. I know I need to keep pushing myself to be more social, even if it feels uncomfortable. It's all part of growing in this business world.

The waiter processes the payments, and we continue chatting, the atmosphere lighter now that the meal's over. I feel a bit of accomplishment for making it through without too much discomfort. I have a long way to go, but each small step counts.

And then . . . the waiter starts handing back the credit cards, reading out the names. When he says "Nathan Williams," everyone stops and looks at him like he just said something shocking.

Fuck. Fuck. Fuck. Fuck. I didn't think this through.

"Uh, yeah, it's me," I say, and everyone at the table stares at me like I've just grown two heads. I take the card and shove it into my purse, praying no one says anything.

But of course . . .

"Why do you have the CEO's credit card?" Addison asks. I feel my cheeks flush as everyone literally stares at me.

"Um, I ran into him on my way down to the ground floor. He tried to make small talk, and I might've mentioned I was waiting for my paycheck because I was, um, a bit broke . . . financially. So he offered his card for me to pay my part of the lunch. I'm gonna pay him back." *Wow, that's some solid bullshit.*

"But that's so unlike him to help someone he doesn't know. That's out of character," she says.

Wrong, that's totally like him.

"Well, look at her, she's beautiful. It's no wonder," Hillary chimes in, and I can hear the jealousy in her voice.

"He told me to pay him back once I get my paycheck, so it has nothing to do with me being beautiful or him being mean to people," I say, trying to keep my voice steady.

I hear them mumbling, but I shut off again. *Fuck.* Nate is going to kill me.

We gather our things and stand up to leave.

When we get back to the office, Ailly and I settle at our desks, and she closes the door behind us.

"Why the fuck do you have Nathan Williams's credit card?" she whisper-yells.

"I told you, it's a coincidence. I ran into him when I came out of the bathroom, and then we ended up in the elevator together, and we just . . . talked."

"He hit on you?" she asks, suspicious.

"Nooooo!" I reply, too defensive. I hate lying to her, especially since I actually like her. But my relationship and Nate's reputation come first.

"Okay, okay. Let's get back to work before you leave for the day," she says. I pull out my phone and send Nate a text.

> **Delilah:** *You're going to kill me.*
> **Nate:** *I know.*

Oh fuck . . . the rumor's already out.

> **Delilah:** *How do you know???*
> **Nate:** *What are you talking about?*

That's confusing.

> **Delilah:** *What are YOU talking about?*

My phone rings, and "I Want To Fuck You" flashes on the screen. *Not the right time.*

I hit Decline. I can't talk to him with Ailly right here.

> **Nate:** *When I call, you answer!*
> **Delilah:** *I'm not alone! Ailly's here! I'll come up at 2 PM.*

I go back to work. Only half an hour left. Ailly doesn't press me about the credit card thing. She probably believes me because, seriously, why on earth would Nathan Williams have anything to do with me?

You're a joke, Delilah. He's too good for you. He's out of your league. He'll realize it soon enough.

"It's 2:30. I've kept you too long today. Go home, girl. We'll finish this tomorrow," Ailly says. Time flies when I bury myself in work. I've got a ton left to do, plus I have to deal with Nate before I leave.

"Hum, yeah, okay. I'll go. I have to study at home anyway."

"You're brave, Delilah. Working here is no joke, and you do it well. The fact that you're able to study in your spare time is incredible. Go do your homework, and I'll try to take care of the rest."

"No, I'm the one who's supposed to help you here, not the other way around," I say, winking at her.

"Yeah, well, let's help each other. That'll be better. Let's go out Friday night, have some fun, drink fine cocktails, and go dancing! What do you think?"

Oh . . . how do I say no? But I don't want to say no. I want to try. The whole point of not dying is trying to live. I want to become a normal girl. I want to go out and have some fun. I've never done this before. Determined to avoid repeating my reaction with Jenna from the last time we discussed such a sensitive topic, when my emotions and my past overwhelmed my reason, I decide to smile and say . . .

"Why not."

The voices in my head still urge me toward destructive actions, but as the days pass, I find myself growing stronger and more resilient. Saying I'm fully recovered would be a lie, but at least I'm trying.

"Friday night it is! We'll talk more about it later. Now, go home!" she says, and I leave the office with a huge smile on my face and bigger worries in my head. *I'll be okay.*

I head upstairs to Nate's office. I hate that I have to go through Chloe first, but I don't want people to be more suspicious than they already are.

"I'm here to see *Mr. Williams*," I say, emphasizing his name to keep it formal.

"*Nathan's* not available," she says, teasing me mischievously. *Ugh. I hate her.* I decide to ignore her and go straight to his office, opening the door without knocking.

But holy shit, I should have waited.

"Oh, hi—shit. I mean, sorry, I didn't know you were busy. Well, I knew you were because Miss Queen Bee-tch told me, but I didn't believe her—"

"Delilah, it's fine. You can come in; I was expecting you. This is James, you haven't met him yet," Nate says, gesturing toward Mr. Kingston. *Shit, shit, shit.*

"James, this is Delilah," he says, wrapping his arm around my waist and kissing the top of my head. This is sooo awkward. *So he didn't tell him.*

"Nice to meet you, Mr. Kingston," I say, smiling big because I want to make the best of it.

"Ms. Rose," he says curtly, but stays polite because Nate's right here.

"I know we're at the office, but you can call him James when it's just us," Nate says.

"Huh, James it is, then," I say, smiling even more, sensing that James is irritated but can't say anything. I love this. He's so embarrassed.

"So, what did you want to tell me?" Nate asks. I frown, not understanding what he means. "Earlier, you texted me thinking I wanted to kill you. I'm listening," he says.

Oh, right.

James sits down, a big smile on his face. Well, screw me, I'm fucked.

I tell Nate everything that happened at the restaurant during lunch and how his credit card came up. Now I'm the one embarrassed.

"Baby, that's fine. I'll deal with any rumors. I'm not mad," he says, all reassuring.

My Nate . . .

"Oh, and Ailly asked me to go out on Friday night. She mentioned cocktails and dancing. I said yes," I admit.

"You're ready for that?" he asks, glancing at James, making me feel uncomfortable talking in front of him.

"It's okay, babe. James is my best friend. He'd never judge you. I trust him," Nate says.

"Wouldn't he?" I tease, cutting James off before he can speak. "It's fine. We'll talk about it tonight. I'm heading home; I have to study, make dinner, and take care of the dogs, so I'd better go now."

James interrupts. "I absolutely need to see Nathan Williams with dogs for myself. This is so unlike you, and I need to make sure it's real."

"Fuck you," Nate says, affronted. "Well, you know what? Why don't you come over tonight and have dinner with us? Delilah is an amazing cook."

Fuck me.

"It's okay with you, babe?" he asks, all smiles. Shit. I want to say "fuck no," but I have no right. Nate has given me everything. Literally. So if he wants me to welcome his best friend into his home and cook for him, then I'll do it. I can't show my disgust.

"Sure, come. I'll make something good."

"That I don't doubt. I'll be there," James says, pleased. *Fucker.*

"Great!" Nate says, hugging me and planting a fat kiss on my lips. He slaps my ass, as usual, and then I'm out the door.

When I get home, I head straight to the kitchen, needing to do *something*. I yank open the pantry and grab the first things I see — olive oil, onions, garlic, canned tomatoes, potatoes. My hands move quickly, almost on their own, pulling out whatever I can find. The fridge yields more: ground lamb, eggplants, a block of feta. Moussaka.

I'll make moussaka. It's complicated. It'll be perfect.

He'll leave you. They all leave you.

I ignore the voice and lay everything out on the counter, arranging it as if I were lining up soldiers for battle. I pick up the knife and slice the eggplants into thin rounds, too fast, too uneven, but I don't care. I sprinkle salt on each piece with shaky hands, watching the grains scatter like tiny crystals. My chest tightens, but I force myself to keep going. Chop onions. Chop garlic. Focus on the rhythm—the steady *thunk-thunk-thunk*—anything but the whispers clawing at my mind.

James saw right through you. He knows you're trash. Nate will know it too.

The knife slips, nicking my finger. I hiss, staring at the tiny bead of blood. It doesn't matter. I grab a paper towel and wrap it tight, then toss the onions and garlic into a hot skillet, letting the sizzle drown out everything else. The smell hits me—sharp, comforting, familiar. I throw in the lamb, breaking it apart with a spoon, watching the pink meat turn brown. The kitchen fills with sound and scent, layers of noise and smells that I desperately pile on, hoping it'll be enough to drown them out.

You should have jumped.

No! Stop! I stir harder, almost attacking the pan as if I could push the voices out through sheer force. As the sauce thickens, I turn to the potatoes, slicing them too thin, my hands shaking. I boil them, watching the water bubble up, steam clouding my face.

Layer the dish. Focus. Potatoes, eggplant, sauce. Potatoes, eggplant, sauce. Keep going. I smooth the béchamel over the top, my knuckles white around the spoon. Feta crumbles between my fingers, scattering over the creamy surface. Done. Into the oven it goes.

But it's not enough. It's never enough.

I whip around and grab for the cheesecake ingredients, hands moving on their own. Cream cheese, sugar, eggs—everything blends together into a smooth batter as I mix furiously. I can't stop. Not yet. I pour it over the crust, slide it into the oven beside the moussaka. Then I start the berry sauce—raspberries, strawberries, blackberries—mashing them down, watching the colors bleed together like bruises. The voices buzz louder, my head spins.

But I don't stop. I can't. I strain the sauce, watching the seeds get caught in the mesh, bits of pulp clinging desperately, trying to break free.

You can't run from who you are.

But I can try. The kitchen is warm, filled with the scents of lamb, cheese, and sweet berries. I'm trembling, my body tired, but I keep moving. Anything to hold the darkness back for just a little longer.

With both the moussaka and cheesecake in the oven, I take a deep breath, feeling a sense of accomplishment. Ignoring the voices in my head is tough, but I won't let them win. I settle at the kitchen island, books and notes spread out before me. The SATs are less than a week away, but as I review my material, I feel confident.

The comforting smells of dinner and dessert baking give me a sense of calm and readiness, knowing I've prepared not just a delicious meal but also myself for the challenges ahead. I feel ready.

I take some time to play with Cowboy and Sheriff, my babies, the light of my life. The penthouse is so big that I can throw balls and they'll still run a long way to catch them. I snuggle them, brush them, and talk sweetly to them. I realize the voices in my head—my demons—haven't shown up in a while. *Cool.*

The door opens, and I see Nate come in first. I don't even think; I'm just so happy to see him that I jump on him like I always do. He hugs me tight and kisses me like we haven't seen each other in weeks. I feel weak in the knees when he puts me down, so I grab his tie and pull him in for one more kiss. I do this every day, at least five times a day whenever I can. I love it.

Then James comes into view. He looks a bit shy but hides it well. Finally, Sheriff and Cowboy run toward us, jumping on Nate.

"Hey, buddy! Hey, you!" Nate greets them warmly.

James steps inside, looking slightly tense but managing a smile. "Thanks for inviting me. The place smells incredible."

"Thanks, James," I say, giving him a polite smile. "I hope you're ready for some homemade moussaka and cheesecake."

I take the wine from Nate.

"Perfect timing. This will go great with dinner. Let's go," I say.

We move to the living room, where Nate pours the wine. I sit close to him, leaning into him, and he wraps an arm around my shoulders. James sits opposite us, his eyes darting around, taking in the comfortable setting.

"So, babe," Nate starts, "how's the SAT prep going?"

"It's going well. I feel pretty ready, just a bit nervous," I admit.

"You'll do great." Nate kisses my temple. "You've been working so hard. No matter the results, I'm proud of you, baby," he says, his words cutting right through my broken heart. I lean in and give him a soft kiss, thanking him.

James clears his throat.

"I hope you do well on your test, Delilah. Nate mentioned how dedicated you are," he says. *Hypocrite.*

I nod, smiling.

"I'm trying my best. It's been a lot of late nights and coffee," I say, keeping my smile. *Douche.*

Soon the conversation shifts to the dogs. Sheriff jumps onto the couch, nuzzling against my leg.

"So, it's true—you adopted Cowboy and Sheriff," James says, looking at the dogs and making jokes about their names. *Jackass.* It pisses me off that he seems like a nice person.

"Yes, they've brought so much joy," I say, scratching Sheriff behind the ears.

"Cowboy might be missing an eye, but he's got the biggest heart. And Sheriff, well, he's the mischievous one," Nate says, making me laugh. "Sheriff loves to chew on anything he can find. We're constantly trying to keep up with him."

The timer dings in the kitchen, signaling that dinner is ready. I get up to check on the moussaka, feeling James's eyes on me. I can sense his discomfort, and it gives me a small, private satisfaction.

"Dinner's ready," I announce, bringing the steaming dish to the table. Nate helps with the salad.

We sit down, and I serve generous portions of moussaka.

"Dig in, James. Delilah really outdoes herself back there."

James takes a bite, closing his eyes for a moment.

"This is amazing, Delilah. Honestly," he says.

"Thank you, James. I'm glad you like it," I say sweetly, enjoying his awkwardness.

We talk about work, with Nate mentioning some recent projects at Williams Holdings. I chime in occasionally, and it's clear how much Nate values my input. James seems to relax a bit, probably realizing how close Nate and I are, always a hand on each other.

As the evening goes on, James tries to throw a few subtle digs at me—comments about my lack of a traditional background—but I handle them with grace, turning his comments into jokes. Nate either doesn't notice or brushes them off, thinking James is just being playful.

We move on to dessert, and the cheesecake with red berry coulis is a hit. Nate praises my baking skills, and even James seems genuinely impressed.

"Delilah, this cheesecake is divine. You really have a talent for this. I think I'll take some home," James says, seeming more at ease.

"Thank you. Cooking is therapeutic for me," I reply, watching him closely.

By the end of the night, there's a strange sense of camaraderie. James seems to have dropped his guard a little, maybe realizing that Nate is truly happy with me.

Impossible. He can't be. You're a burden.

But I can't forget what he tried to do. Despite the laughs and the seemingly pleasant evening, I still dislike him.

As James leaves, Nate walks him to the door. "Thanks for coming, James. It was a great night."

"Yes, thanks for having me," James replies. "Delilah, you were a wonderful host. I guess I'll see you at the office."

"Thank you. Have a good night," I say, closing the door behind him.

Nate pulls me into a hug.

"You were amazing tonight. I'm so lucky to have you. Thanks for being great with him."

I smile, hugging him back.

"I'm the lucky one."

As we clean up the kitchen, I can't shake the feeling of satisfaction. I played James at his own game, and tonight, I won. But the battle isn't over, and I'll stay vigilant.

~

Today is Friday. We went to the office this morning, and when I got to Nate's office to say goodbye, he decided he'd work from home and came back with me. I tried to focus on my studies, but I couldn't shake my anxiety. Tonight, I'm supposed to go out with Ailly and have fun. I'm stressed, scared, and feel like I can't even breathe.

People still scare me. Even though working at Williams is good practice for mingling with others, I still feel uncomfortable. I feel like I can't do it, but I have to try.

I don't want to stress Nate with my doubts and fears, so I don't bother him and let him work. I don't even know what to wear. What if she asks questions? What if I'm too weird, and she ends the night early?

My phone rings, and Ailly's name pops up.

"Hey?" I say, questioningly, since it's still early.

"Hey, I just left a meeting with a client outside of the office. I won't have time to go back to my place. Give me your address so I can catch up with you, and we can get ready together," she says.

Holy fuck!

"Um, okay, why not. Just give me a minute, and I'll text it to you," I manage to say.

She hangs up, and I run to Nate's office. I open the door, and he's on the phone. *Shit.*

He puts his phone aside and looks at me.

"What's wrong, baby?" he asks.

"You're obviously busy—"

"You're more important. What's wrong?" Ugh, he already knows me so well.

"Ailly told me she wanted to come over to get ready together, and I didn't know how to say no, so I kind of didn't . . . and now I don't know what to do," I mumble.

"If you want her to come here, I'm fine with it. This is your home too, it's up to you."

"But then she'll know about us!" I say, feeling the weight of the situation.

"So what? We won't hide forever."

"I guess not . . ." I exhale, trying to let go of my anxiety.

"Call the doorman to let him know and inform Anders too," he says, kissing my temple. He has to get back to his call, so I don't hold him up any longer.

I text Ailly my address, and she immediately replies, "*Park Avenue???*" I don't respond, unsure how to explain it.

Later, Fran, the housekeeper, informs me that Ailly is on her way up. I go to Nate and tell him to give me two minutes with her before he comes in, and he agrees. The door opens, and Ailly steps inside. To say she's shocked is an understatement.

"A penthouse? You live in a penthouse? On Park Avenue?"

"Yes, but that's not all. I live with someone, too. I couldn't say it before, but you can't tell anyone. I'm sorry I lied to you, but I had to."

"Okayyy . . ." she says, clearly puzzled. And then Nate joins us in the foyer. Her mouth drops open when she sees him.

"Mr. Williams," she says, shocked, as Nate offers his hand.

"Please, call me Nate. Outside the office, as Delilah's friend, you can call me Nate."

"I'm not sure I'll be able to, but I'll try," she says, then looks at me. "You sure know how to keep a secret."

"I'm sorry," I say, feeling a bit guilty. Nate pulls me close and kisses the top of my head, reassuring me.

"Ailly, can I offer you something to drink?" Nate asks.

"I'm sure some wine will help me feel better," she says, laughing, putting my heart at ease a little.

We head to the kitchen, and Nate goes to the cellar to pick out what I assume is a good bottle of wine.

"Now I get the credit card thing! Did you two meet at the office?" she asks, chuckling.

"No, we met two months ago, and he suggested I come work at his company. I accepted the challenge while I study," I reply. Nate returns, as usual, touching me and kissing me without caring who's around.

"I think I need some time to adjust. I can't believe you two are in a relationship," she says.

"Hum, no," I correct. "We're not in a relationship."

"We *are* in a relationship," Nate insists while pouring the white wine.

"We're not—"

"Go convince someone else," he says, and I know this isn't a battle I'll win. He's too strong.

"Anyway," I say, "we do live together, and no one knows. I don't want people talking about me. I prefer to remain in the dark."

"Baby, I shine too bright. I'll illuminate your beautiful face someday, you know?" he says, caressing my ass. I push his hand away.

"Oh, come on!" I say, half-irritated and half-amused.

We chat about our evening plans. Nate wants to know what we'll be doing and how closely security will follow us. My phone rings, and I see Sam's name on the screen.

"Excuse me, I have to take this," I say, showing Nate the caller ID before I pick up. "Hello?"

"Hey, *hermosa*, I'm depressed. I need a drink at your fancy place. I'm on my way. I'll be there in five. Tell your doorman so I can have no obstacles between me and your boyfriend's wine cellar," he says, making me laugh.

"Nate is not my boyfriend, and I have a friend from work over. We're going out tonight," I say, trying to dissuade him.

"Perfect! That's all I need—new faces, you, and your wine. I mean, your boyfriend's—"

"He's not my—"

"Okay, see ya in five," he says, cutting me off before hanging up. *What the fuck?*

I go back to the kitchen, where Nate and Ailly are deep in conversation about work. I interrupt and tell Ailly that Sam is on his way up, giving her a brief introduction, without too many details. She seems fine with the idea, and that brings me a lot of relief. I could use some familiar faces tonight. Sam is perfect.

Five minutes later, he arrives in the foyer. He looks a bit down, but when he sees Nate, his mood brightens, and he smiles fondly at him. We all laugh at the sight.

"*Dios mío*, Nate. How do you look more gorgeous every time I see you?" Sam says, only half joking. Nate laughs—nothing embarrasses this man, I swear.

"Delilah keeps me in shape," Nate says with a wink.

"Oh my God, Nate!" I shout, slapping his chest. He laughs harder, grabs my hand, and pulls me close, biting my neck playfully. He's being possessive, enjoying himself. I love that about him.

Nate offers Sam a glass of white wine, and I swear I can see the butterflies in Sam's belly. We chat to introduce everyone. The scene feels surreal to me. I can sense the anxiety, doubts, and fears trying to creep in, but I shut them off. For now, it seems to work.

Sam and Ailly hit it off. They share a similar sense of humor, and I enjoy how their accents sound together—Sam's slight Venezuelan accent, Ailly's strong Southern one. They also bond over their shared passion for clothes. Both are ambitious, having risen from nothing to reach the top. They're still on their way. Nate seems at ease, laughing with them, welcoming them, and getting friendly. It warms my heart to see him like this.

I melt at the sight of him.

"Why don't you call Jenna?" Nate suggests.

"Oh, I didn't think about that. I guess I should. Would you guys be okay with that?" I ask.

Sam says, "I think it's about time I meet this other friend of yours. I'm jealous you have someone else." He pretends to be hurt, making me laugh.

"It's more than okay with me. I love meeting new people," Ailly says.

I text Jenna to see if she's game, and within two minutes, she replies with "Hell yeah."

"Jenna's on her way. I should probably get ready," I say, feeling a wave of anxiety.

I'm glad the people I like are here, but part of me still struggles with it.

"We'll get ready together," Ailly says, and we head upstairs.

Nate grabs my hand and pulls me closer.

"Are you okay, baby?" he asks, his voice low. I exhale, feeling the anxiety build.

"I'm trying. I think this is a step I should take. I want to do this, but I'm shit-scared, Nate," I admit, looking down at my feet, embarrassed. Nate gently lifts my chin with his fingers, making me meet his gaze. I could die for those eyes. His deep, icy blue eyes . . .

"It'll be fine. Don't underestimate your strength. Stand your ground. There's nothing you can't do. And when you don't believe in yourself, remember that I believe in you. And I'm not just anyone," he says, winking at me.

"You're Nathan fucking Williams," I tease.

"That I am," he says, all too proud. I catch the back of his neck and pull him into a deep, heavenly kiss.

"Oh my goood, look at the size of this bed!" we hear the others shouting from upstairs. They're clearly giving themselves a tour of the place. Nate and I laugh together, and then I head upstairs to join them while Nate returns to his home office.

While we're getting ready, Jenna joins us in the dressing room. We all pick outfits from my wardrobe, except Sam, who can't find anything, since Nate's clothes are way too big for him. We get dressed, do our hair, and put on a bit of makeup.

"The man is so in love with you, Delilah," Ailly says.

Hum, no, he's not. He can't be.

"No, he's not. We have great chemistry, sure, but it's not like that between us," I say. Sam chimes in. "Woman, we've seen how he looks at you. There's no mistaking that."

"Guys, please, don't push it. We have an agreement; it's temporary. Nate and I don't stand a chance. He'll realize it soon enough," I say, my voice weakening.

He's too good for you. You'll end up alone.

"Let's drop it," Jenna says. "For now. I found this new bar near Times Square—it's a karaoke bar! What do you think?"

"Did you guys know that Delilah can sing her heart out?" Sam says, grinning.

"Well, that's settled. We're going there!" Ailly decides.

"I've got food in the fridge, if you want to eat before we go," I offer.

We head back to the kitchen, where I prepare something quick. Everyone is chatting, and the mood is light and fun. Even Nate, who joined us about fifteen minutes ago, is getting along with everyone. After we finish eating, I excuse myself to use the restroom.

When I step out, I stop and watch Sam, Jenna, Ailly, and Nate, all laughing together at some joke. My heart stops.

I can't do this. I'm not a normal girl. I don't do friendship. I don't do relationships. This is too dangerous for me—for my heart. I'm too broken, too shattered. I can't do this.

I want to shut down, go back to my dark place. I don't belong here. I don't deserve happiness. What the fuck is happening to me?

My heart races, my blood pumping fast. *I need Nate.*

I walk straight over to him and grab his arm.

"Excuse me, I just need to talk to Nate for a minute," I say to the group. No one seems to notice my discomfort. I lead Nate to the pantry behind the kitchen, pulling him inside with me.

"What the fuck?" he says, confused.

"I don't know if I can do this . . ." I whisper.

"Baby, if you don't want to go, I can tell them to leave. It's your call. But I think it'll be good for you."

"I'm not . . . normal," I say, feeling my heart squeeze with pain.

"No one is, baby," he says, caressing my cheeks.

"I need you," I finally admit.

"I'm right here, baby. I'll always be," he says, but I don't let him finish. I unfasten his belt. I need the connection, the contact. Only he knows how to calm me down, how to make me forget. He doesn't miss a beat as he pulls my black leather skirt up.

"I'm right here, baby," he whispers before kissing me. I pull his pants and boxers down, jump up, and wrap my legs around his waist.

"I need you, Nate," I pant, already burning with desire. He slides into me in one hard thrust. The feel of him inside is beyond ecstatic. I moan into his mouth, and Nate grins, clearly enjoying every second. He can't stop smiling as he fucks me with fervor.

"Harder, baby, please. Harder," I beg. I need it rough. I need the intensity, the brutality of the sex.

"Are you sure? Once I start breaking this delicious pussy, I'm not sure I can stop," he growls.

"Please, baby, I need it," I plead, and he thrusts hard—so hard, and it feels . . . *amazing*.

"What my girl wants, my girl gets," he says, and he fucks me like he's never fucked me before. My back and head knock against the wall, but I need more.

"Please don't stop," I beg, panting heavily. It's perfect—exactly what I need.

"I'll never stop, baby," he groans, thrusting harder, deeper. "I'll never stop fucking you, Delilah."

It's too good. I can feel the wave building inside me, that familiar pleasure swelling.

"Nate," I breathe. "I'm gonna—ah!" I moan, already on the edge.

"I know. I'm there too," he pants, biting my nipples harder. *It's perfect.*

I don't even need his hand on my clit. The orgasm crashes over me, spreading through every nerve in my body. I scream, not realizing it until Nate covers my mouth with his hand. My eyes roll back as I lose myself in the overwhelming pleasure. Nate's cock pulses inside me, and I feel his release—hot, deep. He groans into my mouth, and I kiss him hard, almost with teeth. It's violent, intense, abrupt . . . and perfect.

I open my eyes and see the scratches on his shoulders. I didn't realize I'd hurt him.

"Did I hurt you, baby?" I ask, almost panicking.

"In the very, *very* best way, angel. That was amazing. I'm dead," he says, and we both laugh.

"Thank you. I needed that," I say, climbing down from his waist and grabbing a cloth to wipe my inner thighs as his cum leaks out. Nate watches me, smirking with satisfaction. He grabs my face with both hands.

"Whenever, wherever, baby. You need me, you call me," he says, locking eyes with me. I nod, too overwhelmed to speak. I fix my clothes, and we step out of the pantry.

I feel so much better, ready. I can do this. I can go out and have fun. I'm Delilah fucking Rose, and there's nothing I can't do.

We return to Sam, Jenna, and Ailly, who are completely unaware of what just happened.

"Tyler will take care of your rides in the limo," Nate says, and everyone is excited by the idea.

"Thank you," I mouth to him, and he winks at me. I've never seen a more beautiful human being in my entire life.

What a man. Damn.

CHAPTER 18

Nate

Delilah left about an hour ago, and I already fucking miss her. But I know she needs this time for herself. It's still hard for her to go out there and face the world. Yet she goes anyway, and I'm amazed by the resilience and strength that pulses within her.

I'm extremely happy, satisfied, content, proud, and empowered to know she finds her strength in me. I take some time to reflect on the evolution of our relationship and the dynamics in our exchanges.

Delilah, like the most beautiful flower, is flourishing, blossoming. At first, she was a branch with thorns, and whoever dared to touch her would hurt themselves. The thorns are getting smaller every day, the bud of the flower is starting to show, and you can almost smell the floral scent all around. Sometimes, she needs water; sometimes, she needs sun. I like to think she relies on me for that. I realize how much she needs stability, a strong routine so she doesn't get lost.

Often, when I come home or just step out of the bathroom at night, I take some time to observe her—how she tidies, how she cleans, how she cooks, how she organizes her notes for her job or her study. She's so goddamn beautiful, and I see how much she needs the routine. She doesn't like the unexpected, and I realize a little more every day why.

When she told me about her past, how she came into this world and how she lived the first ten years of her life, my heart broke for her. My whole being ached for her. I still can't comprehend why and how people act this way. She lived in filth, surrounded by garbage, and that's why, I think, she can't stand any mess around her. Everything has to be clean.

She doesn't believe people are naturally nice, because that's not how she was introduced to the world. I'm going to avenge her. The second I see she's healed from the past, I'll avenge her. But something tells me there's a lot more to her story, something darker, even evil.

Delilah opens up little by little, step by step, letting me in, but she still keeps her guard up. Her shield is still there, and she doesn't trust me fully.

Earlier tonight, I went upstairs to make sure everything was fine for everyone. I heard my name in a conversation, and I obviously eavesdropped a bit. Delilah said that I couldn't love her and that our relationship wasn't about romance, that I'll realize she's not good enough for me. I hated every word. I was hurt by the way she saw me—us. But maybe that was her way to shut people out, or maybe she felt uncomfortable talking about all this. Maybe she was trying to protect her heart from disappointment.

It's my fucking mission to make her believe she's wrong about me, and about us.

I hear my phone ring and see "Dirty Secretary Fantasy Coming True" on the screen.

I love that game.

"Hey, babe," I answer.

"Hey, sorry to bother you. I just . . . I needed to hear your voice. I'm sorry," she says, and I don't hear any noise behind her.

"Where are you?" I ask.

"In the bathroom. I needed to calm down. It's . . . a lot. I'm trying," she confesses.

"I'm here. Talk to me, baby, you'll be okay." I just love it when she calls and needs me.

"Nothing happened. Everyone's having fun, and I want to be part of their world. They all think I am, but sometimes I look around and I think I'm a farce. I'm a fraud. None of this is me, like I don't deserve any of it. I don't know . . . it's hard to explain."

"Those voices in your head, baby—you gotta find a strategy to shut them up. You *are* part of this world. You're the biggest part of *my* world. You belong here. You deserve happiness, even if you don't believe in it. Would you feel better if I come?"

"You wouldn't mind? I know you have a lot of work to do. I don't want to burden you . . ."

"You're more important. I'm on my way."

I can hear the relief in her voice. "Okay. Thank you, baby. Thank you so much."

"I know ways for you to thank me," I tease her.

"Hurry, then," she says, and hangs up.

What a woman. What a goddess. Just hearing her voice, I'm fucking hard for her.

Earlier, when she grabbed me and dragged me into the pantry because she needed my dick, I felt like Superman—no one could beat me, I was invincible. The urgency in her eyes, the way her hands marked my skin, it all ignited a fire within me. She needed it rough.

We've had rough sex before, but I've never gone harder than I did before Delilah. She's a paradox of fragility and strength, and I know Delilah finds solace in sex, but I think if we do it my way— harder, rawer—she'll find not just solace, but true peace. It's like she's shedding the weight of the world with every thrust, finding a moment of escape in the intensity of our union. And fuck, so do I.

I've done plenty of things with Delilah, pushing boundaries and exploring desires. Now I want to dig deeper into this. I want to see how far she's willing to go, to explore the depths of her sub-mission and my dominance. She'll love it, I know. There's a spark in her eyes when I push her limits, a flicker of something primal and free. I wanted to go slow because I was scared she might leave me. But now? Now I think we're on the same wavelength.

I text Delilah to tell her I'm going to be a bit late. She says it's fine, she'll wait for me. I call James to join me at the bar where Delilah is with her friends. He's quick to agree, always up for a night out.

He suggests we ask Luke, one of our friends who owns a tech company, to come along. Luke's a good guy, a bit of a wild card, and I know he'll add an interesting dynamic to the evening. We meet at my place, since they both live nearby, and we have a little chat to fill Luke in about who Delilah is and what she means to me.

As we sit in my living room, James lights a cigar, the rich aroma filling the air as we talk. James and Luke are my closest friends. We share everything, even our most embarrassing stories. Naturally, I mention Delilah, especially since we're about to meet her. I make sure they understand who she is, what she is to me, how we met, and why she's living with me. But I don't delve into the details of Delilah's private life, her past, or her struggles. That's her story to tell.

James nods but doesn't respond. He's seen me with Delilah. He knows how I feel about her. Luke listens intently, his curiosity piqued.

"I'm falling for her," I say, leaning back in my chair.

"She's incredible—funny, caring, and so fucking sexy. There's a fire in her I've never seen in anyone else."

James takes a drag of his cigar and exhales slowly.

"She has fire, alright."

"Exactly."

Luke looks at me intently.

"I'm sorry to ask this, but does that mean you and Charlotte are over?" Every time I hear her name, my heart tightens. It hurts.

"Charlotte and I broke up when she left. We promised to reunite when she comes back, but we both knew there was a risk of meeting someone else. I didn't tell Delilah about Charlotte because she'd leave me, and I can't bear the thought. I haven't told Charlotte either because she'd rush back home, and I need more time to explore what I have with Delilah before I decide where my heart truly lies.

"I still love Charlotte. Deeply. But Delilah . . . it's like she's shaken up my world, turned it upside down, and made me open

my eyes and feel . . . everything. She makes me question everything I've ever known. I've never felt more alive. And the sex . . .
fuck, it's incredible. I'm lost, guys. Completely lost," I confess,
burying my face in my hands.

"Looks like you're fucked," Luke says emphatically. I simply
nod in response.

We talk some more, and then I feel it's time to go see my girl.
Since Tyler is at Delilah's service tonight, and because there's
a good chance I might end up drunk at some point, we go with
James's private driver. We leave to join my girl, anticipation buzzing through my veins. The city lights blur past as we make our
way to the bar, the hum of the car's engine a background to our
conversation.

When we arrive, the bar is alive with energy. I spot Delilah immediately—surrounded by her friends, laughing—and I feel relieved. She looks stunning in her high-waisted black leather
miniskirt and that black tank top that's way too revealing. As
we approach, she sees me, and her eyes light up, her smile radiating across the room. She abandons her friends and runs to me.
My heart skips a beat at the sight of her, at the way she needs me.
Baby . . .

When she reaches me, she jumps on me, legs wrapped around
my waist, arms tight around my neck. I breathe her in, needing her
more.

"Finally," she whispers, and I can smell the alcohol on her.

"I'm here, baby," I say, giving her a deep kiss, tasting her drink.
I introduce her to Luke and point out James. They don't shake
hands because Delilah doesn't like to be touched by people she
doesn't know. Then she turns to James.

"Is he like you?" she asks, and I'm confused.

"No," James says with a laugh. "I'm worse."

"What are you talking about?" I ask, just as Sam calls for us, his
face lighting up when he sees me. It makes me laugh as we go to
join them at their table, and I place Delilah on my lap.

"Mr. Williams, did you know Delilah is a singer?" Ailly asks.

"You can call me Nate when we're not at the office, Ailly, don't worry. And yes, I knew," I say, turning my gaze to my beautiful girl.

"Did you sing, babe?" I ask, and she nods with a smile. She loves to sing, and I love watching her do it.

We all order drinks. I ask Delilah quietly if she's sure about having another one. She tells me she just needs to loosen up a little more, and since I'm here, she feels at ease. I agree with her, and the waiter takes our orders.

"So, are you guys ready to sing? We're next!" Sam says.

"You're all going to sing together?" James asks.

"Hell yeah," Jenna says, and I see a flicker of desire in James's eyes when he looks at her. *No way.*

"What are you going to sing, baby?" I ask, curious.

"It's a surprise," Delilah says, and kisses me with her tongue. I'm so fucking hard for her, it's almost embarrassing.

Some guy takes the mic and calls for Delilah, Sam, Jenna, and Ailly to come up to the stage. I slap Delilah's ass—which, honestly, is mine—and then they're on.

The first note of the song starts, and I immediately recognize it from *Moulin Rouge:* "Lady Marmalade." *Fuck me balls deep.*

The lights dim, and I watch as Delilah steps onto the stage with Sam, Jenna, and Ailly. My heart skips a beat. Delilah looks stunning, her presence instantly commanding the room. I lean forward, my eyes fixed on her.

The music starts, and Delilah takes Christina Aguilera's part. Her voice is powerful, beautiful, hitting every note perfectly. She's not just singing; she's performing. She moves in a seductive yet classy way, her hips swaying, her hands caressing the microphone stand. Her eyes are half-closed, lost in the music, and it drives me fucking wild.

She dances with a confidence that's both arousing and mesmerizing, every move deliberate and sensual. The way she flicks her hair, the subtle roll of her shoulders, the slight arch of her back—it all fucking excites me. I'm harder than I've ever been. A surge of heat rushes through me, a primal response to her allure. My body reacts instinctively, a mix of desire and possessiveness stirring within me.

I glance around and notice the men in the bar staring at her. Their eyes are hungry, full of admiration and lust. A surge of jealousy hits me.

"SHE'S MINE!" I shout to every fucker around. I glare at them, my jaw tightening. *I don't like it.* She's mine, and I hate the way they look at her. They have no right to fucking fantasize about her. She'll end up in *my* bed and my bed *only.*

James and Luke are watching the performance too, but James seems particularly entranced by Jenna. He hasn't taken his eyes off her since she stepped on stage. Jenna has this playful energy, and it's clear James is already under her spell, even though they've just met. Luke notices this and nudges me, smirking. I just shake my head, focusing again on Delilah.

The song reaches its climax, and Delilah's voice soars. Everyone in the bar is mesmerized, completely taken by her performance. The final note hangs in the air, and for a moment, there's complete silence. Then the room erupts. People are screaming, shouting, clapping. They loved the show, but it's Delilah who truly had the spotlight.

She transcended the typical karaoke performance. She was out of their league.

"That's my girl!" I shout, clapping my hands, cheering for her at the top of my lungs.

I feel a swell of pride. She's amazing, and everyone knows it. As she steps off the stage, our eyes meet. I smile, trying to convey everything I feel—admiration, desire, possessiveness. She smiles back, and it's like the whole world fades away for a moment. I stand up, ready to go to her, still feeling the electric charge from her performance.

The night is just beginning, and I know one thing for sure: Delilah has turned this ordinary evening into something unforgettable.

She runs to me and jumps on me again, and I get a good hold on her ass. I hope every fucker in the room sees she's mine.

"You're fucking amazing, baby. You are fucking incredible. I'm so fucking proud of you," I say into her neck, and I feel her relax at my words. She gets back on her feet, her arms around my waist, raising her lips to mine, and we kiss deeply. *That's my girl.*

We get back to our table, and the conversation flows easily. The funny part is James trying to talk to Jenna and Jenna being completely indifferent. She looks almost bored when he tries it. I laugh hard, remembering that's exactly how Delilah treated me the first time we met. And now? Look at us—inseparable. I laugh again, happy with how far we've come. *What a journey.*

Delilah looks better now, even fine. She talks, she laughs, but she never gets off my lap. Not that I'd let her anyway.

"You look better, *hermosa,* now that your man's here," Sam says.

"He's not my man," Delilah answers.

"I *am* her man." I nod, silently contradicting her by closing my eyes and grinning like a teenager. Delilah turns around to face me.

"You're not—"

"Go convince someone else." I cut her off, playfully. We all laugh and get back to having fun. Which we do.

After some time, the girls stand up to go to the restroom, and Luke uses the opportunity to address me directly, discreetly.

"I've never seen you like this. *Ever,*" he says.

"Like what?" I ask, not understanding.

"This close to someone. You guys can't keep your hands off each other. You're like . . . smiling all the time, without a care in the world. Usually, you're . . . distant. Cold, even. But now? I don't even recognize you."

"You make it sound like a bad thing," I say, bemused.

"It's not. It's good to see you happy. I don't even recall you being this close with—"

"Don't," I reply, widening my eyes. I know he was about to say "Charlotte," but Sam is still here. I don't need anyone revealing my secret to Delilah.

"Looks like your girl is being courted," James says, and that draws my immediate attention. I look around and see a man—more like a fucker—hitting on Delilah. She steps back—*that's my girl*—but she's still listening to him.

Two seconds later, I step between them. I don't even need to speak. I just glare at him, and he steps back. *Good boy.*

"Oh, you're Nathan Williams, right?" he asks, but I don't answer. I feel Delilah's hand on my arm.

"Babe, relax. The guy works in the music industry. He just asked if I had representation or something," she explains.

"I'm David Vence. I work with SoundEskape Production. Delilah has an incredible talent, and I'd love to work with her," the fucker says.

"Are you on top of the business? Is your label the number one in the country?"

"Um, no, but—"

"Then no," I reply. I can feel Delilah rolling her eyes without even looking at her.

"Maybe Delilah would like to speak for herself," he dares to say. I close the distance, towering over him with my size. I don't say a word, and he breaks eye contact first. *Coward.*

"Babe," I ask without turning my head, "do you want to work in the music industry?"

"Hard no," she answers, as if I didn't already know what my girl wants.

"Then I guess this means good night," I say, my harsh tone fully intended. The guy takes a card out of his inside pocket and hands it to Delilah. She looks at it and then takes it—hopefully out of respect.

"If you ever think about becoming a singer, I'd be happy to work with you. It'll be my mission to help you conquer the world with your voice," he says before leaving.

I turn to face Delilah, expecting an explanation.

"What? I didn't do anything!" she says, raising her hands defensively.

"Why did you take his card?"

"What if someday I wake up and decide I want to sing for a living?" she retorts, placing her hands on her hips.

"Then I'll introduce you to the best agent and the top label in the industry. Not some fucker," I respond.

"And you just happen to know people in the music industry?" she asks, clearly shocked.

"Baby, you seem to forget—I'm Nathan fucking Williams. I don't need to know anyone. Everyone already knows me," I reply with a wink. She rolls her eyes again, and I grab her in my arms, biting her sweet face and pinching her perfectly rounded ass.

We're enjoying ourselves at the table again when a woman— someone I've met before—shows up.

"Hey, guys! It's been a while!" she says, her gaze locking onto James.

"Victoria," we say in unison. Victoria was one of James's regulars, pre-Hayley.

"I hope we can catch up soon. I heard you were back on the market," she says, winking at James. I can feel him getting uncomfortable.

"Will do," he says, uneasy. She flaunts her purse for everyone to see.

"I've always loved your presents," she says, and James looks away. They exchange a few more words before she leaves.

"You bought her a Birkin?!" Sam asks, and James nods.

"What's a Firkin?" Delilah asks, making everyone laugh.

"*Birkin*, babe. It's a very expensive purse," I explain.

"How much does one cost?" Jenna asks.

"Around $25K," James answers.

"For a purse?" Delilah says, shocked. "Damn, you really need to put your money to better use," she tells James.

"I'm sure you have ideas," James snorts.

"That I do. My office is on the twenty-seventh floor, in case you didn't know," Delilah answers, a huge grin on her face.

"That I did," James retorts.

I sense something deeper here, something's missing. *I'll dig into it later.*

"I'll buy you one," I say to her, sincerely.

"If the day ever comes when you think spending that kind of money will bring me joy, let me know ahead of time," she says, and I melt for her even more. She couldn't care less about things like that. I love how simple she is. And now I see the rest of them—faded, dull, shallow.

Our conversation shifts to *what to sing next*. Of course, all eyes are on Delilah. Everyone in the fucking bar is begging her to sing again. I understand why—she has a voice that could kill hearts. But I want to keep her for myself. I've never felt like this before.

"Let's sing Disney songs!" Jenna says. She's drunk. No further explanation needed.

"I wanna sing *The Lion King!* 'Oh, I just can't wait to be kiiiiiii-ing!'" Sam chimes in, equally drunk.

"I'm going with *Hercules* and the Muses!" Ailly says. Also drunk.

"I only know one," Delilah whispers, and I see Sam rushing to her. I can't hear what he says, but Delilah answers him with "It's fine." I watch them, questioning their exchange, but they both ignore me.

They go to the karaoke organizer and tell him their picks. When they return, I notice Delilah's mood has shifted. I pull her onto my lap.

"What's wrong, baby?" I ask quietly so only she can hear.

"Nothing. The alcohol is messing with me, don't mind me," she says, kissing the tip of my nose. I look into her eyes, waiting for more, but nothing comes.

I know better than to push her, so I let it go for now. I caress her thighs with my hand, wanting her to feel me, to feel all my affection. I feel her connecting with me—her eyes, her touch . . . her heart. We don't need words; we just need to feel each other.

"What are you doing?" she asks, half laughing.

"Rubbing my confidence all over you," I answer, rubbing my head against her side.

She bursts out laughing, and I know she feels lighter now. *Good.*

Jenna gets up on stage first, and I see James watching her, mesmerized. I laugh at the scene—*James has a crush.*

Jenna sings "Let It Go" from *Frozen.* I'm lucky I've never heard it before. Everyone in the bar—mostly women—is singing along, making my ears bleed.

Delilah smiles, but that's it. I hold her tight and murmur in her ear, "You're way too talented for all of them." She chuckles and whispers back.

"That's why they wanted me to go last."

I don't know if it's her breath, her hand on the back of my head, or the sound of her voice, but I'm instantly fucking hard for her. I grab her hips and press her against my very erect cock. Delilah gasps and turns around with wide eyes. I grin at her. "I want to fuck you," I mouth, and she bursts out laughing.

All her friends have performed, and now it's Delilah's turn. I see Sam holding her hand, offering silent encouragement, providing emotional support—which only deepens my confusion.

Delilah steps on stage, and everyone in the bar is shouting, excited to hear her sing again. The first notes of the music play, but I don't recognize the song.

"What's the song?" I ask Sam.

"'Part of Your World' from *The Little Mermaid,*" he answers, his eyes focused on Delilah. *Never heard of it before.*

The melody is gentle, almost like a lullaby, but the moment Delilah starts to sing, it's clear that this is something more. Her voice, which I know so well, takes on a new depth. The words she sings seem to pull something from deep within her, something she's kept hidden. She's not just performing; she's living the song, embodying every note, every word.

As the lyrics flow, I see her becoming one with the music. It's as if the notes wrap around her, and she's no longer just Delilah standing on a stage—she's the very essence of the music itself. Her voice is powerful, but there's a vulnerability in it too. Each word seems to reveal a piece of her past, her dreams, her pain. I've heard her sing many times, but never like this. This is different. This is raw.

"What's the deal with the song?" I ask Sam, noticing Delilah becoming emotional.

"Ashley . . ." he exhales.

"Her sister?" I ask, and he nods.

"The song was theirs—hers and Delilah's. I didn't think she had the guts to sing it. She's so fucking strong," he says. *That she is . . .*

The bar, usually filled with the hum of conversation, falls into a hush. Everyone is watching her, captivated by the emotion she pours into every note. Her voice, usually so controlled and precise, is a little unsteady now, but that only makes it more real. It's as if she were allowing herself to be seen, truly seen, for the first time. *My sweet, sweet Delilah . . .*

As she reaches the final verses, tears begin to well in her eyes. She doesn't stop, doesn't falter, even as the tears spill over. Her voice carries on, strong and clear, but I can see the struggle within her. It's as if the song were pulling something out of her that she's not ready to let go of, and it breaks my heart to watch.

She's so fucking beautiful when she sings. She's a goddess, the epitome of beauty. I can't look away; I'm drawn to her, completely mesmerized. I'm caught under her spell.

When the last note fades, she lowers the microphone, her hand trembling. She quickly turns away, trying to hide the tears she can't control. My chest tightens.

The room remains silent, the weight of her performance hanging in the air. I've heard her sing so many times, but this . . . this was different. It was more than just a song. It was a glimpse into her soul, a soul that's been through more than I can imagine. And as much as it hurts, I can't help but feel grateful that she let us see it, even for just a moment.

I immediately go to her and carry her off the stage, my mind racing, my heart aching. I murmur in her ear, "It's okay, baby. I'm here. You were fucking perfect, like always." But she keeps crying, and Delilah *never* cries. Never. Sometimes her eyes get a little wet, but that's it.

Now she's fucking crying, and it breaks me.

"We're going home," I say, and she simply nods.

I text Tyler, and he comes within five minutes. I text the others to let them know we left, and they all understand.

When we arrive home, we're greeted by the boys, which is comforting, and I know it puts some balm on Delilah's soul. I settle her on the bed and tell her not to move. I prepare a hot bubble bath, adding salts and whatever other stuff I find on the shelves. I light some candles and then go back to take care of my girl. I undress her, getting hard as I do, then help her into the water.

"Come with me," she asks, and I oblige. I undress and get in right behind her. I use the cloth to pour hot water over her delicate body, making her fair skin glow.

"I'm sorry," she says.

"For what?" I ask softly.

"Ruining the night," she whispers, her voice barely audible.

"You didn't ruin anything. Everyone had a blast. Hearing you was insanely good for everyone. Plus, they were all drunk," I say, laughing. "They probably won't remember shit."

"I hope you're right. I feel guilty for the way we left," she admits.

"You don't need to be. *I* made the decision," I say, and Delilah laughs a little. "Do you want to talk about it?"

"No," she says simply. It hurts, but I remain silent. "How will they get home?" she asks after a pause.

"James and Luke called their personal drivers. They'll take care of Sam, Jenna, and Ailly. Don't worry," I say, kissing her neck. She relaxes, and I can feel my girl coming back to me.

I add, smiling, "And I think James will be more than happy to take care of Jenna, if you know what I mean." But Delilah turns to face me, appalled.

"No, I don't know what you mean," she says.

"I think James has a crush on Jenna," I say, raising an eyebrow.

"What?!" she asks, clearly not happy with the news. "That can't happen."

"Why not?"

"Jenna is a great woman. She's kind, she's funny, she's real, and I don't want to jeopardize the friendship we're building. You know how hard it is for me to 'open up,' if I may say. Please tell James she's off-limits," she says, angry. But I'm even more confused.

"You don't like James?" I ask, not sure I want to know the answer.

"No, I didn't say that."

"You didn't have to. What's going on?" I press.

"Nothing. Let's drop it. I'm not in the mood to fight."

"Baby, we're not fighting. We're talking. Sometimes we agree, sometimes we don't. But we talk anyway," I say, but she doesn't reply.

"I thought you and James got along," I add. I want them to be friends. They're the two most important people in my life right now. I don't want them to hate each other.

"What I think of James is irrelevant," she says, and I swear I can feel her shutting down.

"What's that supposed to mean?"

"It means that *this*"—she gestures between us with her hand—"is temporary. It will end someday, at some point. James has been, is, and will always be part of your life. I'm just a passenger. I don't like or dislike any of your friends, Nate. I'm just here, enjoying the ride while it lasts."

I don't respond. I fall silent again. I don't want to say something I might regret later. Delilah is fragile; she tested her limits tonight and broke. She needs to rest and deal with other issues another time. I want to spare her, protect her, and make her feel better.

After the bath, we slip into our pajamas, though I'm not sure they'll last long. We crawl into bed, finding each other without hesitation, and I pull her close, spooning her, feeling her. There's a deep contentment in this moment, just having her here beside me.

Every day she stays feels like a win.

"You wanted to fuck?" she asks, her voice teasing.

"I always want to fuck," I admit with a chuckle, tightening my hold around her. "But I'm also fine doing this." And I am. The feel of her body against mine, the way she fits so perfectly into me, is its own kind of satisfaction. That makes her laugh, and it's a sound almost as beautiful as when she sings.

"Nate?" she whispers.

"Yes, baby?" I respond, nuzzling into her hair, breathing in the familiar scent that's become so comforting.

"Tell me something about the stars," she asks, her voice carrying a note of despair that always catches me off guard. I pause, thinking for a moment, then remember something.

"Many stars have names originating from ancient Arabic, Greek, or Latin," I begin, wanting to share something meaningful with her.

"For instance, 'Betelgeuse' comes from the Arabic phrase *Yad al-Jawza*, meaning 'the hand of the giant,' referring to the constellation . . . *Orion*."

"Where we met . . ." she murmurs softly, the memory hanging in the air between us.

"Where we met," I echo, pressing a kiss to her neck, feeling her relax even more into my embrace.

"So we met at the hand of the giant," she says with a small laugh, the kind that comes from realizing something unexpectedly sweet.

"Some might say God himself has put us on the same path," I reply, the thought coming naturally, as if it were always meant to be said.

"Do you believe in God?" she asks, and there's a seriousness in her tone that makes me pause.

"Sometimes I do, sometimes I don't," I answer honestly.

She doesn't respond, and I can feel her slipping into sleep, her breathing slowing, her body growing heavier in my arms.

"Good night, angel mine," I murmur, my words almost swallowed by the quiet of the room. I hold her just a little bit tighter, as if to keep the moment from slipping away, before letting sleep take me too.

CHAPTER 19
Delilah

I sit at my desk, my fingers hovering over the paperwork in front of me, but my mind is somewhere else. The office is far from quiet today, yet I can't hear anything beyond the noise in my own head. I glance at the clock on my screen—1:17 p.m. I should be working on the project Ailly asked me to help with, but my thoughts keep drifting back to the last few days.

I took the SATs. Finally, after all those weeks of intense studying, it's over. But now the waiting—this awful, endless wait for the results—is killing me. I think I did well, or at least I hope I did. I answered the questions with as much focus as I could muster, but as the days pass, my confidence wavers. What if I messed up the math section? What if my essay wasn't as strong as I thought? The anxiety rises in me like a slow, unstoppable tide, and I can't shake it.

Letting out a breath, I try to refocus on the task in front of me. I need to help Ailly with this report, but she's been off all morning. She didn't even eat lunch. She looks sick—pale, tired. I wonder if she's okay. I make a mental note to check on her when she gets back from her meeting, maybe see if she needs anything. She's been a good friend to me lately, especially since that night at the karaoke party.

Karaoke . . . I wince at the memory. It was unexpected, how much fun I had, and how much hurt I felt. Ailly, Jenna, and Sam— they made it better, and somehow we got closer. I didn't expect to deepen my relationships with them so quickly, especially not with Sam, since I thought we couldn't get closer than we already were. He's different from the others—there's something about the way he listens, really listens, that makes me feel seen. And how much he understands too. And Nate . . . my thoughts drift to him, as they often do.

Nate and I have grown closer too, in ways that surprise me. I'm happy—or at least I should be. But there's that nagging voice in my head, whispering that it won't last. That it never does. How long before it ends? How will I feel when it does? I hate that I think this way, but the voice is persistent, always there, casting shadows over every good thing.

I shake my head, trying to push the thoughts away. Every day feels like a small victory, a win over the part of me that wants to give up. I've settled into something comfortable with Nate, something real, but I can't shake the feeling that it's all temporary. I opened up to him more, told him things about my past, things I've kept hidden from others. It feels good, in a way, to let someone in, but it also scares me.

What if he leaves? What if he takes a piece of me with him when he goes?

I feel a lump forming in my throat, but I swallow it down. I can't fall apart right now, not here. I glance over at Ailly. She's hunched over her desk, her face drawn and pale. She really doesn't look well. Maybe I should say something.

"Ailly, you okay?" I ask, keeping my voice low so I don't disturb anyone else.

She looks up at me, her eyes tired.

"Yeah, just a bit under the weather. Nothing serious."

"You sure? You look like you could use a break."

She gives me a weak smile.

"I'll be fine, thanks. Just need to finish this up."

I nod, but I don't quite believe her. She's always been the type to push through, even when she shouldn't. I can relate to that more than I'd like to admit.

I turn back to my screen, but the words blur in front of me. My mind keeps wandering, circling back to the same thoughts, the same worries. I want to believe that things will be okay—that I'll get my SAT results, that I'll keep my friendships, that Nate and I can last—but it's hard. The voice in my head doesn't let up. It tells me I'm not worth it, that everyone will leave eventually. It's been with me for so long that it's hard to ignore.

But I have to try. I force myself to focus on the project, on helping Ailly. Maybe if I keep busy, if I keep moving, I can drown out the noise in my head. One day at a time, I tell myself. *One day at a time.*

"Delilah?" Ailly's voice breaks through my thoughts. I look up, startled. She's standing by my desk, holding a cup of tea.

"Here," she says, offering it to me. "I thought you might need a pick-me-up." I take the cup, surprised.

"Thanks, Ailly. But aren't you the one who needs this more?"

She shrugs. "Maybe, but I figured we could both use a break," she says, and even her voice sounds sick.

I hesitate, then nod. "Yeah, that sounds good."

We sip our tea in silence, but it's a comfortable silence, the kind that doesn't need filling. I still have my doubts, my fears, but standing here with Ailly, I feel a little more grounded. Maybe things won't last forever, but maybe that's okay. For now, I'll take it one day at a time.

There's a knock on the door, and Nate strides in. Damn, he looks so good it almost hurts.

"Hey, babe, got a minute?" he asks, flashing me that irresistible smile.

"Sure, come in. But don't 'babe' me here—someone could hear you!" I scold him, trying to keep it professional, but he just chuckles in response.

"Hello, Mr. Williams," Ailly chimes in from where she's standing, giving him a polite wave. She knows she can't call him Nate at the office.

"You don't look so great," he says, his brow furrowing as he looks at her.

"I'm just a bit sick, nothing serious. Don't worry," she replies with a reassuring smile. Then I turn my attention back to the gorgeous, powerful man standing before me. He starts to move closer, but I raise my hand, signaling that the door is still open. He catches on and closes it before wrapping me in his strong arms and kissing me, not caring that Ailly is still in the room. She discreetly moves behind her desk, giving us a semblance of privacy.

"Hey, you," I say softly after we break the kiss.

"Hi, baby. I missed you," he murmurs.

"You saw me this morning," I tease, the memory of our morning sex still fresh in my mind.

"That I did," he replies with a wink.

"So, what brings you here?" I ask.

"Right, shit. I came to tell you I have to head to Boston—like, right now. There's an emergency meeting that needs my personal touch, you know, to scare the shit out of people," he says with a smug grin. I nod, and he continues, "I'll have to stay the night because there's another important meeting in the morning, but I'll be back by 11 a.m. I can't miss it. Are you okay with that? Wanna come with me?"

"It's just for one night. I have the dogs and the security team, so I think I'll be fine," I say, surprising myself with how much I mean it. I'll miss him like crazy, but I'm confident I can manage on my own. I haven't been alone in so long. I don't miss it.

"Are you sure you don't want to come?" he presses.

"No, baby, it's fine. I have a lot of work to do anyway. It's less than twenty-four hours. I think I can manage." I pause, then ask, "How are you getting to Boston?"

"My jet. Why?" he asks, looking amused.

"Of course." I roll my eyes playfully. He pulls me into a passionate embrace, and we kiss like we're the only two people in the world.

"I have to go now. I miss you already. And don't touch yourself while I'm gone," he says between kisses, making me burst out laughing.

"What the fuck, Nate . . . I sure won't," I reply, running my hands over his body, claiming it as mine. *Mine . . .*

He'll never be yours. You're trash, he'll realize it soon enough. You'll never be good enough. People always leave you behind.

"I'll call you when I land," he promises.

"Yeah, I won't hold my breath," I tease.

"What's that supposed to mean?" he asks, curious.

"The last time you left, you promised to call, and you didn't."

"I *did* call, though it was late. But I *did* call. Anyway, I'll call when I land, I promise," he says, looking deeply into my eyes, like he's holding something back. I give him a questioning look.

"There are things I want to say—" he begins, but I can tell where this is going. He definitely wants to say dirty things, but I'm not comfortable with that while Ailly's still here.

"Don't," I say, holding up my hand to stop him. But he seems upset—hurt, even.

What the fuck?

"Okay. I'll call you," he says, his tone a bit colder now, and then he leaves.

I turn to Ailly, who's watching me closely.

"He's got moods," I say, trying to explain Nate's behavior.

"Fine," she replies simply. I can tell she has more to say, but I'm not going to push her.

After over an hour, I finally get a call from "Hottest Sugar Daddy," a.k.a. Nate. He sounds softer over the phone, so I guess he's back to normal. He tells me he landed okay and headed straight to his meeting. I know he's with James, as usual, so I don't push the conversation, saving the real talk for tonight.

"I'm really not feeling well, shit," Ailly says, snapping me out of my thoughts.

"Just go home, Ailly. I can handle everything here. Honestly, there's not much left to do," I say, trying to convince her.

"I still have to go to Murray Street to deliver some contracts to a client. But I feel like crap. I might even throw up, and it's in the opposite direction. Fuck," she replies, clearly struggling.

"I can go for you if you want. What time do I need to deliver the contracts?" I offer.

"It's not far. You can go in like half an hour if you're sure you can handle it," she says, looking relieved.

"I *can* do it. Just go home, get some rest, see a doctor if you need to, but please, go!" I say with a reassuring smile.

"Alright, alright. Thank you. Here's the envelope with the contracts. Ask for Mr. Peterson and tell him you're coming from me. It'll be fine," she says, handing me the envelope and the address. "I'll call you tomorrow to see how I'm feeling. Though I'm sure the subway won't help with my nausea," she says with a grimace.

"Wait a second," I say, pulling out my phone. I don't think Tyler's back yet, and I'd hate to bother him with all the traffic after his trip to the airport, but Ben and Sophia are in the car; they won't mind. I quickly dial Sophia, and she picks up almost immediately.

"Hey, my friend needs a ride home. She's sick. Can you guys give her a lift? I'm staying at the office."

"Sure, no problem. Just call us before she leaves the building so we can be there on time," Sophia says. I thank her and hang up.

"You didn't have to do that," Ailly says, clearly touched.

"That's what friends are for."

"You really are my friend. Thank you, sweetie. I'll call you," she says, giving me a quick hug from afar before heading out.

I return to my tasks, diving into the work at hand. Time slips away, and I raise my hand to check the clock on the wall. *Shit!* I'm fucking late to deliver the contracts. My phone's battery is almost dead, and I don't even have time to charge it. I need it to find the right location. Grabbing the envelope, my coat, and my purse, I rush out of the office.

Damn, How am I gonna go there? I can't call Tyler—he won't be fast enough. Sophia and Ben aren't back yet, obviously, and

I'm afraid to use my phone in case the battery dies. *Fuck, fuck, fuck.*

I spot a cab, and for the first time in my whole fucking life, I actually hail one. I don't have any other choice. One pulls up almost immediately, driven by a man who looks to be in his fifties.

"Where to, miss?" he asks.

"Murray Street, please. I'm really late—could you speed up a little?" I plead.

"Sure, no problem," he replies. Thank God!

After Nate found out I didn't have any money, he tried to Venmo me an obscene amount, which I declined. I even asked my bank to block any transfers from his account. They were shocked, but they did it. Nate was furious, so instead, every morning, he stashes cash in my purse, my clothes pockets, and my coat. I gave up trying to refuse it, and today, I'm super grateful for it because I actually have the money to pay for this cab. Like a fucking normal person. And it feels damn good. I smile, forgetting for a moment that I'm late. I don't even give a fuck. I'm too happy because today, I feel normal. What a wonderful feeling. I wish Nate could see this. I'll tell him all about it tonight.

I sit in the backseat of the cab, my eyes darting between the dashboard clock and the city speeding by outside the window. The numbers on the clock seem to mock me, moving faster than they should. My heart pounds with each passing second, a frantic rhythm that echoes in my ears. I try to calm myself, but the anxiety claws at my insides, gnawing away at my composure.

"Don't worry, miss," the driver says, his voice cutting through my thoughts. I look up and meet his gaze in the rearview mirror. His eyes are soft, the kind that belong to someone who's seen a lot but hasn't let it harden him. "I'm doing my best to get you to Murray Street on time."

I nod, swallowing hard.

"Thank you," I manage to say, though my voice sounds small, even to me. He's a nice man, I think, the kind you hope for when you're in a hurry and everything seems to be going wrong. There's something reassuring about his calm demeanor, something that makes me believe, even for a moment, that maybe I won't be late.

He makes a quick turn, the tires of the cab hissing against the wet pavement. "We're almost there," he adds, his voice steady. "I know a shortcut."

I glance out the window again. The streets are empty, and the usual gridlock of the city is gone. Instead, the road stretches out before us, wide and open. It's almost eerie, this sudden emptiness, as if the city itself had paused, holding its breath along with me. But I'm relieved—no traffic means we might actually make it on time. I try to relax into the seat, but the tension in my body refuses to ease. I check the time again. The minutes are slipping away, too quickly, always too quickly.

The cab speeds up, taking advantage of the empty streets. I can feel the engine's hum beneath me, a steady vibration that reverberates through the car. I stare at the passing buildings, their shapes merging together in the dim light. My mind jumps from thought to thought, unable to settle. I think about the meeting I'm late for, the way everything depends on me being there. I think about the consequences of missing it for Ailly, the disappointment she'd feel, the frustration. I think about Nate, his smile, the way he'd laugh if he knew how panicked I am right now. He'd tell me to breathe, to calm down. I try to picture his face, to hear his voice in my mind, but the anxiety is too strong, drowning out everything else.

Suddenly, the cab lurches to the side as the driver swerves to avoid something—another car, maybe, or a pothole. I'm thrown against the door, the seatbelt biting into my shoulder. I clutch the door handle, trying to steady myself, but the car straightens out just as quickly as it swerved. The driver glances back at me, his expression apologetic.

"Sorry about that," he says. "Just avoiding a bump."

It's okay," I say, but my voice is shaky, and my heart is pounding even harder now. I force myself to let go of the door handle, my fingers stiff from gripping it so tightly. I glance at the clock again. Time is slipping away, faster and faster.

The road ahead feels endless, a dark path cutting through the city. The buildings on each side rise high like silent guards, their windows catch the streetlights, almost like eyes that watch me. A sense of unease sits heavy in my chest, but I can't figure out why.

I tell myself it's just nerves, just the stress of running late.

The driver makes another turn, and we end up on a narrow street quieter than before. The buildings here stand taller and closer together, the shadows grow darker. I glance around, trying to recognize something, but none of it seems familiar.

"Is this the shortcut?" I ask, my voice tinged with doubt.

He nods, eyes still on the road.

"Yes, miss. It'll take us right to Murray Street, and we'll skip all the traffic. Almost there."

I nod again, but the unease doesn't fade. If anything, it grows stronger, a knot tightening in my stomach. I try to focus on the positives—no traffic means we'll be there soon. But there's something off about this road. It's too quiet, too empty, like the city has been abandoned, and we're the only ones left. I glance at the clock again. Time is slipping through my fingers like sand, and there's nothing I can do to stop it.

And then, out of the corner of my eye, I see it—a flash of headlights, a blur of motion. Before I can fully comprehend what's happening, there's a deafening crash, a sound so loud it feels like it's splitting my head open. The world tilts violently, and suddenly, I'm weightless, floating in the air as the car flips over.

Everything happens in slow motion, each detail searing itself into my mind. The car spins, once, twice, and then slams down onto the pavement with a force that knocks the breath out of me. The impact is brutal, bone-shaking, a jarring collision that sends shock waves through my entire body. I feel the seatbelt tighten across my chest, holding me in place, but my head snaps forward, then back, the force of the crash yanking me like a rag doll.

The windows explode, glass shattering into a thousand pieces that fly through the air like deadly confetti. The sound is a high-pitched, earsplitting screech, mingling with the groan of twisting metal and the dull thud of the car's roof hitting the ground. The world outside the car is a chaotic whirl, spinning and tumbling as the car finally comes to a stop, upside down.

For a moment, there's nothing but silence. The kind of silence that presses in on you, heavy and suffocating. I'm hanging upside down, my body suspended by the seatbelt. I can feel the blood rushing to my head, my vision swimming, dark spots dancing in front of my eyes. My ears ring with a piercing noise that drowns out everything else.

I try to move, but pain shoots through my body, sharp and intense. I gasp, the air catching in my throat. My legs—they're stuck. I try to pull them free, but they won't budge. Panic surges through me, cold and relentless, as I tug at them again, harder this time. The pain is excruciating, like my legs are being crushed in a vise. I can't get out.

I'm trapped.

I turn my head, wincing at the sharp pain that flares in my neck, and look at the driver. He's slumped forward, his body limp, still held in place by his seatbelt. Blood drips from a gash on his forehead, staining his white hair red. His eyes are closed, his face slack. My heart skips a beat, cold dread settling in my chest. *Is he . . . dead?* I can't tell. I can't see if he's breathing, if there's any sign of life. He was so nice, just a moment ago. He promised he'd get me there on time. *He can't be dead. He can't be.*

I can feel my breath coming in short, ragged gasps, my chest tightening with panic. I raise my hands, trying to push away the shards of glass that have fallen around me. But when I look down, I see that my hands are covered in blood—*my* blood. It's smeared across my skin, dark and sticky, dripping onto the shattered glass below. There's so much of it, more than I've ever seen. I stare at it, my mind struggling to process what I'm seeing. Blood, everywhere. *How is there so much?*

The pain in my legs intensifies, a stabbing, searing agony that makes me cry out. It's like fire, burning its way through my body, consuming me from the inside out. I can't think straight. I can't comprehend what's happening. The world around me is spinning, slipping away from me, and I'm powerless to stop it.

My vision darkens at the edges as the pain becomes too much. I can't hold on. I feel myself slipping, my thoughts scattering like the broken glass around me. In the midst of the chaos, one image comes to mind, clear and vivid—Nate's face. His smile, warm and comforting, the way it always is when he looks at me. I cling to that image, to him, the only thing that feels real in this nightmare. I can almost hear his voice telling me it's going to be okay, that I'm going to be okay. But I know it's not true. I feel the tears coming down, there's nothing left to do but cry.

The pain is too much. I can't take it anymore. The darkness closes in, swallowing me whole. I let it take me, sinking into the blackness, holding onto Nate's face for as long as I can.

And then . . . there's nothing.

Am I dead?

~

When I open my eyes, the world is a fog of darkness and pain. My head throbs, the inside of my skull pulsing with each heartbeat. I blink, trying to clear my vision, trying to understand where I am. The smell of gasoline and blood fills my nose, sharp and overwhelming. I remember—there was an accident, the cab flipped. I was in it. *I'm still in it.*

Everything around me is still, eerily quiet. The car is upside down, its roof crushed against the ground. The windows are shattered, jagged edges glinting in the dim light. I look around, my heart pounding. The driver! My gaze shifts to him. He's slumped over the steering wheel, motionless, blood trickling down his face.

He looks dead. I'm not. But I can't shake this feeling deep in my gut that it's not my time. Not yet. I refuse to let this be the end. I promised myself that when I die, it'll be on my terms. And this? This isn't it.

I take a deep breath, the pain radiating from every part of my body. My legs are still trapped, a heavy weight pressing down on them. I try to move, but it feels like my bones are grinding against each other, like my muscles are tearing apart. A cry escapes my lips, sharp and desperate, but I grit my teeth and force myself to push through it. I have to get out. I won't die here.

With all the strength I can muster, I start to push against the twisted metal. My arms shake, my hands slick with blood, slipping on the cold steel. The pain in my legs is unbearable, an agony that makes my vision blur with tears. But I can't stop. I won't stop. I push harder, my breath coming in rough gasps, my body screaming in protest. The metal groans under the pressure, and slowly, painstakingly, I manage to free one leg, then the other. The relief is brief, fleeting—just a moment before the next wave of pain crashes over me.

I collapse back into the seat, panting, the taste of blood sharp in my mouth. The seatbelt is still tight across my chest, digging into my skin. My fingers fumble with the buckle, slick and weak. It takes all my concentration to grip it, to press down and release it. When it finally clicks open, I fall forward, my body limp and exhausted. Tears stream down my face, hot and uncontrollable. I'm sobbing—loud, ugly cries that shake my entire body. But it's not just the pain that brings the tears—it's the memories. The memories that flood back, triggered by the pain, by the helplessness.

I'm not here anymore. I'm back there, back in that dark, suffocating place. I'm a child again, small and scared, trapped in a room with no windows, no way out. The men who kept me there, they come for me every day, dragging me out of the shadows, their faces twisted with cruel smiles. They beat me, over and over, their fists heavy and relentless. The pain was my constant companion, a cruel teacher. It taught me how to survive, how to fight back, how to keep breathing even when I wanted it to stop. The fear, the hurt—it's all coming back now, as vivid as if it were happening all over again.

"Feel the pain, you piece of shit. If you don't do what we ask, you'll die under my bare hands, fucking whore."

I see their faces, the hatred in their eyes, the pleasure they took in my suffering. I remember the feel of their hands, rough and unforgiving, the sound of their laughter as I cried out in pain.

"You little shit. You'll obey and do what we want you to do, you little slut."

I was just a child—so small, so helpless. But even then, I fought. I fought with everything I had. And now, in this twisted, broken car, I feel that same fire ignite inside me. The pain I feel now? It's nothing compared to what I've been through before. If I survived them, I can survive this.

"Look at you crying, you're too weak. You're going to die if you don't do that thing again. Make me lose one more dollar and you'll regret you ever lived, little bitch."

A scream builds in my throat, fueled by the rage and the memories, and I let it out, loud and raw. It echoes in the wreckage, bouncing off the crushed metal and broken glass. I use that rage, that desperation, to force my body to move. I can see my old self— so scared, so defenseless, trying to survive. So, I'll survive too.

I reach for the door, my hands shaking, fingers bloody and bruised. I pull at the handle, but it's jammed, stuck tight from the impact. I scream again, my voice hoarse, and throw my weight against the door. It doesn't budge. But I don't stop. I keep trying, again and again, each attempt more painful than the last, but I won't give up. I can't.

Finally, with one last desperate push, the door creaks open. Cold air rushes in, sharp and stinging against my face. I drag myself out, every inch of movement a battle against the pain. My legs scream in protest, my muscles burning, but I ignore it. I have to get out. I have to survive.

I tumble out onto the pavement, gasping for breath, the ground cold and hard beneath me. I can barely see through the tears, but I force myself to crawl, dragging my body away from the wreckage. My hands scrape against the asphalt, leaving streaks of blood behind. I don't stop until I reach the sidewalk, the rough concrete digging into my palms. I collapse there, my body shaking, the adrenaline starting to fade, leaving me weak and trembling.

As I try to catch my breath, the cold air burns my lungs. My entire body throbs with pain, my mind spinning. But I'm alive. I made it out. *I survived.*

I fumble for my phone, my fingers numb and clumsy. My vision blurs again, but this time it's not from tears—it's from exhaustion, from the sheer effort it took to get out. I finally pull my phone out of my pocket, but before I can dial, I hear a noise—a faint, muffled sound. I freeze, my heart pounding in my chest. Slowly, I raise my head, looking back at the car.

The driver's hand is moving.

For a moment, I just stare, unable to process what I'm seeing. I thought he was dead. He looked dead. But now he's moving—barely, his fingers twitching as if he were trying to reach out for something. He's alive. He's calling for help.

Dread washes over me, followed by a surge of guilt. I'm hurt, I'm in pain, but I can't leave him here. I can't let him die alone in this wreck. I was a survivor then, and I'm a survivor now. And I won't let anyone else suffer if I can help it.

So I force myself to stand, every part of my body protesting. My legs buckle under me, but I catch myself against a wall, leaning on it for support. The pain is unbearable, shooting up my spine, making my head spin. But I push it down, push it all down, and focus on the driver. I have to help him. I have to get him out, just like I got myself out . . . *just like I got Ashley out.*

I stagger back to the car, every step a struggle. The car is crumpled, twisted beyond recognition, the metal sharp and jagged where the frame has collapsed. The driver is still slumped over, unconscious, his breathing shallow. I can see the blood on his face, on his clothes, spreading slowly, too slowly.

"Come on," I whisper, my voice shaking.

"I'm not leaving you. We're both getting out of this."

"Don't worry, Ashley. I'm not leaving you. I'll get us out of here, I promise you, baby girl. You're my sister now. I'll find a way to get us out of here, I promise. Stop crying, baby girl."

I grab hold of him, trying to pull him free, but he's heavy—so much heavier than I expected. My hands slip on his blood-slicked clothes, my fingers aching with the effort. The pain in my body feels like a thousand knives stabbing into me from all angles, but I grit my teeth and keep pulling. I scream again, the sound ripped from my throat, more out of frustration and determination than anything else. I pull and pull until, finally, he starts to move.

It takes everything I have to drag him out of the car. My arms feel like they're going to tear out of their sockets, my back is on fire, but I don't stop. I can't stop. The memory of those men—their faces, their laughter—drives me forward. They wanted to break me, to destroy me. But they didn't. I survived. And I'll survive this too. I'll save him, just like I saved her.

"Don't hurt her, please! I'll do it, I promise. I'll obey, I swear! Please don't hurt her, I'll do anything!"

With one final, desperate effort, I manage to drag the driver out of the car, his body collapsing onto the pavement beside me. I'm sobbing, the tears mixing with the blood on my face, but I don't care. I did it. I got him out.

We're not safe yet—I know it. I can feel it in the air, a tension that hasn't broken. I try to move, try to get him further away from the wreckage, but I'm too weak. My body is giving out, the adrenaline fading, leaving me cold and shivering. I can barely move.

And then it happens.

The car explodes with a deafening roar, the blast wave hitting me like a freight train. I'm thrown backward, my body slamming into a wall. The impact knocks the breath out of me, and I collapse to the ground, my vision going dark for a moment. The heat from the explosion washes over me, searing my skin, filling the air with the acrid smell of burning metal and gasoline.

I can't hear anything but a ringing in my ears, a whine that drowns out everything else. My head is spinning, my body numb from the shock. I force myself to move, to push myself up from the ground, but my limbs feel heavy, unresponsive.

Finally I manage to stand, swaying on my feet. I look around, disoriented, trying to find the driver. He's lying a few feet away, thrown by the explosion just like I was. I stumble toward him, every step agonizing. When I reach him, I collapse to my knees beside him, my hands shaking as I check for a pulse.

He's still breathing. *Thank fuck.*

Relief washes over me, so intense that it brings fresh tears to my eyes. He's alive. I saved him. I did it.

I pull out my phone again, my fingers fumbling over the screen. I manage to dial 911, my voice hoarse and broken as I tell the operator there's been an accident. I don't wait for a response before hanging up. There's nothing more I can do. Help is on the way.

I look down at the driver, his face pale, streaked with blood.

"You're going to be okay," I whisper, though I'm not sure if I'm saying it to him or to myself. I reach out and squeeze his hand, hoping he can feel it, hoping it gives him some comfort.

But I can't stay here. I have to go. I can't let anyone find me like this—covered in blood, broken, and bruised. I know what I look like—I've seen it before, after those men were done with me. I need to get away, to hide, to clean myself up. I'm a survivor.

I've always been a survivor.

I force myself to stand, every part of me screaming in pain. I glance down the street, seeing nothing but darkness and emptiness. The city feels deserted, like it's just me and the ruins of this day. I send a quick text to Sophia, my fingers barely able to type out my location. Then I start to walk, each step a battle, each breath a reminder that I'm still alive.

I'll keep fighting, just like I always have. And no matter what, I'll survive.

Less than ten minutes later, I see Sophia and Ben's car pull up. The moment they spot me, they leap out, rushing over to help.

"What happened? We need to get you to the hospital!" Sophia exclaims, her voice filled with worry.

"No!" I scream, my voice harsher than I intend. I can't even control myself right now; everything is too much.

"Just take me home. I've been in a car accident. But I've been through worse. I can't go to the hospital. I just need to get home, clean up, and rest. I'll be fine," I say, trying to sound firm, even though I feel like I'm unraveling.

"Ms. Rose, you can't—"

"I said no," I snap, my tone sharp enough to cut through the air. People might mistake me for Nate with how commanding I sound.

"Just bring me home."

"I think we should call Mr.—"

"Don't you dare!" I cut him off, my eyes flashing with anger. "I'll call him. Just get me home. I need to clean up and rest. I've been through worse."

I barely recognize myself in this moment, but they don't argue. They know better.

They drive me straight home, avoiding the main entrance by going through the parking lot so no one sees me like this. They help me up to the penthouse, where we're greeted by a very distressed Ms. Frances, the housekeeper.

"I'm fine. It's just blood. I just need a bath," I insist, waving off her concern.

"Ms. Rose, you need to go to the hospital!" she scolds, her voice quaking with fear.

"I can't afford it! I have no insurance. I'm already in debt to the hospital. I can't risk anyone finding out about this!"

"But Mr. Williams has mon—"

"He's already done too much! I won't ask him to cover for me again. I just need a fucking bath and some fucking rest, please!" I plead, my voice cracking under the strain.

"I'll help you," Fran says, giving in with a sigh. She and Sophia guide me to the bathroom and help me undress, all the while I keep assuring them I'm fine. I'm really not, but I will be.

Fran hands me painkillers, and they both start removing the shards of glass embedded in my skin on my right hip.

"I'm okay," I keep repeating, though they clearly don't believe me.

They help me clean up, and I wince with almost every movement, but the painkillers start to take effect, dulling the worst of it.

"We could at least call a doctor?" Fran suggests, her voice gentle but persistent.

"No . . . I don't have health insurance. I have no money, and I don't have any to spare," I reply, exhaustion creeping into my voice.

"But Mr. Williams has money, and he loves you," she says, and the words hit me harder than any physical pain. It hurts more than the car accident itself. Her comment stings, twisting something deep inside me, and I feel nausea rising.

"Mr. Williams has already given me too much. Our living situation is temporary. I don't want to owe him more than I already do. Please, drop the subject," I say, fighting back the tears threatening to spill over. "I'll call him tonight," I add, my voice barely above a whisper.

Once they finish cleaning me up, they begin to bandage my wounds, but one cut is too deep. I've been through this before; I know what to do, how to handle it. My body carries no scars because I learned to take care of myself at a very early age.

"Can you bring me a needle, dental floss, and a lighter, please?" I ask, my voice steady but cold.

"I hope you're joking," Sophia says, her face pale with shock.

"Not at all. Please, hurry," I respond, my tone devoid of any warmth. I'm not being nice, but I can't help it. I have no control over it. My body is on autopilot, and my mind is just trying to keep up.

Fran returns with what I asked for. I don't think, I don't feel, I don't even breathe—I just do. Like I've done before. I thread the dental floss through the needle, sterilize it with the lighter, and pierce my skin to stitch up the wound. I don't register the pain, but the tears start to fall anyway.

Sophia and Fran help me tie up my hair and dress in light night-clothes. They understand I need to be alone, to have some privacy. They promise to stay outside the door, just in case, and that's enough for me. I crawl under the sheets, closing my eyes, but the tears keep coming, silently escaping down my cheeks.

I fucking survived. *Again.*

CHAPTER 20

Nate

I stand in the hallway outside the conference room, the late afternoon light slanting through the tall windows. The air in Boston feels tense, charged with the kind of pressure that makes people nervous. I feel it too, but I've learned to keep it under control. I'm here for a reason, and that reason is to get the Boston office back in line. The Singapore deal is supposed to be their responsibility, but something's gone wrong, and the investors are getting cold feet. That's why I had to fly out here on such short notice. They need to see that I'm not playing around—that this deal is too important to mess up.

James stands beside me, his expression as serious as ever. He knows what's at stake. We've both been through enough of these situations to understand the gravity of it. If we don't get this deal back on track, the ripple effects could be devastating—not just for our company, but for our reputation in the global market. The investors are already wary, and if they sense any more uncertainty, they'll pull out. That's not something I'm willing to let happen.

But even as I prepare to step into this meeting and lay down the law, my mind keeps drifting back to Delilah.

It was only a few hours ago, just before I left New York, that I went to say goodbye to her. I wanted her to come with me, but I knew deep down that it'd be a waste of her time, since it's just a quick business trip. I reflect on how things between us quickly escalated into something deeper, something that caught me off guard. Before I knew it, she and the boys had changed my life in a way I hadn't expected. Never in a million years would I have seen it coming.

At first, I wasn't sure how it would work out. I'm used to being in control, to having things a certain way. But with Delilah, everything is different. She brought a warmth into my life that I didn't know I was missing. The dogs—two energetic bundles of fur—have a way of turning even the most stressful day into something bearable. And Delilah herself, with her quiet strength and kind heart, has become someone I can't imagine living without. I find myself looking forward to coming home, to hearing the dogs bark excitedly as I walk through the door, to seeing her smile when she looks up from whatever she's doing in her favorite place: her kitchen.

It's only been a few months of living together, but it feels like this is how life was always supposed to be. And the thing is, it's not, and never has been, the picture of a family I grew up with or wanted to have—and fuck, it feels perfect that way. Yes, Delilah is still closed off sometimes, but less than before. Yes, she's still hot and cold, but again, not as much anymore. She's so goddamn affectionate and caring; she literally comforts me, brings me peace. When I think about her, I'm so fucking overwhelmed by all these . . . *feelings*.

Earlier this afternoon, when I went to her office to say goodbye, I didn't plan on anything dramatic. I just wanted to see her one last time before I left. I knocked on the door and walked in, seeing her talking with Ailly, her coworker and friend, who looked a bit sick. Nothing special, just a normal day. But when I looked at Delilah, something hit me, hard. It was like all the feelings I'd been pushing aside suddenly rushed to the surface. I realized in that moment just how much she means to me, how much I love this new life we've built together. The thought of leaving her, even just for a night, felt heavier than it should have.

I walked over to her, intending to give her a simple hug goodbye, but as soon as I wrapped my arms around her, the words I hadn't planned to say were on the tip of my tongue. I opened my mouth, ready to tell her how much she means to me, how much I care about her. But before I could get a word out, she pulled back slightly, looking up at me with those soft, concerned eyes. "Don't," she said firmly, almost scared.

It stopped me in my tracks. I think she knew what I was about to say, and she got scared. Maybe she isn't ready to hear it, or maybe she doesn't trust me yet—not completely. I've been trying to show her that I'm serious about us, but I know it's not always easy for her to believe it. She's been through things I don't fully understand, and I can see that she's still holding back, still waiting for the other shoe to drop.

Her "don't" hurt more than I expected it to. I've never been good with emotions, especially when they're as strong as this. But in that moment, I promised myself that I'd do more to earn her trust, to show her that what we have is real, that she doesn't need to be afraid, because I don't want to lose her—not when I've finally found something worth holding onto.

I kissed her, quick, and then I left. I didn't give her time to say anything else, didn't give myself time to dwell on the hurt. I had a plane to catch and a crisis to manage.

Now I stand outside this conference room, ready to scold the Boston office for dropping the ball on the Singapore deal.

"We need to make sure the head of the project hears us loud and clear," James says, bringing me back to the present. "If they don't get their act together, we'll lose the investors, and this deal will fall apart."

I nod, squaring my shoulders as I prepare to walk into the room. The meeting is about to start, and I need to be fully focused on what's ahead.

I push open the door, and the room falls silent as James and I enter. The tension is palpable; everyone knows why we're here. I take my seat at the head of the table, my expression hard and focused. This is what I do best—I handle crises, I make the tough decisions.

My eyes are locked on the group in front of me. The room is too quiet, suffocatingly still, as they all wait for me to speak. I let the silence linger, stretching it out until the tension thickens. I know how to use silence—it's a tool, and right now, it's working. I see their discomfort, the way they avoid my gaze, shifting nervously in their seats. They know they screwed up.

"The Singapore deal was your responsibility," I say, my voice cold and controlled. "It was your job to make sure everything ran smoothly, that the investors felt confident, that the project stayed on track. And now, we're here, dealing with the fallout because you didn't."

They flinch, but no one speaks. *Good.* They need to understand the severity of this. This isn't some minor problem; it's a colossal failure. I didn't want to fly to Boston to clean up their mess, but I will if it means saving this deal.

"I don't care about your excuses," I continue, my tone sharp. "I care about how you're going to fix it. If this deal falls apart because of your incompetence, you'll all be out of a job. Am I clear?"

There's a low murmur of agreement, heads nodding. They're anxious, scrambling to dig themselves out of this hole. They start speaking over one another, offering explanations—political instability, miscommunication with the local team—but their words barely register. Something shifts inside me, a strange unease I can't shake.

It's like a shadow has passed over me, a feeling I can't place. I try to refocus on what they're saying, but their voices are distant, muffled, like I'm hearing them underwater. The room feels smaller, the walls closer, the air heavy. Something is off, but I can't put my finger on it.

What the fuck is happening?

I shift in my seat, trying to push the feeling away, to concentrate on the issue at hand. This deal is too important for distractions. But the uneasiness in my gut grows, gnawing at me. I glance around the room, scanning the faces, but nothing stands out.

They're just as nervous as before, yet no one else seems to feel this . . . whatever "*this*" is.

But I do, and it's getting harder to ignore.

I try to bring the conversation back.

"This deal is critical," I say, my voice steady, though there's an edge of distraction creeping in.

"We need to show the investors we can handle this. If we lose their confidence, we lose everything. Fix it, now." They nod again, more urgently, throwing out suggestions.

I should be listening, analyzing their ideas. But the feeling . . . it's like a dark cloud hovering over me, pressing down. I can't shake it. It's like something is lurking, just out of sight.

And then, suddenly, a memory jolts through me. That night I met Delilah. The instant I sensed something was wrong, danger in the air. I barely knew her then, just a stranger in a bar, but I knew I had to get her out. It didn't make sense at the time, but I followed my gut.

I feel my phone buzzing and I instinctively reach for it. The meeting continues around me, but I know that whatever's coming, it's not good. I'm surprised to see the caller ID.

"Gentlemen, I need to take this," I say, my voice steady despite the turmoil brewing inside me. I look at James, signaling for him to take over. His jaw tightens, and I can see the frustration in his eyes—he thinks the call can wait, that this meeting is more important. But I don't give two fucks. I can't.

I don't even leave the room. I just step aside, my back to the others, blocking out the noise. I focus on the phone in my hand, the device that suddenly feels like both a lifeline and a noose all at once.

"Tyler?" I say as I pick up the call. He knows I'm in Boston; he drove me to the airport. It's not like him to call unless it's about picking me up. There's something wrong. I feel it in the pit of my stomach.

"Mr. Williams, I'm so sorry to bother you, but it's important . . ." Tyler's voice shakes with anxiety. I can hear it, feel it, like static in the air.

"Speak," I order, though my voice is already laced with dread. A cold sweat breaks out across my skin.

"Ms. Rose was in a car accident—" he starts, and in that instant, the world stops. Everything around me blurs, the sounds of the room fading into a distant hum. I can't breathe. My chest tightens like a vise, and the air seems to thin out, slipping from my grasp.

"How is she?" I manage to choke out, each word a struggle as panic grips my throat.

My mind is racing, screaming.

Please, God, don't take her away from me. Please, Lord, don't take her from me.

"Sir, she was severely wounded . . ." Tyler's words hit me like a freight train. I'm gasping, trying to suck in air that won't come. My heart pounds against my ribs, my blood roaring in my ears. The pain in my chest is unbearable, like a physical wound tearing through me. I can't lose her. I can't live without her. She's everything to me—my heart, my soul, my home.

James's eyes are on me, the entire room falling silent as they sense the shift in my demeanor. But I couldn't care less about them right now. All I can think about is Delilah and the overwhelming fear that I'm about to lose her.

Please, baby, please, don't leave me. I beg you, baby, please don't leave me. I can't live without you.

"Which hospital is she in?" I ask, my voice barely above a whisper. It hurts to breathe, every breath a jagged edge slicing through my chest. I'm terrified of what he's going to say next, terrified of the words that might shatter my world completely.

"Sir, Delilah is not at the hospital . . ." Tyler's voice trails off, and my worst fear slams into me with brutal force. She's dead. My Delilah is gone. The realization crashes over me, drowning me in a tide of grief and despair. I won't see her beautiful face again. I won't hear her laugh, or feel her warmth beside me. My baby is gone.

That's impossible, it can't be real, this can't be happening.

The tears well up in my eyes, and I can't stop them. I fall to my knees, the strength leaving my body as the weight of this unbearable loss pulls me down. The ground meets me with a dull thud, but I don't feel the pain. All I feel is the gaping hole in my chest where my heart used to be.

I know people are around me, probably staring, trying to figure out what's happening. But they don't matter. None of it matters. I can feel everyone leaving the room on James's orders, but I don't even see. *This isn't real. It's a nightmare, obviously, I'll wake up soon.* My Delilah can't be gone. I never got to tell her what she really means to me. She can't leave this world without knowing that I love her. I love her more than anything. I love her more than life itself.

My world collapses in on itself, the grief swallowing me whole. I can't breathe. I can't think. I can't accept this. All I can do is cry out silently to the universe, to whatever power is out there, begging for it to be a mistake, for this to be some kind of nightmare that I'll wake up from. But deep down, I know the truth. My Delilah is gone, and with her, she's taken every last piece of me.

I put the phone back to my ear, desperate to hear the frightening words clearly.

"Where is she?" I ask as panic claws at my throat.

"She's home, that's why I called you." *What?*

"How the hell was she in a car accident, died, and then went home?" I ask, my voice unsteady.

"No, sir, you misunderstood me. I'm sorry. She *was* in a car accident, called her security team to pick her up, and begged them to drive her straight home, not to the hospital. She refuses to go to the hospital and refuses to see a doctor. Frances called me because she doesn't know how to deal with the situation," he says, his words rushing out. Thank FUCK! The relief I feel right now is indescribable. But now anger starts to rise in my body.

"How the fuck is that possible?! How is she? What the fuck is going on? What the fuck happened?!" I say, my voice rising, uncontrollable. I glance at James, furious, and tell him to call for the jet as we leave the building, still on the phone with Tyler.

"Sir, Delilah said she didn't want to go to the hospital and took care of herself, but she's not okay. I fear she might not—"

"Why the fuck did you all listen to her? How come none of you had any fucking sense? What the hell happened? You better start talking because I'm on my way back home," I say, seething with anger.

"I'm sorry. It's hard to make Ms. Rose do something she doesn't want. She said she has no health insurance and was already indebted to the hospital. She didn't want to ask for your money."

Okay, the little act about the good girl who doesn't want her man's money has to fucking end. I'm in the car that'll drive us back to the airport, and fury is growing inside me. I'm going to fire every one of them. I'll make sure every one of them is out of a job forever.

"Where are you?" I say, cold as ice, with disgust in my tone.

"I'm at your penthouse. I came as soon as I heard."

"Put Delilah on the phone. Now."

"Sir, she's sleepi—"

"Don't make me repeat myself," I say, my tone menacing. I hear some noise over the phone, doors creaking open. I'm so furious, but at the same time, so relieved she's alive. I hear him calling her, trying to wake her, and after a few attempts, she answers him, and I can hear everything.

"Ms. Rose, I'm so, so sorry to wake you up, but Mr. Williams wants to talk to you."

"I'll see him in the morning, please, I need to sleep," she mumbles. God, I thought I'd never hear her voice again.

"Ms. Rose, if you don't take the phone, I'll be out of a job. I beg you to take the phone," he says.

That's right—you will. All of you.

"Nate," she exhales into the phone.

"You have ten fucking seconds to go to the hospital before I drag you there myself."

"I'm fine, Nate. Don't be dramatic," she says, and her voice is unsteady, trying to smile through the phone. *She's lying.*

"Listen to me while you still can. You'll go with Tyler straight to the hospital, and I'll meet you there. Don't you dare open your fucking mouth to me right now, or I swear the fucking car accident will be a treat compared to what's coming. You scared the shit out of me. I'm on my way. I'll see you there." I hang up, not giving her time to answer.

I was fucking terrified of losing her. The kind of fear that rips through your chest and leaves you gasping for air, drowning in the thought of a world without her in it. But now that fear has twisted into something else, something darker. I'm so fucking furious.

The rage is like fire in my veins, burning through the terror and leaving only one thought in its wake—I need someone to fucking pay for this.

I grab my phone, my fingers trembling with barely contained fury, and dial the number. It rings once before they pick up.

"Explain," I command, my voice cold and sharp, like a blade poised to strike.

"Sir, I'm sorry—"

"I don't need your sorry," I snap, my voice rising. "I need your explanation."

There's a brief pause, and I can hear the nervousness on the other end. *Good.* They should be fucking scared.

"She texted us, asking if we could give a lift home to her sick friend or coworker. She said she wouldn't leave the building while we were away. There was a lot of traffic, and then we came back and told her we were there, but she didn't answer. We thought she was deep in her work. We didn't know . . . Then we received a geolocation point via a text message without any explanation. We went there and saw her . . . covered in blood, barely standing. We rushed out of the car and helped her. She begged us to take her home. She said she couldn't afford to go to the hospital. She said you couldn't help. She was in distress. We didn't want to argue too much because we feared she'd pass out. I'm sorry. I know we shouldn't have listened to her and should've driven her to the hospital anyway, but—"

"There is no but!" I scream. The image of Delilah—my Delilah—covered in blood, standing alone on the street, flashes in my mind, and it feels like someone's squeezing my heart with a fist made of iron. *What the fuck happened?*

"I know, sir—"

"Who was driving? Whose fucking car was she in?" I cut him off, my voice dangerously low, like the calm before the storm.

"We don't know, sir. She won't say. We've done some research, and there was a car accident in the area. It was a cab. We don't know for sure if it was Delilah's . . ."

"Why would she need a fucking cab? Where was Tyler? Where the fuck was she going?" I demand, my voice rising with each question. I need answers. I need to know who to blame.

"She didn't say, sir. I'm sorry."

"You're not. But you will be," I say, and hang up before they can respond. The words taste bitter in my mouth, but I can't stop. I need to fucking know what happened.

The rest of the flight is a haze of rage and desperation. I call everyone I can think of—anyone who might have seen something, who might know where she was going, what the fuck happened. But no one has answers. It's like she just disappeared, leaving nothing but blood and fear behind.

I'm fucking hurt. I'm fucking angry. I want to destroy everything around me, to make the world feel the pain that's tearing through me. James doesn't even dare ask what's going on. He can see the storm brewing in me, and he knows better than to step into its path. *Good.* I need space. I need to focus on finding out what the fuck happened. I need to see her. I need to know she's okay, that she's still here with me.

And then the text comes in like a punch to the gut. Delilah won't budge. She won't leave the bed. She's asleep, and no one dares move her against her will, to carry her to a fucking car and drive her to the fucking hospital where she fucking should be.

Looks like I'm going to do it myself.

The plane lands, and I see Tyler waiting for me on the tarmac, standing by the car. I look him straight in the eyes so he can feel my wrath. My rage is a living thing, coiling inside me, ready to strike. I don't speak as I get into the car. I don't need to. He knows.

He knows I'm about to unleash hell.

He drives straight to the penthouse, not saying a word. The tension is thick enough to cut with a knife. As soon as we pull up in front of the building, I turn to him.

"Wait here," I order, my voice ice-cold. "I'll be back with Delilah in less than five motherfucking minutes."

I don't wait for a response. I'm already out of the car, heading straight for the elevator. The ride up feels like an eternity, my heart pounding in my chest like a war drum. When the doors open, I'm practically running toward the bedroom. I throw open the door, my eyes locking onto the bed where she lies.

There she is—my Delilah, my love, my life—lying there, pale and fragile, but alive. Relief crashes over me, almost knocking me off my feet. But it's mixed with so much anger, so much fury at what she's gone through, at what could have happened, that I can barely contain it. I want to hold her, to protect her, to never let her out of my sight again. More than anything, I need to understand. I need to know why. I need to know how to make it right.

But for now, all I can do is stare at her, my heart breaking and mending all at once.

And I know, whatever it takes, I will never let this happen again.

I get closer and pull the blanket off her, carefully placing one hand under her knees and the other under her back to carry her. She slowly opens one eye, and the second she sees me, she smiles.

"Am I dreaming?" she says. *Smart-ass.* I shake my head in response as I walk toward the door, still carrying her.

"I hope to God you didn't come home for me," she grumbles. "I can walk, I'm fine." She's trying to get down. *Wrong decision.*

I hold her tighter. She winces and decides to let me do it. I still can't speak.

"Nate, I'm okay," she repeats. I know she's trying to soothe me, but I'm too overwhelmed by the whole fucking thing. I reach the elevator, waiting for the damn thing to arrive at last.

"Oh, so now I get the silent treatment," she says, realizing I don't want to talk. I'm so fucking mad at the situation. She rests her head on my neck. I know her. I know that's her way of telling me she's happy to see me, but she'll never say it. She'll never admit it. Little does she know how happy *I* am to see her. Alive.

Tyler opens the door when he sees us coming. We settle into the car and head straight to the hospital.

We make it there in twenty minutes. I step out of the car, cradling Delilah in my arms. Tyler opens the door, and I stride toward the emergency room entrance. Delilah tries to protest, saying she's fine, but I don't listen. She's pale, too pale, and her breathing is shallow. I feel the weight of her in my arms, lighter than she should be, fragile.

The automatic doors slide open, and I shout for a doctor. The nurses stop what they're doing and rush toward me like I'm running the place. Their eyes widen when they see Delilah, and I don't need to explain.

A doctor approaches us, a man in his early forties with tired eyes but a steady demeanor. He steps forward, looking between me and Delilah with a quick, assessing glance.

"She was in a car accident," I say quickly, my voice tight. "She's pretending to be fine, but she's in a lot of pain."

The doctor nods, gesturing to a nurse to bring over a gurney.

"Let's get her checked out. Can you tell me her name?"

"Delilah Rose," I reply, my voice softening as I say her name. "She's twenty-six."

The doctor jots down the information, then looks up at me, his expression turning serious.

"Are you a family member?"

"I'm her husband," I say without hesitation.

Delilah, despite the pain she's in, suddenly bursts out laughing, the sound unexpected and sharp. It catches the attention of the nearby nurses. I roll my eyes, a mix of frustration and affection swirling inside me. This woman, even now, still finds a way to tease me.

The doctor looks between us, a hint of confusion on his face, but he doesn't press the issue. He motions to the gurney, and I set Delilah onto it, though my hands are reluctant to let go.

As they wheel her toward the examination area, I stay by her side, holding her hand.

She's still chuckling, even as pain flashes across her face again.

"You're impossible, you know that?" I murmur, squeezing her hand lightly.

She just smiles weakly at me, her eyes half-lidded as the pain edges back in. It's more intense now that the adrenaline is wearing off. While they examine her, she tries to smile, to reassure me, but her face is a mask of pain. A nurse checks her vitals; the numbers flash on the monitor—blood pressure too low, heart rate too fast.

A surgeon arrives, eyes sharp behind his glasses. He scans Delilah, his hands moving over her ribs, her abdomen. He frowns, then his expression turns urgent. He calls for an immediate OR. I don't understand what's happening, why everything shifts from tense to frantic.

"What the fuck is going on?" I demand, my voice rough, almost a growl. The surgeon doesn't answer me directly. He just says Delilah needs surgery right now, and they push me back, telling me I can't be in the room.

"No, I'm not leaving her," I say, stepping forward. But a nurse places a hand on my chest, gently but firmly stopping me.

"Sir, please. We need to act fast."

"I said, I'm. Not. Leaving. Her."

"If you want her to live, you have to let the doctors operate. Your wife is in good hands, sir." *Your wife . . .*

I want to fight, to throw them aside and stay with her, but the look in their eyes stops me. They're scared too, I realize. They're scared for her. And that terrifies me.

I'm left standing in the hallway, the doors swinging shut in front of me. The cold air bites at my skin, the fluorescent lights buzz overhead—too bright, too harsh. I feel lost, like the walls are closing in, squeezing the breath out of me.

I find a corner, lean against the wall, and slide down to the floor. My hands cover my face, and then I do—once more—something I hardly ever do: I pray.

Please, I beg you, please, keep Delilah safe, let her come back to me. I beg you, please.

My chest tightens with fear, a fear I can't control, a fear that eats away at my insides like acid.

Time drags, each second an eternity. The sounds of the hospital—footsteps, beeping machines, hushed voices—blend together. I'm alone, completely alone, and I don't know if she's going to make it. My mind races, imagining the worst. I try to push the thoughts away, but they keep coming, relentless.

I grip the edge of my jacket, knuckles white, and whisper her name. I can't lose her. Not now, not ever. She's everything. I close my eyes, forcing myself to breathe, to keep it together. But it's so damn hard when all I can do is wait and hope and pray.

I sit in the cold hallway, my elbows on my knees, my head in my hands. Time feels like it's stretching, each minute an hour, each second a minute. My heart pounds in my chest, and I can't shake the fear gnawing at me.

Finally, after what feels like forever, I see the doctor coming toward me. I stand up quickly, my legs stiff from sitting so long. His face is calm, but I search his eyes for any sign of what's to come.

"She'll be fine," he says, and I feel the air rush out of my lungs in a shaky breath. "Delilah is going to be okay, but she was very, very lucky."

"Thank God," I whisper, running a hand through my hair, the tension in my body starting to loosen just a bit.

"She's in the recovery room now," the doctor continues, nodding down the hallway. "I can take you there."

I follow him, my footsteps heavy but steady. When we reach the recovery room door, he turns to me, a sympathetic look on his face.

"You can't come in just yet," he says softly. "She needs to rest. You can wait outside, or if you prefer, go home. We can call you once she wakes up."

I shake my head, not even considering the option.

"I'm not leaving. I just want to be with her."

The doctor nods, as if he expected my answer.

"I understand. But she's stable, and she won't need much time to come around."

"What did you do in the OR?" I ask, needing to know what they found, what they had to fix.

The doctor hesitates for a moment, then says, "Delilah had an abnormality in her ribs. It's something we rarely see—a malformation caused by the accident that made them more fragile. One of her ribs punctured a small blood vessel, causing internal bleeding. We repaired it, reinforced the weakened ribs, and she should heal well, but she'll need to be careful." I nod, absorbing the information, but it feels like there's more.

"Is that all?" I ask, my voice edged with worry.

"She'll need to tell you the rest," he says, his tone firm but reassuring. "It's important she hears it first from us, but don't worry. Delilah is fine. She's going to live."

I try to let his words sink in, to hold on to the relief they're supposed to bring. But the knot in my chest doesn't completely unravel. I thank him, and he gives me one last nod before leaving me alone outside the recovery room.

I sit down again, this time on the floor, my back against the wall, and stare at the door. I'm so close to her, yet I still feel so far away. I'm exhausted, but I don't even think about closing my eyes. I sit there and just wait, focusing on the thought of her waking up, of seeing her again, and knowing she's going to be okay.

Out of the corner of my eye, I notice movement. I turn my head and see a man in a wheelchair being pushed by a nurse. He's wounded—his face is pale, lined with age, maybe in his fifties, and his arm is in a cast. They're getting closer to Delilah's room, and they don't seem to notice me sitting there.

The nurse stops in front of Delilah's door. She glances down at the man in the wheelchair and says, "This is her room, but I don't know if she's awake yet."

The man looks at the door, his expression tense but soft, like he's carrying some heavy burden.

"Can I stay and wait until she does?" he asks, his voice quiet and almost pleading.

A surge of protectiveness and anger flares up inside me. I push myself off the floor, my muscles tense, and step toward them.

"Who the hell are you?" I demand, my voice sharp, cutting through the quiet hallway.

The man looks up at me, surprised, and the nurse blinks, startled by my sudden appearance. I don't care. All I can think about is Delilah lying in that room, and this stranger wanting to see her.

"Why do you want to see her?" I ask again, my tone hard, eyes locked on the man.

He looks like he's been through hell, but I don't let that soften my suspicion.

The man hesitates, glancing at the nurse before he looks back at me. There's something in his eyes—regret, pain, something I can't quite place. But I don't lower my guard. Not until I know what's going on.

"I . . . I just want to make sure she's okay," he finally says, his voice low, almost pleading.

I narrow my eyes, still not satisfied with his answer.

"How do you know her?"

The nurse steps in, trying to calm things down.

"Maybe we should talk about this somewhere else," she suggests, but I don't move.

"I'm not going anywhere until I know who this guy is and why he's here," I say firmly, my gaze never leaving the man in the wheelchair.

He sighs, looking worn out, and meets my eyes.

"I'm someone who owes her my life," he says, his voice heavy with something deeper. "I know you don't know me, but I'm not here to cause trouble. I just want to see her, to know she's okay. And thank her," he says.

Still, I'm not ready to let him in.

"You can wait here," I say, keeping my voice firm. "But you're not going in until I know more."

The man nods, accepting my terms without argument, and the nurse steps back, giving us space. I stand there, watching him closely, still on edge, trying to figure out what the fuck is going on. The only thing I know for sure is that I'm not letting anyone near Delilah until I know exactly who they are and what they want.

"I'm . . . the driver," he says in a shaky voice. My heart stops. The words hang in the air like a death sentence. This is the man responsible for why Delilah is lying in that room, broken and battered. Rage surges through me, burning hot and fierce. I feel my fists clenching, my whole body tensing, ready to lash out.

He sees the anger in my face, the way it twists and hardens my features, and he starts speaking quickly, his words stumbling over each other as tears stream down his face.

"She saved me," he says, his voice cracking, tears spilling freely now. "I need to thank her, to make sure she's okay . . . just like she made sure I was."

I'm shaking, trying to hold myself together, but his words are like ice in my veins.

"What happened?" I ask, my voice cold, barely controlled.

He looks at me, broken, guilt-ridden.

"She was late . . . She needed to get to Murray Street. She asked me to drive fast, so I took some shortcuts I know. It all happened so fast . . . A car came out of nowhere and crashed into us. It hit the side where the young lady—where Delilah—was sitting. I remember the car flying through the air, flipping over, and then . . . nothing. It all became a blur."

He sobs, his whole body shaking with the force of it, but he keeps talking. He needs to get it all out.

"I was stuck. I couldn't move, I couldn't speak, but I was aware. I heard her scream and cry, and I couldn't do anything. My body just . . . stopped working. She fought to get out of the car, and I . . . I couldn't help her. I couldn't even speak." He's crying harder now, the memories tearing him apart.

"She made it to the sidewalk. The street was empty . . . I was scared. I tried to scream, to call her, but nothing came out. Somehow, the next minute, she was back. She managed to break the door open, she screamed and cried even more, but she promised to help me. She was in a terrible state, but she didn't leave me."

I listen, frozen, as he continues, the words barely getting through the fog of my own emotions.

"She pulled the seatbelt with her own strength, tore through the airbag, held me, dragged me out of the car . . . She kept saying, 'I'm here, don't worry, you'll make it, I promise,' and her words . . . they soothed me. She had barely any time, and then the car exploded. Our bodies were thrown away, and I blacked out. When I woke up, I was here, in the hospital. I asked for her, and they said I was the only one there. She was the one who called 911 too . . . And then a nurse came and said a woman had arrived, had been in a car accident earlier in the day. I had to come and see her. I'm so, so sorry," he finishes, his voice breaking as he cries his heart out.

I don't move. I don't comfort him. I can't. My mind is reeling, trying to process what he's just told me.

Delilah came back for him. She saved him. She risked her life for a man she didn't even know. That says everything about the woman I share my life with.

I've always known Delilah had a good soul, even if she doesn't like to admit it. She loves to pretend she's not as kind as she is, that she's tougher, harder. But she is good. She's better than good. And hearing what she did, how she fought through her own pain to save this man . . . Delilah is the bravest, most incredible person I've ever known. I think I just fell in love with her all over again.

The nurse tells the man that he needs to rest and offers him the chance to come back in the morning to see Delilah. I don't respond, I don't even look at them. I just need to see her. Fuck. I'm going in, I don't give a shit what people say, I just need to be right beside her.

I step into the room, and there she is—Delilah. Lying on that hospital bed, surrounded by tubes and wires, machines beeping quietly around her. Her body, usually so full of life, now seems impossibly fragile, wrapped in the cold sterility of the hospital. But even in this state, she radiates strength. It's in the quiet rise and fall of her chest, the way her brow is slightly furrowed as if she were still fighting, even in her sleep. How did I get so fucking lucky to walk into that bar that day? To find her? To have her in my life?

I move closer, and every step feels heavier, like the weight of the fear I've been carrying is settling deeper into my bones. I take her hand—her fingers are cold, but her skin is soft, like silk beneath my thumb, just like always. The contrast of her softness against the harshness of this place makes me ache inside.

"Hi, baby, it's me. I'm here," I whisper, squeezing her hand gently. My voice cracks a little, betraying how shaken I am, but I keep holding on, willing some of my warmth, my strength, to transfer to her. I tell myself she's safe now, that the doctors did their job, but the fear still grips me like a vise. I'm scared—no, I'm fucking terrified. She's lying there, so beautiful, so goddamn beautiful it physically hurts to look at her.

"I miss you, baby," I murmur, my voice low. "I'll stay right here, and I'll wait for you to wake up." I lower myself into the chair beside her bed, never letting go of her hand. The silence between us feels too loud, the hum of machines the only sound, but I don't care. I'll wait here as long as it takes.

The emotions are building inside me, threatening to spill over. There's nothing I can control right now—not her pain, not her recovery, not the storm inside me. It's all out of my hands, and it's driving me insane. With one hand still gripping hers, I fumble for my phone with the other. My fingers are clumsy, shaking, but I manage to fire off a few texts—James, Chloe, Anders, and Danny, the head of my PR team.

I make it clear that I need privacy. I tell them to handle the press, to make sure that no one, absolutely no one, dares to leak any information about Delilah or me. I'm ready to sue anyone who tries. I also need a lie—a good one, something to tell my family if they start asking where I've disappeared to. They won't understand. No one can. I tell them I'm cutting my phone off for the next few days. My only focus is on Delilah and her health, nothing else.

As I hit Send, the weight of everything presses down on me all at once. The adrenaline starts to fade, replaced by exhaustion I didn't even realize I was carrying. I lean forward, resting my head on the bed next to her, still holding her hand, my face inches from hers. I don't even feel myself slipping into sleep—my body just gives in, the only thing anchoring me to the world being the touch of her hand in mine.

~

I feel it before I fully wake up—Delilah's hand threading through my hair, soft and warm. It's the kind of touch that pulls me out of the fog of sleep slowly, gently, like she's trying not to break the moment. I don't want to open my eyes yet; I just want to stay here, feeling her fingers in my hair grounding me in her presence. But I can't help it. I open my eyes, and there she is.

She's smiling at me. That damn smile. It hits me like a punch to the chest, and I melt. She's been through hell, and yet somehow, she's still so fucking beautiful, still has that look in her eyes that makes me forget how to breathe.

"Hi," she murmurs, her voice a little raspy but alive, and I could cry just hearing it. Her fingers keep moving through my hair, and I just stay there, staring at her like an idiot, because I can't believe she's awake, she's here, she's okay.

"You didn't have to do all this," she whispers. "But I feel better now, so thank you. I'm ready to go now." That hits me like a truck.

"No," I say, a bit too sharply, but I can't help it. I sit up straight, looking at her like she's just said the most dangerous thing in the world.

"No, you're staying right here."

Her smile falters, and I can see the stubbornness in her eyes, the way she's about to argue, and I can't fucking do this right now.

"Delilah, please. I'm not ready to have that conversation. Not ready to talk about why the hell you didn't want to go to the hospital in the first place or why the fuck you were in an accident with a stranger while we have all the staff in the world. I'm not ready for a fight." My voice is tight, almost begging. I feel like if I let go of this moment, I might lose her all over again.

I say, "Can we just . . . can we just sit here? Let me have this. Let me appreciate that fucking smile of yours for a second."

She looks at me, the fight draining out of her eyes, and instead, there's something softer, something that makes me feel more at ease.

I reach for her hand, holding it tight, feeling the warmth of her skin under mine.

"The doctors said you're going to be alright," I tell her, my voice low, almost a whisper. "But . . . there's something they need to tell you. Something I don't know about."

Her eyes search mine, and for the first time, I see a flicker of fear in them. It's small, but it's there, and it breaks something in me. I want to protect her from everything, but I can't protect her from this. I don't know what the doctors are going to say, and that terrifies me.

"I don't know what it is," I admit, my voice shaking just a little. "But whatever it is, we'll face it together, okay? I'm not going anywhere."

She doesn't respond as she looks at the ceiling. I don't push it; I don't have the fucking energy to do so.

"I'm sorry," she says, her voice barely audible. I nod, not able to formulate words.

The door to Delilah's hospital room swings open, and two doctors walk in, their faces serious but calm. I feel my body tense immediately. I'm holding Delilah's hand, trying to stay cool, but fuck, this has been the longest night of my life. They start speaking, their voices steady, clinical.

"Ms. Rose, the surgery went well," one of them says, flipping through some papers.

"We managed to stop the internal bleeding, and we addressed the malformation in your hip. It was more complicated than we initially thought, but it's stable now. You're going to need some time to heal, but everything looks good."

I glance over at Delilah, watching her absorb the information. Her face doesn't give away much, but I can tell she's relieved. I am too, but not fully. Something in me still feels like a coiled spring.

The doctor continues, looking between us.

"If you hadn't come to the hospital when you did, Ms. Rose, you wouldn't have survived the night. You would have died in your sleep."

Those words hang in the air and hit me in the gut. My chest tightens, my grip on her hand reflexively tightens. But then Delilah looks at them, calm as hell, and says:

"It wasn't my time."

I swear my heart stops. What the fuck did she just say? I snap my head toward her, the shock running through me like an electric current.

"Because I stepped up!" I say, my voice low, but it's loaded with anger, fear, everything I've been holding in.

"That's why you're alive. Because I fucking made sure you'd come here."

She meets my eyes and just says, "Things come in threes."

I stare at her, completely confused. What the fuck does that even mean? The doctors look at each other but don't interrupt. I don't know whether to scream or break down, but the look in her eyes tells me she's not ready to explain it, not yet.

One of the doctors clears his throat and looks back at Delilah.

"Ms. Rose, you shouldn't have tried to sew your own wound. That was a deep laceration. You could've caused an infection or further damage to the tissue. Internal stitching like that requires precise work."

I snap my head back toward her, my eyes wide.

"You tried to sew your own fucking wound?" I say loudly. I can't believe what I'm hearing.

She just shrugs, completely nonchalant, like it's nothing.

"Wasn't my first time."

I'm floored. I can't even find the words. My mind is racing, and my throat tightens. There's a mixture of outrage, sadness, and a deep, gnawing fear in me. What the hell has she been through? And why does she think this is normal?

Before I can say anything else, a psychologist steps into the room. The doctor turns to me and says, "Mr. Williams, we need to speak with Ms. Rose privately. It's important she has a safe space to talk about . . . well, everything." I feel my body go rigid.

"I'm not fucking leaving," I say, my voice cold. "You'd need the fucking military to get me out of here."

The doctor opens his mouth, but Delilah interrupts with a soft laugh.

"He's my *husband,* so I guess he can stay. I don't mind."

The word *"husband"* hits me like a warm wave, and for a second, I forget the shitstorm we're in. I look at her, and something tight in my chest begins to loosen.

She called me her husband for the sake of the joke, but fuck, I already know right then and there, I'll make sure it's real. Soon.

The doctor sighs and nods.

"Alright, Mr. Williams. You can stay."

He pulls up a scan on his tablet and points to the screen.

"Ms. Rose, during your MRI, we found an alarming number of cracked bones—some of which look like they've been healing for years. It's not situated in one zone but everywhere in your body. In my thirty years of practice, I've never seen this many fractures in one body. And with no visible scars."

What the fuck? I'll burn them all, I will fucking burn them to the ground when I get my hands on whoever *they* are.

"You're either incredibly lucky or . . ." He pauses, glancing at the psychologist.

"This will need immediate treatment to promote bone regeneration. We have a process that uses specialized injections to help speed up healing here at the hospital—one every month—but it's costly."

Before the doctor even finishes, I cut in.

"Money isn't a problem." I turn to Delilah, giving her a hard look.

"Don't fucking try to say anything."

She doesn't. She just looks down, silent. The room feels heavy. The doctor clears his throat again.

"Ms. Rose, would you like to explain how your bones ended up in this condition? We have a psychologist here if you'd like to talk about it."

Delilah stays quiet, her head lowered. She doesn't even look at me. My heart fucking breaks in that moment. I squeeze her hand, trying to reassure her.

"It's okay," I whisper. But she doesn't respond.

After a long, uncomfortable pause, I turn to the doctors.

"Maybe she needs more rest. Maybe tomorrow we can try again." The doctor nods.

"That's reasonable. We'll keep her overnight for observation, but her vitals look strong. She should be able to leave the hospital tomorrow."

Relief washes over me, but it's mixed with a deep sense of unease. As the doctors file out, I sit back down next to Delilah, still holding her hand. There's so much I want to say, so much I don't even know how to say it. But right now, I'm just grateful she's here. Grateful she's alive.

The rest . . . we'll figure out.

CHAPTER 21
Delilah

We left the hospital about half an hour ago and went straight home. As soon as we step inside the apartment, the dogs rush to us, their tails wagging, tongues out, barking like crazy. I can't help but smile. God, I missed them. I kneel down, and they're all over me, licking my face, nudging my hands. It's like they knew something was wrong, but now that I'm back, they're happy. I'm happy too. For a moment, everything feels *"normal."*

Nate stands nearby, quiet. He doesn't join in, just watches. He's been like this since we left the hospital. Silent. Not a word, not even when I tried to make a joke in the car.

He's tense, like he's holding something back. I try not to think too much about it.

He's going to leave you. You'll soon be left alone.

We go into the kitchen. I settle at the counter, the dogs following me, while Nate leans against the wall, arms crossed, eyes on me. He doesn't say anything, and the silence feels heavy. Too heavy. I keep myself busy, stroking the dogs, but my mind is all over the place.

I met my new doctor before we left. He talked about the treatment for my bones, the injections I'll need. I listened, nodded, but honestly? I feel fine. My body doesn't hurt anymore. The doctor acts like I'm still broken, but I'm not. I've been through worse. I don't need this extra fuss.

But Nate . . . he hasn't left my side since we got to the hospital. Even now, he's hovering, watching. Silent. I can't take it anymore.

I look at him, taking a deep breath.

"You're quiet," I say. Simple. Direct.

He doesn't answer right away. His jaw tightens, and he looks away for a second, like he's thinking. Then he looks back at me, his eyes dark, like he's trying to figure out what to say.

I decide to push a bit.

"Nate, if you want to say something, just . . . say it, okay?"

He stiffens, his eyes narrowing. For a moment, I think he's going to snap, but he just stays there, silent. The tension in the room is thick.

"I'm fine," I say, my voice firm. "I'm not hurt anymore."

His eyes flash, and I can see the anger, the fear bubbling under the surface. He's not fine. Not even close.

"You're not fine, Delilah," he finally says, his voice low but harsh. "You almost died."

I don't know what to say to that. It's true. I could've died. But I didn't. And now I just want to move on.

"I don't need all this," I say, trying to sound calm. "The doctors, the injections . . . I'm okay."

Nate shakes his head, pushing off the wall and stepping closer.

"You're not okay. You think this is nothing, but you don't get it. You could've died because you didn't go to the hospital right away. You don't get to brush this off." I stare at him, my heart pounding. I hate admitting it, but he's right.

"I know, but I'm fine, I swear," I say, my voice barely above a whisper.

He sighs, running a hand through his hair, clearly frustrated.

"What happened? I know some parts, but I need to hear it from you," he says, his eyes locked on mine.

I take a deep breath and tell him everything. From the moment I left the office to why I decided to skip the hospital, how I thought I could handle it. Nate doesn't interrupt. He just listens, stone-faced, not saying a word.

"So, that's it. That's what happened," I say, my voice low, trying to gauge his reaction. Nate exhales sharply.

"This never should have happened," he mutters, his voice tight.

"It's no one's fault . . ." I start, but that only makes him angrier.

"It's everyone's fucking fault!" he yells, his voice booming.

"Tyler should have been there, Ben and Sophia never should have left you, and YOU should never have left work!" His face is flushed with anger, and before I can respond, he cuts me off, eyes blazing.

"The fact that both of those imbeciles saw you covered in blood and drove you home instead of the hospital is fucking beyond me. The fact that neither Frances nor Tyler called an ambulance after they saw you hurt—are you fucking kidding me? And then fucking Sophia and Fran stood there and watched you fucking sew yourself up? That's insane. And you? The motherfucking fact that you chose not to go to the hospital is just—" He pauses, his voice ragged with rage. "I'm fuming. They're all fired, Delilah, so if I were you, I'd rethink my behavior."

"What?!" I can barely believe what I'm hearing. "Nate! That's not fair! You can't fire them for a decision I made!"

"The fuck I can't," he snaps, stepping closer, his voice dripping with authority.

I feel the anger rising in my chest.

"If that's how you want to make things work, then I'm leaving. I'm not staying here if they're not." My voice shakes, but I mean every word.

"Try," he says, his eyes narrowing, a mischievous gleam in them.

"Am I held captive now?" I ask, my voice laced with disbelief. But as I say it, I see a flicker of realization in his face. He's coming back to his senses. *Thank God.*

"No, you're not," he mutters, softer now, but still agitated.

"I don't want to fucking lose you, Delilah. You don't get it," he says, louder, his voice strained.

"Then call them back!" I shoot back, desperate. "And I swear, I won't do it again. Okay? I promise. But only if you call them back. Or I'm fucking leaving you."

"Delilah—"

"What?" I snap.

"Why didn't you go to the hospital?" His voice is quieter now, but there's still an edge to it. I can't dodge the question anymore. I have to tell him the truth. There's no way out of this.

I sigh.

"Before I met you, I went to the hospital once, and I didn't pay the bill. I don't have insurance. I was scared to go there again. I just . . . I can't afford it, okay?" I look him straight in the eyes as I admit it. He seems confused, like he's struggling to understand.

"You know . . . and I mean *you know* that I have money, you *know* it." His voice is calmer, but I can hear the frustration creeping back. "I don't just have money, Delilah. I'm a fucking billionaire. You *knew* that information, and yet . . ." He pauses, exhaling. "I know you don't want me to think you're here for the money and, baby, I get it. I know for a fact that you're not interested in my money. I need to understand," he pleads.

"I don't want to be indebted to you," I say, my voice small. "I owe you too much already."

"But I don't want you to fucking pay me back!" His voice rises again, more exasperated now.

"For now!" I shoot back, my heart racing.

"What the fuck is that supposed to mean?" he shouts.

"It means that you may think that now you're gifting me the money, but when this ends, you'll come back and ask for your money back. And I can't take that fucking risk!"

Nate stares at me, stunned.

"I'm right here, Delilah. I'm not going anywhere."

"Until when?" I scream, my worst fear spilling out. My voice cracks, and I feel exposed. Vulnerable.

He's quiet for a second, his eyes softening.

"You don't get it, do you?" he asks, and now I'm the one confused. I shake my head. I *don't* get it.

"I love you, Delilah," he says, and my world tilts. My heart stops, my breath catches in my throat.

No, this isn't happening. He can't mean it.

I shake my head again, almost in disbelief.

"You can't," I whisper, my voice barely audible.

"Why not?" he asks, his voice gentle now, softer than I've ever heard it.

"You don't know me," I say, my voice shaking, almost pleading. *He can't love me.*

He doesn't even know the half of it.

"Don't I?" he replies, his tone calm, almost reassuring. But I just shake my head.

This is impossible. I'm spiraling, the walls closing in.

This can't be real.

I freeze, my breath catching in my throat. He moves closer, his gaze soft but unyielding, his hands reaching out, gingerly holding mine. The weight of his touch is grounding, but I'm spinning. *I don't want to hear this. I can't.*

"I know you, Delilah," he says quietly. "I know you think I don't, that there are parts of you hidden away. But I see you, baby. I see everything that matters."

I open my mouth to argue, to push him away, but he squeezes my hands a little tighter, holding me there, in this moment.

"Let me explain," he starts. "I love the way you care," he says, his voice thick with emotion. "How you take care of everything—the dogs, the house, how you take care of me . . . You don't even realize it, but you've turned this cold penthouse into a home.

"You've given it life. You've given *me* life."

My heart stutters, but I can't speak. I don't know how to respond. *How can he say these things? How can he mean them?*

Nate continues, his voice quiet, but the emotion in it is like a tidal wave crashing over me.

"It's the simple things. The way you laugh when you're watching TV, the way you keep everything so clean, like it gives you some control over the chaos. Sometimes I even mess up a little on purpose, just so I can watch you more. I love the way you hum under your breath when you're cooking, how you always outdo yourself just to please me. The way your voice sounds when you sing—God, when I hear you sing, Delilah, it's like I'm flying. The way you make everything around you . . . brighter. You don't even see it, but your smile? It lights up the darkest room."

I feel a lump forming in my throat. I don't want to believe any of this. I don't want to let it in. But his words, they're burrowing deep.

"And it's how you are with others, too," Nate says, his voice catching. "I love how you try to see the good in people who've been shitty to you. And the other day, even after the accident, when you could barely stand, you still went and saved that old man. You didn't know him. You could've left, but you didn't. You put him first, like you always do, and that's what defines you, sweet Delilah. I love the fact that you have this strength, this resilience that amazes me every single day."

My chest tightens, and I shake my head, trying to fight back the emotions threatening to spill over.

"Nate . . ." I manage to whisper, but he keeps going, his voice more intense now. "And when you look at me . . ." He pauses, his eyes searching mine.

"When you look at me like I'm something worth loving . . . it undoes me, Delilah. You make me want to be better. You make me want to come home every day. I count the seconds until I can see your smile. Until I can be near you."

I can't breathe. The words are too much. Too big. Too real.

This can't be happening. He's lying.

Nate reaches up, brushing a tear from my cheek that I didn't even realize had fallen. His touch is so gentle, and it only makes it harder to keep my emotions at bay.

"I also love you because you're a fucking survivor. You rose from the dust when the world tried to break you. You didn't just survive—you fought, you pushed through every bit of pain, and you came out stronger. And that strength, Delilah . . . it amazes me all the time." *I can't breathe.*

"I love how you fight," he says, his voice softening again. "How you're fighting for school, for work, for a life you don't even realize you're already a part of. You try so hard, Delilah, but you're already there. You belong, baby. You belong with me."

I shake my head again, more tears slipping down, my chest tightening with a mix of fear and disbelief.

"I don't—" I start, but my voice cracks, and I can't finish the sentence.

Nate leans forward, his forehead resting against mine, his breath warm on my skin.

"You do. You belong with me. I don't need to know your past to love you. I love who you are right now. I love you every morning when I wake up next to you, feeling like the luckiest man in the world. And I love you every night when I fall asleep by your side, feeling finally complete. Like I've found the one person in this world I can't live without."

I close my eyes, trying to block it out, trying to stop the flood of emotions I can't handle. But his voice keeps pulling me back, wrapping around me like a lifeline.

I open my eyes, and the look in his is so raw, so full of . . . of . . . *love,* it breaks something inside me. I can't breathe. I can't believe any of this. It's too much. It's not true.

I feel like I'm drowning.

"I'm scared," I whisper, admitting my truth, my voice breaking. "I'm so scared, Nate."

"I know," he says, his voice comforting. "I know you are. And that's okay. You don't have to be ready right now. I'll wait for you, Delilah. For as long as it takes. I don't expect anything from you. I just needed you to know how I feel because . . . because I can't keep it inside anymore."

I close my eyes, squeezing his hands tight, trying to hold on to something solid as my world tilts. *It's impossible. It can't be real.*

"Every day I'm with you, I feel like the luckiest man in the world," he murmurs, his voice thick with emotion. "And when I'm inside you, Delilah . . . it's like I'm dancing among the stars. I feel alive in ways I never did before you. You've given me everything without even realizing it."

Tears are streaming down my face now, and I can't stop them. I don't know what to say. I don't know how to be in this moment.

"I love you," he whispers again, his voice shaking now. "I love everything about you. Your strength, your beauty, your heart. You are perfect to me. You don't have to hide anything from me. I'm here, and I'm not going anywhere."

I let out a shaky breath, overwhelmed by the weight of his words. I want to say something, anything, but *I can't.*

I can't admit this is real because if I do, if I let myself believe it, I'll never survive when it all falls apart.

Nate must see the fear in my eyes, because he cups my face, his thumb stroking my cheek.

"I'll wait for you," he says softly. "I'll wait as long as you need. I don't need you to say anything. Just know that I'm here. I'm yours, baby."

I can't speak. I can't move. All I can do is stare at him. I don't even know what to think anymore. Because for the first time, I *want* to believe him. But I'm so scared.

"Nate," I finally whisper, my voice quivering, but I don't know what else to say.

He smiles, brushing another tear from my cheek.

"It's okay," he whispers. "I got you."

"Nate . . . stop, please. You're hurting me," I manage to say, because it's true. I know for a fact that this isn't meant to be. It's too beautiful to be true. He's too fucking perfect to be mine.

I can see the pain caused by my words. His face changes—he's confused, just like I am.

"What can I do to make you believe me?" he insists.

"There's nothing you can do," I say, feeling defeated.

"You're right. There's only one thing *you* can do," he says, and that confuses me.

"What?" I reply. Little did I know what he was about to say.

"Marry me."

Oh. My. God. Oh my God, OH MY GOD!

It's like he shot me, the bullet going straight to my heart. I'm fucking dead right now.

No, no, no, no, no. This CANNOT happen.

If I was speechless before, now I'm completely mute. There is absolutely nothing that can come out, as there is absolutely nothing going right in my head. And so I laugh. Really laugh.

But he doesn't, and then I realize he wasn't joking. *What the fuck?*

"Please tell me you're joking right now."

"I'm not. I want you to trust me when I say that I'm all in. I've been all in from the start. You'll only trust me completely once you're sure that I'm here for the long run. You'll relax. I love you, Delilah. I love you too fucking much," he says, like it's some kind of revelation.

"Oh my God, Nate, no! We can't! This is *so* wrong. When will you realize you deserve better than this?"

"No, baby, when will *you* realize *you* deserve better than this?"

"Nate, let's just drop it, okay? Let's forget about it. I just . . . I don't know, I need a bath." My mind is a mess right now. I don't even know what I say. He's just upset about everything that happened. He thought I was going to die. He's scared, and he's overreacting. That's what he does. Nate listens, his face softening, like he's realizing how absurd his idea was. *Fucking accident.*

He offers to chill on the couch and watch some movies. I want to cook us something, but he insists I should just relax while he orders pizza. I try to tell him I'm fine, that I'm feeling more than okay, but he won't hear it, so I let it go.

After the movie, we slide into the bathtub, Nate having

prepared the perfect bubble bath for us. We debate the last movie we watched, and I'm surprised at how easily the conversation flows, despite everything — despite the fight, despite what he . . . *said.*

Nate makes the bed, but I can't watch him do it wrong. I fight him over the details, telling him how to get it right, scolding him for messing it up. I win that battle, of course.

When we finally settle into bed, relaxed, I'm shocked by how . . . at home I feel. *I shouldn't think of it like that. This isn't mine. This isn't supposed to feel like home.*

Nate pulls me into a warm hug, but he's too gentle. Way too careful.

"Nate, I'm fine, you can hold me tighter," I say with a light smile.

"You just got out of the fucking hospital after a fucking car accident," he grumbles.

"And yet I'm fine," I reply, but Nate just puffs out a breath, still unconvinced.

"Nate?" I ask, my voice soft now.

"Yeah, baby?"

"Can I ask you a favor?"

"Anything."

"Can you make sure Ailly doesn't get in trouble for losing the contracts? It was *my* fault, not hers. Please, I'm so scared for her. This job is everything to her, and I'd feel awful for ruining it."

"It's already taken care of. Ailly won't be held accountable for it. Don't worry," he says, kissing the top of my head while spooning me. I let out a relieved breath and thank him.

We stay silent for a while. Not an awkward silence, far from it. We're just enjoying the comfort of falling asleep next to each other, in each other's arms. Nate kisses my shoulder while I caress his forearm.

"I thought I died," I whisper after a long pause. Nate sits up, listening intently, and I feel his attention pull me into the moment.

"It was after the car flipped. I remember the blood, the smell, the pain . . ." I pause, the memory creeping in too vividly.

"But then . . . I saw your face. I saw your smile. I heard you telling me everything was going to be okay. I felt the darkness closing in, and I felt myself . . . dying. The last thing I remember seeing . . . was you." My voice breaks and goes quiet.

Nate pulls me tighter, his breath warm against my skin as he buries his nose beside my face.

"I love you," he whispers in my ear.

Though I can't respond, held back by fear.

If I let myself feel, I'd fall apart,

For love, once opened, can break the heart.

And then, finally, I fall asleep.

~

A few days have passed since the accident. Nate stayed home with me, working from his home office. I begged him to let us go back to work. I feel extremely good, I don't feel any pain anymore, so he accepted on one condition—that for a whole week, I work with him in his office so he can keep an eye on me.

I still don't know how to feel about this. I've never been taken care of. Not when I was a child and not in my adult life. I want to say I feel like I'm a little girl, yet I don't know what that would be like. Nate taking care of me feels incredibly good to my broken soul, that's a fact. But I know better than to believe any of this is going to last forever. I don't want to think it's true.

When this ends, I'll only suffer more.

Anyway, I accepted his proposition, and today we're at the office together. I won't even begin on his PA's attitude—she's rude, she's offensive, but really, she's just fucking jealous.

I'm seated at the small table by the great window, working on some files while Nate is focused on his own work at his too-big desk.

"Your PA is in love with you," I say, annoyed.

"She's not," he answers, still looking at his computer.

"Wow, and here I thought you were a smart man . . ."

"Smart-ass," he fires back, making me chuckle.

"Anyway, I don't want people to know that, you know, we . . . hum . . . live together," I manage to say, but that only makes him smile.

"That we're a couple, you mean."

"No, not . . . we're not . . . you and . . . oh fuck you," I say, and he bursts out laughing.

Everywhere I look, it's polished, immaculate, and cold, just like the man sitting behind that desk. Except I know the heat that lives under his exterior.

I sit quietly, pretending to be busy with my files, but I can't focus. Not when Nate commands the room with such force. Throughout the day, people come and go, knocking timidly on the door. Executives, partners, and high-ranking managers—each of them seems to shrink in his presence. The moment they step inside, their voices lower, their eyes flicker nervously, as if afraid to breathe wrong. Nate listens, nods, gives them his instructions, and they leave with the kind of briskness that tells me they'd rather be anywhere but here.

And the whole time, I sit on the side, like a shadow. But I'm watching him. Really watching him. I've never seen him like this before, not fully. This isn't just Nate, the man who holds me at night or kisses my scars. This is Nathan Williams, the most powerful man in the building. No, in the city. Hell, maybe even the world.

He moves with precision, his fingers skimming effortlessly over papers, signing documents with a steady hand. He's in total control, his every word commanding attention. I've always known he was good at his job, but this . . . this is another level. I can see now why he's revered, why people fear him. It's not just his position; it's the way he owns every inch of this space.

He looks incredible. The charcoal suit he wears clings to his broad shoulders, tailored perfectly to his body. Every time he shifts in his chair, the fabric stretches over his muscles, and I have to bite my lip to keep from staring too hard. His crisp white shirt peeks through the jacket, and he's wearing my favorite black silk tie. His hands, those strong hands, move confidently over the desk, gripping a pen or shuffling papers, and I can't stop imagining them on me instead.

My body reacts, slowly at first, a soft hum building deep inside me. I cross my legs, pressing them together as the heat starts to pool between my thighs. Every time he speaks, his deep, commanding voice sends shivers down my spine. I try to focus on the screen in front of me, but it's impossible. He's too much. The man is practically oozing power and sex, and it's doing things to me I can barely control.

A few hours later, Nate has a lunch meeting with clients. He glances at me before we leave.

"I'll tell people you're a trainee for the week, as you requested. You're ready?" he asks, his lips curving into that devilish smile I know so well.

"Absolutely, sir," I tease, pretending to really be a trainee. He chuckles, slaps my butt while giving me a fat kiss, and we head out.

At lunch, I do my best to play the part of the quiet observer, seated next to him and his clients, taking notes as if I were some diligent assistant. But under the table, his hand finds my knee. My breath hitches the moment he touches me. His fingers start to move, slowly sliding up my thigh, teasing the sensitive skin there. I try to maintain my composure, try to act like I'm still paying attention to the conversation happening above the table, but his hand keeps moving, higher and higher.

"Good girl," he mouths to me. *Oh my God.* I don't respond because I don't want anyone to suspect what's going on. We're good.

By the time his fingers brush the edge of my skirt, I'm a mess. I squeeze my thighs together, desperate to stop the throbbing between my legs. My heart races, my breaths come shorter. He knows exactly what he's doing to me, the bastard. He never looks my way, his attention fully on the men across from him, but his hand continues its slow torture, his thumb rubbing small circles on my inner thigh. I swallow hard, fighting the moan building in my throat.

By the time we return to the office, my body is on fire. I'm wet, aching for him, barely able to keep my hands still as I try to return to my desk. But it's impossible to focus. Every time I look at him sitting there in all his CEO glory, I'm reminded of how badly I want him. But I see how busy he is, I don't want to trouble him with my needs . . . just yet.

It's the last meeting of the day, and I'm seated in the corner of the boardroom, pretending to work on my files. There's a team of people in the room, presenting some project, but all I can focus on—yet again!—is Nate. He's standing up against the wall, facing the men, one hand in his pocket. *Damn.* I swear I'm drooling right now.

His attention is on the presentation, but all I can think about is how good he looks. His jaw is clenched in concentration, lips parted. Every time he moves, I feel that tug deep in my core, that ache that's been building all day.

But then I notice something else.

Chloe, the bitch, stands next to him, her body angled toward his. At first, I don't think anything of it. She's just doing her job, handing him a document, whispering something in his ear. But then I see her hand. It lingers on his arm for just a second too long. It's not professional. It's intentional.

My stomach twists, and I sit up a little straighter. She's touching him. Not just handing him papers, but actually touching him. Her fingers graze his sleeve, sliding down his forearm as she speaks to him in a low voice. And Nate, oblivious as ever, doesn't seem to notice. But *I* notice. And it pisses me the hell off.

My body tenses as I watch her, trying to stay calm. I grip the edges of my laptop, my nails digging into the sides. Her hand is still on his arm, and I swear she's doing it on purpose. There's no fucking reason for her to be that close to him. Nate's focused on the meeting, unaware of her little game, but I see it. I see the way she looks at him, the way her body leans into his personal space.

Jealousy flares up in my chest, hot and sharp. I can feel my heart pounding in my ears, my body on edge, a mix of desire and anger swirling inside me. She needs to back the fuck off. I bite my lip, forcing myself to stay in my seat, but every second her hand remains on him, my blood boils hotter.

That's it. I've had enough. I pull out my phone discreetly and shoot a text to Nate.

Delilah: *You have ten seconds to remove her hand, or I will.*

I decide to talk to him the way he does—it'll show him how serious I am. He'd never tolerate this if the situation were reversed. But the bastard doesn't take out his phone. I wait until he finally glances at me. It feels like forever, but then he looks at me, and I mouth "phone," which he understands. He takes a look at it and literally laughs out loud.

He leans into her ear—and I swear, I feel like I'm going to kill him for being so close—then he tells her something I can't hear. She backs off, looking pissed, but doesn't respond. Bitch. My phone buzzes.

Nate: *I love you jealous.*

I don't answer him. I just smile.

The meeting ends, everyone leaves, and Nate tells me he just needs to finish something in his office before we head home. I follow him, but as I watch him go, my body buzzes with anticipation.

I can barely focus as we make our way back to Nate's office. All day, I've been watching him—the way he commands attention, the power in every movement, every word. The way people around him are scared of his authority, the effortless control he has over everything. It's driving me insane. He doesn't even realize how much I've wanted him, how every glance, every time his deep voice rolls through the room, it ignites something primal in me.

We step into his office, and I close the door behind us, locking it without a word. Nate walks toward his desk, completely unaware of the fire building inside me. I can't hold it back any longer.

"Nate," I say, my voice breathy with need. He turns, surprised by the intensity in my voice. His brow furrows for a second, as if he were about to ask what's wrong, but I don't give him the chance.

I stride across the room, my heels clicking against the floor. I reach him in an instant, and before he can react, I push him back against his desk, crashing my lips against his. The kiss is fierce, desperate, and he tenses under my touch, caught off guard. But then he responds, his hands gripping my waist, pulling me against him.

"Delilah—" he starts, but I cut him off by biting down on his bottom lip, a playful smile teasing my lips.

"I can't wait anymore," I whisper against his mouth.

"You've been driving me crazy all day, Nate. Watching you like this, in charge, so fucking powerful . . . I need you."

His eyes darken instantly, and I can feel the shift in his body. The tension, the hunger. He's always been able to switch from calm to commanding in an instant, and I know I've just unleashed that side of him.

"You've been thinking about fucking me all day, haven't you?" he growls, gripping my hips tighter, his fingers digging into my flesh.

"Watching me work, getting all hot and bothered like the needy little slut you are."

I shudder at his words, the heat between my legs intensifying. I want him. God, I want him so bad. I nod, unable to form words as my breath comes out in short, needy gasps.

"I bet you could hardly concentrate, sitting there pretending to work," he continues, his voice dripping with authority.

"You've been wet for me this whole time, haven't you?"

I bite my lip and nod again, feeling the throbbing ache inside me building. My body is on fire, every nerve alight with desire.

"I want you, sir," I breathe, my hands running up his chest, feeling the hard muscles under his suit.

"I've been good all day, but now . . . I want to be bad for you."

His eyes flash with something dark and dangerous, and he grabs my chin, forcing me to look up at him.

"You want to roleplay, huh?" he asks, his voice low, seductive.

"You think you can be a little slut for your boss and get away with it?"

I whimper at his words, my body reacting instantly. The heat between my thighs becomes almost unbearable, my skin tingling with need. I can't stop myself from leaning into him, my body aching for more.

"Yes, sir," I whisper, playing along with the game.

"I've been bad. I need you to punish me."

Nate chuckles darkly, spinning me around and pressing me against the edge of his desk. My breath catches in my throat as he leans over me, his hand sliding down my back, tracing the curve of my spine.

"You've been teasing me all day," he growls into my ear, his breath hot against my skin. "Now you're going to learn what happens to bad girls."

I moan softly, my body shaking with anticipation. His hand moves lower, lifting the hem of my skirt. The fabric brushes against my thighs, and I feel the cool air on my heated skin. I bite my lip, trying to stifle the whimper that escapes me.

"Look at you," Nate murmurs, his hand sliding over the curve of my ass. "Already so desperate. You've been aching for me, haven't you?"

"Yes," I gasp, arching my back as his hand moves over me. "Please, sir . . ."

He chuckles again, his fingers trailing along the edge of my panties. I can feel his control, his dominance, and it only makes me want him more. He's teasing me, knowing exactly how to drive me crazy.

"You want me to fuck you, don't you?" he says, his voice dripping with authority.

"You want me to take you right here, on my desk."

"Yes," I breathe, my voice shaky with need.

"Please, Mr. Williams, I need you . . ."

Without warning, he grabs my hips, pulling me closer to him. I gasp as he presses himself against me, his body hot and hard through his suit. I can feel him, every inch of him, and my body responds instantly.

"Beg for it," he growls, his lips brushing against my ear.

"Tell me how much you want it."

I bite my lip, my body shaking with desire.

"Please, Mr. Williams." My words are barely a whisper.

"I need you. I've been thinking about this all day, about you inside me. Please, fuck me . . ."

He groans, his grip tightening on my hips.

"Good girl," he murmurs, his hand sliding down to cup my ass.

"You're going to get what you've been begging for."

I feel him move behind me, his body pressing against mine, and my heart races in anticipation. Every part of me is aching for him, every nerve on fire. I can barely think, barely breathe—all I can feel is the heat building between us.

Nate pushes my head onto the desk, hikes up my skirt, and expresses his joy when he sees I'm wearing stockings.

"Fuck, Delilah, watching your bare ass parted by this string, and these stockings squeezing your thighs—fuck, you're killing me," he says. His words send a rush of heat through me, so I deliberately shake my ass, inviting him closer. But then he spanks me. The line between pleasure and pain is delicious, and I can't help but lean into it, loving every second. It gives me chills. I gasp at his teasing.

"Stop shaking that perfect ass. I'll give it to you, don't worry, but not just yet," he says. *What?*

Then I feel him kneeling behind me, and I see his beautiful head popping between my legs. With his bare teeth, he tears off my panties like an animal, and *oh my God*, the scene almost gives me a premature orgasm.

He doesn't wait before grabbing my pussy with his mouth, kissing it as if he were kissing my lips. Every time, it's pure fucking pleasure like nothing else compares. My whole body claims it. I feel like I no longer exist—just lust personified.

Nate keeps going with his tongue, playing with my clit, biting my lips. His hands rip my blouse in one swift move, exposing the breasts still confined in my bra. I don't waste a second before undoing it and throwing it away.

I look Nate directly in his eye. He's kneeling before me, fucking me with his tongue. He pinches my tits even though they're already hard. This fucking scene is incredible.

A wave is building inside me, but Nate decides to play a little more. I feel one of his fingers sliding into my ass, and that sensation undoes me. The heady mix of pleasure from both parts of my body is a melody of sex itself. I feel like I'm dissolving into the moment, like my whole body is tuned into nothing but him. My breath catches, and I tremble, unable to think of anything but how much I want him.

"I love feasting on this exquisite pussy," he says between two tongue strokes. But I can't hold it any longer. The wave inside me is so powerful it sweeps me away, and I feel it with my whole being. A bolt of pleasure, electrifying, perfectly mixed with a tsunami, devastates me. I moan with all my soul, thanking the universe for this moment.

Thanking Nate.

"You're so beautiful," he murmurs, his voice thick with desire. "I could stay here all day, watching you fall apart for me."

"Sounds like a plan," I say, barely breathing.

But I don't even have time to catch my breath as Nate picks me up and places me on his desk, spreading my legs wide. I realize I didn't even see him undo his belt or pull down his boxers. I only see his big, perfect, immaculate cock fully erect as he slides inside me with fierceness and rage. *I. Fucking. Love. It.* I live for this. I try to scream, but he covers my mouth with his hand.

"Be a good trainee and shut up, or I'll fire you, you dirty slut," he says, and damn, that one sends shivers down my core.

"Please don't fire me, sir. I really need the job. I only screamed because your dick is doing magic, sir. I apologize," I say, fully knowing I'm teasing him—two can play at this game. Then I feel him fucking me harder and harder, so much that we ruin his desk. He grabs me and crushes me against the wall, my legs wrapped around his waist and his cock buried deep inside me.

"If you want to keep seeing those paychecks, you better give me that ass," he says, pinching my butt so hard I swear I'm going to bleed. But does that bother me? Not in the least. I love it. I crave it. I moan yet again, this time in his mouth, trying to keep quiet. I see he still has his shirt on, and I need the rawness of our connection right now.

"Baby, please, I've been drooling over your body all fucking day. Please let me see your skin under that shirt," I say. I need to see him. All of him. He laughs a bit and gestures for me to undo it myself, which I do. Then I literally lick his torso as I take his cock in my hand. I lick every inch of him. His natural scent is exhilarating, mixed with his cologne—it's too much for me. I lick it, all the while jerking him off.

"Good God, baby, that's sexy as fuck. You want it, don't you? Such a good girl, baby, keep licking and jerking me off like the good slut you are. It's all yours, my love. All yours," he says, and I dive deep.

I stand up, then face the wall, placing my hands on both sides, and I feel Nate questioning.

"What are you doing?" he asks.

"Giving the boss what he wants," I say, pushing my ass toward him. That undoes him completely, and within two seconds, he slams his huge dick inside my ass. I hear him groan and swear under his breath. I love the power I have over him. I love the fact that he's in this state because of me. He fucks me so hard it hurts, but in the best way possible.

I know Nate is on the verge of coming when I feel his hand on my pussy urging me to come with him. I'm so deep in lust that I follow him. And then it happens. The explosion, the pleasure, the electricity, the shock — all at once.

We're both panting, barely breathing.

Wow. That was fucking intense. Nate turns me to face him and kisses me with ultimate passion.

"Fuck, baby. That was amazing," he says, and it makes me smile genuinely.

"It really was. Thank you," I reply. He shakes his head, never losing that beautiful smile of his. We try to get dressed, but then I see my blouse — it's ruined. I can't wear it!

I show it to him, my face shocked, and he bursts out laughing.

"I'm not even sorry," he says, and I know how much he means it. He offers me his suit jacket to cover myself, and it works.

Nate tries to reorganize his desk that we both destroyed. I laugh a lot and help him put it back together, remembering how it started.

Then we hear someone trying to open the door. I jump at the noise, but Nate doesn't even react. I swear the man never gets scared. He goes to open the door, and then James comes into view. *Urgh.*

"Hey, you okay? Why did you lock the door?" he asks Nate, and then he sees me. "Oh, sorry! Hey Delilah, how are you since, you know, the accident?" he asks.

"Fine, thank you for asking, Mr. Kingston," I say. I see Nate's gaze lock on me as if he wanted me to explain something.

"Why are you calling him Mr. Kingston?" he asks. Both James

and I try to say something, but Nate raises his finger at James, suggesting he shut up, not breaking eye contact with me, urging me to answer.

"Because we're at the office," I say, which is true.

"You can call me James."

"Thank you, James," I reply. Then Nate's phone rings.

"Fuck, I have to answer this, it's my mother," he says, leaving to go to his private bathroom, leaving James and me alone.

"I'm sorry about the accident. I mean it," James says.

"Yeah, I know. You don't want me to die, you just want me to leave," I whisper to him. He smiles, shaking his head.

"I'm starting not to," he says, and I laugh because I know he's lying. *Of course he's lying.*

"I've been receiving letters," he murmurs, and my heart stops. *What letters?* He sees my face, then explains.

"I'm receiving letters from women. From The Voices of Women Shelter. They're thanking me for my donation. They tell me how much I saved a bunch of them from the streets, from abusive men, from death . . ." He exhales.

"I've read one letter that says a mother and her child now have a temporary home where her ex-husband can't find them. He tried to kill them both in the past. Her child is only five." he says, unable to contain his emotions.

"That's good, James. You should be happy about it," I say, even though I know.

"But I *didn't* do it," he says, and I smile.

"I don't know what you're talking about," I tell him. But he only puffs at me, and it makes me burst out laughing.

Nate walks out of the bathroom, smiling as he sees me and his best friend laughing. "What's so funny?" he asks.

"I asked Delilah for Jenna's phone number," James says. *What the fuck?*

Nate looks at me.

"Hard no," I say, and they both laugh.

"Heard the lady," Nate says, grabbing his stuff to bring home. "Let's go."

James tells him something about a client on our way to the elevator, and then we leave.

Nate and I step into the penthouse, both of us quiet after the long day. We've only known each other for a few months, but it already feels like we've settled into a comfortable rhythm. The night seems wrapped in a thick, calm blanket as we head straight for the shower without a word. It's more about washing away the day—and the mess we made of each other earlier.

The hot water does wonders. I let it roll down my shoulders, feeling refreshed as I step out and wrap myself in a towel. Nate's already in the kitchen, flipping through some files he brought home. I feel light, almost buzzing with energy, and the idea of making something delicious pops into my head.

"I'm cooking," I say, opening the fridge.

"You're the boss," Nate replies, glancing up briefly with that half-smile I've started to notice more lately. He pulls a pen from behind his ear and jots something down.

I grab some ingredients—chicken, bell peppers, garlic, and a bit of cream. I'm going to make a creamy chicken pasta, something I know will hit the spot. While I start chopping, Nate is tapping keys on his laptop. He's still deep in work mode, but I like that we're sharing this space—me cooking, him working.

We keep exchanging small jokes as we go. It's nice, easy. I like how we've come back to being us again despite the whole accident drama.

When the food is ready, I set the plates on the table, and we sit down across from each other.

"Alright, dig in," I say, watching as Nate takes his first bite.

His eyes widen.

"This is . . . really good."

I grin, twirling some pasta on my fork. "I know."

We eat slowly, and the conversation drifts between work and

random things we've noticed today. It's not deep or heavy, just simple and relaxed. Every time he laughs, I feel a bit lighter.

After dinner, we decide to take the dogs out. They've been restless all day, and it's a perfect excuse to stretch our legs. We walk down to Central Park, the air cool but not too cold. The dogs trot ahead, pulling slightly at their leashes, excited to explore.

We keep walking, the conversation flowing easily between us, our footsteps syncing up without us even trying. It's funny how natural it feels.

By the time we get back to the penthouse, I'm feeling a bit tired, but in a good way. Nate heads to the bathroom to brush his teeth, and I start tidying up the bedroom, fluffing the pillows and pulling the covers back. I make the bed neat, the way I like it. It's still strange to think that I'm sharing this space with him, even though it doesn't feel strange at all when I'm actually doing it.

Nate joins me in bed a few minutes later, sliding in beside me. He leans back against the headboard, and I curl up on my side next to him, resting my head on his chest. His arm wraps around me, and I feel completely comfortable.

"You think you'll ever get tired of all these late nights?" I ask, tracing random patterns on his arm with my finger.

He shifts, looking down at me.

"Not if they end like this."

I smile and close my eyes for a moment, enjoying how easy it feels to be here with him. We talk for a little while longer, about nothing too important, just enough to wind down. Nate shifts onto his back, and I nestle closer, resting my head against his shoulder.

"Babe," I say.

"Yes?"

"I probably should get back to my floor tomorrow. You'd still be in the same building with me, but I should go back to the twenty-seventh floor."

"We didn't agree on that. Why do you want to go back? I thought you loved our day together."

"I did! A little too much, don't you think?" I say, sitting up to face him, and he laughs hard at the memory. I slap his chest playfully.

"I love that you want me," he says, wiggling his eyebrows.

"That's your ego speaking."

"No, baby, that's my *heart* speaking. Bared to you," he says, and I feel my heart break. *That's not possible, that's not possible, that's not possible.*

"Still. I don't like Chloe, nor do I like you with her. I don't like the way it makes me feel. Brings back bad memories," I say, admitting something I dread talking about.

"What are you talking about? I'm not into her, nor have I ever been, and neither will I ever be. It's only you, baby. I promise I'll put distance between us. I thought you were joking about the Chloe thing. I don't ever want to be responsible for you feeling sad, baby. I'll fire her," he says.

"No, no, don't. I need to face my trust issues. But I just don't want to see it right now. I'm working on it," I manage to say.

"I need you to at least try to explain this to me. What did I do wrong? What memory were you talking about?" he asks, suddenly concerned, and I hate myself for ruining the good mood.

"I'm not ready to talk about it, and I don't want to develop the subject more, okay? But . . . Eric . . ." *Fuck,* saying his name is difficult. "Eric was married when he and I . . . you know. Anyway, I was dragged into a love triangle, and I *hated* it. Eric was never meant to be mine. I allowed myself to hope, and he promised me he would be with me exclusively. Forever. He said he loved me. But all that time, he loved her too. It broke me. I felt like Icarus. I burned my wings trying to fly high. He was just another liar," I say, the memory bringing back pain I do not wish to revisit. I feel like I can't breathe.

"Can we please not talk about it anymore?" I ask softly, praying for him to agree.

"Sure," he says. "Come here." And he takes me into a warm

embrace. A reassuring touch mixed with delicate kisses. Nate understands me so well. He knows exactly when it's time to just let go of his eagerness to know more, giving me the time to recover, to heal.

"Thank you," I say, my voice barely above a whisper.

"I love you, Delilah. I swear to you, I love you so fucking much," he insists, and as usual, I choose not to give in. Not to believe. Not to hope. *I'm so fucking scared.*

Then I fall asleep.

CHAPTER 22

Nate

It's Wednesday morning, and the dogs are sick. Cowboy, the massive, one-eyed monster, and Sheriff, our tiny ball of fur, both look miserable. Delilah is pacing in front of the kitchen counter, glancing over at them like they're two helpless children. I stand there with my arms crossed, watching the scene unfold, already knowing where this is headed.

"Nate, we have to take them with us. We're their parents; we can't just leave them here," she says, almost pleading. She's wearing one of my old shirts, and it's hard to focus on anything but her bare legs, but I manage.

"I like the mommy talk, babe. Turns me on. Call me daddy," I say while walking towards her and grab her ass. She bursts out laughing, but truthfully, that sounds so fucking right in my ear.

"They're gonna spend the day in your office with you," she says, still looking at Cowboy.

"Why me?" I ask, even though I know the answer. "They're your dogs too."

"I have a full schedule of meetings today, and my office is tiny. They won't fit," she says, hands on her hips, giving me that look that tells me she's about to win this argument before it even starts.

I point toward Cowboy, who's half-sprawled across the floor.

"Cowboy takes up half a room by himself, Delilah. He's like a small horse." Delilah rolls her eyes.

"Exactly. Which is why they need to go to your office. You have the space."

"My office is not a petting zoo."

"And mine is? Come on, Nate," she says, her tone softening a bit. "Look at them. They're miserable. You can't just leave them here. You're the fucking CEO, no one would dare say anything. Me, on the other hand? Not so much."

I glance over at Cowboy, who gives me a pitiful look with his one good eye, then at Sheriff, who's curled up like a tiny ball of sadness. I sigh. She's right, of course, but I don't want to admit it.

"Fine," I say, running a hand through my hair. "But they stay inside my office. I don't want them roaming the building."

Delilah grins, her eyes lighting up with victory.

"Deal. Thank you."

"Yeah, yeah," I mutter, grabbing my briefcase and heading toward the door. "But you owe me for this."

She steps closer, biting her lip like she always does when she knows she's pushing her luck.

"Maybe I'll collect tonight?" I smirk, shaking my head.

"You better." I say, kissing her firmly on those delicious lips I love so much. Then I slap her perfect bare ass. Obviously, I end up fucking her before going to work. *Best morning ever.*

By the time I get to the office, I have Cowboy lumbering behind me like he's on patrol, and Sheriff trotting along, sniffing everything in sight. The lobby is its usual buzz of activity, but it slows down the second people see me walking in with the dogs. Eyes widen, conversations stop. Some people try to act casual, like they see their CEO walk in with a giant one-eyed dog every day. Others just stare.

I don't give two fucks. I own the company. I own the damn building. I could bring the entire Bronx Zoo in if I felt like it.

We head straight to my private elevator. Cowboy barely fits inside, and Sheriff insists on standing in the middle of the door like he's guarding it. The ride up is quiet, except for Cowboy's heavy breathing, which sounds like a wheezing engine.

When we reach my floor, the usual bustling comes to a halt as soon as the doors open. My assistants glance up, wide-eyed. A few employees exchange nervous glances.

I walk past, not acknowledging the stares. Let them wonder.

As soon as we get into my office, I lead the dogs over to the far corner where I've already had a blanket set up. Cowboy collapses immediately, and Sheriff curls up beside him. I make sure they've got water, then sit down at my desk, glancing at the clock. It's not even 9 a.m., and I've already had more chaos than most people have in a day.

The morning drags on in a blur of meetings. I've got a video conference with the London office, a catch-up with the finance team, and then a call about a potential partnership in France. Every time I look up, Cowboy and Sheriff are still there, snoozing away like they own the place.

Chloe knocks on the door before entering with a stack of papers. She's been a bit distant since our last conversation—since I told her we needed some clear boundaries. Delilah was right; she was getting too familiar, too . . . close. After that talk, she's been colder, more professional. And honestly, it's a relief. I don't need any more complications.

"Here are the documents for the afternoon board meeting," she says, placing them neatly on my desk. Her voice is clipped, her expression neutral. No unnecessary small talk. Just business.

"Thanks," I say, glancing up at her before turning back to my computer. She lingers for a moment, but I ignore it. I'm not interested in reopening that conversation.

Then my mind drifts to the other night when Delilah told me how she didn't want anyone to drag into a love triangle like the last fucker did. She implied Chloe was the third member. Little does she know how far from the truth she is. I immediately thought of Charlotte, and if Delilah ever finds out before I tell her, she'll leave me on the spot.

I can't bear the idea, but now I know I have to tell Delilah about

Charlotte. I want to be with her. I'm going to marry her whether she likes it or not. But I'm fucking scared she'll discover the truth.

Pushing the thought aside, I dive back into my work.

Halfway through a budget review with James, my phone buzzes. It's Delilah. I check the message.

> **Delilah:** *How are my babies?*

I smirk and glance over at Cowboy and Sheriff.

> **Nate:** *Cowboy is snoring like a chainsaw. Sheriff is judging me. Business as usual. Did you include my dick in "my babies"?*

Her reply comes quickly.

> **Delilah:** *I did not. Did Cowboy drink water?*

I roll my eyes, but it's endearing. I stand up, walk over, and check the water bowl.

It's half-full.

> **Nate:** *Yes, mother, he drank.*

Her response makes me grin.

> **Delilah:** *Watch it, Mr. Williams. I might have to reward you later. (Dick included)*
> **Nate:** *Is that a promise?*
> **Delilah:** *Only if you're good.*

~

By late morning, I'm knee-deep in financial reports when James walks in, looking more stressed than usual.

"You're ready for that meeting with the governor this afternoon?" he says, flipping through his tablet.

I blink, caught off guard. "Governor? Of New York?"

James gives me a look. "Yes, Nate. You have to finalize the deal for the tax incentives on the new project. It's at the Executive Chamber."

I curse under my breath. The meeting is important—vital, actually—but I completely forgot about it.

"And I can't exactly bring the dogs with me," I mutter, glancing over at Cowboy and Sheriff.

"No," James says, deadpan. "I don't think the governor would appreciate that."

I sigh, pulling out my phone. I text Delilah again.

Nate: *I have to meet the governor. Can't bring the dogs. Where are you?*

I wait. No reply.

I grab my coat and prepare to leave. I walk out of my office, the dogs following behind, and just like earlier, people stop and stare as I walk down the hall. Cowboy's size alone draws attention, but it's the one-eyed look that really gets people. Sheriff, despite his size, skips along like he's leading the charge.

We take the elevator down to Delilah's floor. Once again, the whispers start the second I step out. A few employees quickly step aside, not wanting to get in the way of their CEO and his intimidating duo.

I glance around, but I don't see Delilah anywhere. Finally, I stop one of the interns rushing by.

"Where's Ms. Rose?"

The guy practically jumps out of his skin before stammering, "Uh, she's . . . she's in a meeting, sir. With all the managers."

I curse again. I turn on my heel and head straight for the conference room. When I push the door open, the room falls silent.

All the managers stand up, their eyes wide, like deer caught in headlights. And there's Delilah, sitting with her coworkers at the table, staring at me with a mix of surprise and embarrassment on her face. Cowboy and Sheriff stroll in behind me like they own the place, despite being sick just hours ago.

"Babe, I have a meeting with the governor. I need to leave. You take the dogs."

Everyone stays frozen. Delilah's cheeks flush, and damn, I love that color on her.

"I'm in a meeting!" she says, widening her eyes. I sigh, while the others look like they're trying to figure out how to breathe again.

"I won't outright say that what you do is less important than what I do, but really what I do is more important than what you do. So, take the dogs."

"Oh my God," she mutters, flustered. She turns to the woman sitting closest to her. "Um, Mrs. Rutherford, is it okay if . . . sorry, if my dogs stay here? They're sick."

"Yeah, Addison, is that okay?" I ask, fully aware that she'll agree if I'm the one asking.

She beams at me.

"Of course, no problem at all! We don't mind."

How I love being the CEO.

I crouch to say a quick goodbye to Cowboy and Sheriff, then glance at Delilah. Her eyes are narrowed, shooting daggers my way. Smart enough to read the room, I back off with a grin.

As I leave, I notice dog hair all over my suit. *Fuck.* But I know Delilah always carries a lint roller in her purse.

I spin around, heading back to the conference room. I step in, and once again, everyone stands up like they're on autopilot. I don't bother telling them to sit.

"Do you have the lint roller?" I ask, looking directly at Delilah. She looks pissed, but she's even more stunning when she's mad. It's almost worth the trouble.

"In my purse. In my office," she says through clenched teeth, her glare sharp enough to cut glass.

I thank her and head to her office, finding the lint roller easily.

But as I try to clean the dog hair off my suit, I realize I can't reach my back. Looks like I'll need her help again.

So I walk back into the conference room for the third time, immediately telling everyone, "Don't stand up."

I look straight at Delilah.

"Babe, can you help me? I can't reach everywhere," I say, keeping my tone casual, though I'm clearly enjoying myself. I love messing with her. And honestly, I don't give two fucks about outing us. I'm going to marry her, so people better start getting the image in their head. So does she.

"You can't be serious right now."

"I'm dead serious. I have to meet the governor, and the dogs are only here because *you* insisted they come with us this morning," I reply, a smile tugging at my lips.

She sighs, standing up and stalking over to me. She yanks the lint roller from my hand with more force than necessary, but I let her. I turn around, feeling every roll as she drags the sticky surface over my suit. She's likely trying to scrub off more than just dog hair.

"Done. Goodbye, Nate," she snaps, clearly ready to be rid of me.

But I'm not quite done yet. Screw the governor—I want to stretch this out just a little longer.

"Wait," I say, turning to her again. "Can you fix my tie? Is it straight?"

I ignore the fact that the room is full of people. Right now, it's just Delilah and me. I can see she's even more furious, and that only makes her more irresistible. She makes me want to fuck her more, if that's possible.

"You'll pay for this," she mutters, stepping closer to adjust my tie with quick, sharp movements.

"I better," I say, winking at her. I lean in for a kiss, but she dodges, leaving me grinning at nothing.

I laugh softly.

"I'll call you when I'm back," I say, just loud enough for the room to hear. "To pick up the dogs, of course."

She doesn't answer, and I leave the room, still laughing under my breath.

Damn, that woman. She's going to kill me. But it was time. And she'd never have agreed to this. So I took the best decision for both of us. She'll come to that realization soon enough.

I step out of the car, adjusting my tie as I approach the governor's office. The Executive Chamber is grand, with towering pillars and sleek marble floors. As soon as I enter, I'm greeted with a level of respect that's almost royal. People stand taller, offering polite nods as I walk past. I'm not just another businessman here—everyone knows who I am. I'm the CEO of Williams Holdings, a figure who commands power, and they treat me accordingly.

The governor himself is waiting at the entrance. I have to say I like the old man.

He's always shown a wise side in politics. He offers his hand with a welcoming smile.

"Nathan," he says, shaking my hand firmly. "It's always a pleasure."

"Likewise, Governor," I reply, keeping my tone even, though the tension in the air is hard to ignore. I know this meeting isn't just about business.

We walk down the hallway to his private office. Inside, it's as impressive as you'd expect—dark wood paneling, heavy curtains, and a large desk that dominates the space.

A secretary brings us coffee, but I barely touch mine. My mind is focused.

Once we're seated, the governor leans back in his chair, his expression serious.

"Nathan, I want to get straight to the point," he says, his voice lower than before.

"Your brother, Jake, came to see me a few days ago."

I feel a flicker of anger, but I force myself to stay calm. I lean forward.

"Jake?"

He nods, his eyes narrowing.

"He tried to sabotage you."

I don't move, but inside, the fury is building. *Jake, again.*

"How so?" I ask, my voice steady, but my mind racing.

"He presented a proposal to redirect some of the funds we've been negotiating for the project. He suggested diverting them to a new venture—one under his control. A false project, of course, but on paper, it looked good. If I hadn't checked the details, I might have considered it."

I clench my fists under the table, the anger simmering just beneath the surface. Jake is reckless, always has been, but this—this is more than that. This is calculated. It's a direct attack.

"What did he say about me?" I ask, knowing Jake wouldn't just stop at a proposal.

The governor's eyes don't leave mine.

"He claimed you were mismanaging the company. That your focus was scattered. He implied you weren't fit to lead anymore, and that he should take over."

For a moment, I see red. My own brother, trying to take everything I've built and turn it into his plaything. But I can't let this show. *Not here.*

"Governor," I say calmly, keeping my voice even, "thank you for telling me. And thank you for your loyalty." The governor nods.

"Nathan, I've known you a long time. I trust you, not him. But I thought you should know. You need to be careful. Jake is . . . dangerous."

I stand up, shaking his hand again.

"I appreciate that. And don't worry—I'll handle this."

We exchange a few more pleasantries before I leave, but my mind is already working through possibilities. Jake crossed a line, and now I need to stop him.

~

Back at my office, I shut the door behind me. The sound of it closing feels final, like the beginning of something I can't avoid. I sit
at my desk, staring at the city skyline for a moment before pulling
out my phone. Jake's betrayal isn't just personal—it's a threat to
everything I've built, everything I've worked for.

I run through scenarios in my mind. Jake is reckless, but he's
not entirely stupid. He'll be expecting me to react, but I can't come
at him head-on. That's what he wants—he thrives in chaos, and if
I confront him directly, he'll twist the situation, make himself look
like the victim.

So I need to be smarter. I need to isolate him, cut off his re-
sources, make sure he has nowhere to turn. I can pull strings quietly, get some of my team to start investigating his connections.
Jake always surrounds himself with the wrong people, and if I dig
deep enough, I'll find something to use against him.

I pick up my phone and make a few calls. I don't give away
too much, just enough to get the ball rolling. People I trust, people who owe me favors, they'll handle the details. The plan starts
forming, piece by piece, in the back of my mind. I'll strike when
Jake doesn't expect it. This time, he's gone too far.

I'm still deep in thought when the door to my office swings
open, and there's Delilah, standing in the doorway with the dogs
at her feet and the biggest smile on her face. I blink, a bit surprised,
because I was sure as fuck she was still mad at me for earlier.

She walks in, Cowboy and Sheriff walking happily behind her.
I stand up, my mind still half in strategy mode, half trying to figure out what's going on. Before I can say anything, she practically
bounces toward me, her smile so wide it's contagious.

"I got the SATs!" she shouts, and before I can react, she jumps
into my arms. I catch her easily, holding her up like she weighs
nothing. She wraps her arms around my neck, and I can feel her
excitement buzzing through her. I'm grinning now too.

She's been working for this for so long. It's a huge deal, and I know how much it means to her. My heart swells for her, not just because of what she's accomplished, but because of how hard she's worked for it.

"Delilah," I say, my voice soft but full of pride. "I knew you'd nail this. I'm so fucking proud of you, but it's no surprise."

She pulls back just enough to look at me, her face glowing with happiness.

"I couldn't have done it without you," she says, her eyes shining.

I chuckle.

"You did all the hard work, babe. I'm just here to catch you when you jump on me."

She laughs, and it's the kind of sound that melts away the stress of the day—the kind of sound that makes everything else seem small and distant. I hold her for a moment longer, not wanting to let go. This, right here, is what matters.

I set her down gently, still smiling like an idiot.

"I'm so proud of you," I tell her, my hands still resting on her waist. "You deserve this."

She beams up at me, and for a second, the whole mess with Jake fades into the background. The dogs wag their tails, oblivious to the whirlwind of emotions in the room.

"So what's next?" I ask.

"Well, I thought I could apply to college. A distance program. We talked about this, remember? Will you help me look into this?" she asks, and I fall for her all over again.

My sweet, sweet Delilah.

"We will, baby," I say as I kiss her firmly, but she fucking bites my lip and slams my chest.

"Ouch! What the fuck was that for?" I ask.

"I'm still mad at you! Take care of the boys, I have to go back to work. We'll discuss this at home," she says, and maybe I'm sick, but that sounded like hot, dirty talk to me.

"I love you," I say like a revelation. She laughs, almost mocking me, and then she's out the door.

I sit at my desk, flipping through the latest reports. I'm supposed to be reviewing the new marketing projections for our international expansion, but my mind is only half on the task. My focus keeps drifting back to the situation with Jake. I need to figure out how to deal with him, but that can wait. For now, I push the papers aside and pick up my pen, jotting down a few notes.

Suddenly, my phone buzzes. I glance at the screen and see "Mother" flashing on it. I sigh, hesitating for a moment. I know what she wants to talk about—Jake. She always wants to talk about Jake. But I can't avoid her forever. With a deep breath, I swipe to answer.

"Mother," I say, trying to sound casual.

"Nathan, darling, how are you?" Her voice is sweet, but there's an edge to it. She's fishing for something.

"I'm fine, busy," I reply, keeping my tone even.

"Busy as always," she says with a little laugh. "Well, I wanted to remind you about the gala honoring the New York police in a few weeks. You're going, right? You're always invited."

I rub my temple, already knowing where this is headed.

"Yeah, I'll be there."

"And will you be bringing a plus-one this year?" she asks, her voice light but pointed. She's being intrusive, as usual.

"I always have a plus-one," I say, keeping it vague. I'm not about to mention Delilah. That's none of her business.

There's a pause, then she drops the comment I've been waiting for.

"Until Charlotte comes back, right?" I clench my jaw, refusing to bite.

"I always bring a plus-one, Mother," I repeat, keeping my voice steady. I don't want to get into this now—or ever, really.

She doesn't push further, thankfully. Instead, she changes the subject.

"Well, I just heard some exciting news. James has been nominated for the Philanthropist of the Year award." That catches me off guard.

"Really?" I didn't know anything about this.

"Yes, and between you and me," she says, lowering her voice like she's sharing a big secret, "he's going to win. I'm friends with the organizer and the head of the jury. They told me."

A rush of pride fills me. James is one of the hardest-working people I know, and he deserves the recognition.

"That's incredible," I say, genuinely excited. "James will be thrilled."

"He's one generous man," she continues. "I just thought you'd want to know."

"Thanks for telling me."

"Of course, darling. I'll see you on Sunday."

"Yeah, see you then." I end the call, relieved that it didn't spiral into a conversation about Jake or Charlotte.

I toss the phone back onto the desk and return to my work. My thoughts briefly linger on James. It's impressive. He never mentioned being up for an award, but that's typical James—humble, always focused on the job.

As I'm organizing some documents, the door opens, and James walks in, holding a stack of financial reports. He looks like he's ready for business, but I can't help the grin that spreads across my face.

"James," I say, standing up. "The man of the year."

"What are you talking about?" he asks, acting clueless, but I see something shift in his eyes.

"The philanthropist award. I heard your name is on the list," I say, expecting him to smile, but instead, his face falls. He looks like he's been punched, and I don't understand why.

"Fuck," he mutters, barely audible. Now I'm confused as hell.

"Man, this is great news. I don't get your reaction," I say, trying to figure out what's going on.

"Nate, I gotta tell you something, but you're going to fucking kill me." His tone changes, and now I'm intrigued—and a little pissed.

"What are you talking about, James?" I press.

"I fucked up, man. Big. You're really going to lose it when I tell you." He runs his hands through his hair, looking everywhere but at me.

"Okay, get to the point. Stop with the suspense."

He takes a deep breath.

"Nate, you're my best friend. You know that, right? You're not just a friend—you're like a brother to me. Everything I've done has been with your best interests at heart. The company's best interests."

I narrow my eyes, getting a bad feeling about where this is headed.

"James, just spit it out."

"It's about Delilah," he says, and just like that, my heart skips a beat. Everything in me tightens, every muscle on edge. When it comes to Delilah, I don't play. She's off-limits. I bite down on the urge to snap at him.

"Go on," I say, my voice low.

"The day she started working here . . . I, uh . . . I went to see her." He looks away as soon as the words leave his mouth.

"What the fuck are you talking about? I introduced you to her," I say, my patience wearing thin.

"No, we met before. She was covering for me when you introduced us. I went to her office on her first day."

I step closer, already wanting to punch him for lying to me, the tension rising in my chest.

"You better start explaining yourself, James."

"I didn't think she was right for you, okay? I thought she was a distraction. You were too wrapped up in her, and it wasn't good for you or the company. I didn't want you screwing things up, especially with Charlotte. So, I went to her. I may have . . . offered her money to leave."

"What the fuck did you just say?" My voice comes out in a growl. My fists tighten, and I feel the rage bubbling up, threatening to explode.

"I offered her five million dollars to disappear," he admits, his voice shaky. "I thought it was for the best, man. I went to her, I apologized for the time not being good enough, I might have been offensive to her, but I offered her a check to . . . disappear."

WHAT THE FUCK?! I'm fucking stunned. Five million? The fucker just shocked the hell out of me. He tried to pay her off like some problem to be dealt with. I step even closer, ready to break his nose, but I hold back. Barely.

"When did you say this happened?" I ask through clenched teeth.

"Her first day."

A memory hits me, hard. Her first day . . . *No way.*

"On her fucking birthday?" I yell, fury burning through my veins.

James looks horrified.

"What? No, I didn't know that. I swear!"

I can't stop myself. My fist connects with his face, and he goes down. Blood pours from his nose as he lies on the floor. The dogs start barking, and I know they feel my anger too. He insulted their mom.

"I'm sorry, Nate. I didn't know. I thought I was doing you a favor!" James says, struggling to sit up, holding his bleeding nose.

"That wasn't your fucking decision to make! If you knew Delilah even just a little, you'd know she doesn't give a fuck about money!" I shout. "She's been through hell with people abandoning her, rejecting her. You fucking broke her, James!"

I kick him once more, the dogs growling in the background. James winces in pain but forces himself to stand.

"Unfortunately, that wasn't the end of my story," he says.

What the fuck?! My blood runs cold. There's more?

"Keep talking," I demand, my voice low and dangerous.

"She took the check," he says. "She took the check and asked me not to write her name on it, and told me to give her a few days before disappearing," he says.

She took the check?

"The five million was cashed," he says. "By the charity The Voices of Women Shelter. Apparently, my assistant—who never heard any of it—made the donation in my name, since I'm a busy man. But it was Delilah. She went to the charity and gave them the check on my behalf, pretending to be my assistant. When I went to confront her, she denied ever meeting me, nor taking any money to this very day. I felt like shit.

"I started receiving letters from women I apparently saved. Thanks to my money, they are now opening a new shelter for women and children, and my fucking name will appear even though I told them not to use it. And now I'm on the fucking list for Philanthropist of the Year. What a joke. I'm sorry, Nate, I swear to God, I'm fucking sorry. I've changed my mind about her, and I truly think she's a great person." I stare at him, shocked.

"She gave it all away?"

James nods, looking ashamed.

"Yeah. I never told anyone. I confronted her, and she denied ever meeting me or taking the money. She acted like nothing ever happened."

"And now you're nominated for Philanthropist of the Year because of her?" I ask, barely able to process this bullshit.

"Yeah," he says, wiping the blood from his face.

"I'm sorry, Nate. I swear, I've changed my mind about her. She's amazing, and I realize that now. But I screwed up."

That's not enough. I'm fuming. I can't even look at him. My anger is boiling over, but I manage to hit the intercom.

"Chloe, get Delilah in here. Now!"

James looks at me, beaten and bloodied.

"I'm so sorry."

"It's not me you should be apologizing to," I say, sitting back, my blood still pumping with rage.

"I'll apologize to her," he says.

"You better."

Less than two minutes later, I hear a knock at the door. I shout, "Come in," and Delilah walks in, the dogs rushing to greet her. She takes one look at James, covered in blood, and then notices the fury etched across my face.

"What's going on?" she asks, her eyes darting between the two of us.

"Do you have something to tell me?" My voice is laced with anger. I'm so fucking mad she never mentioned any of this to me. How could she still not trust me? Why keep this from me?

Her gaze flickers between James and me, confusion and suspicion in her eyes.

"You sold me out?" she directs at James, her tone sharp and accusatory.

"Delilah, I'm so sorry. I never should have done what I did to you. You never deserved any of it. I'm sorry. I had to tell him," James says, his voice trembling.

"Why now?" She looks at him in disbelief.

"I . . . I was fucking nominated for the philanthropist award. Nate heard about it, and I couldn't keep lying anymore. I'm sorry," he pleads.

But then, to my utter shock, Delilah's face breaks into the biggest smile. *What the actual fuck?*

"Why didn't you tell me?" I ask, and this time, she can hear the hurt in my voice.

"He's your *best* friend," she says quietly.

"Not anymore. Why didn't you tell me?" I repeat, more forcefully this time.

"Nate, he *is* your best friend. He always has been, and he always will be. Honestly, he didn't tell me anything I didn't already know. From the start, I've known . . . I'm not right for you. Of course your life would be better without me. This thing with us? It's temporary. I told you before, I'm just a passenger in your life, enjoying the ride. The friendship you have with James is something special. I never want to be the reason you two aren't close anymore. He did it for you, and he was right to."

Her words are ripping me apart. She's hurting me so deeply. When will she understand that I want her forever? When will she realize that there's no *"temporary"* when it comes to us?

"Why didn't you take the check?" I ask, almost desperately. As much as I'm angry, I'm also relieved that she didn't.

"I don't give a fuck about the money, and you know that," she replies.

"Well, she accepted the check," James interjects, "She just didn't cash it for herself."

"Shut the fuck up. I'm not done with you," I snap at him.

Delilah exhales, her voice firm.

"I took the check, yes. Because I wanted to teach him a lesson. I was tired of men thinking they could control my life. I wasn't going to let anyone decide for me whether I should stay or go. I *wanted* to make that choice. So I took it, then I searched for a cause worthy of it.

"I took his PA's identity and went to the Voices of Women Shelter while you were in L.A. I fell in love with the charity. Nate, you have no idea how much these women need help to free themselves from their abusers. Do you know how many women are on the streets? Do you know how many women are being beaten? Do you know how many mothers are looking to protect their children? Thanks to his money, those women are going to be saved! That's incredible! All thanks to James—"

"All thanks to *you*, Delilah. You're the one who made it happen, not him!" I insist, raising my voice.

"No," she counters, "I didn't have the money. He did."

"But once you took that check, it was *yours*. Why didn't you make the donation under *your* name?"

"Oh, baby, no, it wouldn't have worked out. I'm a nobody, Nate. I'm not part of your world."

My heart shatters, her words cut deep. How can she still believe that? I need her to understand how much she belongs.

"I still don't get why you didn't come to me," I say, my frustration mounting.

"I didn't want to come between you and James. You love him, you *need* him. You've told me so many times what a great friend he's been. I wanted to protect you from all of this," she says, and I swear, I fall for her all over again.

"No, Delilah. I love *you*, I need *you*, and I want to fucking protect you from everything including fucking James!" I scream, feeling I can't bear her words any longer.

"But he was right, Nate. I'm not right for you. No matter how much we want to rewrite the stars, we can't," she says, and now, I can hear the hurt in her voice.

I pull her close, holding her tight, and murmur into her ear:

"You seem to forget something. I'm Nathan fucking Williams, and I rewrite the stars if I damn well please. And in that realm, I'm the expert here, not you." I take her face in my hands and look deep into her eyes. "I love you, Delilah Rose. I love you, and I'm not going anywhere. Neither are you."

James steps in again, his voice heavy with regret.

"Delilah, I'm so sorry. I didn't know who you really were. I didn't understand. I'm sorry."

I glare at him, my anger simmering just beneath the surface.

"I can't believe you tried to take her away from me . . ." The disgust is evident in my voice.

"I didn't know. I'm sorry," he pleads again.

"Leave," I say, my tone final. He hesitates but doesn't argue.

As Delilah tries to lighten the tension, she jokes, "I have a lot of work to do . . . and the CEO here doesn't seem to be in the best mood. I don't want to push it."

I pull her into my arms, kissing her softly. She leaves my office, but my heart feels heavy. Broken.

This only fuels my resolve. I'm going to make things right.

"Get ready, baby," I whisper to myself. "You're about to have the *ride* of your life."

The dogs look at me with curious eyes, and I chuckle, "I'm talking about your mom, guys. Not you."

It's going to be a wild ride, alright.

CHAPTER 23
Delilah

S itting in the back of the limo, I can't stop my mind from racing, replaying everything that's happened in the last few days. It's been a rollercoaster, and I'm still trying to catch my breath.

It all started when Nate, without so much as a conversation, outed us at work. One moment we were navigating our "relationship" in private, and the next, it was public knowledge. He didn't even ask me how I felt about it—he just dropped the bomb. Now, everyone at work knows I live with the CEO.

The shift in how people treat me is undeniable. I used to feel like I was starting to become part of the team. I was Delilah, just like everyone else. Now, when I walk into the office, it's like the air changes. People stop talking when I enter a room; their eyes flicker to me like I'm some kind of threat. No one argues with me, no one even debates anymore. It's not respect—it's something else. A quiet fear. They know I'm with Nate, and that has put this heavy, invisible barrier between me and the rest of them.

I was furious with Nate for that. He didn't get it. He's always been in power, always had control, and he didn't understand what it's like to suddenly be viewed differently because of who you're with. It made me feel . . . isolated. Ailly was been my rock and a very good friend, but I still hated him for it, for taking that choice away from me.

But then something unexpected happened. In the middle of all that anger and frustration, I got my SAT results. I passed. *I passed.*

It's hard to describe how I felt when I saw those scores. All the late nights spent studying, the doubts that constantly whispered in my ear, the fear that maybe I wasn't smart enough, that maybe I was wasting my time—it all disappeared in that moment. *I did it*. I actually achieved something for myself, and for the first time in a long time, I felt proud.

I've spent so much of my life thinking I wasn't good enough, that I didn't deserve good things, but passing the SATs? It felt like a turning point. Like maybe, just maybe, I could do this. I could actually have a future I never thought was within reach.

For a moment, everything else—Nate, work, the tension—it all faded. I was just . . . *happy*. Purely, simply happy.

That happiness didn't last long before reality came rushing back. Nate found out about the check James offered me, and he lost it. I had already forgiven James—I understood why he did what he did. It wasn't right, but I saw the guilt in his eyes, heard the sincerity in his apology. He's trying to make things right, and I believe he regrets it.

But Nate? Nate can't let it go. He's furious with James, and no matter how much I try to talk to him, to make him see that I've forgiven James, it's like talking to a wall. Nate's proud. Too proud. I keep hoping he'll come around, but he's a tough man. He's not easy to sway, and forgiveness isn't something that comes naturally to him.

Despite all of that, I still have faith. I have to. Nate's done so much for me already, more than anyone has ever done. He's helped me apply to colleges so I can pursue a degree while continuing to work for his company. He believes in me in a way that no one else ever has. When I told him about passing the SATs, the look of pride on his face—it was like he was more excited for me than I was. And that meant everything to me.

The last few days have been hard, emotionally draining, but somehow, Nate and I have grown closer. We've fought, sure, but there's something between us that feels solid, unbreakable. Even when we're mad at each other, there's this undercurrent of affection that pulls us back together. It's not always easy, but it feels real, and that's what matters. Maybe that's the silver lining. Maybe that's what makes it all worth it.

Nate left for work a couple of hours ago, and now I'm here, in the limo, with Tyler driving me to the office. The city blurs by outside the window, but I barely notice. I'm too wrapped up in my thoughts, in everything that's happened. The tension at work, the frustration with Nate, the relief of passing the SATs—it's all swirling inside me, mixing together and hard to untangle.

I think about the future. About what it'll be like going to college, studying for a degree while still working at Nate's company. It's a big step, a huge step, really, but it's exciting. It's been too long since I've felt like I have control over my life, like I'm moving forward instead of being stuck in place. It's terrifying and thrilling all at once.

Leaning back in the seat, I sigh, glancing over at Tyler, who's focused on the road. He's quiet, as usual, and I'm grateful for it. I don't want to talk right now. I just want to sit with my thoughts, sort through everything that's been happening, and try to find some sense of calm.

The limo slows to a stop, and I glance out the window, expecting the familiar sight of the office building. But instead, I see something that makes my heart skip a beat. This isn't the office. This is . . . the airport.

I blink, confused, trying to make sense of what I'm seeing. The long stretch of runway, the sound of distant planes taking off, and the sleek, private jets lined up—it all hits me at once. My stomach twists in knots.

"Tyler?" I say, my voice soft but tense. "What's going on? Why are we here?"

He turns to me, his face calm, almost unreadable. "You just need to get on the plane, miss. You'll see for yourself."

My heart starts to race, my palms suddenly damp with sweat. *Get on the plane?* What is he talking about? Why would I get on a plane without knowing where it's going? Cold fear washes over me. My mind races to a thousand different places, none of them good. *Are they trying to get rid of me? Is this some kind of punishment for the accident?* That near-death experience left scars I didn't even realize were there, and now this . . .

I take a deep breath, forcing myself to stay calm. I can't let Tyler see the fear swirling inside me. I keep my face neutral, a skill I've perfected over the years, even when my mind is screaming at me to run. I don't ask any more questions, don't push for answers. Instead, I just nod and open the door.

My legs feel shaky as I step out of the limo, and the cool breeze hits my face. I scan the area, trying to understand what's happening. A private jet sits on the tarmac, gleaming in the sunlight, and my breath catches in my throat. I know that jet. It belongs to Nate.

There's a man standing near the stairs leading up to the plane. He's tall, dressed in black, and I recognize him as part of Nate's security team. He doesn't say anything, just gestures for me to go up the stairs. My stomach twists even tighter, but I force myself to move forward, each step heavy with uncertainty.

As I approach the stairs, the man steps aside, giving me space.

"Go on in, miss," he says in a low voice.

I nod but say nothing. My heart pounds so hard I can feel it in my throat. The stairs to the jet loom before me, each step feeling like it could be the last. My fear grows with every step upward. *What if something's wrong? What if this is a trap, some way of getting rid of me quietly, far away from anyone who could help?*

Just before stepping inside, I stop, glancing back. Tyler is still by the limo, watching me. I swallow hard and take the final step inside the jet.

And then I freeze.

The sight in front of me knocks the air from my lungs.

Nate is there, standing there with a rose in his hand, smiling like he doesn't have a care in the world. Our dogs are at his feet, wagging their tails happily as if this were just another normal day.

"Nate?" My voice comes out in a whisper, all my confusion

and fear suddenly hitting a wall. I don't understand. I don't know what's happening, why he's here, why the dogs are here. My head is spinning, and I feel like I'm about to collapse under the weight of everything I've been holding in.

"What's going on?" I ask, my voice unsteady now, all the control I'd been clinging to slipping away. "Why are we here? Why didn't you tell me?"

Nate laughs, his smile warm and easy. He walks over to me, his eyes soft as he offers me the rose.

"Happy belated birthday, baby," he says quietly, pulling me closer. "Welcome aboard. We're taking a vacation."

I stare at him, completely lost for words. *Vacation?* He's smiling at me like this is normal, like I should have known. But I didn't. I had no idea. I look around, still trying to make sense of it all. The dogs are here, wagging their tails like they're already excited for whatever comes next. Nate's hand is warm in mine, steadying me as my thoughts spin out of control.

"I . . . I don't understand," I finally manage to say, my voice small, almost fragile.

He chuckles, pulling me into a gentle hug.

"You don't need to understand right now," he murmurs into my hair.

"Just relax. We're going somewhere far away from everything, just us."

I press my face against his chest, breathing him in, feeling the warmth of his embrace, but my mind is still reeling. I wasn't prepared for this. Not after everything that's happened. Not after the fear that's been hanging over me these past few days. But as Nate holds me close, his heart beating steadily against mine, I feel some of that fear begin to loosen its grip.

I don't know where we're going. I don't know what's waiting for us. But for the first time in a long time, I let myself lean into him, into the comfort of not knowing, into the surprise that maybe—just maybe—this is exactly what I need.

"I didn't take anything. I don't have any clothes," I say in a moment of panic.

"Who said we'll need clothes?" he answers with a wink. Yep, Nate is still Nate.

"Where are we going?" I ask.

"I know you don't like surprises, but this is a surprise. I planned it for your birthday, but then I thought I should wait for your SAT results to come out. And now is the perfect time. Don't worry, Ailly knows—she's got you covered at work." *All of this . . . for me?*

"I'm speechless," I admit.

"I hope it's a good thing," he says, raising an eyebrow.

"Yeah, yeah, of course, it is. I'm so happy the dogs are with us." And damn, I am. I love my babies.

"It's going to be a long flight. We have a bedroom and a TV. I have to work on something I couldn't get rid off, and then I'm all yours," he says. Wow. *Is this real life?*

"Of course, yeah, sure. Can I stay with you while you work? I don't feel like being alone," I tell him in a whisper, and Nate grabs my hand and sits me on his lap.

"Talk to me. What's going on?" he asks. He knows me so well. Let's just say it; maybe the feeling will disappear.

"I got scared. When I saw the airport, I thought it was a trap or something. I thought it was revenge from the staff after the car accident and you fired them all. I'm sorry, I don't know how to explain it."

"I hired them back, though. Baby, you don't ever have to fear anything for as long as I live. I'll protect you, my love. I'd die before I let anything happen to you," he says.

It reassures me, but it scares the shit out of me. *Until he leaves me . . .*

I smile at him, thinking I just need to sit next to him with the dogs. Nate gets into work mode, and I love watching him do what he does.

We've been flying for hours, and I still have no clue where

we're going. We've eaten a meal you'd expect at a five-star restaurant, I've slept a lot, I've watched some movies, and now I wait. Nate finishes his work and joins me.

"Wanna join the mile-high club?" he asks, winking at me.

"What's that?"

"Come and see," he says, taking my hand and leading me to the bedroom.

Softly, he starts to kiss me. Tender, slow, beautiful.

"Do you know how much I love you?" he asks between kisses, and I'm always uncomfortable hearing it. I'm so fucking scared to think about it. I don't answer.

"I love you so hard that sometimes, I feel like I can't even breathe. It's like my heart forgets how to beat when I'm around you, and my thoughts blur into nothing but the sound of your voice and the warmth of your touch," he says, before deepening the kiss, and then he continues.

"I love you not because you make everything perfect, but because you drive me absolutely crazy in the best possible way. You challenge me, you frustrate me, but in that chaos, I find everything I never knew I needed."

I can't hear it, I can't let it be real, this isn't real. He's lying.

"I love you for every fight we've had, every laugh we've shared, every quiet moment we've stolen when the universe felt too big. I love you because even when you drive me to the edge, I know there's no one else I'd want standing beside me. When I'm with you, Delilah, I feel like I'm free, like we could take on the world together," he says, his voice tender, looking deeply into my eyes.

I think I can't breathe. What's that buzzing thing in my belly?

"I don't just love you because you make me happy. I love you because you make me feel—everything, all at once. And that, that's what makes this love so real, so undeniable. You are my madness, my calm, my everything." His words make my heart squeeze in my chest. They both soothe and terrify me. *I can't believe this. This can't be real. I'm not worthy.*

I don't know what to say, nor will I be able to know how to say it. Frustration rises again for not being able to . . . return . . . the . . . feeling. So I kiss him. With everything I have, with everything I am. I kiss him with an urge to connect on a deeper level, the one only we know.

I unbutton his shirt delicately, as if I didn't want to break this moment suspended in time, suspended in the air. Nate and I know how to rush things, how to be brutal, how to be like animals. That's not what's happening now.

From the moment he kisses me, from the moment he enters me, from the moment he murmurs in my ear how beautiful I am, how much he . . . l . . . lo . . . how much he . . . loves . . . *me*, until the moment we both reach the stars together, it's nothing but delicacy, tenderness, courtesy, warmth. And fuck, I didn't realize how much my heart needed this. Then I fall asleep in his arms.

~

I wake up to Nate's soft voice and his touch on my arm. My eyelids flutter open, and I realize I'm still on the jet. The hum of the engines is gone, replaced by a stillness as if we'd stopped moving. I blink a few times, disoriented, the light of the cabin casting long shadows around us.

"Hey, sleepyhead," Nate whispers with a smile, brushing a strand of hair from my face. "We've landed."

I sit up quickly, rubbing my eyes and looking around.

"What time is it?" I ask, my voice groggy.

"12:30 a.m., New York time," he replies, his smile widening as he sees the shock on my face.

"12:30? Are you serious?" I can't believe it. It feels like we've been flying forever, but I don't even know how long I was asleep. The excitement that was bubbling in my chest before comes rushing back. I look around, trying to spot our things, but quickly realize there's no luggage. We didn't bring anything because this trip is a complete surprise.

Nate chuckles, clearly amused by my confusion.

"Don't worry. Everything we need is already here."

We gather a few small things—my phone, his jacket that I'd borrowed on the flight—and head toward the exit. My heart pounds with anticipation, but there's also a nervous flutter in my chest. I still have no idea where we are, and the mystery of it all makes my mind race.

As we step out of the jet, the warm air hits me with a soothing breeze, wrapping around me in an embrace. I take a deep breath, and the scent of saltwater and tropical flowers fills my lungs. The sky is dark, but there's a soft purple hue on the horizon, hinting at the sun that just set. I stand there for a moment, trying to take it all in, my eyes wide as I stare at the stunning view. Palm trees sway in the breeze, and in the distance, I can see the faint outline of mountains against the sky.

I turn to Nate, completely overwhelmed.

"Where . . . where are we?" My voice is barely above a whisper, my heart racing with excitement and disbelief.

He laughs that warm, affectionate sound that always makes me feel safe. "Bora Bora," he says, his eyes sparkling as he watches my reaction. "Surprise." I scream, my hands flying to my face as I jump up and down.

"Are you fucking serious?!" I can't stop laughing. I feel like I'm floating, like this can't possibly be real. Bora Bora? We talked about this place when we were in the Hamptons. He suggested we go, but at the time, I didn't know I'd live this long. "I can't believe this! Is this real life?!" It can't be.

Nate pulls me into his arms, kissing the top of my head as he holds me close.

"Yeah, baby, this is real life," he whispers against my hair. I can hear the smile in his voice, and it makes my heart swell. "And it's just the beginning." *Please, God, let it be true . . .*

We walk toward the dock, where a small boat waits for us. The night is warm, the kind of warmth that wraps around you like a blanket. The water beneath us is crystal clear, even in the dim light, and it sparkles as the boat gently rocks with its movement. I can't help but smile like a fool the entire time.

Is this real life, for real?

We climb in, and Nate takes the seat beside me, his hand finding mine as we begin to glide over the water. I lean my head against his shoulder, still buzzing with disbelief and happiness. The stars above us shine so brightly, and for a moment, everything feels perfect—like the whole world has slowed down just for us.

After a short ride, we approach a small private island, and my breath catches in my throat. The property in front of us looks like something out of a dream. The house is beautiful, with wide, open spaces and walls made of glass that allow you to see everything around you. Lights from inside spill out onto the sand, illuminating the lush greenery and the wooden deck that stretches out over the water. It's peaceful, quiet, and completely secluded. I feel like we're the only two people in the world right now.

As we step off the boat and onto the dock, I feel a rush of gratitude and joy so overwhelming that I almost can't speak. The house looks like it belongs in a magazine—a gorgeous blend of nature and luxury. The roof is made of thatched palm leaves, and the walls are a combination of wood and glass, blending perfectly with the surroundings. The deck wraps around the entire house, leading to a private infinity pool that seems to merge with the ocean beyond. Lanterns are lit along the pathways, adding a delicate, romantic glow to the entire space.

I can't believe this is Nate's place. It's like something you see in a dream, a place that feels too perfect to be real. Well, just like Nate.

"Oh my god, Nate," I whisper, staring in awe at everything around us. "This is . . . this is unreal."

Nate grins, his hand still holding mine as we walk toward the house.

"I wanted to bring you here when we were in the Hamptons,

remember? What a ride, huh?" He says it with pride, and I kiss his perfect mouth. Hard. He smiles his perfect smile.

"I thought we could just be together, away from everything."

"It's perfect, baby. It's perfect," I manage to say.

As we step inside the house, my heart swells even more. The entire space is open, with floor-to-ceiling windows that look out onto the water. The furniture is simple yet elegant—white couches, wooden tables, and tropical plants placed throughout. But what get my attention are the clothes scattered around the room.

There are dresses, swimsuits, and everything I could possibly need for the trip, all laid out and ready. Nate has thought of everything. Even the dogs are here, already running around happily, their tails wagging as they explore the space. It's like this entire place was waiting for us.

Tears prick the back of my eyes as I look at Nate. I don't know what to say. I've never felt this . . . *happy*, this lucky, in my entire life. I feel overwhelmed by the thoughtfulness, the . . . *love*, and the care he's put into this surprise.

I walk toward him, my heart bursting with emotions I can't even put into words. "Nate," I say in a trembling whisper. "I . . . I don't even know how to thank you. This is . . . everything."

He wraps his arms around me, holding me tight, and I bury my face in his chest.

"You don't need to thank me, Delilah," he murmurs into my hair. "I just want you to be happy. That's all I care about."

I pull back, looking up at him, my heart pounding in my chest. In this moment, standing here with him in this beautiful place, I feel something I haven't let myself fully admit until now.

I think I'm . . . No. I can't.

The thought makes my breath catch in my throat, and I feel a warmth spread through me that has nothing to do with the tropical air. This moment, this place—it feels like something out of a dream. But it's real. It's all real. *Isn't it?*

Nate leans down, kissing me softly, and for a moment, every-thing else fades away.

There's only us, and the quiet sound of the ocean in the distance.

I don't know what's going to happen next, but for the first time, I don't feel scared. I feel . . . ready. Ready for whatever comes, as long as I'm with him.

It was already late by the time Nate and I stepped off the boat and into the warmth of Bora Bora, but neither of us feels tired. The air is thick with the scent of saltwater and flowers, and the gentle breeze makes the palm trees sway.

After a quick freshen-up, we decide to take a walk around the property with the dogs.

As we stroll, Nate takes my hand, his thumb brushing over my skin, and starts talking.

"I bought this place a few years ago," he says, his voice low and calm. "I needed somewhere to disappear to, a place that felt far away from everything."

I listen closely, hanging onto every word as he tells me about how he fell in love with the island. "There's something about this place," he continues. "It's peaceful, almost untouched. The way the sun sets over the water, the way the stars light up the sky at night . . . It made me feel like I could finally breathe here, like I could escape the noise of the world."

His words sink deep into me. I understand now—why he chose this place, why it means so much to him. As he speaks, I can hear the passion in his voice, the way this island gave him something he was searching for. And the more he talks, the more I fall for not just the island, but for him, too. The way he opens up, the way he shares these moments with me—it makes my heart ache in the best way possible.

The dogs run ahead of us, exploring the paths that weave through the property, and Nate stops to point out certain spots—a hidden corner by the water where he likes to sit, the hammock hanging between two trees that he says is the best place to nap.

I can see how much he loves it here, how much this place has be-come a part of him. And I love that he's sharing it with me.

Eventually, we head back to the house. Nate has another sur-prise waiting, and as we step inside, I feel a flutter of excitement again. We get dressed quickly—he hands me a beautiful light dress he had ready for me, and I slip into it, feeling the soft fabric against my skin.

I watch him as he changes into a linen shirt and pants. He doesn't realize how beautiful he is, how powerful he looks with-out even trying. But it's not just his looks. It's something deeper, something that shines from the inside. His kindness, his warmth, the way he cares so deeply about the people and things he loves—it makes him more beautiful than anything on the outside ever could.

Once we're both ready, Nate takes my hand again, leading me out of the house. We walk down to the beach, and as we get closer, I notice something that makes my breath catch in my throat.

There, near the water, is a table set for two, surrounded by twin-kling string lights hanging from tall bamboo poles. Rose petals are scattered all over the sand, and the moonlight reflects off the ocean, creating a shimmer that seems to stretch on forever. Two waiters stand nearby, quietly waiting for us, but I barely notice them. All I can see is the magic that Nate has created.

I stop in my tracks, my eyes filling with tears. I can't believe this is real. I can't believe he did all of this for me. My hands fly up to cover my mouth as I try to hold back the emotion that's threaten-ing to spill over. I feel like I'm in a dream, but everything around me is so real, so vivid. The sand beneath my feet, the breeze against my skin, the warmth of Nate's hand in mine—it's all perfect.

"Nate," I whisper, my voice shaky. "I don't even know what to say . . . This is . . . it's beautiful."

He pulls me into his arms, holding me close, and I bury my face in his chest. I don't need to say anything else. I think he knows ex-actly how much this means to me.

"Happy birthday, baby," he says quietly, kissing the top of my head. "Come on. Let's sit down and enjoy it."

We walk to the table, and as I take my seat, I feel like I'm floating. The table is simple but elegant, with candles flickering in the center and plates set out with polished silverware. The waiters come over, and Nate tells them we'd like something traditional.

They nod and disappear for a moment, leaving us alone in this paradise.

I look across the table at Nate, and my heart swells with something. He's sitting there, the light from the candles dancing across his face, and he looks so calm, so happy. His blue eyes catch mine, and for a second, I feel like the world has stopped turning. Everything about him is perfect—the way he smiles at me, the way his hand rests casually on the table, his fingers playing with the edge of the napkin. I can't believe this man is . . . "*mine*," and I feel like the luckiest person in the world.

The waiters return with our food, and I can't help but smile at the sight. They've brought us a traditional Polynesian feast— grilled fish marinated in coconut and lime, breadfruit roasted until it's golden, and a salad made with fresh tropical fruits. There's a side of taro root, mashed and seasoned with herbs, and a sauce made from local spices that smells incredible. I don't think I'd be able to reproduce this recipe.

I take a bite of the fish, and the flavors explode in my mouth— rich, fresh, and unlike anything I've ever tasted. Nate watches me, his eyes full of admiration, and we both start laughing. I don't even know why, but it feels like the most natural thing in the world.

"So, you never stay at hotels or something?" I ask.

"Why would I?"

"I don't know, the cost might be less than buying a property, maybe. So why not?" That makes him laugh.

"Because I'm Nathan fucking Williams," he says, winking at me. *Of course.*

We spend the rest of the meal talking and laughing, the

conversation flowing easily between bites of food. We share stories, memories, and little moments that make us laugh until our
sides hurt. The moon hangs high above us, lighting up the ocean,
and the sound of the waves lapping at the shore creates a rhythm
that feels like it's keeping time with my heartbeat.

As the night stretches on, I look at Nate sitting there across from
me, and I realize something. I don't need anything more than this.
Just being here, in this moment, with him—it's all I've ever dared
to want. The world feels right, and for the first time in my whole
damn life, I feel like I'm exactly where I'm meant to be.

After dinner, Nate and I walk along the beach, the dogs running
ahead of us, acting wild as usual. The night is warm, the sound of
the ocean rhythmic as it kisses the shore. The sand feels soft beneath my feet, and I can't stop smiling. Everything feels so light, so
easy. I don't remember the last time I felt like this, like nothing in
the world mattered except this moment.

Nate bursts forward, catching me off guard, grabbing my hand
and pulling me along with him. I laugh, stumbling as we run down
the beach like kids. He spins me around, and I push him back, pretending to escape, but we're both laughing too hard to care who's
chasing whom. The dogs run in circles around us, barking and
jumping, as if they were part of the game.

I catch my breath and stop for a second, but Nate doesn't let up.
He grabs me by the waist and pulls me down into the sand, both
of us collapsing in a giggling fit. I don't even care that the sand is
sticking to my dress, that my hair is probably a mess. None of that
matters right now. We're just . . . *happy*. Ridiculously happy.

We play with the dogs, tossing sticks and watching them chase
after them. It's like nothing exists but us and the quiet of the beach,
the stars scattered across the sky like tiny diamonds. The world
feels endless, like this night could stretch on forever.

But then Nate stops. He stands still, his eyes locking onto mine,
and I feel something shift in the air. He reaches for my hand,
pulling me closer to him. His touch is warm, familiar, and yet,

right now, it feels like everything is about to change. "Delilah," he murmurs, his voice steady but filled with something deeper, something I can't quite name yet. He holds my hand tighter and looks at me with those eyes that always seem to see right through me. I can't look away. "I'd like to finish what I started on the plane," he says.

"You *did* finish what you started on the plane," I reply with a wink.

"Smart-ass. I wasn't talking about that," he says, and I'm surprised. I look at him, puzzled, and then he speaks.

"I love you like the stars love the night sky, endless and unwavering, always finding their way back no matter how far apart they seem. I love you like the ocean loves the shore, constant, steady . . . even when the waves crash violently, they always return. I love you with a force that pulls me, like gravity, binding me to you in ways I can't always explain, but always feel, deep in my bones," he says, and blood rushes in my veins.

I feel the tears building behind my eyes, but I don't move. I just stare at him, my heart pounding in my chest.

"I love you like the universe loves its mysteries, endless and full of wonder. Every day with you, I find something new, something that amazes me, something that makes me want to know more. You *are* my mystery, Delilah, the one thing in this world I can't ever stop wanting to understand, to be close to."

My breath hitches, and the tears spill over. I can't stop them. I don't want to stop them. I've never heard anything so beautiful in my life. His words seep into the cracks I've spent so long hiding, and it's like he's reaching into the deepest part of me, pulling out the pieces I've been too scared to show anyone.

"I love you because you're fierce and soft, all at once. You don't see it, but I do. I see how strong you are, even when you're scared. I see how you push yourself, even when you don't think you can. And I love you for every bit of it, even the parts you think are unlovable."

By now, I'm crying harder, my hands shaking in his. I don't even know how to breathe. My chest feels tight, my heart aching in a way that's both beautiful and terrifying.

"I love you like the first breath of air after a storm — fresh, necessary, full of promise. You are my calm and my chaos, my safe place and my greatest adventure. Every part of you is etched into me, like you were meant to be there, like we were written in the stars long before we even met."

This can't be real.

"When I look at you, I see everything I want, everything I need. It's in the way your eyes find mine in a crowded room, like I'm the only thing that matters. It's in the way your laughter fills the spaces inside me that I didn't even know were empty. You make me believe in something bigger than just the two of us. You make me believe in forever."

I can't breathe.

"Nate —" I try to say, but he doesn't let me.

"I'm not done. I love you like the dawn loves the morning, with a quiet, unshakable certainty that no matter how dark the night gets, we'll always find the light. You *are* my light, Delilah. And I don't need to 'rewrite the stars' like you once said — because for me, you've already written everything I'll ever need."

Nate pulls me close for a second, his lips brushing against my forehead as he holds me. I feel like I'm about to break apart, like I don't know how to hold myself together anymore. But he doesn't let go.

Then, without warning, Nate drops to one knee.

Everything inside me stops.

I watch, unable to move, unable to even think, as he reaches into his pocket and pulls out a small box. My heart is racing, panic flaring up inside me as I try to understand. *Is this real? Is this really happening?*

He opens the box, and inside is the most delicate, stunning diamond ring I've ever seen. The diamond sparkles under the moon's glow, its edges catching the light, almost unreal. The band is thin and elegant, with small diamonds circling around it, every detail so perfect it takes my breath away. It's beautiful in the way that feels timeless, like it was meant to be worn, like it was made just for me.

I can't breathe. I can't even think straight.

"Delilah Rose," Nate says, his voice just barely cracking, but he stays steady, his eyes never leaving mine.

"Will you marry me? Will you be my forever? Because I can't imagine this life without you in it. I don't even want to."

I stand there, frozen, my tears falling silently down my cheeks. My heart is pounding so loud I think it might break through my chest. I'm terrified. Absolutely terrified. I've spent so long being scared to love him, scared to let myself believe this could be real. But now, looking at him, seeing the way he's kneeling there, vulnerable and open, it's like everything inside me is fighting to accept that maybe, just maybe, this is real.

"I know you're scared, baby, I know you don't think that any of this is real. But it *is* real, my love. I want to be with you. I know you think that just because you have a past I don't know anything about, my feelings for you can't be true. But you're wrong, baby.

"You're so wrong, my love. If you told me right now that you killed people in the past, I'd help you bury the bodies. That's how fucking much I love you. I want to love you, to cherish you, to adore you, to protect you. Let me, baby. I beg you. Let me. Marry me, Delilah."

What do I do?

CHAPTER 24

Nate

She said yes.

We're engaged.

But I don't plan on staying engaged. I want to marry the woman as fast as possible.

The one problem is . . . convincing her.

"What's the rush?" she says, her voice rising slightly. We're back at the house, in the bathroom, trying to brush our teeth. Trying.

"Because it's right. I love you. I don't want you to be my girl-friend anymore; I want you to be my wife," I say simply, my mouth filled with foam.

"I was never your girlfriend," she tries to argue.

"You were sooo my girlfriend," I say, rolling my eyes. "But you know I'm right when I say that this thing between us is bigger, deeper. We live together, we work together, we even have dogs. I'm not waiting. I'm done waiting."

"What are you talking about? When did you start waiting?" she says, putting her hands on her hips. She's so fuckable right now. What was she saying? Right, shit, I was making a reference to Charlotte. *Fuck.*

"Waiting for you to admit that I'm right," I say. I'm not even surprised by my smart move. That's what I do. I spill the foam and rinse my mouth. I grab a towel while she tries to apply her face cream, then stop her and rub the day cream on her face for her. She lets her hand fall, looks at me, and I smile at her.

"I love you. I love taking care of you."

"Nate—"

"I'm not done. Damn, woman. More seriously, there's a place here where we can get married, just the two of us. It's like an official private ceremony. We'll just need to have our marriage validated in the United States once we return. Otherwise, our marriage will only be valid here or in France."

"Can I at least think about it?" she asks.

"No," I answer. I mean it. Once we're married, she'll trust me. She'll know I'm in this for the long run. She'll feel safer. And she's fucking perfect for me.

She slaps my chest, and I grab her by her perfect ass, which makes her laugh. And to think she was pissed at me ten seconds ago . . .

"You're impossible, Mr. Williams," she says.

"I know, Mrs. Williams." Wow, that felt right.

"Oh, fuck you!" she says, and we burst out laughing together. I love seeing her wearing my ring. It feels perfect.

She catches me watching, and now she's the one staring at it.

"Please tell me this isn't a real diamond."

"The fuck it isn't," I say, winking at her.

"Please don't tell me it cost a lot of money," she begs.

"It didn't."

"Liar."

"Busted," I say, laughing again as I push her onto the mattress. I jump on her, nuzzling my nose into her neck, my hands roaming as usual.

Then I add, "We're meeting the officiant in the morning. We better get some rest."

"What?!" she shrieks. That makes me laugh, really.

"Just to organize the ceremony. We'll meet with other service providers—the dress, the suits, the meal—for just the two of us. You'll decide on everything."

"Will I?" she shouts again, scandalized.

"Of course! This wedding is for us only. Just like we met. Don't worry, we'll have another reception in New York whenever you want."

"Do you hear yourself right now?" she says, sitting up on the bed, pushing me aside.

I don't like it, so I take her hand and force her to come back to me.

"Baby, I'm dead serious. But if after tomorrow you feel like you don't want any of this, then I'll drop it. I'll come up with different ideas, but I'll listen to you. I'll always put you first. I just want . . . I just want you to put *me* first too," I finally say, and her face literally lights up. She understands everything I'm saying. She wants to please me too. *I love her.*

"Okay . . ." she says, and I don't waste a second before I grab her for the most perfect kiss. And the most perfect, exhausting sex.

~

The next day, we sit in the small, cozy office of the wedding officiant in Bora Bora. Delilah is beside me, looking around like she's trying to take it all in. I can't stop staring at her. I swear, she's fucking beautiful, even in a stuffy office like this. I reach over, grab her hand, and squeeze it. She gives me that soft smile that makes my chest feel too tight.

The wedding officiant, a middle-aged guy with a calm voice, starts explaining the process. He's polite and formal, but I'm just trying to get this thing done so we can get married and celebrate. I mean, I love this woman more than anything, and I don't need anyone dragging this out.

"So," the officiant says, "for a private ceremony, you have a few options. We can arrange something on the main beach at sunset, or there's a beautiful garden nearby. It's secluded, very peaceful. Some couples choose to do it there."

Delilah and I look at each other, and I already know what she's thinking. We decided this last night.

I cut the guy off. "No, we're doing it at a private beach near a restaurant I know." I glance at Delilah, and she nods, like we're totally in sync. "That place is perfect. We want it there, just us." The officiant nods, writing something down.

"Alright, that's fine. Now, before we go further, do you have your prenup ready?"

I blink. "No, we don't have a prenup."

Delilah squeezes my hand. "What's a prenup?" she asks, frowning.

The officiant clears his throat.

"A prenuptial agreement is a legal document that outlines how assets will be divided in the event of a divorce. It's common for couples to establish one before marriage, especially when there are significant assets involved." Delilah's eyes go wide.

"Wait, so . . . it's like insurance? To protect . . . Nate?"

I can't help but laugh. She's so damn cute when she's all worried like that.

"Yeah, baby, it's like that. But we don't need it."

She pulls her hand back, turning to face me fully.

"No, Nate. You need to do it. I want to protect you. You've worked so hard for everything, and I don't want you to lose it if something happens."

I lean back in my chair, grinning like an idiot. She's serious. She really thinks I need this. It's endearing as fuck.

"Delilah, baby, listen to me," I say, grabbing her hand again. "I love you. I don't need a fucking prenup. You can take every last dollar from me if that's what it comes to. Hell, I'll give it all to you. I don't care. You think I'm marrying you for fun? You're stuck with me, gorgeous."

She stares at me, all wide-eyed and shocked.

"Nate, I can't—"

I cut her off with a laugh. "You're not taking my things, babe. Not because you can't, but because we're never getting divorced. End of story. No prenup, no bullshit."

The officiant looks a little uncomfortable, but I don't care. All I care about is Delilah, who's sitting next to me worried about my damn money when all I want is to be with her forever.

Then we step into the tiny wedding planner's office. The air smells like flowers and the ocean, a mix I'm starting to get used to around here. Delilah is next to me, and I can't help but feel like we're on top of the world. We've spent the day running around, picking out clothes for the wedding and tasting the food at the restaurant I suggested—like we're just two random people, not a couple about to get hitched.

We sit down across from a tiny woman with glasses and a clipboard who looks like she could either organize the best day of your life or tear your head off if you cross her.

"So," she says, getting nervous, "you've only given me eighteen hours to plan everything?"

I grin, and Delilah takes the lead.

"Yes. Just white everywhere. We don't need fancy things, just white on the beach. Anything that comes to mind, we trust you," she says.

I add, "And make sure it's private—no one gets through. It's gotta be locked down tight."

The planner looks at me like I'm crazy, but then her eyes light up. She loves a challenge, I can tell.

"Alright," she says, jotting things down. "White flowers, white linens, white chairs . . . And you want the private beach near that restaurant, correct?"

Delilah smiles and nods. "Yes, I love the spot. It feels perfect. But no chairs, there won't be any guests."

I squeeze her hand under the table, and she gives me that look, the one that makes me wanna marry her all over again, every damn day.

"Do you have a witness for the ceremony?" the planner asks, flipping through her notes.

"Anders," I say, without missing a beat. "Our head of security. He'll be our witness."

The planner blinks but doesn't say anything. She's probably not used to the groom's security guy being the witness, but hey, it's our day. Anders has been with me for years; he's seen all my highs and lows, so he damn well deserves to stand there when I'm at my best.

"Alright, then. Let's move on to finalizing the details."

The next day comes faster than I expect. Delilah's off getting ready with the staff, probably looking like a beautiful angel, while I'm here with Anders and the dogs. We're in this small bungalow by the beach, and I'm putting on my suit. The dogs are watching me like they know something big's happening. Damn, even Anders looks more excited than usual.

I straighten my tie and look at myself in the mirror. I feel good. Confident. I've been through a lot of shit, made deals that were life-changing, but none of them compare to this. Marrying Delilah? It's the best fucking decision I've ever made. She's the one, no question about it.

"Anders," I say, glancing at him. "How do I look?" He gives me a rare smile.

"Like a man who's about to make the best deal of his life."

"Damn right."

We head down to the beach. When I get there, my breath catches in my throat. The place looks even better than I imagined. The wedding planner knocked it out of the park. The private beach is covered in white—white flowers, white drapes blowing in the breeze, small lights all around. It's simple, clean, and somehow, it feels like magic. The ocean is calm, just lapping at the shore, and the sun's starting to set, casting this warm golden glow over everything.

Underneath a wooden arch, covered in white roses and lilies, is where we'll say "I do." The smell of the flowers mixes with the salt in the air, and it hits me how perfect this moment is. It's like the world faded away, and it's just us. My heart's pounding, and I can't wait to see her.

"Let's begin," the officiant says, and I've never been this ready in my life.

I hear the soft notes of "Saturn" by Sleeping at Last—the first music I ever heard with Delilah. It's the same music we made love to for the first time. The sound floats on the air, and I know it's Delilah's doing. A surprise for me. Damn, I'm gonna love her forever. My throat tightens, and I feel a tear threatening to fall, but I blink it back. Not yet. Not until I see her.

And then I do.

Delilah steps onto the sand, and everything around me goes quiet. She's in this simple, elegant white dress, lace and silk flowing around her like a dream. Her long veil catches the breeze, and it's like she's glowing. She's let her hair fall naturally, just like I love it. I've never seen her look so beautiful in my life. Every time I look at her, I fall in love all over again, but today? Today, it's different. It's deeper. It's forever.

She walks toward me, and my heart's beating out of my chest. The music plays in the background, and I feel that damn tear again. I can't stop it this time. It slips down my cheek, but I don't care. I'm about to marry the love of my life, and nothing else matters.

When she reaches me, I take her hand, and for a second, the whole world is just me and her, standing on this perfect beach, about to start our lives.

The wedding officiant stands under the arch, smiling at both of us as the sound of the waves fills the background. He clears his throat and begins to speak, steady and calm, but with a warmth that makes the moment feel even more special.

"Today, we are gathered here on this beautiful beach to celebrate the union of two souls who have chosen to walk through life together. Nathan and Delilah, you stand before us not as two individuals, but as a couple who have found in each other the partner, the friend, the lover, and the confidant you've always been looking for." He glances between us, then continues.

"This ceremony isn't about promises made out of duty or tradition. It's about the vows you choose to make because you believe in the love that has brought you here today. Marriage is about partnership, about facing life's challenges together, and about celebrating life's joys side by side. It's about love, trust, and respect. The two of you have built a foundation on these values, and today, you're choosing to build on that foundation for the rest of your lives.

The officiant smiles lightly at Delilah, then at me.

"Nathan and Delilah, marriage is more than just a legal bond; it's a commitment that runs deep, that asks for patience, understanding, and a lot of laughter. It's about waking up each day and choosing to love one another, even when it's hard. It's about creating a life together that reflects who you are as individuals and as partners."

He pauses for a moment, letting his words sink in, then turns his gaze fully on us again.

"Now, before we move forward with your vows, I ask you both to take a moment. Look at one another. Remember the journey that brought you here. Remember why you fell in love, and let that love be your guide for the vows you are about to make."

We do as he says, and I look into Delilah's eyes. I see everything—every laugh, every tear, every moment we've shared, and everything I want in our future. My chest tightens, and I squeeze her hand. This is it.

The officiant nods, satisfied with the weight of the moment.

"Nathan, Delilah, as you exchange your vows, remember that the words you speak today hold the power to shape your future together. Speak from your hearts, for it is your love that brings us all here today, and it is your love that will carry you forward."

The air feels thick with emotion as he takes a step back and invites us to share our vows.

"I'd like to go first, if that's okay?" she says, and I don't have the voice to speak. I simply nod.

Delilah stands before me, and I can already see the tears welling up in her eyes. Her hand shakes just slightly, but she's trying to hold it together, and I'm barely holding it together myself.

"Nate . . ." she begins, her voice already faltering, barely above a whisper. Her breath hitches as she swallows hard trying to push through the emotion.

"I wasn't born into a world of love. I've never had a family, never had real friends, never known what a normal life feels like. I didn't know what light was, or love, or what it meant to have a home."

Her voice cracks, and I can see her chin quiver. Tears start to fall freely now, but she doesn't stop. She looks at me, her eyes glistening. I can tell this is hard for her, but she's pushing through.

"I used to think that people who dared to hope for happiness were foolish. That happiness wasn't real, and believing in it was a waste of time. Until I met you. On the darkest day of my life, when I didn't think living was worth it anymore, when breathing was hard . . . I met you."

Her voice wavers, and a sob escapes her, but she catches herself, wiping a tear away with her shaking hand.

"And from the moment our eyes met, something inside me shifted, even if I was too scared to admit it at the time."

She pauses, taking a shaky breath, her tears streaming down her cheeks. She lets them fall now, not bothering to stop them. And I swear I'm going to lose it.

"You saved me, Nate. You healed parts of me that I thought were broken forever. Because you're Nathan fucking Williams, and you can do anything." Her lips twitch into a small, soft smile between the tears.

"You gave me everything I thought I could never have—friendship, stability, comfort, warmth, protection . . . and love. Real love."

Her voice is so quiet now, almost like she's afraid the words will break her completely.

"I didn't want to believe it was real. I thought you'd leave, that I didn't deserve you. But here we are, standing in front of each other, marrying each other. You helped me silence the demons I've lived with for so long."

She takes another breath, her voice shaking more as she fights back another wave of emotion.

"You've been patient with me. You've understood my boundaries when even I didn't know them. You've never pushed me, never rushed me, and you've always guided me, always let me take my time. You put me first, always. And for that . . . I thank you, Nate."

Her tears fall harder now, her voice breaking with nearly every word, but she keeps going, because this is us. This is her heart.

"You are the best human I know. Your heart is pure, your soul is gentle, and your mind is brilliant. It's not just about how you look, Nate, it's everything inside you that made me realize something I've never said before."

Her voice softens, her tears slowing but her eyes still shining with all the emotion she's trying so hard to hold in.

"I love you, Nathan Williams. You showed me light, you showed me love, you showed me what home is. You are my light, you are my love, and you are my home. You've always put me first . . . and from this day forward, I vow to put you first, always.

"Thank you for being my everything."

Her voice falters as she finishes, and she's crying again, but this time she's smiling through the tears. And me? I'm a wreck. Watching her break and then rise again, watching her say those words, there's no way to explain what's happening inside me. All I know is, I'm the luckiest damn man in the world. I know I'm not supposed to kiss her now, but I don't give a fuck. I take off her veil and press my lips to hers. Everyone laughs at my need—let them.

"You're not supposed to kiss me just yet," she says, scolding me.

"I don't care," I answer simply, putting her veil back on.

"Nathan, it's your turn," the officiant says. Fuck.

I look at her standing in front of me, her eyes still red from crying during her vows. Her face is delicate, glowing in the light, but I can see the weight of her emotions, the love she poured into every word she said. I need to do the same. I need to let her know just how much she means to me.

I take a deep breath, but my voice comes out shaky.

"Delilah," I begin, and my throat tightens immediately. I pause, my hands trembling harder, and I laugh softly, trying to steady myself.

"I didn't think I'd be this nervous."

She smiles at me through her tears, and it's the most beautiful thing I've ever seen. Her lips quiver, and her eyes are locked on mine, filled with so much love it makes me weak.

"I've spent my whole life thinking I knew what love was. Thought I understood everything about it, but I was wrong. I was so wrong," I say, my voice faltering. I clear my throat, trying to keep myself together, but I feel the tears welling up. "Before I met you, I didn't know what it meant to love someone so much that it hurt. That the idea of losing them . . . of living without them . . . was more terrifying than anything else."

I look at her, and I see the tears start to fall down her cheeks again. She tries to keep it together, but I know she feels what I feel. My chest tightens, and I can barely breathe, but I keep going.

"*You* saved *me*, Delilah," I whisper, and my voice breaks. "You walked into my life and turned everything upside down. You made me question everything I thought I knew. You showed me that love isn't about control or perfection or always having the answers. It's about trust. It's about vulnerability. It's about letting someone see every broken piece of you and knowing that they'll love you anyway."

She brings her hand to her mouth, trying to hold back a sob, and I feel the tears spill over my own cheeks now. I've lost the battle to stay composed.

"I've always tried to protect you. To give you everything you need. But the truth is, you're the one who saved me. You're the one who taught me what it means to love and to be loved, really loved, without limits, without conditions. You healed parts of me I didn't even know were broken."

I wipe at my face, laughing a little at myself because I'm a wreck. I've never felt this vulnerable in my life.

"You've made me a better man, Delilah. A man who knows that

nothing, and I mean nothing, in this world is more important than you. And the dogs, of course. I love our life together. Thank you for choosing me to fall asleep next to, and to wake up next to." I look down at my shaking hands, trying to pull myself together for the last part.

"I vow today to always put you first, to love you more, to always listen, and to always come home to you. I promise to protect you, to love you, to be there in every way that matters. You are my world, Delilah. You are my light."

I meet her eyes again, and she's crying, her face wet with tears, but she's smiling, and I can't stop myself anymore. I take her hands, my voice barely more than a whisper now.

"You are my everything. And I will spend the rest of my life proving it to you."

Her tears fall harder, and I can feel the weight of the moment between us, like nothing else in the world exists but her and me. I squeeze her hands, my voice shaking as I say, "I love you, Delilah. Always."

Now it's time to exchange the rings. I chose one before leaving New York. It's thin, gold, and discreet.

The wedding officiant steps forward, clearing his throat, a gentle smile on his face.

"Nathan, do you take Delilah to be your lawfully wedded wife, to have and to hold, in sickness and in health, until death do us part?" I barely pause.

"I do," I say, my voice steady, filled with certainty. It's the easiest thing I've ever said.

He turns to Delilah, who looks at me like I'm her whole world.

"Delilah, do you take Nathan to be your lawfully wedded husband, to have and to hold, in sickness and in health, until death do us part?" Her voice is soft, but unwavering.

"I do."

The officiant smiles. The rings have been exchanged. My hands are still trembling, but I feel steady, locked into this moment like nothing can break it. Delilah's eyes are on mine, kind and shining, and all I can think about is how much I love her.

"By the power vested in me, I now pronounce you husband and wife. Nathan, you may kiss your bride." *Thank fuck.*

For a moment, time stops. Everything around us—the rustling of the palm trees, the distant sound of the waves lapping the shore, the delicate notes of the music—fades away. All I see is her.

Delilah stands there, her face radiant in the light of the setting sun, her veil blowing delicately behind her. Her eyes—full of tears, full of love—are locked on mine, and I feel like I'm falling all over again. Every part of me aches to be closer to her.

I step toward her, my heart pounding in my chest. Her breath catches, and my hands, quaking with emotion, cup her face as if she were the most fragile, precious thing in the world—because to me, she is.

I look into her eyes, and everything we've been through, every moment that led us here, flashes between us. What a wild ride. She's my home, my universe, and in this moment, it's like nothing else matters. Just her. Just us.

I lean in slowly, my lips barely brushing hers at first, a soft, tender touch. The warmth of her breath mingles with mine, and the world seems to shift beneath us. I press closer, my lips sinking deeper into hers, and suddenly, everything I've ever wanted, everything I've ever needed, is right here in this kiss.

It's not just a kiss. It's a promise. A promise of forever. It's the embodiment of every vow we just made, every unspoken word of love we've shared. Her lips are warm, and the way she kisses me back—so gentle, so full of emotion—makes my heart swell until I think it might burst.

I feel her hands come up, fingers sliding into my hair, pulling me closer, and I can't hold back anymore. I kiss her with everything I have, pouring all the love, all the gratitude, all the devotion I feel into that one moment. Her body presses against mine, and the warmth of her touch sends shivers down my spine.

When we finally pull apart, our foreheads rest against each other, both of us breathing heavily. Her eyes are still closed, her lips parted, like she's savoring the moment just as much as I am. I brush my thumb across her cheek, wiping away a tear, and whisper:

"I love you, Delilah Williams. Forever."

She opens her eyes, her lips curving into that soft, perfect smile, and whispers back, "I love you."

I can't believe I'm finally married.

We go straight to the restaurant. It's filled with people, strangers, just like Delilah requested. She didn't want to privatize the establishment, and what my wife wants, my wife gets. We're still wearing our wedding clothes, and I can't stop smiling. Just the two of us.

We talk, we laugh, we drink, we eat, and I still can't believe she married me.

"Now we have to prepare our wedding in the States," I say, my mouth full of that amazing chocolate cake.

"Do we have to?" she asks.

"Baby, this wedding was the wedding of my dreams. I loved it. But . . . don't you want to get married surrounded by your friends? Maybe Ashley?" I ask, knowing it's dangerous territory, but I have to ask. I see her face shift.

"No. Not now, I mean. This wedding was perfect, but I want to keep it for ourselves. I need some time to . . . adjust," she says, and I understand her. I take her hand in mine and kiss it.

"So, we'll just get our marriage license, then," I say.

"Hum, about that. I thought we could wait on that too." *What the fuck?*

"Why?" I ask.

"Because it all feels like a dream. I'm scared to wake up. I took a step here, a very beautiful one. But it's still hard. I need some time. We'll have a real wedding later. Just please give me time," she pleads.

"That *was* a real wedding. But okay, I understand. We'll take it slow," I say to comfort her. I don't want to ruin the night.

She smiles and gets back to eating her piece of cake.

"Will you at least change your name?" I ask.

"Nate, come on," she says, and she sees my face turning red. "If it means that much to you, okay, I will."

"Thank you. Yes, it does mean a lot. I want those fuckers out there to know that you are not available."

"There are more women wanting you than men wanting me," she says.

"Is my wife jealous? Does my wife need reassuring? I'd love to fulfill all your needs," I say with a huge grin, and Delilah bursts out laughing.

"I have a surprise for you," she says. I'm intrigued.

"Does that surprise include nudity?"

"Hum, no. Sorry." And I pout. She laughs again and then asks me to wait here.

After a moment, I hear a melody throughout the terrace where I'm seated, and then Delilah comes into view, with a mic, starting to sing. I know the song.

> *When the rain is blowing in your face*
> *And the whole world is on your case*
> *I could offer you a warm embrace*
> *To make you feel my love*
> *When the evening shadows and the stars appear*
> *And there is no one there to dry your tears*
> *I could hold you for a million years*
> *To make you feel my love*
> *The storms are raging on the rolling sea*
> *And on the highway of regret*
> *The winds of change are blowing wild and free*
> *You ain't seen nothing like me yet*
> *I could make you happy, make your dreams come true*

Nothing that I wouldn't do
Go to the ends of the earth for you
To make you feel my love
To make you feel my love

If I thought I couldn't love the woman more than I already did, I was completely wrong. She stuns me. Wow. What a beautiful sight. What a goddess. My wife.

I stand up, rush to her, and give the people what they want. I kiss my bride as if it were our last day on earth.

"I love you," she says. I didn't know how much I needed those words until she finally said them at our wedding. I vow to never tire of hearing them for as long as I live.

~

I sit in the backseat of the car, my head leaned back, Delilah nestled against me, her hand resting on my leg while the dogs snore like little chainsaws. Tyler's driving us through the jungle of Manhattan traffic, and everything feels surreal. The city's its usual loud, chaotic self—horns blaring, people jaywalking like they've got a death wish.

But I'm just sitting here, staring out the window, grinning like an idiot because I'm still coming down from the high of the last few days. Bora fucking Bora.

Man, we lived it up. I'm talking about the kind of trip that ruins every vacation after.

We hiked up that mountain—volcano, actually—sweating like pigs, but the view? Insane. We dove into water so clear, I swear I could see my future in it. Jet skiing? Oh yeah, we tore through those waves like maniacs. Delilah's laugh when we hit that big-ass wave and nearly flipped? Priceless. The drinks, the food, the sun . . . everything felt like it was out of a dream. But nothing beat the moment we said, "I do."

Simple, real, and perfect. I've never felt so connected to another human being in my life. I'm not talking about the fun kinky stuff, though that was amazing. I'm talking about how we really connected. The kind of closeness where you feel like you're in each other's heads. We had these long, deep talks, and then we'd go quiet, just holding each other, like there was nothing else in the world. I never thought I could feel like this. Not with anyone.But now we're back in New York, and reality's slapping me in the face—except I've got one more trick up my sleeve. Delilah doesn't know it yet, but I'm about to blow her mind.

Tyler pulls the car up to the curb, right near Central Park. Delilah lifts her head off my shoulder, stretching. She looks around, confused. I can feel her body tense up as she scans the street. We're parked in front of this old house. Not one of those modern, glass-and-steel monstrosities. No, this place has character. It's ancient, though it was renovated.

Delilah blinks at the house, then at me, like I've finally lost it.

"Nate, what are we doing here?" she asks, with this nervous edge in her voice. She's got that look, the one where she's trying to figure out if I'm serious or pulling some elaborate prank.

I just grin and step out of the car, feeling that little jolt of excitement in my chest. I reach into my pocket and pull out a key. Delilah gets out too, but she's still looking around, glancing at the house, then back at the street like she's expecting someone to pop out and start robbing us. Her arms are crossed, and I can tell she's anxious.

"Are you sure we should be here?" she asks, her voice tightening. "Like, this doesn't look . . . safe. What if people think we're breaking in?"

I smirk and hold up the key, dangling it in front of her face. "Relax, babe. I think we're good."

She narrows her eyes at me, totally not getting it.

"What the hell is going on, Nate?"

I walk up to the door, my heart pounding a little harder now. I can feel Delilah's eyes on me, and she's starting to get frustrated, which just makes this even better.

I slide the key into the lock and turn it, feeling that satisfying click. Then I push the door open. It creaks, because of course it does—it's that kind of house. There's an enclosed foyer with two doors. One leading to the staff's home and the other to *ours*.

As I open the door, I turn back to her, leaning against the doorframe with a grin plastered on my face.

"Happy belated birthday," I say, drawing it out for dramatic effect.

"And congratulations for the SATs. Oh, and wedding present."

Delilah's standing there, her mouth half-open, staring at me like I've just spoken in a different language.

"Whaaaaat?" She drags out the word, her eyes wide, looking between me and the house, trying to process what I've just said. I chuckle.

"Yeah, I bought the house. *Our* house."

Her jaw drops even more. She looks at the house again, then back at me. Her eyes get watery, and I can see her brain trying to catch up with her emotions. And that's when I know I've got her— hook, line, and sinker.

"You told me once that you hoped the dogs were happy because, in your head, dogs lived in a house with a garden."

"So you bought the dogs a house," she says, smirking at me. I love her attitude.

"I bought *us* a house. I put your name on it and faked your signature. You're welcome."

"What the fuck?" she shouts.

Damn, how I love my wife.

CHAPTER 25

Delilah

It's been a few weeks since the wedding. We haven't officially registered it, and honestly, I don't think we ever will. We know we're married, and we act like a married couple—at least, I think we do. But that's it. No paperwork, no grand announcements. We told our closest friends, but Nate's family? They have no idea. I haven't even met them yet, and frankly, I'm not in a rush to. It just feels . . . overwhelming.

The house is almost finished. We didn't change much—it's too charming to mess with. Just a few decorations here and there, nothing major. The dogs are living their best lives, running around the garden and loving how close we are to Central Park. There's even an attached apartment for the security team and staff, giving Nate and me some much-needed privacy. If someone rings the bell, security handles it first, then lets us know. It's nice. I feel . . . *safer*.

I applied to a bunch of distance programs, and now I'm waiting to hear back. I'm trying not to dwell on it because if I do, I'll spiral into a funk. Nate left for work early this morning—he has meetings lined up. Meanwhile, I took the morning off to keep unpacking and sorting through clothes. We left some stuff at the penthouse, which Nate wants to keep as an investment for the company. *His decision, not mine.*

Ailly suggested we have lunch at the house before heading to work together with my new security team, Michael and Sienna. I threw together something quick in the kitchen. Honestly, I love cooking here. This kitchen feels like home. The house is stunning—teal shades, dark wood, and massive windows that flood the space with sunlight. It feels . . . alive.

We're sitting at the kitchen counter, eating and discussing marketing strategies for a project at Williams. She casually mentions visiting her mom, Angie, in Alabama for a few days, meaning I'll be left to handle things solo at work.

"I think I'll be fine. If I get stuck, Nate can help," I tell her.

She raises an eyebrow. "You do know he's not supposed to hear about this project before the head manager presents it at the exec meeting next month, right? It's gotta be perfect for the CEO."

"Oh, okay, no problem. I won't tell him."

Ailly laughs, shaking her head.

"No, no. What I mean is don't let *anyone* know you're asking the CEO for advice on the project. But between us? He's your husband. Of course you can ask him. Just . . . keep it out of the office."

That word—*husband*—still feels weird.

"He's not my real husband," I say. "We're only married in France and French Polynesia. It's not . . . official." Ailly gives me a look.

"Girl, *he's* your husband. I've never seen a marriage more real than yours." I smile but don't dive deeper into that.

We get to the office, and I slip off my wedding ring. Everyone knows Nate and I are together, but no one dares to ask questions. We settle into work mode, and before I know it, my phone buzzes. "Husband Cockband" flashes on the screen, and I pick up the call with a grin.

"Hey," I say, still smiling.

"Hey, babe. You at the office?"

"Yeah, why? Everything okay?"

"Yeah, just busy. Can't you come up to my office? Work with me?"

I laugh. "And why's that?" I ask.

"Because I want to fuck you," he says, completely deadpan. *Of course.* I burst out laughing.

"I have work to do too, sir."

"Keep talking dirty to me," he teases, making me laugh harder.

"I'll come up in ten, alright?"

"Okay, wife. Love you. See you in ten." I hang up, still smiling like an idiot.

"Wow, I wish I had a reason to smile that big," Ailly jokes, and I stick my tongue out at her before gathering my stuff to head upstairs.

When I reach Nate's office on the ninetieth floor, I'm greeted with a death stare from Chloe Lenly—the office bitch. I ignore her and walk straight in.

Nate's face lights up the second he sees me. He rushes over, pulling me into a tight embrace and kissing me until I can't breathe. I run my fingers across his face, feeling this weird sense of disbelief that he's . . . *mine*. I smile so hard it hurts.

He kisses my palm and leads me to his desk.

"I told you I have to work," I remind him, already heading toward the small table I usually use.

"No, no," he says, grinning. "I've made room for you. My desk is big enough for both of us."

Working at Nate's desk? Now, *that* is a treat. I settle into the chair, glancing around.

"Wow, I feel like I'm in charge behind this massive thing," I joke. But when I look at Nate, I realize the innuendo I just made, and we both laugh.

People come in and out of his office, and I stay out of his business, just working quietly. No one dares ask who I am, *thank God*.

"Babe, I have to work on some files, alone, because Ailly is off for a few days. I told you she's going to visit her mom. I need some help just to make sure I'm heading in the right direction with this—"

"Sure, show me."

"I wasn't done," I say, fake smiling. "The team is supposed to present this project to you in a month during the exec meeting to get your approval. So technically, you *can't* look into it."

"Where are you going with this?" he asks.

"Well, I need you to look at it not as Nathan Williams, my CEO, but as Nate, my . . . you know."

"Husband," he finishes for me. I swallow, still processing the word. It still feels unreal.

"Yeah," I say quietly, not wanting to hurt his feelings.

"I swear, I'm gonna get our marriage license here and now if you keep denying what we are."

"I'm not denying it, I'm just saying . . . it's not real."

"The fuck it's not—" Nate starts, but Chloe interrupts.

"Mr. Williams, Mr. Kingston is here to see you," she says. For once, I'm actually relieved she interrupted.

James enters the office, and the tension is thick. Nate still hasn't forgiven him since their fight.

"Hey, Nate," James says first, glancing quickly at him before noticing me.

"Oh, hi, Delilah." His voice is tight, awkward. He shifts his attention back to Nate, trying to keep things professional.

"I just came to grab the revisions on the Hudson deal you suggested. Everything's looking good."

Nate doesn't even respond. Not a word. He just takes the file from James, his face expressionless. He scribbles some notes in the margins, his focus completely on the paper, and after a couple of minutes, he hands it back without even looking up. Silent, cold. Nate seems to be an expert at holding a grudge.

James awkwardly says goodbye, but it's like talking to a wall. He leaves quickly, clearly uncomfortable, and I can't help but let out a small chuckle.

Nate turns to me, eyebrows raised.

"What?"

"You're really good at holding a grudge," I say, smiling.

"And why does that make you smile?" He sounds genuinely curious, but there's a hint of amusement in his eyes.

"Because I think I just discovered something we have in common."

Nate leans back a bit, tilting his head.

"What do you mean?"

"Well, I'm unable to forgive. If I care about you and you screw me over, I literally can't forgive."

"But you forgave James."

"I never cared about James."

"So if I screw up, you'll never forgive me?" he asks, almost terrified. "That's unfair, I'm your husband. I hope to God you'll come to your senses and see that I love you and I'm worth forgiving after everything we've been through. Don't you think?" *What the fuck is he talking about?*

"Nate, what are you talking about?" I ask, completely confused. He exhales but doesn't answer.

I think the James thing is too much for him. I don't know what happened with James since their fight, but I can see Nate isn't ready to talk about it. He doesn't want to focus on James—he must be hurting. I decide to get back to my worksheets and give him some space, without considering his last little concerning intervention.

"I'm never divorcing you, Delilah," he says. "Never."

I look up to meet his gaze, not understanding what he's implying. Does he think the demons in my head are speaking? They're always speaking, but right now, they aren't.

What the fuck is going on? I don't answer. He's holding something in, so I decide to give him space, turning back to my work as I feel Nate's hand on my thigh.

I glance over at Nate after a while. He's been staring at the same document for hours, completely lost in it. His concentration is impressive—every page gets his full attention, as if nothing else existed. I can't help but smile. He's always like this: dedicated, relentless.

I should be focusing too, but it's hard when I'm sitting here, right next to him, at the same desk. We're working on different things—me on a marketing campaign, him on who knows what—but just being here, side by side, makes everything better.

Chloe announces Nate's next meeting and two men from the executive floor walk in. He looks up, frowning slightly as they greet him. I decide to give them some privacy, so I slide out of my chair and move over to the table by the big window. The sunlight pouring in feels warm against my skin as I sit down trying to focus on my work, but I can't help listening to the conversation.

"We don't think we should keep investing in his business," one of the men says. I don't catch the name. Nate leans back in his chair, considering.

"I know him. He's a good guy, solid reputation," Nate replies.

"Business is business," the other man says with a shrug.

Nate says, "It's too bad for him, but he's Paul Davis. He'll find someone to inject money. He's resourceful."

My heart stops. I freeze. *Did I hear that right?*

Without thinking, I interrupt, my voice shaky.

What did you say the name was?"

All eyes turn to me, and Nate's expression shifts to concern. He repeats the name carefully.

"Paul Davis. Why?"

I don't answer. I freeze again.

"Leave. I'll see you later," Nate says, before joining me by the windows. He looks into my eyes, searching for answers.

"Is Paul Davis okay?" I ask.

"His business is in great difficulty. How do you know Paul?"

"Is he going to be okay?" I ask.

"I don't know, baby, why?"

"He's . . . he's Ashley's husband," I say, feeling tears threaten my eyes. Talking about Ashley is still so fucking hard for me.

"What? Paul's wife is your sister?" he says, almost incredulous. *My sister.* I nod to him.

"Do you know him . . . personally?" I ask, unsure.

"No, I wouldn't go as far as 'personally,' but he's part of my circle. He's a respected man, a good one. We've met dozens of times and shared polite business conversations.

"I've never met Ashley. He never brought her to any event."

"That's no wonder. Ashley hates being around people. I thought she'd change that. Being with Paul . . . So, you work with him?"

"No, I'm an investor. But the situation is . . . critical. We can't invest anymore or we'll lose money," he says. I understand, I swear I do. But my heart breaks for Ashley. I hope she's okay. I hope everything is fine with her.

"What do you want to ask me?" Nate says softly.

"Nothing, I don't want to talk about this anymore. I'm still . . . well, me. I'm sorry. It's hard." But Nate is completely shocked, and I don't understand why. Is it because I married him he thought I *had to* open up?

"Why aren't you asking me to still invest to save his ass?" he asks, almost incredulous. *What?*

"That's not what I do, Nate. That's what you do. You're the expert. I'll never tell you to invest in something I know nothing about. I'll never drag you into this," I say, a bit offended. Then I see relief in his eyes.

"You're so different. I'm so fucking happy I married you. I love you." He kisses me. "But I'll invest if you want me to," he says, and I don't answer. I can feel my heart break. *All I want is to see her. Hear her voice. I miss her.*

"I think I just need to go home. I'm sorry." I can feel myself shutting off. I'm flooded with the unwelcome memory of the last day I saw Ashley. I'm so hurt. *Why do people always leave?*

"Wait, baby, no, stay with me. I still have a couple of files I need to work on, and then I'm all yours, okay?" *All yours . . . What a joke. Until he leaves me, just like everybody else.*

"It's fine, Nate. You stay, I'll go. I just need to be alone." Alone and safe.

"That's the thing about marriage, baby. You'll never get to be alone ever again."

Okay, I need to get things straight right now.

"That's not a real marriage. We got too excited on a beach and rushed into a wedding we both knew was fake. Let's stop pretending it's something it isn't," I say, and I see Nate's face turning red. He's furious. I hurt him, I know. But I have to protect myself.

"Don't you dare, Delilah," he says fury in his eyes, but I'm not even hearing him anymore. I think he's shouting, but all I can think about is leaving.

The next second, I feel Nate's hand grabbing me, turning me to face him as he places both his hands on my face.

"I'm sorry. I shouldn't have yelled at you. You're hurt. But your words, Delilah . . . I don't deserve them," he says. No, he doesn't. But I can't think straight.

"I'm sorry. I just need . . . I just need to be alone. I'm sorry."

"I won't let you. Come on, let's go. We're going home."

"Nate, you have work to do. You're not just anyone. You need to stay and run the business or it'll all fall down. I'll be fine. Don't worry."

"Being the CEO comes second. Being your husband comes first," he says, and these words go straight to my broken heart. *Protect yourself, Delilah.*

I hear my phone buzz. I take it out of my pocket and see Sam calling. *What are the odds?*

"Hey," I answer.

"Hey, *hermosa*, have you finished working?"

"Um, yeah. Yes, I have. Why?"

"Needed some good beverage from your HUSBAND'S cave," he says, laughing at his own joke. I see Nate smiling. *He's proud.*

"Hold on a minute," I say before I grumble, directing my gaze to Nate, "You okay with that?"

"Babe, that's literally your house. Everything that is mine is yours. Literally. Don't ask for permission. Ever."

"I wasn't asking for permission. Just making sure *we*'re okay with this," I say, making an extra effort to talk about *us* rather than just me.

"Of course, baby. I'm coming with you," he says.

"It's unnecessary. You have work to do. I know I come first, but right now, I don't need to, okay?" I say in a measured tone. I need distance. Nate exhales; he's pissed, but he doesn't push me.

"Fine," he says, and I feel some relief.

I take my purse, and I haven't even reached the door when Nate calls me.

"You're not even kissing me goodbye? Delilah, what the fuck?" he says, and now he's upset.

"I'm sorry," I say, my voice barely audible. I go to him and hug him tight. His scent reassures me, his body anchors me, and I can feel myself relaxing in his embrace, but I'm scared. I hate myself for it. I still have no control over my reactions and natural instinct to just . . . flee. I rise onto my tiptoes and press my lips against his.

"I love you," he says, and I simply nod in response.

I know it's hard for him, being with someone who's as closed off as I am. But it's just as hard for me to open up and let him in.

~

Sam and I sit in the living room, the late afternoon light filtering through the windows. He swirls his glass of white wine, staring at it like it holds answers. Sheriff and Cowboy come near us, resting their heads on Sam's lap.

"Hey, hey, *mis niños guapos*," Sam coos, petting them, his face softening for a moment. "You love me, huh?"

"More than me, apparently," I joke, sipping my Diet Coke.

"They have taste," he quips back, but it feels forced. I can see it in his eyes. Sheriff's head is still resting on Sam's knee, and Cowboy is now lying on his back for belly rubs.

Sam takes a long sip of his wine, staring at the glass for a moment before he speaks.

"Today was . . . it was bad," he says.

I glance at him, my stomach tightening. I can feel the shift in the air around us.

"What happened?"

He lets out a shaky breath, like he's been holding it in all day.

"There was this kid, seventeen years old." He pauses, his eyes darting to the floor.

"Tried to hang himself."

The words hit me like a punch to the gut. I feel myself start to slip, my own memories clawing their way to the surface, but I push them down. *Not now, Delilah.*

Focus on Sam. I take a deep breath and nod, staying quiet, letting him talk.

"We got there in time, or at least I thought we did," Sam continues, his voice breaking a little. "He was unconscious, but we cut him down. Got him to the hospital. I kept thinking, 'Okay, he's gonna make it. He's gonna be fine.' But . . . he wasn't." He swallows hard, and I see the tears welling in his eyes.

"His heart stopped on the way. They tried, Delilah. We all tried so damn hard, but we lost him. I lost him."

He presses his palms to his eyes, shaking his head.

"Seventeen. He was just a kid. I . . . I don't understand how someone so young can feel like they have no other way out."

I feel the words stick in my throat because I *do* understand. I know exactly how someone can feel that lost. The darkness, the weight of everything pressing down until you can't breathe. But I can't go there. Not now. Not with Sam sitting here, broken.

"Sam," I murmur, placing my hand on his arm. "You did everything you could." He pulls his hands away from his face and looks at me, his eyes red.

"But it wasn't enough. I wasn't enough." He lets out a bitter laugh. "I hate this part of the job. I hate that sometimes no matter what we do, it doesn't matter. I couldn't save him."

Sheriff nudges his leg, as if he could sense the pain in Sam's voice. Cowboy lifts his head and gives a whine.

"I guess you can't save everyone," I say, knowing how hollow it sounds, but it's the truth. "It's not on you."

He takes another sip of wine, his hand starting to shake.

"I keep thinking about his parents. How they'll never get their son back. And I just keep wondering, how did it get that far for him? How did no one see it?"

The familiar ache in my chest threatens to pull me under. I glance at the dogs, at Sam's wine glass, at anything to keep myself from falling back into that place. I know that darkness. I've been in that same hole, but right now, I need to stay here, in this room, with Sam.

"You can't always see it," I say, my voice faltering. "Sometimes people are really good at hiding how bad it is."

He looks at me, and there's something in his eyes, like he knows. Sam knows my story. He knows enough, anyway. He doesn't push, though. He just nods, letting the silence stretch between us for a moment.

But he's watching me now, and I can feel his gaze. He winces.

"You seem off. What's going on?"

I sigh. Sam knows me too well.

Though I hesitate, not wanting to add to his pain, I trust Sam.

"I heard something today. About Paul Davis," I say, and his eyes widen.

"What did you hear?" Sam leans forward, curious now.

I swallow hard.

"He's . . . he's having financial problems. Big ones."

"*Dios mío . . .*" he says, his voice low. *Weird.*

"Did you know?" I ask.

"Oh, no, I didn't, I swear. I haven't heard from Ashley since she . . . left. I never got close to any of the other girls at my other jobs. You were the only one. And Ashley, of course. It hurt when she told me she didn't want to stay in touch. I can't even imagine how you felt when she did."

His words are hard to hear. I'm not healed. I'm not ready to talk about what happened, how it happened.

"I don't want to talk about it."

"Of course, *hermosa,* I'm sorry. Let's change the mood. I don't want to be in depressive mode. Where's your husband? I need a peek at his body to mend my broken self," he says, and I burst out laughing. *Impressive.* But yeah, that's accurate.

Ugh, I feel so guilty about how I left his office.

I tell Sam what happened earlier and how I shut down with Nate. Sam is one of the best friends anyone could have. He always tries to see everyone's point of view. But it's the way he feels people's emotions and their journeys—the way he understands others—that makes him extraordinary.

"Nate's a smart man. You've been together for months now. He lives with you, he knows you. He'll understand it was a reaction linked to your past trauma. I know it's hard for you to believe what I'm gonna say, but he loves you for real, Delilah. He'll understand," he says, and my heart breaks. *It can't be true.*

"If worse comes to worst, give him the best blow job, and you'll be forgiven," he says with a wink, and again, he makes me laugh. Hard.

Sam and I are still on the couch, mid-conversation, when I hear the front door creak open. Before I even see him, I know it's Nate. The dogs go wild, barking and scrambling toward the door like their tails are on fire. My heart leaps into my throat, and I'm on my feet before I can stop myself. *Nate's home.*

I barely hear Sam chuckling beside me as I rush to the entryway. Nate's standing there, holding his duffel bag, his hair as always perfectly brushed. He looks up, and the second our eyes meet, I don't think—I just move.

"Baby!" I yell, practically launching myself at him.

He drops his bag, laughing as I throw my arms around his neck and wrap my legs around his waist. His hands instinctively go to my hips, holding me tight. I feel his body shaking with laughter as he spins me around, his warmth immediately chasing away the cold edges of the day.

"Hey, babe," he says, his voice low and full of that soft affection he always has for me.

I press my face into his neck, breathing him in, feeling that rush of happiness that comes every time he walks through the door.

"You're home early."

"Yeah, couldn't wait to see you," he murmurs, squeezing me a little tighter before setting me down.

I tell him, "I'm so sorry for earlier. I'm fucked up. I'm sorry."

"It's okay, baby. I get it. Don't worry," he replies.

Sam, standing in the doorway, watches the whole scene with a dramatic groan.

"Oh, *Dios mío.* Nate, why can't you look at me like that?"

Nate chuckles as he brushes a strand of hair behind my ear, leaning down to kiss my forehead.

"Sorry, Sam. I'm taken."

Sam dramatically throws his arms up, walking over to Nate.

"It's so unfair! Can I at least get the same greeting?"

Nate grins—I know he likes Sam.

"Of course," he says, opening his arms.

"Oh *Dios mío,* yeeeah!" Sam screams like a teenage girl and jumps into Nate's arms just like I did. I burst out laughing, and I think I love Nate even more than I did before.

After what feels like forever, Sam gets back on his feet, looking way too happy.

"I'm not giving up, though. You keep playing hard to get, but one day, you're gonna realize what a great catch I am." He winks at Nate, who just laughs, clearly used to Sam's antics by now.

"Just keeping me on my toes, huh?" Nate jokes, glancing down at me with that smile that always makes my heart race a little faster.

I laugh, taking Nate's hand and squeezing it, loving how natural it feels. The warmth between us is always there, like a constant hum that I never take for granted. He squeezes my hand back, and I can feel how happy he is to be here too.

"Actually, I wanted to ask you something," Nate says, turning his attention to me, his eyes softening.

"Yes?" I ask, tilting my head.

"I got a call from Adam, my friend from college—you remember me mentioning him, right? He's in town with his wife, Annie," Nate explains, his voice careful.

"They wanted to see me, and I was thinking . . . after what happened today, maybe it would be a good opportunity to cool down and go meet them? I'd really like to see them, but I wanted to check with you first."

I blink, taking it in. Meeting Nate's college friends—it feels like a lot. But Nate's looking at me with that hopeful expression, and I know how much it means to him.

"For you?" I smile, squeezing his hand again. "Of course. We can have them over here. I'll cook."

Nate's face lights up, and before I can blink, he's pulling me into his arms again. He lifts me off the ground, spinning me around, just like he did when he first walked in.

"You're the best," he says, laughing as I hold on to him.

"Put me down, you giant," I say between laughs, my head spinning but my mind at ease.

Nate sets me down, his hands still on my waist, and he leans in, pressing a kiss to my lips. It's delicate and filled with everything I love about him. I kiss him back, feeling warmth spread through my chest.

"Okay, okay, stop," Sam groans from behind us. "You're going to make me cry, and I don't look good when I cry."

Nate laughs, turning to Sam.

"Well, you're welcome to stay for dinner too. You can meet Adam and Annie, and we'll make sure there's enough food." Sam raises an eyebrow.

"Are you inviting me to your little dinner party? I thought you'd want to keep me away from Adam so I don't steal him, too."

I snort, shaking my head. "Better him than Nate."

Sam beams. "You guys are too good to me. Fine, I'll stick around. But if this Adam guy is as cute as Nate, I'm claiming him."

Nate grins. "I'll warn him."

Sam just winks. "You do that."

I head back into the kitchen to start prepping, feeling lighter somehow. The house is full of laughter, and it helps ease the knot that's been sitting in my chest all day. But as I prepare everything, my mind can't help but drift back to Ashley.

The thought of her feels like a shadow lurking at the edges of my mind. I try to push it away, but it's always there. The sounds from the living room—Sam making Nate laugh, the dogs barking—grounds me for now. I focus on the meal, on the idea of meeting Adam and Annie. It's enough to keep me from slipping too far into my own thoughts.

For now, at least.

It's almost 7 p.m., and I'm standing in the kitchen, finishing up the final touches for dinner. Nate is helping however he can while Sam leans back on the couch casually sipping his drink like he lives here. I try to stay composed and shut down the voices in my head because I really want to make a good impression.

We're told by the staff that Adam and Annie have arrived, and Nate is already heading out to greet them. I take a deep breath, smoothing down my dress. I'm so nervous. These people probably have staff to do everything for them, and here I am playing hostess like it's the 1950s.

Nate swings the door open, all smiles.

"Adam! Annie! Come on in, it's been a while." His voice is warm and welcoming.

I'm just not sure how to approach, so I timidly walk toward them and stop halfway.

"Come in," Nate gestures toward the living room. He's in his element with these people, and I'm . . . well, I'm *me*.

I offer a quiet "hello," giving them a wave and a smile. I'm trying. My distance isn't missed, though, because Sam, lounging on the couch with a smirk, chimes in.

"Delilah doesn't like human touching," he teases, grinning at me. "You'll have to wave at her."

I roll my eyes but smile anyway. He's not wrong.

Adam laughs, and Annie just smirks, flicking her beautiful brown hair over her shoulder as she steps inside.

"That's no problem at all," she says in a way that makes me wonder if she's ever really been around someone who doesn't want to be touched. She's very chic and classy, very New York-like.

Then I see a woman behind them carrying something. And that's when I notice the baby. *Oh dear God*. It's cradled in the woman's arms, bundled up in a plush blanket.

"I'm sorry we had to bring the baby and the nanny. It's a long story. She's only two months old, I hope you don't mind," Adam says. Something inside me freezes for a second, then shifts. I can't explain it, but my eyes are glued to the baby.

"Congratulations again to you both. I'm happy to finally meet her," Nate says.

She's tiny, with delicate little hands peeking out of the blanket. I don't know what it is, but I can't stop staring at her. My heart feels tight, like it's wrapped in something warm and unfamiliar.

"What's her name?" I ask before I can stop myself.

"Millie," Annie replies, sounding distracted, like it's a detail that barely matters.

Millie. The name echoes in my head. I feel something heavy and soft settle in my chest. The hard memories are trying to creep in.

I can't take my eyes off her. There's a pull, something magnetic, something . . . powerful. I swallow hard, feeling emotions swirl inside me, but I keep my face neutral.

I'm used to keeping things under control.

Millie lets out a coo, and my heart just . . . melts. But Annie and Adam don't seem all that affected. It's the nanny who holds her close, rocking her. It's like Millie is just another part of the background to them, something to manage. I feel a pang of something—I don't know what. Sympathy? Sadness? Maybe both?

"We'll get settled at the table," Nate says, ushering everyone to the dining room. I move to the kitchen, carefully carrying out the dishes I made.

When I set the food down in front of Annie, she blinks at it like it's an alien object.

"You . . . made all this?" she asks, her voice tinged with surprise.

I nod, unsure of what she's getting at.

"Yeah, I like cooking."

"Really?" She raises an eyebrow, almost incredulous. "You don't have staff for that?"

I feel my face flush, but I force a small smile.

"Yes, we do, but I like doing it myself." I can hear the subtle judgment in her tone, like she can't believe someone like me—meaning Nate—wouldn't have a team of people waiting on us. I wonder what she'd say if she knew I used to wait on people, in a much different way.

We settle around the table, and everything is going smoothly enough until Annie's eyes fall on the rings on my finger.

"Oh," she says, her voice sharp as she tilts her head, "what is that on your hand?" she asks, almost disgusted. *What?*

Nate's face lights up with the biggest grin, and I can almost feel the joy radiating from him.

"Yes, we're married," he says, his voice full of pride.

But before he can bask in the moment too long, I speak up.

"Only in France and French Polynesia."

The words slip out of my mouth before I can stop them, and I know the second I say them, it's a mistake. I don't even have to look at Nate to know the fury is burning in his eyes. His body tenses beside me, but he doesn't say a word. His silence is worse than any explosion of anger. My chest tightens, and I wish I could take it back. *Why did I say that? Why couldn't I just let him have this?*

"It was a small private ceremony, but we *are* going to have one

in the States sometime in the future," he says, and I don't contradict him.

Dinner continues, but the atmosphere is tense. Annie doesn't
seem to notice, or maybe she just doesn't care, because she's too
busy picking at her food like it's something she's never seen before. Sam, of course, is busy cracking jokes under his breath, trying
to break the awkwardness, but I can feel the weight of Nate's gaze
on me.

Then a small cry pierces the air. Millie is crying. The nanny
comes into view holding the baby, rocking her, trying to calm her
down.

"Marietta, this is rude. What is going on?" Annie asks.

"I'm sorry, I can't seem to calm her down."

"We pay you to calm her down, Marietta," Annie fires back.

"Maybe I can try?" I say, not even thinking things through.

"You sure?" Adam asks.

"Oh, yeah, absolutely. I'm never going to be a mom, so at least
I'll have this," I say, smiling awkwardly.

The room falls silent. Everyone is staring at me, and I feel the
weight of their shock. Even Sam, who never takes anything seriously, looks stunned. I don't know what made me say it, but the
truth is out there now, hanging in the air like a thick cloud.

Sam, ever the one to fill the silence, stands up.

"I'll help her," he says quickly, his voice light, trying to brush
off the heaviness of what I just said.

But before he can even move, Nate's voice cuts through the air.

"No. I'll go with her." His tone leaves no room for argument.

I meet his gaze, and there's something in his eyes I can't quite
read. My heart pounds in my chest as I nod.

The nanny approaches me slowly, holding Millie close to her
chest. My heart races as she steps forward, her eyes questioning, waiting for confirmation that I truly want this. I nod, unable
to speak. My hands, quivering, reach out. As the nanny gently
transfers the tiny, delicate weight into my arms, something shifts

inside me—something deep, something I didn't even know was there.

Millie's body settles against mine, and the world around me seems to disappear. Everything fades—the sounds of conversation, the clinking of silverware, even the subtle tension that lingered between me and Nate. It's just me and her now. I look down at her, and my breath catches. Her tiny, perfect face, her fingers curling ever so slightly near my chest—she is absolutely mesmerizing.

I start to rock her, just a bit. A natural, instinctive motion I didn't even think I had in me. The warmth of her small body, her steady breathing—it's like she's put a spell on me, pulling me into this strange, beautiful moment I never thought I'd experience. I feel a tightness in my chest, but not the kind that hurts. It's a different kind of tightness, something almost too big to hold.

Before I know it, a quiet melody escapes my lips. I don't even think about it. My voice trembles at first, but then it grows steady, comforting. I'm singing—for her, for me, for whatever this feeling is that's blooming inside me.

And then I feel it—Nate's arm, strong, slipping quietly behind my back. He's not saying anything, but he's there, his presence solid and real, grounding me. His hand rests lightly on my waist.

"She looks so innocent." My voice trembles a little more. "I can't believe I used to be one . . . a baby," I say, and I feel the tears threatening to spill.

"You must have been the prettiest baby back then," Nate murmurs as I feel his lips near my ear.

"I don't think the mother would agree," I say, my voice barely above a whisper, and I can't believe I just spoke about *her*.

"I love you," Nate whispers in my ear, and I turn my face to him just enough to kiss him softly.

"Wow, you calmed her down! Thank you, I'll put her back in her crib," Marietta says, and I reluctantly give Millie back to her. Nate takes my hand firmly in his, and we go back to our guests, who are deep in conversation about hospitals, I think. Nate doesn't release my hand, or my thigh, or my shoulder, until everyone leaves.

It was a good night overall, but I'm exhausted. I clean the kitchen, and Nate tries to convince me to let the staff do it. He tries, but fails. So he ends up helping me clean everything while telling me all about Annie and Adam. They were New York elites, but had to move to L.A. a few months ago for business matters. Apparently, the ruder you are, the better it is in New York.

Once the kitchen and living room are clean, we go take a shower together, and things heat up fast in there. Nate loves shower sex, and I think I love it even more.

Tonight, I need it rough, raw, and brutal. I beg for it, and Nate immediately responds, working his magic on me. His dirty talk knows no bounds, but I wouldn't have it any other way.

Today, we had many fights—we were frustrated and pissed at each other. This is how we make our point. I bite him, I scratch him, he slaps my ass, my pussy, and pinches my tits. I swear I almost orgasm at every point. Nate's groans are my favorite melody down this Earth. He carries me up against the shower tiles, my legs wrapped around his waist, still under the shower jet.

"Stick your tongue out," I say, panting.

He raises an eyebrow and smirks. Nate doesn't take orders when he fucks. *Never*. That's a first for him, for sure. But he does it anyway. He puts his tongue out, and I take it in my mouth, sucking it like I suck his dick, all the while having his cock deeply buried in me. And *dear lord*, can the man moan with pleasure. I melt.

"You're so fucking sexy, baby. You're going to unman me, gorgeous." I see and feel the power *I* have over him. He *gave* it to me.

And then I feel it. Not my orgasm, but the wave of emotion and feelings I feel toward this man. The very same I felt during the exchange of our vows. I don't control anything anymore; I can't hold it.

"I love you, Nate. I love you so fucking much," I say, and I embrace the words I just spoke. Nate stops. He literally stops and looks me deep in the eye.

He smiles, and I don't think I've ever seen him smile so wide. He takes my chin between his fingers and plants a soft kiss on my lips, a strong contrast to the rawness of our sexual expression.

"I love you more," he says. And we forget the rest as we lose ourselves in each other.

Now we're both silent in bed, spooning as we wait to fall asleep. I can feel myself drifting. But then Nate speaks.

"Why did you say you're never going to be a mom?" he asks.

But I can't answer him. I pretend to already be asleep, as I can't face yet another part of my past that still hurts too much today.

CHAPTER 26
Nate

It's been a few days since that impromptu dinner party, and I can't stop thinking about Delilah with that baby. Every time I close my eyes, I see her holding it. Every time I let myself drift for a second, there she is again—Delilah, cradling that baby. It's not just a passing thought; it's vivid, sharp. The way she looked . . . it almost physically hurt. She was *beautiful* in a way that twisted something deep in my chest.

I've seen plenty of women holding babies. Hell, I've even seen Charlotte with one before, and I felt *nothing*. But seeing Delilah? It did something to me. Something I can't shake. I don't know why—actually, I do know, but I'm not going to dwell on it. Not yet. I'll stash that image away somewhere in the back of my mind. I'll come back to it when the time is right.

I tried digging a little deeper after she made that comment about never wanting to be a mom. I asked a few times. Each time, she dodged it. She's not ready to talk, and I know better than to push. When Delilah's not ready, you wait.

There's a knock on my office door, pulling me out of my thoughts.

"Come in," I say, already half-annoyed because I'm not in the mood for interruptions.

Chloe steps in, clipboard in hand, her usual professional smile plastered on.

"The gala honoring the NYPD is this Friday, and I wanted to check if you needed a plus-one."

Fuck. I completely forgot about the gala. I clench my jaw for a second. She's waiting for an answer, eyes on me.

"I already have one, thanks," I say, barely glancing up.

"Is it that Ms. Rose?" she asks. *Wrong move.*

"It's *Mrs.* Williams," I correct, my voice going cold. Her smile falters, but she tries to recover.

"Oh, right. I heard your mother will be attending as well."

"I'm not talking about my mother." I look her dead in the eye, making sure she feels the weight of every word. "I'm talking about my *wife*. Now, close the door on your way out."

Her face pales, and there's this tiny, barely audible gasp, like she's just realized she's stepped into a minefield. But she doesn't say anything. She just turns and leaves, closing the door behind her. *Good.* Message received.

I lean back in my chair, exhaling sharply. Chloe's nosy, but not stupid. She won't make that mistake again.

Now I need to find Delilah. I haven't mentioned the gala yet, and there's no way I'm showing up without her. Time to head up to the twenty-seventh floor.

I reach Delilah's office, but I don't see her. *Where is my wife?* I see a woman passing by, ask her, and she says she's at the coffee machine. The woman was so scared of me, it almost made me care. *Almost.*

I walk into the break room, and there she is—Delilah. She stands by the coffee machine, talking to some guy. They're laughing. *Laughing.* My heart pounds in my chest, and I can feel the heat rise in my neck. I stop right in my tracks, fists tightening at my sides.

She's too close to him. He's too close to *her*.

The guy, some clueless intern, says something, and she leans in, smiling. My blood boils, and before I even realize it, I'm moving toward them. My whole body tenses. My jaw locks.

Delilah notices me first, her smile faltering as she catches the look on my face. The guy turns, still grinning like a fool—until he sees me. His smile disappears. Good. He knows exactly who I am.

"Nate—" Delilah starts, her voice too soft, too calm.

I ignore her. My eyes are locked on him, the idiot who thinks he can cozy up to *my* wife.

"What the fuck are you doing?" I growl, stepping right into his space. He stumbles back, eyes wide.

"Nate! Stop it!" Delilah tries to grab my arm, but I don't move.

The guy swallows hard, his face pale. "Nothing—we were just—"

"Just what?" I snap, taking another step forward. He flinches, practically backing into the coffee machine. "Just flirting with my wife?"

His eyes go even wider. He looks like he's about to pass out.

"I—I didn't know—"

And then I realize that we don't wear our wedding rings at the office. *That's going to change now.*

"Nate, *stop!*" Delilah's voice cuts through, sharp now. She steps between us, her eyes blazing with anger. She pushes against my chest, trying to make space between me and the guy.

"He's an intern!" she hisses at me, keeping her voice low. "We were *talking.*" I finally turn to her, my eyes narrowing.

"Talking, huh? Looked like a hell of a lot more than that."

"Oh my God, you're being ridiculous!"

"I'm being ridiculous?" I glare at her, but my voice stays low, dangerous. "You think I'm gonna stand here while some little shit gets all cozy with you?"

"He was asking about the project, Nate! That's all!" Her voice rises with frustration, but I'm still too pissed to care.

I glance at the guy, who's standing there, shaking, like he might pass out at any second.

"Don't you dare ever try to get close to my wife ever again. Believe me, you won't like it."

His mouth opens and closes like a fish out of water. He nods quickly, eyes darting toward the door like he's desperate to escape.

Delilah's face flushes with anger.

"Nate! What the *fuck* is wrong with you? You didn't need to—"

"Didn't need to what?" I snap. "Didn't need to let him know that you're mine? That he's out of his goddamn mind if he thinks he can flirt with you?"

She crosses her arms, her eyes furious. "You just told him we're married! In front of the whole office! You promised—"

"I don't give a shit who knows, Delilah. Not when it comes to this."

The guy finally bolts, slipping past us like he's running from a burning building. Delilah glares at me, fists clenched at her sides.

"You always do this," she hisses, her voice low with fury. "I've never given you reasons to be jealous, Nate. I told you over and over again, I. Don't. Like. People! You didn't need to act like this and worse, tell everyone we're married without—once again—telling me first so we can decide together. I'm really disappointed." *The woman can hit hard with her words.*

"You know I don't like it when men approach you, Delilah. It drives me crazy, okay? I'm sorry."

Her eyes flash, and she steps even closer, her voice barely above a whisper.

"You think that's helpful?"

"I think it's helpful to let everyone know you're mine." My voice rumbles, and I stare down at her, unrelenting. "I don't share."

Her eyes narrow, and she leans in, her voice cold as ice.

"You are such a caveman."

"And you love it."

She lets out an exasperated breath, shaking her head, eyes still blazing. The tension crackles between us, her anger matching mine, but I don't regret a single word.

We step into her very tiny office, she closes the door and I get closer, because I need a hug, a kiss, whatever, she's too beautiful to be true.

"What the fuck do you think you're doing?!" she says. I'm trying to hold her, but she steps back.

"Greeting my wife?" I say, unsure.

"No. I'm too fucking mad at you right now."

"Don't you dare push me away, Delilah. I don't like it."

"Do you think I like being exposed? Without my consent?"

"I apologized for it."

"Whatever. Why did you come down?"

"I need a hug first," I say, I know I'm acting like a kid, but that's true, I need the physical contact. I pout a little, I know Delilah can't resist me when I do that.

She rolls her eyes and I know I got her. *Yes!* She slightly opens her arms and I catch her in a strong, hard embrace. I bite her neck and she giggles.

"Stop making me laugh, I'm mad at you!" I love her so much I give her a fat kiss on her plush lips that I love so much.

"Friday night, there's a gala honoring the Police of New York. I have to be there, since I'm probably gonna be a candidate for the Senate. I want you to come with me."

"Wow, that's a lot. But, yeah, sure. I'll do it for you."

"That's not all. My family will be there. Jake won't, though, he's avoiding me."

"More Williams, huh? Under what identity am I going?"

"What do you mean?"

"Well, you're not going to say 'that's Delilah, my wife,' so, who am I going to be?"

"Delilah, my wife," I say deadpan, but she bursts out laughing. *What the fuck?*

"Why aren't you laughing?" she says.

"'Cause there is nothing funny."

"Come on, Nate, outing us in front of your friends: okay. At the office? Why not. Your fucking family? No way! This is serious!"

"My love for you *is* serious. We'll talk more about it tonight. I have to go, I have a meeting. Get the dress of your dreams, my love," I say, kissing her, leaving her stunned.

And I leave her office.

After the meeting, I head back to my office, and James follows, carrying the reports. We go over the numbers, discussing the few risks and potential issues. It's business as usual, but the air between us is tense, thick with things left unsaid. I can feel it. When I've heard enough, I glance at him, then turn my head—my usual signal. He knows it's time to go.

But instead of leaving, he stands there, fidgeting. I can feel his hesitation before he even speaks.

"Nate, I'm sorry. I really am," he starts, his voice quieter than usual. I don't look at him. I'm already bracing myself for whatever he's about to say.

"I heard from Adam that you got married. I'm happy for you, even though . . . I don't understand why you didn't invite me. It really hurt. I hope someday we can get back to where we were before all this."

I turn my head slowly, glaring at him.

"Why would I invite you? So you could stand there and *witness* the love between Delilah and me? If you had it your way, there wouldn't be a wedding. You *tried* to get her away from me. Do you even realize—"

"Nate, I'm sorry!" he interrupts, his voice pleading. "I do realize what a mistake it was. I apologized. Even Delilah has forgiven me. Of course I would have wanted to be at your wedding!"

I scoff, leaning back in my chair, shaking my head in disbelief.

"I *told* you, James. The second I saw her, everything in me changed. I fell for her the moment I laid eyes on her. I *told* you I'd never been this happy in my fucking life. I haven't felt like myself in so long—until I met her. And you *knew* that. Yet you decided it wasn't 'right'? Who the fuck do you think you are? And I'm supposed to just be okay with that?"

James's face falls. He looks genuinely torn up, but I'm still pissed.

"You're absolutely right, Nate," he says, his voice strained. "I'm so fucking sorry. If I could go back in time, I'd never have done it. But I was worried about Charlotte—"

"Don't," I snap, my voice a warning. The second he says her name, it's like a match being struck inside me. Fury floods my veins, fast and hot. I can't talk about *her*. I can't *think* about her.

James looks at me, realizing he's pushed too far. His shoulders slump, and for a second, the room is filled with nothing but the sound of my breathing.

"I need more time," I manage to say through clenched teeth, trying to hold back the rage simmering inside me.

"Of course," he says quickly, his voice quiet now. He doesn't argue. He just nods and quietly leaves my office, shutting the door behind him.

As soon as he's gone, I run a hand through my hair, gripping it hard for a moment.

My chest feels tight, and my head is pounding.

Fuck.

The week speeds past. Every day, it's meetings, calls, deadlines. I'm drowning in work, and Delilah—she's working her ass off too. It's like we're racing against time, but somehow, we manage to put each other first. We always find time to eat together, no matter how hectic the day is. We talk for hours before bed, and at work, I sneak glances at her whenever I can. But still, it's not enough.

I miss her. I miss having her all to myself, like when we were on vacation. No distractions, no work, just *us*. I need that again.

Now I'm standing in the bedroom, leaning against the door-frame, watching her.

She's finishing up her outfit for the gala, and my heart stops. Delilah is breathtaking. She's wearing this black dress—long, classy, but just revealing enough to drive me insane. The way the fabric hugs her body, it's like the dress was made just for her. Her hair is loose, flowing down her back in soft waves, and she's wearing the lightest makeup. She doesn't need much; she's already perfect. She looks like a dream, like she's stepped right out of some fantasy.

And here I am, falling in love with her all over again, like an idiot. Every time I think I can't love her more, she does this—just *exists*—and it hits me like a freight train.

But she's fidgeting. She keeps adjusting her dress, smoothing it out, messing with her earrings, shifting her weight from foot to foot. She lets out little grunts under her breath, like she's annoyed at everything. It's endearing as fuck.

She checks her reflection again, grumbling about something I can't even hear, and I just stand there, grinning like a fool.

"You good?" I finally ask, trying to keep my voice casual, but my chest seizes up just looking at her.

She huffs, turning to me with a frustrated look.

"This dress—it doesn't sit right. And my hair is . . . ugh, I don't know. Maybe I should change. I feel like I'm not pulling this off."

I chuckle, stepping closer.

"Delilah, you look perfect."

She rolls her eyes, but I can see a small smile tugging at her lips.

"You have to say that."

"No, I really don't," I say, shaking my head.

"You're beautiful, and I'm not just saying it. You're killing me over here."

She pauses, finally looking at me. Her eyes soften, but she still fidgets with the strap of her dress.

"You're just being nice."

"I'm not nice, remember?" I smirk, taking her hand and pulling her closer. "I'm honest. And I honestly don't know how I'm supposed to focus on anything tonight with you looking like this."

She blushes, biting her lip, and I feel that tug in my chest again. I don't care how many weeks or months pass in a blur—I could look at her like this forever.

Grumbling again, she straightens her dress one more time. "Fine. But if I trip over this thing or my hair gets all frizzy, I'm blaming you." I laugh, pressing a kiss to her forehead.

"Deal. But trust me, you'll be the most beautiful person there, no matter what."

She groans, but I can see the smile she's trying to hide. And in that moment, I don't just feel like I love her—I feel like I'm the luckiest man alive.

"What are you afraid of?" I ask, watching her fidget again with the strap of her dress.

"You want the list?" she replies, her voice light but serious.

"There's a *list*?" I say, genuinely shocked, and that makes her laugh—exactly what I was hoping for.

But then she sighs, and the laughter fades.

"First, I'm scared of embarrassing you. I know how important public appearances are for you, and I'm scared I'll mess up just by . . . being *me*. Second, I know it sounds irrational, I know it doesn't sound like me, but I'm also a bit freaked out about facing the women in your circle. They're gorgeous as hell, and I can't help but wonder if you'll see me and realize what a mistake it was to even talk to me in that bar. And . . . of course, meeting your family . . ." She pauses, running a hand through her hair, her voice tight. "I don't even know what a family *is*. I don't know how families talk, how they act. I'm completely fucked up, Nate. And yeah . . . well, I'm scared."

Her words rush out like she's been holding them in, and hearing all of it at once . . . Wow. This woman needs a clear reminder. I step closer, taking her face gently in my hands, making sure she looks me in the eye.

"Delilah," I say, my voice low and firm. "First of all, I *thank God* every day that I had the guts to walk up to you in that bar. You've changed my life in ways I didn't even think were possible. I'd do it all over again in a heartbeat. Second—" I take a breath, making sure she hears every word. "I don't see the women around me. I *only* see you. You're so goddamn beautiful that the rest of them might as well not exist. I'm going to be looking at you—*just you*—for the rest of my life. I vowed that. But . . ." I smirk, giving her a playful wink. "Keep being jealous. It turns me on."

Her lips twitch into a smile, and I know I'm getting through to her. The tension in her shoulders loosens a little.

"And about my family," I continue, leaning in so she feels the weight of my words. "You have *nothing* to worry about. I love you just the way you are, Delilah. I don't want you to change, and I don't want you pretending to be someone you're not. You're perfect to me. If the rest of them don't see it, that's their loss and my win."

I finish with a soft kiss on her lips, lingering just enough to remind her how serious I am. When I pull back, I see her eyes glistening, wet with emotion.

"You always say the right things," she whispers. "Thank you." I grin, feeling that warm satisfaction spread through me.

"Remember," I say, keeping my tone light, "I always know ways for you to thank me properly."

She rolls her eyes but laughs at the same time. That sound, her laugh, it does something to me every time.

"Of course," she says, teasing me now. "Don't worry, you're getting laid. You're too hot in that suit to go unnoticed."

I raise an eyebrow, stepping even closer, my voice dropping to a low growl. "Keep talking dirty to me."

She playfully pushes me away, laughing harder now, the tension gone.

That laugh is everything I needed to hear. *Mission accomplished.*

"Alright," I say, holding out my arm for her to take. "Off we go. Oh, I forgot to tell you, we're going to the Hamptons after the party, just the two of us."

"Really?" she says, really excited by the news. Then she frowns. "What about the dogs? I don't want to leave them alone."

"Tyler will bring the dogs at the end of the party, don't worry," I say in a mocking tone.

And then we're off.

The gala is in full swing, and as expected, I'm one of the most important people in the room. Everyone wants a piece of me—politicians, business leaders, donors. I'm used to it. It's part of the game, and frankly, it's no challenge for me. I navigate the crowd effortlessly, making all the right moves, saying all the right things. I know exactly how to command attention.

Delilah stays by my side, and she's handling everything like a pro. She smiles, makes small talk, and follows my lead, but I can tell she's nervous. I always step in when needed, guiding her through the conversations, and together we make a damn good team. It feels natural—like we've done this a hundred times. She gives me a look every now and then, her eyes saying *thank you* without words.

But as much as I try to focus, I can't ignore the way the men in the room look at her.

Their eyes linger on her, drawn to the way that black dress hugs her body, the way her hair cascades over her shoulders. It annoys the hell out of me. She's *mine,* and I make sure everyone knows it. I keep her close, my hand resting on the small of her back, pulling her in just a little tighter than necessary. When someone looks at her too long, I lean in, kiss her temple, or whisper something in her ear that makes her laugh. I can tell she knows what I'm doing, and she finds it funny, but I don't care. I want every single man in this room to know she's with me, and only me.

The night goes smoothly, better than I expected. We're doing great. But then the music changes. The lights dim, and the announcement comes through the speakers, inviting the guests to dance.

I turn to Delilah, holding out my hand.

"Dance with me."

Her eyes go wide.

"Are you serious?"

"Completely," I say, not backing down. I've made up my mind.

The first notes of "You Are The Reason" by Calum Scott play. She hesitates for a second, then slowly places her hand in mine. I pull her close, and the second we start moving, everything around us fades.

I'm not even thinking about the people watching, the conversations, or the deals being made. My focus is entirely on her. I hold her firmly but gently, one hand on her waist, the other holding hers. She looks up at me, and for a moment, it's like the world stops spinning.

I stare into her eyes, deep, unblinking, feeling everything at once. Her breath hitches, her body melts into mine, and the music feels like it's playing just for us. The lyrics wrap around us, but it's the way she looks at me that gets me. There's this fierce intensity in her gaze, like she's letting me see every piece of her, every fear, every hope, every part of her that's mine. And I feel it, deep in my chest—the weight of how much I love this woman. It's strong, it's raw, and it's real.

As we move together, it's like nothing else exists. The way our eyes lock, it says everything. The song flows around us, but the only thing I hear is her heartbeat, the warmth of her body, the softness of her hand in mine. There's no need for talking—every emotion is there in her eyes, in the way she clings to me.

I see her swallow hard, her eyes glistening. Then, near the end of the song, a single tear slips down her cheek. My chest tightens, and before I can say anything, she whispers, her voice shaking, "I love you."

It hits me like a tidal wave. Without thinking, I lean down and kiss her—deep, slow, pouring everything I feel into that kiss. And when I pull back, I notice the room has gone completely silent.

Everyone's watching us.

They're not just looking—they're in *awe*. Like they've just seen something rare, something they don't see every day: pure love, raw and unfiltered. It's written on their faces—stunned, almost reverent.

But I don't care about them. All I care about is her.

And I've never loved her more.

After the dance, it's nearly impossible to get a moment alone. Everyone wants to know who Delilah is and how we met, but I dodge their questions like a pro. No one's getting into my private life, not tonight.

We're mid-conversation with another couple when my mother interrupts us.

"Well, well, I finally get to greet my son," she says, her voice dripping with that subtle edge she always has.

"Mother," I say, leaning in to kiss her cheek. Nicole Williams is still as striking as ever in her sixties—tall, blonde, blue-eyed, and in perfect shape. Her smile looks warm, but I can sense the tension underneath. She's not pleased.

"Nathan, you look handsome, my son," she says, her eyes flicking over to Delilah.

"And who is this?"

She stiffens next to me, and I feel her nerves spike. I take her hand firmly in mine, squeezing it.

"This is Delilah. Delilah, this is my mother, Nicole Williams," I say smoothly. My mother reaches out, probably to shake hands, but I spot an old friend across the room and make a quick diversion by pointing them out. It works, and Delilah doesn't have to touch her.

"Nice to meet you," Delilah says quietly, sounding timid.

"So, you're the plus-one?" my mother says, her voice dripping with curiosity.

"Oh, yeah, I guess I am," Delilah replies, awkwardly playing along.

"She's not just my plus-one, Mother, Delilah is—"

"His coworker." Delilah cuts me off, her voice suddenly firm. "I work at Williams, in the marketing department."

I blink, my eyes going wide. *What the fuck?*

Before I can say anything, James walks up to greet my mother, and the conversation shifts. I spot Luke approaching with his date. I'm hoping their presence will help Delilah feel more comfortable.

Luke grins and looks at James. "Did you come alone tonight?"

James shrugs. "Yeah. I invited Jenna, but she turned me down. I'm not giving up, though." *What?* So, he's actually serious about her. That's unexpected.

Delilah catches James's eye and mouths "I'm sorry" to him. But before I can react to that, my mother suddenly gasps, loud enough to turn heads.

"Oh my God!" she practically screams, staring at Delilah.

"What is *that* on your hand?"

Delilah flushes bright red, trying to cover it, but it's no use.

"It's a wedding band," I say proudly.

"What?!" my mother shrieks, causing even more heads to turn. Delilah's face is burning now, and she hides behind her hands, but that only makes the diamond on her ring finger more obvious. I can't help but laugh at the sight.

"Please tell me this is a joke, Nathan," my mother says, her voice a mix of disbelief and frustration.

"What's going on?" my father interrupts, walking over.

"Your son got *married!*" my mother yells, in shock.

"What? I didn't know Char—" my father starts, but I cut him off before he can dig myself a deeper hole.

"Father, this is *Delilah*. My *wife*," I say firmly, making sure he understands. *Thank fuck* Delilah didn't catch that near disaster.

My dad looks at Delilah and smiles warmly. "Oh, well well, she's very beautiful. Nice to meet you. I'm Grant Williams," he says, offering his hand, though Delilah seems a bit lost in the moment.

Before things can settle down, my mother starts up again.

"Please tell me you made an ironclad prenup, Nathan."

I open my mouth to answer, but Delilah beats me to it.

"We did, yes," she says, and I'm already shocked by her confidence. But then she keeps going. "But don't worry, Nate hasn't spoiled me." *What the fuck is she doing?*

My mother narrows her eyes, expecting more. Delilah doesn't miss a beat.

"I swear. I asked him for a Firkin bag, but he got me one from a thrift shop. I wanted a diamond ring, but he got me a zirconium one instead. I even asked for a puppy, and he gave me a one-eyed dog from a shelter named Cowboy. Don't worry, your son's not spending too much on me. Plus, we got married in Bora Bora, so the marriage isn't valid in the U.S.," she says with a deadpan face, and I immediately understand what she's doing.

I burst out laughing. And so are James and Luke, who both understand Delilah's little game.

"A *Birkin* bag," my mother corrects, her face tight with irritation.

"What?" Delilah asks, blinking innocently.

"You meant a *Birkin* bag," my mother presses.

Delilah turns to me, and I laugh even harder.

"Yeah, that," she says, finally breaking into a sheepish grin.

"Well, at least I'm relieved to know my son hasn't lost all his senses." My mother sighs.

"Nathan, I thought you were more generous than that," my father adds, shaking his head.

Before I can respond, Luke's date pipes up. "That's no zirconium, honey. That's a diamond," she says, pointing at the wedding ring.

Delilah's eyes widen, and she gasps.

"What? Is it?" she shouts, looking genuinely surprised. And that's when I lose it completely, laughing so hard I have to hold on to the back of a chair to keep from doubling over.

Just as I'm catching my breath, the mayor of New York calls me over. I figure the scene has been entertaining enough, and it's time to move on to more important things.

"Well done, baby," I whisper in Delilah's ear as I lean in for a kiss.

She shoots me a smirk.

"Fuck you," she whispers back, but there's love in her eyes.

And yeah, I love her for it.

Delilah needs to go to the restroom and I understand she has cramps, again. We really need to get her to a professional. Every time she eats something she doesn't know, she needs to go to the toilets. I go with her. I don't want her to be alone, and truth be told, I like to make fun of her in these situations. She doesn't spend half as long in there when she's home, but I still think she's the cutest of them all.

We're laughing in the corridor, on our way back to the party, when we hear someone.

"Delilah," a male voice says.

I feel her freeze at the sound. We turn to see who it is.

"Delilah, I knew it was you," he says, and I automatically take her hand in mine.

"Eric . . ." she says, and I can feel my heart stop. *That's the fucker.*

I step between them, keeping him from getting closer to her.

"I thought you were dead," he says. *That sounds familiar.*

"I was . . ." Delilah replies. *Too familiar.*

"You're . . . you're not pregnant anymore?" he says.

WHAT THE FUCK?

"No . . ."

"You were pregnant?" I ask, shocked.

"What happened, sweetheart?" Eric asks, his voice softer, but I don't let it slide.

"If I were you, I'd be very careful how you address my wife in front of me," I fire back.

"Your *wife?* You're *married?*" he asks, looking more surprised than I'd like.

"It's not a real marriage," Delilah suddenly says.

WHAT THE FUCK?

"Careful." My eyes are wide with fury.

"You're Nathan Williams, right?" he asks, not even bothering to look at me. His gaze is fixed on Delilah, like he can't pull himself away from her.

I'm Delilah's *husband*," I growl, but the bastard is still focused on her. I see Anders and his two men coming, but I discreetly signal for him to leave us because I'm handling the situation and there's no danger.

"What happened to our baby?" he asks, his voice wavering. *I'm going to kill him.*

That's it.

Delilah starts crying, tears streaming down her face as she begins to speak.

"After our last discussion, I left the apartment. I walked too far and got lost in a bad neighborhood. A group of men approached me, and I woke up in the hospital. Empty. I lost it," she says, her voice breaking.

WHAT THE ACTUAL FUCK?

"How?" he presses.

"They were calling to me, trying to make me talk to them. They were rude. I . . . I was desperate, lost, and so hurt that I provoked them. I insulted them, and they jumped on me. They beat me—on my face, my stomach. They tried to rape me, and I blacked out. When I woke up in the hospital, they told me I miscarried," she says, her tears falling freely now.

"Sweetheart, I'm so sorry," Eric says, his voice full of regret.

"Second warning. There won't be a third. Watch your mouth when you talk to my wife," I growl, my anger barely under control.

But he doesn't even flinch.

"I came back for you, Delilah. I realized I made the biggest mistake of my life when I left. I went to the police station. They told me there had been an assault, but I thought they caught you. When I went back to the apartment, all your things were packed, even your phone. I thought it was a setup. I've been looking for you everywhere. I thought you were dead, but now I see you . . . I'm so, so happy. I came back for you, sweetheart. It was always you. She lost the baby too, but I didn't even care. I'm getting a divorce, I swear it. I can't lose you."

That's fucking enough. I lunge forward, grabbing him by the throat, slamming him against the wall, my voice low and deadly.

"The next time you try to get my wife back, I'll kill you with my bare hands."

"Nate, it's okay, please. Let him go," Delilah pleads, trying to pull my arms away. She's crying, and I see the pain in her eyes. It hits me like a punch to the gut. There's so much I don't know about her past, so much she's never told me. "I'm so sorry, Delilah. I'm so sorry. It's all my fault. But I still love you. I'll love you until I die," Eric says, his voice desperate.

I'm about to punch him, but Delilah steps between us.

"It's okay, Nate. Stop, please," she says, her voice rough as she looks up at me, her eyes filled with tears. Then she turns back to Eric.

"The girl I was *died* that day, Eric. I'm a different person now. I've changed. I met Nate, and I fell in love with him. I've moved on. You should too. Thank you for coming back. It soothes me to know I wasn't completely abandoned."

"I did abandon you and you didn't deserve it. But I regretted it. I still love you, Delilah. What we had was magical, and you know it. We can still have our happy ending," Eric says, his voice pleading.

I'm going to beat the shit out of him.

"No," Delilah says, first to me, then turning back to him. "No. What we had was a strong friendship, and I wish we'd never ruined it. But . . . loving Nate made me realize that you and I never really loved each other. I'm sorry."

"Delilah!" a voice says, cutting through the tension. "You're alive, oh my God, it's so good to see you!" *Who the fuck is that?*

"Marty, hey. Yes, I am," she says, forcing a smile.

Another man walks over. "Hey, aren't you Nathan Williams?" Marty asks.

"I am," I say, my tone sharp, not in the mood for any more interruptions.

"We should go. Thank you, and I'm sorry," Delilah says to

both of them. I'm so hurt and furious right now I can hardly see straight. We barely take two steps before Eric speaks again.

"I know about the letter," he says, his words hanging in the air like a bomb about to go off.

What the fuck is he talking about? I look at Delilah, and she freezes. The dread in her eyes is unmistakable.

"Ashley got one too," Eric says, and Delilah gasps.

"What is he talking about?" I ask her, my voice tight with confusion.

"How is she?" Delilah asks, ignoring me completely, her voice shaky.

"I told her husband and asked for extra security around her house. She's going to be okay," Eric answers.

Delilah turns toward me. "I have to see her," she says, her body trembling. I wrap my arms around her protectively.

"You shouldn't," Eric warns, his voice serious.

"We'll go together, okay?" I interrupt, trying to bring Delilah some peace.

"Does he know?" Eric asks, his eyes still fixed on Delilah. She shakes her head.

"I don't need to know," I say, as much as it kills me. I see how scared and hurt she is, and my only mission is to make her feel safe. I'll deal with my feelings later.

"Can I see you again?" Eric asks, but I give him a death stare that makes it clear: *over my dead body.*

"No," I say firmly, and I take Delilah away from him.

I send a quick text to Tyler, telling him to meet us at the back entrance so we don't have to face anyone on our way out.

"I'm so sorry, Nate. This was supposed to be your night. I swear I'll behave. I don't want to ruin this for you. Let's go back, I can do it. I'm so sorry," Delilah says, her voice breaking.

"I don't give a fuck about anything but your well-being and your safety. We're going to the Hamptons *now*," I say, my voice sharper than intended, but I don't care.

We climb into the limo, the silence suffocating. I can't speak, can't even bring myself to ask questions. I'm too lost. Too furious at everything.

As soon as we get inside, our dogs greet us eagerly, tails wagging, their bodies wiggling with excitement. They've been waiting for us, sensing the tension, trying to bridge the gap between us. Their presence softens the blow, just a little. Delilah scratches behind their ears, murmuring gentle words, but it doesn't break the heavy silence between us.

Delilah is the first to speak.

"I'm sorry."

"For what?"

"For . . . everything."

I don't respond. The silence stretches between us, thick and heavy. A few minutes later, she tries again.

"Do you . . . do you want to leave me?" she whispers, her voice shaky. *What the fuck?*

"No, Delilah. I don't want to leave you," I say as I exhale. She nods, biting her lip.

"If you do, I just—I don't want you to worry. I'll be okay."

"Fuck you, Delilah," I snap. I can't hold it back.

"Excuse me? Who do you think you are?" Her eyes narrow.

"I'm your fucking husband, Delilah, that's who I am. You keep saying this isn't real, like I'm some joke, while I'm over here telling everyone you're my world! I'm the husband who loves you so much that, unlike you, I will *never* be okay if you leave me!" I shout, my chest tight with anger and pain. She just stares at me, silent.

"You know what hurts the most?" I continue, my voice shaky. "I keep giving you space, letting you take your time to open up, to trust me. And then he asks a few questions, and you just . . . spill it all. I knew it was hard for you to talk about, but you told *him,* just like that. You didn't think. You didn't hesitate. You just . . . *told* him. While I'm standing here, still waiting. That's what hurts most, Delilah."

"I'm sorry . . ." she murmurs, looking down.

"For what?" I snap.

"For everything," she repeats, her voice breaking.

I grit my teeth, trying to calm down. Then I feel her unfasten her seatbelt. Before I can react, she climbs onto my lap, wrapping her arms around my neck. I let her. *God, I need this.*

She cups my face, her touch gentle, and presses a soft kiss to my lips.

"I'll always choose you," she whispers, looking right into my eyes. I nod slowly, swallowing hard.

We stay like that for the rest of the ride, holding onto each other in silence, with the dogs curled at our feet, until we finally pull up to the Hamptons.

The dogs leap out first, racing toward the front door as if they already knew this place, tails wagging furiously. Delilah's face lights up at the sight of the house.

"I can't believe I'm back here. I love your house."

"It's yours too, now," I say quietly, kissing the top of her head. The tension in my chest starts to ease.

We follow the dogs inside, watching them explore like they've always belonged here. We change into comfortable pajamas—both of us opting for cozy, simple outfits.Delilah says she's not tired yet, so I suggest watching the stars together. She smiles and agrees eagerly.

I set up the telescope outside while she prepares a bunch of snacks: chips, nachos, soda, marshmallows, cookies. It feels almost normal. Like the fight never happened. Or like it was ages ago. All I know is, I'm here with my wife, we're close, and we're about to share a quiet, peaceful moment.

She settles next to me on the grass, handing me a soda. I show her Jupiter through the telescope, and we laugh, shoulders brushing together. The dogs are lying beside us, already curled up comfortably on the lawn, as if they, too, were at peace.

"Do you remember our first time here?" she murmurs.

"I'll never forget it."

"Do you regret it?"

I turn to her, my voice gentle.

"Just because we argue doesn't mean I regret anything, Delilah. No, I don't regret a second of it."

She looks down, fiddling with a marshmallow.

"I thought about leaving in the middle of the night to go see Ashley."

I sigh, shaking my head. "I'd be lying if I said I didn't think you might."

"Really?" Her eyes widen.

"Yeah. I actually texted Anders. There's a security team at her house right now, and they'll follow her everywhere. But . . . thank you for telling me."

She looks at me, something vulnerable and raw in her gaze.

"I want to trust you."

"I know," I say quietly, my eyes holding hers. "And I'll wait as long as it takes."

She leans her head on my shoulder, and we fall back into the easy silence we both need.

Just us. Together, under the stars, with our dogs close by.

CHAPTER 27
Delilah

I think I'm in love with the Hamptons.

The ocean is close enough that I can smell the salt in the breeze, the sky above us endless and full of stars. We came here for the weekend with the dogs, to escape the city, to find some kind of peace. And so far, everything is fine. More than fine. We've revived our first weekend together, and it's almost like time rewinds, bringing us back to those moments when everything between us felt simple and full of wonder.

This morning, we walked along the beach, side by side, our hands entwined. I ran ahead, laughing, the dogs racing past me and barking at the waves as they crashed onto the shore. I bathed in the ocean, the water cool and fresh, waking up something deep inside me. I felt alive. More alive than I did the first time I came here. The waves moved over me like time itself, pulling me forward into a future I didn't believe I could have. A future I didn't even want back then.

Later, we went to the Ermont Club. I remember that first night so well—the way we danced, the way I let myself fall into him, even though I was afraid. We danced again, the same way. But this time, it was different. I fell into Nate more easily, without that fear holding me back. I feel closer to him now than I ever did before. Our bodies moved together, and for a moment, it felt like nothing else existed. Just the music, just him, just us.

We watched movies too, curled up on the couch, and I could feel the steady rhythm of his breathing next to me. Later, we lay on the deck, looking up at the stars. They spread out across the sky like a map of everything I've ever known and everything I've yet to learn.

The stars used to remind me of the vastness, the emptiness of life, how small and insignificant I felt. But now they're different. Now they shine like a promise, like a path leading forward instead of a reminder of all the places I used to be trapped. Each star is a small flicker in the dark, but together they make the night beautiful. They remind me that even in darkness, there's something worth holding onto.

I think about the first time I came here. How broken I was. How I was always thinking about dying, about letting go of this life that had only ever brought me pain. But now I'm thinking about living. I'm thinking about what it means to breathe, to feel, to wake up each morning and know there is still something left to experience. The past feels like a distant place, another version of myself that I can barely recognize. I am still her, but I am more now. I am someone who wants to stay.

Nate tried to talk to me about what happened on Friday night. He wanted to open that door, to have a real conversation about it. I could see the hurt in his eyes when I told him I wasn't ready. The way his shoulders tightened, how his gaze softened, as if he were holding something back, something heavy. He respects my choice, always does, but it doesn't change how much it hurts him. I see it, the weight of it pressing on him, but I can't help myself. I don't have the strength to open up that part of me, not yet.

Maybe soon. But not now.

Now we're at the restaurant where I sang that first weekend. The place hasn't changed much—soft lights, quiet conversations, the distant sound of glasses clinking. We're having a good time, laughing, talking about everything and nothing. There's a lightness to the evening, a kind of ease I didn't expect to feel. The past lingers, as it always does, but it doesn't overwhelm me like it used to. I can breathe here. I can enjoy this moment, with Nate, with this life I've somehow found myself living.

And for now, that's enough.

"Are you ready to go to work tomorrow?" I ask.

"I'm always ready to work. But I love having you to myself. I miss you when we're in New York."

"Baby, we live together, we work together, we do everything together. How can you miss me?" I ask, even though I feel the butterflies stirring in my belly.

"I just miss you. I never have enough of you. Don't you feel the same?" he asks, and I can see he's being serious.

"I think I'm too scared to let myself feel that way. I don't think about it, though I don't take any day with you for granted. But yeah, when I'm in my office, I can't wait to see you and be with you, and when I'm home, I can't wait for you to come home. And it's nice to come here, to your house, and just have this time together."

"*Our* house," he corrects me quietly.

"That's one of the things that made me fall for you, the first time we came here," I say.

"What are you talking about?" he asks, curious now.

"Well, you barely knew me. I was a stranger, and I was weird, but you kept saying words like '*home*' and '*us*,' and it made me feel like . . . like I belonged," I say, my voice fragile as I remember that moment.

"You do belong, my love. You belonged the moment I first laid eyes on you," he says, and I squeeze his hand to show him how much I appreciate it. I can't bring myself to say the words out loud, but I hope he knows.

"Delilah," he starts, and I know this is serious now. His tone shifts.

"I need to ask you something. And I can't leave it unsaid before we head back to New York."

"Oh?" I reply, feeling unsure.

"The fucker—I mean, Eric—said you got a letter. And so did Ashley. You froze, and you were so fucking scared. You wanted to sneak out and find her. I need to ask you, baby. I know you don't want to talk about what happened, and I know you're not ready to tell me who's behind all this shit, but I just need to ask . . . are you safe?"

I freeze again. I can feel my heart racing. I'm scared, more scared than I've ever been. He can't know what's really beneath the surface. *He can't. He'll leave me.* But I can't lie to him. I just shake my head.

"I'm reinforcing your security at home, at work, and anytime we're outside. Starting tomorrow, I'll train you every morning for self-defense, just like the classes you had at The Rex, only I'm a better teacher. I'm not scared, not in the least. You need to know that. Bring it on, whoever they are. I just want *you* to *feel* safe."

"I do feel safe when I'm with you. But I don't want to be a burden to you . . ."

"You could never be a burden when you're the light of my life. But I need to ask something else," he says, and I nod, waiting.

"The fucker said he wanted to see you again . . . but do you?" he asks, and I can see a flicker of insecurity in his eyes. It's rare to see him like this.

I laugh a little, because seeing Nate, the man who never breaks, feeling unsure is almost absurd.

"No. I don't. I believe we could have been friends, and I'll always be grateful for what he did for me. But he also hurt me. And I'm not one to forgive."

"He said he's getting a divorce. He wants you."

"Then he'll get a divorce. It has nothing to do with me. I don't care. I've moved on. Like I said, the woman he knew is dead. I'm not her anymore. I don't want him. I . . . I want you," I say, looking him in the eye.

"I love you," he says, standing up and leaning over to kiss me gently on the lips. I smile at him. It's me saying "I love you too" in my coward language.

"You have nothing to worry about," I say, trying to reassure

him, and I can see him start to relax. Nate is such a powerful figure, always so composed, always in charge. But with me, he lets
himself be vulnerable, and I never thought I could fall harder for
him . . . but here I am.

"I was thinking we could invite Ashley and Paul over to the
house," he says casually, but I freeze. No. I shake my head, and I
know I need to explain, at least a little.

"When Ashley left, she made it clear that seeing me would be
too hard for her. Even though our circumstances are different now,
even though we're free from the nightmare we were trapped in, it
would still be too much for her. She won't want to pretend like
nothing happened, and she can't face what we went through without breaking. She doesn't want Paul to see her like that.

"I'll call her during the week. I don't know when or how I'll be
able to talk to her, to hear her voice without falling apart myself . . .
but I'll do it. I do need to know that she's okay. And I trust you
when you say you've got your team involved. I'm forever grateful
for that. But that's all I can handle right now. I'm sorry if I don't
express myself well," I say, and I feel a lump rising in my throat.

Nate takes my hand, kisses it, and buries his face in my palm.

"I understand. If you need me when you'll call her, I'll be there,"
he says softly. But I know he doesn't. Not really.

~

The week flies by faster than I expect, and then Nate and I are back
in New York.

Every morning, before we even set foot in the office, we take an
hour for my self-defense training. Nate insists on it, saying I need
to be able to protect myself, and though I complain about the intensity, I know he's right. These sessions are no joke—Nate is an
excellent teacher. He's patient but pushes me to my limits. Every
punch, every kick, every move is about focus, strength, and control. But it's hard to focus sometimes when Nate is standing right
in front of me.

He's too damn sexy for his own good. His body is all hard

muscle, his broad shoulders straining against his fitted workout shirt, and his biceps flex every time he moves. His chestnut hair is always just a little messy, falling across his forehead in a way that drives me crazy. And those blue eyes—deep and intense, like the ice in the middle of the ocean—always watching, always guiding me, making me feel both safe and distracted at the same time. When we train, sweat glistens on his skin, making him look like some kind of Greek god, and every time he corrects my stance or shows me a new move, I can't help but lose my focus for a second. I have to remind myself why we're doing this.

It's hard, though. It's hard not to notice how perfect his jawline is when he clenches it in concentration, or the way his lips curl into that teasing smile when he knows I'm not giving my all. But I push through, because I want to be strong. For him, and for me. And every morning, when we're done, I feel a little more capable. A little more ready to face the day. Even though eighty percent of the time we end up fucking in the ring.

Can't help it.

After training, the day flies by. Nate and I are both buried in work. My role has expanded—I'm now working with the marketing team on a new project. I'm helping Ailly pull together all the pieces for the new product launch, organizing meetings, reviewing copy, and tracking social media campaigns. It's a lot to handle, but I love the pace. It keeps me focused, keeps my mind sharp.

Nate, on the other hand, is buried under even bigger tasks. As CEO, he's in the middle of negotiations for a massive deal that could change the entire investment landscape. He's working with clients from London, Tokyo, and New York all at once, constantly bouncing between meetings and conference calls. I can see how much pressure is on him, yet he manages it with that same calm confidence he always has. It's part of why I admire him so much. He makes the impossible look effortless.

Despite how busy we both are, we still find time for each other. Every night, after the chaos of the day settles, we reconnect. We laugh, talk, and it's like the world slows down for just a moment. Nate has this way of making me crack up like no one ever has before. He teases me, makes silly jokes, and sometimes we laugh so hard I feel tears rolling down my cheeks. And when we're not laughing, our connection grows in other ways. I feel closer to him, emotionally and physically, every day.

There's this unspoken energy between us, and lately, it's become even more intense. Nate explores the edges of my body in ways I didn't know were possible, pushing limits, always making sure I feel safe. I love every moment of it, being completely vulnerable with him. It's something I never thought I'd be able to do, but with him . . . it's different. I trust him in a way that's deeper than anything I've ever known.

Today, I'm at my desk, working with Ailly. Our heads are deep in the details of the next meeting we're setting up, and the office is buzzing with the usual chaos. Papers are scattered across my desk, emails are pouring in, and my fingers fly across the keyboard as I try to keep up. Ailly is beside me, muttering something about missing files when my email dings. I glance at the screen, not expecting anything, but then I see it: *NYU Admissions Office.*

My heart skips a beat, and for a moment, I can't breathe. I click on the email, my fingers shaking, and the words jump out at me:

Subject: *Congratulations on Your Admission to NYU*

Dear Ms. Rose,

We are pleased to inform you that you have been admitted to the NYU Distance Learning Program for the upcoming Fall semester, starting in October 2022. Your application stood out among a competitive pool of candidates, and we believe you will be a valuable addition to our program.

Please find attached the next steps regarding your enrollment process.

We look forward to welcoming you to NYU.

Sincerely,
NYU Admissions Office

My vision blurs, and before I even realize it, tears are streaming down my face. I'm crying, but it's not just tears—it's something deeper, something that's been locked inside me for so long. My chest tightens, my breath catches, and suddenly I'm on autopilot. I stand up, barely aware of Ailly asking if I'm okay. I don't answer. I can't. I just run. I'm running through the office, dodging people, not caring who I bump into.

My feet carry me straight to Nate's office.

His assistant tries to stop me, tells me he's in a meeting, but I don't care. I push open the door.

Nate is sitting at the head of the table, surrounded by at least a dozen people. They're all important, all here to discuss something big, but none of it matters right now. Not to me.

"Nate!" I almost shout, breathless, my voice breaking as I run to him.

He looks up, startled, and in an instant, I see his face soften, worry flickering in his eyes.

"What's wrong?"

I can barely get the words out between the sobs.

"I did it. NYU. I got in."

There's a moment of stillness, like the world has paused, and then Nate's face breaks into the biggest smile I've ever seen. Without a second thought, he jumps up from his chair, runs over to me, and scoops me into his arms. He spins me around, lifting me off the ground as we both laugh, scream, cry—every emotion pouring out of us all at once.

He twirls me in the air, my legs dangling as I cling to him, my tears soaking his shoulder. The room disappears. The people disappear. It's just us, and I feel like I'm floating. His laughter vibrates through his chest, his happiness so strong I can feel it in my bones. It hurts how happy we are in this moment, like our joy is so big it doesn't fit inside our bodies.

I don't even register the people around us until I hear James. "Congratulations, Delilah." But I can't turn to acknowledge him. I'm too lost in Nate's deep blue eyes, those eyes that always make me feel safe, that make me feel like I belong somewhere.

Nate puts me down but keeps his hands on my waist, pulling me close, his forehead resting against mine. I'm crying, but it's not the same tears of fear and sadness that I used to cry. This is differ-ent. I'm overwhelmed, full, my heart bursting with more than I ever thought I could feel.

"Thank you," I whisper, my voice shaky. "For everything you've done. For making this possible."

Nate shakes his head, his eyes softening as he looks at me.

"That's all on you, Delilah. *You* made this happen. I'm just here for the ride."

I laugh a broken sound between tears, and he kisses my fore-head, bringing me back to reality.

And right now, nothing else matters. Not the people watching, not the meeting Nate just abandoned. It's just us, wrapped in this happiness so big it almost hurts.

"Looks like tonight we're going out to celebrate, baby." he says.

"Really?" I shout.

"I'll handle everything, I'll meet you home at 7 p.m." He kisses me, not giving a fuck about the people around us.

I go back to my office and tell the news to Ailly, who screams out how happy she is for me. I can't believe that in few weeks I'll be starting college. Me. I'm so fucking proud and happy that even the demons in my head are shutting up. *Good.*

~

"How do I look?" I ask Nate, standing in front of the mirror while he leans against the doorframe watching me.

"It's too short, too revealing, too tempting . . . way too sexy for

my liking. You look too goddamn beautiful, as always," he murmurs, his voice low and filled with something deep. I can't help
but giggle.

"You want me to change?" I tease, glancing over my shoulder at
him.

"No, wear whatever makes *you* feel good. I'll never tell you not
to wear something. Besides, I'll be by your side the entire time," he
replies firmly.

"Okay," I whisper, turning back to the mirror, admiring how
the little red dress clings to my body. I do look sexy. I love it.

"I have something for you," he says, his tone softer now. I turn
to see him holding a small box. My curiosity is piqued as he hands
it to me and flips it open. My heart nearly stops.

"Please tell me those aren't real," I breathe, but deep down, I already know the answer. He chuckles, that sound I adore.

"It's just a small gift to say congratulations for getting into NYU.
I'm so damn proud of you and the incredible woman you've become."

"Nate . . . it's so beautiful. I've never—I mean, you know . . . I—
oh, God," I stammer, completely lost for words. He smiles, his eyes
warm, then gently lifts the necklace out of the box, putting it on
around my neck.

"It's a diamond rivière necklace . . . with matching earrings," he
explains quietly, his fingers brushing against my skin as he fastens it.

"There's a card too. But . . . I'm too shy to read it out loud. Even if
they're my own words," he admits, a faint blush coloring his cheeks.

My curiosity deepens. I reach for the card and start to read.

> *Time had stopped when I met you,*
> *Our love a diamond bright and true.*
> *Like stars that shine in endless night,*
> *Your heart's my gem, my guiding light.*
> *Love, N.*

I'm speechless.

"Baby . . ." I say. "This is so romantic. Thank you, baby. I love you," I say as I feel my heart squeezing inside my chest. *He's too shy* . . . I just melt for the man. I grab his perfect mouth and give him a fat kiss. *I love him.*

We eat at a very romantic restaurant in Tribeca. The place is perfect for an intimate night, just the two of us. We talk about NYU, how we're going to get through this together as a team. The distance program had to be under a solid contract with a company, and Nate is my sponsor. I'm going to work part-time again. I'm happy, even though I'm going to miss him.

Nate tells me he has another surprise for me, so it's time we leave the restaurant.

We're in the limo now, with Tyler driving us to I-don't-know-where. Nate toys with my legs, his touch driving me crazy, turning me on so bad. But two can play this game.

So I stand to straddle him, grinding down hard as I bite his lower lip.

"Stop teasing me!" I whisper fiercely.

But I should have known better. Never challenge Nate Williams—he's always one step ahead. In an instant, he flips me onto the limo floor, his mouth crashing down on mine as he slides two fingers inside me. If I was laughing a second ago, I'm not anymore. A desperate moan escapes my lips, and I crave more. I fumble with his belt, and he pulls out his massive cock, positioning himself right at my entrance. I'm breathless, urging him to take me, but he only nudges the tip inside.

"Oh, wait—looks like we've arrived. Sorry. Rain check, babe," he says with a smirk, and chuckles at his own joke.

"Are you *fucking* kidding me? Get back here! We're not done!" I shout, my voice filled with frustration. But that only makes him burst into full-on laughter.

"Come on, we're late," he says, fastening his belt and placing a teasing kiss on my pussy. *Bastard.* "I hate you," I mutter, meaning every word.

"You love me," he replies, flashing that infuriating grin. *Well . . . yeah.*

We step out of the car and I immediately feel the energy of the city pulse around us. The building in front of me is sleek and modern, all glass and dark steel, towering above the street like it's part of the sky. The neon lights outside flash in soft blues and purples, casting a glow on the perfectly dressed crowd waiting to get inside. This isn't just any nightclub—it's a high-end, luxury club, the kind where only the most exclusive people are allowed in. The music hums through the walls, low and bass-heavy, vibrating under my feet as we walk toward the entrance.

Nate's hand rests on the small of my back, guiding me, and as we approach the door, the staff greets us with wide smiles and open doors. *No waiting in line for us.*

He leans down, his lips close to my ear. "I own this place," he says casually, like it's no big deal.

I smile to myself. *Of course he does.* I'm not even surprised. Nate practically owns the city—this club is just another piece of his empire.

We glide through the entrance, the velvet ropes parting for us like we're royalty. The interior is even more impressive than I imagined. The lighting is dim, with golden accents highlighting the edges of the walls and ceiling. Modern chandeliers hang overhead, sparkling like diamonds. The floor is polished, reflecting the lights, and the DJ is set up in the center, already spinning tracks that make the whole room pulse with energy. The bar stretches along one wall, glowing with backlit bottles, and every surface is smooth and black, like the night itself.

The staff guides us upstairs to the VIP section, and as we walk, I can feel the curious eyes on us. Whispers follow us through the club, but I ignore them. We step into the private lounge, and the second we enter, the entire room erupts into cheers.

"Congratulations!"

I freeze for a second, my eyes widening. In front of me, I see

Jenna, Sam, and Ailly grinning from ear to ear, waving me over. But it's not just them—James is here too, along with Luke and a few others I don't quite know but I've seen before. Nate's shown me pictures. They're his friends, people from his world.

Stunned, I turn to look at Nate, and he gives me that devilish smile I love so much.

"Surprise," he says, his voice low and playful.

Before I can respond, he leans down again, his breath warm against my skin.

"I invited some of my friends to celebrate with us," he murmurs in my ear. "I wanted to make tonight special."

Excitement bubbles up inside me. I can't help but smile. Tonight, I'm going to let go of everything. I'm going to have the night of my life.

Sam walks over, his eyes twinkling with mischief.

"*Mira, chica, estás increíblemente* sexy," he says, his Venezuelan accent thick. He winks at me, and I can't help but laugh.

"Thank you, Sam," I say, feeling the confidence surge through me. I can feel the heat in my cheeks, and it's not just from his comment—it's from the way Nate is looking at me, his eyes full of pride.

Nate wraps an arm around my waist, pulling me close.

"Everyone," he says, his voice clear over the music, "I want you to meet my wife."

The word hits me like a shock wave. My heart flutters, and I can feel the butterflies swirl in my belly. *His wife.* I look up at him, and he's smiling down at me, like it's the most natural thing in the world.

The room cheers again, and I feel like I'm floating, like nothing else matters but this moment. Nate squeezes my waist gently, his hand resting there, grounding me. I lean into him, feeling the warmth of his body, and for the first time in a long time, I feel completely, utterly free.

This night is ours. And I'm going to make sure it's unforgettable.

Nate doesn't leave me on second. I'm on his lap all the time, and we kiss like there's no one else around us. I whisper in his ear that I need to talk to Jenna and he reluctantly releases me. I signal to her and she moves to meet me.

"So, James is here!" I say, raising an eyebrow at Jenna.

"Yeah, when he heard Nate planned a surprise for you, he went to see him and asked if he could come. Nate's still tough on him, but he agreed, so I think that's progress."

"Well, you sure know a lot. You and James talk often, huh?" I ask, my curiosity piqued.

"He comes to Orion a lot . . . and well, he talks, I listen. But I'm not falling for it. He's not a good guy. After what he did to you—"

"That was a long time ago. He was just trying to protect his best friend, and that's between me and him. It has nothing to do with you, Jenna. Listen, I'm not here to give advice—I'm awful at it. But whatever happens between you two is your business. No matter what decision you make, it has nothing to do with me. I'll support you in every way I can, I'll always be here for you. Just . . . don't let me be the reason you make a choice," I say firmly, making sure she hears me. It's already complicated enough with Nate, I don't need to drag Jenna into that mess too.

"Yeah, you're right. I'll see how things going. One day at a time, I guess," she replies. I smile, glad she understands.

Just then, Nate calls me over. I move back to him, climbing onto the couch and wrapping my arms around his shoulders from behind. He strokes my thighs, and I smile.

I love this feeling because, for once, I'm on the same level as him. Usually, he towers over me like a giant. I kiss his neck and lean my head against his shoulder, feeling the way his body relaxes under my touch. Now I get it—why he loves resting his head against mine. It's the best place to be. I run my nose along his neck, nuzzling closer. He turns his head, meeting my lips, and I kiss him softly.

"So, you and James are . . . okay?" I ask cautiously.

"I wouldn't go that far, but I'm trying. It's hard, though. He really hurt me." His voice tightens with old pain.

"I know," I whisper, leaving it at that. I don't want to dig up the past. I want him to relax tonight.

"Wanna play a little game?" I murmur in his ear, letting my lips brush against his skin. He turns his head, his eyes locking onto mine, intrigued. I have his attention now.

"I'll be dancing down there. Meet me, stranger," I whisper with a playful wink before sliding off the couch and heading down.

As I make my way over, I motion for the girls—and Sam—to join me. It's time to heat up the dance floor.

The music pounds through the floor, pulsing up through my body, matching the rhythm of my heartbeat. I'm dancing in the middle of the floor with Sam, Jenna, and Ailly. The lights are dim, flickering in time with the beat, and everything else around us fades away. It's just the music, the movement, and the heat of the dance. The song the DJ chose is the remix of "Crazy in Love" from Beyoncé herself. Very sensual, very sexy, *perfect*.

I let myself move freely, my body flowing with the music like it's second nature. I've danced professionally for years, so I know exactly how to carry myself, how to move in a way that's sensual without crossing a line. My hips sway, my arms rise above my head, and I let my body roll with each beat, smooth and controlled, but still undeniably suggestive.

But I'm not just dancing for me. I'm dancing for *him*.

I look up, searching through the haze of lights until my eyes find Nate. He's still in the VIP section with his friends, but he's not paying attention to any of them. His eyes are locked on me. I can feel his gaze like it's burning into my skin. There's something dangerous in the way he's watching me, something intense and primal, and it sends a shiver down my spine.

Smirking, I tease him from across the room with the way I move, my hips swaying in time with the music, my body arching in just the right ways. I know exactly what I'm doing. And so does he.

In the next moment, Nate's on his feet. I see him start to move, pushing past his friends, his eyes never leaving mine. He's coming toward me, fast, like he can't stand to be away for another second. My heart races, the excitement building in my chest. I keep dancing, my movements slower now, more deliberate, waiting for him to reach me.

The tension between us builds as he crosses the room, his powerful stride cutting through the crowd like nothing else exists. My breath catches when I see the look on his face—like he's barely holding himself back, like he's on the verge of losing control. His eyes are dark, intense, and locked on mine with an intensity that makes my knees weak.

Finally, he reaches me. His hands slide around my waist, strong and sure, pulling me back against him. His body presses close, so close I can feel the heat radiating off him. He doesn't say anything at first, just lets his hands move over my hips, guiding me to move with him. His touch is electric, sending sparks through me, and I melt into him, my body falling naturally into the rhythm of the dance.

He leans down, his lips brushing the shell of my ear, his breath hot and teasing.

"You like dancing like that in front of me, don't you?" he murmurs, his voice low and rough, filled with a hunger that makes my pulse race.

I tilt my head, giving him a playful smile as I whisper back, "Hey, stranger. I've seen you watching me. Liked what you saw?" My voice is light, playful, and I know he understands instantly what I'm doing. I'm not just his Delilah right now. I'm someone else—a stranger at a club, someone he's meeting for the first time, someone who's caught his attention in a way that's impossible to ignore.

Nate chuckles, a dark sound that vibrates against my neck. His grip on my hips tightens slightly, his hands pulling me even closer, our bodies moving together in perfect sync. His lips graze my ear again, and I feel a heat roll through me.

"Liked what I saw? Baby, you have no idea what you do to me," he says, his voice dripping with desire. "The way you move . . . fuck, it's like you're asking for trouble."

I shiver at his words, feeling the fire build between us. His hands slide down my sides, slow and deliberate, leaving a trail of heat everywhere he touches. He's not just touching me—he's claiming me, owning every inch of my body as we move together, our movements getting more sensual with each beat of the music. My heart pounds in my chest, and every nerve in my body is alive, buzzing with the tension between us.

He leans in again, his lips brushing against my neck as he murmurs, "You think you can tease me like that and walk away untouched?" His voice is rough, on the edge of control, and it sends a thrill through me.

I turn my head, looking up at him through my lashes.

"Who says I'm walking away?" I tease back, my voice breathless.

His eyes darken even more, and I can feel the barely controlled need radiating off him. He presses his hips against mine, and I can feel how hard he is, how much he wants me, and it takes everything in me not to let go completely. The heat between us is unbearable, and I can tell he's on the verge of exploding. His breath comes faster, more ragged, and I know he's fighting to hold on.

"Fuck," he growls, his hands gripping me tighter, pulling me even closer. "You're driving me insane."

I smile, feeling the power I have over him, the way he's unraveling because of me. I arch my back slightly, pressing myself against him in a way that makes his grip tighten even more.

"Good," I whisper, my lips brushing his ear. "I want you crazy."

He lets out a low growl, his hands sliding up my body, his fingers digging into my skin just enough to send a thrill through me.

His mouth is so close to mine, but he doesn't kiss me. Not yet. He's holding back, just barely, letting the tension between us build to a breaking point.

"You have no idea what you're asking for, baby," he says, his voice low and dangerous, filled with promise. "But you will."

He whispers back in my ear. "What would your wife say if she knew you were dirty dancing with a stranger? What would your husband say if he knew a stranger is about to fuck you?"

The music continues to pulse around us, but it's like we're in our own world. Our bodies move together, perfectly in sync, every touch, every glance filled with heat and tension. My heart races, my skin tingles, and I feel like I'm on the edge of something explosive, something I'm not sure I can control.

And right now, I don't want to.

"Truth or dare?" I ask him.

"Dare," he answers. *Of course.*

"Fuck me in the restroom."

By the look of his face, I think I just shocked the fuck out of him. Nate is wayyy too easy to play with when it comes to my body. How I love it is indescribable. He doesn't even wait for me to laugh as he grabs my hand and lead me to the said restroom. We don't even wait in line. He pushes the door open, gets me inside with him and kisses the fuck out of me.

"Now, stranger, what are you going to do?" he dares me. *Pfff, oh please.*

I lock eyes with him as I slowly lower myself until I'm faced with his cock. I kiss it through his pants, and Nate is going to lose it.

"You want to suck my dick, baby? Show me if you're a good girl, or a good slut," he says. It turns me on plenty. I unfasten his belt, push down his boxers and free his beautiful dick—that looks so hard I fear it might hurt him.

"You're hard, stranger. Is that for me? Or are you thinking about your wife right now?" I say, fully teasing him. He chuckles.

"You're playing dirty here. Don't make me talk about my wife," he says, and I spit on his cock just like he loves it. He growls, and I know he's as turned on as I am.

"Why? Is she beautiful? Is she a good wife to you?" I ask with a smile. He laughs again and slams his dick in my mouth, shutting me up as he fucks my mouth.

"My wife is the most desirable creature on this planet. Fuck, the galaxy, even. She's the best wife a man could ask for," he says, panting, but I'm too focused on my task as I lick him and suck him like the good slut that I am. Then Nate grabs me by the arms and carries me up against the wall. I wrap my legs around his waist, and he thrusts into me so fiercely it almost makes me cry with pleasure.

"What about your husband, stranger?"

"My husband is Nathan fucking Williams. He'd kill you if he knew what you're doing to his wife," I say, provoking him. But he bursts out laughing while fucking me.

"Damn right he will," he says, and I can feel his dick hardening, growing in me. But I'm not far behind, so it happens almost at the same time. We come hard together, and I think we're loud right now, but who cares?

We arrived home less than twenty minutes ago. We took a quick shower, we kissed the dogs, we brushed out teeth, and now we're in bed, about to pass out from the night.

"You're the best fucking wife in the history of wives," he says as he's spooning me.

"Really?" I say, feeling extremely proud.

"Sucking my dick while roleplaying with me? Well done, you unmanned me. I love you," he says, and I laugh hard.

"Nate?"

"Yes?"

"You're the best fucking husband in the history of husbands," I confess.

It's a huge step for me to say these kinds of things, but it felt right. Nate holds me even closer and kisses my neck, but I'm so tired I don't even feel it, losing myself to sleep.

~

I'm sitting at my desk, the office quiet now that most people have gone home. My head is buried in the new marketing campaign, and I can't stop thinking about how much I want this to be perfect. It's no longer about not disappointing people, or worrying that I won't live up to their expectations. Now it's about impressing them—about showing them what I can do, proving that I belong here, that I'm not just Nate's wife. I've done hours of research, digging deep into social strategies, looking at trends, influencers, and audience engagement. My fingers fly over the keyboard as I type out the plan, outlining every step of the campaign.

I've got ideas for new posts, collaborations with influencers, and an entire strategy for how we'll build momentum over the next month. I'm planning interactive stories, engaging polls, and behind-the-scenes content that will make people feel like they're part of something bigger. I've studied the analytics, gone over the numbers, and every piece of the puzzle is starting to fit together. There's still so much to do, but I'm excited about it. My mind is buzzing with possibilities.

Ailly had to leave earlier, something about an emergency at home. She told me I should go too, but I'm not ready. There's still so much to finish, and I want everything laid out before I head home. I don't even feel the time slipping away, not when I'm this focused.

Then I hear a knock on the door. It startles me, pulling me out of my work. My fingers stop typing, and for a second, I just stare at the door, confused.

"Come in," I say, my voice steady but curious.

The door opens slowly, and a man steps into the room. I sit up straighter, my eyes scanning him as he steps into the light. He's fairly tall, and his build is lean, but there's something solid about him, a confidence in the way he holds himself. His hair is dark—black, almost—and neatly styled. He's wearing a suit, a fine, expensive one. I've developed an eye for these things, thanks to Nate. The cut, the material, the way it fits him perfectly—it's all high-end.

But it's his eyes that really catch my attention. Striking blue. The color almost shocks me, and for a second, my breath catches in my throat. Those eyes . . . they're like *ice*. Sharp, clear, and cold. Just like Nate's. My heart skips a beat, a strange feeling creeping up my spine as I stare at him. There's something familiar about him, and yet I can't quite place it.

He stands there for a moment, watching me, before a slow smile curves his lips.

"We meet at last," he says, his voice smooth, with just a hint of amusement.

I blink, tilting my head. My heart is pounding now, my mind racing to catch up.

"Who are you?" I ask, my voice coming out quieter than I expect.

The man steps closer, and for a moment, the room feels too small, too tight. My palms grow clammy, and I can feel a cold sweat starting at the back of my neck. There's something about him, something intense, like he's not just a man walking into my office. There's a weight to his presence that I can't shake, a tension that makes my skin prickle with unease.

"I'm Jake Williams," he says, his smile widening, and suddenly, it clicks.

My stomach drops. *Oh my god.*

Nate's brother.

CHAPTER 28

Nate

It's been a week since Delilah got into NYU, and I swear, it's like I'm seeing her transform right before my eyes. She was always beautiful, but now . . . now there's something more. It's like she's blooming, unfurling, like a flower opening its petals to the sun after a long, dark night. She's always been this hardworking, fierce spirit, but since she got the acceptance letter, something has shifted. I watch her become more confident with each passing day.

She works late into the night, studying, pushing herself, and now, for the first time, she's starting to see that all of her efforts are paying off. It's like watching the dawn spread across a sky that was once covered in clouds. She's brighter, stronger, more assured. And I love it. I love seeing her grow, seeing her finally stand a little taller, speak with more conviction. She's finding herself, piece by piece, and it's breathtaking to witness.

But it's not all gone. The shadows still linger. I can see them lurking behind her eyes when she thinks I'm not paying attention. There are moments when I see the doubt creep back in like tendrils of darkness that haven't quite let go of her heart. She still has those fears, those demons that claw at her from the inside. She's not free from them, not yet.

Something is different, though. Ever since that encounter with the fucker . . . there's been a subtle shift. She's more open, more . . . I don't know, light, maybe? There's a calmness in her that wasn't there before, a sense of relief. But at the same time, the mystery, the part of her that closes off, it's still there too.

She hasn't called Ashley. And I don't understand. She said she would. But she hasn't, and every time I ask, she brushes it off. There's something in her silence that troubles me, something I can't quite reach.

I want to be there for her. I want to understand. But I know some things can't be forced. So, I wait, hoping that she'll let me in when she's ready.

Right now, I'm at my desk, working on an important file. Something is wrong. The financial reports in the document seem inaccurate, and no one had noticed it before. Until me. I'm trying to gather the names of the managers on the project when the my office door opens.

"Hey, babe," Delilah says. How the woman is even more beautiful than the day before is beyond me.

"Hey, wife," I say, standing up to meet this incredible creature. I grab her perfect mouth and smooch her. She carries in some grocery bags, and I help her set them down.

"What you got in there?" I ask.

"Food, I'm hungry. I ordered some Thai food and it just arrived. I thought we could eat together. I'm sorry I didn't ask," she says, realizing she decided all of her own.

"Never apologize for that. You come first, always. What my wife wants, my wife gets."

"Oh, come on! Can you take your lunch break now, or do you have to wait?" she asks, and she's serious.

"Cute thing," I answer.

"What?"

"I'm Nathan fucking Williams. I do what I want whenever it pleases me. Period," I say as I sit down next to her. She rolls her eyes at me, still unpacking our food, and I slap her ass. Just because I can.

We eat and talk about work and social strategies that she's been working on. I gotta say, I'm so happy to see her so passionate about her work, and I realize that this was exactly what I wanted for her.

She has some sauce at the corner of her mouth, and I clean it with my thumb, then lick my thumb. The gesture itself is sexy as fuck but also so intimate.

This woman is my wife. But she's more than that. She's my home, she's my family. I feel a surge of love within me. It's so fucking intense that I can't contain it, so I take her sweet face and kiss her softly.

"What was that for?" she asks, surprised.

"I just had a surge of love for you. Had to let it out," I say, and she smiles, she smiles so bright it's contagious.

"I'm happy," she murmurs, and that electrifies me. I remember the Delilah I met over four months ago, how she didn't believe in happiness, her cynical view of it. Wow, she did bloom well.

"I ate too much, I need to lie down just a little. Do you think it's okay?" she asks.

"Of course, come," I say as I grab her hand and lead her to my couch. She lies down, and I take off her shoes and start massaging her tiny foot after I kiss it.

"Have you ever fucked one of your coworkers?" she asks completely out of the blue.

What?

"No, never, why?"

"Why haven't you?"

"I don't mix business with pleasure. Where did that come from?"

"You're mixing business and pleasure right now," she says, smirking at me.

"Smart-ass. I met you before I hired you. And you're my wife, it doesn't count."

"I wasn't your wife when I started," she says with a smile, but it pisses me off.

"Honestly, I think you became my wife the moment I first kissed you. The rest were technicalities. What's that all about?"

"I don't know . . . I just thought about it and thought I should ask you. I trust you to tell me the truth."

"Delilah, what the fuck are you talking about?"

"Nothing, baby, I'm sorry, I didn't want to upset you." She gets up, takes my head in her hands and kisses me. "I should get back to work," she says, but I hold her a little tighter.

"Not yet, please," I say, not wanting to let her go. She's my breath of fresh air. I need her.

She stays for another fifteen minutes, but then Ailly calls her, says she needs her, so Delilah leaves.

Something is off. I don't know what it is, but something tells me something bad is about to happen.

I sit in my office, staring at the schedule on my desk. My next meeting is coming up, and it's about something much bigger than Williams Holdings — my potential candidacy for the Senate.

I've been going back and forth on it, weighing the pros and cons, but today, the team will present the steps, the strategy, and the stakes. This isn't just about running a campaign; it's about whether I'm ready to step into a role that could change everything.

I hear a knock at the door. My assistant pops her head in.

"Mr. Gregory and the team are here for the meeting."

I nod, straightening in my chair as the group walks in. Thomas Gregory, the strategist who's been managing high-profile political campaigns for years, leads the way. Behind him are my PR managers, Elaine and Danny, and two other members of my advisory team. They settle into the chairs across from me, their expressions serious.

This isn't just another business meeting. I can feel the weight of it already.

Thomas doesn't waste any time.

"Nathan," he says, his voice firm but calm, "we've put together the outline for your candidacy. If you decide to move forward, we need to start soon."

He spreads a folder across the table filled with charts, polling data, and projections. But it's not the numbers that get to me. It's the way Thomas speaks—like this is a done deal, like I've already made up my mind.

"We've done a thorough analysis," he continues. "You're the perfect candidate. Your influence in the country is undeniable. With over fifty thousand employees in your workforce in the city alone, you already have a significant voter base. You own half this city, and that kind of power demands respect. People know you, they trust you, and frankly, some fear you. That balance is crucial in politics."

I try to keep my face neutral, but inside, I'm conflicted. It's true—I've built an empire. I've worked my way to the top. But politics? That's a different beast.

Danny leans forward, his expression more cautious. "Nathan, your public image is impeccable. You've always played it right—polished, professional, never stepping out of line. But with this campaign, everything will be under scrutiny. Every aspect of your life will be analyzed, dissected, and reported on. That's why we need to address something sensitive."

I feel a shift in the room. The tension grows, and I know what's coming.

"It's about Delilah," Danny says softly, his eyes flicking to Thomas for support.

He continues, "She's not from our world. She didn't grow up in these circles. We're concerned about how voters might react. The elite of New York expects certain things from their candidates, and we're worried Delilah might complicate that narrative."

I stiffen. My hands clench into fists beneath the table, but I keep my voice calm.

"What exactly are you suggesting?"

Thomas steps in, taking control.

"We're suggesting that, for now, you keep your relationship with Delilah private. Don't legalize the marriage until after the campaign. It's not about how you feel—it's about strategy. Right now, you need to maintain the image of a man fully committed to the voters, with no distractions."

The words hit me like a brick. *Keep Delilah hidden?*

Pretend like she isn't part of my life? The thought makes my chest tighten, anger bubbling just beneath the surface.

"Let me get this straight," I say, my voice low but firm. "You want me to put my marriage on hold. To hide Delilah like she's some kind of liability?"

Danny tries to soften the blow. "It's not about her, Nathan. We know how much she means to you. But this is a campaign. Voters—especially in this city—are sensitive to appearances. Delilah . . . doesn't fit their expectations."

The room feels like it's closing in on me. I love Delilah. She's strong, real, someone who grounds me in ways these people could never understand. And now they're asking me to hide that? To pretend like she doesn't exist?

"I need time to think about this," I say finally, my voice tight. "I haven't made any decisions about running yet."

Thomas nods, his expression unreadable.

"Of course. Take the time you need, but we'll need to move quickly if you decide to go ahead. The campaign window is closing soon."

They start to gather their things, but I barely notice. My mind is spinning, thoughts of Delilah, of everything we've built together, clashing with this new reality. How am I supposed to tell her this? How can I even begin to explain that the people advising me think she's a liability to my political career?

As they leave, I sit back in my chair, the silence in the room deafening. I feel lost.

The idea of running for Senate should be exciting, but all I feel is a deep sense of conflict. I think I might want this. But not at the cost of Delilah. Not at the cost of pretending she's not part of my life.

I need to talk to her. I need to hear her voice, to figure this out together, because right now, I don't know which way to turn. I take out my phone and I laugh as I see Delilah's name on my phone, "Eatable Wife."

Nate: *I miss your face.*
Delilah: *Just my face?*
Nate: *Haha, no. What are you doing?*
Delilah: *I'm finalizing the details on the project. You?*
Nate: *Thinking of you.*
Delilah: *Wow. You're sooo getting laid tonight.*
Nate: *I better.*

"Sir, your mother is here to see you," Chloe says through the intercom. I did not have her on my schedule.

"Let her in," I say. And here it goes.

I hear the familiar sound of her heels on the marble floor before she enters.

"Mother," I say, trying to keep my voice steady as she steps into my office. She doesn't sit. Instead, she stands in front of my desk, looking down at me with that familiar, icy stare. I already feel my stomach tighten.

"We need to talk, Nathan," she says, her voice sharp, a blade slicing through the air.

I already know that this is about Jake. Here we go again.

I sigh.

"What is it this time?"

"Don't play dumb with me." She crosses her arms, her gaze never leaving mine.

"You know exactly what I'm talking about. This . . . *situation* with Delilah." *That*, I didn't expect. I brace myself.

"You mean my *marriage* with Delilah."

"Marrying her was a mistake," she says, coldly, each word hitting me like a punch. "And it's not too late to undo it."

I stare at her, the anger rising in my chest.

"Undo it? What are you talking about?"

"You haven't legalized the marriage in the States yet," she continues, as if I were a child she's scolding. "That's good. You should keep it that way. Don't make it official." The room feels smaller again, like the walls are closing in around me.

"I won't *undo* anything. If I had it my way, I'd already be legally married to her."

Her expression hardens, her lips pressed into a thin line.

"She doesn't belong in your life, Nathan. She's not one of us. She's not from our world, and she never will be."

"I don't care," I say, my tone even. "What you think, or what the rest of the world thinks is irrelevant. Are you done?"

"When will you open your eyes?" she snaps, leaning forward, her eyes cold and hard. "I've seen women like her before. She's using you, Nathan. She's a gold-digger, clinging to you because she sees your wealth, your power. She's after your money and your status, nothing more."

I feel my hands clench into fists, my nails digging into my palms.

"So what if she is?"

"What has she done with you? I don't recognize my son!" she says, her voice dripping with contempt.

My chest tightens, anger and hurt twisting inside me.

"And yet I've never felt more like myself," I say, quiet, but firm.

"She's not good enough for you," she insists, her voice rising. "She doesn't belong in this family. And if you think for one second that she's going to help you with your career—your future— you're delusional. She's going to ruin everything you've worked for."

I stand up from my chair, the tension between us thick.

"This isn't about my career or the Senate. This is about *me*, Mother. And I answer to no one."

She scoffs, shaking her head.

"You're blind. You're throwing everything away for some girl who will never understand what it means to be part of this world. Charlotte—"

I feel a wave of discomfort wash over me at the mention of her name.

"Don't go there," I warn her.

"*She*'s the one you should be with," my mother says, her tone shifting, as if she were trying to reason with me. "Charlotte loves you. She's always loved you. She's the perfect match. For you, for the company, for the Senate. She understands this life, this world. She knows how to navigate it."

I shake my head, the confusion growing. My mind spins, a whirlpool of emotions.

I'm not ready to hear this.

"Mother, this isn't about Charlotte. Delilah is my wife now."

"She's nothing!" Her voice cuts through the air like a whip.

"She's *nothing* compared to Charlotte. You could have it all—the perfect life, the perfect future. Delilah is a distraction. A mistake. And if you go through with this, you will regret it."

I take a deep breath, my heart pounding in my chest.

"She's not a mistake. And she's not going anywhere."

My mother stares at me, her eyes cold and hard, but I don't back down. The silence between us stretches, thick and heavy, until she finally speaks again.

"You'll ruin everything," she says quietly. "Your reputation, your career, the company . . . everything you've worked for. All because of her."

I look away, unable to meet her gaze. The doubt creeps in, but I push it aside.

She straightens, her eyes narrowing.

"Think about what you're doing, Nathan. Before it's too late."

And with that, she turns and walks out, leaving me alone with the weight of everything she's just said.

~

It's the weekend, and the world outside feels far away. Delilah and I are curled up on the couch, our legs tangled together under the blanket. The dogs are sprawled across us like two extra cushions, their warm bodies pressing down, adding to the coziness. The TV hums in the background, playing a movie we randomly picked, but it's just noise. We're talking more than we're watching, and that's how I like it.

Delilah leans into me, her head resting on my chest. Her fingers absentmindedly trace small patterns on my arm, and I can feel the softness of her touch. It's moments like this, when it's just us, that I feel the most at peace. Everything about this—about her—feels right. Like it's exactly where I'm supposed to be.

"I can't believe you made all these snacks," I say, glancing at the small tray on the coffee table. She made homemade chips and dip earlier, the smell still lingering in the air.

"Hey, don't act so surprised," she teases, looking up at me with a mock-offended expression. "I'm full of hidden talents."

I chuckle, leaning down to kiss the top of her head.

"I know you are. Just didn't expect a full spread for movie night."

"Well, I wanted to make it special," she says, smiling. "Besides, you deserve it."

My heart swells at her words. She has this way of making even the simplest things feel like they're wrapped in love.

I glance down at her hand, noticing her wedding ring. It catches the light, and I take a moment to admire it—the simple band that means so much more than the gold it's made of. I look at my own ring too, remembering the quiet ceremony we had, just the two of us. We haven't taken them off in a while now. I'll never take it off.

"This," I murmur, "this is perfect. You, me, the dogs, our quiet weekends like this. I wouldn't trade it for anything." She looks up at me, her eyes warm.

"Me neither," she whispers, and I know she means it.

I stroke her hair, feeling the strands slip through my fingers. She feels like home.

And yet there's this tug inside me—this small nostalgia about how things used to be before the world knew about us. When it was just me and her, in our own little bubble. No outside pressures, no expectations. Now, with the candidacy looming over us, my family's pressure, it feels like the world is closing in, and I miss the days when I didn't have to share her with anyone else.

"What's going on in that beautiful head of yours?" she asks, her voice breaking through my thoughts.

I shake my head, trying to smile.

"Just thinking how lucky I am. How much I love this life with you."

She grins, snuggling closer. "You're such a softie, you know that?"

"Only for you," I say, leaning down to kiss her.

We sit there for a moment, quiet, just enjoying the closeness. The dogs shift, Cowboy letting out a small sigh as he settles deeper into the blanket.

She smiles, but then her face shifts, her brow furrowing just a bit.

"Hey," she says, her voice softer now, "didn't you have a meeting this week? About the candidacy?"

I feel my stomach twist at her question. I knew this was coming, but I'm still not ready to talk about it. I don't want to ruin this moment, but I can't avoid it forever.

"Yeah," I say quietly, my hand still resting in her hair. "I did." She sits up a bit, looking at me with those wide, curious eyes.

"You didn't mention it to me. What happened?"

I hesitate, not sure how to explain everything. How do I tell her about the pressure, the suggestions to keep her out of sight, like she's some secret I need to hide?

"It's complicated," I finally say, my voice barely above a whisper. "I haven't made up my mind yet. People just kept pressuring me into running, but, I never cared this much. Politics is another level of shit."

She watches me closely, her fingers still resting on my arm.

"You don't have to do this if it doesn't feel right, baby," she says. "You don't owe anyone anything."

I nod, but the weight of it all feels heavy. I can't hide the truth from her, but I don't know how to tell her everything without breaking her heart.

"I know," I say, my voice strained. "I just . . . I need to figure some things out."

Delilah leans back into me, her hand slipping into mine, her thumb tracing over my wedding band.

"Whatever happens, we'll figure it out together," she whispers.

"Always," I answer.

I squeeze her hand, feeling a mixture of love and guilt swirl inside me. She's right. But the thought of the world trying to tear us apart . . . that's what scares me the most. *I need to change the subject.*

"You still haven't called Ashley," I finally say, the words hanging heavy between us. I've been waiting for the right moment, but maybe there never really is one. I can feel the tension rise as soon as I bring it up.

"No . . ."

"You still don't want to talk about Ashley with me, huh?" I ask, trying to keep my tone steady, but it hurts. It cuts deep, knowing that we haven't reached that place in our relationship yet—the place where she can trust me completely, with everything. It stings, and I feel a small crack in my heart, but I don't push. I don't want to push.

Delilah doesn't say anything. She just shakes her head, her lips pressed tightly together, and I can see she's holding something in, shutting me out. *Again.* I don't answer. I don't react. What can I say? This isn't something I can fix with words.

She stands up, not looking at me, and I let her go. I stay where I am on the couch, watching her leave the room. She needs space, I get that. But fuck, it still hurts. I know she's fighting something inside herself, and it's killing me that I can't reach her.

Less than five minutes later, she's back, phone in hand. She sits down on my lap, straddling me, her legs wrapping around me, and I instinctively grab her thighs, pulling her closer. Of course, the second she's on top of me, my body reacts. How could it not? But there's more to this moment, something deeper. Her eyes are focused, but there's a storm behind them.

Without a word, she starts dialing. I don't know what she's doing, and I don't ask. I just sit there, holding her, trying to be her anchor. She puts the phone on speaker.

"Hello?" A voice crackles through the speaker. And in that moment, I realize that voice belongs to Ashley, and I see it—Delilah's eyes gleam, her breath catches. She's scared, vulnerable, and strong all at once. This breaks her and she's allowing me in.

Delilah is letting me in!

"Hi, Ashley. It's me. Delilah," she says, her voice starting to tremble, and I reach up to stroke her thighs, trying to let her know I'm here. I'm with her. This is hard for her—fucking hard—and it breaks me to see her like this. But she's letting me in, letting me see this part of her, and that means everything.

"Oh, you *are* alive. I thought you were dead," Ashley's voice is shaking. There's history there, weight in every word. The bond they share—it's complex, tangled, and I don't fully understand it, but I know it's deep.

"I was . . ." Delilah's voice wavers, and I lean in, kissing her shoulder, her neck, anywhere I can reach, desperate to soothe her, to give her some comfort. She's breaking, right here in front of me, and I feel helpless. *What happened that led her to think she died?*

"How?" Ashley's voice is barely above a whisper, but it's still laced with uncertainty.

"It's a long story," Delilah murmurs, her voice soft. "I just wanted to make sure you were . . . you know. Okay."

There's a long pause on the other end, and I can hear Ashley's sigh.

"Women like us will never be okay, Delilah. Never." *What?*

"I know," Delilah whispers in a sob, and I can feel her body shudder against mine. She sobs quietly, and it's too fucking much. I can't take it. I gesture to her, trying to tell her to end the call. This is tearing her apart. I can see it.

But before Delilah can hang up, Ashley speaks again.

"I'm so sorry, Delilah, but I need . . . distance. I'm just . . . too fragile, too vulnerable. I feel like I'm gonna break. I'm so sorry, Delilah, I . . . I just can't." *What the fuck?*

I can feel the heat rising in my chest, anger and confusion swirling inside me. How can she reject her like that? After everything? After all Delilah has been through? How can she turn her back on her own sister?

But Delilah—*my Delilah*—she stays calm, even though she's falling apart.

"I understand. Don't worry. I'll forever love you, Ashley. I'll wait for you to come to me," she says, her voice cracking as tears stream down her face.

I fucking hate this. I hate seeing her like this, so broken, so hurt. I hate that Ashley can just reject her like that and leave her hanging. It's like a punch to the gut, watching Delilah cry over someone who can't see how amazing she is, how strong she is.

I scoop her up in my arms, lifting her easily as I stand, carrying her up to our bedroom. She's still sobbing, her tears wetting my shirt, and all I can do is hold her tight.

"I love you, I'm sorry, I love you," I keep whispering, over and over, because what else can I say? I feel guilty for pushing her to call Ashley. I thought it would help her, thought it would unlock something, help her heal. But it's done the opposite. It fucking broke her.

I lay her down on the bed, wrapping my arms around her, holding her close. She curls into me, her body trembling, and all I can do is kiss her hair, her forehead, anything to try and make her feel safe again.

"I thought it would help," I whisper, my voice tight. "I'm sorry, Delilah. I thought it would help."

She doesn't say anything, just buries her face in my chest, and we stay like that, wrapped around each other, until the world fades away.

~

The weekend rushes by, and I barely notice it slipping through my fingers. It feels like I didn't have enough time to just be with Delilah, to hold her and help her heal after everything with her sister. There's this ache inside me, knowing she's still carrying that weight. No matter how much I want to take it from her, I can't. I wish I could do more, wish I could protect her from the pain that still lingers in her heart.

Every moment I spend with her feels like it's too short, like we're racing against time. When she's in my arms, it's like the world stops, but only for a while. I crave more of those moments, when it's just the two of us, no outside pressure, no expectations. But the world keeps pulling me away from her. My family and my PR team are pressing me and I can't form a coherent thought in my head. And now the weekend is over, and I'm back in my office, diving headfirst into work.

I stare at the numbers on the financial report in front of me, but my mind is only half focused. The figures blur as I think about Delilah. The weight of her past, her relationship with Ashley—it all feels so heavy. Her secrets with the fucker and everything my mother said . . . *Fuck,* I should focus on my task at hand.

A knock at the door snaps me out of my thoughts. It's James. He steps into the office, and the air between us grows cold and awkward instantly. Things have been tense for a while now, and I'm not ready to forgive him—not yet. I don't know when, or if, I'll ever be able to. But for now, we keep things professional. That's all I can manage.

"Hey," he says, nodding stiffly as he approaches my desk.

"Hi," I respond, my tone flat. I don't bother looking up from the report just yet. I know why he's here. The room feels heavy, like we're trying too hard to act like everything's fine when we both know it's not.

James sets a folder on the desk, his movements rigid.

"Here's the financial data you asked for," he says, his voice clipped.

"Thanks," I reply, glancing at the folder before looking back at my computer screen. I don't offer more than that, and the silence between us stretches, thick and uncomfortable. I know he wants to talk about more than just the reports, but I'm not ready for that conversation. *Not yet.*

James shifts, like he's going to say something, but then he stops. He clears his throat instead.

"Let me know if you have any questions," he mutters, before turning on his heel and heading for the door.

I don't watch him leave. I can't. The tension in my chest is too tight, and I'm not ready to face whatever emotions might come up if we start talking about what happened between us.

As soon as James leaves, Chloe walks in. She steps in confidently, clipboard in hand, always organized, always efficient.

"Nathan," she says, "your driver is waiting. You have a meeting with Mr. Cooper in an hour."

I nod, standing up and stretching slightly.

"Thanks, Chloe. I'll head down in a few."

She leaves the room, and I grab my phone. I need to call Delilah before I go. It's not that I need to check in with her—it's more that I *want* to hear her voice. I dial her number and see "Perfect Wife in the History of Wives" on the screen. How I love her . . . And after a couple of rings, she picks up.

"Husband," she says softly, and instantly, everything feels a little lighter.

"Wife," I reply, a small smile tugging at my lips. "Just wanted to let you know I'll be out of the office for a few hours. Got a meeting with a client."

"Okay," she says, her voice warm. "The Cooper one?"

"Yes, that one. You do listen, baby! If I'm not done by the time you're done, I want you to go home. I'll send Tyler to get you."

"Of course I listen! And I'll be fine, thanks," she reassures me, but the last time she left the building on her own, she had a fucking accident and I nearly lost my heart. "Good luck with the meeting," she adds, and I can hear the smile in her voice.

I chuckle. "I'm not the one who needs luck, babe. They'll all bend to me. I make negotiations, not the other way around."

She laughs that sound I love so much, the kind that makes everything else fade away.

"So full of yourself," she teases.

"Oh baby . . . you know exactly how that feels, don't you?"

"That I do, baby."

"Fuck, I'm hard."

"I'll deal with that tonight."

"Of course you will," I say, and I feel like I'm on the verge of losing my shit. I just want to get down to the twenty-seventh to take care of my wife.

We say our goodbyes, and as I hang up, I feel a bit more grounded. I grab my briefcase and head downstairs to meet my driver. The car ride is smooth, and I go over the details of the negotiation in my head, knowing that this meeting with Mr. Cooper is a big one. He's a client we've been courting for months, and today is the final push to lock things in.

When I arrive at his office, I'm greeted by his assistant, who ushers me into the large, sleek conference room. Mr. Cooper is already there, along with two of his senior executives. They stand as I walk in, extending formal greetings.

"Mr. Williams," Mr. Cooper says, shaking my hand firmly. "Good to see you again."

"Likewise," I reply, taking a seat at the head of the table.

The meeting begins, and we dive into the negotiations. The conversation is professional, calculated. Every word is measured, every sentence chosen carefully. This is what I'm good at—controlling the room, guiding the conversation in the direction I want it to go.

For hours, we go back and forth on numbers, terms, and conditions. Mr. Cooper and his team push hard, but I push harder. This is my territory, and I know how to play the game. By the time we reach the final stages, it's clear who's in control. They're bending, just like I knew they would.

"Mr. Williams," Mr. Cooper says, his tone respectful, almost deferential now. "I believe we can reach an agreement here."

I nod, glancing at the final proposal in front of me.

"I think we can too."

We sign the necessary papers, shake hands again, and as I leave the office, I can't help but feel that familiar rush of satisfaction. Another deal closed, another success.

I stand at the entrance of the building, the weight of the meeting still lingering in my chest, but I try to shake it off. The air is cool, and I let myself breathe it in deeply. The world seems distant, blurred by the constant rush of people and cars around me. I check my phone, waiting for Tyler to pull up with the car, my mind already drifting to what comes next. I'm just about to send Delilah a text when I hear a voice.

"Nate," the voice calls, quiet but unmistakable.

The sound of it freezes me in place. My fingers stop over the screen, and I feel my pulse quicken. I can barely breathe. It's a voice I know, one that I haven't heard in so long. Slowly, I turn around, my body tense, my heart hammering in my chest. And then I see her.

Charlotte.

She's standing there, right in front of me, like a ghost from a past I thought I'd buried. I forgot how *fucking beautiful* she is. The sight of her knocks the air right out of my lungs. Her fair skin is almost glowing under the sunlight, as perfect as I remember. Her bright-blue eyes, the same eyes that always felt like they could see straight into my soul, pierce through me like they used to. They match the ocean, endless and deep, and I can't help but feel like I'm drowning in them all over again.

Her smile—it's so beautiful, so familiar, and it hits me in the gut. She's smiling at me, and for a moment, I feel like nothing's changed. Her long blonde hair falls over her shoulders, catching the sunlight in a way that makes it look like *gold*, like the sun itself, warming everything it touches, including the part of my heart I'd tried to shut off. I can't speak. I can't think. All I can do is stare at her, *speechless*.

We're standing on the sidewalk, but it feels like the world around us fades away. It's just her and me, like it's always been. My heart beats so hard in my chest I swear she can hear it. I try to force words out, but nothing comes. Instead, I just laugh, a nervous, awkward laugh, and she laughs with me. That laugh—it's like we're eighteen again, like nothing has ever pulled us apart.

Before I know what's happening, she jumps into my arms, her arms wrapping around my neck, and I catch her, holding her tight. And the second she's in my arms, something shifts inside me. It's like muscle memory. It's *her*. It's *Charlotte*.

Holding her . . . it's something I haven't done in years. Yet somehow, I know exactly how to hold her, how to *breathe* her in. I bury my face in her neck, closing my eyes, letting the scent of her fill my lungs. I missed her more than I ever let myself admit. She's been a part of my life for over twenty-five years, and standing here, with her back in my arms, it feels like I'm holding a piece of my past, a piece of me that I'd forgotten.

My mind spins, caught between the present and all the time we spent together. There's something about her, something I've tried to ignore, tried to push down. I don't know what to do with it. I don't know what to feel. But right now, in this moment, all I feel is her.

After what feels like forever, she pulls back just a little, just enough to meet my eyes. She's still smiling, her blue eyes soft as they search my face. Her hand comes up to my cheek, her fingers gentle as they graze my skin. It's a touch I know too well, and yet it feels so foreign after all this time. I can't look away.

She takes a breath, and then she says it.

"I'm back."

Her voice is so calm, like this was inevitable, like it was always going to be her standing here in front of me. And all I can do is nod, because I can't find the words. My throat is tight, my mind racing, but no thoughts are clear. I'm paralyzed in this moment with her, and the weight of those words sits heavy in my chest.

Then, before I can even process what she's just said, she whispers the next words that change everything.

"Let's get married."

It's like time has stopped. The world outside of us completely vanishes. Her words echo in my mind, and I don't know how to respond. My body freezes, my breath catches, and I feel my heart slam against my ribs.

Without thinking, I nod again, the word slipping out of my mouth before I can stop it.

"*Yes.*"

To be continued . . .

ABOUT THE AUTHOR

L.S. River, Lysa, is a romance writer living in the south of France. At thirty-three, she balances many roles—English literature teacher, wife to her high school sweetheart, mother to her daughter Alabama and son Romeo, and devoted pet mom to Kala, Nala, and Maui.

For as long as she can remember, Lysa has dreamed of becoming a writer. A true Gemini at heart, she embraces duality and passion in everything she does, and her debut novel, *Souls Collide*, was written with her whole heart and soul. Deeply inspired by the works of Mia Sheridan, she strives to craft stories that are both epic and intimate, exploring themes of healing, love, and resilience.

Romance novels have been her lifelong companions, and she hopes her own work will give readers the same sense of hope and beauty she has always found in the genre. *Rewriting Our Stars* marks the beginning of her author journey—a dream realized, and the first step into a world of stories she has always carried inside her.